RED
SQUARE
&
GYPSY
IN AMBER

Also by Martin Cruz Smith

THE INDIANS WON

CANTO FOR A GYPSY

NIGHTWING

STALLION GATE

GORKY PARK

POLAR STAR

ROSE

HAVANA BAY

MARTIN CRUZ SMITH

RED SQUARE & GYPSY IN AMBER

PAN BOOKS

Red Square first published in Great Britain 1992 by Harvill
Gypsy in Amber first published 1973 by Arthur Barker Ltd

This omnibus edition published 2002 by Pan Books
an imprint of Pan Macmillan Ltd
Pan Macmillan, 20 New Wharf Road, London N1 9RR
Basingstoke and Oxford
Associated companies throughout the world
www.panmacmillan.co.uk

ISBN 0 330 41515 8

1 3 5 7 9 8 6 4 2

A CIP catalogue record for this book is available from
the British Library.

Printed and bound in Great Britain by
Mackays of Chatham plc, Chatham, Kent

RED
SQUARE

For Em

Part One

MOSCOW

6 August–12 August 1991

Chapter One

In Moscow, the summer night looks like fire and smoke. Stars and moon fade. Couples rise and dress and walk the street. Cars wander with their headlights off.

'There.' Jaak saw an Audi passing in the opposite direction.

Arkady slipped on headphones, tapped the receiver. 'His radio's out.'

Jaak U-turned to the other side of the boulevard and picked up speed. The detective had askew eyes set in a muscular face and he hunched over the wheel as if he were bending it.

Arkady tapped out a cigarette. First of the day. Well, it was one a.m., so that wasn't much to brag about.

'Closer,' he said, and pulled the phones off. 'Let's be sure it's Rudy.'

Ahead were the lights of the ring road that circled the city. The Audi swung on to the ramp to merge with ring road traffic. Jaak edged between two flatbed lorries carrying steel plates that clapped with every undulation of the road. He passed the lead lorry, the Audi and a tanker. On the way, Arkady had caught the driver's profile, but there were two people in the car, not one. 'He picked someone up. We need another look,' he said.

Jaak slowed. The tanker didn't pass, but a second

3

later the Audi slid by. Rudy Rosen, the driver – a round man with soft hands fixed to the wheel – was a private banker to the mafias, a would-be Rothschild who catered to Moscow's most primitive capitalists. His passenger was female, with the wild look achieved by Russian features on a diet, somewhere between sensual and ravenous, with short, stylishly cut blonde hair brushed back to the collar of her black leather jacket. As the Audi passed, she turned and sized up the investigators' car, a two-door Zhiguli 8, as a piece of trash. In her thirties, Arkady thought. She had dark eyes, and a wide mouth and puffy lips, parted slightly as if starving. As the Audi swung in front, it was followed by the sound of an outboard engine and the appearance of a Suzuki 750 that inserted itself between the two cars. The motorcycle rider wore a black dome helmet, black leather jacket and black hightop shoes that sparkled with reflectors. Jaak eased off. The biker was Kim, Rudy's protection.

Arkady ducked and listened to the headset again. 'Still dead.'

'He's leading us to the market. There are some people there, if they recognize you, you're dead.' Jaak laughed. 'Of course then we'll know we're in the right place.'

'Good point.' God forbid anyone should exercise sanity, Arkady thought. Anyway, if anyone recognizes me it means I'm still alive.

All the traffic squeezed off the same exit ramp. Jaak tried to follow the Audi, but a line of 'rockers' – bikers – swarmed in between. Swastikas and tsarist eagles decorated their backs, all wreathed in the rising smoke of the exhaust pipes stripped of silencers.

At the end of the ramp, construction barriers had been pushed to one side. The car bounced as if they were crossing a potato field and yet Arkady saw silhouettes that loomed high against the faint northern sky. A Moskvitch went by, its windows crammed with swaying rugs. The roof of an ancient Renault wore a living-room suite. Ahead, brake lights spread into a pool of red.

The rockers drew their bikes into a circle, announcing their stop with a chorus of roars. Cars and lorries spaced themselves roughly on a knoll here, in a trough there. Jaak killed the Zhiguli in first; the car had no neutral or parking gear. He emerged from the car with the smile of a crocodile who has found monkeys at play. Arkady got out wearing a padded jacket and cloth cap. He had black eyes and an expression of bemusement, as if he had recently returned from a long stay in a deep hole to observe changes on the surface, which wasn't far from the truth.

This was the new Moscow.

The silhouettes were towers, red lights at the top to warn off planes. At their bases were the chalky forms of earthmovers, cement mixers, stacks of good bricks and mounds of bad, metal-reinforced bars sinking into mud. Figures moved around the cars and more were still arriving, an apparent convention of insomniacs. No sleep-walking here, though; instead, the swarming, purposeful hum of a black market.

In a way it was like walking through a dream, Arkady thought. Here were cartoons of Marlboros, Winstons, Rothmans, even despised Cuban cigarettes stacked as high as walls. Videotapes of American action or Swedish porn sold by the gross for distribution. Polish glassware glittered in factory crates. Two men in tracksuits arranged not windscreen wipers, but whole windscreens, and not merely carved out of some poor sod's car but new, straight from the assembly line. And food! Not blue chickens dead of malnutrition, but whole sides of marbled beef hanging in a butcher's lorry. Gypsies lit kerosene lamps beside attaché cases to display gold tsarist rubles in mint condition, sealed and sold in plastic strips. Jaak pointed out a moon-white Mercedes. Further lamps appeared, spreading the aura of a bazaar; there might be camels browsing among the cars, Arkady thought, or Chinese merchants unrolling bolts of silk. An encampment to themselves was the Chechen mafia, men with pasty, pocked complexions and black hair who sprawled in their cars like pashas at their ease. Even in this setting, the Chechens enforced a space of fear.

Rudy Rosen's Audi was in a choice central location near a lorry unloading radios and VCRs. A well-behaved queue had formed outside the car under the gaze of Kim, who stood, one foot on his helmet, about ten metres away. He had long hair that he pushed away from small, almost delicate features. His jacket was padded like armour and open to a compact model of the Kalashnikov called Malysh, 'Little Boy'.

'I'm getting in line,' Arkady told Jaak.

'Why is Rudy doing this?'

'I'll ask.'

'He's guarded by a Korean vampire who'll be watching every move you make.'

'Make a note of numberplates, then watch Kim.'

Arkady joined the queue while Jaak loitered by the lorry. From a distance, the VCRs seemed solid Soviet goods. Miniaturization was a virtue for consumers of other societies; generally, Russians wanted to show what they bought, not to hide it. But were they new? Jaak ran his hands along the edges, searching for the telltale cigarette burns of a used machine.

There was no sign of the golden-haired woman who had come with Rudy. Arkady felt himself being scrutinized and turned towards a face whose nose had been broken so many times it had developed an elbow. 'What's the rate tonight?' the man asked.

'I don't know,' Arkady admitted.

'They twist your prick here if you have anything but dollars. Or tourist coupons. Do I look like a fucking tourist?' He dug into his pockets and came out with crumpled notes. He held up one fist. 'Zlotys.' He held up the other. 'Forints. Can you believe it? I followed these two from the Savoy. I thought they were Italian and they turned out to be a Hungarian and a Pole.'

'It must have been pretty dark,' Arkady said.

'When I found out, I almost killed them. I *should* have killed them to spare them the pain of trying to live on fucking forints and zlotys.'

Rudy rolled down the window on the passenger side and called to Arkady, 'Next!' To the man waiting with zlotys, he added, 'This will take a while.'

Arkady got in. Rudy was well wrapped in a double-breasted suit, an open cashbox on his lap. He had thinning hair combed diagonally across his scalp, moist eyes with long lashes, a blue cast to his jowls. A garnet ring was on the hand that held a calculator. The back seat was an office of neatly arrayed file boxes, laptop computer, computer battery, and cases of software, manuals and computer disks.

'This is a thoroughly mobile bank,' Rudy said.

'An illegal bank.'

'On my disks I can hold the complete savings records of the Russian Republic. I could do a spreadsheet for you some other time.'

'Thanks. Rudy, a rolling computer centre does not make for a satisfying life.'

Rudy held up a Game Boy. 'Speak for yourself.'

Arkady sniffed. Hanging from the rearview mirror was something that looked like a green wick.

'It's an air freshener,' Rudy said. 'Pine scent.'

'It smells like armpit of mint. How can you breathe?'

'It smells cleaner. I know it's me – cleanliness, germs – it's my problem. What are you doing here?'

'Your radio's not working. Let me see it.'

Rudy blinked. 'You're going to work on it here?'

'Here is where we want to use it. Behave as if we're conducting a normal transaction.'

'You said this would be safe.'

'But not foolproof. Everybody's looking.'

'Dollars? Deutschmarks? Francs?' Rudy asked.

The cashbox tray was stuffed with currencies of different nationalities and colours. There were francs that looked like delicately hand-tinted portraits, lire with fantastic numbers and Dante's face, oversized Deutschmarks brimming with confidence, and, most of all, compartments of crisp-as-grass green American dollars. At Rudy's feet was a bulging briefcase with, Arkady assumed, much more. Tucked by the clutch there was also a package wrapped in brown paper. Rudy lifted the hundred-dollar notes from the tray to reveal a transmitter and micro-recorder.

'Pretend I want to buy rubles,' Arkady said.

'Rubles?' Rudy's finger froze over the calculator. 'Why would anyone want to buy rubles?'

Arkady played the transmitter's power switch back and forth, then fine-tuned the frequency. 'You're doing it, buying rubles for dollars or Deutschmarks.'

'Let me explain. I'm exchanging. This is a service for buyers. I control the rate, I'm the bank, so I always make money and you always lose. Arkady, nobody buys rubles.' Rudy's small eyes swelled with sympathy. 'The only real Soviet money is vodka. Vodka is the only state monopoly that really works.'

'You have some of that, too.' Arkady glanced at the rear floor, which was littered with silvery bottles of Starka, Russkaya and Kuban vodka.

'It's Stone Age barter. I take what people have. I help

9

them. I'm surprised I don't have stone beads and pieces of eight. Anyway, the rate is forty rubles to the dollar.'

Arkady tried the 'On' button of the recorder. The miniature spools didn't move. 'The official rate is thirty rubles to the dollar.'

'Yes, and the universe revolves around Lenin's arsehole. No disrespect. It's funny, I deal with men who would slit their mother's throat and are embarrassed by the concept of profit.' Rudy became serious. 'Arkady, if you can just imagine profit apart from crime, then you have business. What we're doing right now is normal and legal in the rest of the world.'

'He's normal?' Arkady looked in the direction of Kim. His eyes fixed on the car, the bodyguard had the flat face of a mask.

Rudy said, 'Kim's there for effect. I'm like Switzerland, neutral, everybody's banker. Everybody needs me. Arkady, we're the only part of the economy that works. Look around. Long Pond mafia, Baumanskaya mafia, local boys who know how to deliver goods. Lyubertsy mafia, a little tougher, a little dumber, just want to improve themselves.'

'Like your partner, Borya?' Arkady tried tightening the spools with a key.

'Borya's a great success story. Any other country would be proud of him.'

'And the Chechens?'

'Granted, Chechens are different. If we were all a pile of skulls, they wouldn't mind. But remember one thing, the biggest mafia is still the Party. Never forget that.'

Arkady opened the transmitter and slapped out the batteries. Through the window he noticed customers growing restless, although Rudy seemed in no hurry. If anything, after his initial nervousness, he was in a serene, valedictory mood.

The problem was that the transmitter was militia goods, never strong cause for confidence. Arkady twisted the connecting jacks. 'You're not scared?'

'I'm in your hands.'

'You're only in my hands because we have enough to put you in a camp.'

'Circumstantial evidence of non-violent crimes. Incidentally, another way to say "non-violent crimes" is "business". The difference between a criminal and a businessman is that the businessman has imagination.' Rudy glanced at the rear seat. 'I have enough technology here for a space station. You know, that transmitter of yours is the only thing in this car that doesn't work.'

'I know, I know.' Arkady lifted the contact prongs and gently slipped the batteries back in. 'There was a woman in your car. Who is she?'

'I don't know. I *really* don't know. She had something for me.'

'What?'

'A dream. Big plans.'

'Is greed involved?'

Rudy let a modest smile shine. 'I hope so. Who wants a poor dream? Anyway, she's a friend.'

'You don't seem to have any enemies.'

'Chechens aside, no, I don't think I do.'

'Bankers can't afford enemies?'

'Arkady, we're different. You want justice. No wonder you have enemies. I have smaller aims like profit and pleasure, the way sane people live around the world. Which of us helps other people more?'

Arkady hit the transmitter with the recorder.

'I love to watch Russians fix things,' Rudy said.

'You're a student of Russians?'

'I have to be, I'm a Jew.'

The spools started to roll.

'It's working,' Arkady announced.

'What can I say? Once again, I'm amazed.'

Arkady laid transmitter and recorder under the notes. 'Be careful,' he said. 'If there's trouble, shout.'

'Kim keeps me out of trouble.' When Arkady opened the door to leave, Rudy added, 'In a place like this, you're the one who has to be careful.'

As the line outside pressed forward, Kim pushed it back with rapid shoves. He gave Arkady a black stare as he brushed by.

Jaak had bought a short-wave radio that hung like a space-age valise from his hand. The detective wanted to stow his purchase in the Zhiguli.

On the way to the car, Arkady said, 'Tell me about this radio. Short wave, long wave, medium wave? German?'

'All waves.' Jaak squirmed under Arkady's gaze. 'Japanese.'

'Did they have any transmitters?'

They passed an ambulance that offered vials of morphine in solution and disposable syringes still in sterile American cellophane. A biker from Leningrad sold acid from his sidecar; Leningrad University had a reputation for the best chemists. Someone Arkady had known ten years before as a pickpocket was now taking orders for computers; Russian computers, at least. Tyres rolled out of a bus straight to the customer. Women's shoes and sandals were arrayed on tiptoe on a dainty shawl. Shoes and tyres were on the march, if not into the daylight, at least into the twilight.

There was a white flash and a gust of glass from behind them, in the middle of the market. Perhaps a camera bulb and a broken bottle, Arkady thought, though he and Jaak started to return in the direction of the disturbance. A second flash erupted like a firework that caught each face in recoil. The flash subsided to an everyday orange, the sort of fire men start in an oil can to warm their hands on a winter's eve. Little stars rose and danced in the sky. The acrid smell of plastic was tinged by the heady bouquet of petrol.

Some men staggered back with sleeves on fire and, as the crowd spread and Arkady pushed through, he saw Rudy Rosen riding a blazing phaeton, upright, face black, hair aflame, hands clasped to the wheel, brilliant in his own glow but motionless within the thick, noxious storm clouds that whipped from the interior and out of the gutted windows of his car. Arkady got near enough to look through the windscreen at Rudy's eyes sinking into the smoke. He was dead. There was that silence, that gutted gaze in the middle of the flames.

Around the burning car other cars were moving. Spilling rugs, gold coins, VCRs, a mass evacuation flowed to the gate. The ambulance lumbered off, ploughing over a figure in its headlights, followed by a Chechen motorcade. Motorbikes split into several streams, searching for gaps in the site fence.

Yet some men stayed and, as the stars drifted overhead, fought to catch them. Arkady himself leaped and plucked from the air a burning Deutschmark, then a dollar, then a franc, all lined with worms of burning gold.

Chapter Two

Although the ground was still in shadow, Arkady could see that the site was a layout of four twenty-storey towers around a central square – three of the towers were faced in pre-cast concrete while the last was still in a skeletal girders-and-crane phase that in the hopeful light of dawn appeared both gargantuan and frail. On the ground floors he supposed there would be restaurants, cabarets, perhaps a cinema, and in the middle of the square, when the earthmovers and cement mixers were gone, a view of coaches and taxis. Now, however, there were a forensic van, the Zhiguli and the black shell of Rudy Rosen's Audi sitting on a black carpet of singed glass. The Audi's windows were hollow and the heat of the fire had exploded and then burned the tyres, so at least it was the stench of burnt rubber that was strongest. As if listening, Rudy Rosen sat stiffly upright.

'Glass seems to be evenly distributed,' Arkady said. Polina followed with her pre-war Leica and took a picture every other step. 'Glass is melted closer to the car, which is a four-door Audi 1200. Left doors shut. Bonnet shut, headlights burned out. Right doors shut. Boot shut, rear lights burned out.' There was nothing to do but get on his hands and knees. 'Fuel tank is blown. Silencer separated from exhaust pipe.' He got up.

'Numberplate black now but a Moscow number is legible and identified as property of Rudik Rosen. By the wide spread of glass, origin of fire seems to have been inside the passenger compartment, not out.'

'Pending expert reports, of course,' Polina said to maintain her reputation for disrespect. Young and tiny, the pathologist wore one coat and one smirk summer and winter, her hair piled high and stabbed ferociously with pins. 'You should get the thing up on a lift.'

Arkady's comments were written down by Minin, a detective with the deep-set eyes of a maniac. Behind Minin a cordon of militia marched across the site. Arson dogs dragged their handlers around the towers, racing from pillar to post, raising their legs.

'Exterior paint is peeled,' Arkady went on. 'Chrome on the door handle is peeled.' There go prints, he thought; nevertheless, he wrapped a handkerchief around his hand to open the front passenger door.

'Thank you,' Polina said.

At Arkady's touch the door swung open, spilling ash on his shoes.

'Interior of the car is gutted,' he continued. 'Seats are burned down to frames and springs. Steering wheel seems to have melted and disappeared.'

'Flesh is tougher than plastic,' Polina said.

'Rear rubber floor mats melted around what appears to be puddled glass. Rear seat burned to springs. Charred computer battery and residue of non-ferrous metal. Flecks of gold probably from conductors.' Which was all that was left of the computer Rudy was so proud of.

'Metal shuttles from computer disks.' The megabytes of information. 'Covered with ash.' The file boxes.

Reluctantly, Arkady moved to the front. 'Flash signs by the clutch. Fragments of charred leather. Plastic residue, batteries in dash compartment.'

'Naturally. The heat was intense.' Polina leaned in to snap a shot with her Leica. 'Two thousand degrees, at least.'

'On the front seat,' Arkady said, 'a cashbox. The tray is empty and charred. Under the tray are small metal contacts, four batteries, perhaps the remains of a transmitter and tape recorder. So much for surveillance. Also on the seat is a metal rectangle, perhaps the back of a calculator. Key in the ignition is turned to "Off". Two other keys on the ring.'

Which brought him to the driver. This was not where Arkady excelled. In fact, this was where he could have used a long walk and a cigarette.

'With the burned ones you have to open the camera aperture all the way just to get any detail,' Polina said.

Detail? 'The body is shrunken,' Arkady said, 'too badly charred to be immediately identifiable as male or female, child or adult. Head is resting on the left shoulder. Clothes and hair are burned off; some skull shows through. Teeth do not appear salvageable for moulds. No visible shoes or socks.'

Which didn't really describe the new, smaller, blacker Rudy Rosen riding on the airy springs of his chariot. It didn't capture his full transformation into tar and bone, the particular nakedness of a belt buckle hanging in the pelvic cavity, the wondering sockets of the eyes and the molten gold of his fillings, the trousers stripped for speed, the way his right hand gripped the steering wheel as if he were cruising through hell, and the fact that the pearlized wheel had melted like pink toffee on his fingers. It didn't convey the mysterious way bottles of Starka and Kuban vodka had liquefied and pooled, how hard currency and cigarettes had vanished in a puff. 'Everybody needs me.' Not any more.

Arkady turned away and saw that as black as Rudy Rosen was, Minin's face registered nothing but satisfaction, as if this sinner had suffered barely enough. Arkady took him aside and aimed him at some of the searchers among the militia who were stuffing their pockets. The ground was strewn with goods abandoned in the panic of the evacuation. 'I told them to identify and chart what they found.'

'You didn't mean for them to keep it.'

Arkady took a deep breath. 'Right.'

'Look at this.' Polina probed a corner of the back seat with her hairpin. 'Dried blood.'

Arkady went over to the Zhiguli. Jaak was in the back seat, questioning their only witness, the same unlucky man Arkady had met when he was waiting to talk to Rudy. The mugger with too many zlotys. Jaak had tackled him just inside the fence.

According to his ID and work papers, Gary Oberlyan was a Moscow resident and hospital orderly, and, by the looks of his coupons, due for a new pair of shoes.

'You want to see his ID?' Jaak said. He pulled back

Gary's sleeves. On the inside of the left forearm was the picture of a nude sitting in a wine glass and holding the ace of hearts. 'He likes wine, women and cards,' Jaak said. On the right forearm was a bracelet of spades, hearts, diamonds and clubs. 'He loves cards.' On the left little finger, a ring of upside-down spades. 'This means conviction for hooliganism.' On the right ring finger, a knife through a heart. 'This means he's ready to kill. So let's say Gary did not wash up in a basket of reeds. Let's say Gary is a multiple offender who was apprehended at a gathering of speculators and who should cooperate.'

'Fuck you,' Gary said. In the daylight his broken nose looked welded on.

'Still have your forints and zlotys?' Arkady asked.

'Fuck you.'

Jaak read from his notes. 'The witness states that he spoke to the fucking deceased because he thought the deceased was someone who owed him money. He then left the fucking deceased's car and was standing at a distance of approximately ten metres about five minutes later when the fucking car exploded. A man the witness knows as Kim threw a second fucking bomb into the car and then ran.'

'Kim?' Arkady asked.

'That's what he says. He also says he burned his fucking hands trying to save the deceased.' Jaak reached into Gary's pockets to pull out handfuls of half-burned Deutschmarks and dollars.

It was going to be a warm day. Already the dewiness

19

of dawn was turning to beads of sweat. Arkady squinted at a sunlit banner that hung limply across the top of the western tower. 'NEW WORLD HOTEL!' He imagined the banner filling with a breeze and the tower sailing away like a brigantine. He needed sleep. He needed Kim.

Polina knelt on the ground on the passenger side of the Audi.

'More blood,' she called.

As Arkady unlocked the door to Rudy Rosen's flat, Minin pressed forward with a huge Stechkin machine pistol. Definitely not standard issue.

Arkady admired the weapon but he worried about Minin. 'You could saw a room in half with that thing,' he told him. 'But if someone's here, they would have opened the door or blown it off with a shotgun. A pistol won't help now. It just scares the ladies.' He dispensed a reassuring nod to the two street sweepers he'd gathered as legal witnesses to the search. They answered with shy glimpses of steel teeth. Behind them, a pair of forensic technicians pulled on rubber gloves.

Search the home of someone you don't know and you're an investigator, Arkady thought. Search the home of someone you do know and you're a voyeur. Odd. He'd watched Rudy Rosen for a month but never been inside before.

Upholstered front door with peephole. Living/dining room, kitchen, bedroom with TV and VCR, another bedroom turned into an office, bathroom with whirlpool. Bookcases with hardback collections of culture (Gogol, Dostoyevsky), biographies of Brezhnev and Moshe Dayan, stamp albums and back issues of *Israel Trade, Soviet Trade, Business Week* and *Playboy*. At once, the forensic technicians began a survey, Minin one step behind them to make sure nothing disappeared.

'Don't touch a thing, please,' Arkady told the street sweepers, who stood reverentially in the middle of the room as if they had stepped into the Winter Palace.

A kitchen cabinet held American scotch and Japanese brandy, Danish coffee in aluminium-foil bags; no vodka. In the refrigerator, smoked fish, ham, pâté and butter with a Finnish label, a cool jar of sour cream and, in the freezer, a chocolate bar and an ice-cream cake with pink and green frosting in the shape of flowers and leaves. It was the sort of cake that used to be sold in common milk shops, and was now a fantasy found only in the most special buffets – a little less rare, say, than a Fabergé egg.

Kilims on the living-room floor. On the wall, matched portrait photographs of a violinist in formal clothes and his wife at a piano. Their faces had the same roundness and seriousness as Rudy's. The front window looked down on Donskaya Street and, over rooftops, north towards the giant Ferris wheel slowly rolling nowhere in Gorky Park.

Arkady moved on to an office with a Finnish maple desk, Stairmaster, telephone and fax. A power-surge protector at the outlet, so Rudy had used his laptop computer in the flat. The drawers held paper-clips, pencils, stationery from Rudy's hotel shop, savings book and receipts.

Minin opened a closet and slapped aside American tracksuits and Italian suits. 'Check the pockets,' Arkady said. 'Check the shoes.'

In the chest of drawers in the bedroom even the underwear had foreign labels. Bristle brush on the television set. On the night table, travelogue videotapes, satin sleep mask and alarm clock. A sleep mask was what Rudy needed now, Arkady thought. Safe but not foolproof, was that what he had told Rudy? Why did anyone ever believe him?

One of the street sweepers had followed him as silently as if she moved in felt slippers. She said, 'Olga Semyonovna and I share a flat. We have Armenians and Turkmen in the other rooms. They don't speak to each other.'

'Armenians and Turks? You're lucky they don't kill each other,' Arkady said. He unlocked the bedroom window for a view of a courtyard garage. Nothing hanging outside the sill. 'The communal apartment is death to democracy.' He thought about it. 'Of course democracy is death to the communal apartment.'

Minin entered. 'I agree with the chief investigator. What we need is a firm hand.'

The sweeper said, 'Say what you want, in the old days there was order.'

'It was rough order but it was effective,' Minin said and they both turned to Arkady with such expectation that he felt like a mad dog on a pedestal.

'Agreed, there was no shortage of order,' he said.

At the desk, Arkady filled in the Protocol of Search: date, his name, in the presence of – here he entered the names and addresses of the two women – according to search warrant number, entered Citizen Rudik Abramovich Rosen's residence, apartment 4A at 25 Donskaya Street.

Arkady's eye was caught by the fax again. The machine had buttons in English – for example, 'Redial'. Gingerly he lifted the phone and pushed the button. The receiver produced tones, a ring, a voice.

'Feldman.'

'I'm calling for Rudy Rosen,' Arkady said.

'Why can't he call himself?'

'I'll explain when we talk.'

'You didn't call to talk?'

'We should meet.'

'I don't have time.'

'It's important.'

'I'll tell you what's important. They're going to shut the Lenin Library. It's collapsing. They're turning off the lights, locking the rooms. It's going to be a tomb like the pyramids at Giza.'

Arkady was surprised that anyone associated with Rudy cared about the state of the Lenin Library. 'We still have to talk.'

'I work late.'

'Anytime.'

'Outside the library, tomorrow at midnight.'

'Midnight?'

23

'Unless the library comes down on top of me.'

'Let me just check the phone number.'

'Feldman. F-e-l-d-m-a-n. Professor Feldman.' He recited the number and hung up.

Arkady set the receiver down. 'Terrific machine.'

Minin had a bitter laugh for one so young. 'The forensic bastards will strip this place and we could use a fax.'

'No, we leave everything, especially the fax.'

'Food and alcohol, too?'

'Everything.'

The second sweeper's eyes grew larger. The magnetic force of guilt made her stare at pearls of vanilla ice cream that traced a trail in the oriental carpet to the refrigerator and back.

Minin whipped open the freezer door. 'She ate the ice cream while our backs were turned. And the chocolate's gone.'

'Olga Semyonovna!' The first sweeper was also shocked.

The accused lifted her hand from a pocket and seemed to sink at the knees as if the weight of the incriminating chocolate bar were too much. Tears coursed down the folds of her cheeks and dropped from her trembling chin as if she had stolen a silver cup off an altar. Terrific, Arkady thought, we've made an old woman cry over chocolate. How could she not succumb? Chocolate was an exotic myth, a whiff of history, like the Aztecs.

'Well, what do you think?' Arkady asked Minin.

'Should we arrest her, not arrest her but beat her, or just let her go? It would be more serious if she had taken the sour cream, too. But I want to know your opinion.' Arkady really was curious to learn how zealous his assistant was.

'I suppose,' Minin said finally, 'we can let her go this time.'

'If you think so.' Arkady turned to the women and said, 'Citizens, that means you both will have to help the organs of the law a little more.'

Soviet garages were mysteries because steel siding was not legally for sale to private citizens, yet garages constructed of such siding continued to appear magically in courtyards and multiply in rows down backstreets. Rudy Rosen's second key opened the mystery in the courtyard. The hanging bulb Arkady left untouched. In the sunlight he could see a tool kit, cases of motor oil, windscreen wipers, rearview mirrors and blankets kept to cover the car in winter. Under the blankets there was nothing more unusual than tyres. Later Minin and the technicians could dust the bulb and tap the floor. The sweepers had stood timidly in the open door the entire time; the old dears hadn't tried to make off with even a lug wrench.

Why wasn't he tired or hungry? He was like a man with a fever but no diagnosed disease. When he caught up with Jaak at the Intourist Hotel lobby, the detective was swallowing caffeine tablets to stay awake.

'Gary's full of shit,' Jaak said. 'I don't see Kim killing Rudy. He was his bodyguard. You know, I'm so sleepy that if I find Kim, he's going to shoot me and I won't even notice. He's not here.'

Arkady looked around the lobby. To the far left was a revolving door to the street and the outdoor Pepsi stand that had become a landmark for Moscow prostitutes. Inside stood a line of security men who scrupulously let in only prostitutes who paid. Camped within the grotto darkness of the lobby, tourists waited for a bus; they had been waiting for some time and had the stillness of abandoned luggage. The information stands were not only empty but seemed to express the eternal mystery of Stonehenge: why were they built? The only action was to the right, where a semi-Spanish courtyard under a skylight invited attention to the tables of a bar and the stainless-steel glitter of slot machines.

Rudy's lobby shop was the size of a large armoire. A case displayed postcards with views of Moscow, monasteries, the fur-trimmed crowns of dead princes. On the back wall hung ropes of amber nuggets and the bunting of peasant shawls. On the side shelves, wooden, hand-painted dolls of ascending sizes crowded around plaques for Visa, MasterCard, American Express.

Jaak unlocked and opened the glass door. 'One price for credit cards,' he said, 'half price for hard currency, which, when you consider that Rudy bought the dolls from idiots for rubles, still gave him a profit of a thousand per cent.'

'Nobody killed Rudy over dolls,' Arkady said.

Handkerchief on his hand, he opened the counter drawer and flipped through a ledger. All figures, no notes. Minin and forensics would have to come here, too.

Jaak cleared his throat and said, 'I have a date. See you in the bar.'

Arkady locked the shop and wandered across the courtyard to the slot machines. They displayed draw poker or revealed plums, bells and lemons on wheels of chance under instructions in English, Spanish, German, Russian and Finnish. All the players were Arabs who circulated joylessly, setting down cans of orange 'Si Si' soda to stack tokens. In the middle of the machines an attendant poured a silvery stream of tokens into a mechanical counter, a metal box with a crank that he kept in furious motion. He jumped when Arkady asked him for a light. Arkady caught his own reflection on the side of a machine: a pale man with lank, dark hair in desperate need of sunshine and a shave, but not frightening enough to account for the way the attendant wrestled with his lighter.

'Did you lose count?' he asked.

'It's automatic,' the attendant said.

Arkady read the numbers off the counter's tiny dials. Already 7950. Fifteen canvas bags were full and tied shut, five empty bags to go.

'How much are they?' he asked.

'Four tokens for a dollar.'

'Four into . . . well, I'm not good at mathematics, but it seems enough to share.' When the attendant started around looking for help, Arkady said, 'Just joking. Relax.'

Jaak was sitting at the far end of the bar, sucking sugar cubes and talking to Julya, an elegant blonde dressed in cashmere and silk. A pack of Rothmans and a copy of *Elle* were open beside her espresso.

Jaak pushed a cube across the table as Arkady joined them. 'Hard-currency bar, they don't take rubles.'

'Let me buy you lunch,' Julya offered.

'We're staying pure,' Jaak said.

She gave him a rich smoker's laugh. 'I remember saying that myself.'

Jaak and Julya had once been man and wife. They had met on the job, so to speak, and fallen in love – not a unique situation in their callings. She had gone on to bigger and better things. Or he had. Hard to say.

The buffet had pastries and open sandwiches under banners for Spanish brandy. Was the sugar the product of imported Cuban sugar cane or the plain but honest Soviet sugar beet, Arkady wondered. He could become a connoisseur. Australians and Americans traded monotones along the bar. At nearby tables, Germans wooed prostitutes with sweet champagne.

'What are they like, the tourists?' Arkady asked Julya.

'You mean, special kinks?'

'Types.'

She allowed him to light her cigarette and took a thoughtful drag. She crossed her long legs in slow motion, drawing eyes from around the bar. 'Well, I specialize in Swedes. They're cold but they're clean and they're regular visitors. Other girls specialize in Africans. There's been a murder or two, but generally Africans are sweet and grateful.'

'Americans?'

'Americans are scared, Arabs are hairy, Germans are loud.'

'What about Russians?' Arkady asked.

'Russians? I feel sorry for Russian men. They're lazy, useless, drunk.'

'But in bed?' Jaak asked.

'That's what I was talking about,' Julya said. She looked around. 'This place is so low-class. Did you know that there are fifteen-year-old girls working the street?' she asked Arkady. 'At night girls work the rooms, knocking on doors. I can't believe Jaak asked me here.'

'Julya works at the Savoy,' Jaak explained. The Savoy was a Finnish venture around the corner from the KGB. It was the most expensive hotel in Moscow.

'The Savoy says they don't have any prostitutes,' Arkady said.

'Exactly. It's very high-class. Anyway, I don't like the word *prostitute*.'

Putana was the word most often used for high-class hard-currency prostitutes. Arkady had the feeling that Julya wouldn't like that word either.

'Julya's a multilingual secretary,' Jaak said. 'A good one, too.'

A man in a tracksuit set his sports bag on a chair, sat down, and ordered a cognac. A few sprints, a little cognac; it sounded like a good Russian regimen. He had

29

the knotty hair of a Chechen, but worn long at the back, short at the sides, with a curly fringe dyed an off-orange. The bag looked heavy.

Arkady watched the attendant. 'He doesn't seem happy. Rudy was always here when he counted. If Kim killed Rudy, who's going to protect him?'

Jaak read from a notebook. 'According to the hotel, "Ten entertainment machines leased by TransKom Services Cooperative from Recreativos Franco, SA, show total average reported receipts of about a thousand dollars a day." Not bad. "The tokens are counted daily and checked daily against meters in the backs of the machines. The meters in the slot are locked in; only the Spanish can get into them and reset them." You saw . . .'

'Twenty bags,' Arkady said.

Jaak calculated. 'Each bag holds five hundred tokens and twenty bags is two and a half thousand dollars. So that's a thousand dollars for the state and fifteen hundred a day for Rudy. I don't know how he did it, but by the bags he beat the meters.'

Arkady wondered who TransKom was. It couldn't be just Rudy. That kind of import-and-lease needed Party sponsorship, some official institution willing to be a partner.

Jaak turned his eyes to Julya. 'Marry me again.'

'I'm going to marry a Swede, an executive. I have girlfriends in Stockholm who've already done it. It's not Paris, but the Swedes appreciate someone who's good with money and knows how to entertain. I've had proposals.'

'And they talk about the Brain Drain,' Jaak said to Arkady.

'One gave me a car,' Julya said.

'A car?' Jaak was more respectful.

'A Volvo.'

'Naturally. Your bottom should touch nothing but foreign leather.' Jaak implored her, 'Help me. Not for cars or ruby rings, but because I didn't send you home the first time we took you off the street.' He explained to Arkady, 'The first time I saw her she was wearing gumboots and a mattress. She's complaining about Stockholm and she came from somewhere in Siberia where they take anti-freeze to shit.'

'That reminds me,' Julya said, unfazed, 'for my exit visa I may need a statement from you saying you don't have any claims on me.'

'We're divorced. We have a relationship of mutual respect. Can I borrow your car?'

'Visit me in Sweden.' Julya found a page in her magazine that she was willing to deface. She wrote three addresses in curly script, folded the margin and tore it along the crease. 'I'm not doing you a favour. Personally, Kim is the last person I'd want to find. You're sure I can't buy you lunch?'

Arkady said, 'I'll just treat myself to one more cube before we go.'

'Be careful,' Julya told Jaak. 'Kim is crazy. I'd rather you didn't find him.'

On the way out, Arkady caught another glimpse of himself in the bar mirror. Grimmer than he thought, not the kind of face that woke up expecting sunshine. What was that old poem by Mayakovsky? 'Regard me, world, and envy: I have a Soviet passport!' Now everyone just wanted a passport to get out, and the government, ignored by all, had collapsed into the sort of spiteful arguments that erupted in a whorehouse where no customers had come to call in twenty years.

What could explain this shop, this country, this life? A fork with three out of four tines, two kopecks. A fishhook, twenty kopecks, used, but fish weren't choosy. A comb as small as a seedy moustache, reduced from four kopecks to two.

True, this was a discount shop, but in another, more civilized world wasn't this trash? Wouldn't it all be thrown away?

Some items had no discernible function. A wooden scooter with rough wooden wheels and no pole, no bars to hang on to. A plastic tag embossed with the number '97'. What were the odds someone had ninety-seven rooms, ninety-seven lockers or ninety-seven anything and was only missing the number '97'?

Perhaps it was the *idea* of buying. The idea of a market. Because this was a cooperative shop and people wanted to buy . . . something.

On the third table was a bar of soap, shaved and shaped out of a larger, used bar of soap, twenty kopecks.

A rusty butter knife, five kopecks. A blackened light bulb with a broken filament, three rubles. Why, when a new bulb was forty kopecks? Since there were no new light bulbs for sale in the shops, you took this used bulb to your office, replaced the bulb in the lamp on your desk and took the good bulb home so that you wouldn't live in the dark.

Arkady slipped out of the back door and walked across the dirt towards the second address, a milk shop, cigarette in his left hand, which meant that Kim had not been inside the cooperative. Up the street, Jaak seemed to be reading a newspaper in a car.

There was no milk, cream or butter in the milk shop, though the chill rooms were stacked with boxes of sugar. The empty counters were staffed by women in white coats and caps who wore the boredom of a rearguard. Arkady lifted a sugar box. Empty.

'Whipped cream?' Arkady asked an assistant.

'No.' She seemed startled.

'Sweet cheese?'

'Of course not. Are you crazy?'

'Yes, but what a memory,' Arkady said. He flashed his red ID and walked around the counter and through the swinging door into the rear. A lorry was in the bay and a delivery of milk was being unloaded, directly into another, unmarked lorry. The manager of the shop came out of a chill room; before the door snapped shut, Arkady saw wheels of cheese and tubs of butter.

'Everything you see is reserved. We have nothing, nothing!' she announced.

Arkady opened the chill room door. An elderly man huddled like a mouse in a corner. In one hand, he clutched a certificate naming him a volunteer citizen inspector to combat hoarding and speculation. In his other hand was a bottle of vodka.

'Staying warm, uncle?' Arkady asked.

'I'm a veteran.' The old man touched the bottle to the medal on his sweater.

'I can see that.'

Arkady walked around the storeroom. Why did a milk shop need bins?

'Everything here is special order for invalids and children,' the manager said.

Arkady opened a bin to see sacks of flour stacked like sandbags. When he opened another, pomegranates rolled around his feet and over the storeroom floor. A third bin, and lemons poured over pomegranates.

'Invalids and children!' the manager shouted.

The last bin was stacked with cigarettes.

Arkady stepped carefully around the fruit and exited through the bay. The men loading the milk tucked their faces away.

From the back of the shop, his cigarette still in his left hand, Arkady walked across a yard seeded with broken glass to the main street. On it, apartment buildings rusted in seams along drainpipes and window casings. Cars had the creased and rusted look of wrecks. Kids hung on to a rust-orange roundabout without seats. The school seemed to be built of bricks of rust.

At the end of the street, the local Party headquarters was sheathed like a sepulchre in white marble.

At Julya's last address for Kim, Arkady dropped the cigarette as he approached a pet shop whose plaster had fallen from its façade in large, geographic sections. He heard Jaak and the car rolling close behind.

The only animals for sale seemed to be chicks and cats peeping and mewing in wire cages. The shop assistant was a Chinese girl carving what looked like liver for a customer. When the liver stirred Arkady saw that it was actually a spreading mound of bloodworms. He stepped behind the counter and into a back room as the girl followed with her cleaver and warned, 'This is no entry.'

In the back were sacks of wood shavings and chicken pellets, a refrigerator with a calendar for the Year of the Sheep, shelves with tall glass jars of teas, mushrooms and fungi, man-shaped ginseng and items labelled only in Chinese characters, but which he recognized from the herbal shops he had seen in Siberia. What looked like tar in a jar was black-bear bile; a larger bottle held a lumpish mass of coagulated pig's blood, good for soup. There were dried seahorses and deer penises that resembled peppers. Bear paws, another illegal delicacy, were stacked on a rope. An armadillo stirred, half-alive, on a string.

'No entry,' the girl insisted. She couldn't have been more than twelve and the cleaver looked as long as her arm.

Arkady apologized and left. A second door led up

stairs littered with birdseed to a metal door. He knocked and pressed himself against the wall. 'Kim, we want to help you. Come out so we can talk. We're friends.'

Someone was inside. Arkady heard the careful easing of a floorboard and a sound like rustling sheets. When he pounded the door, it popped open. He walked into a storeroom that was dark except for a shoebox that was burning from the top down in the middle of the floor; he smelled the lighter fluid that had been poured on to it. Around the walls were television cartons, on the floor a bare mattress, tool kit, hot plate. He pulled the curtains aside and looked out of the open window at a fire escape leading down to a yard knee-deep in pet-shop junk: birdseed bags, steel netting, dead chicks. Whoever had been here was gone. He tried the switch. The light bulb was gone, too. Well, that showed forethought.

Arkady made a complete circuit of the room, looking behind the cartons, before he returned to the burning box. The sound of the flames was soft and furious at the same time, a miniature firestorm. It wasn't a shoebox. The side of it said 'Sindy' and showed a doll with a blonde ponytail sitting at a table, pouring tea. He recognized it because Sindy dolls were the most popular import in Moscow, displayed in every toy-shop window, non-existent on the shelves. The box's illustration also showed a dog, perhaps a Pekingese, that sat at the doll's feet and wagged its tail.

Jaak rushed in to stamp out the fire.

'Don't.' Arkady pulled him back.

The fire line edged down into the picture. As Sindy's hair burst into flame, her face darkened in alarm. She seemed to raise the teapot, then stand as her upper half was consumed. The dog waited faithfully as paper burned down around him. Then the entire box was black, twisted, spider-webbed with red, turning grey and gauzy, with a layer of ashes that Arkady blew away. Inside was a land mine, lightly charred, its two pressure pins up, triggered, still waiting for Jaak's foot to push them down.

Chapter Three

Arkady drew a cartoon car on a piece of paper. Crayons, he thought, were about the only thing he lacked. Amenities for rehabilitated Special Investigator Renko included desk and conference table, four chairs, files, and a closet that held a combination safe. Plus two 'Deluxe' portable typewriters, two red outside phones with dials and two yellow intercoms without. He had two windows dressed with curtains, a wall map of Moscow, a rollaway blackboard, an electric samovar and an ashtray.

On the table Polina spread a black-and-white 360-degree panorama of the construction site and approaching shots of the Audi, then detailed colour shots of the gutted car and driver. Minin hovered zealously. Jaak, forty hours without sleep, stirred like a boxer trying to rise before the count of ten.

'It was vodka that made the fire so bad,' Jaak said.

'Everyone thinks of vodka,' Polina sneered. 'What really burns are seats because they're polyurethane. That's why cars burn so quickly, because they're mostly plastic. The seat adheres to the skin like napalm. A car is just an incendiary device on wheels.'

Arkady suspected that not so long ago Polina had been the girl in pathology class with the best reports, illustrated and footnoted in punctilious detail.

'In these photographs, I first show Rudy still in the car, then after we've peeled him off and removed him, then a shot through the springs to show what fell through from his pockets: intact steel keys, kopecks melted with floor rubbish, hardware from the seat, including what was left of our transmitter. The tapes burned, of course, if there ever was anything on them. In the first photographs you'll notice that I have circled in red a flash mark on the side wall by the clutch.' She had indeed, right by the charred shinbones and shoes of Rudy Rosen's legs. 'Around the flash mark were traces of red sodium and copper sulphate, consistent with an explosive incendiary device. Since there are no remains of a timer or fuse, I assume it was a bomb designed to ignite on contact. There was also petrol.'

'From when the tank blew,' Jaak said.

Arkady drew a stick figure in the car and, with a red pen, a circle around the stick feet. 'What about Rudy?'

'Flesh in that condition is as hard as wood, and at the same time bones break as soon as you cut. It's hard enough to pick the clothes off. I brought you this.' From a plastic bag Polina produced a newly buffed garnet and a hard puddle of gold, what was left of Rudy's ring. The cool pride on her face reminded Arkady of the sort of cat who brings mice to its owner.

'You checked his teeth?'

'Here's a chart. The gold ran and I haven't found it, but there are signs of a filling in the second lower molar. This is all preliminary to a complete autopsy, of course.'

'Thank you.'

'Just one thing,' she added. 'There's too much blood.'

'Rudy was probably pretty cut up,' Jaak said.

Polina said, 'People who are burning to death don't explode. They're not sausages. I found blood everywhere.'

Arkady squirmed. 'Maybe the assailant was cut.'

'I sent samples to the lab to check the blood type.'

'Good idea.'

'You're welcome.' Chin up, contemptuous from then on of the proceedings, she even sat just like a cat.

Jaak diagrammed the market on the blackboard, showing the relative positions of Rudy's car, Kim, the queue of customers, then, at a distance of twenty metres, the lorry with VCRs. A second grouping was arranged in a loose orbit of ambulance, computer salesman, caviar van; then more space and half an orbit that included Gypsy jewellers, rockers, rug merchants, the Zhiguli.

'It was a big night. With Chechens there we're lucky the whole place didn't erupt.' Jaak stared at the board. 'Our only witness states that Kim killed Rudy. At first I found it hard to believe, but looking at who was actually close enough to throw a bomb, it makes sense.'

'This is from a memory of what you saw in the confusion in the dark?' Polina asked.

'Like much of life.' Arkady searched his desk for cigarettes. No sleep? A little nicotine would take care of that. 'What we have here is a black market, not the usual daytime variety for ordinary citizens, but a black market at night for criminals. Neutral territory and a

40

very neutral victim in Rudy Rosen.' He remembered Rudy's description of himself as Switzerland.

'You know, this was like spontaneous combustion,' Jaak said. 'You get together enough thugs, drugs, vodka, throw in some hand grenades and something's going to happen.'

'A type like that probably cheated someone,' Minin suggested.

'I liked Rudy,' Arkady said. 'I forced him into this operation and I got him killed.' The truth was always good for embarrassment. Jaak looked pained by Arkady's lapse, like a good dog that sees his master trip. Minin, on the other hand, seemed grimly satisfied. 'The question is, why two fire bombs? There were so many guns around, why not shoot Rudy? Our witness—'

'Our witness is Gary Oberlyan,' Jaak reminded him.

Arkady continued, 'Who identifies Kim as an assailant. We saw Kim with a Malysh. He could have emptied a hundred bullets into Rudy more easily than throwing a bomb. All he had to do was pull the trigger.'

Polina asked, 'Why two bombs instead of one? The first was enough to kill Rudy.'

'Maybe the point wasn't just to kill Rudy,' Arkady said. 'Maybe it was to burn the car. All his files, every piece of information – loans, deals, paper files, disks – were on the back seat.'

Jaak said, 'When you kill someone, you want to leave the area. You don't want to have to start moving files.'

'They're all smoke now,' Arkady said.

Polina changed to a happier subject. 'If Kim was

close to the car when the device ignited, maybe he was injured. Maybe it was his blood.'

'I alerted hospitals and clinics to report anyone coming in with burns,' Jaak said. 'I'll add lacerations to that. I just find it hard to believe that Kim would have turned on Rudy. If nothing else, Kim was loyal.'

'How are we on Rudy's place?' Arkady asked while he followed the at once tantalizing and repellant smell of stale tobacco to a bottom drawer.

Polina said, 'The technicians lifted prints. So far they've only found Rudy's.'

In the back of a drawer, Arkady found a forgotten pack of Belomors, a true gauge of desperation. He asked, 'You haven't finished the autopsy?'

She said, 'There's a wait for morgue time, I told you.'

'A wait for morgue time? That's the ultimate insult.' The Belomor lit with a puff of black fumes like diesel exhaust. Hard to smoke it and hold it away at the same time, but Arkady tried.

'Watching you smoke is like watching a man commit suicide,' Polina said. 'No one has to attack this country, just drop cigarettes.'

Arkady changed the subject. 'What about Kim's place?'

Jaak reported that a more complete search of the storeroom had turned up more empty cartons for German car radios and Italian running shoes, the mattress, empty cognac bottles, birdseed and Tiger Balm.

'All the fingerprints from the storeroom matched the

militia file on Kim,' Polina said. 'The prints on the fire escape were smudged.'

'The witness identified Kim throwing a bomb into Rudy's car. You find a land mine in his room. How much doubt can there be?' Minin asked.

'We didn't actually *see* Kim,' Arkady said. 'We don't know who was there.'

'The door opened and there was a fire inside,' Jaak said. 'Remember when you were a kid? Didn't you put dog shit in a bag and set the bag on fire to see people stamp it out?'

No, Minin shook his head; he'd never done anything like that.

Jaak said, 'We used to do it all the time. Anyway, instead of dog shit there was a land mine. I can't believe I fell for it. Almost.' A photo in front of Jaak showed the mine's oblong case, the two raised pins. It was a small army anti-personnel mine with a trinitrotoluol charge, the kind nicknamed 'Souvenir for . . .' The detective lifted his eyes and regained his poise. 'Maybe it's a gang war. If Kim went over to the Chechens, Borya will be looking for him. I bet the mine was left for Borya.'

Polina had never removed her coat. She stood and buttoned the top with quick fingers that expressed both decisiveness and disgust. 'The mine in the box was left for you. The bomb in the car was probably meant for you, too,' she told Arkady.

'No,' he said and was about to explain to Polina how backwards her reasoning was when she left, shutting the door as her last word. Arkady killed the Belomor and regarded his two detectives. 'It's late, children. That's enough for one day.'

Minin rose reluctantly. 'I still don't see why we have to keep a militiaman at Rosen's flat.'

Arkady said, 'We want to keep it the way it is for a while. We left valuable items there.'

'The clothes, television, savings book?'

'I was thinking of the food, Comrade Minin.' Minin was the only Party member on the team; Arkady fed him 'comrade' as occasional slops to a pig.

Sometimes Arkady had the feeling that while he had been away, God had lifted Moscow and turned it upside down. It was a nether-Moscow he had returned to, no longer under the grey hand of the Party. The wall map showed a different, far more colourful city drawn with crayons.

Red, for example, was for the mafia from Lyubertsy, a workers' suburb east of Moscow. Kim was unusual in that he was Korean, but otherwise he was typical of the boys who grew up there. The Lyubers were the dispossessed, the lads without elite schools, academic diplomas and Party connections, who had in the last five years emerged from the city's metro stations first to attack punks and then to offer protection to prostitutes, black markets, government offices. Red circles showed Lyubertsy spheres of influence: the tourist complex at Izmailovo Park, Domodedovo airport, video hawkers on Shabalovka Street. The racetrack was run by a Jewish clan, but they bought muscle from Lyubertsy.

Blue was for the mafia from Long Pond, a northern dead-end suburb of barrack housing. Blue circles marked their interest in stolen cargo at Sheremetyevo airport and prostitutes at the Minsk Hotel, but their main business was car parts. The Moskvitch car factory, for example, sat in a blue circle. Borya Gubenko had not only risen to the top of Long Pond but had also brought Lyubertsy under his influence.

Islamic green was for the Chechens, Moslems from the Caucasus Mountains. A thousand lived in Moscow, with reinforcements that arrived in motorcades, all answering to the orders of a tribal leader called Makhmud. The Chechens were the Sicilians of the Soviet mafias.

Royal purple was reserved for Moscow's own Baumanskaya mafia, from the neighbourhood between Lefortovo Prison and the Church of the Epiphany. Their business base was the Rizhsky Market.

Finally, there was brown for the boys from Kazan, more a swarm of ambitious hit-and-run artists than an organized mafia. They raided restaurants on the Arbat, moved drugs and ran teenage prostitutes on the streets.

Rudy Rosen had been banker for them all. Just following Rudy in his Audi had helped Arkady draw this brighter, darker Moscow. Six mornings a week – Monday to Saturday – Rudy had followed a set routine. A morning drive to a bathhouse run by Borya on the north side of town, then a trip with Borya to pick up pastries at Izmailovo Park and meet the Lyubers. Late-morning coffee at the National Hotel with Rudy's Baumanskaya contact. Even lunch at the Uzbekistan with his enemy, Makhmud. The circuit of a modern Moscow businessman, always trailed by Kim on the motorcycle like a cat's tail.

The night outside was still white. Arkady wasn't sleepy or hungry. He felt like the perfect new Soviet man, designed for a land with no food or rest. He got up and left the office. Enough.

There was grillwork at each landing of the stairwell to catch 'divers', prisoners trying to escape. Maybe not only prisoners, Arkady thought on the way down.

In the courtyard, the Zhiguli was parked next to a blue dog van. Two dogs with bristling backs were chained to the van's front bumper. Ostensibly Arkady had two official cars, but petrol coupons enough for only one because the oil wells of Siberia were being drained by Germany, Japan, even fraternal Cuba, leaving a thin trickle for domestic consumption. From his second car he'd also had to cannibalize the distributor and battery to keep the first one running, because to send the Zhiguli to the shop was equivalent to sending it on a trip around the world, where it would be stripped on the docks of Calcutta and Port Said. Petrol was bad enough. Petrol was the reason defenders of the state slipped from car to car with siphon tube and can. Also the reason dogs were leashed to bumpers.

Arkady got in through the passenger side and slid over to the wheel. The dogs shot the length of their chains and tried to claw through his door. He prayed and turned the key. Ah, at least a tenth of a tank of petrol. There was a God.

Two right turns put him in Gorky Street's gamut of shop windows, still lit. What was for sale? A scene of sand and palm trees surrounded a pedestal surmounted by a jar of guava jam. At the next shop, mannequins fought over a bolt of chintz. Food shops displayed smoked fish as iridescent as oil slicks.

At Pushkin Square, a crowd spilled into the street. A year before there had been exhilaration and tolerance between competing loud-hailers. A dozen different flags had waved: Lithuanian, Armenian, the tsarist red, white and blue of the Democratic Front. Now all were driven from the field except for two flags, the Front's and, on the opposite side of the steps, the red banner of the Committee for Russian Salvation. Each standard had its thousand adherents trying to outshout the other group. In between there were skirmishes, the occasional body down and being kicked or dragged away. The militia had discreetly withdrawn to the edges of the square and to the metro stairs. Tourists watched from the safety of McDonalds.

Cars were stopped, but Arkady manoeuvred up an alley into a courtyard of plane trees, a quiet backwater to the lights and horns on the avenue outside. A playground's chairs and a table were set into the ground, waiting for a bear's tea party. At the far end, he drove up a street narrowed by lorries straddling the pavement. They were heavy, with massive military wheels, the backs covered by canvas. Curious, Arkady honked. A hand drew aside a flap, revealing Special Troops in grey gear and black helmets, with shields and clubs. Armed insomniacs – the worst kind, Arkady thought.

The prosecutor's office had offered him a modern flat in a suburban high-rise of apparatchiks and young professionals, but he had wanted to feel he was in Moscow. That he was, in the angle formed by the Moscow and Yauza rivers, in a three-storey building behind a former church that produced liniment and vodka. The church spire had been gilded for the '80 Olympics, but the interior had been gutted to make way for galvanized tanks and bottling machinery. How did the distillers decide which part of their production was vodka and which was rubbing alcohol? Or did it matter?

While he was removing windscreen wipers and rear-view mirror for the night, Arkady remembered Jaak's short-wave radio, still in the boot of the car. Radio, wipers and mirror in hand, he considered the food shop on the corner. Closed, naturally. He could either do his job or eat; that seemed to be the option. If it was any consolation, the last time he had made it to the market he'd had a choice of cow head or hooves. Nothing in between, as if the bulk of the animal had disappeared into a black hole.

Since access to the building could be gained only by

punching numbers into a security box, someone had helpfully written the code by the door. Inside, the letter boxes were blackened where vandals had shoved newspapers in the slots and torched them. On the second floor, he stopped by a neighbour's for his mail. Veronica Ivanovna, with the bright eyes of a child and the loose grey hair of a witch, was the closest thing to a guard the building had.

'Two personal letters and a phone bill.' She handed them over. 'I couldn't get you any food because you didn't remember to give me your ration card.'

Her flat was illuminated by the airless glow of a television set. All the old people in the building seemed to have gathered on chairs and stools around the screen to watch, or rather to listen, with their eyes closed, to the image of a grey, professorial face with a deep, reassuring voice that carried like a wave to the open door.

'You may be tired. Everyone is tired. You may be confused. Everyone is confused. These are difficult times, times of stress. But this is the hour of healing, of reconnecting with the natural positive forces all around you. Visualize. Let your fatigue flow out of your fingertips, let the positive force flow in.'

'A hypnotist?' Arkady asked.

'Come in. It's the most popular programme on television.'

'Well, I *am* tired and confused,' Arkady admitted.

Arkady's neighbours leaned back in their seats as if from the radiant heat of a fireplace. It was the fringe of beard from ear to ear and under the chin that gave the hypnotist a serious, academic cast. That and the thick glasses that enlarged his eyes, as intense and unblinking as an ikon's. 'Open yourself up and relax. Cleanse your mind of old dogmas and anxieties because they only exist in your mind. Remember, the universe wants to work through you.'

'I bought a crystal on the street,' Veronica said. 'His people are selling them everywhere. You place a crystal on the television set and it focuses his emanations directly on you, like a beacon. It amplifies him.'

In fact, Arkady saw a row of crystals on her set.

'Do you think it's a bad sign when it's easier to buy stones than food?' he asked.

'You will only find bad signs if you're looking for them.'

'That's the problem. In my work I look for them all the time.'

From his refrigerator Arkady took a cucumber, yoghurt and stale bread that he ate standing at an open window, looking south over the church towards the river. The neighbourhood had ancient lanes on real hills and an actual wood-burner's alley hidden behind the church. Behind the houses were yards that used to hold dairy cows and goats, which sounded good now. It was the newer parts of the city that looked abandoned. The neon signs above the factories were half dark, half lit, delivering illegible messages. The river itself was as black and still as asphalt.

Arkady's living room had an enamel-topped table with a coffee can filled with daisies, armchair, good brass lamp and so many bookshelves that the room seemed to have been built against a dam of books, a paperback bulwark from the poet Akhmatova to the humorist Zoschenko, and including Makarov – the .9mm pistol he kept behind the Pasternak translation of *Macbeth*.

The hall had a shower and WC and led to a bedroom with more books. His bed was made, he gave himself credit for that. On the floor were a cassette player, headphones and ashtray. Under the bed he found cigarettes. He knew he should lie down and close his eyes, yet he discovered himself wandering back through the hall. He still wasn't sleepy or hungry. Merely as an occupation he looked into the refrigerator again. The last items were a carton of something called 'Berry of the Forest' and a bottle of vodka. The carton demanded a mauling to permit a stream of brown, gritty juice to plop into a glass. To judge by taste, it was either apple, prune or pear. Vodka barely cut it.

'To Rudy.' He drank and filled the glass again.

Since he had Jaak's radio he placed it on the table and turned on a garble of short-wave transmissions. From distant points of the earth came spasms of excitable Arabic and the round vowels of the BBC. Between signals the planet itself seemed to be mindlessly humming, perhaps sending those positive forces the hypnotist had talked about. On a medium band he heard a discussion in Russian about the Asian cheetah. 'The most magnificent of desert cats, the cheetah claims a range that extends across southern Turkmenistan to the tableland of Ustyurt. Distribution of these splendid animals is uncertain since none has been seen in the wild for thirty years.' Which made the cheetah's claims about as valid as tsarist banknotes, Arkady thought. But he liked the concept of cheetahs still lurking in the Soviet desert, loping after the wild ass or the goitered gazelle, gathering speed, darting around tamarisk trees, leaping skyward.

He found he had gravitated to the bedroom window again. Veronica, who lived below, said he walked a kilometre from room to room every night. Just claiming his open range, that's all.

A different voice on the radio, a woman's, read the news about the latest Baltic crisis. He half listened while he considered the land mine at Kim's address. Arms were stolen from military depots every day. Were army lorries going to set up shop at every street corner? Was Moscow the next Beirut? Filmy smoke hung over the city. Below, the same smoke swirled around empty vodka cases.

He drifted back to the living room. There was a strange slant to the broadcast, yet the voice itself sounded vaguely familiar. 'The right-wing organization "Red Banner" stated that it planned a rally tonight in Moscow's Pushkin Square. Although Special Forces are on the alert, observers believe the government will once again sit on its hands until chaos escalates and it has the excuse of public order to sweep away political opponents on both the right and the left.'

The indicator needle was between 14 and 16 on the medium wave and Arkady realized he was listening to Radio Liberty. The Americans ran two propaganda stations, the Voice of America and Radio Liberty. VOA, staffed by Americans, was a buttery voice of reason. Liberty was staffed by Russian émigrés and defectors, hence offered vitriol more in character with its audience. An arc of jamming arrays had been built south of Moscow simply to block Radio Liberty, sometimes chasing the signal up and down the dial. Although full-time jamming had stopped, this was the first time since then that Arkady had heard the station.

The broadcaster talked calmly about riots in Tashkent and Baku. She reported new findings on the poison gas used in Georgia, more thyroid cancer from Chernobyl, battles along the border with Iran, ambushes in Nagornyy Karabakh, Islamic rallies in Turkestan, miners' strikes in the Donbas, rail strikes in Siberia, drought in the Ukraine. In the rest of the world, Eastern Europe still seemed to be rowing its lifeboats away from the sinking Soviet Union. If it was any consolation, the Indians, Pakistanis, Irish, English, Zulus and Boers were making hells of their parts of the globe. She finished by saying that the next news would be in twenty minutes.

Any reasonable man would have been depressed, yet Arkady checked his watch. He got up, assembled cigarettes and took the next vodka straight. The programme between newscasts was about the disappearance of the Aral Sea. Irrigation for Uzbek cotton fields had drained the Aral's rivers, leaving thousands of fishing boats and millions of fish foundered in slime. How many nations could say that they had wiped out an entire sea? He got up to change the water for the daisies.

The news came on at the half-hour for only one minute. He listened to the blissful chirping of Byelorussian folk songs until the news returned again at the hour for ten minutes. The stories didn't change; it was her voice he sat forward to attend to. He laid his watch on the table. He noticed he had lace curtains. Of course he knew his windows had curtains, but a man can forget these niceties until he sits still. Machine-made, of course, but quite nice, with a floral tracery fading into the pale light outside.

'This is Irina Asanova with the news,' she said.

So she hadn't married, or else she hadn't changed her name. And her voice was both fuller and sharper, not a girl's any more. The last time he had seen her she was stepping across a snowy field, wanting to go and wanting to stay at the same time. The bargain was that if she went, he stayed behind. He had listened for her voice so many times since, first in interrogation when he was afraid she had been caught, later in psycho wards where his memory of her was grounds for treatment. Working in Siberia, he sometimes wondered whether she still existed, had ever existed, was a delusion. Rationally he knew he would never see or hear her again. Irrationally he always expected to see her face turning the next corner or hear her voice across a room. Like a man with a condition, he had waited every second for his heart to stop. She sounded good, she sounded well.

At midnight, when programming started to repeat, he finally turned the radio off. He had a last cigarette by the window. The church spire blazed like a golden flame against the grey, under the arch of the night.

Chapter Four

The museum had a catacomb's low ceiling and compressed atmosphere. Unlit dioramas were spaced down the walls like abandoned chapels. At the far end, instead of an altar, open crates held unpolished plaques and dusty flags.

Arkady remembered the first time he had been granted admittance twenty years before, and the ghoulish eyes and sepulchral tone of his elderly guide, a captain whose only duty was to instil in visitors the glorious heritage and sacred mission of the militia. He tried the light switch on a display. Nothing.

The next switch did work and illuminated a foreshortened Moscow street circa 1930 with the hearselike cars of that period, model figures of men striding importantly, women shuffling with bags, boys hiding behind lamp-posts, all apparently normal except for, lurking on the corner, a doll with his coat collar turned up to his hat brim, a miniature paranoid. 'Can you find the undercover officer?' the captain had proudly asked.

The younger Arkady had arrived with other high-school boys, a group picture of sniggering hypocrisy. 'No,' they chorused with a straight face while they traded smirks.

Two more dead switches, then a scene of a man

skulking into a house to reach for an overcoat hanging in the hall. In an adjoining parlour a plaster family listened contentedly to the radio. A caption revealed that when this 'master criminal' was captured he had a thousand coats in his possession. Wealth beyond compare!

'Can you tell me,' the captain had asked, 'how this criminal, without drawing suspicion, carried these coats home? Think before you answer.' Ten blank faces stared back. 'He wore them.' The captain looked each boy in the eye so that everyone understood the sheer brilliance and inventive deceit of the criminal mind. 'He *wore* them.'

Other models continued the historical survey of Soviet crime. Not a tradition of subtlety, Arkady thought. See photos of slaughtered children, see the axe, see the hair on the axe. Another display of disinterred bodies, another murderer with a face half erased by a lifetime of vodka consumption, another carefully preserved axe.

Two scenes in particular were designed to draw gasps of horror. One was of a bank robber who made his getaway in Lenin's car, equal to stealing an ass from Christ. The other featured a terrorist with a home-made rocket that had narrowly missed Stalin. Find the crime, Arkady thought: trying to kill Stalin or missing him.

'Don't dwell in the past,' Rodionov said from the door. The city prosecutor delivered his warning with a smile. 'We're the men of the future, Renko, all of us, from now on.'

The city prosecutor was Arkady's superior, the all-seeing eye of Moscow courts, the guiding hand of Moscow investigators. More than that, Rodionov was also an elected deputy to the People's Congress, a barrel-chested totem of the democratization of Soviet society at all levels. He had the frame of a foreman, the silvery locks of an actor, and the soft palm of an apparatchik. Perhaps a few years ago he'd been just one more clumsy bureaucrat; now he had the particular grace that comes from performing for cameras, a voice modulated for civil debate. As if he were bringing together two dear friends, he introduced Arkady to General Penyagin, a larger, older man with deep-set, phlegmatic eyes, whose blue summer uniform was marked by a black armband. The chief of criminal investigation had died only days before. Penyagin was now head of CID and though he had two stars on his shoulder boards he was distinctly the new bear in the circus, taking his cue from Rodionov. The city prosecutor's other companion was a different type altogether, a jaunty visitor named Albov who looked less Russian than American.

Rodionov dismissed the displays and cartons with a wave and told Arkady, 'Penyagin and I are in charge of cleaning out the Ministry archives. These will all be junked, replaced by computers. We joined Interpol because, as crime becomes more international, we have to react imaginatively, cooperatively, without outdated ideological blinkers. Imagine when our computers here are hooked up to New York, Bonn, Tokyo. Already

Soviet representatives are actively assisting in investigations abroad.'

'No one could escape anywhere,' Arkady said.

'You don't look forward to that prospect?' Penyagin asked.

Arkady wanted to please. He had once shot a prosecutor, a fact that lent relations a certain delicacy. But was he thrilled by that prospect? The world as a single box?

'You've worked with Americans in the past,' Rodionov reminded Arkady. 'For which you suffered. We all suffered. That's the tragic nature of mistakes. The office suffered the loss of your services during crucial years. Your return to us is part of a vital healing process that we all take pride in. Since this is Penyagin's first day at CID, I wanted to introduce him to one of our more special investigators.'

'I understand you demanded certain conditions when you returned to Moscow,' Penyagin said. 'You were given two cars, I hear.'

Arkady nodded. 'With ten litres of petrol. That makes for short car chases.'

'Your own detectives, your own pathologist,' Rodionov reminded him.

'I thought a pathologist who wouldn't rob the dead was a good idea.' Arkady glanced at his watch. He had assumed they would leave the museum for the usual conference room with baize table and double sets of aides taking notes.

'The important point,' Rodionov said, 'is that Renko

wanted to run independent investigations with a direct channel of information to me. I think of him as a scout in advance of our regular forces, and the more independently he operates, the more important the line of communication between him and us becomes.' He turned to Arkady and his tone became more serious. 'That's why we have to discuss the Rosen investigation.'

'I haven't had time to review the file,' Penyagin said.

When Arkady hesitated, Rodionov said, 'You can talk in front of Albov. This is an open, democratic conversation.'

'Rudik Abramovich Rosen.' Arkady recited from memory. 'Born 1952, Moscow, parents now dead. Diploma with distinction in mathematics from Moscow State University. Uncle in the Jewish mafia that runs the racetrack. During school holidays, young Rudy helped set the odds. Military duty in Germany. Accused of changing money for Americans in Berlin, not convicted. Came back to Moscow. Carpool dispatcher at the Commission on Cultural Work for the Masses, where he sold designer clothes retail out of cars. Freight-yard director at the Moscow Trust of the Flour and Groats Industry, where he stole wholesale by the container load. Up to yesterday, managed a hotel souvenir shop from which he ran the lobby slot machines and bar, which were sources of hard currency for his money-changing operation. With the slot machines and the exchange, Rudy made money at both ends.'

'He lent money to the mafias, that's it?' Penyagin asked.

'They have too many rubles,' Arkady said. 'Rudy showed them how to invest their money and turn it into dollars. He was the bank.'

'What I don't understand,' Penyagin said, 'is what you and your special team are going to do now that Rosen is dead. What was it, a Molotov cocktail? Why don't we leave Rosen's killer to a more ordinary investigator?'

Penyagin's predecessor at CID had been that rare beast who had actually risen from the detective ranks, so he would have understood without having everything explained. The only thing Arkady knew about Penyagin was that he had been a political officer, not operational. He tried to educate him gently. 'As soon as Rudy agreed to put my transmitter and recorder in his cashbox, he became my responsibility. That's the way it is. I told him I could protect him, that he was part of my team. Instead I got him killed.'

'Why would he agree to carry a radio for you?' Albov spoke for the first time. His Russian was perfect.

'Rudy had a phobia. He was hated in the Army. He was Jewish, he was overweight and the sergeants got together and put him in a coffin filled with human waste and nailed him in for a night. Since then he had a fear of close physical contact or dirt or germs. I only had enough to put him in camp for a few years, but he didn't think he could survive. I used the threat to make him carry the radio.'

'What happened?' Albov asked.

'The militia equipment failed, as usual. I entered

Rudy's car and tinkered with the transmitter until it worked. Five minutes later he was on fire.'

'Did anyone see you with Rudy?' Rodionov asked.

'Everybody saw me with Rudy. I assumed no one would recognize me.'

'Kim didn't know that Rosen was cooperating with you?' Albov asked.

Arkady revised his opinion. Although Albov had the physical ease and blow-dried assurance of an American, he was Russian. About thirty-five, dark brown hair, soulful black eyes, charcoal suit, red tie, and the patience of a traveller camping with barbarians.

'No,' Arkady said. 'At least I didn't think he did.'

'What about Kim?' Rodionov asked.

Arkady said, 'Mikhail Senovich Kim. Korean, twenty-two. Reform school, minors colony, Army construction battalion. Lyubertsy mafia, car theft and assault. Rides a Suzuki, but we expect him to take any bike off the street and of course he wears a helmet, so who knows who he is? We can't stop every biker in Moscow. A witness identifies him as the assailant. We're looking for him, but we're also looking for other witnesses.'

'But they're all criminals,' Penyagin said. 'The best witnesses were probably the killers.'

'That's generally the case,' Arkady said.

Rodionov shuddered. 'The whole thing is a typical Chechen attack.'

'Actually,' Arkady said, 'Chechens are more partial to knives. Anyway, I don't think the point was only to kill Rudy. The bombs burned the car, which was a computerized mobile bank stuffed with disks and files. I think that's why they used two bombs, in order to make sure. They did a good job. It's all gone now, along with Rudy.'

'His enemies must be happy,' Rodionov said.

'There was probably more incriminating evidence about his friends on those disks than about his enemies,' Arkady said.

Albov said, 'It sounds as if you liked Rosen.'

'He burned to death. You could say I sympathized.'

'You would describe yourself as an unusually sympathetic investigator?'

'Everyone works in a different way.'

'How is your father?'

Arkady thought for a moment, more to adjust to this shift of ground than to search for an answer.

'Not well. Why do you ask?'

Albov said, 'He's a great man, a hero. More famous than you, if you don't mind my saying so. I was curious.'

'He's old.'

'Seen him lately?'

'If I do, I'll tell him you asked.'

Albov's conversation had the slow but purposeful motion of a python. Arkady tried to catch the rhythm.

'If he's old and sick, you should see him, don't you think?' Albov asked. 'You select your own detectives?'

'Yes.' Arkady was trying to answer the second question.

'Kuusnets is an odd name – for a detective, I mean.'

'Jaak Kuusnets is the best man I have.'

'But there aren't that many Estonians who are Moscow detectives. He must be especially grateful and loyal to you. Estonians, Koreans, Jews – it's hard to find any Russians in your case. Of course some people think that's the problem with the whole country.' Albov had the meditative gaze of a Buddha. Now he let it incline towards the prosecutor and the general. 'Gentlemen, your investigator seems to have both a team and a goal. The times demand that you let initiative have its head, not bring it to a halt. I hope we don't make the same mistake with Renko that we made before.'

Rodionov could tell the difference between a red light and a green. 'My office is totally committed to our investigator, of course.'

'I can only repeat that the militia wholeheartedly supports the investigator,' Penyagin said.

'You're from the prosecutor's office?' Arkady asked Albov.

'No.'

'I didn't think so.' Arkady added up the suit and the air of ease. 'State Security or Ministry of the Interior?'

'I'm a journalist.'

'You brought a *journalist* to this meeting?' Arkady asked Rodionov. 'My direct channel to you includes a journalist?'

'An international journalist,' Rodionov said. 'I wanted a more sophisticated point of view.'

Albov said, 'Remember, the prosecutor is also a people's deputy. There's an election to consider now.'

'Well, that *is* sophisticated,' Arkady said.

Albov said, 'The main thing is I've always been an admirer. This is a turning point in history. This is Paris in the Revolution, Petrograd in the Revolution. If intelligent men can't work together, what hope is there for the future?'

Arkady was still stunned after they left. Maybe Rodionov would show up next time with the editorial board of *Izvestia* or cartoonists from *Krokodil*.

And what would become of the crates and dioramas of the militia museum? Were they really going to be replaced by a computer centre? And what would become of all the bloody axes, knives and threadbare overcoats of Soviet crime? Would they be stored? Of course, he answered himself, because the bureaucratic mind saved everything. Why? Because we might need it, you know. In case there was no future, there was always a past.

Jaak drove, skipping lanes in the manner of a virtuoso pianist going up and down a keyboard.

'Don't trust Rodionov or his friends,' he told Arkady as he shouldered another car to the side.

'You don't like anyone from the prosecutor's office.'

'Prosecutors are political shits, always have been. No offence.' Jaak glanced over. 'But they're Party members. Even if they leave the Party, even if they become a people's deputy, in their hearts they're Party members. You didn't leave the Party, you were thrown out, that's why I trust you. Most prosecutor's investigators never leave their office. They're part of the desk. You get out. Of course, you wouldn't get far without me.'

'Thanks.'

One hand on the wheel, Jaak handed Arkady a list of numbers and names. 'Plates from the black market. The lorry nearest Rudy when he blew up is registered to the Lenin's Path Collective Farm. I think it was supposed to be carrying sugar beets, not VCRs. There are four Chechen cars. The Mercedes registered in the name of Apollonia Gubenko.'

'Apollonia Gubenko,' Arkady tried it on the tongue. 'There's a round name.'

'Borya's wife,' Jaak said. 'Of course Borya has a Mercedes of his own.'

They looped ahead of a Lada whose windscreen was patched with pins, paper and glue. Windscreens were hard to come by. The driver steered with his head out of the side.

'Jaak, what is an Estonian doing in Moscow?' Arkady asked. 'Why aren't you defending your beloved Tallinn from the Red Army?'

'Don't give me any more of that shit,' Jaak warned. 'I was in the Red Army. I haven't been to Tallinn in fifteen years. What I know about Estonians is that they live better and complain more than anyone else in the Soviet Union. I'm going to change my name.'

'Change it to Apollo. You'd still have an accent, though – that nice Baltic click.'

'Fuck accents. I hate this subject.' Jaak made an effort to cool down. 'Speaking of dumb, we're getting calls from a coach at Red Star Komsomol who says Rudy was such a club supporter that the boxers there gave him one of their trophies. The coach thinks it should be among Rudy's personal effects. An idiot but a persistent guy.'

As they approached Kalinin Prospect, a coach tried to cut in front of Jaak. It was an Italian bus with tall windows, baroque chrome and two tiers of stupefied faces – almost a Mediterranean trireme, Arkady thought. The Zhiguli accelerated with a burst of blue smoke. Jaak tapped the brakes just enough to threaten the finish on the bus's front bumper and raced ahead, laughing triumphantly. 'Homo Sovieticus wins again!'

At the petrol station Arkady and Jaak got into separate queues for meat pies and soda. Dressed like a lab technician in white coat and toque, the pie vendor whisked flies from her wares. Arkady remembered the advice of a friend who picked mushrooms – to stay away from those surrounded by dead flies. He reminded himself to check the ground when he reached the barrow.

A far longer queue, all male, stretched from a vodka shop at the corner. Drunks sagged and leaned like broken pickets on a fence. Their clothes had the greyness of old rags, their faces were striped red and blue, but they clutched empty bottles in the solemn knowledge that no new bottle would cross the counter except in exchange for an empty. Also, it had to be the right size empty bottle: not too big, not too small. Then they had to pass militiamen stationed at the door to check coupons for out-of-towners trying to buy vodka marked for Moscow. As Arkady watched, a satisfied patron left the store, cradling his bottle like an egg, and the queue inched forward.

There was a selection, which was what was holding up Arkady's queue: meat or cabbage pies. Since the filling was sure to be no more than a suggestion – a delicate *soupçon* of ground pork or steamed cabbage, a fine line within dough first steeped in boiling fat and then allowed to cool and congeal – it was a choice that demanded a fine palate, not to mention hunger.

The vodka queue also stalled, held up by a customer who had swooned on his way into the shop and dropped his empty. The bottle rang as it rolled to the gutter.

Arkady wondered what Irina was doing. All morning he had denied to himself that he was thinking about her. Now, with the chiming of the bottle, the very strangeness of the sound, he saw her having her midday meal not on the street but in a Western cafeteria of gleaming chrome, brightly lit mirrors, smoothly rolling trolleys bearing white porcelain cups.

'Meat or cabbage?'

It took him a moment to return.

'Meat? Cabbage?' the vendor repeated and held up identical-looking pies. Her own face was as round and coarse, her eyes sunk in a crease. 'Come on, everyone else knows what they want.'

'Meat,' Arkady said. 'And cabbage.'

She grunted, sensing indecision rather than appetite.

Maybe this was his problem, Arkady thought, lack of appetite. She got his change and handed over two pies embellished by paper napkins dripping grease. He checked the ground. No dead flies, but the ones buzzing around looked depressed.

'You don't want them?' the vendor asked.

Arkady was still seeing Irina, feeling the warm pressure of her and smelling not the rancid fumes of grease but the clean crispness of sheets. He seemed to be moving quickly through progressive stages of insanity, or else Irina was moving from oblivion to the unconscious, then to the conscious areas of his mind.

As the vendor leaned over the barrow, a transformation took place. In the middle of her face appeared what was left of a girl's embarrassment, of sad eyes lost between jowls, and she shrugged apologetically with round shoulders.

'Eat them, don't think about it. It's the best I can do.'

'I know.'

When Jaak brought the sodas Arkady awarded him both pies.

'No, thanks.' Jaak recoiled. 'I used to like them before I started working with you. You ruined them for me.'

Chapter Five

On Butyrski Street, past a long shopfront of lingerie and lace, was a building of barred windows with a driveway that dipped by a guardhouse down to entrance stairs. Inside, an officer issued numbered aluminium tags to Arkady and Jaak. A grille with a heart-shaped pattern slid open and they followed a guard across a parquet floor, down a stairwell with rubber treads and into a corridor of calcified stucco lit by bulbs in wire cages.

Only one person had ever escaped from Butyrski Prison and that was Dzerzhinsky, the founder of the KGB. He had bribed the guard. In those days a ruble meant something.

'Name?' the guard asked.

A voice behind the cell door said, 'Oberlyan.'

'Article?'

'Speculation, resisting arrest, refusal to cooperate with proper organs – what the fuck, I don't know.'

The door opened. Gary stood stripped to the waist, his shirt tied turban-style around his head. With his rakishly broken nose and torso of tattoos, he looked more like a pirate marooned on a desert island for a dozen years than a man who had spent one night in jail.

'Speculation, resisting and refusal. Great witness,' Jaak said.

The interrogation room had a monastic simplicity: wooden chairs, metal desk, ikon of Lenin. Arkady filled out the protocol form: date, city, his own name under the grand title 'Investigator of Very Important Cases under the General Prosecutor of the USSR', interrogated Oberlyan, Gary Semyonovich, born 3/11/60, Moscow, passport number RS AOB 425807, Armenian nationality . . .

'Naturally,' Jaak said.

Arkady went on, 'Education and specialization?'

'Vocational. Medical industry,' Gary said.

'Brain surgeon,' Jaak said.

Unmarried, hospital orderly, not a Party member, criminal record of assault and possession of drugs for sale.

'Government honours?' Arkady asked.

Both Jaak and Gary laughed.

'It's the next question on the protocol,' Arkady said. 'Probably just looking to the future.'

After he wrote out the exact time, the questioning began, going over the same ground Jaak had covered at the site of the crime. Gary had been walking away from Rudy's car when he saw it blow up, and then Kim threw in a second bomb.

'You were walking backwards from Rudy's car?' Jaak asked. 'How did you see all this?'

'I stopped to think.'

'*You* stopped to *think*?' Jaak asked. 'What about?'

When Gary fell silent, Arkady asked, 'Did Rudy change your forints and zlotys?'

'No.' Gary's face went dark as a cloud.

'You were pretty mad.'

'I would have twisted his fat neck.'

'Except for Kim?'

'Yeah, but then Kim did it for me.' Gary brightened.

Arkady drew an 'X' in the middle of a page and handed Gary the pen. 'This is Rudy's car. Mark where you were, then mark what else you saw.'

With concentration, Gary drew a stick figure with trembly limbs. He added a box with wheels: 'Lorry with electronic goods.' Between him and Rudy, a blacked-in figure: 'Kim.' A box with a cross: 'Ambulance.' A second box: 'Maybe a van.' Lines with heads: 'Gypsies.' Smaller squares with wheels: 'Chechen cars.'

'I remember a Mercedes,' Jaak said.

'They were already gone.'

'*They*?' Arkady asked. 'Who were *they*?'

'A driver. I know the other one was a woman.'

'Can you draw her?'

Gary drew a stick figure with a big bust, high heels and curly hair. 'Maybe blonde. I know she was well-stacked.'

'A real careful observer,' Jaak said.

'So you saw her out of the car, too,' Arkady said.

'Yeah, coming from Rudy's.'

Arkady held the paper a couple of ways. 'Good drawing.'

Gary nodded.

It was true. With his blue body and busted face, Gary looked just like the stick figure on the page, rendered more human by his picture.

The South Port car market was bounded by Proletariat Prospect and a loop of the Moscow river. New cars were ordered in a hall of white marble. No one went inside; there were no new cars. Outside, gamblers laid cardboard on the ground to play three-card monte. Construction fences were papered with offers ('Have tyres in medium condition for 1985 Zhigulis') and pleas ('Looking for fan belt for '64 Peugeot'). Jaak wrote down the number for the tyres, just in case.

At the end of the fence was a dirt lane of used Zhigulis and Zaporozhets, two-cylinder German Trabants and Italian Fiats as rusty as ancient swords. Buyers moved with eyes that scrutinized tyre tread, mileometer, upholstery, dropping to one knee with a torch to see whether the engine was actively leaking oil on the spot. Everyone was an expert. Even Arkady knew that a Moskvitch built in far-off Izhevsk was superior to a Moskvitch built in Moscow, and that the only clue was the insignia on the grille. Around the cars were Chechens in tracksuits. They were dark, bulky men with low brows and long stares.

Everyone cheated. Car sellers went to the market sales assistant's wooden shack to learn – depending on model, year and condition – what price they could demand (and on which they would pay tax), which bore no resemblance to the money actually passed between seller and buyer. Everyone – seller, buyer and sales assistant – understood that the real price would be three times higher.

Chechens cheated in the most devious way. Once a Chechen had the title in his hand, he paid only the official price, and there was as much chance of a seller getting the rest of his money as taking a bone from the jaws of a wolf. Of course the Chechen turned around and sold the car for full price. The tribe amassed fortunes at the South Port market. Not off every sale – that would destroy the incentive that brought fresh cars – but off an intelligent percentage. Chechens culled the market as if it were a flock of sheep that was all their own.

Jaak and Arkady dropped halfway down the queue and the detective nodded towards a car parked by itself at the end of the lane. It was an old, black, once-official Chaika sedan with a scalloped chrome grille rubbed to a mirror finish. Curtains were drawn across the side windows of the back seat.

'Fucking Arabs,' Jaak said.

'They're no more Arab than you are,' Arkady said. 'I thought you were free of prejudice. Makhmud is an old man.'

'I hope he's got the strength to show you his collection of skulls.'

Arkady went on alone. The last car for sale was a Lada so dented that it looked as if it had been rolled to the market end over end. Two young Chechens with tennis bags stopped to ask where he was headed. When Arkady mentioned Makhmud's name, they escorted him to the Lada, pushed him into the back, felt his arms, legs and torso for a gun or a wire and told him to wait. One went to the Chaika; the other got in front, opened his bag and turned to slide a gun between the two front seats so that the muzzle nestled in Arkady's lap.

The gun was a new single-barrel 'Bear' carbine cut to half-length and retooled for shot. The visors of the car were fringed with beads, the dash decorated with snapshots of grape vines, mosques, and decals of AC/ DC and Pink Floyd. An older Chechen got in behind the wheel, ignored Arkady and opened the Koran, droning aloud as he read. He had a heavy gold ring on the little finger of each hand. Another got in beside Arkady with a skewer of shashlik wrapped in paper and handed pieces of meat to everyone, including Arkady, not in a friendly fashion, more as if he were a despised guest. All they needed were mustachios and bandoliers, Arkady thought. The Lada pointed away from the market, but in the rear-view mirror he occasionally caught sight of Jaak examining different cars.

Chechens had nothing to do with Arabs. Chechens were Tartars, a western tide of the Golden Horde that had settled in the fastness of the Caucasus Mountains. Arkady studied the postcards on the dash. The city with the mosque was their mountain capital of Grozny, as in 'Ivan Grozny' – 'Ivan the Terrible'. Did that twist the Chechen psyche a little bit, growing up with a name like that?

Finally the first Chechen returned, accompanied by a boy not much bigger than a jockey. He had a heart-shaped face with raddled skin and eyes full of ambition. He reached into Arkady's jacket for his ID, studied it and slipped it back. To the man with the shotgun he said, 'He killed a prosecutor.' So by the time Arkady got out of the car, he was accorded some respect.

Arkady followed the boy up to the Chaika, where the rear door opened for him. A hand reached out and pulled him in by the collar.

Vintage Chaikas had a stately Soviet style: upholstered ceiling, elaborate ashtrays, banquette seats with corded piping, air conditioning, plenty of room for the boy and driver up front and Makhmud and Arkady in the back. Also bulletproof windows, he was sure.

Arkady had seen pictures of mummified figures dug from the ashes of Pompeii. They looked like Makhmud, bent and gaunt, no lashes or eyebrows, skin a parchment grey. Even his voice sounded burned. He turned stiffly, as if hinged, to hold his visitor at arm's length and stare with eyes as black as little coals.

'Excuse me,' Makhmud said. 'I had this operation. The wonder of Soviet science. They fix your eyes so you don't have to wear glasses anymore. They don't do this operation anywhere else in the world. What they don't tell you is from then on you only see at one distance. The rest of the world is a blur.'

'What did you do?' Arkady asked.

'I could have killed the doctor. I mean, I really could

have killed the doctor. Then I thought about it. Why did I have this operation? Vanity. I'm eighty years old. It was a lesson. Thank God I'm not impotent.' He held Arkady steady. 'I can see you right now. You don't look very good.'

'I need some advice.'

'I think you need more than advice. I had them keep you down there while I asked some questions about you. I like to have information. Life is so various. I've been in the Red Army, White Army, German Army. Nothing is predictable. I hear that you've been an investigator, a convict, an investigator again. You're more confused than I am.'

'Easily.'

'It's an unusual name. You're related to Renko, that madman from the war?'

'Yes.'

'You have mixed eyes. I see a dreamer in one eye and a fool in the other. You see, I'm so old now that I'm going around a second time and I appreciate things. Otherwise you go crazy. I gave up cigarettes two years ago for the lungs. You have to be positive to do that. You smoke?'

'Yes.'

'Russians are a gloomy race. Chechens are different.'

'People say that.'

Makhmud smiled. His teeth looked oversized, like a dog's. 'Russians smoke, Chechens burn.'

'Rudy Rosen burned.'

For an old man, Makhmud changed expression quickly. 'Him and his money, I heard.'

'You were there,' Arkady said.

The driver turned. Though he was big, he was almost as young as the boy beside him, with acne clustered at the corners of a pouty mouth, hair long at the back, short at the sides, bangs a spray-painted orange. It was the athlete from the Intourist bar.

Makhmud said, 'This is my grandson Ali. The other is his brother Beno.'

'Nice family.'

'Ali is very fond of me, so he doesn't like to hear this sort of accusation.'

'That's not an accusation,' Arkady said. 'I was there, too. Maybe we're both innocent.'

'I was at home asleep. Doctor's orders.'

'What do you think might have happened to Rudy?'

'With this medication I have and oxygen tubes, I look like a cosmonaut and I sleep like a baby.'

'What happened to Rudy?'

'My opinion? Rudy was a Jew, and a Jew thinks he can eat with the devil and keep his nose from being bitten off. Maybe Rudy knew too many devils.'

Six days a week, Rudy and Makhmud had taken Turkish coffee together while they bargained over exchange rates. Arkady remembered seeing the fleshy Rudy across the table from the bone-thin Makhmud, and wondering who would eat whom.

'You were the only one he was afraid of.'

Makhmud rejected the compliment. 'We had no

problem with Rudy. Other people in Moscow think the Chechens should go back to Grozny, back to Kazan, back to Baku.'

'Rudy said you were out to get him.'

'He was lying.' Makhmud dismissed the idea like a man used to demanding belief.

'It's hard to argue with the dead,' Arkady noted as tactfully as he could.

'Do you have Kim?'

'Rudy's bodyguard? No. He's probably looking for you.'

Makhmud said to the front of the car, 'Beno, could we have some coffee?'

Beno passed back a thermos, small cups and saucers, spoons and a paper bag of sugar cubes. The coffee came out of the thermos like black sludge. Makhmud's hands were large, fingers and nails curved; the rest of him might have shrunk with age, but not the hands.

'Delicious,' Arkady said. He felt his heart fibrillate with joy.

'The mafias used to have real leaders. Antibiotic was a theatrical promoter, and if he liked a show he'd hire the whole hall for himself. He was like family to the Brezhnevs. A character, a racketeer, but his word was good. Remember Otarik?'

'I remember he was a member of the Writers' Union even though his application had twenty-two grammatical errors,' Arkady said.

'Well, writing was not his main occupation. Anyway, now they're replaced by these new businessmen like

Borya Gubenko. It used to be that a gang war was a gang war. Now I have to watch my back two ways, from hit men *and* militia.'

'What happened to Rudy? Was he part of a gang war?'

'You mean a war between Moscow businessmen and bloodthirsty Chechens? We're always the mad dogs; Russians are always the victims. I'm not addressing you personally, but as a nation you see everything backwards. Could I give you a small example from my life?'

'Please.'

'Did you know that there was a Chechen Republic? Our own. If I bore you, stop me. The worst crime of old people is to bore young people.' Even as he said this, Makhmud clutched Arkady's collar again.

'Go on.'

'Some Chechens had collaborated with the Germans, so in February 1944 mass meetings were called in every village. There were soldiers and brass bands; people thought it was a military celebration and everyone came. You know what those village squares are like – a loudspeaker in each corner playing music and announcements. Well, this announcement was that they had one hour to gather their families and possessions. No reason given. One hour. Imagine the scene. First the pleading, which was useless. The panic of looking for small children, for grandparents, forcing them to dress and dragging them out of the door to save their lives. Deciding what you should take, what you can carry. A bed, a chest of drawers, a goat? The soldiers loaded everyone into lorries. Studebakers. People thought the Americans were behind it and Stalin would save them!'

In Makhmud's stare, Arkady saw black irises locked like the lens of a camera. 'In twenty-four hours there wasn't a Chechen left in the Chechen Republic. Half a million people gone. The lorries put them on trains, in unheated freight carriages which travelled for week after week after week in the middle of winter. Thousands died. My first wife, my first three boys. Who knows at what siding the guards threw their bodies out? When the survivors were finally allowed to climb down from the carriages they found themselves in Kazakhstan, in Central Asia. Back home, the Chechen Republic was liquidated. Russian names were given to our towns. We were removed from maps, histories, encyclopedias. We disappeared.

'Twenty, thirty years went by before we managed to return to Grozny, even to Moscow. Like ghosts, we make our way back home to see Russians in our houses, Russian children in our yards. And they look at us and they say, "Animals!" Now you tell me, who has been the animal? They point fingers at us and shout, "Thief!" Tell me, who's the thief? When anyone dies, they find a Chechen and say, "Murderer!" Believe me, I would like to meet the murderer. Do you think I should feel sorry for them now? They deserve everything that's happening to them. They deserve us.' Makhmud's eyes became their most intense, dead coals come alive, and then dimmed. His fingers unclenched and released Arkady's lapel. Fatigue folded into a smile across his face. 'I apologize, I wrinkled your jacket.'

'It came wrinkled.'

'Nevertheless, I got carried away.' Makhmud smoothed the jacket. He said, 'I'd like nothing more than to find Kim. Grapes?'

Beno handed back a wooden bowl overflowing with green grapes. By now, Arkady could see not so much a family resemblance among him, Ali and Makhmud as a likeness of species, like the bill of a hawk. Arkady took a handful. Makhmud opened a short knife with a hooked blade to slice off a bunch carefully. When he ate, he rolled down the window to spit the seeds on the ground.

'Diverticulitis. I'm not supposed to swallow them. It's a terrible thing to grow old.'

Chapter Six

Polina was dusting Rudy's bedroom for prints when Arkady arrived from the car market. He had never seen her out of her raincoat before. Because of the heat, she wore shorts, had knotted her shirt into a halter and tied her hair up in a kerchief, and with her rubber gloves and little camel's-hair brush she looked like a child playing house.

'We dusted before.' Arkady dropped his jacket on the bed. 'Aside from Rudy's prints, the technicians got nothing.'

'Then you have nothing to lose,' Polina said cheerfully. 'The human mole is in the garage tapping for trapdoors.'

Arkady opened the window over the courtyard and saw Minin in his hat and coat in the open door of the garage. 'You shouldn't call him that.'

'He hates you.'

'Why?'

Polina rolled her eyes, then climbed a chair to dust the mirror on the chest of drawers. 'Where's Jaak?'

'We've been promised another car. If he gets it, he'll go to the Lenin's Path Collective Farm.'

'Well, it's potato time. They can use Jaak.'

At a variety of odd locations – on hairbrush and

headboard, inside the medicine-cabinet door and under the raised toilet lid – were the shadowy ovals of brushed prints. Others had already been lifted with tape and transferred to slides lying on the night table.

Arkady pulled on rubber gloves. 'This isn't your job,' he said.

'It isn't your job, either. Investigators are supposed to let detectives do the real work. I have the training for this and I'm better than the others, so why shouldn't I? Do you know why no one wants to deliver babies?'

'Why?' Immediately he was sorry he asked.

'Doctors don't want to deliver babies because they're afraid of AIDS, and because they don't trust Soviet rubber gloves. They wear three or four at a time. Imagine trying to deliver a baby wearing four pairs of gloves. They don't do abortions either, for the same reason. Soviet doctors would rather set women out about a hundred metres away and watch them explode. Of course, there wouldn't be so many babies if Soviet condoms didn't fit like rubber gloves.'

'True.' Arkady sat on the bed and looked around. Though he had followed Rudy for weeks, he still knew too little about the man.

'He didn't bring women here,' Polina said. 'There are no crackers, no wine, not even a condom. Women leave things – hairpins, make-up pads, face powder on a pillow. It's too neat.'

How long was she going to be up on the chair? Her legs were whiter and more muscular than he would have expected. Perhaps she had wanted to be a ballerina at one time. Black curls escaped from the discipline of her kerchief and coiled at the nape of her neck.

'You're working room by room?' Arkady asked.

'Yes.'

'Shouldn't you be out with your friends playing volleyball or something?'

'It's a little late for volleyball.'

'Did you lift prints from the videotapes?'

'Yes.' She bounced a glare off the mirror.

'I got you more morgue time,' Arkady said to mollify her. Isn't that the way to soothe a woman, he thought, by offering her more time in a morgue? 'Why do you want to go back inside Rudy?'

'There was too much blood. I did get laboratory results on the blood from the car. It was his type, at least.'

'Good.' If she was happy, he was happy. He turned on the television and VCR, inserted one of Rudy's tapes, pushed the 'Play' and 'Fast Forward'. Accompanied by high-speed gibberish, images rushed across the screen: the golden city of Jerusalem, Wailing Wall, Mediterranean beach, synagogue, orange grove, high-rise hotels, casinos, El Al. He slowed the tape to catch the narration, which was more glottal than Russian.

'Do you speak Hebrew?' Arkady asked Polina.

'Why in the world would I speak Hebrew?'

The second tape showed in rapid succession the white city of Cairo, pyramids and camels, Mediterranean beach, sailing boats on the Nile, muezzin on a minaret, date grove, high-rise hotels, Egyptair.

'Arabic?' Arkady asked.

'No.'

The third travelogue opened in a beer garden and raced through etchings of medieval Munich, aerial views of rebuilt Munich, shoppers on the Marienplatz, beer cellar, polka bands in lederhosen, Olympic stadium, Oktoberfest, rococo theatre, gilded angel of peace, autobahn, another beer garden, nearby Alps, vapour trail of Lufthansa. He rewound to the Alps to listen to a narration that was both ponderous and exuberant.

'You speak German?' Polina asked. The dusted mirror was starting to look like a collection of moth wings, each one an oval of whorls.

'A little.' Arkady had spent his Army years in Berlin listening to Americans and had picked up some German in the truculent fashion that Russians approach the language of Bismarck, Marx and Hitler. It wasn't only that Germans were a traditional foe; it was because the tsars for centuries had imported Germans as taskmasters, not to mention that the Nazis had regarded all Slavs as sub-human. There was a certain accretion of national ill will.

'Auf wiedersehen,' said the television.

'Auf wiedersehen.' Arkady turned the set off. 'Polina, auf wiedersehen. Go home, see your boyfriend, go to a film.'

'I'm almost done.'

So far, Polina seemed to have sensed more about the flat than Arkady had. He knew he was missing not so much clues as essence. Rudy's phobia about physical contact had created a flat that was solitary and sterile. No ashtrays, not even dog-ends. He craved a cigarette, but didn't dare upset the flat's hygienic balance.

Rudy's single weakness of the flesh appeared to be food. Arkady opened the refrigerator. Ham, fish and Dutch cheese were still cool, in place and overwhelming even to a man who had just eaten an appetizer of Makhmud's grapes. The food was probably from Stockmann's, the Helsinki department store that delivered complete smorgasbords, office furniture and Japanese cars for hard currency to Moscow's foreign community; God forbid they should have to live like Russians. In its rind of wax, the cheese shone like a mushroom cap.

Polina stepped into the bedroom doorway, one arm already thrust into her raincoat. 'Are you examining the evidence or consuming it?'

'Admiring it, actually. Here is cheese from cows who graze on grass that grows on dykes a thousand miles away, and it's not as rare as Russian cheese. Wax is a good medium of prints, isn't it?'

'Humidity is not the best atmosphere.'

'It's too humid for you?'

'I didn't say I couldn't do it, I just didn't want to get your hopes up.'

'Do I look like a man with high hopes?'

'I don't know; you're different today.' It was not characteristic of Polina to be uncertain about anything. 'You—'

Arkady put a finger to his lips. He heard a barely

audible noise, like the fan of a refrigerator, except that he was standing by the refrigerator.

'A toilet,' Polina said. 'Someone's relieving themselves on the hour.'

Arkady went to the water closet and touched the pipes. Usually pipes banged and rang like chains. This sound was fainter, more mechanical than liquid, and inside Rosen's flat, not out. It stopped.

'On the hour?' Arkady asked.

'On the dot. I looked, but I didn't find anything.'

Arkady went into Rudy's office. The desk was undisturbed, phone and fax silent. He tapped the fax and a red 'alert' light blinked. Tapped harder and the button winked as regularly as a beacon. The volume had been turned all the way down. He pulled the desk forward and found facsimile paper that had scrolled between the desk and the wall. 'First rule of investigation: pick things up,' he said.

'I hadn't dusted here yet.'

The paper was still warm. On top was the transmission date and time, one minute ago. The message, typed in Russian, read: 'Where is Red Square?'

Anyone with a map could answer that. He read the previous message. The transmission time on it was sixty-one minutes ago: 'Where is Red Square?'

You didn't need a map. Ask anyone in the world – up the Nile, in the Andes or even in Gorky Park.

There were five messages in all, each sent on the hour, with the same insistent demand: 'Where is Red Square?' The first also said, 'If you know where Red

Square is, I can offer contacts with international society for ten per cent finder's fee.'

A finder's fee for Red Square sounded like easy money. The machine had automatically printed a long transmitting phone number across the top. Arkady called the international operator, who identified the country code as Germany and the city as Munich. 'Do you have one of these?' he asked Polina.

'I know a boy who does.'

Close enough. Arkady wrote on Rudy's stationery, 'Need more information.' Polina inserted the page, picked up the receiver and dialled the number, which answered with a ping. A light flashed over a button that said 'Transmit' and when she pushed the button the paper started to roll.

Polina said, 'If they're trying to reach Rudy, they don't know he's dead.'

'That's the idea.'

'So you'll get pointless information or find yourself in an embarrassing social situation. I can't wait.'

They waited an hour without an answer. Finally Arkady went downstairs and visited the garage, where Minin was tapping the floor with the butt end of a shovel. The hanging light bulb had been replaced by one with greater wattage. Tyres had been moved to the side and stacked according to size, rubber belts and oil cans enumerated and tagged. Minin's only concession to the heat had been to remove his coat and jacket; his hat stayed on his head, casting an umbra across the middle of his face. The man in the moon, Arkady thought. When he saw his superior, Minin came to sullen attention.

Arkady thought the problem was that Minin was the classic dwarf child. Not that he was small, but Minin was the unloved creature, the sort who always felt despised. Arkady could have him removed from the team – an investigator didn't have to accept everyone assigned to him – but he didn't want to justify Minin's attitude. Also, he hated to see an ugly man pout.

'Investigator Renko, when Chechens are on the loose, I think I would be of better use on the street than in this garage.'

'We don't know if we're after Chechens, and I need a good man doing this. Some people would slip the tyres under their coat.'

Humour seemed to give Minin a wide berth. He said, 'Do you want me to go upstairs and watch Polina?'

'No.' Arkady tried human interest. 'There's something new about you, Minin. What is it?'

'I don't know.'

'That's it.' On Minin's sweat-darkened shirt was the enamel pin of a red flag. Arkady would never have noticed it if he hadn't taken off his jacket. 'A membership pin?'

'Of a patriotic organization,' Minin said.

'Very stylish.'

'We stand for the defence of Russia, for the repeal of so-called laws that steal the people's wealth and give it to a narrow group of vultures and money-changers, for a cleansing of society and an end to chaos and anarchy. You don't mind?' It was a challenge as much as a question.

'Oh, no. On you it looks right.'

Driving to Borya Gubenko's, it seemed to Arkady that the summer evening had fallen like a silence. Streets vacant, taxis camped outside hotels, refusing to carry anyone but tourists. One shop was besieged with shoppers, while those on either side were so empty they seemed deserted. Moscow looked like a cannibalized city, without food, petrol or basic goods. Arkady felt like a cannibalized man, as if he might be missing a rib, a lung, some part of his heart.

It was oddly reassuring that someone in Germany had asked a Soviet speculator about Red Square in English. It was confirmation that Red Square still existed.

Borya Gubenko picked a ball from a pail, set it on his tee, cautioned Arkady about the backswing, concentrated, drew the club back so that it seemed to encircle his body, uncoiled and lashed the ball on a line.

'Want to try it?' he asked.

'No, thanks. I'll just watch,' Arkady said.

A dozen Japanese teed up on squares of plastic grass, drew back their clubs and drove golf balls that sailed as diminishing white dots the interior length of the factory. The irregular pop of balls sounded like small-arms fire – appropriately since the factory used to turn out bullet casings. During the White Terror, Patriotic War and Warsaw Pact, workers had manufactured millions of brass and steel-core cartridges. To convert to a golf range, assembly lines had been scrapped and the floor painted a pastoral green. A couple of immovable metal presses were screened by cut-out trees, a touch appreciated by the Japanese, who wore golf caps even indoors. Besides Borya, the only Russian players Arkady could see were a mother and daughter in matching short skirts taking a lesson.

On the far wall, balls thudded against a green canvas marked in ascending distances: two hundred, two hundred and fifty, three hundred metres.

Borya said, 'I confess, I overestimate a little bit. A happy customer is the secret of business.' He posed for Arkady. 'What do you think? The first Russian amateur champion?'

'At least.'

Borya's big frame was tamed by a plush pastel sweater, his unruly hair wetted into sleek golden wings around a watchful, angular face with eyes of crystal blue.

'Look at it this way.' Borya plucked another ball from the pail. 'I spent ten years playing football for Central Army. You know the life: terrific money, flat, car, as long as you can perform. You get injured, you start to slip and suddenly you're on the street. You go right from the top straight to the bottom. Everyone wants to buy you a beer, but that's it. That's the payoff for ten years and your busted knees. Old boxers, wrestlers, hockey players, same story. No wonder they go into the mafia. Or worse, start playing American-style football. Anyway, I was lucky.'

More than lucky. Borya seemed to have crystallized into a new, successful persona. In the New Moscow, no one was as transcendentally popular and prosperous as Borya Gubenko.

Behind the driving range, slot machines sang beside a bar decorated with Marlboro posters, Marlboro ashtrays and Marlboro lamps. Borya lined up his shot. If possible, he looked more robust than in his playing days. Also sleek, like a well-groomed lion. He swung and froze, studying a drive that faded as it rose.

'Tell me about this club,' Arkady said.

'It's hard-currency, members only. The more exclusive you make it, the more foreigners want in. I'll tell you the secret,' Borya said.

'Another secret?'

'Location. The Swedes have poured millions into an eighteen-hole resort outside town. It's going to have conference facilities, communications centre, super security so that businessmen and tourists can come without ever really staying in Moscow. But that sounds stupid to me. If I was going to invest money somewhere, I'd want to see what it's really like. Anyway, the Swedes are way out of town. In comparison, we're central, right on the river, practically across from the Kremlin. Look what it took – a little paint, Astroturf, clubs and balls. We're in guidebooks and foreign magazines. And all of it was Rudy's idea.' He looked Arkady up and down. 'What sport did you play?'

'Football in school.'

'Position?'

'Mainly goal.' Arkady wasn't going to claim any athletic distinction in Borya's company.

'Like me. The best position. You study, see the attack, learn anticipation. The game comes down to a couple of kicks. And when you commit, you commit, right? If you try to save yourself, that's how you get hurt. For me, of course, playing was a way to see the world. I didn't understand what food was until we went to Italy. I still referee some international games just to eat well.'

'To see the world' had to be a mild description of Borya's ambition, Arkady thought. Gubenko had grown up in the concrete 'Khrushchev Barracks' of Long Pond. In Russian, 'Khrushchev' rhymed with 'slum', giving bite to the title. Borya would have been raised on cabbage soup and cabbage hopes, and here he was talking about Italian restaurants.

Arkady asked, 'What do you think happened to Rudy?'

'I think that what happened to Rudy was a national disaster. He was the only real economist in the country.'

'Who killed him?'

Without hesitating, Borya said, 'Chechens. Makhmud is a bandit with no concept of Western style or business. The fact is he holds everyone else back. The more fear the better – never mind that it closes a market down. The more unsettled everyone else is, the stronger the Chechens become.'

On the tees a tier overhead, the Japanese hit a unified salvo, followed by excited shouts of 'Banzai!'

Borya smiled and pointed his club up. 'They fly from Tokyo to Hawaii for a weekend of golf. I have to throw them out at night.'

'If Chechens killed Rudy,' Arkady said, 'they had to get past Kim. For all his reputation – muscle man, martial arts – he doesn't seem to have been much protection. When your best friend Rudy was looking for a bodyguard, didn't he come to you for advice?'

'Rudy carried a lot of money and he was concerned about his safety.'

'And Kim?'

'The factories in Lyubertsy are closing down. The problem with interacting with the free market, Rudy always said, is that we manufacture shit. When I suggested Kim to Rudy, I thought I was doing them both a favour.'

'If you find Kim before we do, what will you do?'

Borya aimed the club at Arkady and dropped his voice. 'I'd call you. I would. Rudy was my best friend and I think Kim helped the Chechens, but do you think I'd endanger all this, everything I've achieved, to take some sort of primitive revenge? That's the old mentality. We have to catch up with the rest of the world or we're going to be left behind. We'll all be in empty buildings and starving to death. We have to change. Do you have a card?' he asked suddenly.

'Party card?'

'We collect business cards and have a drawing once a month for a bottle of Chivas Regal.' Borya controlled a smile, barely.

Arkady felt like an idiot. Not an ordinary idiot, but an out-dated, socially uninformed idiot.

Borya put down his driver and proudly led Arkady to the buffet. In chairs upholstered in red and black Marlboro colours were more Japanese in baseball caps and Americans in golfing shoes. Arkady suspected that Borya had hit upon the exact decor of an airport lounge, the natural setting of the international business traveller. They could have been in Frankfurt, Singapore, Saudi Arabia – anywhere – and for this very reason felt at home. Above the bar a television showed CNN. The crowded buffet offered an array of smoked sturgeon and trout, red and black caviar, eggplant caviar, German chocolates and Georgian pastries around bottles of sweet champagne, Pepsi, pepper vodka, lemon vodka and five-star Armenian cognac. Arkady was dizzy from the smell of food.

'We also have karaoke nights, putting tournaments and corporate parties,' Borya said. 'No prostitutes, no hustlers. It couldn't be more innocent.'

Like Borya? The man had not only gone from football to the mafia but had made the second, steeper evolutionary leap to entrepreneur. The way his Western sweater draped his shoulders, the directness of his eyes, the freer gestures of clean hands all said: businessman.

Borya gave a discreet, proprietary wave and a uniformed waitress immediately arrived from the buffet and set a plate of silver herring on the table in front of Arkady. The fish seemed to swim before his eyes.

Borya asked, 'Remember unpolluted fish?'

'Not well enough, thanks.' Arkady dug a last cigarette from a pack. 'Where do you get the fish?'

'Like anyone else. I trade this, barter that.'

'On the black market?'

Borya shook his head. 'Direct. Rudy said there wasn't a farm or fishing collective that wasn't willing to do business if you could offer more than rubles.'

'Rudy told you what to offer?'

Borya held Arkady's eyes with his. 'Rudy started out as a football fan. He ended up as an older brother. He simply wanted to see me happy. He gave me advice. That doesn't sound like a crime to me.'

'It depends on the advice.' Arkady wanted to provoke a reaction.

Borya's eyes were clear as water, without a ripple. 'Ruby always said there was no need to break the law, just to rewrite it. He looked ahead.'

'Do you know an Apollonia Gubenko?' Arkady asked.

'My wife. I know her well.'

'Where was she the night Rudy died?'

'What does it matter?'

'There was a Mercedes registered in her name at the

black market about thirty metres from where Rudy died.'

Borya took a little longer to answer. He glanced at the television, where an American tank was rolling through a desert. 'She was with me. We were here.'

'At two in the morning?'

'I often close after midnight. I remember we went home in my car because Polly's was in a garage being repaired.'

'You have two cars?'

'Between Polly and me, two Mercedes, two BMWs, two Volgas and a Lada. In the West people can invest in stocks and bonds. We have cars. The trouble is, as soon as a nice car goes to the garage, someone borrows it. I can try to find out who.'

'You're sure she was with you? Because a woman was seen in it.'

'I treat women with respect. Polly is her own person, she doesn't have to answer to me for every second of her time, but that night she was with me.'

'Did anyone else see you here?'

'No. The secret of business is you stay close to the cash register and lock up yourself.'

'There are a lot of secrets in business,' Arkady said.

Borya leaned forward and spread his hands. Although Arkady knew he was a big man, he was surprised at the wingspan. He remembered how Borya the player used to roar out of the Central Army goal to stop penalty kicks. Gubenko let his hands fall. His voice was soft. 'Renko?'

'Yes?'

'I'm not going to kill Kim. That's your job. If you want to do society a favour, kill Makhmud, too.'

Arkady looked at his watch. It was eight p.m. He had already missed the first broadcast and his mind was starting to wander. 'I have to go.'

Borya steered Arkady through the bar. Another discreet signal had been sent because the waitress caught up to them with two packs of cigarettes which Borya stuffed into Arkady's jacket.

The mother and daughter made their way around the tables. They shared the same fine features and grey eyes. When the woman spoke, she had a faint lisp; Arkady was relieved to hear an imperfection.

'Borya, the teacher's waiting for you.'

'The pro, Polly. The pro.'

'Armenian nationalists attacked Soviet Internal troops again yesterday, inflicting ten deaths and as many wounded,' Irina said. 'The object of the Armenian attack was a Soviet Army depot, which they ransacked, removing small arms, assault rifles, mines, a tank, a personnel carrier, mortars and anti-tank guns. The Moldavian Supreme Soviet yesterday declared its sovereignty, three days after the Georgian Supreme Soviet did the same.'

Arkady set the table with brown bread, cheese, tea and cigarettes and sat facing the radio as if it had come to dinner. He should have returned to Rudy's flat; yet here he was, a man with no will, in time for her broadcast. What apocalyptic news she had, but it didn't matter.

'Rioting continued in Kirgizia between Kirgiz and Uzbeks for the third straight day. Armoured personnel carriers patrolled the streets of Osh after Uzbeks took control of the downtown tourist hotels and directed automatic fire at the local offices of the KGB. Deaths in the unrest now total two hundred and the question of draining the Uzgen Canal to find more bodies has been raised.'

The bread was fresh and the cheese was sweet. A breeze drifted in at the open window and the curtain stirred like a skirt.

'A Red Army spokesman admitted today that Afghan insurgents have penetrated the Soviet border. Since Soviet troops withdrew from Afghanistan, the border has become accessible to drug runners and to religious extremists who are urging Central Asian republics to begin a holy war against Moscow.'

The sun hung on the northern horizon, onion domes and chimneypots. Her voice was a shade huskier and her Siberian accent sounded more schooled and sophisticated. Arkady remembered her gestures, sometimes flamboyant, and the colour of her eyes, like amber. Listening, he found himself leaning towards the radio. He felt ridiculous, as if he should be holding up his side of the conversation.

'Miners in Donetsk yesterday demanded the resignation of the government and the removal of the Party, and announced the start of a new strike. Work stoppages

have also begun in all twenty-six mines in the Kara-
ganda Basin and in twenty-nine mines in Rostov-on-
Don. Mass rallies in support of the strikers were held
by miners in Sverdlovsk, Chelyabinsk and Vladivostok.'

The news was not important; he hardly heard it. It
was her voice and breath transmitted across a thousand
miles.

'Last night in Moscow, the Democratic Front rallied
outside Gorky Park to call for the "de-legalization" of
the Communist Party. At the same time, members of the
right-wing "Red Banner" met to defend the Party. Both
groups demanded the right to march in Red Square.'

She was Scheherazade, Arkady thought. Night after
night she could tell tales of oppression, insurrection,
strikes, and natural disaster, and he would listen as if
she were spinning stories of exotic lands, magical spices,
flashing scimitars and pearl-eyed dragons with scales of
gold. As long as she would talk to him.

Chapter Seven

At midnight, Arkady waited across from the Lenin Library, admiring the statues of Russian writers and scholars that hovered along the roofline. He remembered what he had heard about the building being ready to collapse. True enough, the statues looked ready to jump. When a shadow emerged and locked the door, Arkady crossed the street and introduced himself.

'An investigator? I'm not surprised.' Feldman wore a fur hat, carried a briefcase and looked like Trotsky, down to a goat's beard of snow white. He started a vigorous shuffle towards the river and Arkady fell in step beside him. 'I have my own key. I didn't steal anything. You want to search?'

Arkady ignored the invitation. 'How do *you* know Rudy?'

'It's the only time to work. I thank God I'm an insomniac. Are you?'

'No.'

'You look like one. See a doctor. Unless you don't mind.'

'Rudy?' Arkady tried again.

'Rosen? I didn't. We met once, a week ago. He wanted to talk about art.'

'Why art?'

'I'm a professor of art history. I told you I was a professor on the phone. You're a hell of an investigator, I can tell already.'

'What did Rudy ask?'

'He wanted to know everything about Soviet art. Soviet avant-garde art was the most creative, most revolutionary period in history, but Soviet man is an ignoramus. I couldn't educate Rosen in half an hour.'

'Did he ask about any paintings in particular?'

'No. But I catch your point and it is amusing. For years, the Party demanded Socialist Realism and people hung paintings of tractors on their walls and hid avant-garde masterpieces behind the toilet or under the bed. Now they're dragging them out. Suddenly Moscow is full of art curators. You like Socialist Realism?'

'Socialist Realism is one of my weakest areas.'

'Are you talking about art?'

'No.'

Feldman regarded Arkady with a more wary, interested eye. They were in the park behind the library, where steps ran between trees down to the river near the southwest corner of the Kremlin. Spotlights made the lower branches into lattices of gold that turned to black.

'I told Rosen that what people forget is that there actually was idealism at the beginning of the Revolution. Starvation and civil war aside, Moscow was the most exciting place in the world to be. When Mayakovsky said, "Let us make the squares our palettes, the streets our brushes," he meant it. Every wall was a painting.

There were painted trains, boats, aeroplanes, balloons. Wallpaper and dinner plates and gum wrappers were all created by artists who genuinely thought they were making a new world. At the same time women were marching for free love. They all believed anything was possible. Rosen asked how much one of those gum wrappers would be worth now.'

'The same question occurred to me,' Arkady admitted.

Feldman stomped down the stairs in disgust.

'Since avant-garde art was not approved, you chose a fairly suicidal speciality. Is that how you got used to working late at night?' Arkady asked.

'Not a totally stupid observation.' Feldman stopped short. 'Why is red the colour of revolution?'

'It's traditional?'

'Prehistoric, not traditional. The two earliest habits of the apeman were cannibalism and painting himself red. Soviets are the only ones who still do it. Look what we did to the genius of the Revolution. Describe Lenin's tomb.'

'It's a square of red granite.'

'It's a Constructivist design inspired by Malevich. It's a red square on Red Square. There's more to it than just Lenin laid out like a smoked herring. Art was everywhere in those days. Tatlin designed a revolving skyscraper taller than the Empire State Building. Popova drew high fashions for peasants. The artists of Moscow were going to paint the trees of the Kremlin red. Lenin did object to that, but people thought that anything was possible. Those were days of hope, days of fantasy.'

'You lecture on this?'

'No one wants to hear. They're like Rosen, they only want to sell. I spend all day authenticating art for idiots.'

'Rosen had something to sell?'

'Don't ask me. We were supposed to meet two days ago. He didn't come.'

'Then why do you think he had something to sell?'

'Today everyone is selling everything they have. And Rosen said he'd found something. He didn't say what.'

At the embankment Feldman looked around with such fervour that Arkady could nearly imagine painted trees in the Kremlin gardens, amazons marching on Gorky Street, dirigibles towing propaganda posters under the moon.

'We live in the archaeological ruins of that new world that never was. If we knew where to dig, who knows what we would find?' Feldman asked and trudged on alone across the bridge.

Arkady wandered along the embankment wall towards his flat. He didn't feel sleepy, but he didn't feel like an insomniac. Just the word made him restless.

He found no amazons along the river. There were fishermen baiting hooks. A couple of years of his exile had been spent on a Pacific trawler. He had always appreciated how at dusk the rustiest, most nondescript ship became a dazzling and intricate constellation of stars, with fishing lights on masts, booms, gunwales, bridge, ramp and deck. It occurred to him now that the same could be done for Moscow's nocturnal fishermen, with batteries and lamps on their hats, belts and the tips of their poles.

Maybe the problem wasn't insomnia. Maybe he was crazy. Why was he trying to find out who killed Rudy? When an entire society was collapsing like so many rotten beams, what difference did it make who murdered one black-market speculator? Anyway, this wasn't the real world. The real world was out there where Irina lived. Here he was one more shadow in a cave, where he couldn't sleep anyway.

Straight ahead the silhouette of St Basil's stood like a crowd of turbaned Moors backlit by the all-night floodlights of the square. In shadow at the stone base of the cathedral were about a hundred soldiers from the Kremlin barracks in full field gear with radio packs and submachine guns.

Red Square itself rose as a vast hill of cobblestones. To the left, the Kremlin was illuminated, bricks nearly white, with swallowtail battlements that were grace notes on a fortress that seemed to stretch as far as the Chinese Wall. The spires above the gates looked like churches that had been captured, roped, dragged from Europe and erected as trophies to a tsar, topped now by ruby stars. Shimmering in upturned lights, the Kremlin was midway between reality and dream, an immense, oppressive vision. From the gate at Spassky Tower a black sedan issued like a bat and flitted across the stones.

Far off, at the head of the square, a four-storey banner for Pepsi covered the façade of the Army Museum. To his right the classical stone face of GUM, the world's largest and emptiest department store, shrank into the dark. From the roof of GUM and from the Kremlin wall, cameras constantly monitored the square, but no floodlights were bright enough to penetrate the valley of shadow in the centre of the square, where Arkady was. No individual there would be more than a blip on a grey screen. The sheer size of scale and awesome vacuum of the square didn't so much uplift the soul as both hide it and suggest how inconsequential it was.

Except for one soul. When Lenin lay dying, he begged for no memorials. The mausoleum Stalin built for him was a vengeful pile of crypts, a squat ziggurat of red and black under the battlements of the Kremlin wall. Empty tiers of white marble flanked it, the area where dignitaries would sit for the May Day parade. Lenin's name was inscribed in red letters above the door of the tomb. At the door, two guards of honour, boy sergeants with white gloves and faces as pale as waxworks, swayed with fatigue.

Ordinary traffic was barred from the square, but as Arkady turned away from the tomb a black Zil rolled out of Cherny Street and, racing at official speed, crossed in front of GUM towards the river and sank into the dark around St Basil's. Tyres squealed, a sharp sound of protest that reverberated the length of the square.

The Zil came back. Because the car's headlights were

dark, it was too late when Arkady realized it was coming straight at him. When he started to run for the museum, the Zil followed, its bumper almost on his heels. He darted left towards the tomb and the big car roared by and cut in front. He dodged the rear bumper and headed for Cherny Street. The Zil tipped, settled and lumbered towards him in a wider circle, the car's centrifugal force accelerating.

When his escape intersected the car's arc, Arkady dove. He rolled, rose and started dizzily back towards St Basil's but slipped on the stones. Headlights rose up. He fell to one knee and raised his arm across his eyes.

The Zil stopped directly in front of him. Four uniforms emerged from the halos exploding in his eyes. General's dark-green dress uniforms with brass stars, fringed shoulder boards and mosaics of medals behind ropes of golden braid. As his vision returned, Arkady saw that the men inside the uniforms were strangely shrunken, holding each other up. As the driver got out he almost fell. He wore a civilian sweater and jacket, topped by a sergeant major's cap. He was drunk and his eyes were leaking tears that rolled from his eyes to his jowls.

'Belov?' Arkady asked as he stood.

'Arkasha.' Belov's voice was as deep and hollow as a barrel. 'We were at your address and you were not at home. We went to your office and you weren't there. We were just driving around when we saw you, and then you ran.'

Arkady dimly recognized the generals, though they

were grey and stunted versions of the tall, impressive officers who used to trail behind his father. Here were the staunch heroes of the Siege of Moscow, the tank commanders of the Bessarabian offensive, the vanguard of the push to Berlin, each of the four properly wearing an Order of Lenin awarded for 'a decisive action that significantly altered the course of the war'. Except that Shuksin, who had always slapped his boots with a crop, was now so shrivelled and bent that he was hardly much higher than the top of those boots, and Ivanov, who had always claimed the privilege of carrying his father's field case of plans, was as stooped as an ape. Kuznetsov had turned as round as a child, whereas Gul was a skeleton, his vigour and ferocity reduced to bristles of hair jutting from his eyebrows and ears. Though Arkady had hated them all his life – despised them, really, because they abused him out of sycophancy rather than evil – he was astonished at their feebleness.

Boris Sergeyevich was different. He had been Sergeant Belov, his father's driver, the very same bodyguard who had escorted the young Arkady to Gorky Park. Later Boris became Investigator Belov, though his gift was less for legal scholarship than for devotion to orders and iron-clad loyalty. His attitude towards Arkady had never been less than adoration. Arkady's arrest and exile was something Belov had never grasped – like, say, French or quantum mechanics.

Belov removed his cap and placed it under his left arm as if reporting for duty. 'Arkady Kyrilovich, it is my painful task to inform you that your father, General Kyril Ilyich Renko, has died.'

The generals advanced and shook Arkady's hand.

'He should have been Marshal of the Army,' Ivanov said.

Shuksin said, 'We were comrades in arms. I marched into Berlin with your father.'

Gul waved a rusty arm. 'I marched here in this same square with your father and laid a thousand Fascist flags at Stalin's feet.'

'Our most sincere condolences for this immeasurable loss.' Kuznetsov sobbed like an aunt.

Belov said, 'The funeral is already arranged for Saturday. That's soon, but your father left instructions for everything, as usual. He wanted me to give you this letter.'

'I don't want it.'

'I have no idea of the contents.' Belov tried to push an envelope inside Arkady's jacket. 'Father to son.'

Arkady knocked Belov's hand away. He was surprised by his own brusqueness to a good friend and by the depth of his revulsion towards the others. 'No, thanks.'

Shuksin took a wobbly step towards the Kremlin. '*Then* the army was appreciated. Soviet power meant something. *Then* the Fascists shit in their pants whenever we blew our nose.'

Gul picked up the theme. 'Now we crawl to Germany to kiss their arse. That's what we get for letting them get off their knees.'

'And what do we get for saving Hungarians and Czechs and Poles except the spit on our face?' The passion of his question was too much for Ivanov; the ancient bearer of the field case slumped against the fender of the car. They were all so thoroughly soaked with vodka, Arkady realized, that a match would set them off like rags.

'We saved the world, remember?' Shuksin demanded. 'We saved the world!'

Belov pleaded. 'Why?'

'He was a killer,' Arkady said.

'That was war.'

Gul asked, 'Do you think *we* would have lost Afghanistan? Or Europe? Or a single republic?'

'I'm not talking about the war,' Arkady said.

'Read the letter,' Belov begged.

'I'm talking about murder,' Arkady said.

'Arkasha, please!' Belov's eyes were as pleading as a dog's. 'For me. He's going to read the letter!'

The generals rallied, regrouped and crowded round. One push and they would probably collapse and turn to piles of dust, Arkady thought. Who did they see, he wondered? Him, his father, who? This could be his moment of vindictive triumph, a child's long-awaited fantasy. But it was too pathetic, and the generals, grotesque as they seemed, were also at their most human in this last stage of fangless dotage. He took the letter. It had a luminous quality and his name printed in spidery letters. It felt light, as if empty, to the hand.

'I'll read it later,' Arkady said and walked away.

'The Vagankovskoye Cemetery,' Belov called after him. 'Ten a.m.'

Or I'll throw it away, Arkady thought. Or burn it.

Chapter Eight

The following day was the final one of so-called 'hot investigation', the last day of official alerts at travel points, a peak time for frustration and argument. Arkady and Jaak chased false sightings of Kim north, west and south at all three Moscow airports. On the fourth tip, they headed east towards the dead end known as Lyubertsy.

'A new informant?' Arkady asked. He was driving, which was always a sign of bad humour.

'Totally new,' Jaak insisted.

'Not Julya,' Arkady said.

'Not Julya,' Jaak maintained.

'Borrow her Volvo yet?'

'I will. Anyway, it isn't Julya, it's a Gypsy.'

'A Gypsy!' With an effort, Arkady stayed on the road.

'You always say *I'm* prejudiced,' Jaak said.

'When I think of Gypsies, I think of poets and musicians, I don't think of reliable informants.'

Jaak said, 'Well, this guy would sell out his brother and that's what I call a reliable informant!'

Kim's motorcycle was there. An exotic, midnight-blue Suzuki, sculpture that linked two cylinders to two wheels, propped on a chrome kickstand at the back of a five-storey block of flats. Arkady and Jaak walked around the machine and admired it from every angle, taking an occasional glance at the building. The upper floors had balconies that were illegally enclosed. The ground was littered with refuse that seemed to have rained down from the windows: paper cartons, mattress springs, broken bottles. The next block was a hundred metres away. It was an incomplete landscape of buildings set far apart, sewer pipes lying in open trenches, concrete walkways that intersected among weeds. No one was walking. The sky was soiled with that particular kind of smog which expressed both industrial poison and despair.

Lyubertsy was all that Russians feared, which was to be outside the centre, not to be in Moscow or Leningrad, to be forgotten and invisible, as if the steppes started here, only twenty kilometres from the Moscow city limit. This was the vast population that moved on a straight track from day care to vocational school to assembly line to the long vodka queue to the grave.

Lyubertsy was also what Muscovites feared because its young factory workers took the train into Moscow to beat up privileged urban kids. It was only natural that Lyubers developed into a mafia with a special talent for tearing up rock shows and restaurants.

Jaak cleared his throat. 'In the cellar,' he said.

'The cellar?' That was the last thing Arkady wanted to hear. 'If we're going into the cellar, we should have bulletproof vests and lamps. You didn't order those?'

'I didn't know Kim was going to be here.'

'You didn't really believe your reliable informant, did you?'

'I didn't want to cause a lot of fuss,' Jaak said.

The trouble was that Lyubertsy cellars were not ordinary cellars, because until recently the private practice of unarmed oriental self-defence was against the law. In response, Lyuber muscle men had gone underground, refitting coal bins and boiler rooms as secret gymnasiums. Wandering alone around a Lyubertsy basement was not a prospect Arkady looked forward to, but he knew it would take a day to get special gear out of Moscow.

Three babushkas sat on the steps of the apartment building and watched over a playground where toddlers climbed into a sandbox that was made from rotting boards. The women had grey heads and black coats that made them look like crows.

Jaak asked, 'Remember the Komsomol club that called about a trophy for Rudy?'

'Vaguely.'

'Did I mention they keep calling?'

'Is this a good time to mention it?' Arkady asked.

'What about my radio?' Jaak asked.

'Your radio?'

'I bought it, I'd like to listen to it. You keep forgetting to bring it in.'

'Come by my place tonight and pick it up.'

They couldn't stand around the bike all day, Arkady thought. They had already been seen.

Jaak said, 'I have the gun, so I'll go in.'

'As soon as someone goes in, he's going to run. Since you have the gun, you wait here and stop him.'

Arkady walked up to the steps. The women regarded him as if he had arrived from a different solar system. He tried a smile. No, they didn't accept smiles here. He looked at the playground. It was empty; the kids were chasing cottonwood fluffs across the ground. He glanced back at Jaak, who was sitting on the bike and watching the building.

He moved along the base of the house until he found stairs leading down to a steel door. The door was unlocked and the other side of it was as black as an abyss. He called, 'Kim! Mikhail Kim! I want to talk to you!'

The answer was a profound hush. This was the sound of mushrooms growing, Arkady thought. He didn't want to enter the cellar. 'Kim?'

He felt around until he found a chain. When he pulled it a dozen dim light bulbs appeared, hanging from an electrical line tacked directly to bare support beams, not so much illumination as markers in the dark. As he stooped down it was like slipping into shallow water.

Clearance from floor to ceiling was a metre and a half, sometimes less. It was a crawl space excavated into a tunnel that worked its way over and around exposed pipes and valves. The underside of the house creaked overhead like a ship. He peeled cobwebs from his face and held his breath.

Claustrophobia was an old friend come along for the trip. The main thing was to keep moving from one tiny, shivering light bulb to the next. To breathe more evenly. Not to think about the weight of the building pressing down on his back. Not to consider the low quality of Soviet construction. Not to imagine for a moment that the tunnel resembled a mouldering grave.

At the last light bulb, Arkady squeezed through a second hatch and found himself on his hands and knees inside a low, windowless room that was smoothly plastered and painted and lit by a fluorescent tube. On the floor were mattresses, barbells and pulleys. The barbells were home-made from steel wheels crudely slotted to fit over bars. The pulleys were boiler plates cut up and strung with wire. On the walls were a full-length mirror and a picture of Schwarzenegger in total flex. A heavy bag hung by a chain from the ceiling. The air was pungent with sweat and talc.

Arkady got to his feet. Behind was a second room with benches and weights on blocks. Books on body-building and nutrition lay on a mattress. One bench was slick and showed the imprint of a sneaker. Set in the ceiling above the bench was a metal plate. There was a switch on the wall. Arkady turned the light off so that he wouldn't be a silhouette. He stood on the bench, lifted the plate and slid it back. He was beginning to hoist himself up when a gun pressed against his head.

It was dark. Arkady's head was halfway through the floor behind the stairs of the building foyer. The bench was a million miles below his swaying feet. The odour

of stale urine wafted from the foyer floor. He could see
a tricycle with no wheels, the corner detritus of cigarette
packs and condoms and, on the other end of the automatic, Jaak.

'You scared me,' Jaak said. He pointed the gun up.

'Really?' Arkady felt as if more than his feet were
dangling.

Jaak pulled him up. The foyer faced the opposite
street from the way they had approached the building.
Arkady leaned against the letter boxes. They were
torched, as usual. The foyer light was broken, of course.
No wonder people got killed.

Jaak was embarrassed. 'You were taking forever, so I
came around to see if there was another way in just as
you popped up.'

'I won't do it again.'

Jaak said, 'You should have a gun.'

'If I had a gun, we'd be a suicide pact.'

Arkady still felt dizzy when they went outside.

'Let's just watch the motorcycle,' Jaak suggested.

When they came around the building, Kim's beautiful
bike was gone.

The militia towed vehicular wrecks to a dock near the
South Port, handy for the metal stamps and car factories
of the Proletariat Borough. Whatever was remotely re-
usable had been stripped from them. These were the
bones of cars, and they had a kind of dignity, like dried
flowers. The dock had a vista of the entire southern end

of Moscow; it was not Paris, granted, but it possessed a certain sweep, the occasional gold cap of a church flashing in the shadow of industrial chimneys.

The evening sky was still lit. Arkady found Polina at the end of the dock working with a brush, cans of paint and squares of pressed wood. She had unbuttoned her raincoat, a concession to the balmy weather.

'Your message sounded urgent,' Arkady said.

'I thought you should see this.'

'What?' He looked around.

'You'll see.'

He was losing patience. 'There's no emergency? You're just working?'

'You're working, too.'

'Well, I lead an obsessed but empty life. Don't you want to go dancing or see a film with a friend?' Irina's newscasts had begun and he knew there was something he would rather be doing.

Polina daubed green paint on a square of wood balanced on the fender of a Zil from which doors and seats had been removed. She herself made rather a pretty picture, Arkady thought. If she had an easel and a little more technique . . . But she just slapped the paint on.

She seemed to sense his mind wandering. 'How did you do with Jaak?'

'It was not a day covered in glory.' He looked over her shoulder. 'Very green.'

'You're a critic?'

'Artists are so temperamental. I meant, as in

119

"expansively, generously green." ' He stood back to study the cityscape of black river, grey cranes and chimneys melting into a milky sky. 'What exactly are you painting?'

'The wood.'

'Ah.'

Polina had four different pots of green paint labelled CS1, CS2, CS3, CS4, separated from four pots of red labelled RS1, RS2, etc. Each pot had its own brush. The green paint had an infernal reek. He searched his pocket, but he had left Borya's Marlboros in his other jacket. When he did find Belomors, Polina blew the match out.

'Explosives,' she said.

'Where?'

'Remember, in Rudy's car we found traces of red sodium and copper sulphate? As you know, that's consistent with an incendiary device.'

'Chemistry wasn't my strong point.'

'What we couldn't understand,' Polina went on, 'was why we didn't find a timer or remote receiver. I did some research. You don't need a separate source of ignition if you combine red sodium and copper sulphate.'

Arkady looked at the pots at his feet again. RS: red sodium, marine-paint red, a deep carmine with an ochre tinge. CS: copper sulphate, a vile, stewpot green with a sniff of the devil. He put his matches away. 'You don't need a fuse?'

Polina set the wet board down on the Zil's front seat and brought out another on which the green paint was dry. Over the board she taped brown paper. 'Red sodium and copper sulphate are relatively harmless individually. Together, however, they react chemically and generate enough heat to ignite spontaneously.'

'Spontaneously?'

'But not immediately and not necessarily. That's the interesting part. It's a classic binary weapon: two halves of an explosive charge separated by a membrane. I'm testing different barriers such as cheesecloth, muslin and paper for time and effectiveness. I've already put painted boards in six cars.'

Polina took the brush from a can marked RS4 and started painting the paper in broad strokes of red sodium. Arkady noticed that she started with a 'W', like a house painter. 'If they did ignite immediately, you'd know by now,' he said.

'Yes.'

'Polina, don't we have militia technicians with bunkers and body armour and very long brushes to do this sort of thing?'

'I'm faster and better.'

Polina was quick. She kept red drips from falling into green cans and in less than a minute covered the papered board so that it had a completely scarlet surface.

Arkady said, 'So when wet red sodium soaks through the paper and makes contact with the copper sulphate, they heat up and ignite?'

'That's the idea, put very simply.' Polina took a notepad and pen from her raincoat and jotted the paint numbers and the time down to the second. With finished board and brush in hand, she started to stroll down the line of wrecks.

Arkady walked with her. 'I can't help thinking you'd be better off skipping through a park or sharing an ice-cream sundae with someone.'

The cars on the dock were crushed, rusted and stripped. A Volga was so twisted that its axle aimed at the sky. A blunt-nosed Niva wore its steering wheel through the front seat. They passed a Lada with its engine block resting ominously in the rear. Around the dock were darkened factories and military depots. Out on the river, the last hydrofoil of the evening slid by like a snake of lights.

Polina laid the red board by the brake pedal of a four-door Moskvitch and painted a '7' on the left front door. When she saw Arkady begin to approach the other six cars on the end of the dock, she said, 'You'd better wait.'

They sat in a Zhiguli from which windscreen and wheels had been removed, affording a low, clear view of the dock and the far bank.

Arkady said, 'A bomb inside the car, Kim outside. It seems a little redundant.'

Polina said, 'At the assassination of Duke Ferdinand, which started World War I, there were twenty-seven terrorists with bombs and guns at different points along the procession route.'

'You've made a study of assassinations? Rudy was only a banker, not an heir to the throne.'

'In contemporary attacks by terrorists, especially

against Western bankers, the car bomb is the weapon of choice.'

'You *have* made a study of this.' It made his heart sink.

'I'm still confused about the blood in Rudy's car,' Polina admitted.

'I'm sure you'll figure it out. You know, there's more to life than ... death.'

Polina had the dark curls of a girl painted by Manet, Arkady thought. She ought to be in a lace collar and long skirt, sitting at a wrought-iron table on sun-dappled grass, not in a wreck on a dock talking about the dead. He noticed her eyes observing him. 'You really do lead an empty life, don't you?' she said.

'Wait a second,' Arkady said. Somehow the conversation seemed to have been, without any warning or logic, reversed.

'You said so yourself,' she pointed out.

'Well, you don't have to agree.'

'Exactly,' Polina said. 'You can lead your empty life, but you criticize how I lead mine, even though I'm working day and night for you.'

The first car blew with a muffled sound like a damp drum. A white flash mixed with the explosion of wind-screen and windows. After a blink, and while crystallized glass was still raining down, the car interior filled with flames. Polina entered the time in her notepad.

Arkady asked, 'That didn't have a blasting cap or a fuse? Just chemicals?'

'Just what you saw, although with solutions at

different concentrations. I have others with phosphorus and aluminium powder. Those need a cap or some sort of blow to detonate.'

'That one seemed pretty effective,' Arkady said.

He had expected some sort of spontaneous combustion, but not an explosion of such strength. Already the fire had taken root, the front seat and dash covered with lapping flames that produced dark, noxious smoke. How did anyone ever escape car fires? 'Thanks for not letting me take a closer look,' Arkady said.

'Entirely my pleasure.'

'And I apologize for criticizing even by suggestion your professional dedication, since you're the only member of the team who has shown any competence. I'm in awe, really.'

While Polina scrutinized him for sarcasm, he lit a cigarette. 'I'd roll down the window if there were a window,' he said.

The second car burst into flames without the explosive force of the first, and the bomb in the third car was even weaker – hardly a blast at all, though it was followed by a steady, hard-working flame. The fourth met the initial standard. By now Arkady was a veteran observer and could appreciate the sequence: the initial eruption of crystallized safety glass, the blinding flare of ignition, the whump of compacted air, and then the two-step flowering of roseate flames and brown, toxic smoke. Polina jotted down notes. She had delicate hands made even smaller by the rolled cuffs of her coat. Her rapid writing was as neat as type.

Belov had said there would be a funeral for his father. Were they going to bury the body or a pot of ashes? They could skip the crematorium and bring the old man out here for a glorious post-mortem ride in one of Polina's flaming chariots. Irina could report it on the news as one more Russian atrocity.

It occurred to Arkady that cars were not meant for Russians. First of all, Russians didn't have enough roads free of frost heaves and mud wallows. More important, vehicles capable of any speed should not be placed in the hands of people given to vodka and melancholy.

'Did you have something else planned tonight?' Polina asked.

'No.'

The fifth and sixth cars exploded almost simultaneously, then burned very differently, one developing into a bowl of fire and the other, already a burnt-out shell, subsiding into guttering flames. No fire engines had arrived yet. The era of nightshifts was long over, and at this hour the factories around the dock were empty except for watchmen. Arkady wondered how much of the city he and Polina could torch before anyone noticed.

As she leafed through her notes, Polina said, 'I wanted to put dummies in the cars.'

'Dummies?'

'Mannequins. I wanted thermometers, too. I couldn't even find oven thermometers.'

'Everything's so hard to find.'

'Because chemical combustion is inexact, especially in the lead time to ignition.'

'It's my impression that it would have been more exact for Kim to spray Rudy with a sub-machine-gun. Not that I'm not having a wonderful time watching cars blow up. It's sort of like suttee. You know, how Indian women immolate themselves on their husbands' funeral pyres? This is like a grand suttee on the Ganges, except that we're on the Moscow and it's not the middle of the day, it's the middle of the night and we neglected to bring any widows. Even dummies. Otherwise, it's practically romantic.'

Polina said, 'That's hardly an analytical approach.'

'Analytical? I wouldn't need an oven thermometer. I smelled Rudy. He was done.'

Polina was stung. Arkady was shocked at himself. What could he say now? That he was tired, upset, wanted to be home cupping his ear to the radio? 'I'm sorry,' he said. 'That was mean.'

'I think you'd better get a different pathologist,' Polina said.

'I think I'd better go.'

As he got out, the seventh car exploded, shooting fountains of glass high into the air. After the clap of detonation, the glass rang like chimes as it fell and scattered in crystals around his feet. The Moskvitch burned like a furnace at full blast, white flames leaping excitedly from window to window, broadcasting a circle of heat that made Arkady flinch and step back. As the seat burned, the nature of the flames changed into roiling purplish smoke rich with toxin. Paint bubbled and the whole dock glowed with shining glass, like coals.

He noticed that Polina was making notes again. She would have made a good assassin, he thought. She was a good pathologist. He was an idiot.

Chapter Nine

'It's sad about Rudy. He was very human, warm, concerned about Soviet youth.' Antonov winced as one boy backed another into a corner and knocked out his mouthpiece. 'Many's the time he was here, encouraging the kids, telling them to mind the straight and narrow.' Antonov bobbed sympathetically as the beleaguered fighter slipped free. 'Stick him, stick him, *move*! Well, that's a good imitation of a propeller! Anyway, Rudy was like an uncle. This is not the centre of Moscow. These kids are not going to special schools for ballerinas. Hit him! But youth is our most precious possession. Every boy and girl in Komsomol gets a fair chance. Model planes, chess, basketball. I bet Rudy sponsored every club here. Backpedal! Not you! *Him!*'

Jaak hadn't checked in yet. Polina had called, but the last place Arkady had wanted to start the day was the morgue. Didn't she ever get her fill of gore? On the other hand, watching boys pummel each other was proving no cure for a headache. Master of Sport Antonov gave the impression of a man whose brains had long since been pounded into more solid stuff. He had a grey crewcut and flat, utilitarian features, and in his fists, so knotted that he seemed to have extra knuckles, he held a bell mallet and a watch. The boys in the ring wore leather helmets, tank tops, shorts. Their skin was as pale as potato flesh except where they'd been hit. Sometimes they looked like they were boxing, the next moment as if they were dancing badly. Besides the ring, the Leningrad Borough Komsomol gymnasium also gave room to wrestling mats and weights, so the walls resounded with the puffing of wrestlers and lifters. There were two different psychological types, Arkady thought: weightlifters were soloists of grunts, while wrestlers couldn't wait to get tangled. A dim light penetrated whitewashed windows, and an ancient reek clung to the air. Wrestling and boxing ladders framed the door and a sign that said CIGARETTES AND SUCCESS DON'T MIX!, which reminded Arkady he had unwittingly put on the jacket with Borya's two packs of Marlboros, so there was a bright side to things.

'Rudy was a sports enthusiast – that's why you asked me to come? You had a trophy for him?'

Antonov asked, 'He's really dead?'

'Absolutely dead.'

'Follow up, follow up!' Antonov shouted up at the ring. To Arkady he said, 'Forget the trophy.'

'Forget the trophy?' Antonov had called the office twice a day about the trophy.

'What's Rudy going to do with a trophy now?'

'That's what I wondered,' Arkady said.

'I don't want to be disrespectful, but I had a question. Say, in a cooperative, the person who signs the cheques dies. Does that mean the other partner in the cooperative gets whatever money is left in the account?'

'You were partners with Rudy?'

Antonov sneered as if the question were ridiculous. 'Not me personally, no. The club. Excuse me. Don't switch leads! If you're right-handed, stay right-handed!'

Arkady started to wake up. 'The club and Rudy?'

'Local Komsomols are allowed to be in cooperatives. It's only fair, and sometimes it helps to have an official partner involved when you want to bring in certain stuff.'

'Slot machines?' Arkady took the happiest guess.

Antonov remembered his watch and whacked the mallet on a pail. The fighters reeled away from each other, neither able to raise a glove.

'It's perfectly legal,' Antonov said and lowered his voice. 'TransKom Services, with a capital K.'

TransKom. The Young Communist League plus Rudy equalled the Intourist slot machines. Seen in the light of Rudy's talent, this dingy little Komsomol club was dross turned to gold. For Arkady it was a minor victory, admittedly inconsequential compared to finding Kim.

Antonov said, 'You'll see, the club's on the cooperative papers. There were the names of the partners, statement of services, bank accounts, everything.'

'You have the papers?'

'Rudy had all the papers,' Antonov said.

'Well, I think Rudy took them with him.'

The dead were perverse.

In the morgue they were patient. Stretcher trolleys lined the hall, the bodies under soiled sheets waiting their turn on the table with a final, supine lack of urgency. No matter to them if they rotted for lack of formaldehyde. There was no offence taken if an investigator lit an expensive American cigarette to mask the stench. Rudy was in a drawer, internal organs in a plastic bag between his legs. Polina, however, was gone.

Arkady found her midway in a queue of a thousand people queueing for beets in the small park next to Petrovka. Rain fell as a steady, insinuating drizzle that sparkled around lamplights. Some umbrellas were up, though not many, because people needed both hands free for bags. At the head of the queue soldiers piled sacks in the mud. With her raincoat buttoned to her chin, drops beaded on her dark hair, Polina looked as if she were being borne forward by a centipede of pinched eyes and mouths. There were other queues for eggs and bread, and a queue that wound around a kiosk for cigarettes. Food vigilantes patrolled the queues to make sure no one switched. Arkady didn't have his coupons, so all this plenty was wasted on him.

Polina said, 'I came here after the dock to finish up Rudy. I told you there was too much blood. He's all yours now.'

Arkady doubted there could ever be too much blood for Polina, but he maintained an attitude of appreciation. Obviously she had worked all night.

'Polina, I'm sorry about the dock. I'm terrible about forensic medicine and pathology. You have more nerve than I do.'

Behind Polina, a woman with a grey shawl, grey

eyebrows and moustache leaned towards him to demand, 'Are you trying to cut in?'

'No.'

The woman said, 'They should shoot people who cut in.'

'Watch him,' advised the man behind her. He was a short, bureaucratic type with an impressive briefcase, the kind that could hold a lot of beets. All the way down the queue, Arkady saw faces regarding him with suppressed fury. They moved one lock step forward, crowding to make a wall he couldn't breach.

'How long have you been queueing?' Arkady asked Polina.

'Just an hour. I'll get some beets for you,' she said and glared at the pair behind her. 'Fuck them.'

'What do you mean, "too much blood"?'

Polina shrugged; she had offered. 'Describe the explosions when Rudy died,' she said. 'What you saw, exactly.'

'Two bursts of flame,' Arkady said. 'The first was a surprise. It was brilliant, white.'

'That was the red sodium-copper sulphate device. The second burst?'

'The second was bright, too.'

'As bright?'

'Less.' He had run them together in his mind before. 'We didn't have a clear view, but maybe more orange than white. Then we saw burning money rising in the smoke.'

'So two bursts of flame, but only one hot enough to

leave a flash point in the car. Did you smell anything after the second burst?'

'Petrol.'

'The petrol tank?'

'That blew later.' Arkady watched a brawl at the kiosk, where a customer claimed he had been given only four packs for the month, not five. A pair of soldiers carried him like a suitcase, one arm around his neck and one around his crotch, and threw him into a van. 'Gary told us that Kim threw a bomb in the car. It could have been a Molotov cocktail, a bottle of petrol.'

'It was better than that,' Polina said.

'What's better?'

'Gelled petrol. Gelled petrol sticks and burns and burns. That's why there was so much blood.'

Arkady still didn't understand. 'Before, you said burning didn't cause bleeding.'

'I went over Rosen again. He simply didn't have the number or kind of cuts to produce all that blood inside the car and out. I know that the lab said it was his blood type, but this time I checked it myself. It wasn't his type. It wasn't even human blood. It was cattle blood.'

'Cattle blood?'

'Drain the blood through a cloth and use the serum. Mix it with petrol and a little coffee or baking soda. Stir until it gels.'

'A bomb of blood and petrol?'

'It's a guerrilla technique. I would have caught on

faster if the lab result had been correct,' Polina said. 'You can thicken petrol with soap, eggs or blood.'

'That must be why they're in short supply,' Arkady said.

The couple behind Polina were listening intently. 'Don't get eggs,' the woman warned. 'The eggs have salmonella.'

The bureaucrat countered, 'That is a baseless rumour started by persons who intend to keep all the eggs to themselves.'

The queue shuffled forward another step. Arkady wanted to stamp his feet to keep warm. Polina was in open sandals, but she could have been a plaster bust for her reaction to rain, blood and the insanity of the wait. Her entire attention was focused on the nearing scales. The rain fell harder. Drops ran along the contour of her temple and webbed the pagoda curve of her hair.

'Are they selling by weight or by count?' she asked her neighbours.

'Dear,' the old woman said, 'it all depends whether they have rigged scales or little beets.'

'Do we get beet greens, too?' Polina asked.

'There's another queue for greens,' the woman said.

Arkady said, 'You did a good job. I'm sorry it had to be so gruesome.'

Polina said, 'If it bothered me, I'd be in the wrong profession.'

'Maybe *I'm* in the wrong profession,' Arkady said.

Most of the transactions at the scales were mute and sullen exchanges of rubles and ration chits for beets, though every fourth or fifth erupted into an accusation of cheating and a demand for more, denunciations that sang with frustration, hysteria and rage, which drew the people anxiously closer until soldiers pushed them back and the customer on, so that there was a constant eddy and pulse within the queue. At least the rain washed the beets, showing their scarlet under a lamp-post. In its light Arkady could see that the sacks heaped behind the scales exhibited the effects of their rough passage from the country, dirt and bruises staining the wet burlap. The wetter sacks were smeared bright red; the ground around was steeped red, and the scales were dyed a winey vermilion speckled with the skins of beets. In the reflection off the water running from the sacks, the entire park glowed in a spreading lens of red. Polina stared down at her toes and open sandals, which were already stained pink. Arkady watched her face turn to wax and he caught her as she dropped.

'Not the morgue, not the morgue,' she said.

Arkady put her arm over his shoulder and half carried, half walked her out of the park and down Petrovka Street in search of somewhere she could sit. Across the street an ambulance was leaving the gate of a buff-coloured mansion, the sort of pre-Revolutionary building the Party loved to use for offices. It seemed to be some kind of clinic.

As soon as he got her into the courtyard, though, Polina insisted, 'Not a doctor.'

On one side of the courtyard was a rustic wooden entrance whimsically painted with crowing roosters and dancing pigs. They went through into an empty café. Small tables were surrounded by leather-upholstered benches, and a row of stools stood along a padded bar. In back of the counter was an arsenal of orange-juice presses.

Polina sat on a bench, put her head between her knees and said, 'Shit, shit, shit, shit, shit.'

A waitress appeared from the kitchen to chase them away, but Arkady held up his ID and asked for brandy.

'This is a medicinal clinic. We don't serve brandy.'

'Then medicinal brandy.'

'For dollars.'

Arkady put a pack of Marlboros on the table. The waitress stared, unmoved. He added the other pack.

'Two packs.'

'And thirty rubles.'

She disappeared, returned a moment later and in one circular motion set down a flask of Armenian cognac with two glasses and scooped up the cigarettes and money.

Polina sat up and let her head loll back. Her hair hung in sad ringlets. 'That's half your weekly salary,' she said.

'What was I going to save it for? Beets?'

He poured her a glass that she downed in one swallow.

'I don't think you really wanted borscht, anyway,' he said.

'That lousy body. Once you know what happened, it's worse, not better.' She tried long, deliberate breaths.

'That's why I went outside. Then I saw the food queues and joined the nearest one. No one makes you go back to work if you're shopping.'

At the bar, the waitress dug under her apron for a lighter, lit a cigarette and exhaled with a sensuality that hooded her eyes. Arkady envied her.

'Excuse me,' he called. 'What kind of clinic is this? A café with leather seats and soft lighting, it's rather fancy.'

'It's for foreigners,' the waitress said. 'It's a diet clinic.'

Arkady and Polina shared a glance. There must be hysteria in the air, he thought, because she seemed ready to laugh and cry at the same time, and he felt the same way himself. 'Well, Moscow is certainly the right place,' he said.

'They couldn't come to a better place,' Polina said.

Arkady saw colour return to her cheeks. It was interesting how quick recovery was in someone young, like roses. He poured her another glass and one for himself. 'It's insane, Polina. It's Dante's *Inferno* with breadlines. Maybe there's a diet centre in hell.'

'Americans would go,' she said. 'They'd do aerobics.' There was a real smile on her face, perhaps because there was a real smile on his. It merely took appreciating insanity together. 'Moscow *could* be hell. This *could* be it,' she said.

'Good cognac.' Arkady poured two more glasses. It had a terrific impact on an empty stomach. 'To hell,' he added. He could feel the damp in his clothes rising like steam. He called to the waitress, 'What kind of food is on this diet?'

'Depends.' She screwed her lips around the cigarette. 'Whether you're on a fruit diet or a vegetable diet.'

'Fruit diet? Do you hear that, Polina? Like what?' he asked.

'Pineapples, papayas, mangoes, bananas.' The waitress rattled them off casually as if she were intimately acquainted with them.

'Papayas,' Arkady repeated. 'Polina, you and I would be willing to queue for seven or eight years for a papaya. I'm not sure I know what a papaya looks like. They could give me a potato and I'd probably be happy. Then I wouldn't lose weight. Luxury is wasted on people like you and me.' He asked the waitress, 'Could you show us a papaya?'

She studied them. 'No.'

'She probably doesn't even have a papaya,' Arkady said. 'She just says it to impress her friends. Feel better?'

'I'm laughing, so I must feel a little better.'

'I've never heard you laugh before. It's a nice sound.'

'Yes.' Polina slowly rocked back and forth. Her smile sank. 'At medical school we used to ask each other, "What is the worst way to die?" After Rudy, I think I know. Do you believe in hell?'

'There's a question out of the blue.'

'Well, you're like the devil. You take a secret glee in your work, like you've come to grab the damned. That's why Jaak likes to work with you.'

'Why do you work with me?' He didn't think she was going to quit now.

Polina took a moment. 'You let me do things right. You let me get involved.'

Arkady knew this was the problem. The morgue was a simple theatre of black and white, dead or alive. Polina had been full of analytical detachment, a blind determinism perfect for labelling the dead as so many cold and inert specimens. But a pathologist who became involved in the investigation outside the morgue started seeing bodies as living people, and then the cadaver on the table became the picture of someone's worst and ultimate breath on earth. He had robbed her of professional distance. In a way he had corrupted her.

'Because you're smart.' Arkady left it at that.

She said, 'I've been thinking about what you said last night. Kim had a gun. Why use two different kinds of bombs on Rudy? It was such a complicated way to kill him.'

'The point wasn't just to kill him; the point was to burn him. Or burn all the records and computer disks and every piece of information that would connect him to someone else. I'm more sure of that all the time.'

'So I am a help.'

'A Hero of Red Labour.' He toasted her.

Polina drank her cognac and levelled her gaze.

'I heard that you left once,' she said. 'There was a woman, I heard.'

'Where do you hear all these things?'

'You're avoiding the question.'

'I don't know what people say. I was out of the country for a short time and then I came back.'

'The woman?'

'Did not come back.'

'Who was right?' Polina asked.

Now that, Arkady thought, was a question only asked by the very young.

Chapter Ten

Irina said, 'The Soviet Defence Minister conceded that Soviet troops attacked civilians in Baku to prevent the overthrow of the Azerbaijan Communist regime. The Army had stood aside when Azeri activists rioted against Armenians in the capital, but went into action when an Azeri crowd threatened to burn down Party head-quarters. Tanks and troops broke through blockades set up by anti-Communist militants and stormed into the city, firing dumdum bullets and spraying apartment buildings without provocation. Hundreds, perhaps thousands of civilians are estimated to have died in the assault. Although the KGB had spread rumours that Azeri militants would be armed with heavy machine guns, only hunting rifles, knives and pistols were found among the dead.'

Arkady had left Polina and hurried home in time to catch Irina's first broadcast. Drinks with one woman, then rushing to the voice of another. What a sophistic-ated life, he thought.

'Official justification for the military operation was the mob violence against Armenians by militants who showed documents identifying themselves as leaders of the Azeri Popular Front. Since the Front does not issue such documents, a KGB provocation is once again suspected.'

While Arkady listened, he changed into a dry shirt and jacket.

Who was right? She was. He was. There was no choice, no right or wrong, no black or white. He wished for one blinding ray of certainty; even to be wrong would be relief. He had stepped back in his memory so many times his tracks would have worn through stone, and he still didn't know what else he could have done. He had told Polina, 'We'll never know.'

Irina said, 'Increasingly, Moscow has cited nationalist tensions to justify the continued presence of Soviet Army troops in different republics, including the Baltic states, Georgia, Armenia, Azerbaijan, Uzbekistan and the Ukraine. Tanks and missile launchers that were supposed to be scrapped in the arms-control agreement with NATO have instead been moved to bases in the dissident republics. At the same time, nuclear missiles have been removed from those republics to the Russian republic.'

He hardly heard her words. Every rumour he heard was worse than her reports; reality was worse than her reports. So, like a beekeeper separating honey from a comb, he was able to hear only her voice and not the words. She had a darker sound tonight. Had it rained in Munich? Were there traffic jams on the autobahn? Was she with anyone?

She could have said anything and he would have gone on listening. Sometimes he felt as if he were going to fly out of the window, and wheel in the sky above Moscow. He would home in on that voice like a beacon, which would lead him, lead him, lead him away.

When the news switched to a tape, Arkady left his flat not with wings but wipers, attached them to his car and plunged into the midnight traffic. Night and rain combined to make disoriented streets and paint smears of light across the windscreen. At the embankment road he had to stop for a convoy of Army lorries and personnel carriers as long and slow as a freight train. While he waited he felt his jacket for cigarettes, found an envelope and winced when he recognized the letter Belov had given him in Red Square. His name was written across the face of the envelope with a fine nib in letters that started in slashes and ended in sprawls, as if the hand had been too weak to wield a pen or a knife.

Polina had asked what the worst way to die was. Holding the letter, letting it rest lightly across his palm with the shadow of water running over his name, Arkady knew the answer. It was to realize that when you died no one would care. It was to realize that you were already dead. He didn't feel that way now; he would never feel that way. Just hearing Irina made him come so alive his heart shook with every beat. What had his father written? The wise course, he thought, would be to leave the letter on the street. The rain would wash it down a storm drain, the river would carry it to the sea, where the paper would unfold and fall apart and the ink would run and fade like poison. Instead, he slipped it back into his pocket.

Minin let him into Rudy's flat.

The detective was agitated because of the rumour that speculation would become legal. 'This undermines the basis of our investigation,' he said. 'If we can't go after money-changers, who can we arrest?'

'There are still murderers, rapists and violent thieves. You'll always be busy,' Arkady reassured him and gave him his hat and coat. Getting Minin out of the place was like unearthing a mole. 'Catch some sleep. I'll take over here.'

'The mafia's going to open banks.'

'Very likely. I understand that's how they start.'

'I searched everything,' Minin said and stepped reluctantly on to the threshold. 'Nothing hidden in books, cupboards, under the bed. I left a list on the desk.'

'It's suspiciously clean, isn't it?'

'Well . . .'

'That's what I thought, too,' Arkady said as he started to shut the door. 'And don't worry about a lack of crime. In the future we'll have a better class of criminal – bankers, brokers, businessmen. You'll need lots of sleep for that.'

Alone, the first place Arkady went to was the office desk to see whether anything new had come on the fax. The paper was clean and bore the same faint pencil dot on the reverse side that he had left after tearing off the messages about Red Square. He picked up Minin's list. The detective had cut open Rudy's mattress and springs, inspected cupboard and drawers, unscrewed switches, tapped skirting boards, disassembled and assembled the flat again, and found nothing.

Arkady ignored Minin's list. What could be found, he thought, would be more obvious. Sooner or later a flat fitted a man like a shell. He might be gone, but his outline stayed in a worn chair, a photo, a crust of food, a forgotten letter, in the smell of hope or despair. In part, Arkady took this approach because technological support for investigations was so weak. The militia had invested in German and Swedish gear, spectrographs and haemotypers, which lay unused for lack of parts for dearth of funds. There was no computer matching of blood or numberplates, let alone of something so laughably out of reach as 'genetic fingerprints'. What Soviet forensic labs possessed were archaic chemistry sets of blackened test tubes, gas burners and curlicues of glass piping that the West hadn't seen in fifty years. Polina had extracted answers from the body of Rudy Rosen in spite of her equipment, not because of it.

Since the chain of hard evidence tended to be thin, a Soviet investigator was more dependent on softer clues, on social nuance and logic. Arkady knew investigators who believed that with a sufficiently clear understanding of the scene of a homicide they could deduce a murderer's sex, age, occupation and hobbies. The only place in the Soviet Union where psychological analysis was allowed to thrive was criminal investigation.

Of course Soviet investigators had always relied on confession, too. Confession solved everything. But confession really worked only with amateurs and innocents. Makhmud or Kim would no more confess to a crime than suddenly burst into Latin.

What had this flat said so far? One thing: 'Where is Red Square?'

Was Rosen religious? There were no menorahs, Torahs, prayer shawls or Sabbath candles. The portraits of his parents were the bare minimum of family history; generally Russian homes were photo galleries of sepia ancestors in oval frames. Where were Rudy's pictures of himself or of friends? He was hygienic. The walls were smooth, scrubbed clean, not a nailhole to mar the blank space, as if he had effaced himself.

Arkady pulled books and magazines from the shelves. *Business Week* and *Israel Trade* were in English and indicated an international breadth of ambition. Did the stamp album speak of a solitary youth? Inside was a regular aquarium of outsize stamps of tropical fish issued by miniature nations and islands around the world. In a paper sleeve were loose stamps of nondescript variety: tsarist two-kopecks, French 'Libertés', American 'Franklins'. No valuable red squares.

He stacked the books and moved to the bedroom, where he balanced the pile on the night table. The sleep mask had a poignant quality, suggesting that a combination of rich food and diet pills made for uneasy nights.

There was no chair in the bedroom. Arkady removed his shoes, sat on the bed and at once had the shock of hearing the complaint of springs that anticipated Rudy's weight. He packed the pillows behind his back, the way Rudy would have, and flipped through the books.

Every home had a few classics just to prove literacy. Rudy read his. Arkady found underlined the humorous passage in the immortal Pushkin's *The Captain's Daughter* in which a Hussar offers to teach a young man the game of billiards: 'It's quite essential to us soldiers,' he said. 'One can't always be beating Jews, you know. So there is nothing to it but to go to the inn and play billiards; and to do that one must be able to play.'

'Or beat Jews with cues' was scribbled below the line. Arkady recognized Rudy's handwriting from the bank book.

Deep in Gogol's *Dead Souls*, Rudy had marked, 'For some time, Chichikov made it impossible for smugglers to earn a living. In particular, he reduced Polish Jewry almost to despair, so invincible, so almost unnatural, was the rectitude, the incorruptibility which led him to refrain from converting himself into a small capitalist.' In the margin, Rudy had added, 'Nothing changes.'

There had to be more, Arkady thought. Thanks to Jewish emigration, the Moscow mafia had good connections with Israeli criminals. He put on the television set and replayed the Jerusalem videotape, skipping from place to place, from Wailing Wall to casino.

His mind wandered to what Polina had said: 'Too much blood'.

He agreed. If petrol could be thickened with blood, it could also be thickened with a dozen other agents easier to get hold of. He'd seen blood in some other strange form recently, but couldn't remember where.

He looked at the Egyptian tape again. It was warming to see the tawny hues of the Sinai desert while rain tapped on the windows, and he crowded closer, like a man to a fireplace. He reached into his jacket for cigarettes, and before he remembered that he had given them away he had pulled the letter from his pocket. He could count the number of letters he had received from his father. One a month while Arkady was in Pioneer camp. One a month when the general was in China, at a time when relations with Mao were fraternal and deep. All those missives were brisk, military-like reports that ended with instructions for Arkady to be hardworking, responsible and worthy. About twelve letters altogether. He received one more after choosing the university over officers' school. He was impressed because his father cited the Bible, namely the episode in which God demanded from Abraham the sacrifice of his only son. This was where Stalin improved on God, the general said, because he not only would have allowed the execution but would have been glorified by Abraham all the more. Besides, there were some sons, like weak calves, that were fit only for sacrifice. Too much blood? For his father there was never enough.

The father renounced his son, the son renounced his

father, one cutting off the future, the other the past, and neither daring to mention, it occurred to Arkady now, the one point in time where they would always dwell together. At the dacha, boy and man had stared from the dock at feet caught in the drowsy, warm river that ran by the edge of the dacha's lawn. The feet were bare, and they neither floated up nor plunged down to deeper water; instead, they lazed underneath the surface like underwater flowers. Further down, Arkady could make out his mother's white dress billowing and swaying in the current, to his child's mind waving goodbye.

Dhows tipped and cruised the waters of the Nile. Arkady realized that he had stopped consciously watching the television. He replaced the letter in his jacket as delicately as if he were handling a razor, then punched the Egyptian tape out of the VCR and pushed in the one from Munich. He paid more attention now because in a rudimentary way he understood German, and because he needed to focus on something besides the letter. Of course he watched with Russian eyes.

'Willkommen zu München...' the tape began. On the screen was an etching of medieval monks watering sunflowers, turning a spitted boar, pouring beer. It didn't look like such a bad life. The next image was of modern, rebuilt Munich. The narration managed to be boastful of this phoenix-like accomplishment without directly mentioning any world wars, suggesting that a 'sad and tragic' plague had reduced the city to rubble. Munich had been liberated by Americans, and there was the plastic feel of an American mall to the images on the screen. From the figure of the belled jester turning in the Marienplatz clock tower to the chequerboard walls of the Old Court, every historical site was sterilized to quaintness. Virtually every other image was of a beer garden or a beer hall, as if brew were an anointing oil of innocence – Hitler's beer hall putsch aside, of course. Yet Munich was undeniably attractive. People looked so wealthy and well dressed that they seemed to be shopping on a different planet. Cars looked inexplicably clean and sounded like the brass horns of a hunt. Swans and ducks flocked to the city's lakes and river; when was a swan last seen on the Moscow?

'Munich is a city with the stamp of royal builders,' the narrator intoned. 'Max-Joseph-Platz and the National Theatre were built by King Max-Joseph, Ludwigstrasse by his son, King Ludwig I, the "Golden Mile" of Maximilianstrasse by Ludwig's son, King Max II, and Prinzregentenstrasse by his brother, Prince Regent Luitpold.'

Ah, but do we get to see the beer hall where Hitler and his Brown Shirts started their first premature march to power? Will we see the square where Goering took the bullet meant for Hitler and in so doing captured der Führer's heart forever? Will we tour Dachau? Well, Munich's history is so packed with people and events that we can't see everything on one tape. Arkady admitted his attitude was unfair, jaundiced and corroded with envy.

'At last year's Oktoberfest, celebrants drank over five million litres of beer and consumed seven hundred thousand chickens, seventy thousand pork knuckles and seventy roasted oxen . . .'

Well, they could come to Moscow to diet. The nearly pornographic display of food glazed Arkady's eyes. After opera in the National Theatre – 'built by a tax on beer' – refreshment in a romantic beer cellar. After a spin on the autobahn, a pit stop in the beer garden. After an Alpine hike up the Zugspitze, well-earned beer at a rustic inn.

Arkady stopped the tape and rewound to the hike. Vista of Alps leading to stone-and-snow escarpment of the Zugspitze. Hikers in lederhosen. Tight shot of edelweiss. Silhouettes of mountaineers high above. Drifting clouds.

Beer garden of the inn. Honeysuckle climbing yellow plaster. The engraved stillness of Bavarians after lunch, except for one woman in short sleeves and sunglasses. Cut to a vapour trail leading from clouds to a Lufthansa jet.

Arkady rewound and ran the scene in the garden again. The tape quality seemed the same, but both the narrator's voice and the music were absent. In their place was the scraping of chairs and the off-screen sounds of traffic. The sunglasses were a mistake; in a professional tape they would have been off. He went back and forth from Alps to airliner. The clouds were the same. The beer garden scene had been inserted.

The woman raised her glass. Blonde hair was brushed back like a mane from her broad eyebrows and broader cheeks. Short chin, medium height, mid-thirties. Dark sunglasses, gold necklace, black short-sleeved sweater, probably cashmere – contrasts that were more sensual than pretty in any ordinary sense. Red nails. Fair skin. Red lips half open in the same slack, reckless study she had once given Arkady through a car window – lifting a corner of a half-smile, she mouthed, 'I love you.'

Her lips were easy to read because her promise was in Russian.

Chapter Eleven

'I don't know,' Jaak said. 'You saw her better than I did. I was driving.'

Arkady drew the curtains so that his office was lit only by the glow of the beer garden. On the monitor a glass was lifted and held by the 'Pause' button of the VCR.

'The woman who was in Rosen's car looked at us.'

'She looked at you,' Jaak said. 'My eyes were on the road. If you think she's the same woman, that's good enough for me.'

'We need stills. What's the matter?'

'We need Kim or the Chechens; *they* killed Rudy. Rudy as good as told you they would. If she's German, if we drag foreigners in, we have to spread the circle and share with the KGB. You know how that goes: we feed them and they shit on us. You told them?'

'Not yet. When we have more.' Arkady turned off the monitor.

'Like what?'

'A name. Maybe an address in Germany.'

'You're going to run this one around them?'

Arkady handed Jaak the tape. 'We just don't want to bother them until we have something definite. Maybe the woman is still here.'

Jaak said, 'You've got brass balls. You must ring when you walk.'

'Like a belled cat,' Arkady said.

'The bastards would just take all the credit anyway.' Jaak reluctantly accepted the tape, then brightened and waved a pair of car keys. 'I borrowed Julya's. The Volvo, naturally. After I run your errand, I'm headed for the Lenin's Path Collective. Remember the lorry that sold me the radio? It's possible they saw something when Rudy was killed.'

'I'll bring the radio,' Arkady promised.

'Bring it to Kazan Station. I'm meeting Julya's mother at the "Dream Bar" at four.'

'Julya won't be there?'

'She wouldn't be caught dead at Kazan Station, but her mother's coming in on the train. That's how I got the car. Unless you want to keep the radio.'

'No.'

When he was alone, Arkady opened his closet and locked the original Munich tape in his safe. He had come to the office early to make a duplicate. Who was paranoid?

He opened the windows. The rain had stopped, leaving weepy stains around the windows of the courtyard. The skyline was a ring of damp chimneypots upraised like spades. Perfect weather for a funeral.

The man at the Ministry of Foreign Trade said, 'A joint business venture requires a partnership between a Soviet entity – a cooperative or a factory – and a foreign company. It helps if there is sponsorship from a Soviet political organization—'

'Meaning from the Party?'

'Yes, to be plain, but it's not necessary.'

'This is capitalism?'

'No, this is not pure capitalism; this is an intermediate stage of capitalism.'

'Can the joint venture take rubles out?'

'No.'

'Can it take dollars out?'

'No.'

'This is a very intermediate stage.'

'It can take oil. Or vodka.'

'We have that much vodka?'

'For sale abroad.'

Arkady asked, 'All joint ventures must be approved by you?'

'They should be, but sometimes they aren't. In Georgia or Armenia they tend to make their own arrangements, which is why Georgia and Armenia don't ship anything to Moscow anymore.' He giggled. 'Fuck them.'

His office was on the tenth floor with a view of squalls moving east to west. No factory smoke, though, because parts hadn't arrived from Sverdlovsk, Riga, Minsk.

'What did TransKom register as its purpose?'

'Importation of recreational equipment. It is sponsored by the Leningrad Borough Komsomol. Boxing gloves, things of that nature, I suppose.'

'Like slot machines?'

'Apparently.'

'In trade for what?'

'Personnel.'

'People?'

'I guess so.'

'What kind of people? Olympic boxers, nuclear physicists?'

'Tour guides.'

'Touring where?'

'Germany.'

'Germany needs Soviet guides?'

'Apparently.'

Arkady wondered what else the man would believe. That the baby Lenin left coins under pillows in exchange for teeth?

'TransKom has officers?'

'Two.' The man read from the file in front of him. 'Many positions, but all filled by two people, Rudik Abramovich Rosen, Soviet citizen, and Boris Benz, a resident of Munich, Germany. TransKom's address is Rosen's. There may be any number of investors, but they're not listed. Excuse me.' He covered the file with *Pravda*.

'The Ministry has no names for the tour guides?'

The man folded the newspaper in halves and quarters. 'No. You know, people come here to register a venture to import penicillin, and the next thing you know they're bringing in basketball shoes or building hotels. Once conditions exist here for a free market, it will be like watering the ground.'

'What will you do when capitalism is in full swing?'

'I'll find something.'

'You're inventive?'

'Oh, yes.' From a drawer he took a ball of string, bit off an arm's length and put it and *Pravda* in his jacket. 'I'll walk you out. I was on my way to lunch.' Bureaucrats survived on the butter, bread and sausage they took home from cafeterias. The jacket was loose and its pockets were jowls dappled with grease.

Vagankovskoye Cemetery was lovingly but casually tended. A coverlet of wet leaves lay unswept around limes, birches, oaks; dandelions were allowed to line the walk, and overall spread the soft embrace of natural decay. Many of the gravestones were busts of Party stalwarts hewn from granite and black marble: composers, scientists, writers of Socialist Realism with broad brows and commanding gazes. More timid souls were represented by photographs set like cameos on their stones. Since the graves were surrounded by iron fences, the faces on the tombstones seemed to peer from black birdcages. Not all, though. The first grave inside the gate belonged to the roughneck singer-actor Vysotsky, and was heaped so high with daisies and roses freshly watered by the rain that it stirred with the hum of bumblebees.

Arkady found his father's funeral procession halfway down the central path. Cadets bearing a star of red roses and a cushion with medals were followed by a porter pushing a handcart and coffin, then a dozen shuffling generals in dark-green dress uniforms and white gloves, two musicians with trumpets and two with dented tubas playing a funeral march from a sonata by Chopin.

Belov was in the rearguard, wearing civilian clothes. His eyes lit when he saw Arkady. 'I knew you would come.' Solemnly he pumped Arkady's hand with both of his. 'Of course, you couldn't stay away, it would have been disgraceful. You saw *Pravda* this morning.'

'Being used as food wrap.'

'I knew you'd want this.' He gave Arkady an article that seemed to have been meticulously torn from the newspaper with a ruler.

Arkady stopped to read the obituary. 'General of the Army Kyril Ilyich Renko, a prominent Soviet military commander . . .' It was a long piece and he read it in small handfuls '. . . after completing the M. V. Frunze Military Academy, K. I. Renko's active involvement in the Great Patriotic War was a brilliant page in his biography. Commander of a tank brigade, he was cut off by the first rush of the Fascist invasion but joined partisan forces and mounted raids behind enemy lines . . . fought successfully in battles for Moscow, in the Battle of Stalingrad, the campaign in the steppes and operations around Berlin . . . After the war, he was responsible for stabilizing the situation in the Ukraine and then for command of the Urals Military District.' Or to put it another way, Arkady thought, the general, now numbed to slaughter, was responsible for a mass execution of

Ukrainian nationalists so bloody that he had to be exiled to the Urals. '. . . Twice awarded the title Hero of the Soviet Union and awarded four Orders of Lenin, the Order of the October Revolution, three Orders of the Red Banner, two Orders of Suvorov (First Class), two Orders of Kutuzov (First Class) . . .'

Belov had pinned a plaque of fading ribbons on his jacket. His white crewcut was a sparse stubble and badly-shaved wattles covered his collar.

'Thanks.' Arkady put the obituary in his pocket.

'You read the letter?' Belov asked.

'Not yet.'

'Your father said it would explain everything.'

'That would be quite a letter.' It would take more than a letter, Arkady thought; it would take a heavy tome bound in black leather.

The generals marched ahead in creaky lock step. Arkady had no desire to catch up. 'Boris Sergeyevich, do you remember a Chechen named Makhmud Khasbulatov?'

'Khasbulatov?' Belov adjusted slowly to the change of subject.

'What's interesting is that Makhmud claims he's been in three armies: White, Red, and German. According to the records, he's eighty. In 1920, during the Civil War, he would have been ten years old.'

'It's possible. There were plenty of children on each side, White and Red. Those were terrible times.'

'Let's say that at the time of Hitler Makhmud was in the Red Army.'

'Everyone served, one way or another.'

'I was wondering: in February 1944, was my father in the Chechen military district?'

'No, no, we were pushing to Warsaw. The Chechen operation was completely rear echelon.'

'Hardly worth the time of a Hero of the Soviet Union?'

'Not worth a second of his time,' Belov said.

Wasn't it wonderful, Arkady thought, how completely some people retired? Belov had only recently left the prosecutor's office; now Arkady had asked him about the head of the Chechen mafia and the old sergeant had not made the connection at all, as if his mind had already retreated forty years.

They started walking again in silence. Arkady felt watched. In marble and bronze the dead stood over their graves. A dancer whirled dreamily in white stone. An explorer paused, compass in hand. Against a bas-relief of clouds, a pilot pulled aviator goggles from his eyes. They shared a sombre, communal gaze, restless and restful at the same time.

'It was a closed coffin, of course,' Belov muttered.

Arkady was distracted because moving in the opposite direction on a parallel path was another, longer procession with an empty cart, a larger battery of horns and tubas and, among the mourners, some familiar faces. Bolstering a widow on either side were General Penyagin and Rodionov, the city prosecutor, both of them with black bands on their sleeves. Arkady remembered that Penyagin's predecessor at CID had died only days ago; presumably the woman was the dead man's wife. The three were trailed by a slow-moving entourage of militia officers, Party officials and relatives parading fixed expressions of boredom and grief. None of them noticed Arkady.

His own cortege had turned down an alley of shaggy pines and stopped at a gate open to a fresh hole in the ground. Arkady looked around. Since Soviet tombstones were not anonymous slabs, he felt introduced to his father's new neighbours. Here was a statue of a singer listening to music inscribed in granite. There, a sports-man with bronze muscles shouldered an iron javelin. Behind the trees gravediggers hunkered over cigarettes, hands on their shovels. Beside the open grave was a small marker of white marble almost flush with the ground. Space was tight in Vagankovskoye, and some-times husbands and wives were stacked on top of each other, but not this time, thank God.

As the generals formed ranks by the grave, Arkady recognized the four he had seen in Red Square. Shuksin, Ivanov, Kuznetsov and Gul looked even smaller in the daylight, as if the men he had feared and detested as a child had been magically bent and shrunk into beetles with carapaces of green serge and gold brocade, their sunken chests stiffened by tiers of campaign medals, honours and orders, a dazzling clatter of ribbons, brass stars and coins. They were all weeping bitter vodka tears.

'Comrades!' Feebly Ivanov unfolded a piece of paper and began to read. 'Today we say goodbye to a great Russian, a lover of peace, yet a man forged . . .'

Arkady was constantly amazed at people's faith in lies. As if words had the remotest relationship to the truth. This band of veterans were nothing but little butchers bidding a mawkish farewell to a great butcher. Take the arthritis from their joints and they would drive the knife home as vigorously as in their glorious youth, and they believed every lie they uttered.

By the time Shuksin took Ivanov's place, Arkady wanted his own cigarette and shovel.

' "Not one step back!" Stalin ordered. Yes, Stalin. His name is still sacred to my lips . . .'

'Stalin's favourite general' was what his father had been called. When they were surrounded and without food and ammunition other generals would dare surrender their men alive. General Renko never surrendered; he wouldn't have surrendered if he'd had nothing but dead to command. Anyway, the Germans never caught him. He broke back through the lines to join the defence of Moscow, and a famous photograph showed him and Stalin himself, like two devils defending hell, studying an underground map to plot the shifting of troops from station to station.

The round Kuznetsov took his turn and balanced on the lip of the grave. 'Today, when every effort is made to libel our Army's glorious duty . . .'

Their voices had the hollow tremor of busted cellos. Arkady would have felt sorry for them if he didn't remember how they would troop into the dacha, like so many lesser shadows of his father, for the midnight dinners and drunken songs that ended in the Army roar, 'Arrrrrrrrraaaaaaaaagh!!!'

Arkady wasn't sure why he had come. Perhaps for the sake of Belov, who had faithfully maintained the hope of a reunion between father and son. Perhaps for his mother. She would have to lie side by side with her own murderer. He stepped forward to brush dirt off the white marker.

'Soviet power, built on the holy altar of twenty million dead . . .' Kuznetsov droned on.

No, not metamorphosed into beetles, Arkady thought. That was too kind, too Kafkaesque. More like hoary, three-legged dogs, senile but rabid, baying at a pit.

Gul wavered, his green tunic weighted with medals and hanging from his bones. He removed his hat, revealing hair the colour of ashes. 'I recall my last encounter with K. I. Renko a very short time ago.' Gul laid his hand on the coffin of dark wood with brass handles, slim as a skiff. 'We remembered comrades in arms whose sacrifices burn like an eternal flame in our hearts. We talked of the present period of doubt and self-mortification so different from our own iron resolve. I give you now the words the general gave me then. "Those who would shovel dirt on the Party. Those who forget the Jewish historical sins. Those who would distort our revolutionary history, debase and vulgarize our people. To them I say, my banner was, and is and always will be red!"'

'Well, that's about as much as I can take,' Arkady told Belov and started back down the path.

'There's more.' Belov caught up.

'That's why I'm going.' Gul was still ranting on.

'We were hoping you would say a few words now that he's dead.'

'Boris Sergeyevich, if I had been the investigator of my mother's death, I would have arrested my father. I gladly would have killed him.'

'Arkasha – '

'Just the idea that this monster died quietly in his bed will haunt me for the rest of my life.'

Belov's voice dropped. 'He didn't.'

Arkady stopped. He forced himself to be calm. 'You said it was a closed coffin. Why?'

Belov had trouble drawing breath. 'At the end the pain was so great. He said the only thing holding him together was cancer. He didn't want to die that way. He said he preferred the officer's way out.'

'He shot himself?'

'Forgive me. I was in the next room. I . . .'

As Belov's knees gave way, Arkady eased him on to a bench. He felt incredibly stupid; he should have seen what was in the old man's face before this. Belov dug into his jacket, twisted around and gave Arkady a gun. It was a black Nagant revolver with four squat bullets as polished as old silver. 'He wanted you to have this.'

'The general always had a good sense of humour,' Arkady said.

*

There was brisk business at a kiosk beside Vysotsky's grave when Arkady got back to the gate. Now that the sun was out, fans were buying pins, posters, postcards and cassettes of the singer, dead ten years and more popular than ever. The number 23 tram stopped right across the street; it was the handiest souvenir run in Moscow. Around the gate were beggars, peasant women with white kerchiefs and sun-browned faces, legless men with crutches and carts. They congregated around worshippers leaving the cemetery's little yellow church. Coffin lids dressed in crepe and wreaths of sharp-smelling evergreens and carnations rested against the church front. Seminarians sold Bibles from a card table, asking forty rubles for the New Testament.

Carrying his father's gun in his pocket, Arkady felt a little dizzy and had some difficulty in discriminating. As much as he saw the ceremonies of human grief – a widow polishing the photo on a headstone – he saw just as clearly a robin wrestling a worm from a grave. He had no sense of focus. A funeral bus pulled inside the gate and the family clambered down its front steps. A coffin was slid out of the rear, slipped and hit the ground with a bang. A girl in the family made a comic grimace. That was the way Arkady felt. Outside the gate, the Rodionov–Penyagin party was still milling around the pavement. Arkady didn't feel in decent enough shape to talk to either the prosecutor or the general, so he slipped into the church.

Inside there was a crowd of the worshipful, the bereaved and the spiritual tourists. All standing, no pews. The atmosphere was like a crowded, colourful train station, with incense for cigarette smoke, and instead of a loudspeaker an unseen choir whose voices hovered in the vaulted ceiling singing about the lamb of God. Ikons – Byzantine, age-darkened faces in cutouts of bright silver – tipped down from the walls painted like pages of an illuminated manuscript. Ikon candles were wicks suspended in glass cups of oil. Strategically placed on the floor were cans of oil to keep the flames alight. Votive candles came in thirty-kopeck, fifty-kopeck and one-ruble sizes. Candles burned and sputtered in pools of pearly wax; candle stands glowed like softly burning trees. Lenin had described religion as a hypnotic flame for a reason. Women in black gathered contributions on brass plates covered with red felt. To the left, a shop sold postcards of miraculous relics. To the right, three women, also in black dresses and scarves, hands crossed on their breasts, lay in open coffins surrounded by candles on arms of wrought iron dripping wax.

In a chapel next to the coffins, a priest taught a boy how to bow by pushing down his head, then led him through the Orthodox manner of crossing himself, with three fingers, not two. Arkady found himself forced by the sheer press of bodies into the 'devil's corner', where confessions were heard. A priest in a wheelchair looked up expectantly, his long beard as white as rays of the moon. Arkady felt an interloper because his disbelief was not an institutional attitude, but the fury of a son who had deliberately and in a rage left his father's camp.

Yet his father had not been a believer; for all the good it had done her, it was his mother who had secretly slipped like a bird into the few churches open in Stalin's Moscow. Kopecks dropped. Wax dripped. Collection plates circulated around the faithful as the glorious music unfolded, descant climbing over descant, appealing to the Almighty: *Hear us and watch over us.* No, Arkady thought, better to beg that He was deaf and blind. The voices pleaded, *And be merciful, be merciful, be merciful.* At least mercy was the last thing the general ever wanted.

Arkady looped around the horsetrack to Gorky Street, stuck the blue light on the car roof, leaned on his horn and raced down the middle lane while traffic officers, like so many semaphores in oilskins and batons, cleared the way ahead. The rain had started again, marching in gusts up the street, raising umbrellas with flower patterns on the pavement. He wasn't going anywhere in particular. It was the sound of water tearing under the wheels, the blur of a windscreen without wipers, the gondola flow of running lights, and the melting of shop windows that he pursued. At the Intourist Hotel, prostitutes fluttered for cover like pigeons.

Without braking, Arkady swung into Marx Prospect. Rain turned the wide square into a lake that taxis surged through like motorboats. Move fast enough and you could move through time, he thought. Gorky Street, for example, had been given back its old title of Tverskaya,

Marx Prospect was being renamed Mokhovaya, and Kalinin, just ahead, was once again New Arbat. He imagined Stalin's ghost wandering the city in confusion, lost, looking into windows, frightening babes. Or, worse, seeing the old names and not being confused at all.

Through the rain Arkady saw that a traffic officer had stopped a taxi in the middle of the square. Lorries blocked him on the right; to his left were oncoming cars. He hit his brake pedal and fought the squirming wheels as the faces of the officer and the taxi driver gaped in the lights. The Zhiguli skidded up to their trouser legs.

Arkady jumped out. The officer wore a plastic cover on his cap. A licence was in one hand and a blue five-ruble note in the other. The taxi driver had a narrow face with eyebrows frightened to his hairline. Both looked as if they had been struck by lightning and were waiting for the thunder's clap.

The militiaman stared at the car bumper, miraculously stopped. 'You almost killed us.' He waved the ruble note, which was damp and limp. 'Excellent, it's a bribe. A lousy five rubles. You can take me off and shoot me, you don't need to run me down. Fifteen years and I make two hundred and fifty rubles a month. You think my family can live on that? I have two bullets in me and they gave me a traffic light, as if that made up for it. Now you want to kill me over a bribe? I don't care. I no longer care.'

'You're not hurt?' Arkady asked the taxi driver.

'No problem.' The man snatched his licence back and dove into his car.

'You, too?' Arkady asked the officer; he wanted to be sure.

'Yes, fuck, who cares? Still on duty, comrade.' The officer saluted. He became braver when Arkady turned his back. 'As if you never saw a little extra. The higher you go, the more you get. At the top, it's a golden trough.'

Arkady sat in the Zhiguli and lit a Belomor. He was soaked – soaked and probably crazy. As he put the car in gear he noticed that the officer had stopped all traffic for him.

He drove more carefully along the river. The major question was whether he should pull over to put the windscreen wipers on. Was it worth getting even more wet just so he could see? Was he a good enough driver for it to make a difference?

Clouds drifted in his way as the road dipped south by the swimming pool where the Church of the Saviour used to stand, and he found himself forced to drive on to the pavement and stop. It was stupid. Stalin had torn down the church. How many Muscovites actually remembered the Church of the Saviour? Yet that was how they identified the pool. Once Arkady got out to put the wipers on, he lost interest in the task. The car looked like a jar draped with wet leaves on the outside and airless as a grave within. He needed to walk.

Was he in an emotional state? He supposed so. Wasn't everybody, all the time? Had anybody ever, awake or asleep, experienced a totally *non*-emotional state? To his right, a clump of trees sank into steam flowing from the pool. He climbed down and then up through the trees using branches as handrails until he came to a real handrail of metal, cold and sweaty to the touch, and pulled himself on to an apron of concrete.

He walked around the locked and shuttered changing rooms until he came to the edge of the water. Vapour rose not in wisps but as white and dense as smoke off the surface of the water. This was the largest swimming pool in Moscow, a perfect factory for the fog that wrapped around him and made his eyes smart from chlorine. He knelt. The water was heated, warmer than he had expected. Although he had assumed the pool was closed, the lamps were on, sodium halos hanging in the mist. He heard the slap of water against the sides, and then not words but perhaps someone humming. He wasn't sure of the direction, but he thought he heard feet strolling around the pool's perimeter. Whoever it was hummed not so much tunelessly as idly and in snatches, in the manner of someone who believes himself or herself totally alone. Arkady guessed from the lightness of the step and voice that it was a woman, probably an attendant or a lifeguard who felt herself at home.

Fog was a great confuser. On a trawler, Arkady remembered a veteran seaman who had listened to a distant foghorn for an hour before discovering that the sound came from an open bottle ten metres away. 'Chattanooga Choo-Choo' – that's what she was humming. A classic. Unless no one was there, because suddenly she was silent. Waiting for her to start again, he tried to light a cigarette but the match was dowsed instantly and the cigarette crumpled into wet paper and tobacco. How hard was it raining? He heard her from a new direction, straight ahead and higher, nearly level with the lamps. Her voice faded, paused, and he heard the flexing of a diving board. There was a flash of white dropping through the steam and the swallowed splash of a clean entry.

Arkady resisted the temptation to clap for what was, he thought, an unusual dive at every stage: finding the ladder, climbing the rungs by feel, walking out on to the high board and keeping her balance while locating the board's end with her toes, finally pushing down against the strength of the board and flying off into ... nothing. He expected to hear her surface; he imagined she would be an expert swimmer, the sort who did laps with languid, tireless strokes. But there was no sound besides the steady drumming of rain on the pool and the irregular, barely audible rush of traffic from the embankment road.

'Hello,' Arkady called. He stood and walked along the side. 'Hello.'

Chapter Twelve

The other customers in the 'Dream Bar' of the Kazan Railway Station carried suitcases, duffel bags, cardboard boxes and plastic bags, so Arkady didn't feel out of place with Jaak's radio. Julya's mother was a stocky peasant dressed in discards sent her over the years by a chic, long-legged daughter: rabbit-fur coat, denim skirt and lacy hose. She consumed sausages and beer while Arkady ordered tea. Jaak was half an hour late.

'Julya won't meet her own mother's train. She won't even send Jaak, oh, no. She sends a stranger.' She studied Arkady. His jacket smelled like wet washing and sagged around the gun in his pocket. 'You don't look Swedish to me.'

'You've got a good eye.'

'She needs my permission to go, you know. That's the only reason I'm here. But the princess is too good to come to the train herself. And now we have to wait?'

'Let me get you another sausage.'

'Big spender.'

They waited another thirty minutes before he took her outside to the taxi queue. Clouds smothered the spire lights of the two other railway stations across Komsomol Square. Taxis slowed as they approached the queue, perused the prospects and drove on.

'A tram might be faster,' Arkady said.

'Julya told me in an emergency to use this.' As she waved a pack of Rothmans, a private car skidded to a stop. She hopped in the front and rolled down the window to say, 'I'm warning you, I'm not going back home in any rabbit-fur coat. I may not go home at all.'

Arkady returned to the Dream Bar. Still no Jaak. He was never this late.

Kazan Station was 'the Gateway to the East'. The information hall had walls of flipping destination cards under a brick, mosque-like dome. A bronze Lenin, striding, right hand raised, looked strangely like Gandhi. A Tadzhik girl wore a brilliant scarf over braided hair and a dull raincoat over loose, multicoloured trousers. Gold earrings played at her neck. All the porters were Tartars. Arkady recognized Kazan mafia in black leather jackets making the rounds of their prostitutes, pasty-faced Russian girls in jeans. A shop in the corner dubbed music on cassettes. As an inducement it played the Lambada. Arkady felt like a fool carting the radio around. He had gone to his flat and stared at it for an hour before forcing himself to return it to its rightful owner, as if it were the only one in Moscow that could receive Radio Liberty. He would get one of his own.

On the outdoor platforms, Army patrols searched for deserters. In the cab of a locomotive Arkady saw two engineers, a man and a woman. He was seated at the controls, a muscular man stripped to the waist; she wore a pullover and coveralls. He couldn't see their faces but he could imagine a life on the tracks, the whole country passing by the window, eating and sleeping behind the momentum of a diesel engine.

Arkady returned to the Dream Bar, crossing a waiting room so crowded and still that it could have been a madhouse or a prison. Row after row of faces were raised towards a silent, rolling image of folk dancers on a television screen. Militia prodded sleeping drunks. Whole Uzbek families bedded on huge pillow-like sacks that contained all their earthly possessions. By the bar, two Uzbek boys in knitted caps played a Treasure Box. For five kopecks they manipulated a grip that controlled a robot hand within a glass case. The bottom of the case was covered with sand, and strewn on this miniature beach were prizes that could be, with luck, picked up and dropped to the winner in a sliding tray. A tube of toothpaste the size of a cigarette, a toothbrush with a single row of bristles, a razor blade, a stick of gum, a piece of soap. Each in turn slid out of the grasp of the hand. When he looked more closely, he could see that the prizes had been in the case for years. The yellow bristles, the curling wrappers, the veins in the soap were not so much treasure as trash occasionally sorted, never removed. But the boys played enthusiastically, undeterred, since the idea wasn't the getting as much as the grasping.

After an hour and a half, Arkady gave up. Jaak wasn't coming.

The Lenin's Path Collective Farm was north of the city on the Leningrad Highway. Women bundled in scarves against the rain held up bouquets and buckets of potatoes to cars and lorries passing by.

Where Arkady left the motorway, the road turned immediately to a dirt lane that rose and fell through a village of dark cabins with painted eaves, newer houses of breeze blocks, and gardens of tomato poles and sunflowers. Black-and-white cows wandered on the road and through the yards. At the end of the village the road split into two tracks. He chose the one that was more deeply rutted.

The country around Moscow was flat potato fields. Picking was still done bent over, by hand. Students and soldiers were ordered out for the harvest, straggling behind peasants who tirelessly filled sacks; at any time, scavengers could always glean a few potatoes from a field. But he saw no one at all, only mist, turned earth and a glow in the distance. He followed the road to a burning pile of cardboard boxes, burlap and corn husks. It was a dirty country habit to mix trash with brown coal for incineration. Not usually in the evening, though, and not in the rain. Around the fire were livestock pens, lorries and tractors, water and petrol tanks, barn, garage, shed. Collectives were smaller farms where workers shared according to the time they put in. Someone should be on watch, but no one answered his horn.

Arkady got out and before he was aware of it stepped into water that overflowed the yard from an open pit. The sharp odour of lime overlaid ambient barnyard smells. In the pit, rubbish, slops and animal bones stripped of skin floated in a stew that was pocked by rain. The fire was half as tall again as he was. It blazed in some sections and smouldered in others, individual flames blossoming around newspapers, gnawing on spoiled potatoes. A can rolled from the top of the pyre to the bottom, next to two neatly placed man's shoes. Arkady picked one up and as quickly dropped it. The shoe was hot, literally steaming.

The whole yard glowed. The tractors were ancient models with rusty harrow discs, but both lorries were new, one the lorry from which Jaak had bought his radio. Tractor attachments – reapers, balers, ploughs – were laid out along the shed; morning glories had grown around them, twined around tines, their petals folded for the night. Nothing stirred in the pens; there were no piggish grunts, no nervous clacking of a goatbell.

The garage was open. There were no working switches but the light of the fire was sufficient for Arkady to see a white four-door Moskvitch with Moscow plates squeezed between oil cans and a tyre vice. The car doors were locked.

The barn was cement, with empty stalls on one side. The other side was a slaughterhouse. A coat hung on a wall. It took a while for Arkady to see it was a pig on a hook. The pig was upside down and it droned not with bees but with flies. Below it was a pail covered in cheesecloth black with crusted blood. Beside it was a long tallow paddle for stirring fat. The floor was cement, with blood grooves leading to a central drain. Against one end were butchering blocks, meat grinders and tallow pots as big as kettle drums on hooks standing before a hearth. On the blocks were perfume vials labelled 'Black Bear Bile – Highest Quality', with a label in Chinese on the other side. There were also vials labelled 'Deer Musk' and 'Powdered Horn'; the latter bottles claimed both Sumatran origin and the rejuvenating powers of rhino horn.

The shed's double doors stood ajar, bent where a crowbar had forced the lock. Arkady swung them wide to the light of the fire. Unpacked VCRs, CD players, personal computers, hard disks and video games were stacked to the ceiling. Tracksuits and safari wear hung on racks, and a Japanese copier stood on slabs of Italian marble – all in all, a scene like a customs depot, except it was in the middle of a potato field. The Lenin's Path Collective hadn't worked as a real farm for years, he realized. On the floor was a prayer rug; on a card table were dominoes and a newspaper. The paper's headline was in Arabic script, but the masthead was half in Russian and said *Grozny Pravda*.

Arkady went outside to the fire. It was uneven, blazing through woodshavings here, creeping through damp hay there. Paint rags burned in their own aura of colours. He pulled out a burning hoe shaft, poked in the flames and found nothing but charred brand names, Nike falling over Sony crashing on to Luvs, threatening to collapse over him.

As he stepped back, he noticed that the reflections of the fire betrayed a narrow track of footsteps leading between the slaughterhouse and the shed to a meadow of tall wild grass that obscured two berms, low earthen walls serving no apparent purpose. At the end of one, cement steps went down to a steel hatch with a wheel lock that wore a bar and heavy padlock.

The second berm had a similar hatch without a bar. Arkady opened it and stepped inside, crouching because he felt how tight the space was. His lighter produced a weak glow, enough for him to see that he had stumbled into an Army war bunker. Command bunkers – capsules of buried, reinforced concrete like this – had been built all around Moscow, then mothballed when the nuclear holocaust didn't arrive. Elaborate venting and radiation monitors surrounded the hatch. On a long communications desk were a dozen phones; two of them he recognized from his own service as radio-frequency phones, artifacts of the past. There was even a high-speed Iskra system, phone and code modem intact. He lifted a receiver and got an earful of static, but was astonished that the line was alive at all.

He returned to the yard. There was too much water to make out individual tyre treads. He walked the periphery without finding any other tracks except to the road, and he had come that way. It struck him that since the lorry and tractor tyres weren't smeared with lime, the overflow was recent. There was no flooding anywhere else.

In the reflection of the fire the overflow was molten gold, though Arkady knew that in daylight it would look like watered milk. He guessed the pit was about five metres square. He sank the hoe; the pit was at least two metres deep. An object bobbed to the surface that resembled a cross-section of sausage; it rolled to show the circular jowls, cone ears and snout of a pig, a face made smooth and hairless by corrosive lime, then rolled and sank again. Feathers and hair lay pasted on the scum. A stench deeper and more profound than simple rot pervaded the mist.

Arkady reached into the middle of the pit with the hoe and hit metal. He hit metal and glass. As he walked back and forth along the pit he traced the outline of a car beneath the surface. By now he was breathing in shallow gasps not only because of the smell. He thought he heard Jaak inside the car; he was beating on the roof of Julya's Volvo and screaming. Not that the sound escaped the pit, but Arkady could feel it.

He pulled off his jacket and shoes and dived in. He kept his eyes closed against the lime and felt his way down the side window to the door, found a handle and pulled without success because of the pressure of water. He broke the surface, breathed and dove again. The motion of his dive disturbed the pit and unseen things rose, poking, prodding, as if trying to nudge him from the door. The second time he came up for air, the surface of the pit was crowded with the sweetmeats of the bottom, overwhelming with the smell of death.

On the third dive, he got both legs against the car and opened the door a crack. That was enough. As water leaked in, pressure equalized, faster by the second. He held on because he wasn't going up and down again. As the door opened, water flowed in with a rush, Arkady with it. He swam blindly on to the front seat, then climbed into the back, where Jaak was starting to float.

The door shut with the suction of the water. Eyes still closed, Arkady located the inside handle, but the door wouldn't budge and he couldn't get decent purchase for his feet with Jaak bobbing every which way around him. What a tight, well-made car, Arkady thought. He rolled down the window and, as the car filled up, the door eased open and he kicked himself out, towing Jaak behind him.

He crawled over the lip of the pit and pulled the detective by the arms up on to the yard. Jaak didn't look too bad – wet, eyes wide, curly hair matted like a lamb's – but he was too cold and uncooperative, without a pulse at the wrist or neck, and his irises could have been glass. Arkady tried the kiss of life, lifting Jaak's arms and then beating life into his chest until a raindrop exploded in the centre of one of Jaak's eyes and he didn't blink. Without trying, Arkady's hand found a small entry wound at the back of Jaak's skull. No exit wound. Small calibre; the slug had probably just bounced around the brain.

The pig bobbed to the crowded surface of the pit. No, this head was smaller, ears shorter, followed by the surfacing X-form of outstretched limbs. Arkady realized that his problem getting out of the car had been because there had been two bodies, not one, in the back seat. What a regular fishing hole, this pit! With the hoe he pulled the body close and dragged it up beside Jaak. It was an older man, not Korean or Chechen, the features slack and dirty but familiar. Killed the same way, a hole in the back of the skull that the tip of his little finger fitted in. A black mourning band on the left sleeve was how Arkady recognized him. It was Penyagin.

What was the Chief of Criminal Investigation doing with Jaak? Why was Penyagin at the Lenin's Path Collective Farm? If it was a payoff, since when did generals collect in person? Arkady resisted the temptation to kick him back into the pit.

Instead, he peeled open Penyagin's jacket to remove the dead man's internal passport, Ministry pass and Party card. Inside the vinyl book that held the card a list of phone numbers was pressed against the image of Lenin's damp cheek.

The car keys in Penyagin's pocket unlocked the Moskvitch in the garage. Under the dashboard shelf was a briefcase stuffed with the pasteboard-and-ribbon folders of Soviet officialdom – Ministry directives and memoranda, raw reports and 'correct analyses' – two oranges and a ham wrapped in a copy of the Tass news digest *For Official Use Only*.

Arkady locked the briefcase and car, wiped his prints from the car door, replaced the keys in Penyagin's trousers and radioed from his own car for help. He returned to Jaak and emptied the detective's pockets of keys. Two were house keys, a third was large and looked as if it had been fashioned to open a castle door. The Volvo keys were probably still in the car. Whoever put the car in the pit had probably just set the car in 'Drive'.

He walked around Jaak. Was this worth it? His entire

body stung. He found himself in front of the fire, which blazed away, cartons roaring, ignoring the rain. He remembered Rudy's words: 'legal anywhere else in the world.' Kim had led them on. Jaak had come close. For what? Things were no better, they were worse. A flaming carton tumbled from the top of the pyramid, a rolling cube lit inside and out. It crashed, split and sputtered out on a tide of Russian shit. 'Some things never change'; Rudy had said that, too.

Arkady upended a bucket and let the water flow over his head, chest and back. Waiting for his radio call to be answered, he had built a fire in the hearth of the slaughterhouse using cardboard and coal. Now the yard was lit like a circus with a generator lorry, lamps, breakdown van, fire engine and two forensic vans, and animated by the silhouettes of Ministry troops racing back and forth in combat gear. But the only person in the slaughterhouse with Arkady was Rodionov, the city prosecutor, who kept to the shadow beside the door. As the fire in the hearth shifted, the pig on the hook took on a restless aspect. Water spread in rays from Arkady's feet, the runoff following the blood grooves of the floor.

'Kim and the Chechens are obviously working together,' Rodionov said. 'It seems clear to me that poor Penyagin was abducted and brought here, shot either before or after he arrived, and then the detective was murdered afterwards. You agree?'

'Oh, I understand Kim killing Jaak,' Arkady said. 'But

why would anyone go to the bother of shooting the chief of Criminal Investigation?'

'You've answered your own question. Naturally they'd want to remove someone as dangerous as Penyagin.'

'Penyagin? Dangerous?'

'Some respect, please.' Rodionov glanced at the doorway.

Arkady walked to the butchering block, where a towel lay over the cast-off plain clothes that had been brought from the prosecutor's office. His shoes and jacket were beside them. As far as he was concerned, his own clothes could be burned. He started to dry himself on the towel.

'Why are there Ministry troops out here? Where's the regular militia?'

Rodionov said, 'Remember we're outside Moscow. We got the men who were available.'

'They certainly got here quickly and they look like they're available to go to war. Is there something I'm not aware of?'

'No,' Rodionov said.

'I'd like to add this to the Rosen investigation.'

'Definitely not. The killing of Penyagin is an assault on the entire structure of justice. I'm not going to tell the Central Committee that we added General Penyagin to the investigation of a common speculator. I can't believe that this morning Penyagin and I were together at a funeral. You can't imagine the shock.'

'I saw you.'

'What were you doing at the cemetery?'

'Burying my father.'

'Oh.' Rodionov grunted as if he had expected a more imaginative excuse. 'Condolences.'

Through the door, the yard was so full of incandescent lamps that it looked ablaze. As the Volvo was winched from the pit, water poured in bright fountains from the doors.

'I'll fold the Rosen investigation into the Penyagin investigation.' Arkady pulled on dry trousers.

Rodionov sighed as if a difficult decision had been forced on him. 'We want someone working full-time on Penyagin and nothing else. Someone fresh, more objective.'

'Who are you placing in charge? Whoever it is will have to spend time getting briefed on Rudy.'

'Not necessarily.'

'You're going to bring in someone cold?'

'For your sake.' Rodionov glanced around to demonstrate solidarity with Arkady. 'People will say that if Renko had found Kim, Penyagin would still be alive. They'll blame you for the tragic deaths of both your detective and the general.'

'We have no evidence that Penyagin was abducted. All we know is that he's here.'

Rodionov was pained. 'This sort of innuendo and speculation is uncalled for. See, you're too close to this case.'

The shirt was a sail with sleeves. Arkady tucked it in and slipped his bare feet into the shoes. 'So who are you putting in charge of the investigation?'

'A younger man, someone who can bring more

vigour to this case. In fact, this person is very well versed on Rosen. There should be no problems of co-ordination at all.'

'Who?'

'Minin.'

'*My* Minin? Little Minin?'

Rodionov became firmer. 'I've already talked to him. We're raising him a grade so that he'll have equal authority to you. I think we may have made a mistake by bringing you back to Moscow, by glorifying you and letting you loose on the city. You should be careful or you're going to fall further than you did before. I must tell you that not only will Minin bring more vigour to this case, he will also bring a clearer sense of direction.'

'He'd kill that bucket if you told him to. Is he here now?'

'I told him not to come until you were gone. Send him a report.'

'There'll be overlap between investigations.'

'No.'

Arkady had started to take his jacket from the butchering block. He put it down. 'What are you trying to say?'

As he answered, Rodionov carefully made his way across the floor. 'This is a crisis that demands forceful action. The murder of Penyagin is not just the loss of a single man, it's a blow against the body of the state. Everything we do, our office and militia, must have one overriding goal, finding and arresting the elements responsible. We will all have to make sacrifices.'

'What's my sacrifice?'

The prosecutor lifted a face lined with sympathy. The Party still turned out great actors, Arkady thought.

Rodionov said, 'Minin will take over the Rosen investigation, too. It will be part of this case, as you suggested. Tomorrow I want all your files and evidence on the Rosen case delivered to him – as well as a report on tonight's events, of course.'

'This is my case.'

'The debate is over. Your detective is dead. Minin is reassigned. You don't have a team and you don't have an investigation. You know, I think we've been demanding too much of you. You must have been in an emotional state after your father's funeral.'

'Still am.'

'Take a rest,' Rodionov said. As he handed Arkady his jacket from the block, a pocket rang against a tile.

'My God, an antique,' Rodionov said when Arkady took out the Nagant.

'An heirloom.'

'Don't point that at me.' The prosecutor backed away from the revolver.

'No one's pointing it at you.'

'Don't threaten me.'

'I'm not threatening you. I was just wondering. Penyagin and you were at the cemetery out of respect for . . .' He tapped the gun on his head to remember.

'Asoyan. Penyagin succeeded Asoyan.' The prosecutor edged towards the door.

'Right. I never met Asoyan. I forget, just what did Asoyan die of?'

But the city prosecutor escaped to the blinding lights of the yard.

Chapter Thirteen

On his way into town, Arkady parked behind the apartment complex by Dynamo Stadium, where a blue militia-precinct lamp on the corner announced what looked like an all-night bar. In the street, a drunk and his wife had a domestic conversation. He said something and she slapped him. He said something else and she slapped him again. He leaned into the blows as if he agreed with her point of view. Another drunk, in good clothes lightly dusted, walked in circles as if one foot were nailed to the pavement.

Inside the station, the desk officer was helping to subdue a drunk who, stripped to the waist and blinded by methanol, was trying to fly, beating his tattooed arms against the wall and leading a chorus of drunks who shouted from separate cells. Passing through, Arkady showed his ID, not bothering to open it. He might be dressed in odd sizes, but in this crowd he looked pretty good. Upstairs, where all the doors were padded in grey upholstery, a bulletin board displayed photos of Afghan vets on the force. In the Lenin room – the meeting place for political reinforcement and morale – militiamen were crashed out on long tables, towels across their faces.

Jaak's key opened a door to a room with a linoleum

floor and yellow walls. Since a precinct 'undercover'
room was home to different detectives working different
hours, the furniture was sparse and the decoration was
anonymous: two desks facing each other at the window,
four chairs, four hulking pre-war safes made of iron
plate. A car poster, a soccer poster and a scene of a
world's fair were taped to the wall. A corner door was
open to a pissoir, a foul nosegay to the room.

The desks shared three phones: an outside line, an
intercom and a dispatch connection to Petrovka. The
drawers held old sheaves of wanted faces, car descriptions and calendars that went back ten years. Around the
legs of each desk the linoleum was scarred by cigarettes.

Arkady sat down and lit a cigarette. He realized he
had always believed that one day Jaak would decamp
for Estonia, be reborn as an ardent nationalist and
heroically defend the fledgling republic. He believed Jaak
had the capacity to lead a different life. Instead of this.
The difference between him and Jaak was not so great,
dead or alive.

The first phone call he made was to his own office.
He was answered on the second ring. 'Minin here.'
Arkady hung up.

A naïf might ask why Minin hadn't gone to the
Lenin's Path Collective. Arkady knew from experience
that there were two types of investigations: one that
uncovered information, and the more traditional type
that covered it up. The second was actually more difficult since it demanded someone to cover the crime
scene and someone to control information in the office.

As Arkady's superior, Rodionov had to be the man at the collective. Minin, hard-working Minin, upgraded Minin, would be entrusted with gathering all the evidence and dossiers that showed any connection between the martyred General Penyagin and Rudy Rosen.

Arkady pulled out the short list of phone numbers he had taken from Penyagin's Party book. The first he recognized as Rodionov's; the other two were Moscow numbers but were new to him. He glanced at his watch: two a.m., an hour when all good citizens ought to be home. He picked up the outside line and dialled one of the unfamiliar numbers.

'Yes?' A man's voice answered, calmly coming awake.

'I'm calling about Penyagin,' Arkady said.

'What about him?'

'He's dead.'

'That's terrible news.' The voice stayed well spoken, soft, calmer than before. 'Did they catch anyone?'

'No.'

There was a pause; then the voice corrected itself. 'I mean, how did he die?'

'Shot. At the farm.'

'Who am I talking to?' The very polish of the voice was unusual, Russian birch painted with foreign lacquer.

'There was a complication,' Arkady said.

'What complication?'

'A detective.'

'Who is this?'

'Don't you want to know how he died?'

There was a pause at the other end. Arkady could

almost hear an intelligence becoming fully alert. 'I know who this is.'

The line went dead, but not before Arkady had recognised Max Albov's voice, too. Even if they had only met for an hour, because it was recently and in Penyagin's company.

He dialled the other number, feeling like a night fisherman dropping a hook in black water to see what would bite.

'Hello!' This time it was a woman, wide awake, yelling over a background of television babble. She had a lisp. 'Who is it?'

'I'm calling about Penyagin.'

'Wait a second!'

While he waited, Arkady listened to what sounded like an American relating a tedious story interspersed by explosions and the popping of small arms.

'Who is this?' A man came on the line.

'Albov,' Arkady said. Not that he was nearly as smooth as the journalist, but he modulated his voice a bit and there was that racket at the other end. 'Penyagin's dead.'

There was a pause, not a silence. With a musical segue, the American in the background moved on to a different story. The small-arms fire continued though, with echoes that suggested a luxury of space.

'Why are you calling?'

Arkady said, 'There were problems.'

'The worst thing you can do is call. I'm surprised at a sophisticated man like you.' The voice was strong, with the radiant humour and confidence of a successful leader. 'You don't start panicking in the middle of the game.'

'I'm worried.'

There was the click of a well-hit ball, a burst of applause and enthusiastic shouts of 'Banzai!' By now Arkady could picture a bar of Marlboro colours and contented golfers. He could hear the ringing of the cash register and, in softer tones, the distant chimes of slot machines. He could also see Borya Gubenko cupping the receiver, starting to be concerned.

'What's done is done,' Borya said.

'What about the detective?'

'You of all people know this is not a conversation to have on the phone,' Borya said.

'What next?' Arkady asked.

It was the middle of the night now. The television's American voice had a reassuring mutter. Arkady could almost feel the campfire glow of the screen, an international sameness of news that must accompany businessmen everywhere. Once Americans were going to save Russia. Then the Germans were going to save Russia. Whoever was going to save Russia now would bring their golf clubs to Borya's, Arkady thought: he had said that the Japanese were always the last to leave. 'What do we do?' he asked again.

He heard the launch of another ball. Was it bouncing off one of the cut-out trees standing on the factory floor? Or sailing long and true to the grass-green canvas on the far wall?

'Who is this?' Borya asked, then hung up.

Leaving Arkady with . . . nothing. First, he had not taped the conversations. Second, what if he had? He had captured no confession, nothing that couldn't be explained by sleepiness, noise, misunderstanding, a bad connection. So what if Penyagin had their phone numbers? Albov had been introduced as a friend of the militia, and the militia protected Borya Gubenko's driving range. So what if Albov and Gubenko knew each other? They were sociable members of the New Moscow, not hermits. Arkady had proof of nothing at all except that the Rosen case had taken Jaak to a collective farm, where he was killed and was found in the same car with Penyagin. And Arkady had bungled the Rosen case. He didn't have Kim, and what evidence he did have was being seized at this moment by Minin.

On the other hand, Jaak might be dead, but he was not a bad detective. Arkady looked through all the drawers and under them, and then brought out Jaak's oversized key. Each undercover detective had his own safe, a locked repository of his work. He tried the key on all four ancient safes in turn, fishing for a tumbler, until the last lock yielded and the iron door swung open to the three private shelves of Jaak's life. On the lower shelf were dead files tied in red ribbon, a basement of Jaak's professional memory. On the top shelf were personal items: loose photos of a boy and a man fishing, of the same boy and a man holding a model plane, of that boy now grown into an Army uniform and recognizable as Jaak posing with a happy but self-conscious woman smoothing her apron. They stood on the steps of a dacha. Light covered Jaak's eyes, shade covered his mother's. A picture of soldiers in their tent, singing, Jaak the one with the guitar. Divorce papers, eight years old, torn apart and taped back together. A snapshot of Jaak with Julya in an earlier phase of dark hair, blurred because they were plummeting on an amusement ride, also torn and taped together.

On the middle shelf was a grey criminal code book stuffed with the sloppy addenda of daily changing laws: protocol forms for investigation, search, interrogation; red directory of detectives in the Moscow region; loose Makarov slugs in copper casings. There were a surveillance photo of Rudy, a mug shot of a young Kim, Polina's shots of the black market and the burned shell of Rudy's car. Also an inter-office envelope. Arkady opened it and found the German videotape he had given Jaak along with two developed stills. So Jaak had got the pictures done.

They were individual photographs of the woman in the beer garden. On the reverse side of one, Jaak had written, 'Identified by reliable source as "Rita", emigrated to Israel 1985.'

A romantic name, Rita, short for the flower, marguerite. He guessed Julya was the source. If Rita married a Jew and got out, Julya would remember her.

Israeli? The combination of blonde hair, black sweater and gold chain struck Arkady as a classic German style, added to a full red mouth and line of the cheek that were pure Slav. Why wasn't she in the Jerusalem tape instead of the Munich one? Why had Arkady seen her in Rudy's car and intercepted a glance from her that had read him and his Zhiguli as a man and machine all too familiar? Why had he seen her mouth on the tape, 'I love you'?

The second picture was identical. On its back, Jaak had written, 'Identified by Soyuz receptionist as Mrs Boris Benz. German. Arrived 5/8, departed 8/8.' Two days ago.

The Soyuz Hotel was not one of Moscow's best, but it was the closest to where he and Jaak had sighted her with Rudy.

The outside line rang. He picked up.

'Who's there?' Minin demanded.

Arkady laid the receiver on the desk and softly left.

By now they would be watching his flat. Arkady drove to the south bank of the river, parked and walked to stay awake.

Moscow was beautiful at night. The other day when he was in the café with Polina, he had recited a poem by Akhmatova. 'I drink to our ruined house, to the dolour of my life, to our loneliness together; and to you I raise my glass, to lying lips that have betrayed us, to dead-cold, pitiless eyes, and to the hard realities: that the world is brutal and coarse, that God in fact has not saved us.' Polina, the romantic, had insisted that he recite it again.

Moscow was the ruined house, a cityscape that

looked half burned at night. Yet a streetlamp showed an iron gate opened to a court of graceful lime trees around a marble lion on a pedestal. Another light, askew, shone on a church cupola, azure, studded with gold stars. As if in Moscow anything that wasn't ugly dared display itself only at night.

His own bitterness surprised Arkady. He had been willing to tolerate a background of meanness and corruption if he could carry out his work at a certain level of efficiency, the way a surgeon might be content with setting bones in the middle of an endless catastrophe. His own honesty became a shell for him, a way both to deny and to accept the general misrule. See the contradiction, Arkady told himself – a lie, to be concise. Still, if he'd lost Rudy and Jaak, never even caught sight of Kim and probably been an evil influence on Polina, just how good was he?

What did he want? What he wanted was to be far away. For years he had been patient, yet for the last week he had felt that every second was like another grain of sand rolling through his fingers, ever since he'd heard Irina's voice on the radio.

If he felt this way, maybe he was in the wrong city. Was it possible to escape from the ruins of his old life?

The Central Telegraph on Gorky Street was open twenty-four hours a day. At four a.m. its grand hall was populated by Indians, Vietnamese and Arabs wiring home, and by equally desperate Soviets trying to reach relatives in Paris, Tel Aviv or Brighton Beach.

The air tasted of ashes, and the odour lingered on the teeth. Writers sat with telegram blanks to compose messages at five kopecks a word, men wadding up rejected attempts, women sitting more thoughtfully over one. Family groups collaborated in a circle of heads, usually brown heads with bright scarves. Occasionally a guard wandered in to make sure that no one stretched out on a bench, so the drunks in the hall made every effort to keep their bones assembled in a sitting position. There was an expression: a Russian is not drunk while there's a single blade of grass to hold on to. Maybe it was a law, Arkady wasn't sure. On the other side of a high counter, clerks maintained a quiet hostility. They held their own prolonged and whispered phone calls, turned their backs to read novels in privacy, disappeared for discreet naps. Their understandable grudge was that their shift gave them no chance to shop during working hours. Clocks above the counter showed the time: 0400 in Moscow, 1100 in Vladivostok, 2200 in New York.

Arkady stood at the counter and studied the two identical photographs, one of a Russian prostitute in Israel, the other of a well-dressed German tourist. Was either identification correct? Neither? Both? Jaak probably had the answer.

On the back of a telegram blank, he drew Rudy's car, the approximate positions of Kim, Borya Gubenko, the Chechens, Jaak and himself. On the side, to give her a name, he added Rita Benz.

On a second blank, he wrote 'TransKom' and listed Leningrad Komsomol, Rudy and Boris Benz.

On a third, under 'Lenin's Path Collective': Penyagin, Rudy's killer, maybe Chechens. From the blood, maybe Kim. Rodionov absolutely.

On a fourth, under 'Munich': Boris Benz, Rita Benz and an 'X' for whoever had asked Rudy, 'Where is Red Square?'

On a fifth, under 'Slot Machines': Rudy, Kim, TransKom, Benz, Borya Gubenko.

Frau Benz was the connection between the black market and Munich, and the contact between Rudy and Boris Benz. If Borya Gubenko had slot machines too, was he part of TransKom? Who better to introduce Rudy to his unlikely associates at a Komsomol gym than a former football idol? And if Borya was in TransKom, then he knew Boris Benz.

Finally Arkady drew a diagram of the farm, indicating road, yard, pens, barn, shed, garage, fire, Volvo, pit. He marked it with an estimate of distances and an arrow north, then added a diagram of the barn, with a sketch of the pail and cheesecloth of gore.

He thought of the pet shop under Kim's flat and the shelf of dragon's blood and the blood in Rudy's car. This reminded him of Polina. Public phones took only tiny two-kopeck pieces but he found one in his pocket and dialled her home.

Her voice had the low register of half-sleep, then was instantly awake. 'Arkady?'

'Jaak is dead,' he said. 'Minin is taking over.'

'Are you in trouble?'

'I am not your friend. You have always been suspicious of my leadership. You felt the investigation had strayed on to non-productive paths.'

'In other words?'

'Stay clear.'

'You can't order me to do that.'

'I'm asking you.' He whispered into the phone, 'Please.'

'Call me,' Polina said after a silence.

'When everything is straightened out.'

'I'll take Rudy's fax and put it on my number. You can leave a message.'

'Be careful.' He hung up.

Suddenly exhaustion overwhelmed him. He stuffed the blanks into the pocket with the gun and assumed a semi-upright position at the end of a bench. As soon as his eyes closed he was half asleep. He didn't dream as much as feel that he was falling down a soft, loamy hill in the dark, rolling lazily and without a sound, following the course of gravity. At the bottom of the hill was a pond. Someone ahead dove in and ripples spread in white rings. He hit the water without a struggle, sank, and then really was asleep.

Two eyes stared up from a face of loose, badly shaven cheeks. A hand raised a black pistol. The fingers were filthy and calloused and shaky. Another dirty hand held Arkady's ID. As he came fully awake he saw a plaque of war ribbons sewn on to a stained jacket. He also saw that the man, legless, stood on a wooden trolley. By its casters lay two blocks surfaced with strips of rubber tread for him to propel himself with. The face unveiled steel teeth and a breath like petrol fumes. A human car, Arkady thought.

The man said, 'I was only looking for a bottle. I didn't know I was going to run into a fucking general. I apologize.'

The pistol was the Nagant. Carefully he handed it to Arkady butt first. Arkady took the ID, too.

The man hesitated. 'Spare some coins? No?' He picked up the blocks to push himself away.

Arkady checked the clock; it was five a.m. He said, 'Wait.'

Something had occurred to him. While the idea was fresh, he laid his gun and ID down and pulled out the sketch of the farm. On a fresh blank he drew the interior of the shed as best as he could remember it: door, table, stacks of VCRs and computers, racks of clothes, copier, dominoes, telltale *Grozny* newspaper on the table, prayer rug on the floor. Referring to the farm sketch, he added an arrow north. Now that he thought about it, the rug had been new, with no wear from knees or forehead, and it had been aligned east–west. But from Moscow, Mecca was directly south.

'Do you have a two-kopeck piece?' Arkady asked.

'For a ruble?'

The beggar dug a purse from his shirt and produced a coin. 'You're going to make a businessman out of me.'

'A banker.'

He used the same phone he had called Polina on. For once he felt he had the advantage. Rodionov wasn't used to being confused and in the dark, but Arkady was.

Chapter Fourteen

At Veshki, on the verge of the city, the Moscow river seemed to hesitate among sedges and reeds, reluctant to leave a village where the drumming was the sound of frogs, the water reflected the morning hunt of swallows, and the steam of dawn wreathed beds of lilies.

Arkady had sailed here as a boy. He and Belov would tack back and forth, disturbing the ducks, reverentially trailing the swans that summered in Veshki. The sergeant would draw the boat up on the beach and he and Arkady would walk up to the village through a maze of lanes and cherry orchards to buy fresh cream and sour fruit drops. The sun always seemed to be uphill, beyond the crows that roosted in silhouette on the belfry of the church.

Better, the village was surrounded by the lush tangle and wonderful disrepair of old forest. Tier upon tier of birches, ash, broad-leafed beeches, larches, spruces, oaks, and sky that the sun penetrated only in providential single rays that searched for mushrooms. Everything was still and moving at once: ground litter alive with the tunnelling of shrews and moles, an explosion of needles and leaves when a hare left its cover, warblers and tits cleaning branches of caterpillars, woodpeckers ministering to the trunks, the cello drone of insects.

Veshki was the fantasy of all Russians, the village of perfect dachas.

Nothing had changed. When he slipped into the woods he followed paths that were familiar even in the mist. The same solitary oaks, not quite so dark and grandiose. A stand of birches with pale, trembling leaves. Someone had once tried to set out a lane of pines, but vines and smaller trees had sprung up around them and hauled them down. Everywhere ferns, ivy, the boughs of secondary growth tried to hide the way.

Fifteen metres to the left, a squirrel with tufted ears swayed on a lower branch, hanging upside down to scold an overcoat lying in the leaves. Minin lifted his face, which only annoyed the squirrel more. Arkady counted a windcheater huddled in the bushes and a trouser leg further to Minin's left. He moved right, behind a screen of pines.

He stopped when he caught sight of the road. It was smaller and the macadam more frayed than he remembered. A jogger went by in a tracksuit, a Gypsy with caved-in cheeks and black eyes on the woods. A woman rode by on a bicycle, chased by a terrier. When she was well past, he took the last few steps into the clear.

In one direction, the road continued for fifty metres, then veered right, approaching and then pulling away from a high gate, a black square framed by green trees. In the other direction, only ten metres away, were Rodionov and Albov. The city prosecutor looked surprised to see his investigator, though this was the appointed hour and place. Some people resented missing even a single night's sleep, Arkady thought. Rodionov walked stiffly, angrily, as if it were cold, instead of the pleasant summer day that was unfolding. Albov, however, appeared well rested, in tweed jacket and slacks, with an aura of aftershave. 'I told Rodionov we wouldn't spot you,' he said as a greeting. 'You must have visited here quite a lot.'

Rodionov said, 'You were supposed to return to your office and write your account of what happened at the farm. Instead, first you disappear, and then you call and demand that we meet you in the middle of nowhere.'

'Hardly nowhere,' Arkady said. 'Let's walk.' He started to amble in the direction of the gate.

Rodionov stayed by his side. 'Where is that report? Where did you go?'

The road was still deep in shadow. Albov lifted his eyes appreciatively to sunlight spilling halfway down a wall of trees. 'Stalin had a number of dachas around Moscow, didn't he?' he asked.

'This was his favourite,' Arkady said.

'Your father visited frequently, I'm sure.'

'Stalin liked to drink and talk all night. In the morning, they would walk here. Notice that the larger trees are firs. Behind every fir was a soldier who had to stay absolutely silent and out of sight. Of course times have changed.'

From either side of the road came the sound of crashing, as if heavy-footed mice were trying to keep pace.

Rodionov was exasperated. 'You didn't write a report.'

He jumped back when Arkady reached into his jacket. Instead of the Nagant, however, he produced a folded sheaf of yellow pages neatly filled with handwriting.

Rodionov said, 'It will have to be typed on the proper forms. That's just as well. We'll go over it together at the office.'

'And then?' Arkady asked.

Rodionov was encouraged. A report, even handwritten, was a token of surrender. 'We're all shaken by the death of our friend General Penyagin,' he said, 'and I understand how upset you must be over the murder of your detective. Nevertheless, nothing excuses your disappearance and wild accusations.'

'What accusations?' Arkady kept walking. So far he had made no mention of his first phone calls to Albov and Borya Gubenko. Neither had Albov.

'Your erratic behaviour,' Rodionov said.

'Erratic in what way?' Arkady asked.

'Your disappearance,' Rodionov said. 'Your unprofessional reluctance to cooperate in the Penyagin investigation simply because you will not be in charge. Your fixation on the Rosen case. The pressure of being back in Moscow was too much. For your own sake, a change is in order.'

'Out of Moscow?' Arkady asked.

'It's not a demotion,' Rodionov said. 'The fact is that there are crimes in other cities besides Moscow, real hot spots. I'm always lending investigators where they're needed. Without the Rosen case you are available.'

'Where?'

'Baku.'

Arkady had to laugh. 'Baku is not just out of Moscow, it's out of Russia.'

'They asked for my very best man. This is a chance for you to recoup some honour.'

Between the three-way civil war going on between Azeris, Armenians and the Army, in addition to mafia battles over the drug trade, Baku was a combination of Miami and Beirut. There was no easier place on earth for an investigator to vanish.

Twenty metres back, Minin stepped into the road to brush leaves from his overcoat, which was a signal for other men to emerge from the trees. The Gypsy jogged back to Minin's side.

To Arkady it looked as if the stroll had become a parade. 'A fresh opportunity,' he said.

'That's the way to look at it,' Rodionov agreed.

'I think you're right; it is time for me to leave Moscow,' Arkady said. 'But I wasn't thinking of Baku.'

'Where you go is not up to you,' Rodionov said. 'Or when.'

They had reached the gate. Up close, it wasn't black but dark green, with a guardwalk over double doors of wood backed with steel plates and guard towers on the side. In front was a striped barrier to keep the curious away, but how could anyone resist? Arkady stepped over and ran his hands over the lacquer finish, still lovingly maintained. Through it the long sedans used to roll another fifty metres to the dacha, to the midnight dinners and the after-midnight writing of the lists of names, when men and women passed, even while they slept, from the living to the dead. Sometimes children were brought to the dacha to decorate a lawn party or present a bouquet, but always during the day, as if they were safe only in the sun.

This was the door of the dragon, Arkady thought. Even if the dragon was now dead, the gate should be charred black and the road should be scarred by claws. Bones should be hanging from the branches. The soldiers in greatcoats should at least have stayed on as statues. Instead, watching from the guardwalk, was the solitary wide-angle eye of a security camera.

Rodionov hadn't noticed. 'Minin will—'

'Shut up,' Albov said and looked up at the lens. 'Smile.' He asked Arkady, 'There are other cameras on the road?'

'The entire way. The monitors are in the dacha. They're actively watched and taped. It's a historical area, after all.'

'Naturally. Do something about Minin,' Albov said softly to Rodionov. 'We don't want strong-arm tactics. Get the fool out of here.'

Confused but beaming with goodwill, Rodionov waved to Minin while Albov turned to Arkady with the expression of a man who keeps honest score. 'We're friends who are concerned about your wellbeing. We have every reason to meet you out in the open. So someone is watching a television monitor and wondering whether we're birdwatchers or amateur historians.'

'I'm afraid Minin won't pass as either,' Arkady said.

'Not Minin,' Albov agreed.

Rodionov stepped down the road to shoo Minin off. 'Slept?' Albov asked Arkady.

'No.'

'Eaten?'

'No.'

'It's miserable being on the run.' He sounded sincere. He also sounded in control, as if Rodionov had been allowed to chair the meeting as long as items on the agenda were followed in order. The camera at Stalin's gate had changed that. Albov held his cigarette to his mouth as he spoke. 'The call was clever.'

'Penyagin had your phone number.'

'Then it was obvious.'

'My best ideas are obvious.'

Arkady had also called Borya, as Albov must know by now. The question was implicit: what other phone numbers had Penyagin written down?

When Rodionov returned, Albov lifted the report from the prosecutor's pocket. 'Telegram blanks,' Albov said. 'He was at the Telegraph Centre all night.'

Rodionov glanced at the camera and muttered, 'We were covering train stations, known addresses, the streets.'

'Moscow is a big city,' Arkady said in the prosecutor's defence.

'Did you send any telegrams?' Albov asked Arkady.

'We can find out,' Rodionov pointed out.

'In a day or two,' Arkady agreed.

'He's threatening us,' the prosecutor said.

Albov said, 'With what? That's the question. If he knows anything about Penyagin, the detective or Rosen, he's legally bound to inform his superior, who is you, or the investigator of record, who is Minin. Otherwise, he'll be regarded as a raving maniac. The streets are full of raving maniacs these days, so no one's going to listen to him. He's also obligated to follow orders. If you send him to Baku, that's where he goes. He can stand under this camera all day long. It's a dead end; there aren't any floodlights, so you can pick him up tonight and tomorrow he'll wake up in Baku. Renko, let me tell you something from experience. You don't stop running until you've got something to trade. You have nothing, do you?'

'No,' Arkady admitted. 'But I have other plans.'

'What other plans?'

'I was thinking of pursuing the Rosen investigation.'

Rodionov looked down the road. 'Minin is in charge of that now.'

'I wouldn't be in Minin's way,' Arkady said.

Albov asked, 'How could you not be in Minin's way?'

'I'd be in Munich.'

'Munich?' Albov cocked his head as if a new bird note had issued from the woods. 'What would you look for in Munich?'

'Boris Benz,' Arkady said. He didn't use the woman's name because he wasn't sure of her identification.

In the silence Rodionov stiffened, like a man who had missed a step.

Albov looked down, around and finally raised a smile of astonishment mixed with admiration.

'You know, it's in the blood,' he told Rodionov. 'When the Germans invaded and rolled to the gates of Leningrad and Moscow, and Stalin lost millions of men and the entire Red Army fell into disorder and retreat, one tank commander never stepped back. The Germans thought they had trapped General Renko. What they didn't understand was that he was happy behind their lines, and the bloodier and more confused the action the better. The son is exactly the same. Is he trapped? No, he's here, there. God only knows where he will turn up next.'

'There's a direct flight to Munich at seven forty-five tomorrow morning,' Arkady said.

'You truly believe the prosecutor's office will let you leave the country?' Albov asked.

'I'm absolutely sure,' Arkady said. He was, as soon as he had seen Rodionov's reaction to Boris Benz's name, an instinctive flinch that had expressed the anger and fear of a stuck pig. Until then, the name could have meant nothing, but in an instant Arkady had ascertained, as Rudy might have put it, the high market value of Boris Benz.

'Even if the Ministry wanted to, it's not up to us,' Rodionov said. 'Foreign investigation is the responsibility of State Security.'

'You were saying at Petrovka the other day that, now we're members of Interpol, we work directly with foreign colleagues. I'll only have a holdall bag. No inspection.'

'*I* couldn't go tomorrow, if I wanted to,' Rodionov said. 'There's arranging an external passport and Ministry orders. It would take weeks.'

'There are twelve rooms at the Central Committee. All they do is make up passports and visas on the spot. Lufthansa flight 84,' Arkady said. 'Remember, Germans are punctual.'

'There *is* a way,' Albov said. 'If you don't travel as an investigator, as an official of the prosecutor's office, but as a private individual. If the Ministry can generate a passport and if you have the American dollars or German marks, then you simply buy a seat on the plane and take off. In fact, we've just opened a consulate in Munich; you could make contact and receive travel expenses there. The question is only where you'd get hard currency for the ticket.'

'The answer is . . .?' Arkady asked.

'I could lend it to you. In Munich you could pay me back.'

Arkady said, 'The money has to come from the prosecutor.'

Albov said, 'Then that's the way it will be done.'

'Why?' Rodionov protested.

'Because this is a more delicate investigation than we were first aware of,' Albov said. 'Foreign investors, especially Germans, are sensitive to the messy scandals of the new Soviet capitalism. We want to clear everybody's names, even the names of people we've never heard of. Because, even though the investigator may be chasing phantoms, we don't want to place obstacles in his path. Besides, we don't know everything the investigator knows or what rash steps he thinks he has to take to preserve his independence.'

'He never said what he knew.'

'Because he's only desperate, he's not an utter fool. He stuffed your pocket with telegrams and you didn't even notice. I support Renko. More and more, I'm impressed by his adaptability. Still, I wonder,' Albov said, turning towards Arkady, 'I wonder if you've considered the fact that as soon as you step on to the plane you lose your authority. In Germany you'll be a common citizen – less, a Soviet citizen. To Germans you'll be nothing but a refugee, because to them all Russians are refugees. Secondly, you will lose your credibility here. You won't be a hero to your friends any more. No one will believe any warnings, alarms or information that you left behind, because here too you will be regarded as a refugee. And refugees lie; refugees will say anything to get out. Nothing they say is considered the truth anywhere. The one thing I can promise you is you'll be sorry you ever went.'

'I'm only going for this case,' Arkady said.

'See, already you're lying.' Albov's eyes rested on Arkady sympathetically. He seemed to have to force himself to remember a less interesting man. 'Rodionov, you'd better get to it. You have a great deal to do to make sure your investigator doesn't miss his flight.

Necessary papers, funds, whatever, in a day.' Turning to Arkady again, he asked, 'What about flying Aeroflot?'

'Lufthansa.'

'You want an airline where the seat belts work. I completely agree,' Albov said.

Rodionov backed away, excluded, stealing glances, still watching for some other signal from Albov. Far down the road, Minin and his men had reassembled into a confused, forlorn group.

'Go,' Albov said.

He opened a pack of Camel Lights and lit a match for himself and Arkady. He had a fastidious manner, saving the last lick of the flame for the cellophane, which he let burn and blow away on the morning breeze. Then he returned his attention to the gate. As the sun rose, the trees on either side seemed to grow, come into focus, turn ever more green, shift through stages of ornate light and shade. The light that crept around the guardwalk was white, as if on fire. Simultaneously, the gate itself fell into more shadow and by contrast loomed darker, reflecting the two men.

It occurred to Arkady what Albov had meant about being paid back. 'You will be in Munich?'

'Some of my best friends are in Munich,' Albov said.

Part Two

MUNICH

12 August–18 August 1991

Chapter Fifteen

Federov, the consular aide who picked Arkady up at the airport, pointed out sights as if he had personally built Munich, poured the Isar river, gilded the Peace Angel and balanced the domes on the twin church spires of the Frauenkirche.

'The consulate here is new, but I was in Bonn, so this is pretty much old hat to me,' Federov said.

It wasn't to Arkady. The world seemed to be spinning around him, full of traffic and unintelligible signs. Streets were so clean that they looked plastic. Bikers in shorts and summer tans shared the road without being mangled under the wheels of every passing bus. Windows were glass instead of crusted dirt. There were no queues anywhere. Women in short skirts carried not string bags, but colourful carrier bags emblazoned with the names of shops; in full stride, legs and bags moved with a purposeful, integrated rhythm.

'That's all you brought?' Federov looked at Arkady's holdall. 'You'll have two suitcases on the way back. How long are you staying?'

'I don't know.'

'Your visa's only good for two weeks.'

He searched for some sign from his passenger, but Arkady was looking at walls of Bavarian yellow as smooth as butter, with balconies that had no weepy stains, stucco that was not cracked on bricklines, doors that did not wear graffiti and scars of abuse. In a pastry-shop window, marzipan pigs gambolled around chocolate cakes.

One moment Federov had the cautious attitude of a young man who had been sent to take delivery of dubious goods. The next he was consumed by curiosity. 'Generally when someone like you arrives there's a welcoming committee and an official programme. I want to warn you there's nothing laid on for you at all.'

'Good.'

Pedestrians waited like troops at red lights, whether traffic was coming or not. On green, cars swarmed ahead; it was like being in a hive of BMWs. The street spread into an avenue of stone mansions with steps that were guarded by iron gates and marble lions. Signs announced art galleries and Arab banks. The next square was lined by a row of medieval banners with corporate logos. Arkady watched a walking man who was dressed in lederhosen and high socks despite the heat.

'I just don't understand how you got a visa so fast,' Federov said.

'Friends.'

Federov glanced over again because Arkady didn't look like a man who had friends.

'Well, however you did it, you landed in whipped cream,' he said.

The consulate was an eight-storey building on Seidlstrasse. A wood-panelled waiting room had chairs of bright chrome and black leather. Behind bulletproof glass was a reception desk with three television monitors. Federov slid Arkady's passport on a tray under the glass to a receptionist who looked Russian almost to her fingertips, which were long and polished like mother of pearl. When she started to push a book out, Federov blocked the tray and said, 'He doesn't have to sign.'

He led Arkady on to the lift and up to the third floor, down a corridor of small offices, past a conference room with boxes and chairs still wrapped in blocks of plastic packing, and showed him through a metal door with a plaque that said in German CULTURAL AFFAIRS. Inside was a man with grey hair, a good Western suit and a frown. There were only two chairs in the room and he nodded for Arkady to take the other one.

'I'm Vice-Consul Platonov. I know who you are,' he told Arkady. He didn't offer to shake hands. 'That's all,' he said to Federov, who could have been smoke he was gone so fast.

Platonov had the forward hunch of a chess player. He looked like a man with a problem, something nasty but not too large, something he could resolve in a day or two. Arkady doubted this was his usual office. The walls still gave off the tang of fresh paint. An unhung, wide-angle photograph of Moscow at sunset leaned against the near wall. Against the far wall were posters: dancers of the Bolshoi and Kirov, treasures of the Kremlin Armoury, a cruiser on the Volga. The only other furnishings were a folding table, a phone and an ashtray.

'What do you think of Munich?' Platonov asked.

'It's beautiful. It's very rich,' Arkady said.

'It was rubble after the war, worse than Moscow. That says a great deal about the Germans. You speak German?'

'A little.'

'But you do speak German?' Platonov seemed to think he had a confession.

'In the Army I was stationed for two years in Berlin. I was monitoring Americans, but I did pick up some German.'

'German and English.'

'Not well.'

Platonov was in his mid-sixties, Arkady guessed. A diplomat since Brezhnev? That took a man of both rubber and steel.

'Not well?' Platonov folded his arms. 'Do you know how many years it has taken us to open a Soviet consulate here? This is the industrial capital of Germany. These are the investors we need to reassure. We've not even finished moving in and we have an investigator from Moscow. Are you after someone on the consulate staff?'

'No.'

'I didn't think so. Usually we're ordered back to Moscow before we get bad news,' Platonov said. 'I asked if you were actually KGB, but they don't even want to see you. On the other hand, they're not stopping you.'

'That's decent of them.'

'No, that's suspicious. The last thing anyone wants is an investigator who is out of control.'

'That's been my experience, too,' Arkady had to admit.

'Aside from our staff, there aren't that many Soviets in Munich. Factory directors and bankers training with the Germans, a dance troupe from Georgia. Who are you interested in?'

'I can't say.'

Arkady supposed that representatives of the Foreign Ministry were taught a wide stock of encouraging expressions and public grins, those little gestures that signified they were still human. Platonov, however, seemed content with a direct, hostile stare that never wavered while he opened a case and took out a cigarette for himself.

'Just so we understand each other, I don't care who you're after. I don't care if there's a family lying slaughtered in its blood back in Moscow. No murderer is as important as the success of this consulate. The German people will not give hundreds of millions of Deutschmarks to murderers. We have fifty years of bad history to make up for. We want quiet, normal relations leading to loans and commercial agreements that will rescue *all* the families in Moscow. The last thing we want is Russians chasing each other through the streets of Munich.'

'I can see that.' Arkady tried to be agreeable.

'You have no official standing here. If you contact the German police, they will immediately call us and we will tell them you're simply here as a tourist.'

'I've always been curious about Bavaria, the land of beer.'

'We'll keep your passport. That means you can't travel somewhere else or register at a hotel. We have accommodation for you at a pension. In the meantime I will be working hard to have you recalled to Moscow – tomorrow, if possible. My suggestion is that you forget about any investigation. See the museums, buy some gifts, have your beer. Enjoy yourself.'

The pension was above a Turkish travel agency half a block from the train station. The accommodation comprised two rooms with bed, bare mattress, chest of drawers, chair, two tables and a cabinet that opened to reveal a miniature kitchen. The toilet and shower were down the hall.

'Turks on the third floor,' Federov said and pointed up. He pointed down. 'Yugoslavs on the first. They all work at BMW. You could go and join them.'

The lights worked. The refrigerator light went on when Arkady opened the door and there were no cockroach eggs in the corners. Even the closet had a light, and he noticed when they came into the building that the halls smelled of disinfectant instead of piss.

'So this is paradise. It's not all quite as great as you thought, is it?' Federov asked.

'It's been a while since you were in Moscow,' Arkady said.

He opened the rear window. The view was of the

back of the train station and the tracks, steel ribbons shining in the sun. What was odd was that he felt as disoriented as if he were in a different time zone halfway around the world, when he had made only a four-hour flight.

Federov lingered at the door. 'It occurs to me that you couldn't have a more inappropriate name than "Renko" – for a visitor to Germany, I mean. I've heard about your father. He may have been a hero at home, he was a butcher here.'

'No, he was a butcher at home, too.'

'All I mean is that, with a name like yours, maybe it would be wiser to stay right here and not go out at all.'

'Key?' Arkady put his hand out when Federov started to leave.

With a shrug, Federov gave it to him. 'I wouldn't worry, Investigator. One thing a Russian doesn't have to worry about in Germany is being robbed.'

Alone, Arkady sat on the windowsill and had a solitary cigarette. It was a Russian custom to sit before embarking on a trip, so why not on arrival? To take formal possession of a bare, unlocked room. Especially with a filthy Russian cigarette. Down on the tracks he saw a sleek red and black train inching towards the station. In the locomotive an engineer wore the grey cap of a general. He remembered the train he saw in Kazan Station, with the man in the locomotive stripped to his waist and the way the forearm of the woman with him rested on his shoulder. He wondered where they were now. Pulling carriages around Moscow? Rolling across the steppe?

He returned to the bed and opened his holdall. From the pockets of his rumpled trousers he disinterred Penyagin's handwritten list of three phone numbers, Rudy's fax and the identified still of Rita Benz. From a rolled jacket he took the videotape. The clothes, which represented his complete and travelling wardrobe, fitted on two hangers and in one cupboard drawer. He slipped the numbers, fax and photo into the videotape case with the cassette. They were his treasure and shield. Then he counted the money he had squeezed out of Rodionov. One hundred Deutschmarks. How far would that take the usual tourist in Germany? A day? A week? It would take thrift and paranoia to survive much longer.

The cassette inside his shirt, Arkady went out and ran across a boulevard to the train station, which had the mammoth scale of a modern museum on the outside. Light filtered through frosted glass and pigeon netting on the inside. No gangs of Kazans in black jackets, no somnolently flipping television screen, no Dream Bar. Instead, bookshops, restaurants, wine shops, a theatre with erotic films. A kiosk sold maps with translations in French, English, Italian, none in Russian. With the English version, Arkady headed back for the street and followed a crowd out of the main entrance.

The smell of a café's good coffee and chocolate almost dropped him to his knees, but he was so unused to restaurants or even to eating at all that he kept moving forward in the hope of seeing an approachable ice-cream van. He focused not on shop windows, but on the reflections in their glass. Twice he entered shops and immediately came out to see if anyone was waiting for him. A tourist sees the sights. Arkady, however, had a tunnel vision that excluded crowds, fountains and statues for the sake of spotting a telltale Soviet face, rolling walk or habit, like wearing the wedding ring on the right hand. The sound of German around him was a babble of surf. It was like waking up to notice that he had arrived in a wide plaza surrounded by handsome buildings patterned in brick, with stepped gables that climbed to spires of red tile. On one side of the square was a town hall of grey Gothic stone. Hundreds of people strolled or rested at tables with steins of beer or stared up at the hall's carillon of lifesize clockwork dancers and musicians. Arkady turned around. Businessmen wore muted suits and silk ties. Women wore a stylish, not a grieving black. Boys sported the T-shirts, shorts and backpacks of summer holidays. The volume of their voices swelled. There was a bookshop on a corner with three floors of books. Another shop had the sweet reek of tobacco. The yeasty bouquet of beer issued from this doorway and that. A golden madonna looked down from a marble column.

He bought ice cream in a cone, pantomiming his choice rather than testing his command of German. The ice cream was so rich that it tasted like frosting. He spent four marks on cigarettes. All the same, he had engaged with Munich now. He ran down into the plaza's underground station, bought a ticket and jumped on the first train returning the way he had come.

Hanging on to the bar on either side of Arkady were a pair of Turks, each with a faraway gaze. Filling the seat before him was a woman holding a ham that rocked back and forth on her knee like a baby.

What were the chances of anyone following him? Not great, considering the difficulty of trailing someone in an urban setting. According to Soviet technique, to carry out surveillance of a cautious mobile target demanded five to ten vehicles and thirty to a hundred people. Arkady didn't personally know because he'd never had more than enough manpower and cars to follow someone around a room.

At the train station stop, he returned to the same waiting hall where he had been an hour before. Some call boxes were in the open, but upstairs he found telephone booths and books for different cities on a stainless-steel counter. In Moscow phone books were so rare they were kept in safes, but these weren't even chained.

The books were confusing because of the sameness and strangeness of German names, full of consonants in death throes, and the variety of advertisements that filled more than half the pages. Under 'Benz', the only Boris had an address on Königinstrasse. There was no listing for any business called TransKom.

The phone booth had a rounded clear plastic door. Arkady decided he knew just enough German to talk to an operator. He thought she said she had no number for TransKom.

Then he called Boris Benz.

A woman answered. 'Ja?'

Arkady said, 'Herr Benz?'

'Nein.' She laughed.

'Herr Benz ist im Haus?'

'Nein. Herr Benz ist auf Ferien gereist.'

'Ferien?' On holiday?

'Er wird zwei Wochen lang nicht in München sein.'

Away for two weeks? Arkady asked, 'Wo ist Herr Benz?'

'Spanien.'

'Spanien?' Two weeks in Spain? The news was just getting worse.

'Spanien, Portugal, Marokko.'

'Nein Russland?'

'Nein, er macht Ferien in der Sonne.'

'Kann ich sprechen mit TransKom?'

'TransKom?' The name seemed new to her. 'Ich kenne TransKom nicht.'

'Sie ist Frau Benz?'

'Nein, die Reinmachefrau.' The house cleaner.

'Danke.'

'Wiedersehen.'

As Arkady hung up he thought that this was about as basic as a conversation could get without drawing pictures. So he had talked to a housemaid who said

Boris Benz would be away on summer holiday for the next two weeks and who had never heard of TransKom. The only real information was that Benz had gone south for the Mediterranean sun. Apparently Germans did this. By the time he returned to Munich, Arkady would probably be back in Moscow. From the cassette, he pulled Rudy's fax and dialled the transmitting number shown on the top of the page.

'Hello,' a woman answered in Russian.

Arkady said, 'I'm calling about Rudy.'

After a pause, 'Rudy who?'

'Rosen.'

'I don't know any Rudy Rosen.' There was something slovenly about the voice, as if she wouldn't take a cigarette from her mouth.

'He said you were interested in Red Square,' Arkady said.

'We're all interested in Red Square. So what?'

'I thought you wanted to know where it was.'

'What is this, a joke?'

She hung up. In fact she did what any normal person would, given such a stupid riddle, Arkady thought. Because he had failed was no reason to blame her.

On the same floor he found a bank of self-operated luggage lockers for two Deutschmarks a day. He made another circuit of the hall before returning, putting coins in the slot, placing the cassette in an empty locker and pocketing the key. Now he could return to the flat or go back out on the street without fear of losing the evidence, which seemed a great accomplishment considering his state of confusion. Or a pitiful achievement considering how little time he had – according to Platonov, one day.

He returned to the phone-book counter, opened the Munich book, flipped to 'R' and to 'Radio Liberty–Radio Free Europe'. When he called the number an operator answered only, 'RL–RFE.'

Arkady asked in Russian to speak to Irina Asanova, then waited what seemed forever for her to come on the line.

'Hello?'

He had thought he was prepared, but he was so startled actually to hear her that he couldn't speak.

'Hello. Who is this?'

'Arkady.'

He recognized her voice, but after all he had been listening to her broadcasts. There was no reason for her to remember his.

'Arkady who?'

'Arkady Renko. From Moscow,' he added.

'You're calling from Moscow?'

'No, I'm here in Munich.'

The phone was so quiet he thought that he might have lost the connection.

'Amazing,' Irina said finally.

'Could I see you?'

'I heard they'd rehabilitated you. You're still an investigator?' She sounded as if surprise was rapidly evaporating into irritation.

'Yes.'

229

'Why are you here?' she asked.

'A case.'

'Congratulations. If they let you travel, they must have a lot of faith in you.'

'I've been listening to you in Moscow.'

'Then you know I have a broadcast in two hours.' Papers rustled in the background to emphasize how busy she was.

'I'd like to see you,' Arkady said.

'Maybe in a week. Give me a call.'

'I mean soon. I won't be here long.'

'This is a bad time.'

'Today,' Arkady said. 'Please.'

'I'm sorry.'

'Irina.'

'Ten minutes,' she said, once she had made it clear that he was the last man on earth she wanted to see.

Chapter Sixteen

A taxi took Arkady to a park where the driver pointed out a path that led him to long tables, chestnut trees and a pagoda-shaped, five-storey wooden pavilion. 'The Chinese Tower', Irina had told him to say.

In the shade of beech trees, diners carried giant steins of beer and paper plates that sagged under roast chicken, ribs, potato salad. Even the litter the breeze blew his way smelled good enough to eat. The lapping of the conversation and the steady pace of consumption had an unanticipated, sensual languor. Munich was still unreal to him. He had the sudden apprehension not that he was walking in a dream, but that he was someone's nightmare visiting the real world.

He had feared he might not recognize Irina, but there was no mistaking her. Her eyes were a little larger, seemingly darker, and still possessed a quality that selfishly gathered light only for her. Her brown hair was redder and cut shorter, a starker frame to her face. She wore a gold cross over a black, short-sleeved sweater. No wedding ring showed.

'You're late.' She gave Arkady a handshake.

'I wanted to shave,' he said. He had bought a disposable blade and used it at the train station. Cuts on his chin tracked his haste.

231

'We were about to leave,' Irina said.

'It's been a long time,' Arkady said.

'Stas and I have a newscast to get ready.' She didn't appear to be excited or nervous, just pressed by a heavy schedule.

'Not quite yet.' A man, all bones wrapped in a loose sweater and baggy trousers, with bright, tubercular eyes, arrived with three foaming steins of beer. He was Russian, Arkady knew immediately. 'I'm Stas. Do I call you Comrade Investigator?'

'Arkady is fine.'

The skeleton in the sweater sat by Irina and laid his hand over the back of her chair.

'May I?' Arkady took the chair facing them and said to Irina, 'You look wonderful.'

'You look good, too,' Irina said.

'I don't think anyone is thriving in Moscow,' Arkady said.

Stas raised his stein and said, 'Drink up. The rats are leaving the ship now. Everyone's coming for a visit. Most of them are trying to stay. In fact, most of them are trying to get work at Radio Liberty; we see them every day. Well, who can blame them?' He watched a buxom girl collecting empties. 'Waited on by Valkyries. What a life.'

Arkady sipped for politeness' sake. 'I heard you—'

'So, Arkady, you've had rather a chequered career,' Stas interrupted. 'Member of Moscow's Golden Youth, member of the Communist Party, rising star of the prosecutor's office, hero who saved our dear dissident

232

Irina, years of Siberian exile atoning for that single act of decency, and now not only the prosecutor's pet, but his ambassador to Munich, able to hunt down your lost love, Irina. Here's to romance.'

Irina laughed. 'He's just joking.'

'I understand,' Arkady said.

It was funny; in interrogation he had been naked, hosed down, insulted and hit, yet he had never felt as embarrassed as he did at this table. Besides being badly shaved, his stupid face was probably beet red, he thought, because the evidence seemed to be that he was crazy. Evidently he had been crazy for years, imagining a connection between himself and this woman, who clearly shared no similar memory at all. How much had he imagined – their time hiding in his flat, the shootings, New York? At the psychiatric isolator, when the doctors injected sulphazine into his spine, they used to say that he was crazy; now, over beer, it turned out that they were right. He looked at Irina for any response, but she had the equanimity of a statue.

'Don't take it personally. That's just Stas.' She lit one of Stas's cigarettes without asking. 'Arkady, I hope you have some fun in Munich. I'm sorry I don't have time to do anything with you.'

'That's too bad.' Arkady drank to that.

'But you'll have friends at the consulate and you'll be busy with your case. You always were a dedicated worker,' Irina said.

'A fool for work,' Arkady said.

'It must be a heavy responsibility, representing Moscow. The prosecutor sent his human face.'

'It's kind of you to say so.' He was Rodionov's 'human face'? Was that what she thought?

Stas said, 'That reminds me, we ought to do an update on the crime rate in Moscow.'

'On the deteriorating situation?' Arkady asked.

'Exactly.'

'You work together?' Arkady asked.

Irina said, 'Stas writes the newscasts, I only read them.'

'Mellifluously,' Stas said. 'Irina is the queen of Russian émigrés. She has broken hearts from New York to Munich and all stations in between.'

'Have you?' Arkady asked.

'Stas is a *provocateur*.'

'Maybe that's what makes him a writer.'

'No,' Irina said. 'No, that's what got him beaten at demonstrations in Red Square. He defected to the Americans in Finland, for which the Soviet prosecutor general you work for pronounced him guilty of a state crime with a sentence of death. Amusing, isn't it? An investigator from Moscow can come here, but if Stas ever went back to Moscow, he'd disappear. The same with me if I went back.'

'Even I feel safer here,' Arkady agreed.

'What is this case of yours? Who are you after?' Stas asked.

'I can't tell you that,' Arkady said.

Irina said, 'Stas is afraid that I'm your case. Lately

we've been seeing a lot of visitors in Munich. Family members, friends from before we left.'

'Left?' Arkady asked.

'Defected,' Irina said. 'Dear old grandmothers and former soulmates who keep telling us everything is fine and that we can go home again.'

Arkady said, 'Nothing is fine. Don't go back.'

'It's possible that at Radio Liberty we have a better idea of what's happening in Russia than you do,' Stas said.

'I hope so,' Arkady said. 'People outside a burning house generally have a better view than the people inside.'

Irina said, 'Don't worry. I've already told Stas it hardly mattered what you said.'

The sigh of a tuba marked the start of a waltz. Musicians in lederhosen had appeared on the first floor of the pavilion. Otherwise, Arkady saw little besides Irina. The women at other tables were beer-fed, slim, brunette, white-blonde, in slacks and skirts, and all of a German sameness and safeness. With her wide Slavic eyes and self-possession, Irina was unique, an ikon at a picnic. A familiar ikon. Arkady could have traced in the dark the line from the lashes of her eye, over the curve of her cheek to a corner in the softness of her mouth; yet she had changed, and Stas had put the name to it. In Moscow she had been a flame in the wind, so desperately outspoken that she was a danger to anyone near her. The woman Irina had become was someone colder and in control. The queen of the Russian émigrés was only waiting for Stas to finish his beer so she could leave.

Arkady asked her, 'You like Munich?'

'Compared to Moscow? Compared to Moscow, rolling in broken glass is nice. Compared to New York or Paris? It's pleasant, but a little quiet.'

'It sounds as if you've been everywhere.'

'And you, do you like Munich?' she asked.

'Compared to Moscow? Compared to Moscow, rolling in Deutschmarks is nice. Compared to Irkutsk or Vladivostok? It's warmer.'

Stas set down his empty stein. Arkady had never seen anyone so thin drain beer so quickly. At once Irina rose, in command, ready to hurry back to real life.

'I want to see you again,' Arkady said in spite of himself.

Irina studied him. 'No, what you want is for me to say that I'm sorry you went to Siberia, that I'm sorry if you suffered on my account. Arkady, I *am* sorry. There, I said it. I don't think we have anything else to say.' With that she left.

Stas lingered. 'I hope you are a son of a bitch. I hate it when lightning hits the wrong man.'

Because she was tall, Irina seemed to sail between tables, her hair back like a flag.

'Where did they put you up?' Stas asked.

'Across from the train station.' Arkady mentioned the address.

'Sort of a dump,' Stas said, surprised.

Irina finally disappeared into a crowd arriving on the other side of the tower.

'Thanks for the beer,' Arkady said.

'Any time.' Stas hurried after Irina, manoeuvring around tables with a limp that seemed more a gesture of determination than a handicap.

Arkady stayed seated because he didn't trust himself to walk. He felt he had come a long way to be run over by a lorry. Tables were filling all the time, and he wanted the beer garden to close in over him. Here, beer had a sedative effect leading to calm, reasoned conversation. Couples young and old enjoyed civilized steins. Men with fierce eyebrows poured their concentration into chessboards. The tower with the oompah band was about as Chinese as a cuckoo clock. No matter; he had wandered into a village where he was not known, neither welcome nor rejected. He would settle for invisible. He sipped the good beer.

What was really terrible, truly frightening, was that he did want to see Irina again. Humiliating though the experience had been, he realized he would accept more of it to be with her, which revealed a capacity for masochism that he never knew he had. Their encounter had been so grotesque as to be comic. This woman, this memory he had carried like an extra chamber of the heart and found after so long, seemed barely to recall his name. Well, there was a disproportion of emotion that was – to use her word – amusing. Or evidence of insanity. If he was wrong about Irina, perhaps he was wrong about the history he thought they shared.

Reflexively he touched his stomach and felt the groove of scar tissue through the shirt. Though what did that prove? Maybe he had punctured himself with an umbrella one day on the way to school, or been pinned by a statue of Lenin as it fell. In half his statues Lenin pointed towards the future. It was a well-known dangerous finger.

'What's so hilarious?'

'Pardon?' Arkady came out of his reverie.

'What's so hilarious?' The place across the table had been taken by a large man with a florid face and crisp white shirt. A small wool hat perched on a head as bald as a kneecap. He held a beer in one hand and protected a whole roast chicken with the other. Arkady noticed that the entire table was elbow-to-elbow with people hoisting drumsticks, ribs, pretzels, golden beers.

'You're enjoying yourself?' the man with the chicken asked.

Arkady shrugged rather than unveil a Russian accent.

The man's eyes darted to his Soviet coat. He said, 'You like the beer, the food, the life? It's nice. We worked forty years to have it so.'

The rest of the table paid no attention. Arkady realized he hadn't eaten anything except an ice cream. The table was so awash in food that he almost didn't need to. The band slid from Strauss to Louis Armstrong. He finished the beer. Of course there were beer bars in Moscow, but there were no steins or glasses, so patrons filled cardboard milk cartons. As Jaak would have said, 'Homo Sovieticus wins again.'

Not that everyone recognized the fact. When Arkady opened a map, the man across the table nodded, suspicions confirmed.

'Another East German. It's an invasion.'

Retreating, Arkady headed towards the nearest buildings over the treeline, which proved to be offices of IBM and the tower of Hilton. The lobby of the hotel could have been an Arab tent. Each chair and divan was occupied by a man in flowing white keffiyeh and jellaba. Many were elderly, with canes, walkers and worry beads; Arkady assumed they had come to Munich for medical attention. Dark boys in Western slacks and button-down shirts played tag. Their sisters and mothers were in Arab dress; married women wore ornate plastic masks showing only their chins and brows, and trailed heavy perfume through the air.

In the hotel driveway, one young Arab was photographing another beside a new red Porsche. When the boy posing sat on a fender, the car's alarm erupted with a blaring horn and blinking lights. As the boys chased round the car and beat on the hood, the doorman and porter watched with expressively blank faces.

Arkady found the route he had come by cab, following the east side of the park to the museums on Prinzregentenstrasse. Cars flashed past under streetlamps. The sky, however, was already darker than a Moscow summer night and the classical façade of the Haus der Kunst looked almost two-dimensional.

It occurred to Arkady that the west side of the park was bordered by Königinstrasse, where Boris Benz lived. The houses were appropriately grand for a 'Queen Street', stone mansions set behind gardens of aromatic roses and gates with plaques that warned VORSICHT! BISSIGER HUND!

Benz's address was between two enormous houses done in coquettish *Jugendstil*, the German answer to Art Nouveau. They looked like a pair of matrons peeping over fans. Squeezed in the middle was a garage that had been renovated as medical offices. The second-floor button was for Benz. The lights were out. Arkady pushed the button just in case. No answer.

On either side of the door was a panel of leaded glass for viewing visitors. Inside, on a side table, was a vase of dried cornflowers and three neat stacks of mail.

There was no answer when Arkady pushed the button for the office on the first floor. When he pushed the one for the ground floor, a voice answered and Arkady said, 'Das ist Herr Benz. Ich habe den Schlüssel verloren.' He hoped he'd said that he had lost his key.

The door chimed and opened. Arkady sorted quickly through the post for the doctors: medical journals and advertisements for car care and tanning salons. The only letter for Benz was from the Bayern-Franconia Bank. Someone named Schiller had handwritten his name above the return address.

Whoever had let Arkady in wasn't altogether trusting. The ground-floor door opened and a stern face in a nurse's cap looked out and demanded, 'Wohnen Sie hier?' Her eyes were on the mail.

'Nein, danke.' He backed out the door, surprised she had let him get as far as he had.

Arkady didn't know much about social customs in the West, but it struck him as odd that a housemaid would tell an unknown caller how long her employer would be away from home. Or that she would be so patient with the caller's primitive German. Why was she cleaning the flat if Benz was gone? He wondered about the letter. In Moscow depositors queued with bankbooks. In the West, banks posted statements, but did the envelope usually come personally signed?

He walked a couple of hundred metres up Königinstrasse, crossed to the park and strolled back on a path overhung with maples and oaks to sit on a bench with a view of Benz's house. It was the hour when Müncheners walked their dogs. They favoured small ones – pugs and dachshunds not much larger than their beers. This parade was followed by a promenade of elderly, elegantly dressed couples, some with matching canes. Arkady wouldn't have been amazed to see carriages rolling down Königinstrasse behind them.

People came in and out of the house. The doctors drove away in long, sombre cars. Finally the nurse of the dour countenance emerged, gave the street a parting look that put it on its good behaviour and walked in the other direction.

At a certain point, Arkady became aware that the lamps were brighter, the path darker, the night black. It was eleven p.m. All he was sure of was that Herr Benz had not returned.

It was one a.m. before he returned to the pension. If the rooms had been searched in his absence he couldn't tell; they simply looked as barren as before. He remembered that he should have bought food. There were so many things he forgot to do. Here he was in the lap of luxury and it was as if he craved starvation.

He sat at the window with his last cigarette. The station was still. Red and green switches lit the yard, but no trains were moving. At one corner of the station was a bus terminal. It had shut down too. Empty buses lined the street. An occasional headlight went by, racing after . . . what?

What is the thing we crave most in life? The sense that someone somewhere remembers and loves us. Even better if we love them in turn. Anything can be endured if that idea holds fast.

What could be worse than discovering how fatuous, how ignorant that assumption can be?

So, better not to seek.

Chapter Seventeen

In the morning, Arkady was visited by Federov, who flitted around the flat like a maid on inspection.

'The vice-consul asked me to check on you yesterday, but you weren't around. Not last night, either. Where were you?'

Arkady said, 'Sightseeing, walking around the city.'

'Because you have no proper introduction to the Munich police, no authority and no idea of how to conduct an investigation here, Platonov is concerned that you will get into trouble and make trouble for everyone else.' He looked in the bedroom. 'No blankets?'

'I forgot.'

'I wouldn't bother, actually, if I were you. You won't be here long enough.' Federov opened the closet and pulled out drawers. 'Still no suitcase? You're going to take back everything you buy in your pockets?'

'I haven't actually gone shopping yet.'

Federov marched back to the kitchen and opened the refrigerator. 'Empty. You know, you're such a typical Soviet cripple. You're so unused to food that you can't even buy it when it's all around you. Relax, it's real. This is Chocolateland.' He shot a smile back at Arkady. 'Afraid of being taken for Russian? It's true they despise us so much they're actually paying us millions of marks in moving expenses to leave the DDR, building barracks for us in Russia just so we'll go. All the more reason to buy while you can.' He shut the refrigerator door and shivered as if he had looked into a tomb. 'Renko, you could be gone any minute. You should treat this like a holiday.'

'Like a leper on holiday?'

'Something like that.' Federov tapped and lit a cigarette for himself. Arkady didn't necessarily want a cigarette first thing in the morning, but one thing he could say for Russians at home, even interrogators, was that they shared.

'This must be a bore for you, having to check on what I have for breakfast.'

'This morning I have to take the Byelorussian Women's Chorus to the airport, welcome a delegation of honoured state artists of the Ukraine and get them situated, attend a lunch meeting with representatives of Mosfilm and the Bavarian Film Studios, and then oversee a reception for the Minsk Folkloric Dance Group.'

'I apologize for any complication I've caused.' He offered his hand. 'Please call me Arkady.'

'Gennady.' Federov shook hands reluctantly. 'Just as long as you understand what a pain in the arse you are.'

'Do you want me to check in? I could give you a call later.'

'No, please. Just do what's normal. Shop. Get some souvenirs. Be back here by five.'

'By five.'

Federov strolled to the door. 'Have a beer at the Hofbraühaus. Have a couple.'

Arkady had coffee at a stand-up cafeteria in the train station. Federov was right: outside Russia he didn't know how to conduct an investigation. He had no Jaak or Polina. Without official authority he couldn't enlist local police. Minute by minute, he felt more a stranger than at home. The counter was banked with apples, oranges, bananas, sliced sausage and pig's knuckles, all for sale, yet he found his hand starting to swipe a sugar packet. He stopped. It *was* the hand of a Soviet cripple, he thought.

At the end of the bar was a man almost identical to him, with the same pallor and dishevelled jacket, except that he was stealing both sugar and an orange. The thief gave him a conspiratorial wink. Arkady looked around. At either end of the central hall was a pair of soldiers in grey uniforms with H&K submachine guns. Anti-terrorist troops, he realized; Munich had its troubles, too.

He fell in with a group of Turks walking by the cafeteria towards the underground. At the steps, he turned and joined the crowd climbing up and hurrying to the station exits. Outside, he balanced on the plaza curb, waiting with all the good Müncheners for the light to change, when he suddenly took off on his own against the red, through a gap in the traffic, to an island in the middle of the street, then raced, again alone, toward people who were lined along the far curb and watching him, aghast.

Arkady made a detour through an arcade and came out on the pedestrian mall of the day before. He kept moving, checking each passing telephone booth without success for a directory, until at a sidestreet car park he found a yellow kiosk with a phone, bench and book. A tiny woman whose coat touched her toes stood by the kiosk and looked pointedly at her watch, as if Arkady was late. The phone rang and she glided by him to take possession of the booth.

A sign on the door indicated that this was one of the few German public phones that *accepted* calls. The woman's conversation was explosive but quick, ending with a decisive slap of the receiver on the hook. She slid the door open, announced, 'Ist frei,' and walked away.

The telephone was his hope. In Moscow, public booths were gutted or out of order. Phones, when they rang, were usually ignored. In Munich, booths were maintained like bathrooms – better than bathrooms. When the phone rang, Germans answered.

Arkady looked up the Bayern-Franconia Bank and asked to speak to Herr Schiller. He imagined he would be stirring up some clerk, but there was a certain hush on the other end that let him know his call had gone to another level.

A different operator asked, 'Mit wem spreche ich, bitte?'

Arkady said, 'Das Sowjetische Konsulat.'

He waited again. One side of the street was taken up by a department store whose window offered woollens, horn buttons, felt hats, the paraphernalia of Bavarian identity. On the other side, people headed to and from a garage. Cars rolled up and down the ramps, BMWs and Mercedes bumper to bumper, steel bees in a giant beehive.

An authoritative voice came on the other end of the line and asked in Russian, 'This is Schiller. Can I help?'

'I hope so. Have you ever been to the consulate?' Arkady asked.

'No, I regret . . .' By the sound of it, it wasn't a bottomless regret.

'We're fairly new here, as you know.'

'Yes.' A dry tone.

'We have some confusion at the consulate,' Arkady said.

The answer mixed caution and amusement. 'How so?'

'It may just be a misunderstanding or something lost in the translation.'

'Yes?'

'We were visited by a certain firm that wants to engage in a joint venture in the Soviet Union. Of course that's good; that's what the consulate is here for. What is especially promising is that the firm claims it can produce financing in hard currency.'

'Deutschmarks?'

'Quite a large sum of Deutschmarks. I was hoping

you could give us some assurance that these funds are, in fact, available.'

A deep breath at the other end suggested the effort necessary to explain finances to small children. 'The firm may have a sufficient corporate budget, private funds, a loan from a bank or other institutions, there are many combinations, but Bayern-Franconia can only give you information if it is a partner in the venture. My advice is that you should study their credentials.'

'Precisely what I was getting at. They led us to believe – or we misunderstood them to say – that their firm was associated with Bayern-Franconia, and that all the funding would come from you.'

A new gravity issued from the other end. 'What is the name of this company?'

'TransKom Services. It's engaged in recreational and personnel services—'

'This bank has no subsidiaries involved in the Soviet Union.'

Arkady said, 'I was afraid not. But the bank might have committed itself to such financing?'

'Unfortunately Bayern-Franconia does not believe the economic situation in the Soviet Union is stable enough to recommend investment at this time.'

'Strange. He used the name of Bayern-Franconia freely at the consulate,' Arkady said.

'Which is something we take seriously at Bayern-Franconia. Just who am I talking to?'

'Gennady Federov. We would like to know, today if

possible, whether the bank stands behind TransKom or not.'

'I can reach you at the consulate?'

Arkady paused a suitable length of time to check a schedule. 'I'll be out most of the day. I have a Byelorussian chorus to meet at the airport, then Ukrainian artists, lunch with the Bavarian Film Studios, then some dancers.'

'You do sound busy.'

'Could you call at five?' Arkady asked. 'I will keep that time clear to speak to you. The best line to reach me on is 555–6020.' He was reading the number of the phone booth.

'What was the name of the representative of TransKom?'

'Boris Benz.'

There was a pause. 'I'll look into it.'

'The consulate appreciates your interest.'

'Herr Federov, my interest is in the good name of Bayern-Franconia. I will call at five exactly.'

Arkady hung up. He assumed the banker would verify the call by immediately phoning the listed number of the consulate to ask for a Gennady Federov, who should be safely bearing bouquets to the airport. He hoped the banker wouldn't be inquisitive enough to ask for anyone else at the consulate.

As he stepped out of the booth, he felt something change – a foot withdraw into a doorway or a shopper suddenly transfixed by a window display. He considered slipping back into the department store until he caught sight of himself reflected in the window. Was that him? This pale apparition in a shrinking jacket? In Moscow, he could pass as one scarecrow among many; among the robust sausage-eaters of Munich, he was frighteningly unique. He could no more lose himself among shoppers and tourists in the Marienplatz than a skeleton could hide by wearing a hat.

Arkady turned to the garage and walked up a ramp under a yellow and black sign that said, AUSGANG! A BMW roaring down the chute squealed and rocked on its shocks while he pressed himself against the wall. The driver's beefy head swivelled and shouted, 'Kein Eingang! Kein Eingang!'

On the first level, cars cruised among parked rows and concrete pillars in search of an empty slot. Arkady counted on an exit to the opposite street, but all the signs pointed to a central lift with steel doors and a line of Germans dressed well enough to go to heaven. He found emergency stairs to the next floor, which was a similar scene of cars reverberating to the throaty urgency of gas engines and the deliberate ticking of diesels, circling around a similar congregation at the lift.

Fewer cars reached the next level. Arkady saw a number of parking places and a red door at the other end of the floor. He was halfway to it when a Mercedes rose from the ramp and coasted between open slots. The car was an older model, a white chassis crazed like old ivory, with the tinny resonance of a punctured muffler. It stopped in the dark under a missing light.

Arkady walked with his hand on his pocket, in the manner of a man reaching for keys. As soon as he cleared the last car, he started to trot. He should have studied German more, he thought. The sign on the red door said KEIN ZUTRITT; 'No admittance', he translated, too late. The jamb had a built-in digital lock that he fumbled with for a second before giving up and looking back for the Mercedes.

Which had vanished. But was not gone, because the walls echoed with its rheumatic tremor. Alone on this level, the sound seemed to be amplified. He could hear the knock of cylinders, the chime of a loose tailpipe. The driver had moved behind the lift, he thought, or into one of the parking bays on the side. The bays were unlit, a good place to hide.

His return route to the emergency stairs crossed one open space where there were no pillars or parked cars to protect him. There was a different way out, down the 'Up' car ramp, defying KEIN EINGANG prohibitions painted on either side. He slipped between cars and was at the head of the ramp before he realized his mistake. The white Mercedes was waiting. It had backed down the ramp to watch him.

Arkady raced the car to the stairs. He didn't know what sounded worse, his lungs or the car behind him, although the driver seemed to be keeping pace at Arkady's heels more than trying to run him over. At the first side bay filled by a car, Arkady dove in. The Mercedes stopped, effectively blocking the bay, and the driver got out.

On foot, the odds were different. A fire extinguisher hung on the wall of the bay. Arkady lifted it from its hook and bowled it, making the driver jump in a particularly ungainly fashion. Arkady hit him on the way down. While the man tried to rise, Arkady ripped the rubber hose from the extinguisher, wrapped it around the driver's neck and dragged him out of the bay into the light.

Even with his neck squeezed up around his chin and ears, the driver was obviously Stas. Arkady unwound the hose and Stas sagged against a wheel.

'And a good morning to you.' Stas felt his neck. 'Talk about living up to your reputation.'

Arkady squatted beside him. 'I'm sorry. You scared me.'

'*I* scared *you*? My God.' He swallowed in a tentative manner. 'That's what they say about Dobermans.' He gagged and felt his chest.

At first, Arkady was afraid Stas was having a heart attack until he produced a pack of cigarettes. 'Got a light?'

Arkady held out a match.

Stas said, 'Fuck it. Take one for yourself. Beat me up, steal my cigarettes.'

'Thanks.' Arkady accepted the offer. 'Why were you following me?'

'I was watching you.' Stas cleared his throat. 'You told me where you were staying. I couldn't believe they'd bring their favourite investigator all the way from Moscow to put him up in a hole like that. I saw that weasel Federov leave and followed you to the station. I wouldn't have kept up with you for long in the crowd, but you stopped at the phone. When I came back with the car, you were still there.'

'Why?'

'I'm curious.'

'You're curious?' Arkady noticed a woman who came out of the lift and froze, bags swaying like pendulums, at the sight of two men sitting on the floor beside a car. 'Curious about what?'

Stas shifted on to a more comfortable elbow. 'About a lot of things. You're supposed to be an investigator, but you look to me like a man in trouble. You know, when that shit Rodionov, your boss, was in Munich the consulate made a big fuss about him. He even visited the radio station and gave us an interview. Then you come and the consulate wants to bury you.'

'What did Rodionov say?' Arkady asked in spite of himself.

' "Democratization of the Party . . . modernization of the militia . . . sanctity of the investigator's independence." The usual cock in the usual vigorously moving hand. How would *you* like to do an interview?'

'No.'

'You could talk about what's happening with the prosecutor general's office. Talk about anything you want.'

The lift arrived again and the woman with the bags backed in with the briskness of someone going for the authorities.

'No.' Arkady offered Stas a hand up. 'I'm sorry about the mistake.'

Stas stayed on the floor, as if he didn't mind being a heap of bones, as if he could win an argument from any position. 'It's early. You can hit people this afternoon. Come to the station with me now.'

'To Radio Liberty?'

'Wouldn't you like to see the world's greatest centre of anti-Soviet agitation?'

'That's Moscow. I just came from there.'

Stas smiled. 'Just visit. You don't have to do an interview.'

'Then why would I come?'

'I thought you wanted to see Irina.'

Chapter Eighteen

Now that he was in Stas's Mercedes, Arkady couldn't believe that he had ever thought it was a German's car. The passenger seat was covered by a balding rug. The back seat was hidden under a nest of newspapers. With every curve, tennis balls rolled around his feet and with every bump volcanic clouds rose from the ashtray.

In a magnetic frame on the dashboard was the photo of a black dog. 'Laika,' Stas said. 'Named after the dog Khrushchev sent into space. I was just a kid and I thought, 'Our first achievement in outer space is starve a dog to death?' I knew right then I had to get out.'

'You defected?'

'In Helsinki, and I wet my pants I was so scared. Moscow claimed I was a master spy. The English Garden is full of spies like me.'

'The English Garden?'

'You've already been there,' Stas said.

When they emerged on to a boulevard that ran by the pseudo-Greco museum of the Haus der Kunst, Arkady began to recognize where he was. Left was Königinstrasse, the 'Queen Street' that Benz lived on. Stas turned right, and then along the park. For the first time Arkady noticed a sign that said ENGLISCHER GARTEN. Stas turned on to a one-way street with the red-clay courts of a tennis club on one side and a high white wall on the other. A dark row of beeches that grew along the wall screened whatever was behind it from the street. Bikes rested against a steel barrier that ran the length of the curb.

Stas said, 'When I wake up in the morning, I ask Laika, "What's the most perverse thing I can do today?" I think today will be one of my most interesting ones.'

Parking was on the diagonal in front of the courts. Stas picked up a briefcase, locked the car and led Arkady across the street and through a gate of steel slats that was monitored by cameras and mirrors. Inside was a compound of white stucco buildings, with more cameras clinging to the walls.

Like anyone who had grown up in the Soviet Union, Arkady had two contradictory images of Radio Liberty. All his life the press had described the station as a front for the American Central Intelligence Agency and its loathsome collection of Russian stooges and traitors. At the same time, everyone knew that Radio Liberty was the most reliable source of information about Russia's missing poets and nuclear accidents. Still, though Arkady had himself been accused of treason, he felt uneasy about Stas and where they were heading.

He had half expected American Marines, but the guards in the station's reception foyer were German. Stas showed his ID and gave his briefcase to a guard, who pushed it in the leaded box of an X-ray detector. Another guard motioned Arkady to a desk protected by thick lead-reinforced glass. The desk was bigger, the chairs plusher; otherwise there was a generic sameness to American and Soviet reception areas, an international design to accommodate the travelling pacifist and the bomb-heaving terrorist.

'Passport?' the guard asked.

'I haven't got it,' Arkady said.

'His hotel is still holding it,' Stas volunteered. 'It's that fabled German efficiency we hear so much about. This is an important visitor. The studio is waiting for him right now.'

Reluctantly the guard accepted the trade of a Soviet driver's licence in exchange for a visitor's pass. Stas peeled off the backing and slapped it on to Arkady's chest. A glass door buzzed, and they pushed through into a corridor of cream-coloured walls.

Arkady stopped before they went any farther. 'Why are you doing this?'

'Yesterday, I told you I didn't like it when lightning hit the wrong man. Well, you definitely have all the marks of a singed body.'

'Aren't you going to get in trouble for bringing me in?'

Stas shrugged. 'You're one more Russian. The station is full of Russians.'

'What if I meet an American?' Arkady asked.

'Ignore him. That's what we all do.'

The hall had a thick American carpet instead of a Soviet runner. At a half march, half limp, Stas led him by display cases that illustrated stories Radio Liberty had reported to the Soviet Union: Berlin airlift, Cuban missile crisis, Solzhenitsyn, invasion of Afghanistan, Korean airliner, Chernobyl, Baltic crackdown. All the photographs were captioned in English. Arkady felt he was gliding through history.

If the halls were tidy and American, Stas's office had the anarchy of a Russian repair shop: desk and rolling chair, anonymous furniture wearing a shawl at the window, wooden filing cabinet, huge audiotape splicer and armchair. This was the bottom layer. The desk was covered by a manual typewriter, word processor, telephone, water glasses and ashtrays. On the shawl were two electric fans, two stereo speakers and a second computer monitor. A portable radio and spare computer keyboard stood on the cabinet. On the tape player were reels of tape, both loose and rolled. Everywhere – on desk, window-sill, cabinet, armchair – towered unsteady, ominous stacks of newsprint. A wall telephone dropped from an accordion extender. At a glance, Arkady knew that apart from the typewriter and desk phone not a single item worked.

He leaned over the desk to admire pictures on the wall.

'Big dog.' It was the same dark and hairy beast who rode in the dashboard frame. Here Laika had been captured by the lens in a car, savaging a snowman, sprawled across Stas's lap. 'What breed?'

'Rottweiler and Alsatian. Usual German personality. Make yourself comfortable.' He cleared newspapers off the armchair and followed Arkady's eyes around the room. 'Well, they gave us all this electronic shit with useless software. I disconnected it, but I keep it around because it makes the bosses happy.'

'Where does Irina work?'

Stas closed the door. 'Down the hall. The Russian section of Radio Liberty is the largest. There are also sections for the Ukrainians, Byelorussians, Baltics, Armenians, Turkics. We transmit in different languages for different republics. Then there's RFE.'

'RFE?'

Stas folded himself into the desk chair. 'Radio Free Europe, which serves Poles, Czechs, Hungarians, Romanians. Liberty and RFE employ hundreds of people in Munich. The voice of Liberty to our Russian audience is Irina.'

He was interrupted by a scratch at the door. A woman with bristling white hair, white eyebrows and a black velvet bow waddled in with a handful of bulletins. Her body had gone to fat, but she scrutinized Arkady's pinched suit with the slow-rolling eyes of an aged coquette. 'Cigarette?' Her voice was lower than Arkady's.

From a drawer stuffed with cartons, Stas opened a fresh pack for her. 'Ludmilla, you are always welcome.'

When Stas lit the cigarette for her, Ludmilla leaned forward and closed her eyes. When she opened them, they were on Arkady. 'A visitor from Moscow?' she asked.

Stas said, 'No, the Archbishop of Canterbury.'

'The DD likes to know who comes in and out of the station.'

'Then he should be honoured,' Stas said.

Ludmilla gave Arkady a last sweep of her eyes and went out of the door, leaving a vapour trail of suspicion.

Stas rewarded himself and Arkady with cigarettes. 'That was our security system. We have cameras and bulletproof glass, but they don't compare to Ludmilla. The DD is our deputy director for security.' He looked at his watch. 'At two steps a second, thirty centimetres a step, Ludmilla will reach his office in exactly two minutes.'

'You have security problems?' Arkady asked.

'The KGB blew up the Czech section a few years ago. Some of our contributors have died from poisoning and electrocution. You could say we have anxiety problems.'

'But she doesn't know who I am.'

'Undoubtedly she has seen the identification you left at the desk. Ludmilla knows who you are. She knows everything and understands nothing.'

'I've put you in a difficult situation, and I'm in the way of your work,' Arkady said.

Stas patted the bulletins. 'Because of these? This is the daily budget of wire service reports, newspapers and special monitoring reports. I'll also talk to our correspondents in Moscow and Leningrad. From this flood of information, I will distil about a minute of truth.'

'The newscast is ten minutes long.'

'I make up the rest.' He added quickly, 'Only joking. Let's say I pad. Let's say I don't want to put Irina in the position of telling the Russian people that their country is a rotting corpse, a Lazarus beyond resurrection, and that they should lie down and not even try to get up.'

'You're not joking now,' Arkady said.

'No.' Stas leaned back to release a long sigh of smoke; he actually wasn't much wider than a bent chimneypipe, Arkady realized. 'Anyway, I've got all day to trim the budget, and who knows what newsworthy disasters will happen between now and airtime?'

'The Soviet Union is fertile ground?'

'I must be modest. I only harvest, I do not sow.' Stas fell silent for a moment. 'Speaking of the truth, I can well believe that the bloodiest, most cynical Soviet investigator could fall in love with Irina, jeopardize family and career, even kill for her. Afterwards, as I heard it, you received a Party reprimand, but the only punishment was a short tour in Vladivostok, where you had a soft job with the fishing fleet shuffling papers in an office. Then you were brought back to Moscow to help the most reactionary forces stifle business entrepreneurs. I heard that the prosecutor's office could barely control you because you were such a well-connected Party member. So when you joined us at the beer garden yesterday, you were not the plump apparatchik that I expected. I noticed something else.' He rolled his chair forward; he moved more agilely on casters. 'Give me your hand.'

Arkady did so and Stas spread the hand to look at scars that crossed the palm laterally. 'Those aren't paper cuts,' he said.

'Trawl wires. The fishing equipment is old, so the wires fray.'

'Unless the Soviet Union has changed more than I knew, hauling a bloody net is hardly the usual reward for a favourite of the Party.'

'I lost the trust of the Party a long time ago.'

Stas studied the scars like a palm reader. It struck Arkady that he had that heightened level of concentration that came from years of being either crippled or confined to bed. 'Are you after Irina?' he asked.

'My business in Munich has nothing to do with her.'

'And you can't tell me what that business is?'

'No.'

The phone rang. Although dust seemed to rise with the clamour, Stas equably regarded the phone as if it were waving from a distant shore. He checked his watch. 'That'll be the deputy director. Ludmilla has just told him that a notorious investigator from Moscow has infiltrated the station.' He studied Arkady. 'It just occurred to me that you're hungry.'

The station cafeteria was on the floor below. Stas led Arkady to a table, where a German waitress in a black-and-white dirndl took their orders for schnitzel and beer. Young, fresh-faced Americans went outside to the garden. The tables inside were occupied by an older, largely male émigré population that lingered under a haze of cigarette smoke.

'Won't the director look for you here?' Arkady asked.

'In our own canteen? Never. I usually eat at the Chinese Tower; that's where Ludmilla will head first.' Stas lit a cigarette, gave a preparatory cough and inhaled as he swept the room with his bright gaze. 'It makes me nostalgic to see the Soviet empire. Romanians sit at their own table there, Czech table there, Poles there, Ukrainians over there.' He nodded to Central Asians in white short-sleeved shirts. 'Turkics there. Turkics hate Russians, of course. The problem is that these days they go ahead and say it.'

'Things have changed?'

'For three reasons. One, the Soviet Union started falling apart. As soon as the nationalities there started going for each other's throats, the same thing happened here. Two, the canteen stopped serving vodka. Now you can only have wine or beer, which is thin fuel. Three, instead of the CIA, now we're run by Congress.'

'So you're not a CIA front anymore?'

'Those were the good old days. At least the CIA knew what it was doing.'

The beer came first. Arkady took small, reverent sips because it was so different from sour, muddy Soviet beer. Stas didn't so much drink as pour it into himself.

He set down an empty glass. 'Ah, the émigré life. Just among Russians there are four groups: New York, London, Paris and Munich. London and Paris are more intellectual. In New York there are so many refugees you can spend your life without speaking English. But Munich is the group that's really trapped in time; this is where you find the most monarchists. Then there's the Third Wave.'

'What's the Third Wave?'

Stas said, 'The Third Wave is the most recent wave of refugees. Old émigrés don't want anything to do with them.'

Arkady took a guess. 'You mean, the Third Wave is Jews?'

'Right.'

'This is just like home.'

Not exactly like home. Though Slavic conversation filled the cafeteria, the fare was pure German, and he felt solid food being instantly transformed into blood, bone and energy. Better fed, he looked around with more attention. The Poles, he noticed, had suits, no ties and the expression of aristocrats temporarily short of funds. The Romanians chose a round table, the better to conspire. Americans sat alone and wrote postcards like dutiful tourists.

'You really had Prosecutor Rodionov here as a guest?'

'As an example of New Thinking, of political moderation, of the improved climate for foreign investment,' Stas said.

'You *personally* had Rodionov here?'

'I personally wouldn't touch him with rubber gloves.'

'Then who did?'

'The station president is a great believer in New Thinking. He also believes in Henry Kissinger, Pepsi Cola and Pizza Hut. These allusions are lost on you. That's because you've never worked at Radio Liberty.'

A waitress brought Stas another beer. With her blue eyes and short skirt, she looked like a large, overworked girl. Arkady wondered what she made of her clientele of sunny Americans and contentious Slavs.

A large Georgian broadcaster with the curls and beak of an actor joined the table. His name was Rikki. He nodded abstractedly through an introduction to Arkady, then launched immediately into a tale of woe.

'My mother is visiting. She never forgave me for defecting. Gorbachev is a lovely man, she says; he would never gas demonstrators in Tbilisi. She has a little letter of remorse for me to sign so I can go home with her. She's so gaga she'd take me right to jail. She's having her lungs looked at while she's here. They should look at her brains. You know who else is coming? My daughter. She's eighteen. I've never seen her. She arrives today. My mother and my daughter. I love my daughter – that is, I think I love my daughter, because I've never met her. We talked on the phone last night.' Rikki lit one cigarette from another. 'I have pictures of her, of course, but I asked her to describe herself so I would recognize her at the airport. Growing children change all the time. Apparently, I am going to the airport to pick up a girl who looks like Madonna. When I started to describe myself, she said, "Describe your car." '

'This is when we miss the vodka,' Stas said.

Rikki fell into a trough of silence.

Arkady asked, 'Tell me, when you broadcast to Georgia, do you often think of your mother and your daughter?'

Rikki said, 'Of course. Who do you think invited them here? I'm just surprised they came. And I'm surprised who they're turning out to be.'

'Having a loved one come sounds like a combination of reincarnation and hell,' Arkady said.

'Like that, yes.' Rikki lifted his eyes to the clock on the wall. 'I have to go. Stas, cover for me, please. Write something, whatever you want. You're a lovely man.' He heaved himself up and plodded tragically towards the door.

' "A lovely man",' Stas muttered. 'He'll go back. Half the people here will go back to Tbilisi, Moscow, Leningrad. What's crazy is that we, of all people, know better. We're the ones who tell the truth. But we're Russian, so we like lies too. Right now we're in a state of special confusion. We had a head of the Russian section, very competent, highly intelligent. He was a defector like me. About ten months ago he went back to Moscow. Not just to visit; he re-defected. A month later, he's a spokesman for Moscow appearing on American television, saying how democracy is alive and well, the Party is a friend of the market economy, the KGB is a guarantor of social stability. He's good; he should be, he learned here. He makes such a believable case that people at the station wonder: are we performing a real service or are we fossils of the Cold War? Why don't we all march home to Moscow?'

'Do you believe him?' Arkady asked.

'No. All I have to do is look at someone like you and ask, "Why is this man running?" '

Arkady left the question in the air. He said, 'I thought I was going to see Irina.'

Stas pointed to the lit red lamp above the door and ushered Arkady into a control booth. An engineer with a headset sat at the faint illumination of his console; otherwise, the booth was silent and dark. Arkady sat at the back, below the turning reels of a tape recorder. Needles danced on volume meters.

On the other side of soundproof glass, Irina was at a padded, hexagonal table with a central microphone and overhead light. Across from her sat a man in an intellectual's black sweater. Saliva sprayed like stoker's sweat when he talked. He joked, laughing at his own humour. Arkady wondered what he was saying.

Irina's head was slightly to one side, the pose of a good listener. Her eyes, in shadow, showed as deep-set reflections. Her lips, slightly open, held the promise of a smile, if not the smile itself.

It was not a flattering light. The man's forehead bunched in muscles, his eyebrows two hedgerows over the pits of his eyes. But the light flowed over Irina's even features and outlined in gold the corona of her cheek, her loose strands of hair, her arm. Arkady remembered the faint blue line that used to be under her right eye, a result of interrogation; the mark was gone now and she seemed flawless. An ashtray and a glass of water stood in front of her and the subject of her interview.

She said a few words and the effect was like blowing on coals. At once the man became even more animated, waving his hands like an axe.

Stas leaned across the console and turned on the sound.

'That's my point exactly!' the man in the sweater burst out. 'Intelligence agencies are always drawing psychological profiles of national leaders. It's even more necessary to understand the psychology of the people themselves. This has always been the province of psychology.'

'Could you give us an example?' Irina asked.

'Easily! The father of Russian psychology was Pavlov. He's best known to the world for his experiments with associative reflexes, particularly his work with dogs, accustoming them to associate their dinner with the ringing of a bell, so after a time they began to salivate just at the sound of the bell.'

'What do dogs have to do with national psychology?'

'Just this. Pavlov reported that there were some individual dogs that he could not train to salivate at the sound of the bell; in fact, he could not train them at all. He called them atavistic, throwbacks to their wolf ancestors. They were useless in the laboratory.'

'You're still talking about dogs.'

'Wait. Then Pavlov expanded. He called that atavistic trait a "reflex of freedom". He said that "reflex of freedom" existed in human populations the same as in dogs, but to different degrees. In Western societies the "reflex of freedom" was pronounced. In Russian society, however, he said there was a dominant "reflex of obedience". This was not a moral judgement, only a scientific observation. And since the October Revolution and seventy years of Communism, you can imagine how complete that "reflex of obedience" has become. So I'm simply saying that our expectations of any genuine democracy should be realistic.'

'Define *realistic*,' Irina said.

'Low.' He exuded the satisfaction of a man describing the death of a reprobate.

The engineer broke in from the booth.

'Irina, we get feedback when the professor gets close to the microphone. I'm going to play the tape back. Take a break.'

Arkady expected to hear the conversation over again, but the engineer listened on his headset as sound continued to feed into the booth from the studio.

Irina opened a bag for a cigarette and the professor almost jumped the table to light it. As she shifted, her hair swayed, revealing the glint of an earring. The blue cashmere top was more elegant than anything Arkady would have thought she would wear in a radio station. When she thanked her guest with her eyes he seemed content to squirm in them forever.

'That's a little harsh, don't you think? Comparing Russians with dogs?' she asked.

The professor folded his arms, still wrapped in self-satisfaction. 'No. Think about it logically. Those individuals who wouldn't obey were all killed or left long ago.'

Arkady saw contempt in her eyes, like the dilation of a flame. Or perhaps he was mistaken, because she responded with more amiable small talk. 'I know what you mean,' she said. 'There's a different type leaving Moscow now.'

'Precisely! The people who are coming today are the families who were left behind. They're stragglers, not leaders. This is not a moral judgement, merely an analysis of characteristics.'

Irina said, 'Not only families.'

'No, no. Former colleagues I haven't seen for twenty years are popping up everywhere.'

'Friends.'

'Friends?' It was a category he hadn't considered.

Smoke had collected at the light and turned it into a tactile nimbus around Irina. It was her contrast that was arresting. A mask with full mouth and eyes, dark hair cut severely but gently touching her shoulders. She glowed like ice.

Irina said, 'It can be embarrassing. They're decent people and it's so important to them to see you.'

The professor hunched forward, eager to commiserate. 'You're the only one they know.'

Irina said, 'You don't want to hurt them, but their expectations are fantasies.'

'They've lived in a state of unreality.'

'They've thought about you every day, but the fact is that too much time has gone by. You haven't thought of them for years,' Irina said.

'You've lived a different life, in a different world.'

'They want to pick up where you left off,' Irina said.

'They'd smother you.'

'They mean well.'

'They'd take over your life.'

'And who knows anymore where you left off?' Irina said. 'Whatever it was is dead.'

'You have to be friendly but stern.'

'It's like seeing a ghost.'

'Threatening?'

'More pathetic than threatening,' Irina said. 'You just have to wonder, after all this time why do they come?'

'If they listen to you on the radio, I can just imagine the fantasies.'

'You don't want to be cruel.'

'You're not,' the professor assured her.

'It just seems ... it seems to me that they actually would be happier if they stayed in Moscow with their dreams.'

'Irina?' the sound engineer said. 'Let's re-tape the last two minutes. Please remind the professor not to get close to the microphone.'

The professor blinked, trying to look into the booth. 'Understood,' he said.

Irina twisted her cigarette into the ashtray. She took a drink of water, long fingers around the silvery glass. Red lips, white teeth. Cigarette bright as a broken bone.

The interview started again at Pavlov.

Shamefaced, Arkady sank as far into his chair and as deep into shadow as he could go. If shadow were water he would have drowned happily.

Chapter Nineteen

The phone in the booth rang exactly at five.

'Federov here,' Arkady said.

'This is Schiller at the Bayern-Franconia Bank. We spoke this morning. You had some questions about a firm called TransKom Services.'

'Thank you for calling back.'

'There is no TransKom in Munich. No local bank knows it. I spoke to several state offices and no Trans-Kom is registered in Bavaria for workers' insurance.'

'It sounds as though you've been thorough,' Arkady said.

'I think I've done all your work for you.'

'What about Boris Benz?'

'Herr Federov, this is a free country. It is difficult to investigate a private citizen.'

'Is he an employee of Bayern-Franconia?'

'No.'

'Does he have a bank account with you?'

'No, but even if he did, there are safeguards of depositor confidentiality.'

'Does he have a police record?' Arkady asked.

'I've told you everything I can.'

'Someone who misrepresents an association with a

bank has probably done so more than once. He could be a professional criminal.'

'There are professional criminals even in Germany. I have no idea whether Benz is one. You told me yourself that you might have misunderstood what he said.'

'But now the name of the Bayern-Franconia Bank is in the consulate reports,' Arkady said.

'Remove it.'

'It's not that simple. With such a major contract, there's sure to be an investigation.'

'That sounds like your problem.'

'Apparently Benz showed documents from Bayern-Franconia describing the bank's financial commitment. He took the papers with him, but Moscow will want to know why the bank is pulling out now.'

The voice on the other end spoke as distinctly as possible. 'There was no commitment.'

'Moscow will wonder why Bayern-Franconia isn't more interested in Benz. If the bank is being unfairly implicated by a criminal, why isn't it more cooperative about finding him?' Arkady asked.

'We've cooperated with everything.' Schiller sounded convincing, except there was that letter from him to Benz.

'Then you don't mind if we send a man over to see you?'

'Send him. Please. Just so we can get this over with.'

'His name is Renko.'

*

The third floor of the Soviet consulate was filled with women in such intricately embroidered blouses and full, brightly striped skirts that they looked like Easter eggs rolled pell-mell into the hall. Since each held a bouquet of roses, negotiating the corridor involved force and apologies.

Federov's desk stood among pails of water. He looked up from a stack of visas with a snarl that announced he had already fulfilled his day's quota of diplomacy. 'What the devil are you doing here?'

'Nice,' Arkady said. The office was small and windowless, the furniture modern and slightly miniature. Perhaps the occupant faced a subtle, nightmarish sense of growing larger every time he went to work. And getting wetter. A damp spot on the carpet showed where one pail had been kicked over. Arkady noted the dampness of Federov's trousers and sleeves, pink petals on Federov's lapel and the way Federov's tie had become not looser but tighter and twisted to one side. 'Like a florist's shop.'

'If we want to talk to you, we'll visit you. Don't come here.'

Besides the passports, the desk top bore sheets of consulate stationery, a pen-and-pencil set and a brace of telephones, all new and shiny as a start-up kit.

'I want my passport,' Arkady said.

'Renko, you're wasting your time. First of all, Platonov has your passport, not me. Second, the vice-consul is going to keep it until you get on the plane for Moscow, which will be tomorrow if all goes well.'

'Maybe I could make myself useful. It looks like you have your hands full.' Arkady nodded towards the hall.

'The Minsk Folkloric Chorus? We asked for ten, they sent thirty. They're going to have to sleep stacked like blini. I'll try to help them, but if they insist on tripling their visas they're going to have to suffer.'

'That's what a consulate is for,' Arkady said. 'Maybe I can help.'

Federov took a deep breath. 'No, I think you're about the last person I would choose as my assistant.'

'Maybe we could get together tomorrow, have lunch or tea, even dinner?'

'I'm on the run tomorrow. Delegation of Ukrainian Catholics in the morning, lunch with the Folkloric Chorus, catch up with the Catholics at the Frauenkirche in the afternoon, and an evening revival of Bertolt Brecht. Full up. Anyway, you'll probably be flying home by then. Now, if you don't mind, I'm really busy. If you want to do me a favour, don't come back.'

'Could I at least make a call?'

'No.'

Arkady reached for the phone. 'The lines to Moscow are always busy. Maybe I could get through from here.'

'No.'

Arkady picked up the receiver. 'It'll be quick.'

'No.'

As Federov grabbed the receiver, Arkady let go and the consular attaché stumbled backwards, tipping over another pail of water. Arkady tried from the wrong side of the desk to catch him; instead, he swept all the passports from the desk top. Red booklets landed on the carpet, in puddles, in pails.

'You idiot!' Federov said. He scrambled around the pails to pick up passports before they sank. Arkady used handfuls of stationery to soak water from the carpet.

'That's useless,' Federov said.

'I'm trying to help.'

Federov blotted passports on his shirt. 'Don't help me. Just go.' A thought occurred to him as palpably as the squeal of a brake. 'Wait!' Eyes on Arkady, he gathered all the passports on to his desk. Breathing hard, he counted them out carefully not once but twice, and checked to be positive the contents were, even if damp, still intact. 'Okay. You can go.'

'I'm very sorry,' Arkady said.

'Just leave.'

'On the way out, should I warn people below about the water?'

'No. Don't talk to anyone.'

Arkady regarded the overturned pails, the flood plain of the carpet. 'It's a shame, such a new office.'

'Yes. Goodbye, Renko.'

The door opened and a woman crowned by a felt hat draped with pearls peeped in. 'Dear Gennady Ivanovich, what are you doing? When do we eat?'

'In a second,' Federov said.

'We haven't eaten since Minsk,' she said.

She took a brave position inside the door and other folkloric singers followed. As they flowed into the room,

Arkady went in the opposite direction, squeezing past skirts and ribbons, dodging thorns.

In a Polish secondhand shop west of the train station, Arkady found a manual typewriter with spindly type bars, shabby plastic case and Cyrillic characters. He turned it over. On the base was a stencilled military number.

'Red Army,' the shop owner said. 'They're getting out of East Germany and what the bastards don't want to take, they sell. They'd sell the tanks if they could.'

'May I try it?'

'Go ahead.' The shop owner was already moving to greet a better-dressed, more likely customer.

From his jacket Arkady took folded stationery and rolled a page into the machine. The paper was from Federov's desk. At the top was the embossed letterhead of the Soviet consulate, complete with hammer and sickle set in golden sheaves of grain. Arkady had considered trying to write in German, but he didn't trust his grasp of barbed Gothic letters. Besides, for a certain roundness of style, only Russian would do.

He wrote:

Dear Herr Schiller,

    This note is to introduce A. K. Renko, a senior investigator from the Moscow Prosecutor's Office. Renko has been assigned to enquire into questions concerning a proposed joint venture between

certain Soviet entities and the German firm
TransKom Services, and in particular the statements
of its representative, Herr Boris Benz. Since the
activities of TransKom and Benz may reflect badly
on both the Soviet government and the Bayern-
Franconia Bank, I hope we share a mutual interest
in resolving this matter as rapidly and quietly as
possible.

    With every good wish, G. I. Federov.

The close sounded grandly Federovian to Arkady. He
pulled the sheet out and signed it with a flourish.

'So it works?' the shop owner called.

'Amazing, isn't it?' Arkady said.

'I can give you a good price. An excellent price.'

Arkady shook his head. The truth was, he couldn't
afford anything. 'Do you have many buyers for a Russian
typewriter?'

The owner had to laugh.

The lights were still out in the Benz flat. At nine p.m.,
Arkady gave up. With a little planning, half his route
back lay through parks: Englischer Garten, Finanzgarten,
Hofgarten, Botanischer Garten. He wondered if this was
the solace of rabbits – the whispered tread of paths, the
soft arms of trees, the balm of shadows. From time to
time, he stopped in the dark to listen. A student would
wander by, nose in a book, hurrying to the light of the
next lamp. Or a jogger at a serious, slow-motion pace.

He heard no footsteps that stopped abruptly. It was as if when he had left Moscow he had stepped off the edge of the world. He had disappeared. He was in free fall. Who needed to follow?

He emerged from the Botanical Garden a block from the train station. He was crossing the street to check the videotape in the station locker when he saw pedestrians scatter from a car making an illegal U-turn. The civil outcry was so great that he didn't see the car itself. He stayed on the boulevard's central island and hurried past the station and along the switching yard. It was not an example of good survival planning to be surrounded by a wide boulevard with fast-moving traffic. The approaching street was Seidlstrasse, with his room and, farther on, the Soviet consulate. As tyres slowed behind him he turned to face a familiar, dishevelled Mercedes. At the wheel was Stas.

'I thought you wanted to see Irina.'

Arkady said, 'I saw her.'

'You took off before she even finished her interview. You were in the booth one second and the next second you were gone.'

'I heard enough,' Arkady said.

Stas ignored the HALTEN VERBOTEN signs, blithely waving on the cars backed up behind him in the fast lane. 'I came looking for you because I thought something was wrong.'

'At this hour?' Arkady asked.

'I had work to do. I came when I could. How would you like to go to a party?'

'Now?'

'When else?'

'It's almost ten. Why would I want to go to a party?'

Drivers behind Stas shouted, honked and flashed their lights in a chorus wasted on him. 'Irina will be there,' he said. 'You haven't actually talked to her yet.'

'But I got her message. I got it twice in one day.'

'You think she doesn't want to see you.'

'Something like that.'

'For a man from Moscow, you're very sensitive. Look, in a second we're going to be eaten alive by angry Porsches. Get in the car. We'll just drop in at the party.'

'For another round of humiliation?'

'Have you got something better to do?'

The party was up four flights in a flat full of what Stas called 'Retro Nazi'. The walls were checkered red, white and black with Nazi flags. On the shelves were helmets, Iron Crosses, gas masks in and out of canisters, various sizes of ammunition, photographs of Hitler, his dental mould, a picture of Hitler's niece wearing an evening gown and the wry smile of a woman who knows this is coming to no good end. The theme of the party was the first anniversary of the demolition of the Berlin Wall. Bits of the Wall – grey concrete with aggregate – were tied up with black crepe like birthday presents. People crowded the stairs, chairs and sofas, a mix of nationalities with enough Russians smoking enough cigarettes to make the eyes smart. Out of the haze,

Ludmilla loomed like a long-lashed jellyfish, blinked at Arkady and disappeared.

Stas warned, 'When you see Ludmilla, the deputy director is not far behind.'

At the drinks table Rikki was pouring Coke for a girl in a mohair sweater. 'Since I picked her up at the airport, my daughter and I have been doing nothing but shopping. Thank God the shops closed at six-thirty.'

She was about eighteen, wearing lipstick red as an alarm sign, and had blonde hair with dark roots. 'In America, malls are open all night long,' she said in English.

'Your English is good,' Arkady said.

She said, 'In Georgia no one speaks Russian.'

'They're still Communists; they just play a new flute,' Rikki said.

Arkady asked, 'Was it an emotional moment for you, seeing your father after all this time?'

'I almost didn't recognize his car.' She hugged Rikki. 'Aren't there American bases around here? Don't they have malls?' Her eyes lit at the approach of a young, athletic American in a button-down shirt, bow tie and red braces, who included Arkady and Stas in an incriminating gaze. Ludmilla hovered at his back.

'This must be the surprise guest we had at the station today,' he said. He gave Arkady a firm, democratic handshake. 'I'm Michael Healey, the deputy director in charge of security. You know, your boss, Prosecutor Rodionov, visited the station. We gave him the red carpet.'

'Michael is also the deputy director in charge of carpets,' Stas said.

'That reminds me, Stas, isn't there a security directive that says official Soviet guests have to be cleared in advance?'

Stas laughed. 'Station security is so thoroughly compromised that one more spy could hardly make a difference. Isn't tonight the perfect example of that?'

Michael said, 'I love your sense of humour, Stas. Renko, if you want to visit the station again, just be sure to give me a call.' He wandered off in search of white wine.

Stas and Arkady had scotch. 'What's so special about tonight?' Arkady asked.

'Besides the first anniversary of the tearing down of the Wall? Rumour has it that tonight we will be joined by the former head of the Russian section. My former friend. Even the Americans loved him.'

'This is the one who re-defected to Moscow?'

'The same.'

'Where's Irina?'

'You'll see.'

'Ta-da!' The host of the party entered from the kitchen bearing a cake iced in black chocolate, with a candy Berlin Wall surrounded by lots of burning red candles. 'Happy birthday, End of the Wall!'

'Tommy, you've outdone yourself this time,' Stas said.

'I'm a sentimental fool.' Tommy was the sort of fat man who had to keep tucking in his shirt. 'Did I show you my Wall memorabilia?'

'The candles,' Stas reminded him.

But the first note of the birthday song was interrupted by a commotion on the stairs, a wave of excitement that spread through the flat, and a general movement to greet new arrivals. The first in the door was the professor whom Irina had interviewed at the station. He unwrapped a scarf that looked as if it had been cut from a hair shirt and kept the door wide for Irina, who seemed to glide in on a bubble. Arkady could tell she'd had good food and good wine at a good restaurant. Champagne and something better than borscht. She had probably gone straight from the station, which explained how overdressed she had seemed there. If her eyes noticed Arkady, they registered no interest or surprise. Following her was Max Albov, loose on his shoulders the same elegant jacket he had worn when Arkady had first met him at Petrovka. The three of them were laughing at a joke that had carried them up the stairs.

'Something Max said,' Irina explained.

Everyone leaned towards them, wanting to share.

Max shrugged modestly. 'All I said was, "I feel like the Prodigal Son."'

Immediately came protests of 'No,' explosive laughs, appreciative applause. Max's cheeks glowed from the exertion of the climb and the warmth of the reception. He put Irina's arm through his.

Someone remembered. 'The cake!'

The birthday candles had burned themselves out. The candy Wall sank into a pool of wax.

Chapter Twenty

The cake tasted like ashes and tar. The party, however, took on fresh life and became an event with Max Albov, settled on to a sofa with Irina at the centre. They reigned together, beautiful queen and cosmopolitan king.

'When I was here, people said I was CIA. When I went to Moscow, people said I was KGB. For some minds those are the only conceivable answers.'

Tommy said, 'Maybe you're an American television star now, but you're still the best damn head of the Russian section we ever had.'

'Thanks.' Max accepted a whiskey as a small token of esteem. 'But those days are gone. I'd done what I could accomplish here. The Cold War was over. Not only over, it was passé. It was time to stop being a cheerleader for Americans, friends though they might be. I felt that if I really wanted to help Russia now, it was time to go home.'

'How did they treat you in Moscow?' Rikki asked.

'They wanted my autograph. Seriously, Rikki, you're a radio star in Russia.'

'Georgia,' Rikki corrected him.

'Georgia,' Max conceded. He told Irina, 'You're the most famous radio voice in Russia.' He slipped into Russian. 'What you're really asking is whether the KGB put the screws to me, whether I spilled any secrets that could have harmed the station or any of you. The answer is no. That time is past. I haven't seen the KGB or even met anyone from the KGB. Frankly, people in Moscow don't worry about us; they're too busy trying to survive, and they need help. That's why I went.'

Stas said, 'Some of us have death sentences waiting for us.'

'Those old sentences are being taken off the books by the hundreds. Go to the consulate and ask.' Max switched to English for the larger audience. 'There's probably nothing worse waiting for Stas in Moscow than a bad meal. Or in his case, bad beer.'

Arkady thought that Irina would be repelled by Max's touch, but she wasn't. With the exception of Rikki and Stas, they were all – Russians, Americans and Poles – if not persuaded, at least charmed. Had he suffered from his trip back into the Inferno? Obviously not. No singed hair. Instead, the healthy glow of a celebrity.

'In Moscow what exactly did you do to help the hungry Russian people?' Arkady asked.

'Comrade Investigator,' Max acknowledged him.

'You don't have to call me "Comrade". I haven't been a member of the Party for years.'

'More recently than I have been, though,' Max said pointedly. 'More recently than any of us in Munich has been. Anyway, *former* comrade, I'm glad you asked. Two things, in diminishing importance. One, creating joint ventures. Two, finding the hungriest, most desperate man in Moscow and arranging a loan so he could come here. You'd think that man would be more grateful. By the way, how is your investigation coming along?'

'Slowly.'

'Don't worry, you'll be home soon enough.'

Arkady didn't mind so much being skewered like an insect on a pin as seeing his image in Irina's eyes. Look at this mosquito, this apparatchik, this ape at a civilized party! She listened to Max as if she had no independent memory of Arkady at all. She turned to Albov. 'Max, could you give me a light?'

'Of course. You're smoking again?'

Arkady retreated from the circle of admirers and found himself back at the bar. Stas had followed. He lit a cigarette of his own and inhaled so deeply that his eyes seemed to glow. 'You saw Max in Moscow?' he asked Arkady.

'He was introduced to me as a journalist.'

'Max was an excellent journalist, but he can be what he wants to be, wherever he wants to be. Max is the next step in evolution: Post-Cold War Man. The Americans wanted someone who was knowledgeable about Soviet affairs. Actually, they wanted a Russian who sounded like an American, which is what he is. Why was Max interested in you?'

'I don't know.' Arkady found vodka hiding behind bourbon.

Why do people drink? A Latin to be amorous, an Englishman to unbend. Russians were more direct, Arkady thought; they drank to be drunk, which was what he wanted to be now.

Ludmilla was already there. She emerged from the haze, all eyes and a velvet bow, and stole his glass away. 'Everyone blames Stalin,' she said.

'That does sound unfair.' Arkady searched around the bottles and ice bucket for another glass.

'Everyone is paranoid,' she said.

'Including me.' There were no glasses anywhere.

Ludmilla lowered her voice, which was already a conspiratorial croak. 'Did you know that Lenin lived in Munich under the name "Meyer"?'

'No.'

'You knew that it was a Jew that shot the tsar?'

'No.'

'All the bad things, the purge and the famine, were done by the Jews around Stalin to destroy the Russian people. He was the pawn of the Jews, their scapegoat. It was when he started to move against Jewish doctors that he died.'

Stas asked Ludmilla, 'Did you know that the Kremlin has exactly as many bathrooms as the Temple of Jerusalem? Think about it.'

Ludmilla backed away.

Stas filled a glass for Arkady. 'I wonder if she'll report that to Michael.' He cast a consumptive's sardonic gaze around the room, not sparing anyone. 'A mixed bag.'

The party blossomed into arguments. Arkady took shelter on the stairs with another misanthrope, a German dressed in intellectual black. A girl sobbed at the bottom of the stairs. At any decent Russian party there were arguments and a girl crying at the bottom of the stairs, Arkady thought.

'I'm waiting to talk to Irina,' the German said. He was in his twenties, with furtive eyes and nervous English.

'Me, too,' Arkady said.

There was a silence, comfortable enough to Arkady, until the boy blurted out, 'Malevich was in Munich.'

'And Lenin,' Arkady said. 'Or was it Meyer?'

'The artist.'

'Oh, the artist. *That* Malevich.' The artist of the Russian Revolution. Arkady felt slightly stupid.

'There is a tradition of contact between Russian and German art.'

'Yes.' No one could argue with that, Arkady thought.

The boy examined his nails, which were bitten to the quick. 'The red square symbolized the Revolution. The black square symbolized the end of art.'

'Right.' Arkady downed half his vodka in a swallow.

The boy giggled as if he had remembered something worth sharing. 'Malevich said in 1918 that the footballs of entangled centuries would burn out in the sparks from bubbling light waves.'

'Bubbling light waves?'

'Bubbling light waves.'

'Amazing.' Arkady wondered what Malevich drank.

Irina was never alone long enough for Arkady to approach her. While he manoeuvred between groups, he was snared by Tommy and led to an enormous map of Eastern Europe tacked to a wall, with German and Russian positions on the eve of Hitler's invasion marked by swastikas and red stars.

Tommy said, 'This is terrific. I just learned who your father was. One of the great military minds of the war. What I'd love to do is mark exactly where your father was when the Germans rolled in. If you could point that out, it would be great.'

It was a Wehrmacht map. Place names and rivers were in German. Widely spaced lines climbed the Ukrainian steppe; dashes warned of swamps in Bessarabia, swastikas were massed to sweep on separate fronts to Moscow, Leningrad and Stalingrad.

'I have no idea,' Arkady said.

'Not a hint? Did he leave you any anecdotes?' Tommy asked.

'Only tactics,' Max joined them. 'Hide in a hole and stab your enemy in the back. Not bad tactics when you're overwhelmed and overrun.' He turned to Arkady. 'Are you feeling overwhelmed and overrun? Question retracted. What interests me, however, is that the father becomes a general and the son becomes an investigator. There's a similarity there, an inclination towards violence. What do you think, professor? You're a medical man.'

The psychologist who had arrived with Max was still tagging along. He ventured, 'Perhaps a discomfort with normal society.'

'Soviet society is not normal society,' Arkady said.

'Then you tell us,' Max said. 'Explain to us why you

are an investigator. Your father chose to kill people. That's why men become generals. To say a general hates war is to say that a writer hates books. You're different. You choose to arrive *after* the murder. You get the blood without the fun.'

'Much like the victim,' Arkady said.

'Then, what draws you? You live in one of the worst societies on earth, and then you choose the worst part of it. What is the morbid appeal? Picking over the bodies? Sending one more hopeless soul to jail for the rest of his life? As my friend Tommy would say, what's in it for you?'

They weren't bad questions. Arkady had asked them about himself. 'Permission,' he said.

'Permission?' Max repeated.

'Yes. When someone is killed, for a short time people have to answer questions. An investigator has permission to go to different levels and see how the world is built. A murder is a little like a house splitting in half; you see what floor is above what floor and what door leads to another door.'

'Murder leads to sociology?'

'Soviet sociology.'

'Assuming people are honest. I would assume that people would lie.'

'Murderers do.'

Arkady noticed that Max's retinue had regrouped around them. Stas watched from a corner. Irina was in conversation in the hall that led to the kitchen, her back to this exchange. Arkady regretted ever opening his mouth.

'Speaking of honest answers, how long have you listened to Irina on the radio?' Max asked.

'About a week.'

For the first time Max seemed genuinely surprised. 'A week? Irina's been doing newscasts for a long time. I expected you to say you'd sat devotedly by the radio for years.'

'I didn't have a radio.' Arkady glanced towards the hall. Irina was gone.

'And a week ago you did? And here you are in Munich! At this very party! Now that's an amazing coincidence,' Max said. 'Pure chance hardly explains that.'

'Perhaps it was luck.' Stas joined the conversation. 'Max, we want to hear more about your new television career. What is Donahue really like? And about your joint venture. I always thought of you as an inspirational leader, not a businessman.'

'But Tommy was going to tell me about his book,' Max said.

Tommy said, 'We were just getting to the interesting part.'

Arkady ducked away. He found Irina in the kitchen, taking cigarettes from a carton open on the counter. Tommy was a haphazard chef; carrot shavings and celery greens spilled from chopping boards and around bright plastic appliances. A portable television sat on a shelf of cookbooks. A poster of an Aryan mother hung on the wall. The clock said two a.m.

Irina struck a match. Arkady remembered that the first time they had ever met, she had asked for a light, a test to see how he reacted. She didn't ask now.

That first time, he remembered, he had been unruffled. Now his mouth was dry, his breath stopped, without words. Why was he trying a third time? Was he intent on exploring how many levels of humiliation he could sink to? Or was he a kind of Pavlov's dog that insisted on being kicked?

What was strange was that Irina looked so much the same and yet not at all the same. She wasn't changed so much as an amalgam of someone he knew and of a total stranger who had moved into the familiar body, not recently but long ago. She folded her arms. The cashmere and gold she wore were a long way from the rags and scarves she used to sport in Moscow. The image of her he had carried with him still fitted her, but only as a mask. Different eyes looked through it.

Arkady had been on Arctic ice. It wasn't as cold as this room. That was the trouble with knowing a woman intimately. When you're no longer welcome, you're banished to the dark. You spin around a sun that turns its back.

'How did you get here?' she asked.

'Stas brought me.'

She frowned. 'Stas? I heard he also took you to the station. I told you he was a *provocateur*. He's going a little far tonight—'

'Do you remember me?' Arkady asked.

'Of course I do.'

'You don't seem to.'

Irina sighed. Even to himself, he sounded pathetic.

'Of course I remember you. I simply haven't thought about you for years. It's different in the West. I had to survive, get a job. I met a lot of different people. My life changed, I changed.'

'Don't be sorry,' Arkady said. The way she described it, they were two tectonic plates moving in different directions. She was cold, analytical, correct.

Irina said, 'I didn't set back your career too badly?'

'A Russian hiccup.'

'Don't make me feel bad,' she said, though there was no indication that he could.

'No. I had inflated expectations. Maybe my memory was playing tricks.'

'To tell you the truth, I barely recognized you.'

'I look that good?' Arkady asked. A feeble joke.

'I heard you were doing well.'

'Who told you?' Arkady asked.

Irina lit a second cigarette from the first. Why do Russians need to burn a little all the time, he wondered. She stared at him, the smoke shifting, her face shrouded by her hair. He imagined holding her. No, it wasn't imagination; it was memory. He remembered the weight of her cheek against his hand, the softness of her brow.

Irina shrugged. 'Max was a friend and support for years. It's wonderful to see him here again.'

'I can tell he's popular.'

'No one knows why he went back to Moscow. He helped you, so you have no reason to complain.'

'I wish I'd been here,' Arkady said.

If I stood and crossed the room, he thought. If I crossed the room and simply touched her, could a touch be the bridge? No, her face said.

'It's too late now. You never followed me. Every other Russian here emigrated or defected. You stayed.'

'The KGB said—'

'I would have understood if you'd stayed for a year or two, but you stayed forever. You left me alone. I waited in New York; you never came. I went to London to be closer; you never came. When I found out where you were, you were doing exactly what you did before, being a policeman in a police state. Now here you are, finally, but not to see me. You're here to arrest someone.'

Arkady said, 'I couldn't come without—'

Irina asked, 'Did you think that I'd help you? When I think of the time when I did want to see you and you weren't here, thank God Max was. Max and Stas and Rikki – everybody here had the nerve, one way or another, swimming, running or jumping from windows, to escape. You didn't, so you have no right to criticize any of them, or question any of them or even to be with them. As far as I'm concerned, you're dead.'

She took a pack of cigarettes with her and left the kitchen as Tommy danced in, humming a polka, gathering olives and crisps. His legs were drunk. On his head was a German helmet. In the helmet was a hole.

Arkady knew the feeling.

Chapter Twenty-One

The Bayern-Franconia Bank was a Bavarian palace of limestone blocks under the practical hat of a red tiled roof. The inside was all marble, dark wood and the discreet hum of computers calculating mysterious interest rates and currency exchanges. Led up a lift and down a hall with rococo cornices, Arkady felt intimidated, as if he were trespassing in the church of a foreign rite.

There was something padded and posed about Schiller. He sat rigidly behind his desk, about seventy, with clear blue eyes in a pink face. Silver hair was brushed back from a narrow forehead. A linen handkerchief above the pocket of a dark banker's suit. A man in a windcheater and jeans, with a tan that flowed into blond hair, stood at Schiller's side. His blue eyes and expression of restrained contempt were the same as the older man's.

Schiller scrutinized the letter that Arkady had typed on Federov's stationery. 'You are what a senior Soviet investigator looks like?' he asked.

'I'm afraid so.'

Arkady handed over his red identification book. He hadn't noticed before how much the corners were worn, the bindings torn. At arm's length Schiller scrutinized the picture. Even shaved, Arkady felt he looked as if he had sat on his clothes before dressing. He fought the impulse to pinch a crease in his trousers.

'Peter, will you examine this?' Schiller asked.

'You don't mind?' the other man asked Arkady. It was the sort of courtesy extended to a suspect.

'Please.'

Peter turned on the desk lamp. As he held a page under the light his jacket rode up to show a holster clip and pistol.

'Why didn't Federov come with you?' Schiller asked Arkady.

'He apologizes. He's with a church group this morning, then folk singers from Minsk.'

Peter gave back the ID. 'Do you mind if I call?'

Arkady said, 'Go ahead.'

Peter used the phone while Schiller kept watch on his visitor. Arkady looked up. On the ceiling, fat cherubs with tiny wings were painted in mid-flutter against a plaster sky. Walls of Dresden blue coloured the air a sombre grey. Oil portraits of ancestral bankers hung between engravings of merchant ships. The good burghers looked embalmed, then painted. On a bookshelf were tomes on international law arranged by year and, in a crystal dome, a brass clock with a pendulum that wrapped itself around a pole. He noticed a black and white photograph of rubble and burned walls. A roof had collapsed like a tent on a skirt of bricks. A bathtub was set out on the street as a water trough. People huddled around the tub in the grey uniforms of displaced persons. 'An interesting picture for a bank,' he said.

Schiller said, 'That *is* the bank. That's this building after the war.'

'Very impressive.'

'Most countries have recovered from the war,' Schiller said drily.

Peter finally got someone on the phone. 'Hello,' he checked the letter. 'Is Federov there? Where could I find him? Could you tell me exactly when? No, no, thank you.' He hung up and nodded to Arkady. 'Some religious group and singers.'

'Federov is a busy man,' Arkady said.

Schiller said, 'Your Federov is an idiot if he thinks the Bayern-Franconia Bank considers itself obligated to investigate a German citizen. And only a cretin could imagine Bayern-Franconia joining any venture with a Soviet partner.'

'That's Federov,' Arkady agreed as if the attaché's antics were legend. 'All I know is that I've been told to clear this up quietly. I understand the bank is under no obligation to help.'

Schiller said, 'We have no inclination to help either.'

'I don't see why you should,' Arkady said. 'I told Federov he should inform the ministries and get it out in the open. Bring in Interpol, let it go through the courts, the more public the better. That's the way to protect a bank's reputation.'

'The bank's name could be protected by simply removing it from the reports on Benz,' Schiller said.

'True,' Arkady agreed. 'But the situation in Moscow being what it is, no one at the consulate is willing to take that responsibility.'

'Could you?' Schiller asked.

'Yes.'

'Grandfather, do you want my advice?' Peter asked.

'Of course,' Schiller said.

'Ask him how much he wants to leave the bank alone. Five thousand Deutschmarks? If he splits with Federov, ten thousand? This whole story about TransKom, Benz and Bayern-Franconia – they've cooked it up. There are no reports, there's no connection. I look at him and I know he's lying. I smell it. This is a protection racket. I suggest that we call other banks and ask whether they have been approached by Federov and Renko, whether they have heard a story about joint ventures and investigations. You should call the consul general right now, make an official protest, and then call a lawyer. What do you think of that?'

The banker's mouth had almost no lips at all, not enough to hold a smile. There was nothing old or weak about the eyes, though. They weighed Arkady as if he were small change.

'I agree,' Schiller said. 'You have probably never seen a less genuine-looking article in your life. On the other hand, Peter, you've never met a Soviet banker. It's true that the bank has no knowledge of or connection with any claims made by the individual whom the Soviet consulate has described. Certainly we feel under no obligation to give the consulate any assistance. However, if we've learned anything from history it is that mud makes good paint. Whether we deserve it or not, it never washes off entirely.'

He fell silent, as if he had left the room for a moment. Then he gathered himself and looked at Arkady. 'The bank will not participate in any enquiry, but purely as a courtesy to us my grandson Peter has volunteered to assist you, as long as this affair is kept absolutely quiet.'

The wires of outrage working in Peter's face showed less than wholehearted enthusiasm, Arkady thought.

'On an informal basis,' Peter said.

'How can you help?' Arkady asked.

Peter produced a much nicer ID book than Arkady's. Authentic leather, gold tooling, with a colour photo in green jacket and cap of Lieutenant Schiller, Peter Christian, Münchner Polizei. This was more of a windfall than Arkady wanted. This was a trap of his own devising, though, because if he didn't accept the offer, the Germans would call the consulate again and again until they got through to Federov.

'I'd be honoured,' Arkady said.

Peter Schiller's police car was a green-and-white BMW, radio and phone under the dash, blue flasher on the back seat. He wore a seat belt and always used the indicator, yielding to bikers who left their lane, passing pedestrians massed in docile formations to wait for WALK signs at corners where there was no cross-traffic in sight. He looked a little too big for the car. He also looked as if he would be happy to run down anyone who crossed against the light.

'I bet your radio and phone work,' Arkady said.

'Of course they do.'

Irrationally, Arkady yearned for Jaak's homicidal driving and for the suicidal dashes of Moscow pedestrians. Peter looked as if he kept in shape by lifting small oxen. His windcheater was yellow. Arkady noticed that yellow was the most popular colour worn in Munich. A gold-mustard-diarrhoea yellow.

'Your grandfather speaks Russian well.'

'He learned it on the Eastern Front. He was a prisoner of war.'

'Your Russian is good, too.'

'I think all police should speak it,' Peter said.

They headed south, towards the two bonneted spires of the Marienkirche in the centre of the city. Peter shifted down a gear to let a tram go by that was as well maintained as a toy. You had to work to keep Peter Schiller's kind of tan, Arkady thought. Ski in the wintertime, swim in the summer.

'Your grandfather said you'd volunteered. Volunteer something,' he said.

Peter gave him a couple of level looks before responding. 'Boris Benz has no criminal record. In fact, the only thing we have is that according to the Bureau of Vehicle Registration, Benz has blond hair, blue eyes, was born in 1955 in Potsdam, outside Berlin, and does not need glasses.'

'Married?'

'To a Margarita Stein, a Soviet Jew. Her records are where? Moscow, Tel Aviv – who knows?'

'That's a start. Tax or employment records? Service or medical records?'

'Potsdam is in the DDR. *Was* in the DDR. Understand, we're all one Germany now, but many East German records have not been transferred to Bonn yet.'

'What about telephone calls?'

'Tsk, tsk. Without a court order, telephone records are protected by law. We have laws here.'

'I understand. You also have customs control. Did you check them?'

'Benz could be home, he could be anywhere in Western Europe. Since the EEC, there isn't any real passport control any more.'

'What kind of car does he drive?' Arkady asked.

Peter smiled, getting into the rhythm of the game. 'A white Porsche 911 is registered in his name.'

'Numberplate?'

'I don't think I'm allowed to share any more information.'

'What information? Call Potsdam and order his records from there.'

'For a private matter? That's absolutely against the law.'

At an obelisk cars merged and separated with none of the nebular fury of a Moscow roundabout. There, particularly in the winter, lorries and cars thundered into roundabouts with all the discipline of yaks. Here drivers, cyclists and walkers seemed to have received

301

their orders for the day. It was like a rest home the size of a city. Peter smiled like a man who could play all day.

'Many murders here?' Arkady asked.

'Munich?'

'Yes.'

'Beer murders.'

'Beer?'

'Oktoberfest, Fasching. Drunks. Not real murders.'

'Not like vodka murders?'

'You know what they say about crime in Germany?' Peter asked.

'What do they say about crime in Germany?'

'It's against the law,' Peter said.

Arkady recognized the trees of the Botanischer Garten. As soon as the BMW stopped at a light, he got out and reached back to stuff a piece of paper into Peter's jacket. 'That's a Munich fax number. Find out who it belongs to, if that's not against the law. On the other side is a phone number. You can call me there at five.'

'Your number at the consulate?'

'I won't be there. It's a private number.' My private minute at the booth, Arkady thought.

'Renko!' Peter shouted as Arkady got to the pavement. 'Stay away from the bank.'

Arkady kept walking.

'Renko!' Peter added another warning. 'Tell Federov what I said.'

*

Armed with soap and string, Arkady returned to the pension, washed his clothes and hung them up to dry. From the floor below came the sweet smell of spiced lamb. He wasn't hungry. Such lethargy came over him that he could barely move. He stood by the window looking down the street and towards the station yard, at the trains sluggishly moving in and out. The rails were as silvery as snail tracks, perhaps fifty parallel lines and as many points shunting an engine from this line to that. How easily, without noticing, a man finds himself parallel to the life he meant to have, then arrives, years later, to find the band gone, flowers dead, love past. He should be ancient, bent and bearded, disembarking with a cane, instead of merely being too late.

He dropped on to his bed, and at once fell into a black sleep. He dreamed he was in a locomotive. He was the engineer, stripped to the waist and sitting at a cockpit of gauges and controls. Blue sky sped by the window. A woman's hand rested lightly on his shoulder. He didn't look back for fear that she might not be there. They were running along the seashore. Somehow, without tracks, the engine ploughed through the beach. Faraway waves reflected rows of sunlight, nearer waves curled lazily over each other and collapsed on the sand; perfect gulls plunged into the water. Was it her hand or the memory of her hand? He was happy not to look and keep the train moving by sheer will if necessary. But the wheels ground to a stop. The sun was sinking. Waves mounted in towering black walls that carried along dachas, cars, militiamen, generals, Chinese lanterns and birthday cakes.

In panic, Arkady opened his eyes. He was in bed in the dark. He looked at his watch. Ten p.m. He had slept ten hours, right through the call to the booth from Peter Schiller – if he had ever called.

Someone was knocking at the door. Getting up, he brushed aside the drying shirts and trousers hanging in his way.

He didn't recognize the visitor, a heavy-set American with stringy hair and a tentative smile.

'I'm Tommy, remember? You came to a party at my place last night.'

'The man in the helmet, yes. How did you know where to find me?'

'Stas. I bugged him until he told me; then I just knocked on every door here until I found you. Can we talk?'

Arkady let him in and searched for a shirt and cigarettes.

Tommy wore a corduroy jacket stressed at the buttons. He bounced on his toes and his hands hung in soft fists. 'I told you last night that I was a student of World War II. "The Great Patriotic War" to you. Your father was one of the outstanding generals on the Soviet side. Naturally I'd like to talk some more about him with you.'

'I don't think we talked about him at all.' Arkady sat down to pull on socks.

'That's what I mean. The truth is, I'm writing a book

about the war from the Soviet side. I don't have to tell you about the sacrifices the Soviet people made. Anyway, that's one reason I work at Radio Liberty – for the information. When someone interesting comes through I interview them. I heard you might be leaving Munich pretty soon, so I came over.'

Arkady searched for his shoes. He wasn't following Tommy closely. 'You interview them for the station?'

'No, just for me, for the book. I'm interested in more than military tactics; I'm also interested in the clash of personalities. I was hoping you could give me some insight into your father.'

Out of the window, the station yard was a field of signal lights. Arkady saw torch beams running around freight cars and heard the heavy grip of couplings engaging. 'Who told you I was leaving soon?' he asked.

'People said.'

'Who?'

Tommy rose on his toes. 'Max.'

'Max Albov. You know him well?'

'Max was head of the Russian section. I'm in the Red Archives. We worked together for years.'

'The Red Archives?'

'The greatest library of Soviet studies in the West. It's at Radio Liberty.'

'You were friends with Max.'

'I'd like to think we're still friends.' Tommy held up a tape recorder. 'Anyway, what I wanted to cover to begin with was your father's decision, despite being overrun, to stay behind the German lines and wage guerrilla warfare.'

Arkady asked, 'Do you know Boris Benz?'

Tommy leaned backwards and said, 'We met once.'

'How?'

'Right before Max went to Moscow. Of course no one knew he was going. He was with Benz.'

'You haven't seen Benz since?'

'No. It was purely by chance. Max and I were surprised to see each other.'

'You met Benz only once and yet you remember him?'

'Under the circumstances, yeah.'

'Who else was there?'

As Tommy squirmed, his shirt-tail showed under his jacket. 'Employees, customers. No one I've seen since. Maybe this isn't a good time for an interview.'

'It's the perfect time. Where did your encounter with Benz and Max take place?'

'Red Square.'

'In Moscow?'

'No.'

'Munich?'

'It's a club.'

'Would it be open now?'

'Sure.'

'Show me.' Arkady picked up a jacket. 'I'll tell you all about the war and you tell me about Benz and Max.'

Tommy gulped down a brave breath. 'If Max was still with Liberty, you couldn't get a word—'

'Have you got a car?'
'Sort of a car,' Tommy said.

Arkady had never ridden in an East German Trabant before. It was a fibreglass tub with tail fins. The sound of its two cylinders was a syncopated popping. Fumes flowed not only from the exhaust but from a kerosene heater that sat on the car floor between his feet. They drove with the front windows rolled down; the rear windows were glued shut. Every time an Audi or Mercedes passed, the Trabant bobbed in its wake.

'What do you think?' Tommy asked.

'It's like getting on the road in a wheelchair,' Arkady said.

'It's more an investment than a car,' Tommy said. 'The Trabi is a piece of history. Except for being slow and dangerous and polluting, it's probably the most efficient piece of technology in the world today. It goes fifty miles an hour and it'll run on methane or coal tar – probably even on hair tonic.'

'Sounds more Russian.'

In truth, however, the Trabant made Arkady's Zhiguli look like luxury. It made a Polsak Fiat look good.

'Ten years from now, this will be a collector's item,' Tommy promised.

They'd reached the outer city, a black plain where stakes of light led to different autobahns. When Arkady twisted to see whether anyone was following, the seat almost snapped beneath him.

'The whole German–Russian thing is so incredible,' Tommy said. 'Historically, with the Germans always moving east and the Russians always moving west, and then you add Nazi racial laws, making all Slavs into *Untermenschen* only good for slaves. Hitler on one side, Stalin on the other. Now that was a war.'

His face was creased with a new grin of pride and camaraderie. He was a lonely man, Arkady realized. Who else would ride around late at night with a Russian investigator? When a tanker approached in the passing lane, engulfed the air and roared by, the Trabi vibrated violently in the shock wave and Tommy glowed with pleasure.

'I got to know Max best before I came to the Red Archives, when I ran the Programme Review section. I didn't create programmes; I had a separate staff that reviewed them for content. Radio Liberty has guidelines. Our strongest anti-Communists, for example, are monarchists. Of course we're supposed to be pushing democracy, but sometimes a little anti-Semitism creeps in, sometimes a little Zionism. It's a balancing act. We also translate programmes so that the station president knows what we're putting on the air. Anyway, my life was easier because Max was head of the Russian desk. He understood Americans.'

'Why do you think he went back to Moscow?'

'I don't know. We were all amazed. Obviously he had to be in contact with the Sovs before he went back, and they played it as a feather in their cap when he showed up in Moscow. But nobody here suffered. He wouldn't have been welcome at the party if anyone had.'

'How do the Americans at the station feel about him?'

'To begin with, President Gilmartin was upset. Max was always the favourite. It was a shock to think that the KGB had penetrated Liberty. You met Michael Healey at my party. He's deputy director. He tore the station apart looking for moles. Now it looks like Max went back just to make money. Like a capitalist. You can't blame him for that.'

'Did Michael talk to Benz about Max?'

'I don't think Michael knew about Benz. You don't want Michael messing with your life. Anyway, it all turned out okay. Max came back smelling like a rose.' Tommy made his point stronger: 'He's been on CNN.'

Arkady turned in his seat to look behind them again. If something was impinging on his consciousness, there was nothing in sight but the haze of the city.

Ahead, the road forked north towards Nuremberg, south to Salzburg. Tommy turned right, and as soon as they came off the curve and through an underpass Arkady saw what appeared to be a pink island in the dark. He didn't know what he had expected – Kremlin walls or St Basil's domes rising like phantoms by the autobahn? Whatever, something more than a one-storey building of white stucco framed in red neon, with a square red light bleeding into the air beside a sign that said RED SQUARE and, in more demure cursive, SEX CLUB.

As he got out of the Trabi he thought nothing you dream is as strange as what you see.

The inside of the club was so washed in red lights that it was difficult to focus, but Arkady did notice women in suspender belts, black stockings, push-up bras and corsets. The theme was established by brass samovars on the tables and fluorescent stars on the walls.

'What do you think?' Tommy scooped his shirt back into his belt.

'Like the last days of Catherine the Great,' Arkady said.

It was interesting how intimidated men were at a house of prostitution. They had the money, the choice, the chance to leave. Women were servitors, slaves, mattresses. Yet the power, at least before sex, was inverted. The women, ogled in their lingerie, sprawled on love seats as comfortably as cats; the men betrayed the tics of the undressed. American soldiers stood at a horseshoe bar. Approached by a prostitute, they nervously played out a charade of charm and seduction while she maintained a face so slack and bored that she could have been asleep. What amazed Arkady was that the women actually were Russian. He heard it in their accents and whispers to each other, saw it in the pallor of their skin, the tilt of their eyes. He saw a woman in pink silk as broad-shouldered as a farm girl from the steppe who might have wandered west in her underwear. She whispered to a more delicate friend with huge Armenian eyes and a body stocking of black lace. When he looked at them he couldn't help wondering why. How did imported Russian prostitutes differ from the local German? In wingspread, submissiveness, the ability to heal? They pointed to him. They could spot it; he was Russian, too. He asked himself how desperate was he for love, or at least for a facsimile of it. Did the need shine from him or did he look dead as a charred match?

He reminded Tommy, 'You said that Max Albov came back to Munich smelling like a rose.'

Tommy said, 'If anything, I think we respect Max more. I bet he'll make a million.'

'Doing what? Did he say?'

'Television journalism.'

'He mentioned a joint venture.'

'Properties, assets. He says a man who can't make money in Moscow couldn't find flies on shit.'

'Sounds inviting. Maybe everyone should go back to Moscow.'

'That was the idea.'

Tommy couldn't take his eyes off the women. He looked red-faced and overheated just by proximity, pressing his shirt against his belly, raking his hair with thick fingers, signs of an excitement Arkady did not share. Love was the mountain breeze, sunrise and nirvana; sex was a roll in the leaves; paid sex was the taste of worms. But it had been so long since he knew either sex or love, who was he to judge? One man imagines paid sex to be coarse and deadening, the next man finds it simple and direct. Does the next man have less imagination or more money?

Every race has its catalogue of features. A Tartar heritage of narrowed, upward-slanting eyes. Slavic oval outline and rounded brow. Small lips, skin pale as snow. None of the women looked like Irina, though. Her eyes were broader and deeper, more Byzantine than Mongol, both more open and more hidden in their look. Her face was less oval, lighter in the jaw, her mouth fuller, more articulate. It was curious; in Moscow he heard Irina five times a day. Here, silence.

Sometimes he thought of normal, alternative lives he and Irina could have led. Lovers. Husband and wife. The ordinary way people live and sleep and wake together. Perhaps even grow to hate each other and decide to leave, but in a normal fashion, not with lives cut in half. Not with a dream that degenerated into obsession.

The woman in pink came over with her friend and asked for champagne.

'Sure.' Everything seemed like a good idea to Tommy.

The four of them took a table in the corner. The woman in pink was Tatiana; her friend in the body stocking was Marina. Tatiana had dark roots and an elaborate blonde ponytail; Marina wore black hair brushed over a bruised cheek. Tommy, playing host, introduced, 'My pal Arkady.'

'We knew he was Russian,' Tatiana said. 'He looks romantic.'

'Poor men are not romantic,' Arkady said. 'Tommy is much more romantic.'

'We could have fun here,' Tommy suggested.

Arkady watched a woman walk, hips slowly marching towards another battle as she led a soldier through a beaded curtain to the back rooms. 'Do you see many Russians here?' he asked.

'Lorry drivers.' Tatiana made a face. 'Usually we have a more international clientele.'

'I like Germans,' Marina said in a reflective mood. 'They wash.'

'That's important,' Arkady said.

Tatiana lowered her champagne under the table to reinforce it from a flask and generously did the same for the other three glasses. Vodka once again subverting the system. Marina leaned over her glass and whispered, 'Molto importante.'

'We speak Italian,' Tatiana said. 'We toured Italy for two years.'

Marina said, 'We were with the Bolshoi Piccolo Ballet Company.'

'Not necessarily connected to the original Bolshoi Ballet,' Tatiana giggled.

'We did dance.' Marina sat straighter to emphasize a sinewy neck.

'Small towns. But so much sun, such music,' Tatiana recalled.

'There were ten other so-called Russian ballet companies in Italy when we left, all copying us,' Marina said.

'I think we can say we spread a love of dance,' Tatiana said. She poured Arkady a second shot. 'Are you sure you don't have any money?'

'She's always attracted to the wrong men,' Marina said.

'Thanks,' Arkady said to both of them. 'I'm looking for a couple of friends. One named Max. Russian, but better dressed than me, speaks English and German.'

'We never saw anyone like that,' Tatiana said.

'And Boris,' Arkady said.

'Boris is a popular name,' Marina said.

'His last name was something like Benz.'

'That's a popular name here, too,' Tatiana said.

'How would you describe him?' Arkady asked Tommy.

'Big, good-looking, friendly.'

'Does he speak Russian?' Tatiana asked.

'I don't know. He only spoke German around me,' Tommy said.

Benz was such a nebulous creature, nothing but a name on a registration form in Moscow and on a letter in Munich, that Arkady found himself relieved to meet anyone who might have met the man in the flesh.

'Why would he speak Russian?' Arkady asked.

'The Boris I'm thinking of is very international,' Marina said. 'I'm only saying that his Russian is very good.'

'He's German,' Tatiana said.

'You haven't been to bed with him.'

'Neither have you.'

'Tima has. She commented on it.'

'Commented on it?' Tatiana affected a prissy accent. 'We're friends.'

'What a cow. I'm sorry,' Tatiana added when she saw that Marina was hurt. She told Arkady, 'He's a Polish sausage, what can I tell you?'

'Is Tima here?'

'No, but I can describe her to you,' Tatiana said. 'Red, four-wheel-drive, also answers to the name "Bronco".'

'I know where she means,' Tommy said, eager to get back into the conversation. 'It's right down the road. I'll take you.'

'I wish you did have money,' Tatiana told Arkady. Under the circumstances he thought it was the biggest compliment he could expect.

A dozen Jeeps, Troopers, Pathfinders and Land Cruisers had sat in a turnout off the main road, a prostitute waiting behind the wheel of each car. Clients parked on the shoulder to shop. Once a price was set, the woman turned off the red lamp that announced her availability, the client climbed in and they drove to the far side of the turnout, away from the passing lights of the road. Twenty off-the-road vehicles stood there already, on the verge of a black field.

Tommy and Arkady walked by the lit cars and then down the centre of the turnout, stepping aside as a Trooper eased by. Tommy was becoming a more eager guide all the time. 'They worked out of caravans in the city until residents complained about the late-night traffic. There's less visual impact here. They're safe; doctors check them once a month.'

The back windows of the far cars all had drawn curtains. A Jeep jiggled from side to side as if it were running in place.

'What does a Bronco look like?' Arkady asked.

Tommy pointed out one of the larger models, but it was blue. They were all high off the ground, what a person would want to set off across the tundra in.

'What do you think?' Tommy asked.

'They all look good.'

'I mean the women.'

Arkady caught a different drift. 'Tommy, what do you *really* mean?'

'I mean, I could lend you some money.'

'No, thanks.'

Tommy shifted from foot to foot, then held out his car keys. 'Do you mind?'

'You're serious?' Arkady asked.

'Since we're here, we might as well enjoy it.' Tommy talked in gusts, gathering bravado. 'Christ, it will only take a few minutes.'

Arkady was stunned, and felt stupid for being so. Who was he to judge anyone else? In another second, Tommy would be pleading. He took the keys. 'I'll be in the car.'

The Trabi was parked across the road. From it he saw Tommy head directly to a Jeep, agree instantly to a price and run around to the passenger side. The Jeep backed away into the dark.

Arkady lit a cigarette and found an ashtray, but no radio. What a perfectly socialist car, designed for bad habits and ignorance, and he was its perfect driver.

Headlights swung on and off the road, creating an ad hoc junction. Perhaps it wasn't so much a matter of there being no crime in Germany as how crime was defined. In Moscow prostitution was against the law. Here it was a regulated trade.

A Trooper pulled into the slot that the Jeep had abandoned. The driver turned on her red light, primped her curls in the rearview mirror, made up her mouth, adjusted her bra, pushed up her breasts like muscles and then picked up a paperback. The woman in the car ahead stared with eyes that looked as if they were painted on her lids. Neither of them looked like a Tima. Arkady assumed the name was short for Fatima, so he searched for someone vaguely Islamic. At this distance the lights were softened to candle glow. Each windscreen looked like a separate ikon with a separate virgin bored to distraction.

After twenty minutes he began to get nervous about Tommy. An image of the cars on the far side of the turnout shone in his mind. A car rocking harder and harder on its springs, its curtains closed tight. If ever there was a place where sex and violence could be confused, this was it. The sound of someone being throttled and beaten? From the outside, that could sound like love.

It was an unreasonable fear, but he was relieved to see Tommy darting nimbly back across the road. The American dove into the car and squeezed behind the steering wheel. Breathing hard, he asked, 'Was I gone long?'

'Hours,' Arkady said.

Tommy pressed himself back in his seat to tuck in his shirt and button his jacket. The smell of perfume and sweat invaded the small car with his return, like the aroma of a trip to an exotic land. He was so proud of himself, Arkady wondered how often he got up his nerve to approach a prostitute.

'Definitely worth the money. Sure you won't change your mind?' he asked.

'I'll take your word for it. Let's go.'

Arkady's door opened. Peter Schiller had to crouch to be on a level with them.

'Renko, you didn't answer your phone.'

Peter's BMW stood in the dark far back from the main road. Arkady spread-eagled, leaning against the side of the car while Peter patted him down. They had a clear view of the turnout, of the cars off the road, and of Tommy heading back to Munich alone in his Trabant.

'Moscow's a mystery to me,' Peter said. He ran his hands around the small of Arkady's back, the inside of his thighs, along his wrists and ankles. 'I've never been there and never hope to be there, but it seems to me that a senior investigator shouldn't have to work out of a public phone booth. I checked out the number when you didn't answer.'

'I hate staying by a desk.'

'You don't have a desk. I went by the consulate and talked to Federov. I pried him away from some singers. He doesn't know anything about your investigation, he's never heard of any Boris Benz and I think it's fair to say he wishes he'd never heard of you.'

'We never did develop a rapport,' Arkady conceded.

When he tried to turn, Peter pushed his face against the roof of the car. 'He told me where to find the pension. Your lights were out. I waited and thought about how to deal most effectively with you. It was obvious you picked Bayern-Franconia out of the blue to run a protection racket on. It's also clear you were doing it alone, to make a few Deutschmarks during your holiday. A little Russian free enterprise. I considered the usual protests to different ministries and Interpol until I remembered how sensitive my grandfather is to any publicity attached to the bank. It's a merchant bank, not for the public, and it doesn't need publicity, least of all the kind you'd give it. So then I considered just taking you out somewhere and beating you until you were a bloody pulp.'

'Isn't that against the law?'

'Beating you so badly you'd be afraid to tell anyone what happened.'

'Well, you can always try,' Arkady said.

Arkady didn't have a gun and Peter had a pistol, a Walther from the glimpse he'd had at the bank. He was pretty sure that Peter Christian Schiller wouldn't shoot, at least not until he'd ordered Arkady away from the BMW because a bullet could go right through soft tissue and spread glass and gore all over the interior of his handsome car. If Peter wanted to hit him, Arkady didn't know whether he would resist. At this point what would a little blood or loose teeth matter? He straightened up and turned around.

Peter's yellow jacket was whipping around him in a breeze that came off the field. He held his pistol low. 'Then who should show up but your friend in the Trabi. I thought, here's a poor bastard from East Germany. No one drives a Trabi any more if they can avoid it. Sometimes you see them near the old border, but not here. Ten minutes later he comes out of the pension with you. It made more sense that you had an Ossie as an accomplice.'

'An "Ossie"?'

'East German. He picks the victim, you show up with a phoney letter from the consulate. I called in the numberplate, but the car belongs to a Thomas Hall, American national, Munich resident. Why would an American drive a Trabi?'

'He says it's an investment. You followed us?'

'It wasn't difficult. Nothing else was as slow.'

'So, what are you going to do?' Arkady asked.

The wonderful thing about a German face was that the agony of thought played so clearly on it. Even in the dim light from the road, Peter looked torn by fury on the one side and by curiosity on the other.

'You're a good friend of Hall's?'

'I never met Tommy before last night. I was surprised to see him tonight.'

'You and Hall went to a sex club together. That sounds friendly.'

'Tommy said he'd seen Benz there. The women at the club said we shouldn't look here.'

'You never talked to Hall before last night?'

'No.'

'You never communicated with him before last night?'

'No. What are you getting at?' Arkady asked.

'Renko, this morning you gave me a fax number to find. I did. The machine belongs to Radio Liberty. It's in the office of Thomas Hall.'

There were surprises left in life after all, Arkady thought. Here he had spent the evening with an apparent innocent, only to discover his own stupidity. Why hadn't he checked the Liberty numbers himself? How many other pieces of information had he brushed off his lap?

'Do you think you can catch up with Tommy?' Arkady asked.

Peter wavered, and Arkady watched with interest to see which way he would go. The German stared back so intently that Arkady thought of the old stage routine of one man pretending to mirror the other.

Finally Peter said, 'Right now, the only thing I'm certain of is that I can catch a Trabi.'

*

They returned by the same route Tommy had taken but at a different speed. Peter wound the BMW up to two hundred kilometres, as if he were driving on a familiar racetrack in the dark. He kept glancing at Arkady, who wished he would keep his eyes on the road.

'You never mentioned Radio Liberty at the bank,' Peter said.

'I didn't know Liberty was involved. It may not be.'

'We don't need a Russian civil war here. We'd rather you all went home and killed yourselves there.'

'That's a possibility.'

'If Liberty's involved, Americans are involved.'

'I hope not.'

'You've never worked with Americans?'

'You've worked with Americans,' Arkady assumed from Peter's tone.

'I trained in Texas.'

'As a cowboy?'

'For the air force. Jet fighters.'

On a bend, a sign shot by. Arkady thought there was nothing like high speed to make a man appreciate the camber of a road. 'For the German air force?'

'Some of us train there. There's less to hit if we crash.'

'That makes sense.'

'Are you KGB?'

'No. Did Federov say I was?'

Peter produced a sardonic laugh. 'Federov swore you weren't KGB. God forbid. But if you aren't, why are you interested in Radio Liberty?'

'Tommy sent a fax to Moscow.'

'Saying?' Peter demanded.

' "Where is Red Square?" '

They drove in silence until a pink spot emerged ahead.

'We have to talk to Tommy,' Arkady said. He held up a cigarette. 'Do you mind?'

'Roll down the window.'

Air whistled in and with it came an acrid smell that made his throat close.

Peter said, 'Someone's burning plastic.'

'And tyres.'

The pink spot grew, vanished and reappeared, larger and deeper in colour. It disappeared, then came into sight again at the abutment of a cross-ramp, a torch at the base of thick, roiling smoke that leaned away from the wind. Closer, the torch was a meteor furiously trying to burrow its way into the earth.

'Trabi,' Peter said as they went by.

They walked back from the downwind side, hands covering their noses and mouths. The Trabant was a small car, now compacted even more by its impact with the base of the ramp. Yet the flames were enormous, red scalloped with chemical blue and green, and the smoke was black as oil. The Trabi didn't just burn from the inside; it was all on fire at once, plastic walls, hood and roof melting as they burned so that flames rained on to the seats. The tyres burned as spectral rings.

They circled the wreck as best they could in case Tommy had crawled free.

Arkady said, 'I've seen this kind of fire before. If he isn't out now, he's dead.'

Peter retreated. Arkady tried to get closer, crawling on all fours below the smoke. The heat was too intense, a breath that made his jacket steam.

When the wind shifted he saw in the car the kind of portrait a scissors artist cuts out of black paper. It was burning, too.

Peter returned in the BMW, backing up past the fire and searching the road with his spotlight until he found skid marks. He stopped, got out and set his blue flasher on the roof. He was probably a good policeman, Arkady thought.

Too late for Tommy. In violet hues, a plastic door peeled away. As the plastic roof curled back, a stronger updraft made flames swirl like a passionate flower folding and unfolding.

Chapter Twenty-Two

'You know, in the old days we would have gassed you, tied you up and shipped you home in a crate. We don't do things that way any more. Now that our relations with the Germans have improved, we don't need to,' Vice-consul Platonov said.

'No?' Arkady asked.

'The Germans do it for us. First I remove you from these premises.' Platonov pulled a shirt off the line strung across the room, surveyed a map of Munich spread on the table, the roll and juice by the sink, and then deposited the shirt in Federov's hands. 'Renko, I know it feels like home to you, but since the consulate rents this room, we can do what we want. Right now I want to report you as a vagrant, which is what you are because I have your passport and without it you can't register anywhere else.'

Federov unzipped Arkady's holdall into a yawning mouth, tossed in the shirt and said, 'Germans deport foreign vagrants, especially Russian vagrants.'

'It's a matter of economics,' Platonov said. 'It's bad enough, they think, taking care of East Germans.'

'If you're thinking about political asylum, forget it.' Federov emptied the chest of drawers and bustled around the room like the energetic assistant he was.

'That's out of date. No one wants defectors from a democratic Soviet Union.'

Arkady hadn't seen the vice-consul since his first welcome to Munich, but Platonov had not forgotten him. 'What did I tell you? See the museums, buy some gifts. You could have made a year's salary just buying here and selling when you got back. I warned you that you had no official status, and not to contact German police. So what did you do? You not only went right to the Germans, but you also involved the consulate.'

'Have you been to a fire?' Federov sniffed a jacket.

Arkady had washed the clothes he had worn the night before, and had showered too, but he doubted that his hair or his jacket would ever be completely free of smoke.

Platonov said, 'Renko, twice a week I have tea with Bavarian industrialists and bankers to convince them that we are civilized people they can do business with and safely lend millions of Deutschmarks to. Then you show up and start twisting arms and demanding protection money. Federov tells me he had a difficult time convincing a lieutenant of the Polizei that he was not part of a conspiracy to defraud German banks.'

'How would you like to be visited by the Gestapo?' Federov asked. He poured wallet, purse, toothbrush and toothpaste into the bag. The locker key and Lufthansa ticket he confiscated and put in his pocket.

'Did he mention any bank in particular?' Arkady asked.

'No.' Federov looked into the refrigerator and found it empty.

'Did the Germans make an official protest?'

'No.' Federov folded up the map and threw it into the bag.

'Have you heard from the police since?'

'No.'

Not even since the car accident? That was interesting, Arkady thought. 'I'll need my aeroplane ticket,' he said.

'Actually, you won't.' Platonov dropped an Aeroflot ticket on the table. 'We're sending you home today. Federov will put you on the plane.'

'My visa is good for another week,' Arkady said.

'Consider your visa cancelled.'

'I'd need new orders from the Prosecutor's Office. Until then I can't leave.'

'Prosecutor Rodionov is a hard man to reach. I have to ask myself why he sent an investigator on a tourist visa, giving you no real authority. The whole affair is too odd.' Platonov wandered to the window and looked out towards the station yard. Over the vice-consul's shoulder, Arkady saw trains slide across the tracks, morning commuters poised on the steps. Platonov shook his head in admiration. 'Now there's efficiency.'

'I'm not going,' Arkady said.

'You have no choice. Either we put you on the plane or the Germans will. Think how that would look on your record. I'm giving you the easy way out,' Platonov said.

'All because I'm evicted?'

'As simple as that,' Platonov said, 'and absolutely legal. I really have to appreciate good diplomatic relations.'

'I've never been evicted before,' Arkady said. Arrested and exiled, but never simply evicted. Life was getting subtle, he thought.

'It's the coming thing.' Federov swept the rest of the washing off the line and into the holdall.

The door opened. Standing in the hall was a black dog that Arkady assumed was part of the eviction process; the animal had eyes as dark as agate and, by its size and density of hair, looked crossbred from a bear. It walked in confidently and regarded the three men with equal suspicion.

Unequal footsteps followed from the hall and Stas looked in. 'Going somewhere?' he asked Arkady.

'Being sent.'

Stas entered, ignoring Platonov and Federov, though Arkady was sure he knew who they were; he had studied Soviet apparatchiks all his life, and a man who studies worms all his life recognizes worms. Federov started to drop the bundle in his arms, but when the dog turned he held on to the clothes.

'I sent Tommy around last night. Did you see him?' Stas asked Arkady.

'I'm sorry about Tommy.'

'You heard about the accident?'

'I saw it,' Arkady said.

'I want to know what happened.'

'So do I,' Arkady said.

Stas's eyes shone a little more than usual. When he glanced at Platonov and the burdened Federov, the dog followed suit. He looked at the open holdall again. 'You can't leave,' he said as if it were a decision.

Platonov spoke up. 'It's German law. Since Renko has no place to stay, the consulate is expediting his return home.'

'Stay with me,' Stas told Arkady.

'It's not that simple,' Platonov said. 'Invitations to Soviet citizens have to be submitted in writing and approved in advance. His visa has been cancelled and he already has his new ticket to Moscow, so it's impossible.'

Stas asked Arkady, 'Can you go now?'

Arkady removed his locker key and Lufthansa ticket from Federov and said, 'Actually, I'm almost packed.'

Stas joined the traffic milling around the centre of town. Though it was a grey summer day, the windows were down because the dog's breath condensed on the glass. The animal filled the rear seat of the car, and Arkady had the feeling that he would be allowed in front with his bag only as long as he moved slowly. When he had left, Platonov and Federov had looked like a pair of pall-bearers whose corpse was walking out of the door.

'Thanks.'

'I did have some questions,' Stas said. 'Tommy was a silly man and he drove a stupid car. The Trabi wouldn't go more than seventy-five kilometres per hour and never should have been on a motorway, but I don't understand how he could lose control and hit an abutment so hard.'

'I don't either,' Arkady said. 'I doubt there's enough left of the car to tell the police anything. It burned down to an engine block and axle.'

'It was probably that idiotic heater. A paraffin heater on a car floor? A deathtrap.'

'Tommy didn't suffer long. If the crash didn't kill him, the smoke did. We see the flames, but they die of fumes first.'

'You've seen this kind of thing before?'

'I saw a man in Moscow die in a car fire. It just took a little longer because it was a better car.'

Thinking about Rudy made Arkady remember Polina. Also Jaak. He thought that if he got back to Moscow alive he would be a less critical person, more appreciative of friendship and deathly cautious of all cars and fires. Stas, on the other hand, drove recklessly. At least he watched the road, content to let the dog keep watch on Arkady.

'Did Tommy take you to Red Square?'

'You know about that place?'

'Renko, there are not many reasons to be on that road at that time of night. Poor Tommy. A case of fatal Russophilia.'

'Then we went to a parking lot, sort of a mobile brothel.'

'A wonderful place if you're looking for a wasting disease. German law says the women are checked for AIDS every three months, which means they're more scientific about the beer they drink than the women they sleep with. Anyway, trying to have sex in a Jeep can give you a hunchback and I have enough disabilities as it is. I thought the two of you were going to talk about famous battles of the Great Patriotic War.'

'We did for a little while.'

'Americans always want to talk about the war,' Stas said.

'Do you know Boris Benz?'

'No. Who's he?'

There wasn't a hint of deception or a pause for thought. Children performed clownish, wide-eyed lies. Adults gave themselves away with small gestures, casting the eyes towards memory or couching the lie with a smile.

'Could you stop at the train station?' Arkady asked.

When Stas pulled in among the buses and taxis at the north side of the station, Arkady hopped out, leaving his bag behind.

'You're coming back?' Stas asked. 'I have this feeling that you travel light.'

'Two minutes.'

Federov had brains of stale bread, but he might recognize a station locker key when he saw one, and it was even possible that he could remember the number. Arkady's original deposit had expired and he had to pay the attendant an extra four Deutschmarks to open the locker and retrieve the videotape, which left him with seventy-five Deutschmarks for the rest of his stay.

When he went outside, a traffic policeman was trying

to move Stas's shabby Mercedes out of the way of an Italian coach. The coach was polished like a gondola and had a furious musical horn. The more the bus honked and the policeman shouted, the louder the dog barked back. Stas sat himself behind the wheel and enjoyed a cigarette. 'Not opera,' he told Arkady. 'But close.'

Arkady was getting his bearings. He knew when Stas turned north towards the museums and east towards the Englischer Garten. He noticed that a white Porsche he had seen at the station was half a block behind them.

'So, who is Boris Benz?' Stas asked.

'I don't really know. He's an East German who lives in Munich and travels to Moscow. Tommy said he'd met him. That's who we were looking for last night.'

'If you and Tommy were together, why weren't you in the crash? Why didn't you die too?'

'The police picked me up. I was coming back in a police car when we saw the fire.'

'They didn't mention that you were alone.'

'There was no reason to. An accident report is a short, simple form.'

Peter had identified Arkady as a 'witness who observed the deceased consuming alcohol at a roadside erotic club'. A brief but pungent description, he thought. He added, 'Especially a single-car accident where the car has burned so badly it almost disappears. There's nothing left to report.'

'I think there's more. What did this Benz do in Moscow? Why aren't you investigating on a more official level? Where did Tommy meet Benz? Who introduced them? Why would the police take you out of Tommy's car? Was it an accident?'

'Did Tommy have any enemies?' Arkady asked.

'Tommy didn't have many friends, but he had no enemies at all. Why do I have this foreboding that anyone who helps you immediately acquires enemies? I shouldn't have sent him to you. He couldn't protect himself.'

'You can?'

Although he didn't catch any signal from Stas, Arkady felt a hot canine breath at the back of his neck.

'Her name is Laika, but she's very German. Loves leather and beer, distrusts Russians. She makes an exception in my case. We're almost there.' He waved towards a building that was a vertical garden of geraniums. 'Every balcony a beer garden. Bavarian heaven. Actually, the balcony with cactus is mine.'

'Thanks, but I won't be staying,' Arkady said.

Stas swung in front of the building and killed the engine. 'I thought you needed a place.'

'I needed to get away from the consulate. You're generous. Thanks,' Arkady said.

'You can't just walk off. Look, the truth is that you don't have a place to sleep.'

'Right.'

'And you don't have much money.'

'Right.'

'But you think you can survive in Munich?'

'Right.'

Stas said to the dog, 'He's so Russian.' He told Arkady, 'You think some special destiny is protecting you? Do you know why Germany looks so neat? Because every night the Germans pick up Turks, Poles and Russians and put them in sanitary jails until they're shipped home.'

'Maybe I'll be lucky. You showed up when I needed you.'

'That's different.'

Stas got no further before the Porsche eased alongside. The sports car moved back and forth, eyeballing Arkady and Stas. An electrically controlled window slid down, revealing the driver wearing dark sailing glasses with a red cord. His smile seemed to have more than two rows of teeth.

'Michael,' Stas said.

'Stas.' Michael had the kind of American voice that cut through the sound of a car engine. Arkady recalled a cool introduction to the station's deputy director at Tommy's party. 'Have you heard about Tommy?'

'Yes.'

'Sad.' Michael observed a moment of silence.

'Yes.'

Michael became more businesslike. 'I was just coming to ask you about it.'

'You were?'

'Because I heard that your friend, the visiting Investi-

gator Renko from Moscow, was with our Tommy last
night. And who do I see here but Renko himself?'

'I was just leaving,' Arkady said.

'Good, because the station president would really like
to have a few words with you.' Michael pushed open
the passenger door of the Porsche. 'I just want you, not
Stas. I'll bring you back, I promise.'

Stas said to Arkady, 'If you think Michael is any kind
of salvation, you're insane.'

Michael drove the Porsche with one hand and used a
cellular phone with the other. 'Sir, I have Comrade Renko
in tow.' He gave Arkady a grin. 'In tow, sir, in *tow*. We
hit a gap between radio receivers. These phones work
on line of vision.' He cupped the phone on his shoulder
to shift gear. 'Sir, we'll be there in a second. I wish you'd
wait until I get there. In a second.' He dropped the
phone in a sleeve between the bucket seats and offered
another glimpse of his dark glasses and bright smile.
'Fucking technical incompetent. Well, Arkady, I've been
checking up on you and you're an interesting guy. From
what I hear, you're a maverick. I found you in Irina's
file. It's safe to say that now you're in Tommy's file, too.
Does trouble just follow you, or what?'

'Were you following Stas?'

'I admit I was, and he led me straight to you. The
side trip to the train station gave me a scare. What did
you take out of the locker?'

'A fur hat and an Order of Lenin.'

'It looked like a little plastic box. A familiar kind of box. I can't place it and it's driving me crazy. You know, as deputy director for security I have excellent relations with the local police. I can find out in a roundabout way what you and Tommy were doing last night, or else you can simply tell me. Only one way gets you extra credit.'

'Extra credit?'

'Let me put it more simply: money. What we can't afford is any mystery about one of our employees being killed. We hoped that the bad old days of the Cold War were behind us. I'm betting they are.'

'Why? You might lose your job; they might shut the station.'

'I'm looking ahead.'

'So is Max Albov.'

'Max is a winner. He's a star. Like Irina, if she polished her English a little more and chose her friends a little better.' He glanced over. 'President Gilmartin is going to ask you about Tommy. Gilmartin is head of Radio Liberty and Radio Free Europe. He's the front-line voice of the United States and he's a busy man. So if you're cute, then fuck you and you can eat dog food. If you're honest, then there's a bonus for you.'

'It pays to be honest?'

'Exactly!'

The Porsche surged ahead of the traffic like a speed-boat, and Michael smiled as if Munich were tossing in his wake.

*

They crossed to the east side of the city and the largest houses, short of palaces, that Arkady had ever seen. Some of them were modern, stark Bauhaus plaster and steel tubing. Others looked almost Mediterranean, with glass doors and potted palms. A few were either miraculously surviving or painstakingly reconstructed examples of *Jugendstil*; mansions covered with playful, vinelike façades and curving eaves.

Michael pulled into the driveway of the grandest of the mansions. On the front lawn a man was setting up a combination umbrella and table.

Michael led Arkady across the grass. Although no drops were falling, the man was dressed in a raincoat and rubber boots. About sixty, with a noble brow and jowls, he regarded Michael's arrival with a mixture of exasperation and relief.

'Sir, this is Investigator Renko. President Gilmartin,' Michael said.

'A pleasure.' Gilmartin gave Arkady a firm sportsman's hand and then sorted through a tool box on the table for the shiniest pair of pliers. A wrench and screwdriver had already spilled on to the lawn.

Michael pulled off his sunglasses and let them hang from the cord. 'I wish you'd waited for me, sir.'

'The goddamn Germans are always complaining about my dish. The grief. I have to have a dish, and this is the only place with clear sight of satellites unless I put it on the roof, and then would the Heinies scream.'

Now that Arkady looked he saw that the umbrella was actually camouflage, striped fabric over a satellite dish three metres wide. Dish and table were bolted to the ground.

'The boots are a good idea,' Michael said.

'I've been around broadcasting long enough to know better safe than sorry,' Gilmartin said. He told Arkady, 'I was with the networks for thirty years until I decided I didn't like the direction the medium was going. I wanted to have an impact.'

'Tommy,' Michael reminded him.

'Yes.' Gilmartin fixed Arkady with a stare. 'Dark Ages, Renko. We've had trouble in the past. Murders, break-ins, bombings. You blew up our Czech section a few years back. Tried to stab our Romanian chief to death in his garage. Electrocuted one of our nicest Russian contributors. But we never lost an American, and those were the days when we were admittedly CIA. Prehistoric. We're funded by Congress now.'

'We're a private corporation,' Michael said.

'Delaware, I believe. My point is, we're not secret agents.'

'Tommy was an inoffensive guy,' Michael said.

'The most inoffensive guy I ever met,' Gilmartin said. 'Besides, the days of rough stuff are supposed to be over, so what were you, a Soviet investigator, doing with Tommy when he died?'

Arkady said, 'Tommy had an historical interest in the war against Hitler. He asked some questions about people I knew.'

'There's more to it than that,' Gilmartin said.

'There's a lot more to it,' Michael agreed.

'The station is like a family,' Gilmartin said. 'We watch out for each other. I want to know the whole unvarnished story.'

'Such as?' Arkady asked.

'Was there sex involved? I don't mean you and Tommy. I mean were there women?'

Michael said, 'The president means that if Washington goes through Tommy's laundry, are they going to find dirt?'

Gilmartin said, 'It doesn't matter to them that prostitution is legal in Germany. American standards are set in Peoria. Even a hint of scandal here always brings accusations of corruption and high living.'

'And reductions in funding,' Michael said.

'I want to know everything you and Tommy did last night,' Gilmartin said.

Arkady took a moment to choose his words. 'Tommy came to the pension where I was staying. We talked about the war. After a while I said I'd like some fresh air, so we got into his car and drove around. We did see a group of prostitutes off the motorway. At that point I left Tommy and he drove alone back to the city. On the way he had an accident.'

'Did Tommy have sex with a prostitute?' Gilmartin asked.

'No,' Arkady lied.

'Did he talk to a prostitute?' Michael asked.

'No,' Arkady lied again.

'Did he talk to any Russians besides yourself?' Michael asked.

'No,' Arkady lied a third time.

'Why did you separate?' Gilmartin asked.

'I *did* want to see a prostitute. Tommy refused to stay.'

Michael asked, 'How did you get back to Munich?'

'The police picked me up on the side of the road.'

'A sorry night on the town,' Gilmartin said.

'None of it was Tommy's fault,' Arkady said.

Michael and Gilmartin exchanged looks that made a silent conversation; then the president lifted his eyes and considered the sky. 'It's awfully thin.'

'But if Renko sticks to it, it's not bad. He's Russian, after all. They're not going to have a year to boil it out of him. And remember, Tommy drove an East German Trabant, not a very roadworthy car. That's what we zero in on: the car was a deathtrap.' Michael patted Arkady on the back. 'You're probably lucky to be alive.'

'Losing Tommy must be a blow,' Arkady said to Gilmartin.

'More a personal tragedy. He wasn't in any decision-making role. Research and translations, right?'

'Yes, sir,' Michael said.

'Though they're important,' Gilmartin hastened to add. 'Michael's Russian is better than mine, but I think it's fair to say that without our able translators the Russians on the staff would run amok.'

Gilmartin's attention moved to his other concern. He pointed his pair of pliers at loose bolts that had rolled into a fold of the diagram. 'Know anything about satellite dishes?' he asked Arkady.

'No.'

'I'm afraid I may have moved something out of alignment,' Gilmartin confessed.

'Sir, we'll think about windload, check the signal and make sure you didn't damage any cable,' Michael said. 'Looks like a good job.'

'Think so?' Reassured, Gilmartin stepped back for a better view. 'You know, this would be even more convincing if we brought chairs out and got people to really use this as an umbrella.'

'Sir, I don't think you'd actually want people drinking lemonade under a microwave receiver.'

'No,' Gilmartin said. He scratched his chin with the pliers. 'Maybe just the neighbours.'

Chapter Twenty-Three

Stas lived alone... and not alone. Moving through the hall meant elbowing Gogol and Gorky. Poets from Pushkin to Voloshin resided in a closet. The elevated thoughts of Tolstoy filled shelves above a Swedish sound system, CDs and television set. Newspapers and magazines were stacked by year. The least slip, Arkady thought, and a man could die under an avalanche of stale news, music, fantasy, romance.

Stas said, 'I don't like to think of it as messy. I prefer to think of it as life lived at full tide.'

'It looks like full tide,' Arkady said.

'Hotels are lacking in soul,' Stas said.

Laika sat by the door. Arkady could barely see her eyes through fur, though he felt them following his every move.

'Thanks, I have somewhere to go,' he said.

After the visit to the station president, Arkady had spent the rest of the day watching Benz's house. It was dusk now and light was seeping from the room. He had decided to ride on the underground until it shut down, or to buy a cheap ticket for an early morning train so he could wait at the station. That way he would at least be more migrant than vagrant. He had come to Stas's place only for his bag.

One question kept forcing itself to the front of Arkady's mind. It was so obvious that it was hard work not asking. 'Where is Max staying?'

'I don't know. One drink before you go,' Stas said. 'I suspect you're in for a long night.'

Before Arkady could protest or get around the dog and out of the door, his host was in the kitchen and back with two glasses and a bottle of vodka. The vodka was iced. 'Fancy,' Arkady said.

Stas filled the glasses halfway. 'To Tommy.'

The cold vodka gave Arkady's heart a brief squeeze on the way down. Alcohol didn't seem to affect Stas; he was a frail reed that stood up to the flood. He refilled the glasses. 'To Michael,' he offered. 'And the snake that bites him.'

Arkady drank to that and set the glass on a stack of papers out of Stas's reach. 'I'm just curious. You go out of your way to annoy the Americans. Why don't they fire you?'

'German labour law. The Germans don't want any foreigners on their welfare rolls, so once one has a job it's almost impossible to dismiss him. There are meetings between the American management and the Russian staff at the station. By law, the reports are written in German. It drives the Americans crazy. Michael tries to fire me once a year. It's wonderful, like starving a shark. Anyway, I put good programmes on the air.'

'You like to embarrass him?'

'I'll tell you what real embarrassment is – when the Jews on the staff accused the station of anti-Semitism, took it to a German court and *won*. That's embarrassment. I don't want Michael to forget episodes like that.'

'When Max defected back to Moscow, wasn't that embarrassing?'

Stas took a deep breath. 'It was embarrassing to me and to Irina. Actually, it was embarrassing to everyone. We'd had security problems before.'

'Michael said so. An explosion?'

'That's why we have the gates and big walls now. But to have the head of the Russian section defect back to Moscow is a security problem on a different level.'

'I'd think that Michael would hate Max even more than he hates you.'

'You'd think so.' Stas looked at his empty glass. 'I've known Max for ten years. I was always struck by how he could get along with the Americans and us. He changed, depending where he was and who he was with. You and I are Russians. Max is liquid. He changes shape. He fills the container whatever the container is. In a fluid situation, he's king. He came back from Moscow more of a businessman than he was before. The Americans can't help believing Max because he's like a mirror. To them he looks like another American.'

'What kind of business is he involved in?'

'I don't know. Before he left he used to say a fortune could be made out of the collapse of the Soviet Union. He said it was like any huge bankruptcy; there were still assets and property. What's the biggest landowner in the Soviet Union? Who owns the biggest office buildings, the best resorts, the only decent apartment houses?'

'The Party.'

'The Communist Party. Max said that all it had to do was change its name, call itself a company and restructure. Dump the shareholders, keep the goods.'

Arkady wasn't sure at what point he had set his bag down, but he discovered himself sitting on the couch. Bread, cheese and cigarettes were on the table. A floor fixture pointed light in three directions. The balcony door was open to street sounds and night air.

Stas filled the glasses again. 'I wasn't a spy. The KGB called demonstrators and defectors either spies or mentally ill. Russians understand that. The part I didn't expect was that the Americans would think that it was a KGB plot to insert the dangerous Stas into the unsuspecting West. Some of the CIA believed it. *All* of the FBI believed it. The FBI doesn't believe *any* defectors. Jesus could ride an ass out of Moscow and they'd open a file on him.

'There were real heroes. Not me. Men and women who crawled through minefields into Turkey or ran through gunfire to reach an embassy yard. Who threw away careers and lost their families. For what? For Czechoslovakia, Hungary, God, Afghanistan. Which doesn't mean that they weren't compromised. You understand, but Americans don't. We grew up with informers. Among our friends and families there were always informers. Even among heroes there were informers. It's complex. A woman, an old lover from

Moscow, visits Munich. Michael demands to know why I see her when everyone knows she's an informer. But that doesn't mean I don't still love her. We have a writer at Liberty whose wife worked at an Army base teaching the Russian language to American officers, screwing them and getting information for the KGB so she could live like a decent Western woman. She spent two years in jail. That doesn't mean her husband didn't take her back. We all talk to her. What are we going to do, pretend she's dead?

'Or we arrive compromised. An artist, a friend of mine, was called in by the KGB before he left Moscow. They said, "We never put you in a camp, so no hard feelings. All we hope is you don't slander us to the Western press. After all, we think you're a wonderful artist and you probably don't realize how difficult it is to survive in the West, so we'd like to give you a loan. In dollars. We won't tell anyone and you don't need to sign a receipt. After a few years you pay it back with interest or no interest, when you can, just between us." Five years later he publicly sent them a cheque and demanded a receipt, but it took him that long to realize how cheaply he'd been compromised and cancelled out. How many other loans are out there?

'Or we go crazy. There's the writers who went to Paris. A famous writer who survived the Gulag and wrote under the pen name of Teitlebaum. It was revealed that he informed for the KGB. He wrote a defence and said, no, no, it wasn't him who informed, it was Teitlebaum!

'And occasionally,' Stas said, 'we're killed. We open a letter bomb or get jabbed with the tip of a poisoned umbrella, or drink ourselves to death. Even so, at one time we were heroes.'

Laika stretched like a sphinx in the middle of the floor. Arkady couldn't see the dog's eyes as much as feel their force. Her ear might turn towards the sound of a particularly noisy car on the street four storeys down, but her focus remained on him. He said, 'You don't have to explain yourself to me.'

'I do, because you're different. You aren't a dissident. You saved Irina, but everyone wants to save Irina, that's not necessarily a political act.'

'It was more personal,' Arkady admitted.

'You stayed. People who knew Irina knew about you. You were the ghost. She tried to reach you once or twice.'

'Not that I know of.'

'What I'm trying to say is that we made a sacrifice to be soldiers on the right side. Who knew that history was going to change? That the Red Army would end up as camps of beggars in Poland? That the Wall was going to fall? They thought the Red Army was a danger? Now they're worried about two hundred and forty million Russians eating their way to the English Channel. Radio Liberty isn't quite the front line any more. We're not jammed; we have correspondents now in Moscow; we regularly interview people in the Kremlin.'

'You won,' Arkady said.

Stas finished the bottle and lit a cigarette. His narrow

face was wan, his eyes two bright matches. 'Won? Then why only now do I feel like an émigré? Say you leave your native land because you were forced out, or because you thought you could help more from the outside than in? Democrats of the world applaud your noble effort. But it wasn't because of any effort of mine that the Soviet Union dropped to its knees and stretched out its long neck. It was history. It was gravity. The battle isn't in Munich, it's in Moscow. History has marooned us and gone in a different direction. We don't look like heroes any more; we look like fools. Americans look at us – not Michael and Gilmartin, they're concerned about their jobs and keeping the station alive – but other Americans read headlines about what's happening in Moscow and look at us and say, "They should have stayed." It doesn't matter whether we were forced out or risked our lives or wanted to save the world; now Americans say, "They should have stayed." They look at someone like you and say, "See, he stayed." '

'I didn't have a choice. I made a bargain. They'd only leave Irina alone if I stayed. Anyway, that was long ago.'

Stas peered into his empty glass. 'If you'd had the choice, would you have left with her?'

Arkady was silent. Stas leaned forward and waved smoke away to see him more clearly. 'Would you?'

'I was Russian. I don't think I could have gone.'

Stas was silent.

Arkady added, '*My* staying in Moscow certainly had no effect on history. Maybe *I* was the fool.'

Stas stirred, went to the kitchen and returned with

another bottle. Laika kept her attention on Arkady in case he produced a bomb, a gun or a sharpened umbrella against her master.

'Irina had a difficult time in New York. She was in films in Moscow?' Stas asked.

'She was actually a student until she was thrown out of the university. Then she got work at Mosfilm as a wardrobe mistress,' Arkady said.

'In New York she did stage costumes and make-up, fell in with an artistic crowd and worked in art galleries, first there and then in Berlin, all the time defending herself from saviours. The pattern was always the same: an American would fall in love with Irina and then rationalize it as a political good deed. I think Radio Liberty must have been a relief. To give him credit, Max was the one who recognized how good she was. She wasn't a regular at first, just filling in, but he said there was a quality in her voice on the air, as if she were speaking to someone she knew. People listened. I was sceptical at first because she had no professional training. He gave me the job of teaching her how to hit her marks and watch the clock. People have no idea how fast they talk. Irina could run through a script once and almost have it memorized. With training, she was the best.'

Stas opened the bottle. 'So there we were, Max and I, two sculptors working on the same beautiful statue. Naturally we both fell in love with Irina. We did everything together – Max, Stas and Irina. Dinners, skiing in the Alps, musical sidetrips to Salzburg. An inseparable trio, neither Max nor I ever gaining an edge on the other. I didn't actually ski. I read down in the lodge, secure in the knowledge that Max was making no romantic headway on the slopes because, in fact, our trio was really a quartet.' He poured the vodka. 'There was always that man in Irina's past. The one who saved her life and stayed, the one she was waiting for. How could anyone beat a hero like that?'

'Maybe no one needed to. Maybe she just got tired of waiting,' Arkady said.

They drank at the same time, like two men chained to the same oar.

'No,' Stas said. 'I'm not talking about long ago. When Max went to Moscow last year I thought I was in command of the field. But I was outmanoeuvred to a degree I never anticipated, in a manner that only proves Max's genius. Because you see what Max did?'

'No,' Arkady admitted.

'Max came back. Max loved her and he came back for her. It was what I couldn't do and what you never did. Now he's the hero and I'm demoted to mere "dear friend".'

Stas's eyes looked fuelled by vodka. Arkady wondered if he had ever actually seen the man *eat*. He swirled the vodka in his own glass so that it rolled around like mercury. 'What was Max before he ever came to the West?'

'He was a film director. He defected at a film festival. Hollywood, however, was not interested in his work.'

'What kind of films had he done?'

'War epics, killing Germans, Japanese, Israeli terrorists – the usual. Max did have the tastes of a famous director: custom-made suits, fine wine, beautiful women.'

'Where is he staying in Munich?' Arkady asked again.

'I don't know. What I'm trying to say is that my last hope is you.'

'Max has outmanoeuvred me, too.'

'No, I know Max. He only attacks when he has to. If you weren't a threat he'd be your best friend.'

'Not much of a threat. As far as Irina is concerned, I'm dead.' That was the word she'd used in Tommy's kitchen, like a knife she'd found on the table.

'But did she tell you to go?'

'No.'

'So she hasn't really made up her mind.'

'Irina doesn't care whether I come or go. I don't think she even sees me.'

'Irina hasn't smoked for years. The first time she saw you she asked for a cigarette. She sees you.'

Laika's head turned towards the balcony and she rose to her forepaws, then stood, ears sharp. Stas motioned for Arkady to be quiet, then reached for the light fixture and turned it off.

The room was black. Outside were the percussive noises of Volkswagens and a bell chasing someone from a bike lane. Closer, Arkady heard the toeholds of rubber soles, the easing of a rail, the soft landing of a big man on to the balcony. Laika was invisible but Arkady located her by an anticipatory growl in the darkness. As a step crossed the balcony he felt the dog coil to attack.

There was an audible intake of breath and a voice in pain. 'Stas, please! Stas!'

Stas turned the lights on. 'Sit, Laika. Good girl, sit, sit.'

Rikki staggered through the door. Arkady had met the Georgian actor-turned-broadcaster in the station cafeteria and at Tommy's party. Each time Rikki had appeared distraught, or at the least histrionic. Now he was again. The back of one hand was covered in spines. 'The cactus,' he moaned.

'I rearranged them,' Stas said.

Arkady turned on the outdoor light. Under a hanging lamp were a metal table, two chairs, a bucket of empty beer bottles and a semicircle of various potted cacti, some of them pincushions with short spines and some that resembled serrated bayonets.

'It's an alarm system,' Stas said.

A shock wave went through Rikki with each needle that Stas pulled out. 'Everyone else has geraniums on their balcony. I have geraniums. The geranium is a lovely flower,' he said.

'Rikki lives upstairs.' Stas plucked the final spine.

Red puncture marks dotted Rikki's hand. He looked at them mournfully.

'Do you always visit this way?' Arkady asked.

'I was trapped.' Remembering, he pulled Stas and Arkady away from the balcony. 'They're at my door.'

'Who?' Stas asked.

'My mother and my daughter. All these years waiting to see them and now they're here. My mother wants to take the television. My daughter wants to drive back in the car.'

'Your car?' Stas asked.

'*Her* car, once she gets to Georgia.' Rikki explained to Arkady, 'In a moment of weakness, I said she could. But I have a new BMW. What is a girl going to do with that in Georgia?'

'Have fun,' Arkady said.

'I knew this would happen. These people have no control. They're so greedy it makes me ashamed.' Rikki's face fell tragically.

Stas said, 'Don't answer your door and they'll go away.'

'Not them.' Rikki's eyes lifted to the ceiling. 'They'll wait me out.'

'You can go down the stairs from here,' Arkady said.

Rikki said, 'I told them to wait a minute. I can't simply disappear. I have to open the door sometime.'

Stas asked, 'Then why come here?'

'Do you have any brandy?' Rikki examined his hand, which was already starting to swell.

'No. Vodka,' Stas offered.

'It will have to do.' He allowed himself to be helped to a chair and given a glass. 'This is my plan: let her take a different car.'

Stas said, 'You picked her up at the airport. She knows your car. She loves your car.'

'I'll say it's yours – that I borrowed it from you to impress her.'

'Ah. And what car are you going to let her take?' Stas asked.

'Stas.' Rikki batted his eyes. 'Stas, we're close friends. Your Mercedes is ten years old, bought used – a dog bed, if I may speak frankly. My daughter is a woman of some taste. She'll take one look at your car and will refuse to touch it. I was hoping we could trade keys.'

Stas poured two more vodkas and said to Arkady, 'You wouldn't know it now, but Rikki once swam the Black Sea. He had a wet suit and a compass. He dived through nets and mines and swam under patrol boats. It was a heroic escape. Now here he is, hiding from his daughter.'

'You won't trade?' Rikki asked.

'Life has caught up with you. I think your daughter's going to make you pay for years,' Stas said. 'The car is only a beginning.'

The vodka seemed to stick in Rikki's throat. He drew himself up with dignity, walked out to the balcony and spat over the rail. 'Damn her! And you!' he told Stas. He set the glass on the balcony table and hoisted himself up on the waterpipe that ran down the front of the building. For a man his size he was still agile. Arkady saw his legs swing to the upper balcony. As he thrashed, geranium petals rained.

Arkady awoke on the sofa. It was two a.m. by his watch. There is no hole deeper than two in the morning, the hour when fear rules the world. Stas had avoided the question twice. Where was Max staying?

By nature, Russians did not like hotels. Visitors stayed with friends. Other friends knew where. The idea that Max was lying alongside Irina made Arkady stare into the bluish dark of the room. He could almost see them in bed, as if it were just on the other side of the living-room table. See Max's arm locked around her; hear Max breathe the perfume of her hair.

He lit a match. Chairs, desk and bookshelves crept out of the dark and towards the flame. He threw off his blanket. On the desk he had seen the telephone. Feeling around the top, he found a small address book. He lit another match clumsily with one hand, opened the front of the book and found 'Irina Asanova' and her number. The flame was at his fingers. He pinched it out and picked up the phone. Would he say he was sorry to wake her but they had to talk? She had already made it clear she had nothing to say to him, especially if Max was lying next to her. Arkady could warn her. How jealous and inept that would sound, with Max right there.

Or when she answered he could ask for Max. That would let her know he was aware of how things stood. Or if she asked who was calling, he could say, 'Boris', then see how she reacted to that.

Arkady punched her number, but when he started to lift the phone to his ear, his wrist was clamped. Damp teeth held the hand and phone down. When he made the slightest effort to raise the phone, the jaws tightened.

He moved his other hand to the phone and a growl resonated through his arm.

On the other end of the line he heard the characteristic two rings of a German phone. 'Hello?' Irina said.

Arkady tried to wrench his arm free and the jaws closed.

'Who is this?' Irina asked.

The whole weight of the dog hung from his arm.

A click was followed by a dial tone.

As Arkady let his arm fall, the jaws relaxed. When he replaced the phone on the cradle, the teeth let go. He felt the dog waiting to make sure he left the phone alone.

Save me, Arkady thought. Save me from myself.

Chapter Twenty-Four

The secret was that Stas did all his eating at breakfast: liver, smoked salmon, potato salad and pots of coffee. He also had the VCR and enormous television of an unmarried man.

With a remote control, Arkady played the videotape. On fast forward, the television screen raced through monks, Marienplatz, beer garden, modern traffic, beer hall, swans, opera, Oktoberfest, Alps, beer garden. Stopped. He rewound to the start of the last scene. It was a sun-dappled garden in a wall of honeysuckle tended by bees. Diners sat exhausted by the effort of a heavy lunch, all but the woman at one table. He froze the frame where she raised her glass.

'Never seen her before,' Stas said. 'What amazes me is that I've never been in this beer garden. I thought I'd been in them all.'

The screen came back to life. The woman raised her glass higher. Blonde hair swept back almost ferociously, gold necklace bedded on black cashmere, cat-eyed sunglasses that expressed amusement, red nails and lips that promised in Russian, 'I love you.'

Stas shook his head. 'I'd remember her.'

'Not at Radio Liberty?' Arkady asked.

'Hardly.'

'Around Tommy?'

'Possibly, but I've never met her.'

Arkady tried a different tack. 'I'd like to see where Tommy worked.'

'The Red Archive? The next time I try to sign you in, the guards will call Michael. I don't mind annoying him, but he'll just tell the guards not to give you a pass.'

'Is Michael always at the station?'

'No. Between eleven and twelve he plays tennis at the club across the street. But he takes his phone everywhere.'

'You'll be at the station?'

'I'll be at my desk until noon. I'm a writer. I turn the decline and fall of the Soviet Union into bite-sized words.'

When Stas left, Arkady neatened the couch, washed the dishes and ironed the clothes that Federov had squashed into his bag the day before. Arkady's wrist was ringed with bruises, but the skin wasn't broken; Stas had seen the marks and said nothing. Every step Arkady took, from sofa to sink to ironing board, he was followed by Laika. So far, she found his behaviour acceptable.

While he ironed, Arkady ran the tape again. As the camera panned, he realized he might be looking at a restaurant patio rather than a beer garden. There was indoor dining, though the light outside was too intense to see through the windows.

What did he know about her? She might at one time

have been a Moscow *putana* called Rita. She could be the globe-trotting Frau Benz. The only hard evidence of her existence was this tape. This time he noticed that her table was set for two. She had an almost theatrical presence. The gold necklace was Teutonic, but the angles of her face were distinctly Russian. Thick make-up – that was more Russian, too. He wished that just once she would take off her glasses. Slowly her lips formed a smile and said to Rudy Rosen, 'I love you.'

Laika whined, walked towards the television set and sat again.

Arkady rewound and froze every other frame. Backwards from her glasses. Retreat from her table. Turn from the diners. Embroidery of vines and bees. Trolley of linen, utensils, water carafes. Stucco. Honeysuckle. Window with one pane that reflected the person with the camera standing before a solid wall of green. That was another question: who took the film? A man with distinctively broad shoulders in a sweater that was red-white-and-black. Marlboro colours.

He played it again. Motes floated in the sunlight. Bees stirred and diners came back to semi-life. The woman in the glasses repeated, 'I love you.'

At the Luitpold garage, an elongated Mercedes with a red car phone was parked by the attendant's booth. Remembering the Arabs at the Hilton, Arkady climbed the ramp to the next level, chose a BMW that looked light on its feet and gave it a firm shove. The car woke at once with blinking lights and a sounding horn. He heaved into Mercedes, Audis, Daimlers and Maseratis until the entire level reverberated with an orchestra of alarms. When he saw the attendant come racing up the ramp, he ran down the stairs.

In the booth were ticket punch, register, car tools and a long knife for opening locked car doors. The knife demanded patience that Arkady didn't have time for. He took a lug wrench. As he broke the window of the Mercedes, the limousine's alarm joined the woodwinds, but in five seconds he was walking out of the garage exit with the phone.

In Moscow, he was a senior investigator of the city prosecutor's office; here, after less than a week in the West, he was a thief. He knew he should feel guilty; instead, he felt alive. Even smart enough to turn off the phone.

It was after eleven by the time he got to Radio Liberty. Across the street, and hidden by parked cars and wire fences, were a clubhouse, patio tables and steps leading down to clay tennis courts where players in whites and pastels patrolled the baseline and traded top spin. What a delightful world, Arkady thought. Imagine having the leisure in the middle of the day to pull on shorts, chase a fuzzy ball, work up an athletic sweat. He looked into Michael's Porsche. Its red cellular phone, the plastic sceptre, was gone.

Michael was on a court near the clubhouse. He wore shorts and a V-necked sweater and played with the indolent ease of someone who had been given his first tennis ball in the crib. His opponent, whose back was to Arkady, swung wildly and moved as unsteadily as a man on a trampoline. Behind him and directly in Michael's line of sight was a table with the phone, its antenna fully extended. The other tables were empty.

While Arkady considered an approach, he noticed that life offered its own distractions. Michael's opponent hit balls left and right and over Michael's head to the screen. Other times he missed the ball completely. Sometimes he got tangled up in his shorts. The game seemed not just foreign to him but from a planet with a different gravity.

During a conference at the net, Arkady was surprised to overhear his own name. As the opponent returned to the baseline, he got a good look. Federov. The consular aide's next serve flew over the screen and bounced into a far court where two women were playing. They wore short skirts that displayed scissory, tanned legs, and they regarded the ball as a breach of form. Michael strolled to the fence and apologized with a tone that suggested his empathy. Waving his racquet and making too much noise for a tennis court, Federov ran to join him. By then Arkady had walked by the table and switched phones.

On the far side of the clubhouse were two recycling bins, orange for plastic, green for glass. Arkady tossed the phone into the orange one, then walked back past the tennis courts, through the station gates, under the cameras, by the guard booth in the parking lot and up the steps to the reception area.

Summoned, Stas came to the desk, a little astonished to see him, while the guards tried calling Michael. 'It's ringing.'

Stas said, 'We haven't got all day.'

The guard hung up, welcomed Arkady with a glare and a pass. After a buzz at the door he was back in the cream-carpeted hallway of Radio Liberty. The bulletin boards were changed, a sign of a well-run organization. Glossy photographs showed President Gilmartin leading a tour of Hungarian broadcasters and applauding folk dancers from Minsk. Technicians with audio tape trafficked up and down the corridor. Ludmilla's grey hair bobbed in and out of a doorway.

'Did you come to bomb the director's office or Michael's? How much trouble am I in?' Stas asked.

'Which way is the Red Archive?'

'The stairs are between the drinks and the snack machine. Bomb away.'

When Tommy boasted about the Red Archive being the greatest library of Soviet life outside Moscow, Arkady had pictured the lamps and musty stacks of the Lenin Library. As usual, he was unprepared for reality. There were no lamps in the Red Archive, only the aquarium glow of room-length fixtures. No books either, only microfiche files, motorized steel cabinets that glided on tracks. Instead of a reading room there was a machine that enlarged microfiche to legible size. Arkady ran a hand over a file in awe. It was as if Ancient Rus, Peter and Catherine the Great and the storming of the Winter Palace had been reduced to the head of a pin. He was relieved to see something as primitive as a wooden box with filing cards in Cyrillic.

All the researchers scribbling away at desks were Americans. A woman with a blouse full of bows was delighted to see a Russian.

'Where was Tommy's desk?' Arkady asked.

'The *Pravda* section.' She sighed and pointed to another door. 'We miss him.'

'Of course.'

'There's just so much information coming these days,' she said. 'There used to be none and now there's too much. I wish it would just slow down.'

'I know what you mean.'

The *Pravda* section was a narrow room made smaller by shelves of bound copies of *Pravda* on one side and *Izvestya* on the other. At the end of the room a VCR was taping from a colour television set. The station had to have a satellite dish because, though the sound was low, Arkady realized that he was watching Soviet news. On the screen, a crowd in shabby clothes was pushing over a lorry. When it landed on its side, they swarmed into the back of it. A close-up of the driver showed his bloody nose. A different angle on the lorry displayed the name of a cooperative for rendering tallow. People climbed out of it waving bones and black meat. Arkady realized how much he had been conditioned by a few days of ample German beer and food. Was it this bad, he asked himself. Was it really this bad?

Behind the set was Tommy's desk, covered by newspapers, coffee rings and machine-gun bullets used as paperweights. In the middle drawer were soft pencils, staplers, memo pads and paper clips. In the side drawers, Russian–English and German–English dictionaries, cowboy paperbacks, heavier books on military history, manuscripts and rejection letters. There was not even a phone jack for a fax.

Arkady returned to the file room and asked the woman at the filing cards, 'Did Tommy have a fax when he worked at "Programme Review"?'

'Possibly. The "Review" section is in a different part of town. He could have used one there.'

'How long was he here?'

'A year. I wish we had a fax here. That's one of the executive perks. Privileges,' she said brightly, as if describing awards. 'We do have information here. Anything about the Soviet Union. Any subject.'

'Max Albov.'

She took a deep breath and played with the bows on her collar. 'Well, that's close to home. Okay.' She started to move away, stopped. 'Your name is?'

'Renko.'

'You're visiting?'

'Michael.'

'Then . . .' She lifted her hands. The sky was the limit.

Max was a vein of gold that seemed to work its way through cabinet after cabinet of microfiches. Arkady sat at the enlarger and scrolled through years of *Pravda*, *Red Star* and *Soviet Film* describing Max's career in cinema, his treacherous defection to the West, his service with Radio Liberty, the CIA's mouthpiece of disinformation, his pangs of conscience, his return to the motherland and recent incarnation on American television as a respected journalist and commentator.

An early item in *Soviet Film* caught Arkady's attention. 'For director Maxim Albov, the most important part of the story is the woman. "Get a beautiful actress, light her properly and your film is already halfway a success." '

His films, however, had all been of the action variety, extolling the daring and sacrifices of the Red Army and border guards against Maoists, Zionists and mujahedin.

Another item read, 'One effect of an Israeli tank on fire was particularly difficult because the film crew didn't have the blasting caps or plastic explosives they had requested. The successful shot was improvised by the director himself.

'Albov: "We were filming outside Baku, near a chemical complex. Film-goers don't know that my initial schooling was in chemistry. I was aware that by combining red sodium and copper sulphate we could create a spontaneous explosion without a fuse or a cap. Since the question was timing we tested forty or fifty samples before filming, which we did with a remote camera behind a Plexiglas screen. It was a night shot and the effect when the Israeli tank erupts into flame is spectacular. Hollywood couldn't do better." '

Arkady's head snapped up as the archive door slammed open and Michael and Federov entered. Still in tennis shorts. Federov's legs were a fluorescent white. He carried a racquet. Michael held a phone. They were accompanied by the guards from the reception desk and by Ludmilla, who glowered like a vicious pug.

Ludmilla said, 'Use my office. It's next to yours. That way your secretary won't log him in. He just disappears.'

Michael liked the suggestion. They crowded into a room with black furniture and ashtrays set out like urns of the recently departed. On the walls were photographs of the famous poet Tsvetayeva, who had emigrated to Paris with her husband, an assassin. Even by Russian standards it had been a troubled marriage.

The guards pushed Arkady down on to an ottoman. Federov sank into the sofa and Michael perched on the edge of the desk.

'Where's my goddamn phone?'

'In your hand?' Arkady asked.

Michael let the receiver drop on his desk. 'This is not mine. You know where mine is. You changed the fucking phones.'

'How could I change your phone?' Arkady asked.

'That's how you got past the front desk.'

Arkady said, 'No, they gave me a visitor's pass.'

'Because they couldn't reach me on the phone,' Michael said. 'Because they're idiots.'

'What does your phone look like?'

Michael practised even breathing. 'Renko, Federov

and I got together today to talk about you. You seem to cause problems across the board.'

'He refused an order from the consul to go home.' Federov was happy to be included. 'He has a friend here at the station named Stanislav Kolotov.'

'Stas! I'll interrogate him later. He sent you to the archive?' Michael asked Arkady.

'No, I just wanted to see where Tommy worked.'

'Why?'

'He made his work sound interesting.'

'And the files on Max Albov?'

'He sounded fascinating.'

'But you told the head researcher that you'd come to see me.'

'I did come to see you. Yesterday, when you took me to President Gilmartin, you promised me money.'

Michael said, 'You fed Gilmartin horseshit.'

'Renko does need money,' Federov said.

'Of course he needs money. Every Russian needs money,' Ludmilla said.

'Are you sure that's not your phone?' Arkady asked.

'This is a stolen phone,' Michael said.

'The police should check it for prints,' Arkady said.

'Well, it's got my fingerprints on it now, naturally. The police will be here soon enough. The point is, Renko, that you like to stir things up. It's my job to keep things smooth. I've come to the decision that things here will run a lot smoother if you're back in Moscow.'

Federov said, 'That's the feeling at the consulate, too.'

When Arkady shifted, he felt a guard's hand leaning on each shoulder.

Michael said, 'We've decided to put you on the plane. Consider that done. The communiqué my friend Sergei here sends to Moscow will depend in large part on your attitude, which so far is piss-poor. He could describe your work here as so successful that you went home early. On the other hand, I would guess that an investigator who's sent back for harming relations between the United States and the Soviet Union, for abusing the hospitality of the German Republic and for stealing the property of this station will get a cold reception. Do you want to clean a latrine in Siberia for the rest of your miserable life? That's your choice.'

'I'd like to help,' Arkady said.

'That's better. What are you looking for in Munich? Why have you been poking around Radio Liberty? How is Stas helping you? Where's my phone?'

'I have an idea,' Arkady suggested.

'Tell me,' Michael said.

'Call.'

'Call who?'

'Yourself. Maybe you'll hear a ring.'

There was silence for a moment. 'That's it? Renko, you're worse than an asshole, you're a suicide.'

Arkady said, 'You can't send me back. This is Germany.'

Michael hopped off the edge of the desk. He had the springy step of an athlete, a faint sunglass mask around his eyes and a tarry smell of sweat mixed with aftershave. 'That's why you're going. Renko, you're a refugee. What do you think the Germans do with people like you? I think you know Lieutenant Schiller.'

The guards pulled Arkady to his feet. Quick as a dog, Federov jumped up.

An ashtray, phone and facsimile machine furnished Ludmilla's desk, and as Michael strode across the room and opened the door for Peter Schiller, Arkady saw that, next to its transmit button, the fax had the number that had called Rudy Rosen and asked, 'Where is Red Square?'

Peter said, 'I hear you're going home.'

'Look at the fax,' Arkady said.

This seemed to be an occasion that the lieutenant had waited for. He bent Arkady's arm behind his back and screwed his wrist so that he rose on to the balls of his feet. 'Everywhere I go, you are making a mess.'

'Take a look.'

'Theft, trespass, resisting police. Another Russian tourist.' Peter swung Arkady towards the door. 'Bring the phone you found, please,' he told Michael.

'We're dropping charges to speed the repatriation process,' Michael said.

Federov followed. 'The consulate rearranged his visa. We have a seat for him on the flight today. This can all be done quietly.'

'Oh, no,' Peter said. He held Arkady like a prize. 'If he has broken German law, he's in my hands.'

Chapter Twenty-Five

The cell was like a Finnish bathroom; fifteen square metres of white tiled floor, blue tiled walls, a bed facing a bench, a toilet in the corner. For cleanliness' sake, on the other side of the stainless-steel bars lay a coiled hose. Arkady's belt and shoelaces were in a box by the hose. A uniformed policeman little older than a Young Pioneer came by every ten minutes to make sure Arkady wasn't hanging himself by his jacket.

A pack of cigarettes arrived in mid-afternoon. Oddly enough, Arkady wasn't smoking as much as usual, as if food had cut down the appetite of his lungs.

Dinner came on a compartmentalized plastic tray: beef in brown sauce, dumplings, carrots with dill, vanilla pudding, plastic utensils.

Ludmilla had been the voice on the other end when he called the fax number from the train station. Even if she had known Rudy, though, she didn't know he was dead when she asked, 'Where is Red Square?'

The Soviet quota of living space was five square metres, so this holding cell was a veritable suite. Also, a Soviet cell was manuscript. Plaster walls were scribbled with personal messages and public announcements. 'The Party Drinks the People's Blood!' 'Dima Will Kill the Rats Who Turned Him In!' 'Dima Loves Zeta Forever!' And drawings: tigers, daggers, angels, full-bodied women, free-standing cocks, head of Christ. But the tiles here were glazed, highly fired and unscratchable.

Aeroflot had taken off by now, he was sure. Did Lufthansa have an evening flight?

As he made a pillow of his jacket, Arkady found a wadded envelope in an inner pocket and recognized the shaky, needle-fine writing of his own name. It was the letter from his father that Belov had given him and that he had carried around for more than a week, from a Russian grave to a German cell, like a forgotten poison capsule. He crumpled the paper into a ball and threw it towards the bars. Instead of passing through, it hit one and rolled to the drain in the middle of the floor. He tossed it again, and again it bounced back and rolled to his feet.

The paper rustled. What would the parting words of General Kyril Renko be? After a lifetime of curses, what final curse? In the war between father and son, what last blow?

Arkady remembered his father's favourite phrases. 'Titcalf' when Arkady was a small boy. 'Poet, queer, shitpants and eunuch' were heaped upon the student. 'Coward', naturally, when Arkady refused officers' school. 'Failure', of course, from then on. What extra accolade had been saved? The dead had a certain advantage.

He hadn't talked to his father for years. At this low point in his career, in this tiled hole, was this the right time to allow his father a posthumous stab? There was something funny about the situation. Even dead, the general still had the instincts of an executioner.

Arkady flattened the envelope on the floor. He tugged open the corner of the flap, inserted a finger and cautiously tore open the end, because he wouldn't have been surprised if his father had left a razor. No, the letter itself would be the razor. What were the most hateful, damaging words he could hear? What was worth hissing from the grave?

Arkady blew into the envelope and his breath lifted a half-sheet of onionskin. He smoothed the paper and held it to the light.

The handwriting was so faint and palsied that it was more a wave from the deathbed than a letter, written with a hand that could barely hold a pen. The general had managed only one word: 'Irina'.

Chapter Twenty-Six

Night traffic on Leopoldstrasse was a sinuous flow of headlights, glass, pavement cafés, chrome.

Peter lit a cigarette while he drove. 'Sorry about the cell. I had to put you somewhere where Michael and Federov couldn't get at you. Anyway, you really screwed them. You should be proud. They can't figure out how you switched phones. They kept showing me: car, tennis court, car.'

He shifted down a gear and snaked in front of other cars. Sometimes Arkady got the impression that Peter barely controlled the urge to drive on the pavement to get ahead.

'Apparently Michael's phone is special. It has a scrambler for security. He was upset because he would have to get a new one from Washington.'

'He found his phone?' Arkady asked.

'This is wonderful. This is the *Schlag*, the whipped cream on the cake. He took your advice. After Federov left, Michael put on trousers and called his own number and walked up and down the street until he found his phone ringing just so softly inside a rubbish bin. Like finding a kitten.'

'So there are no charges?'

'You were seen leaving the garage where the first

phone was stolen, but by the time I'd finished with him, the attendant didn't know if you were short or tall, white or black. With better prompting, he might give a more accurate description. The main thing is, you're still here and you have me to thank.'

'Thank you.'

Peter showed a crescent smile. 'See, that wasn't hard. Russians are so touchy.'

'You feel unappreciated?'

'Ignored. It's nice that Russians and Americans get along so well, but that doesn't mean they can ship you back to Moscow when they want.'

'Why didn't you look at Michael's fax when I told you to?'

'I already knew. After your friend Tommy died, I called the number. The woman answered herself. I'm that way, when someone is killed I become more curious, not less.' He handed Arkady the pack of cigarettes. 'You know, I enjoyed your game with the phones. We must be alike. If you weren't such a liar, we could be a good team.'

On the motorway, Peter shifted into overdrive, where he was happiest. 'You admit you made up the story about Bayern-Franconia and Benz. Why did you choose my grandfather's bank? Why call *him*?'

'I saw a letter he wrote to Benz.'

'Do you have the letter?'

'No.'

'Did you read the letter?'

'No.'

Kilometre signs flashed by. Flyovers roared above them.

'Don't you have a partner back in Moscow? Couldn't you give him a call?' Peter asked.

'He's dead.'

'Renko, do you ever feel like the plague?'

Peter must have been keeping track of where they were because suddenly he shifted gear and braked to the footing of a black ramp shaded into ash white. Tommy's Trabant was gone.

Peter let the BMW roll back slowly. 'You can see the concrete is not just burned, it's chipped. I asked myself, how could a feeble little Trabi hit with that kind of force? Doors folded, locked shut. Steering wheel bent. There are only the Trabi's tyre marks and no signs of any broken glass or rear lights. But as we come back on to the road, see the skidmarks.'

Two dark apostrophes tailed away from the road towards the ramp.

'Did you test them?'

'Yes. Poor-quality carbon rubber. You can't even recap tyres like that, can't burn them or recycle them. Trabi tyres. The investigators think Tommy fell asleep and lost control. Fatal one-man, one-car accidents are always the most difficult to reconstruct. Unless it was a two-car accident and a larger vehicle came from behind and smashed the Trabi into the ramp. If Tommy had any family or any enemies, the investigation would still be open.'

'It's closed?'

'Germany has so many road accidents, terrible accidents on the autobahn, we can't investigate them all. If you want to kill a German, do it on the road.'

'Were there any flash marks in the car, any sign of arson?'

'No.'

Peter raced in reverse, and with no more than a tap of the brake snapped the car around so that it followed its nose. Arkady remembered that he had flown jets. In Texas, where there was less to hit.

'When Tommy was burning you shouted that you saw a fire like that before. Who?'

'A racketeer.' Arkady corrected himself. 'A banker named Rudik Rosen. He burned up in an Audi. Audis burn well, too. After Rudy died he got a fax from the machine that we saw at the station.'

'The sender thought he was alive?'

'Yes.'

'What kind of car fire was it? Electrical? Collision?'

'Different from this. It was arson. A bomb.'

'Different? I have another question. Before this Rosen died, were you in his car with him?'

'Yes.'

'Why is that the first thing I completely believe? Renko, you're still lying about everything else. There's more than Benz involved. Who else? Remember, there's a plane leaving for Moscow tomorrow. You could still be on it.'

'Tommy and I were looking for something.'

376

'What?'

'A red Bronco.'

Ahead, rear lights lined the shoulder of the road. On the turnout were the taller outlines of off-the-road vehicles. Peter swerved up among them and coasted to a stop. Figures jumped out of the way, arms shielding their eyes. From the dashboard he took torches for Arkady and himself. When they got out, they were accosted by men angry about the intrusion into turnout privacy. Peter straight-armed one and snarled convincingly enough at another to send him backpedalling between fenders. There seemed to be two sides of Peter Schiller, Arkady thought: the Aryan ideal and the werewolf – nothing in between.

Peter worked through the women waiting for customers while Arkady moved along vehicles that had pulled back to the far side of the turnout to consummate business. Since he didn't know what a Bronco looked like, he had to read the name on each vehicle. Wasn't a bronco a bucking horse? No, that wasn't the sound. It was more like the beating of a damp drum or, in the shells of the vehicles, the mating of turtles.

There were no red Broncos, but Peter returned from the other side of the turnout to say that one had just left with a driver named Tima. He didn't seem discouraged. Maybe he drove a little faster getting back on to the motorway.

Arkady imagined the night trailing behind them like a scarf. The rest of Munich lived quietly to a schedule, ate its muesli, biked to work, paid for sex. Peter moved as if he lived at a higher r.p.m.

'I think when you were in the Trabi waiting for Tommy, somebody saw you. Then poor Tommy started home and someone followed him. It wasn't an accident. It was murder, but they thought they were killing you.'

'You want to drive around until someone tries to kill us?'

'To clear my head. Are you following someone from Moscow? Or has someone followed you?'

'At this point I'd follow anything. I'd pick out one star and aim at that.'

'Like my grandfather?'

'Maybe your grandfather is connected and maybe he's not. I honestly don't know.'

'Have you ever met Benz?'

'No.'

'Have you talked to anyone who's met Benz?'

'Tommy. Slow down,' Arkady said. Walking on the shoulder of the road was a girl in a red leather jacket and boots, and as they went by he saw that she had black hair and a round Uzbek face. 'Stop!'

She was angry and not in the mood for a lift. Her German was a dialect of Russian.

'That *Arschloch* threw me out of my car. I'll kill him.'

'What did your car look like?' Arkady asked.

She stamped her boot. '*Scheisse*, everything I have is in there.'

'Maybe we can find it.'

'Pictures and personal letters.'

'We'll look for it. What kind is it?'

She looked off towards the dark and reconsidered. Uzbekistan is a long way off, Arkady thought. Her legs looked thin and cold. She said, 'Never mind. I'll take care of it myself.'

Peter said, 'If someone stole your car, you should report it to the police.'

She studied him and the BMW, with its extra aerial and spotlight. 'No.'

'What's Tima short for?' Arkady asked.

'Fatima.' Immediately she added, 'I never said my name was Tima.'

'Did he take the car two nights ago?'

She crossed her arms. 'Have you been watching me?'

'Do you come from Samarkand or Tashkent?'

'Tashkent. How do you know so much? I'm not talking to you.'

'How long ago tonight did he take the car?'

She set her face and started walking again, wobbling on her heels. Uzbeks had once been the Golden Horde of Tamerlane that had swept from Mongolia to Moscow. This was the end, stumbling on the autobahn.

They drove into the Red Square car park and cruised through. There was no red Bronco. A contingent of businessmen were trooping loudly from vans into the sex club.

'Slumming,' Peter said. 'The Stuttgart set. They'll only touch the beer here and then they'll go home and fuck their wives silly.' He shot a little gravel at them as he swung by.

Back on the road, Peter was calmer, as if he had reached some internal decision. Arkady relaxed, too, more in tune with the speed.

The city spread as they approached, not like wildfire, more like a battlefield of moths.

A red Bronco sat in front of Benz's flat. The windows were dark. They drove by twice, parked on the next block and returned on foot.

Peter stayed in the shadow of a tree while Arkady walked up the steps and pushed the button to the flat. No voice came over the intercom. No window lit upstairs.

Peter joined him. 'He's gone.'

'The car is here.'

'Maybe he went for a walk.'

'A midnight walk?'

Peter said, 'He's an Ossie, how many cars can he have? Renko, let's act like detectives and see what we can find.'

He gave Arkady a torch, led him to the Bronco and opened the tweezers of a combination knife. The chrome on the front bumper was untouched, but its rubber guard sparkled in the torch's beam. Peter squatted and teased from the rubber what looked like threads of glass.

'One reason it's almost impossible to reprocess a

Trabi is that the fibreglass body breaks up into such sharp splinters.' He dropped pieces into a paper envelope. 'Dead or alive, a Trabi is very difficult to handle.'

Peter radioed in the Bronco's numberplate. While they waited for an answer he shook pieces from the envelope into the ashtray, then turned the flame of his lighter directly on the threads. They lit like yellow kindling; strings of black ash rose on brown smoke, and a familiar, noxious aroma filled the car.

'Pure Trabi.' Peter blew out the flame. 'Proving nothing. There's not enough left of Tommy's Trabi to match to this, but even a lawyer would have to say the Bronco hit something.'

The radio spoke rapid German. Peter wrote on a pad 'Fantasy Tours' and the address of Boris Benz.

Arkady said, 'Ask how many cars are registered in Fantasy's name.'

Peter asked, then wrote on the pad the number '18'. Also, 'Pathfinders, Navahos, Cherokees, Troopers, Rovers'.

He put the phone back in its sleeve. 'You said you never met Benz.'

'I said that Tommy had met Benz.'

'You said that you and Tommy were on the motorway because you were looking for Benz. You went to the sex club first.'

'Tommy saw him there a year ago.'

'Who was the connection? How did they meet?'

Arkady had succeeded in keeping Max's name from Peter because Max was only one step away from Irina. It would be a bitter outcome, he thought, if he came all this way just to drag her into Peter's investigation.

Peter said, 'Why would they meet? Tommy wanted to talk to Benz about the war?'

'I'm sure Tommy told him about it. He was interviewing people for a book about the war. He was obsessed with it. His flat is a museum of the war.'

'I was there.'

'What did you think?'

Peter's eyes looked energized, as if they had picked up electricity from the radio. From his jacket he produced a key. 'I think we should visit this museum again.'

Swastikas stretched across two walls. The Wehrmacht map covered a third. On the shelves were Tommy's collection of gas masks, tin Panzers, a hub cap from Hitler's touring car, assorted ammunition, Goebbels' reinforced shoe. A clock in the shape of an eagle said twelve.

Peter said, 'I was here earlier. In and out. Normally we don't search the flats of traffic victims.'

On the table where the birthday cake for the Berlin Wall had melted, a typewriter was set up with notes, paper and filing cards. Peter wandered about, focusing field glasses, trying on an armband and an SS cap, like an actor let loose in a prop room. He lifted a helmet, the one Tommy had worn at the party.

'Alas, poor Jürgen, I knew him well.'

He laid down the helmet and picked up a dental mould. 'Hitler's teeth,' Arkady said.

Peter opened the mould. 'Sieg heil!'

The short hairs on Arkady's neck rose.

'Do you know why we lost the war?' Peter asked.

'Why did you lose the war?'

'It was explained to me by an old man. We were hiking in the Alps. We were on a high meadow surrounded by wild flowers when we stopped to eat. The subject of the war came up. He said the Nazis had committed "excesses", but the real reason Germany lost the war was because of sabotage. There were workers in the munitions factory who deliberately degraded the gunpowder in the shells to make our weapons ineffective. Otherwise we would have been able to hold out for an honourable peace. He described the grandfathers and boys fighting in the ruins of Berlin, stabbed in the back by those saboteurs. It was years later when I learned that those saboteurs were Russians and Jews, slave labour being starved to death while they worked. I remembered the flowers, the wonderful view, the tears in his eyes.'

He put the mould down, joined Arkady at the table and flipped through the filing cards, notes and pages. 'What are you looking for?' Arkady asked.

'Answers.'

They searched the drawers of the desk and night table, folders that were stuffed in cabinets, address books discovered under the bed. Finally, next to the phone in the kitchen numbers without names were pencilled on the wall. Peter gave a laugh of dark amusement, nailed one number with his finger and dialled the phone.

Considering the hour, the other end answered quickly. Peter said, 'Grandfather, I'm coming over with my friend Renko.'

The older Schiller padded around in a silk dressing gown and velvet slippers. His living room was covered in Oriental carpets. His lamps had shades of stained glass.

'I was awake anyway. The middle of the night is the best time to read.'

The banker seemed to make a firm distinction between work and personal life. Bookshelves accommodated not tomes on banking regulations but art books that ran from Turkish rugs to Japanese ceramics. *Objets d'art* – a Greek bronze of a dolphin, Mexican skulls of sugar and jade, a Chinese alabaster dog – sat under spotlights arranged by someone who had taken great care to display eclectic pieces of modest size but unusual quality. A dark ikon of a madonna was in the traditional place, high in a corner that would have been the 'beautiful corner' of a pre-Revolutionary peasant house. Its thick wood was split and the madonna's face was shrouded by smoke, which made her eyes seem all the more luminous.

Schiller poured tea into a gilded cup. He wore a

brace under his dressing gown, Arkady realized, and leaned stiffly, marble from the waist up.

'I'm sorry, I don't have any jam. I remember that Russians love their tea with jam.'

Peter paced back and forth.

'Walk,' his grandfather told him. 'It's good for the rug.' He turned to Arkady. 'When he was a boy, Peter would march a kilometre on that carpet, back and forth. He always had too much energy. He can't help it.'

'Why did the American have your number?' Peter asked.

'His book, his moronic book. He's the sort who lurks in graveyards and thinks he has a career. He kept pestering me, but I refused to be interviewed by him. I suspect he gave my name to Benz.'

'The bank was not involved?' Arkady asked.

Schiller allowed himself the thinnest suggestion of a smile. 'Bayern-Franconia would no more invest in the Soviet Union than in the far side of the moon. Benz approached me personally.'

Peter said, 'Benz is a pimp. He runs a string of prostitutes on the autobahn. What would he approach you about?'

'Real estate.'

'It was business?' Arkady asked.

Schiller sipped his tea. The cup was porcelain with a gilded rim. 'Before the war, we had our own bank in Berlin. We're not Bavarian.' He cast a concerned eye on his grandson. 'That's Peter's problem; he's not bred to be a drunken lout. Anyway, the family lived in Potsdam, outside the city. We also had a summer home on the coast. I've described them to Peter many times. Beautiful places. We lost them all. Bank and houses, everything ended up in the Soviet sector and then in the Democratic Republic of Germany. We lost them first to the Russians and then to the East Germans.'

Arkady said, 'With reunification I thought private property was being returned.'

'Oh, yes. The former East Germany is haunted now by Jewish ghosts. But we weren't helped because the new law excepted properties confiscated from '45 to '49, which was when we lost ours. Or so I thought until Benz appeared at my door.'

'What did he say?' Arkady asked.

'He represented himself as some sort of estate agent. He informed me that there was some question about exactly when the Potsdam house had been seized. When the Russians were in charge, many estates simply stood empty for years. Records had been lost or burned. Benz said he might be able to provide me with the proper documentation to help my claim.' Schiller turned stiffly in his chair. 'It was for you, too, Peter. He said he might be able to help us with the farm and the summer house, too. They could all be ours again.'

'For how much?' Peter asked.

'No money. Information.'

'Bank information?'

Schiller was offended. 'Personal history.' The banker shook off his slippers. His feet were mottled blue, with yellowed nails. Two toes were missing. 'Frostbite. I should live in Spain. Peter, you know where the brandy is. I feel a chill.'

Arkady asked, 'What did you do on the Eastern Front?'

Schiller cleared his throat. 'I was with a special detachment.'

'How special?'

'I understand what you're saying. Other special detachments rounded up Jews. I did nothing like that. My detachment gathered art. My father wanted to keep me out of the front line, so he got me attached to a group of SS who followed the advance. I was a boy, younger than either of you. He told me that I could protect art. He was right: without us, thousands of paintings, pieces of jewellery and irreplaceable books would have been spirited into knapsacks, been burned, melted down or completely disappeared. We were literally rescuing culture. The lists were already drawn up. Goering wrote one list, Goebbels another. We had teams of carpenters, packers, our own trains. The Wehrmacht had orders to keep the tracks open just to send our cargo back. It was an enormously busy autumn. When winter came we stalled outside Moscow, and that was the war right there, though we didn't know it.'

With brandy, the tea was better. The banker shifted in his chair. It occurred to Arkady that for the older man every movement involved pain.

'This is what Tommy wanted to ask you about?' Arkady asked.

'Some of the same questions,' Schiller said.

Peter said, 'You told me you were captured outside Moscow and spent three years in a camp. You said you surrendered when your rifles froze.'

'My feet froze. To tell the truth, when I was captured I was hiding in a goods wagon. The SS men were shot on the spot. I would have been shot, too, if the Russians hadn't opened some cases and found ikons inside. There was some interrogation, which was not delicate. I agreed to make lists of what we'd taken. Then the whole war went in reverse. I was never in camp, not for a day. I travelled with the Red Army, first searching for what the SS had shipped. Then, as we moved further west, I acted as an advisor to special troops from the Soviet Ministry of Culture, helping to locate and send German works of art to Moscow. Stalin made a list, Beria made a list. We sent back even more because we found what the SS had taken from different countries – the Koenigs drawings from Holland, Poznan paintings from Poland. We stripped the Dresden Museum, the Prussian Royal Library, museum collections from Aachen, Weimar, Magdeburg.'

'In other words, you collaborated,' Peter said.

'I served history. I survived. I was hardly the only one. When the Russians arrived in Berlin, where do you think they went? While the city burned, while Hitler was still alive, they were in the museums. Rubens, Rembrandts, the gold of Troy disappeared, treasures that have never been seen again.'

'Were you there?' Arkady asked.

'No, I was still in Magdeburg. When we were done

there, the Russians gave me a vodka. We'd been together for three years. I even wore a Red Army coat at that point. They took the coat off, marched me a few steps to an alley, shot me in the back and left me for dead. See, Peter, personal history.'

'What was Benz most interested in?' Arkady asked.

'Nothing in particular.' Schiller reconsidered. 'Actually, I had the feeling he was checking his list against mine. At heart he was a crude man, a real barracks bastard. In the end, all we talked about was how to build crates. The SS enlisted carpenters from the Berlin firm of Knauer, the most expert art transporters of the time. I drew him diagrams. He was more interested in nails and woods and documentation than in art.'

'What do you mean, "barracks bastard"?'

Schiller said, 'It's commonplace. How many German girls have had babies by foreign soldiers stationed here?'

Arkady said, 'Benz was born in Potsdam. You're saying his father was Russian?'

'That's what he sounded like,' Schiller said.

Peter said, 'All the stories you told me about defending Germany. You were a thief, first on one side and then on the other. Why didn't you tell me all this before? Why tell me now?'

The banker eased his feet into his slippers. He turned as completely to Peter as he could. He had that deadly combination of age: eggshell frailty and brutal honesty. 'It didn't concern you. The past was gone. Now it does. Everything has a price. If we can get our house and property back, if we can go home, Peter, this is the price for you.'

Peter dropped Arkady off at Stas's flat and tore off into the dark.

Arkady unlocked the door with the house key Stas had given him. Laika sniffed him quietly and let him in. He went to the kitchen and made a late dinner of hard biscuits for the dog, and tea, jam and cigarettes for himself.

Steps shambled up the hall. Stas leaned against the door jamb in mismatched pyjama top and bottom and regarded Laika and the biscuits. 'Slut.'

'I woke you,' Arkady said.

'I'm not awake. If I were awake, I'd be asking where the devil you've been.' At a sleepwalker's pace he staggered to the refrigerator and took out a beer. 'Obviously you think of me as the hall porter, the concierge, the elf who polishes your shoes. So where *have* you been?'

'With my new German partner. He has become wildly enthusiastic. In return, I've misled him as best I can.'

Stas sat down. 'You cannot mislead a German any more than you can lead a German.'

Nevertheless, Arkady had misled Peter by omission, by not mentioning Max because of Irina. By now Peter was convinced that his grandfather was the only connection between Tommy and Benz. 'I traded on his sense of national guilt.'

'If you can find a German with guilt, you should

trade on it. Generally I have found this to be a country of widespread amnesia, but if you have found a guilty German, I can guarantee that no one on earth has ever had a larger sense of guilt. Correct?'

'Close enough.'

Stas tipped the bottle back so that it seemed to balance on his lips, then set it down empty. 'I was awake anyway. I was thinking that if I'd stayed in Russia, I probably would have died in a camp. Or maybe I would only have been pressed as flat as a blini.'

'You were right to get out.'

'As a result of which I've had enormous influence on world events. I make fun of the station, but Liberty's budget is less than the cost of a single strategic bomber.'

'Is that so?'

'Not to mention this is a tax-free situation for me.'

'That sounds good.'

Stas stared at the kitchen clock. The second hand dropped in audible clicks, a sound like a key turning over and over in a lock. Laika moved close to him and laid her shaggy head on his lap.

Stas said, 'Maybe I should have stayed.'

Chapter Twenty-Seven

In the morning a heavy fog brought out headlights. Bicycles appeared and disappeared as wraiths.

Irina lived a block from the park, on a street that mixed town houses, artists' studios and boutiques. All the buildings were dressed in fey *Jugendstil* but hers, which was plain and modern. Though her windows were set back, Arkady located her balcony, a chrome rail before a wall of vines, lush and bright in the wet. He stood at a bus stop at the end of the street, the most logical and least conspicuous place to wait.

Did the balcony lead directly to the kitchen? He could imagine the warmth of lights, the smell of coffee. He could also imagine Max having an extra cup, but he had to eliminate Max from the picture in his mind or slide into crippling jealousy. Irina might drive to the station. Worse, she might leave with Max. He focused on the hope that she was alone, was drying a cup and saucer, was putting on her raincoat, would take the bus.

A delivery van parked in the middle of the block. The driver climbed down from the cab, opened the rear doors, brought racks down to street level with a hydraulic lift and rolled them into a dress shop. The van's windscreen wipers kept time, though rain wasn't falling so much as hanging in the air in fine droplets.

The traffic had a sheen. Arkady stepped off the kerb for a better view of Irina's house when a bus arrived and chased him back. Passengers boarded and cancelled their own tickets in an automatic punch box. Every single one of them – that was the amazing thing.

The bus pulled away and the delivery van drove off. It took Arkady a minute to notice that the vine-covered wall on Irina's balcony was a darker green, which meant that the lights of her flat were off. He watched her door for another minute, before he realized that she had left while the van had been blocking his view. He had expected her to use the bus in this weather; instead she had gone in the other direction towards the park and he had missed her.

Arkady ran the length of the street to the park. In the foreshortened view that accompanies emotion, umbrellas bobbed on either side. A Turk wearing a conical hat of newspaper cycled between the bumpers of limousines. Across the street the Englischer Garten began as a wall of giant beeches. Farther down the street, a woman in a white raincoat entered a park gate.

He darted between cars. The radio station lay diagonally across the park. Where he entered the gate, paths twisted left and right. The Englischer Garten was called the 'green lung' of Munich. It had a river, streams, forest, lakes – all veiled now by mist, giving the park a cold, close breath that made Arkady gather his jacket at his neck.

He could hear her, though; at least, he heard someone walking. Did he remember how she walked? Long strides, always sure of herself. She hated umbrellas, she hated crowds. He hurried after the echo, aware that any hesitation put her farther ahead. If she was ahead. The path kept trying to turn away. Overhead, beeches were monkey bars in a cloud. Oaks were shorter, as bent as beggars. Where the path crossed a stream bed, steam rose from the water, a ghostly floodtide. A creature resembling a large caterpillar sniffed around wet leaves. Closer, it became a wire-haired dachshund. Its owner crept behind, a yellow raincoat with a scoop and bag.

Beyond, Irina had disappeared – if it was Irina. Over the years, at a distance, how many women had he dressed in her features? This was the illusion of his life, the nightmare.

Arkady had the park to himself. He heard the slow condensation of mist on leaves, the thud of nuts from the beeches on to sodden earth, the dash of unseen birds. Where shadows faded, he found he had reached the edge of a wide meadow, completely lost in a circle of green. For a moment on the far side he saw a flash of white.

Running over the grass, he had the laboured breath and heavy feet of a farm horse. When he reached the spot where the brief sight of white had been, she was gone again. Now, though, he knew the direction. A path led along a russet screen of maples and the languid vapour of another stream. He heard steps again and, where the maples ended, saw her, a bag over her shoulder. Her coat was actually more silver than white, with a reflective quality. Her hair was uncovered, darker in the rain. She looked back and then continued walking, faster than before.

They walked at the same pace, ten metres apart, down a dark avenue of firs. Where the path narrowed to a strip that threaded a stand of birches, she slowed, then stopped and leaned against the white, papery column of a birch for him to catch up.

They walked on together in silence. Arkady felt like a man who had approached a deer. A single wrong word, he thought, and she would bolt for good. When she glanced at him he didn't dare to try to hold her eyes or read them. At least they were walking side by side. In itself, that was a victory.

He was sorry that he looked so bad. His shoes were flecked with grass, his clothes damp and moulded to his back. His body was too thin, and probably his eyes had the glower of the chronically starved.

They came to the edge of a lake. The water was black and still. Irina looked down at their reflections, at the man and woman looking up from the water and said, 'That's the saddest thing I ever saw.'

'Me?' Arkady asked.

'Us.'

Birds collected. The park was rich in them; velvet-headed mallards, wood ducks, wigeons and teal appeared out of the mist, breaking the surface of the water into spoons of light. Shearwaters flew as acrobatically as signatures; geese dropped like sacks.

They sat on a bench.

Irina said, 'There are people who come here every day to feed the birds. They bring pretzels the size of wheels.'

It was cool enough for their breath to condense.

'I sympathize with these birds,' she said. 'The difference is that you never came. I will never forgive you.'

'I can tell.'

'And now that you're here, I feel like a refugee all over again. I don't like that feeling.'

'No one does.'

'But I've been in the West for years. I've earned the right to be here. Arkady, go home. Leave me alone.'

'No. I won't go.'

He half expected her to rise and leave the bench. He would follow her; what else could he do? She stayed. She let him light another cigarette for her. 'A bad habit,' she said. 'Like you.'

Despair saturated the air. Cold penetrated his thin jacket. He heard his heart echo across the water. A walking collection of bad habits was what he was. Ignorance, insubordination, lack of exercise, dull razors.

So many birds arrived, some dropping wholesale in flocks, others wheeling individually out of the mist, that Arkady was put in mind of the factory ship he had spent part of his exile on, and how gulls mobbed the air above the stern for the overflow and refuse from the nets. He remembered standing in the breeze above the stern ramp fieldstripping a cigarette and a gull snatching the paper from the air and carrying it away as its prize. 'Find the Russian duck,' he said.

'Where?'

'The one with dirty feathers and a crooked bill smoking a cigarette.'

'There is no such thing.'

'But you looked, I saw you. Imagine when Russian ducks really do hear about this lake, a lake with pretzels, they'll come here by the million.'

'The swans too?'

A line of swans glided imperiously through the ducks. When a mallard resisted, the lead swan stretched out its long and creamy neck, opened its bright, yellow bill and snorted like a pig.

'Russian. He's already infiltrated,' Arkady said.

Irina sat back from Arkady to study him. 'You do look terrible.'

'I can't say the same for you.'

She bent the light her way. Mist sat on her hair like jewels. 'I heard you were doing so well in Moscow,' she said.

'Who did you hear that from?'

She hesitated. 'You're not what I expected. You're what I remembered.'

They walked slowly. Arkady was aware that she walked a critical millimetre closer and that their shoulders occasionally grazed.

'Stas was always curious about you. I'm not surprised

you're friends. Max says you're both artifacts of the Cold War.'

'We are. I'm like a piece of marble you find in an ancient ruin. You pick it up, turn it around in your hand and ask, "What was this? Part of a horse trough or part of a noble statue?" I want to show you something.' He took out an envelope, opened it and showed her the paper and the one word scribbled inside.

'My name,' she said.

'It's my father's writing. I hadn't heard from him in years. This must have been about the last thing he did before he died. You actually talked to him?'

'I wanted to reach you without causing trouble, so I tried your father.'

Arkady tried to imagine this. It sounded like a dove flying into a furnace, though his father had been a fairly cold furnace in his last years.

'He told me what a hero you were, how they tried to break you but you forced the prosecutor's office to take you back, that they gave you the most difficult cases and that you never lost. He was proud. He went on and on. He said he saw you often and that you'd write to me.'

'What else?'

'That you were too busy for women, but women were always chasing you.'

'None of this rang a false note?'

'He said the only problem with you was that you were a fanatic and that sometimes you put yourself in God's place. That some things only God could judge.'

'If I were General Kyril Renko, I wouldn't have been so eager to see the face of God.'

'He said he thought about you more and more. Did you have women?'

'No. I was in psychiatric cells for a while, then I was in Siberia on the move, and then I was fishing. There was limited opportunity.'

She stopped him. 'Please. I remember Russia. There's always opportunity. And when you got back to Moscow, you must have had a woman there.'

'I was in love. I wasn't looking for women.'

'In love with me?'

'Yes.'

'You *are* a fanatic.'

They walked along a pond that bore snowy down and fine drops of rain like little pearls. Was it the same lake as before?

'Arkasha, what are we going to do?'

They left the park for a university café that had stainless-steel machines hissing into pots of milk and posters of Italy – ski slopes of the Dolomites, colourful tenements in Naples – on the walls. The other patrons were students with open books and bowl-sized cups of coffee. They took a table by the window.

Arkady talked about working his way across Siberia, from Irkutsk to Norilsk to Kamchatka to the sea.

Irina talked about New York, London, Berlin. 'Theatre work in New York was good, but I couldn't join the union. They're like Soviet unions – worse. I waited on tables. In New York, waitresses are fantastic. So hard and so old you'd think they waited on Alexander the Great or the pharaohs. Hard workers. An art gallery. They wanted someone with a European accent. I was part of the gallery ambience, and I started getting involved in art again. What no one was interested in then was the Russian avant-garde. You know, you expected to see me in Russia and I expected to see you walk into an art gallery on Madison Avenue, dressed in a proper suit, good shoes, tie.'

'Next time we should coordinate dreams.'

'Anyway, Max was visiting the Liberty office in New York. He produced a show on Russian art and happened to interview me and said if I was ever in Munich and needed work to call him. A year later I did. I still do some work for Berlin galleries. They're always looking for pieces of Revolutionary art because now the prices are phenomenally high.'

'You mean the art of our defunct and discredited Revolution?'

'Is auctioned at Sotheby's and Christie's. Collectors can't get enough. You're in trouble, aren't you?'

'I *was* in trouble. Not now.'

'I mean with your work.'

'Work has its difficult moments. The good people die and the wrong people walk away with the spoils. My career seems to be in a shadow, but I'm thinking of taking a holiday, a vacation from professional pursuits.'

'And do what?'

'I could become a German. Transitionally, of course. First, I'd turn into a Pole, then an East German, finally a fully mature Bavarian.'

'Seriously?'

'Seriously, I will wear different clothes every day and walk into your life until you say, "This is just what Arkady Renko should look like; this is the proper suit." '

'You wouldn't let go?'

'Not now.'

Arkady described how the breath of a reindeer herd crystallized and fell like snow. He talked about salmon runs on Sakhalin, the white-headed eagles of the Aleutians and waterspouts that danced around the Bering Sea. He had never thought before of what a catalogue of experiences his exile had brought to him, how unique and beautiful they were, what clear evidence that on no day could a man be sure he should not open his eyes.

They had a lunch of microwaved pizza. Delicious.

He told her how the first wind of the day approaching through the taiga made the million trees shiver like black birds taking flight. He talked about oilfield fires that burned year-round, beacons that could be seen from the moon. He described walking from trawler to trawler across the Arctic ice. Sounds and sights not afforded most investigators.

They had red wine.

He talked about workers on the 'slime line', the dark hold where fish were gutted in a factory ship, and how each individual was a separate mind with a fantasy unconfined by gunwales or decks – a defender of the Party who took to the sea in search of romance, a botanist who dreamed of Siberian orchids, each person a lamp on a separate world.

After finishing the wine, they had brandy.

He described the Moscow he had found on his return. Centre stage, a dramatic battlefield of warlords and entrepreneurs; behind it, as still as a painted backdrop, eight million people queueing. Yet there were moments, the occasional dawn when the sun was low enough to find a golden river and blue domes, when the entire city seemed redeemable.

The warmth of patrons and the steam of the machines had produced a film of condensation on the window that diffused the light and colour of the street. Something caught Irina's eye and she wiped the glass. Max was outside. How long had he been looking in?

He entered and said, 'You two seem to be getting on like a pair of conspirators.'

'Join us,' Arkady offered.

'Where have you been?' Max asked Irina. His manner was alarmed, relieved, alarmed, in three rapid steps. 'You haven't been at the station all day. People were worried about you; we were out searching for you. You and I were supposed to go to Berlin.'

'Talking to Arkady,' Irina said.

Max asked, 'Have you finished?'

'No.' Irina took one of Arkady's cigarettes and lit it. She made it a drawn-out gesture of unconcern. 'Max, if you're in a hurry, go to Berlin. I know you have business there.'

'We both have business there.'

'My business can wait,' Irina said.

Max was absolutely still for a moment, re-evaluating Irina and Arkady together, then dropped the brusque manner as easily as his hat, which he shook free from rain. Arkady remembered Stas's description of him as liquid, the master of a changing situation.

Max smiled, pulled up a third chair, settled and gave Arkady a nod of acknowledgement. 'Renko, I'm amazed you're still here.'

Irina said, 'Arkady has been telling me what he was doing the last few years. It's different from what I'd heard.'

Max said, 'He was probably modest. People claim he was the darling of the Party. A well-earned status, I'm sure. Who knows what to believe?'

'I know,' Irina said. She blew smoke Max's way.

He brushed it aside, considered his hand as if he had caught a cobweb and raised his eyes to Arkady. 'So how is your investigation going?'

'Not well.'

'No arrests imminent?'

'Far from it.'

'And you must be running out of time.'

'I was thinking of abandoning the entire case.'

'And?'

'Staying.'

'Really?' Irina said.

'You're joking,' Max said. 'You came all the way to Munich to give up? Where's your patriotic duty, your sense of pride?'

'I have very little country left and I certainly have no pride.'

'Arkady doesn't have to be the last man in Russia,' Irina said.

'You know, some people are going back, some people see opportunities,' Max pointed out. 'This is a time to contribute, not run away.'

Irina said, 'That's interesting, coming from someone who has run twice.'

'It's hilarious,' Stas said. He closed the café door and fell back against it, a rain-soaked mime of collapse. 'Irina, the next time you vanish, leave a forwarding address. This is the most exercise I've had since Laika learned to fetch.'

His clothes looked wrung, body and all, but he stayed on his feet and concentrated his attention on Max.

'Are you all right?' Irina asked.

'I may throw up. Or maybe I'll have a beer. Max, you were lecturing on political morality? I'm sorry I missed that. Was it a short lecture?'

Max said, 'Stas doesn't forgive me for going home.

He hasn't accepted that the world has changed. It's sad. Sometimes intelligent men cling to simple answers. Even the fact that you're in Munich proves how things have changed. You don't claim to be a political refugee, do you?' He tilted towards Irina. 'Let Renko come or go, I don't see what it has to do with us.'

Irina said nothing. Like a man who senses a growing gulf, Max edged his chair closer and lowered his voice. 'I want to know what kind of wild stories Renko has been entertaining you with. All of a sudden he seems to have assembled an audience here.'

'They were probably happier without us,' Stas said.

'I only want to remind you that Renko is no unsullied hero. He stays when he should go; he goes when he should stay. He's the master of bad timing.'

'Unlike yours,' Irina said.

'I also want to point out,' Max said, 'that your hero probably just came to you because he was frightened.'

'Why would he be frightened?' Irina asked.

'Ask him,' Max said. 'Renko, weren't you with Tommy when he suffered his fatal accident the other night? Weren't you with him right before it?'

'Is this true?' Irina asked Arkady.

'Yes.'

Max said, 'Stas and Irina and I have no idea what kind of disagreeable business you're involved in. But isn't it possible that Tommy is dead because you dragged him into it? Do you really think you should drag Irina into it, too?'

'No,' Arkady admitted.

'I'm only suggesting,' Max said to Arkady, holding up his hand to stifle Stas's protests. 'I'm only suggesting that you came to Irina simply because you want to hide.'

Stas said, 'Max, you really are a shit.'

Max said, 'I want to hear the answer.'

Water dripped from Stas's chin. Max looked unmeltable. For a moment the only sound was the ring of china on the counter and the slow release of steam.

Arkady said, 'I heard Irina on the radio in Moscow. That's why I came.'

Max said, 'You're a devoted fan. Get an autograph. Go home to Moscow and you can hear her five times a day.'

Irina said, 'We can take him to Berlin.'

Max's voice went flat. 'What?'

She said, 'If you're right, Arkady should get out of Munich. No one connects us to him. He'll be safe with us.'

'No,' Max said in disbelief. Arkady saw that he had come to a totally different conclusion; he had carefully and confidently built a seamless, logical argument with only one way out, a perspective of Arkady disappearing over the horizon. Irina had ignored all of it. 'No, I am not taking Renko to Berlin.'

'Then go without me,' Irina said. 'Arkady and I will do fine here.'

Max said, 'We're not staying at a hotel. We'll be in the new flat.'

'It's a big flat,' she said. 'You can have it all to yourself if you want.'

Max reassembled his composure, but for a moment Arkady recognized one reason why the man had returned from Moscow. The worst of reasons.

Love curls around like a snake and crushes two men at the same time.

Part Three

BERLIN

18 August–20 August 1991

Chapter Twenty-Eight

Max drove a Daimler, a saloon with the woodwork of an antique cabinet and the sound of a muted trumpet. His attitude was friendly, as if they were off on a lark, as if becoming a threesome had been his idea.

The German landscape lay under folds of rain. Sitting in front, Irina was the tangible warmth in the car. She propped her back against the door to include Arkady when she talked, almost as if to exclude Max.

'You'll like the show. It's a Russian show, but some of the pieces have never been seen in Moscow, not publicly.'

'Irina wrote the catalogue,' Max said. 'She really should be there.'

'It's just about the provenance of the painting, Arkady, but the painting itself is beautiful.'

'Are critics allowed to use the word *beautiful*?' he asked.

'In this case,' she promised him, 'it's perfect.'

Arkady enjoyed hearing about this other life of hers, this new and independent mix of knowledge and opinions. He was now, as a benefit of experience, a skilled hauler of nets and gutter of fish. Why shouldn't she be an expert on the arts? Max seemed just as proud.

From the back seat, he couldn't tell at what point

they crossed what had been the old East German border. As the road narrowed they slowed for farm equipment that lunged in and out of the mist. When the road cleared, they raced ahead again, as if the three of them were in a bubble caught in a river fed by the rain.

There was a sense of suspended time in the situation. Part of it was Max's self-control. Arkady thought Max had wanted to kill him in Moscow; instead he let him escape to Munich. He was sure Max had wanted him dead in Munich, yet here he was driving him to Berlin. On the other hand, Arkady couldn't touch Max. With what authority? As a refugee? He couldn't even ask questions without Irina accusing him of using her again, without losing her a second time.

Max said, 'Since Irina is going to be busy tomorrow, let me take you around the city. You've been to Berlin before?'

'In the Army. He was stationed there,' Irina answered for Arkady. He was surprised she remembered.

'Doing what?' Max asked.

Arkady said, 'Listening to the American command, translating for the Soviet command.'

Irina said, 'Like you at Radio Liberty, Max.'

More and more she was given to sarcastic attacks on Max, and the walls of the bubble would tremble. Yet it was Max's luxurious car they rode in, his destination they drove to. 'I'll show you the new Berlin,' he told Arkady.

*

When they reached the city late at night, the rain had stopped. They entered on the Avus, the old racetrack through the Berliner Woods, then drove directly on to the Kurfürstendamm. Instead of the homogeneous affluence of Munich's Marienplatz, the Ku'damm was a chaotic collision of West German shops and East German shoppers. For block after block, crowds in Socialist off-colours milled around display cases of silky Italian scarves and Japanese cameras. Their faces had the tight, poutish look of poor relations. A phalanx of skinheads marched in leather jackets and boots. Street-lamps hung on ornate, Nazi-era poles. Tables sold pieces of the Wall, with graffiti and without.

'It's terrible, it's a mess, but it's alive,' Irina said. 'That's why the art market has always been here. Berlin is the only international city in Germany.'

Max said, 'The city between Paris, Moscow and Istanbul.'

He pointed to a sidestreet vendor with a rack of uniforms. Arkady recognized the grey chest and blue shoulders of a Soviet Air Force colonel's greatcoat. The vendor himself was covered with Soviet military medals and ribbons from his collar to his belt. 'You should have kept your uniform,' Max said.

Stas had forced a hundred Deutschmarks on Arkady before he left Munich; he had never been richer or felt poorer.

They passed the Kaiser Wilhelm Church's shattered, floodlit brow. Looming behind it was a glass tower topped by a Mercedes star. Max left the boulevard and followed a dark, arterial route along a canal. All the same, Arkady's internal compass began to function. Before they even reached Friedrichstrasse, he knew they were in what used to be East Berlin.

Max turned down the ramp of a garage. As they drove in, the garage lights automatically went on. A smell of wet cement hit their nostrils like the chlorine of a pool. Electrical junction boxes hung by wires from the walls.

'How new is this building?' Arkady asked.

Max said, 'It's still under construction.'

Irina said, 'Believe me, no one will know you're here.'

Max unlocked the lift with a key. Inside, it had crystal sconces and an unscratched parquet floor. He toted Irina's overnight bag. Carrying his own holdall, Arkady felt like a workman with a sackful of tools.

They stopped on the fourth floor, where Max opened a door to a two-storey living-room-cum-loft. 'Just a studio. I'm afraid it's not furnished, but the electricity and plumbing are in and it's rent-free.' Ceremoniously he handed the doorkey to Arkady. 'We'll be two storeys up.'

Irina said, 'The main thing is that you'll be safe.'

'Thanks,' Arkady said.

Max gathered Irina into the lift. He had her, which was thanks enough.

The key had freshly stamped, sharp serrations, perfect to unlock the heart, Arkady thought, if you worked diligently in between the ribs.

No bed, bedding, chairs or chest of drawers. Dry walls angled seamlessly into hardwood floors. The bathroom was all tiles gleaming like teeth. The kitchen had a stove but no utensils. If he'd had food, he could have held it in his hands above the flame.

Steps echoed out of proportion to every move he made. He listened for sounds from two storeys above. In Munich he had dreaded the possibility that Irina was sleeping with Max. Now, overhead, he had the certainty. What was Max's flat like? Extrapolating, Arkady pictured the finish on the walls, the polish on the floors. He could imagine the rest.

He asked himself if he should have stayed in Munich.

Choice was the luxury of casting a vote, trying on shoes, lingering over a menu and deciding between red caviar and black.

He'd had to come to Berlin. If he hadn't he would have lost Irina, not to mention Max. This way he had them both. Like a man who's proud he wears so much rope around his neck.

The lift was locked. Arkady took the emergency stairs down to the garage, where he wedged the door open and stepped out on to the street. Though Friedrichstrasse was a major thoroughfare, its streetlamps were as dim as curb lights. Except for himself, the pavement was empty. Anyone awake was in the West.

He spotted the point of a television tower and immediately knew that Alexanderplatz was to his right,

West Berlin to his left. The mental map he had was out of date by a decade or so, but no major city in Europe was as unchanged as East Berlin in the last forty years. The advantage of the Soviet model was that construction and upkeep were kept to a minimum, so Soviet memories tended to be excellent.

Munich had been new territory to Arkady. Not Berlin. Day after day, his military assignment had been to monitor British and American radio patrols as they drove through the Tiergarten to Potsdamer Platz, along Stresemann and Koch to Checkpoint Charlie, then on to Prinzenstrasse and back. He followed them from the moment they left their motor pool. It was his own daily ride.

It didn't matter how fast Arkady walked. Jealousy stayed with him, a shadow that walked ahead in giant steps, shrank at the next lamp, then jumped out again.

On Unter den Linden, office buildings were massive and fragile in the same way Soviet architecture was. The hugest structure was, in fact, the Soviet embassy. Trabis were parked nose in. Figures shifted under the lime trees. A man stepped out and hoisted a hand and cigarette like a question mark. Arkady hurried by, surprised he looked good to anyone.

He was approaching the floodlights of the Brandenburg Gate and the familiar outline of Victory in her chariot when the city opened up into a sudden expanse of stars and grass. It wasn't a park but a wide ridge of green hillocks that stretched north and south. Over them a breeze lifted waves of insect calls. His first impulse was to step back. This is where the Wall had been, he realized, which was like saying, 'This is where the pyramids were.'

Actually, around the Gate there had been two Walls, stranding it like a piece of Greece in the middle, so that it was not a gate but a terminus, with the view on either side brought to a halt. The Wall had been a white horizon four metres high. There had also been a flattened no-man's-land of watch towers both round and rectangular, trip wires, sapper charges, tank traps, dogtracks, brushed fields of anti-personnel mines and seasonal brambles of concertina wire. Everywhere, lights had crackled like an electric charge.

The void left by the destruction of the Wall and this attendant apparatus was more immense than its presence had been. An image returned that was more connection than memory. He had been at this same point one summer night long ago. Nothing special had happened except that he had noticed a handler with a brace of dogs that were trotting excitedly along the base of the inner wall. The handler was East German, not Soviet, and the way he kept the dogs encouraged but in check was exactly the same way the charioteer up on her pedestal lightly reined her horses. The dogs sniffed the ground, then turned, straining on their leads, in Arkady's direction. He had the irrational fear – he was a young officer who had done nothing wrong – that they were tracking him, that they could smell his treasonous lack of fervour. He'd stood his ground and the dogs turned aside before they came near. From then on, though, he never looked at the Gate without seeing in the chariot's silhouette a handler and dogs.

Arkady moved into the lights and crossed in long, cautious steps. On the other side was the Tiergarten, a park of well-behaved flowerbeds and well-illuminated avenues. It took him twenty minutes to walk the length of the Tiergarten and around the Zoological Garden to Zoo Station. There the underground emerged to ride above the street. It was the only train stop that West Berliners had been allowed to use to go east. It was also the station where Soviets had been delivered when they went west.

At street level, much of what Arkady remembered was covered with spray paint. Currency exchange windows were shuttered, though a late-night drug trade flourished in the doorways. Overhead, though, less had changed. The same narrow-gauge tracks ran by the same elevated platforms under the same glass roof. Lockers were still available twenty-four hours a day. He stowed the videotape he'd brought from Munich.

Phones were lined up on the street under the station. Arkady unfolded a wad of paper and called the number Peter Schiller had given him.

Peter answered on the eighth ring, sounding irritable. 'Where are you?'

'Berlin. And you?' Arkady asked.

'You know I'm in Berlin. You called this afternoon to say I had to drive in the damn rain all day to be here. You know this is a Berlin number. Who are you with?'

A train came into the station. The sound travelled down through the girder that supported the phone. 'Good,' Arkady said. 'Then I'll try you tomorrow at noon at this same number. Maybe I'll know more then.'

'Renko, if you think you can lead—'

Arkady hung up. It was a comfort to know that Peter was raging somewhere close by, nearer than Munich but farther than arm's reach.

He took the same route back through the park. Again he anticipated the sight of a cement barrier so intensely lit that it rose like a wall of ice. Again he crossed nothing but rubble covered by springy grass and nodding heads of flowers.

He told himself he should have more faith.

Chapter Twenty-Nine

The morning was bright, dry, with not a cloud in the sky. Arkady and Max strolled the same route he had taken the night before. Irina was at the gallery, helping with the installation of the show.

Max was the sort of animal that basked in the sun. He wore a suit the colour of butter. In the windows they passed he looked as if he were being importuned by his companion for loose change, a meal, a business opportunity. Then he would put his hand on Arkady's arm as if to say, 'Look at this raffish friend I have in tow.' Their eyes would meet, and in the small black centre of his irises Arkady could read that Max had not slept with Irina during the night, and that his bed had been no more comfortable than Arkady's bare floor.

'It's a developers' dream,' Max said. 'This side of Berlin always had the grandeur. University, opera, cathedral, the great museums were always in East Berlin. We Soviets built as many monstrosities as we could, but we never had the money or the energy of capitalist developers. West Berlin has shops with the highest real-estate value in the world. Imagine the value of East Berlin. See, without knowing, we Russians saved it. This is literally metamorphosis, this is East Berlin crawling out of its cocoon.'

Friedrichstrasse was different in the daylight. In the dark, Arkady hadn't seen how many government offices were gutted. One was a wooden front with painted windows around the foundation of a Gallery Lafayette that was taking its place. Another was swaddled in five storeys of heavy canvas. Though the street was relatively empty compared to the Ku'damm, from every direction came the sound of a hidden traffic of earthmovers, pile-drivers, cranes.

Arkady asked, 'Do you own the building we stayed in last night?'

Max laughed. 'You're too suspicious. I look for vision, you look for fingerprints.'

There were still Trabis under the lime trees, but they were outnumbered by VWs, Volvos, Maseratis. Out of open buildings floated the dust of sheet rock and the whine of electric drills. Whitewashed windows bore announcements of future offices of Mitsubishi, Alitalia, IBM. Across the street at the Soviet embassy, the steps were empty and the windows were dark. On a side street, a café had set white chairs and tables on the pavement. They sat and ordered coffee.

Max checked his watch, a diver's chronometer with gold links. 'I have an appointment in an hour. I'm the agent for the building you slept in. For a former Soviet, real estate is almost the redemption of life. Do you have any investments?'

'Aside from books?' Arkady asked.

'Aside from books.'

'Aside from a radio?'

'Aside from a radio.'

'I inherited a gun.'

'In other words, no.' Max paused. 'Something can be arranged. You're intelligent, you speak English and a little German. With decent clothes you'd be presentable.'

A coffee pot came with poppyseed rolls and strawberry jam. Max poured. 'The problem is, I don't think you appreciate how much the world has changed. You're a specimen from the past. It's as if you'd arrived from ancient Rome, chasing someone who offended Caesar. Your idea of a criminal is, to say the least, out of date. To stay, you'd have to let go of all that, to erase it from your mind.'

'Erase it?'

'Like the Germans. West Berlin was levelled, so they started afresh and built it into a showcase of capitalism. Our response? We built the Wall, which of course was a pedestal for West Berlin.'

'Why don't you invest in West Berlin?'

'That's thinking in the past. Frankly, West Berlin is nothing. It's an island, a club for freethinkers and draft dodgers. But a united Berlin will be the capital of the world.'

'That does sound visionary.'

'It is. Forgive me for saying so, but the Wall was an even larger reality than your investigation. Now the Wall has gone and Berlin is finally free to bloom. Think of it: over two hundred kilometres of Wall erased, an extra thousand square kilometres in the centre of Berlin to be developed. It's the greatest real-estate opportunity of the second half of the twentieth century.'

There was such conviction in Max's eyes that Arkady realized he had encountered a salesman. Max was selling the idea of the future, and it was compelling. Evidence of the future lined the street. Urgent sounds of it echoed everywhere. The only silent building was the Soviet embassy hulking like a mausoleum above the trees.

Arkady said, 'Does Michael share this vision of yours? For a man who is the radio station's deputy director for security, he welcomed you back pretty quickly.'

'Michael is a little desperate. If the Americans drop the station he'll be left with a European lifestyle and no particular skills. He doesn't have a graduate degree in business administration; he simply has a Porsche. If he can adapt to a new situation, so should you.'

'How would I?'

'Your investigation got you here. What you do from this point on is an entirely different question. Do you go forward or do you turn back?'

'What do you think?'

'I'll be honest,' Max said. 'It wouldn't matter to me except for Irina. Irina is part of Berlin. She stands to benefit. Why do you want to take that away from her? She's never had a chance to enjoy money.'

'She can do that with you, enjoy money?'

'Yes. I don't describe myself as a completely innocent person, but fortunes are not made with "thank you" and "please". I bet that when the wheel was invented, it rolled over someone.' Max wiped his mouth. 'I understand the hold you have on Irina. Every émigré feels guilty about somebody.'

'Really? Who do you feel guilty about?'

A good salesman was not discouraged by rudeness. Max said, 'It's not a matter of morality. It's not even a matter of you or me. It's just that I have the capacity to change and you don't. Maybe you're a heroic investigator, but you're a figure from the past. There's nothing for you here. I want you to be honest and ask yourself what's best for Irina, going forward or going back?'

'That's up to Irina.'

'See, Renko, that's an admission that you *do* know the right answer. Of course the decision is up to Irina. The point is, you and I know what's best. We just came from Moscow. We both know that, even if she goes back, I can protect her better than you. I doubt you'd survive a day back there. So we're speaking of an emotional regression, aren't we? The two of you as poor but loving refugees? With the Soviet embassy trying to deport you? I think you'd need an influential sponsor and, frankly, no one comes to mind but me. The moment you decide to stay you'd have to drop your investigation. Irina would leave you in an instant if she thought you'd stayed for anything else but her.'

'If you know that, why haven't you told her I was after you?'

Max paid homage with a sigh. 'Unfortunately, Irina still has a high opinion of your abilities. She might think you were right. We're on the horns of a dilemma – you on one horn, me on the other. We're coexisting.

That's why morality is so beside the point. That's why we'll have to work out some arrangement.'

After Max paid the bill and left, Arkady went alone through the trees to the Brandenburg Gate, where Victory wore her daytime tint of verdigris. Swifts circled around her, feeding on insects. He slipped among tourists to the meadow. Although his shoes and cuffs were damp, a summer warmth radiated from the ground. The grass had tassels of white flowers and miniature ripples of insects escaping from each footfall. Bees rushed between balls of clover, making up for the down time of wet weather. A cycle path had been laid out; cyclists in helmets and skin-tight outfits rode in single file, flying like flags on a motorcade. Were they aware that they were trespassing on the site of Max's New Berlin?

Since he had time, Arkady walked the Ku'damm to Zoo Station. He felt as if he had fallen into an army of East Berliners who had invaded in good order but had fallen apart at the first pavement display of running shoes. West Berliners retreated behind the railings of cafés, and even there they were pursued by Gypsies with tambourines and babies. A pair of Russians pushed a rack of uniforms. Arkady picked over an assortment of pieces of the Wall with documents attesting to their authenticity. On another table he found an autopilot and altimeter from a Red Army helicopter. He supposed he might find the entire helicopter if he went up and down the Ku'damm long enough. He arrived at Zoo Station right at noon and called Peter's number. This time there was no answer.

Overhead, a train had arrived, releasing yet more regiments of Ossies down the steps to the street. Out of indecision, Arkady was swept up by the crowd and marched across the street to the base of the memorial church, grey and shattered as a tree trunk struck by lightning, where backpackers sprawled on the stairs to watch a street magician. A Japanese tour bus aimed a broadside of cameras.

The old Berlin had been divided in half and ruled essentially by Russians and Americans. He hardly saw an American tourist now. Maybe he could stay as a statue, he thought: *The Last Russian*, posed as if he were trying to sell a pin of Lenin.

Arkady was returning over the meadow when he saw four sections of the Wall left standing like gravestones. So Max was wrong, he thought; not everyone wanted to erase the Wall and turn without pause to the cash register. Someone thought a memorial was appropriate.

Next to the section was a construction crane with a double-jib for tall buildings. About seventy metres up, at the crown of the top jib, the block and tackle held a square basket. Against the sky Arkady saw a figure climb over the edge of the basket and jump. Arms and legs spread, he plunged through the air and disappeared behind the sections.

Arkady walked over quickly. Closer, the sections were each four metres square and elaborately spray-painted with every colour of peace symbol, and airbrushed with Christs, gnostic eyes, prison bars, names and messages in different languages. Behind the cement slabs people sat at tables set on gravel. A sign said, JUMP CAFÉ.

A van offered sandwiches, cigarettes, sodas and beer. The customers were bikers, some older couples with dogs leashed to their chairs, a pair of businessmen dark enough to be Turks and a circle of teenagers, the sun sparkling on the rivets of their jackets.

The jumper, a boy in a tank top and fatigues, was swaying upside down a few feet above the ground. Arkady realized that he had never hit it and that he was connected by elastic cords running from his ankles to the top of the crane. The jib lowered to let him settle on the earth, hands first. He released the cords and staggered dizzily to his feet to applause from the bikers and tribal whoops from his friends.

Arkady was interested in the two businessmen. Their suits were good, but they had massed bottles of beer on their table in a gluttonous volume. They had thick bodies and slouched with their heads tucked in a familiar attitude. Though they sat looking away from him, one of them had memorably ugly hair, long at the back, short at the sides with an orange fringe on top. Though they didn't clap, they watched with close attention.

A second figure was still in the cage high above the tables. He pulled in the loose cords and seemed to sit down. A moment later, he climbed on to the edge of the cage and balanced himself with one hand on a cable. A schnauzer yapped and its owner plugged its mouth with wurst. The figure on the cage looked as if he was trying to pick a place to land.

'*Dvai!*' shouted the man with the bad hair, fed up with waiting. 'Come on!' The way fishermen shout when someone is slow pulling a net.

The figure jumped. He dropped with his arms and legs windmilling. This time Arkady saw cords playing out loosely behind. He assumed that careful calculations took into account the weight of the jumper, the distance to the ground, the full extension of the cords. The face hurtling down was white, eyes first, mouth peeled open. Arkady had never seen anyone so full of second thoughts. He heard an audible chord as the elastic went taut, then the diver was rising, in reverse, a quarter of the way back. He bounced lower, more slowly and more crazily. Now his face was red and the oval of his mouth resumed human shape. Two girls in leather jackets ran forward to help their hero down. Everyone else applauded except for the two businessmen, who laughed so hard they coughed. The one with the hair leaned back to catch his breath. He was Ali Khasbulatov.

Arkady had last seen Ali with his grandfather Makhmud at the South Port car market in Moscow. Ali smacked the table with his hand like a body hitting the ground and started to roar all over again. When an empty bottle rolled off the table on to the gravel, Ali didn't deign to pick it up. The other man at the table was also Chechen, older with eyebrows brushed like fans. The kids in leather jackets found the laughter offensive, but after some cautious glances left the two men alone. Ali spread his arms like wings, pretended to flutter, then to drop. Waved away praise for his acting from the man across the table. Lifted his glass and lit a cigarette with satisfaction.

No one else wanted to jump for Ali's entertainment. After fifteen minutes, he and the other Chechen left and walked to Potsdamer Platz, where they got into a black VW Cabriolet and drove away. Arkady couldn't follow on foot, but he turned back in the direction of the Ku'damm with a freshened eye.

In front of the Ka-De-We department store he found two Chechens resting on the fender of an Alfa-Romeo. Up the Ku'damm, outside the great glass rectangle of the Europa Centre, four Lyubertsy mafiosos were squeezed together in a Golf. A sidestreet called Fasanenstrasse had elegant restaurants with French doors and wine stands, and also small, hairy Chechens tucked in the booth of one of them. On the next block a Long Pond mafioso patrolled the boutiques.

Arkady went to Zoo Station again. The telephone books and the operator had no listings for TransKom or Boris Benz. There was a number for a Margarita Benz. Arkady called.

On the fifth ring Irina answered, 'Hello?'

'This is Arkady.'

'How are you?'

'I'm fine. I'm sorry to bother you.'

'No, I'm glad you called,' Irina said.

'I was wondering when this event was tonight. And how formal it is.'

'At seven. You'll come here with Max and me. Don't worry about formality. Do what German intellectuals do: when in doubt, wear black. They all look like widows. Arkady, are you sure you're all right? Is Berlin completely confusing?'

'No, actually it's starting to look familiar.'

The address for Margarita Benz was only two blocks away, on Savigny Platz. On the way Arkady passed a short commercial section of electronics shops with notices in Polish. Polish cars were parked in front. Men unloaded aromatic bags of cheap Socialist sausage and loaded VCRs.

He found the address at a genteel doorway just off Savigny. The legend below the third-floor button was GALLERIE BENZ. He hesitated, then turned away.

Savigny Platz itself was a square with two matching mini-parks, each surrounded by a tall box hedge. A formal garden was laid out with marigolds and pansies. Set deep into the hedges were arbours designed for trysts.

Something about the neatly trimmed palisade of the hedge made him walk through the park and to a corner. Across the street were the outdoor tables of a restaurant under a filigree of shade lent by a beech. As he crossed, he heard the clatter of cutlery. A waiter poured coffee at a sideboard framed by honeysuckle grown over a yellow wall. Four tables were occupied, two by executive types efficiently eating, two by students resting heads in hands. The tables inside were hidden by reflections of the street. In the windowpanes the box hedge of the park looked like a solid wall of green.

It was the Bavarian beer garden from Rudy's tape. Arkady had thought it was in Munich because it had been inserted into a travelogue of the city, an assumption so stupid in retrospect that it made his stomach hurt. He was hungry, but it was stupidity that was sharp.

A waiter was staring at him. 'Ist Frau Benz hier?' Arkady asked.

The waiter checked the end table, the same one she sat at in the tape. Her regular table, obviously.

'Nein.'

Why insert Margarita Benz into the tape? The only reason Arkady could think of was identification if she had never met Rudy before and didn't want to give him her name. But she was the sort of woman who had her own table at an attractive restaurant on a stylish plaza in Berlin. What business could a Moscow money-changer have with her?

The waiter was still staring. 'Danke.' Arkady backed away, catching his own image in the glass, as if he had stepped into the tape, too.

On the way back to the flat, Arkady bought blankets, towel, soap and a pullover in intellectual black. At six thirty p.m. he was collected by Max and Irina on their way down to the garage.

'You're thin; you can wear something like that,' Max said. Covered by a jacket with brass buttons, he looked as if he'd stepped off a yacht.

Irina wore an emerald outfit that accented the red in her hair. She was so nervous and excited that in the lift she was like an extra light.

Arkady was fascinated by this whole new life she had. He said, 'This is a big affair. You don't want to tell me what it is?'

'It's a surprise,' she said.

'Do you know anything about art?' Max asked Arkady as if including a child.

Irina said, 'Arkady will recognize this.'

They drove in the Daimler along the Tiergarten to Kantstrasse. Irina turned around to Arkady, her eyes were huge in the shell-like gloom of the saloon. 'You are all right? It worried me when you called.'

Max asked, 'He called?'

'I'm looking forward to this, whatever it is,' Arkady said.

Irina reached back and took his hand. 'I'm glad you came,' she said. 'It's perfect.'

They parked at Savigny Platz. Walking to the gallery, Arkady became aware that he was approaching a cultural event of some size. Men so distinguished that they could have been the kaiser escorted matrons draped in beads and jewels. Academics in black marched with wives in knitted coats. There were even berets. Photographers crowded around the nondescript entrance to the gallery. Arkady slipped in while Irina endured a short bath of flashes. Inside, a queue had formed at a brass lift. Max led the way to the stairs and pushed along the banisters past people inching up.

On the third floor, a throaty voice called out, 'Irina!' Arrivals showed invitations at a desk, but Irina was waved forward by a woman with a broad Slavic face and dark eyes that contradicted a mane of golden hair. She wore a long purple dress that looked like the vestment for a cult. Her make-up shifted when she smiled.

'And your friends.' She kissed Max three times, Russian style.

'You must be Margarita Benz,' Arkady said.

'I hope so, or I'm at the wrong gallery.' She let Arkady touch her hand.

He considered mentioning that they had met before, car to car, she with Rudy and he with Jaak. No, he would be a good guest, he told himself.

The doors were opened. The gallery was a loft with a high ceiling and movable partitions stationed to create an open section on one side, a theatre on the other, and lead the eye in between. Arkady was aware of Irina, Max, waitresses, the alert faces of security guards, the anxious faces of employees right and left.

On a stand in the middle of the gallery was a weathered, rectangular crate of wood. Though the corners were chipped, it was obvious that it was well constructed. Through stains, Arkady could see a blurred stamp of the eagle, wreath and swastika of the postal authority of the Third Reich.

However, his attention had gone to the painting that hung alone on the far wall. It was a small square canvas painted red. There was no portrait or landscape or 'picture' in it at all. There was no other colour, only red.

Polina had painted six almost like it to blow up cars in Moscow.

Chapter Thirty

Arkady also recognized it as *Red Square*, one of the most famous paintings in the history of Russian art. It wasn't large and it wasn't a true square either, because the upper right-hand corner rose in a disorienting manner. And it wasn't just red; as he approached, he saw that the square floated on a white background.

Kazimir Malevich, the son of a sugar-maker, was perhaps the greatest Russian painter of the century, and certainly the most modern, even though he died in the thirties. He was attacked as a bourgeois idealist and his paintings were hidden in museum cellars, but, with the perverse pride that Russia took in the quality of its victims, everyone knew the images of Malevich. Like every other student in Moscow, Arkady had dared to paint a red square, a black square, a white square . . . and produced junk. Somehow Malevich, who did it first, created art, and now the world genuflected to him.

The gallery filled rapidly. A separate room was hung with other artists of the Russian avant-garde, the brief cultural explosion that had started with the last days of the tsar, heralded the Revolution, was stifled by Stalin and was buried with Lenin. There were examples of sketches, ceramics and book jackets, though none of the gum wrappers that Feldman had mentioned. The room was almost empty because everyone was drawn to the simple red square on a white field.

Irina said, 'I promised you the show would be beautiful.' In Russian, the word for 'beautiful' was the same as the word for 'red.' 'What do you think?'

'I love it.'

'You said the right thing.'

The painting reflected Irina. She radiated.

'Congratulations.' Max arrived with glasses of champagne. 'This is a coup.'

'Where did it come from?' Arkady asked. He couldn't imagine the Russian State Museum lending one of its most valuable possessions to a private gallery.

'Patience,' said Max. 'The question is what will it bring?'

Irina said, 'It's priceless.'

'Only in rubles,' Max said. 'The people here have Deutschmarks, yen and dollars.'

Thirty minutes after the doors were opened, security guards herded everyone into the theatre section, where the video artist Arkady remembered from Tommy's party was waiting beside a VCR and a parabolic rear-projection screen. There weren't enough chairs, so people sat on the floor and crowded along the walls. From the back Arkady overheard some of their comments. They were devotees and collectors, far more knowledgeable than he, but one thing even he knew;

there was not supposed to be any *Red Square* by Malevich outside Russia.

Irina and Margarita Benz went to the front of the theatre while Max joined Arkady. Only when the room was absolutely still did the gallery owner speak. She had a hoarse voice with a Russian accent, and though Arkady's German wasn't good enough to catch every word, he understood that she was placing Malevich at the level of Cézanne and Picasso as a founder of modern art, perhaps a little higher as the most relevant and challenging artist, *the* genius of his age. As Arkady recalled, Malevich's problem was that there was another genius residing at the Kremlin, and *that* genius, Stalin, had decreed that Soviet writers and artists should be 'engineers of the human soul', which in the case of painters meant producing realistic pictures of the proletariat building dams and collective farmers reaping wheat, not mysterious red squares.

Margarita Benz introduced Irina as the author of the catalogue, and as she stepped forward Arkady saw her looking over the seated rows at him and Max. Even in his new pullover he was aware that he looked more like an uninvited guest than a patron of the arts, while Max was the opposite, practically a host. Or were he and Max bookends, meant to be a pair?

The lights went out. On the screen was *Red Square*, four times its actual size.

Irina spoke in Russian and German. Russian for him, Arkady knew; German for everyone else. 'Catalogues will be available at the door and they will go into much greater detail than anything I say now. It's important, however, that you have a visual understanding of the study this painting has undergone. There are some details you can see on a screen that you wouldn't be able to find if we allowed you to pick up the painting and examine it by hand.'

It was both comforting and odd to hear Irina's voice in the dark. It was like hearing her on the radio.

The red square was replaced on the screen by a black-and-white photo of a dark man with serious brows, fedora and top coat standing before an intact Kaiser Wilhelm Church, the one that was now a war memorial on the Ku'damm.

Irina said, 'In 1927 Kazimir Malevich visited Berlin for a retrospective exhibition of his paintings. He had already fallen into disfavour in Moscow. Berlin at that time had two hundred thousand Russian émigrés. Munich had Kandinsky. Paris had Chagall, the poet Tsvetayeva and the Ballet Russe. Malevich was considering his own escape. The Berlin show contained seventy Malevich paintings. He also brought with him an undetermined number of other works – in other words, half of his entire life's output. However, when he was summoned back to Moscow in June, he returned. His wife and daughter were still in Russia. Also, the Communist Party's Central Committee's agitation and propaganda section was putting artists under more pressure and Malevich's students appealed to him to protect them. When he boarded the train for Moscow, he left instructions that none of his art be returned to Russia.

'At the end of the 1927 Berlin show, all the works were crated by the art-transport firm of Gustav Knauer and sent for storage at the Provinzialmuseum in Hanover, which waited for further instructions from Malevich. Some works were exhibited there, but when the Nazis came to power in 1933 and denounced 'degenerate art', which included, of course, avant-garde Russian art, the Malevich paintings were returned in their Knauer crates and hidden in the museum cellar.

'We know that they were still there in 1935, when Albert Barr, the director of the Museum of Modern Art in New York, visited Hanover. He purchased two paintings and smuggled them out of Germany rolled in his umbrella. The Hanover museum decided that possession of the rest of the Malevich collection was too dangerous and shipped them back to one of Malevich's original hosts in Berlin, the architect Hugo Haring, who hid them first in his house and then, during the Berlin air raids, in his home town of Biberach in the south.

'Seventeen years later, the war over and Malevich dead, curators of Amsterdam's Stedelijk Museum traced the route of the Knauer crates to Haring, who was still alive in Biberach, and acquired the paintings that now comprise the largest collection of Malevich work in the West. But from photographs of the Berlin show, we know that fifteen major paintings are missing. We also know from the quality of the Amsterdam collection that some of the finest paintings Malevich brought to Berlin were not exhibited in the Berlin show at all. How many of those private works are missing we will never know.

Did they burn during the Berlin Blitz? Were they destroyed in transit by a zealous postal inspector who had discovered 'degenerate art'? Or, in all the confusion of the war, were they simply crated, stored and forgotten in Hanover or in the East Berlin warehouse of the Gustav Knauer transport firm?'

Malevich was replaced on the screen by a battered box covered with stamps and yellowed documents. It was the one standing in the gallery. Irina said, 'This crate came to the gallery a month after the Wall came down. The wood, nails, style of construction and bills of lading are consistent with the Knauer crates. Inside was an oil-on-canvas painting, fifty-three centimetres by fifty-three. The gallery knew at once that it had found either a Malevich or a masterful fraud. Which?'

The crate faded and on the screen the painting reappeared in its actual size, a hypnotic beacon. 'There are fewer than a hundred and twenty-five oil paintings by Malevich in existence. Their rarity, as well as their importance in the history of art, accounts for their extraordinarily high value, especially such masterpieces as *Red Square*. Most of the Malevich paintings were suppressed in Russia for fifty years as "ideologically incorrect" art. They're still being released now, like political hostages finally seeing the light of day. The situation is complicated, however, by the number of counterfeits flooding the Western art market. The same forgers who once produced counterfeit medieval ikons now produce counterfeit works of modern art. In the West, we rely on provenance – exhibition catalogues and bills of sale that provide the dates when art was shown, sold and resold. The situation was different in the Soviet Union. When an artist was arrested, his work was confiscated. When his friends heard of his arrest, they hastened either to hide or to destroy whatever works of his they had. The artworks of the Russian avant-garde that exist today are survivors, with the unlikely stories that survivors have of being stuffed in false bottoms or hidden behind wallpaper. Many genuine works have no provenance at all in the Western sense. To demand the usual Western provenance from a survivor of the Soviet state is to deny its survival at all.'

On videotape, hands in rubber gloves gently turned *Red Square* over and delicately peeled a chip, which was analysed and found to be of German manufacture from the correct time period. Irina pointed out that Russians always used German art materials when they could.

There were paintings within paintings. Under X-ray, *Red Square* was a negative that revealed a rectangle painted over. Under fluorescent light, the border's lower layer of zinc white paint softened to a creamy hue. Under ultraviolet light, the brushwork of lead white turned to blue. Under oblique light, magnified brushstrokes were rapid horizontal commas with variations – a cloud of strokes here, a tidal swell of strokes there in a varying sea of different reds, broken by a crazing called 'craquelure', where red paint had not bonded to the yellow paint hidden underneath.

Irina said, 'While the work is unsigned, every brushstroke is a signature. Brushwork, choice of paints, repainting, lack of signature, even the "craquelure" is characteristic of Malevich.'

Arkady liked the word *craquelure*. He suspected that under the proper light he might show some 'craquelure' of his own.

The screen went white again, moving over a magnified weave of canvas and primer thrown into relief by oblique light to the telltale grain of a fingerprint faintly discernible through the paint. Irina asked, 'Whose hand left this mark?'

A face with deep-set, mournful eyes filled the screen. The camera pulled back to show the blue tunic and sorrowful face of the late General Penyagin. Hardly a person whom Arkady had expected to meet again, least of all in artistic circles. With a pen the general pointed to similar whorls and deltas in the enlargements of two fingerprints, one lifted from the gallery's *Red Square* and the other from an authenticated Malevich in the Russian State Museum. An off-camera voice translated. It occurred to Arkady that a German forensic technician would have been faster, but a Soviet general was more impressive. By now he had recognized the off-camera voice as Max's. It asked, 'Would you conclude these prints are from the same man?'

Penyagin stared straight into the camera and worked up forcefulness, as if he sensed how short his starring role would be. 'In my opinion,' he said, 'these prints are absolutely those of the same individual.'

As the lights of the room came up, the most kaiser-like guest in the audience rose and asked angrily, 'Do you pay a *Finderlohn*?'

'Finder's fee,' Max translated for Arkady.

Margarita answered the question. 'No. Though a *Finderlohn* is perfectly legal, we dealt directly with the owner from the start.'

The man said, 'Such fees are notorious ransoms. You know that I'm referring to the fees paid in Texas for the Quedlinburg treasure, which was stolen from Germany by an American soldier after the war.'

'No Americans are involved.' Margarita almost smiled.

'Only one of numerous examples of German art despoiled by the occupying forces. Like the seventeenth-century painting stored in Reinhardsbrunn castle and stolen by Russian troops. Where is it now? On the auction block at Sotheby's.'

Margarita assured him, 'There are no Russians involved either, except for Malevich. And, of course, I have some Russian background myself. You must be aware that it is absolutely against the law to export art of this period and quality from the Soviet Union.'

The art lover was mollified, though not without a parting shot. 'So it came from East Germany?'

'Yes.'

'Then it's one of the few good things that did.'

He drew general agreement.

Was the painting a Malevich, Arkady wondered. Forget the amateur performance by Penyagin. Could the story of the crate be true? It was a fact that most of the Malevich works in existence had been hidden or smuggled to reach the museum where they now reigned. He was the outlaw artist of the century.

What provenance did Arkady have to show for himself? Not even a Soviet passport.

Margarita Benz played a strict but generous hostess, keeping people at arm's length from the painting, forbidding cameras, steering her guests towards a table of caviar, smoked sturgeon, champagne. Irina circulated from guest to guest, answering questions that sounded like hostile inquisitions. That was the German language to an outsider, Arkady thought; if this audience was unhappy, it would have left. All the same, watching her he was put in mind of a white stork walking among crows.

A pair of Americans in black tie and pumps communed over the plates of food. 'I didn't like that crack about the States. Remember, the Sotheby's sale of Russian avant-garde was a big disappointment.'

'Those were all minor works and mostly fakes,' the other American said. 'A major piece like this could stabilize the whole market. Anyway, if I don't get it, I will still have had a nice trip to Berlin.'

'Jack, this is what I wanted to warn you about. Berlin has changed. It's definitely dangerous.'

'Now that the Wall's down, it's dangerous?'

'It's full of—' He glanced up, took his friend by the arm and whispered, 'I'm thinking of moving to Vienna.'

Arkady looked around for what could have scared them. There was no one but him.

An hour later, a continuing high noise level and a thick cigarette haze signalled the success of the show. Arkady retreated to the video theatre and watched a tape of pre-war Berlin that was part footage of horse-drawn carriages on Unter den Linden, part photographs of Russian refugees. He played with the machine, running the tape forward and back. The figures on the screen were the most exotic and attractive refugees of their time, of course. All of them – writers, dancers and actors – gave off a hothouse fluorescence.

He thought he was alone until Margarita Benz asked, 'Irina was good tonight, didn't you think?'

'Yes,' he said.

The gallery owner stood in the doorway of the theatre with a drink in one hand, a cigarette in the other. 'She has a wonderful voice. You found her convincing?'

'Totally,' Arkady said.

She slipped inside. He heard her shoulder graze the wall as she approached. 'I wanted to get a good look at you.'

'In the dark?'

'You can't see in the dark? What a bad investigator you must have been.'

Her manner was a strange mix, coarse and imperious at the same time. He remembered the two contradictory identifications Jaak had made on her pictures: Mrs Boris

Benz, German, staying at the Soyuz, and Rita, hard-currency prostitute, emigrated to Israel five years ago. She dropped her cigarette into her glass, set it on the VCR and gave Arkady matches so that he could light another for her. The tips of her nails were as hard as tines. When Arkady had first seen her in Rudy's car, he had said to himself, a Viking. Now he thought, a Salome.

'Did you make a sale?' he asked.

'Max should have told you that a painting like that isn't sold in a minute.'

'How long?'

'Weeks.'

'Who owns the painting? Who's the seller?'

She laughed on the exhalation. 'What rude questions.'

'This is my first show. I'm curious.'

'Only the buyer needs to know the seller.'

'If it's Russian—'

'Be serious. In Russia, no one knows who owns what. If it's Russian, whoever has it owns it.'

Arkady accepted the rebuff. 'How much do you think you'll get?'

She smiled, so he knew she would answer. 'There are two other versions of *Red Square*. They're each valued at five million dollars.' The number seemed to roll in her mouth. 'Call me Rita. My close friends call me Rita.'

Malevich appeared on the screen in a self-portrait, with a high collar, black suit and anxious shades of green.

'Do you think he was actually going to leave?' Arkady asked.

'He lost his nerve.'

'You can tell that?'

'I can tell.'

'How did you get out?'

'Dear, I fucked my way out. I married a Jew. Then I married a German. You have to be willing to do that sort of thing. That's why I wanted to see you, to see what you're willing to do.'

'What do you think?'

'Not enough.'

Interesting, Arkady thought. Maybe Rita was a better judge of character than he was. He said, 'I had the idea from some of your guests that they've seen too many Russians since the Wall came down.'

Rita was scornful. 'Not too many Russians, too many other Germans. West Berlin used to be like a special club, now it's just a German city. All those East Berlin kids grew up hearing about Western lifestyles, so now they come over and want to be punks. Their fathers are unregenerate Nazis. When the Wall came down, they poured in. No wonder West Berliners are lifting their skirts and running.'

'Are you thinking of running?'

'No. Berlin is the future. This is what Germany is going to be. Berlin is wide open.'

They sat, a foursome, around a late dinner on the patio of the restaurant on Savigny Platz. Max was enjoying the slow dissipation of excitement the way a director of a theatrical production savours an opening night, and was as doting and admiring of Irina as if she were his star. She carried the glow of celebration; she seemed to be circled by candles and crystal. Rita was in the same chair she had sat in on the videotape. As she looked at Max, Irina and Arkady, she seemed concerned over a basic problem of arithmetic.

For Arkady, Max and Margarita kept fading away; all he could see was Irina. Their eyes would meet as palpably as a touch, so he kept up his part of the conversation even in silence.

The waiter set down his tray next to Max and nodded towards two men in shiny suits approaching along the park. They moved slowly, as if they were walking a dog, but there was no dog.

'Chechens. Last week, they broke up a restaurant down the block, the quietest street in Berlin. They killed a waiter with an axe in front of the customers.' He rubbed one arm. 'With an axe.'

'What happened afterwards?' Arkady asked.

'Afterwards? They came back and said they would protect the restaurant.'

'Outrageous,' Max said. 'Anyway, you're already protected, aren't you?'

'Yes,' the waiter was quick to agree.

The Chechens crossed over to the restaurant. Arkady had seen one eating with Ali at the Jump Café, and the other was Ali's younger brother Beno, who had the size and swagger of a jockey. 'You're Borya's friend, aren't you? We heard you had a place here.'

'Do *you* have a place here?' Max acted amazed.

'A whole suite.' Beno had inherited his grandfather's shrewd eyes and force of concentration, Arkady realized: this was the next Makhmud, not Ali. The way he focused on Max, Arkady doubted that he noticed anyone else at the table. 'You're having a party? Can we join?'

'You're not old enough.'

'Then we'll get together later.'

Beno led the older Chechen down the street, two world travellers at their ease.

When Rita started to sign the dinner bill Max insisted on paying for generosity's sake, and also to demonstrate that he was in control. He wasn't in control, though, Arkady thought. Nobody was.

Chapter Thirty-One

In the middle of the night he woke, aware that Irina was in the room with him. She was in a raincoat, her feet bare in the thin milk of moonlight that covered the floor. She said, 'I told Max I was leaving him.'

'Good.'

'It's not. He says he knew as soon as you came to Munich this could happen.'

Arkady sat up. 'Forget about Max.'

'Max has always treated me well.'

'We'll go somewhere else tomorrow.'

'No, you're safe here. Max wants to help. You don't know how generous he can be.'

'Her presence was overwhelming. On her shadow he could have drawn her face, eyes, mouth. He smelled her and tasted her in the air. At the same time he knew how tenuous his hold on her was. If she caught his slightest suspicion about Max, he would lose her in a moment.

'Why don't you like Max?' she asked.

'I'm jealous.'

'Max should be jealous of you. He's always been good to me. He helped with the painting.'

'How?'

'He brought the seller to Rita.'

'Do you know who the seller is?'

'No. Max knows a lot of people. He can help you if you let him.'

'Whatever you want,' Arkady said.

She stooped and kissed him. Before he could stand up, she was gone.

Orpheus had descended into the underworld to save Eurydice. According to Greek legend, he found her in Hades and led her through endless, slowly rising caverns towards the surface. The only stricture laid by the gods on Orpheus for this second chance was that he not look back until they had reached the surface. On the way, he felt her start to change from a wraith to a warm, living body.

Arkady thought about the logistical problems. Orpheus, obviously, had gone first. As they manoeuvred along the ledges of their subterranean route, had he held her hand? Tied her wrist to his as if he were stronger?

Yet when they failed the fault wasn't Eurydice's. Even as they approached the light of the mouth of the cave through which they could make their final escape, it was Orpheus who turned, and with that backward glance condemned Eurydice to death again.

Some men had to look back.

Chapter Thirty-Two

At first Arkady couldn't tell whether Irina's visit had been real, because outwardly nothing seemed changed. Max led them to breakfast at a hotel on Friedrichstrasse, praised the renovation of the restaurant, poured the coffee and laid out newspapers by importance of reviews.

'The timing was good and the show made both *Die Zeit* and the *Frankfurter Allgemeine*. Two cautious but positive reviews, harking back to the long-standing debt that Russian art owes to German support. A bad review in *Die Welt*, which doesn't like modern art or Russians. A worse one in *Bild*, a right-wing rag that prefers news events about steroids, or sex. It's a good start. Irina, you have interviews this afternoon with *Art News* and *Stern*. You do better than Rita with the press. More important, we're having dinner with some Los Angeles collectors. Americans are only the beginning; the Swiss want to speak to us next. The nice thing about the Swiss is that they don't flaunt the art they buy; they prefer it in a vault. Which reminds me, we'll pull the painting off public exhibition by the end of the week to make it more accessible for serious people.'

Irina said, 'The show was supposed to run a month so the public could see it.'

'I know. It's a matter of insurance. Rita was afraid to show the painting at all, but I told her how strongly you felt.'

'What about Arkady?'

'Arkady.' Max sighed to indicate this was a lesser subject. He wiped his mouth. 'Let's see what we can do. When does your visa run out?' he asked Arkady.

'In two days.' He was sure Max knew.

'That's a problem because Germany doesn't accept political refugees from the Soviet Union any more. There's nothing political to be afraid of.' He turned to Irina. 'I'm sorry, there really isn't. You can go back any time you want to. Even if there's a charge of treason against you, nobody cares. At the worst they won't let you in. If you were with me, there'd be no problem at all.' He returned to Arkady. 'The point is, Renko, that you can't defect, so you'll have to get an extension of your visa from the German Foreign Police. I'll take you. You'll also need a work permit and a resident's permit. This is all assuming, of course, that a Soviet consulate will cooperate.'

'They won't,' Arkady said.

'Oh, then that's a different story. What about Rodionov back in Moscow? Doesn't he want you to stay longer?'

'No.'

'Strange. Who are you after? Can you tell me that?'

'No.'

'Have you told Irina?'

'No.'

Irina said, 'Max, stop it. Someone is trying to kill Arkady. You said you were going to help.'

'It's not me,' Max said. 'It's Boris. I talked to him on the phone and he's very unhappy about you and the gallery getting involved with someone like Renko, especially when we're about to see the culmination of all our work.'

'Boris is Rita's husband,' Irina told Arkady. 'A typical German.'

'Have you ever met him?' Arkady asked.

'No.'

Max seemed pained. 'Boris is afraid that your Arkady is in trouble because he's involved with the Russian mafia. A hint of that and the show would be a disaster.'

'I have nothing to do with the gallery,' Arkady said.

Max went on. 'Boris thinks Renko is using you.'

'To do what?' Irina demanded.

She *had* come during the night, Arkady thought; it wasn't a dream. She watched Max for the least little misstep. New lines had been drawn and Max retreated over them as carefully as he could.

'To stay, to hide – I don't know. I'm only telling you what Boris thinks. As long as you want Renko here, I'll do my best to keep him here. That's a promise. After all, it seems that, as long as I have him, I'll have you.'

They played at being a Western couple. Their names could have been George and Jane. Tom and Sue. They shopped, buying a sports shirt for Arkady that he wore from the shop. Wandered through the Tiergarten to the zoo, where they ignored the lions and watched the pony carts. Saw no Chechens or art collectors. Neither tried to say anything exceptional. Normalcy was a spell too easily broken.

At two, Arkady delivered her to the gallery, then went to Zoo Station and put more coins in his locker. He tried calling Peter, but there was no answer. Peter was fed up or had lost interest. Either way Arkady had lost contact.

As soon as he put the phone back on the hook it rang. Arkady stepped back. Along the pavement, Africans were selling Ossies what appeared to be French luggage. Backpackers with long hair queued sleepily at the currency exchanges. No one came forward to answer the phone. He picked it up.

Peter said, 'Renko, you'd make a terrible spy. A good spy never calls from the same place twice.'

'Where are you?'

'Look across the street. See the man in the nice leather jacket talking on the phone? That's me.'

In good weather, the drive out of the city was like a summer jaunt. They went south through the evergreens of the Grünewald, then by the waters of the Havel and hundreds of small boats, their sails catching as much sun as breeze, at a distance looking like gulls.

'There are some benefits to being German. In the middle of your first call I heard a train on your end of the line. Being efficient people, the transport organization was able to tell me at what underground and surface stations around the city trains were arriving at exactly that time. I narrowed the list to Zoo Station because, of course, you're Russian. Zoo was the one station you were sure to know. You were bound to head to familiar places.'

'You're brilliant. It's undeniable.'

Peter didn't argue the point. 'When you called yesterday from Zoo Station I was there waiting for you. I followed you around Berlin. You noticed the city has changed?'

'Yes.'

'When the Wall came down there was such an intensity of celebration. East and West Berlin back together. It was like a wild night of lovemaking. Afterwards was like waking in the morning and finding this woman you had yearned for so long was going through your pockets, your wallet, taking the keys to your car. The euphoria was gone. That's not the only change. We were ready for the Red Army. We weren't ready for the Russian mafia. I was behind you yesterday. You saw them.'

'It's like Moscow.'

'That's what I'm afraid of. Compared to your gangsters, German criminals are a Salzburg choir. German killers clean up after themselves. Russian mafias just shoot each other on the streets. Boutiques are keeping doors locked, hiring private guards, moving to Hamburg or Zürich. It's bad business.'

'You don't seem upset.'

'They haven't reached Munich yet. Life was boring until you came along.'

Arkady felt that once again Peter had taken flight, and all that he could do was see where he would land. He didn't know how long Peter had followed him, and waited to hear the names of Max Albov, Irina Asanova, Margarita Benz.

Somewhere in the woods, among the cottages and country lanes, the road crossed the former East German border and Potsdam came into view. At least the part of Potsdam that was proletariat housing and might have appeared promising in an architectural rendering, but in reality was ten storeys of anonymous balconies with fractured cement.

Old Potsdam was hidden in a canopy of beech trees. Peter parked on a leafy avenue in front of a three-storey town house. This was the kaiser's kind of mansion, with a wrought-iron gate and a portico wide and high enough for a carriage, marble stairs to double doors, classical stone facing, carved scrollwork above the windows that were high enough to show coffered ceilings, an artist's tower rising above a tiled roof. Except that so much of the facing had fallen off the bricks that a makeshift scaffolding covered the second floor. A wooden ramp ran down one side of the stairs; the other side was broken. Some windows were bricked in, some boarded up. A stunted tree and tall grass grew from the caved-in turret of the tower. The grounds had long been abandoned to rubble and weeds of opportunity. A ferrous powder compounded of rust, soot and the dust of decaying bricks covered the gate. But the building was inhabited; from head to foot, the balconies and surviving windows wore boutonnières of red geraniums, and dim lights and slow movement showed through the glass. By the gate was a sign that said MEDICAL CLINIC.

'The Schiller house,' Peter said. 'This is it. This is what my grandfather sold out for, this ruin.'

Arkady asked, 'Has he seen it?'

'Boris Benz brought him a photograph of it. Now he wants to move back in.'

On both sides, the block was lined with mansions similar in design and disrepair to the Schiller house. Some worse. One was as masked by ivy as an ancient tomb. Another was posted VERBOTEN! KEIN EINGANG!

Peter said, 'This used to be Bankers' Row. Every morning they would all go to Berlin, every evening return. These were cultured, intelligent people. They had a modest portrait of the Führer. They closed their eyes when the Meyers disappeared from this mansion over here or the Weinstein family vanished from that house over there. Later, they could get those houses for a good price. Well, you can't tell where the Jews lived today, can you? Now my grandfather wants us to trade with the devil again for this.'

A balcony door opened and a woman in a white cap and apron backed out with a wheelchair that she turned around. She put on the brake and sat down for a cigarette, mistress of all she surveyed.

'What are you going to do?' Arkady asked.

Peter pushed open the gate. 'I should take a look, don't you think?'

The driveway had once been laid in cobblestones and led to a reception arch of pillars. Now two ruts cut through the weeds, and one of the pillars had long since suffered a collision and been replaced by a standing sewer pipe. The front door had a red cross and a RUHIG! sign for quiet, but it was open and the sound of radios and the smell of antiseptic drifted out. There was no reception desk. Peter's inspection tour took them down a hall of dark mahogany to a ballroom turned into a mess hall and an enormous kitchen divided by breeze blocks into a small kitchen with steaming vats and a second area of tiled baths and toilet cubicles.

Peter tried the soup. 'Not bad. They have good yellow potatoes in East Germany. I was in Potsdam last night, but I didn't get here.'

'Where were you?'

'In the archives of the Potsdam City Hall, looking for Boris Benz.' He let the ladle drop and moved on. 'There's not enough of him,' he said. 'I tap into the federal computer and I see his driver's licence, Munich residence, marriage licence. I see his registered ownership of a private company called "Fantasy Tours", with work, insurance and medical records in order, because his employees are examined for venereal disease once a month by law. What does not show up is his local education or work history.'

'You told me that Benz was born here in Potsdam

and that many East German records weren't transferred yet.'

Peter bounded up the stairs. 'That's why I came here. But there are no records at all here for Boris Benz. It's one thing to plug a name into a computer file; you're only adding one more blip to the screen. It's more difficult to insert a name on an old, meticulously written school roll. As for work or military records, they don't matter if you're not looking for work or a loan from the bank. It only proves that Boris Benz has more money than personal history. Ah, this must have been the master bedroom.'

They looked into a ward with five beds on one side. Some of the beds were occupied by patients attached to IVs. Family photographs and crayon drawings were taped to the walls. The sheets looked clean and the parquet floor was mopped to a shine. Four elderly women in housecoats were playing cards. One of them looked up. 'Wir haben Besucher!' Visitors!

Peter nodded approvingly at each resident. 'Sehr gut, meine Damen. Schönen Foto. Danke.' They beamed as he waved and backed away.

The other bedrooms had been turned into wards and more zinc-lined baths. Cigarette smoke travelled out of the open fanlight of an office. They climbed to the third floor. In the ceiling of the stairwell where a chandelier had once hung was a fluorescent ring.

Peter said, 'I asked myself, if Benz didn't grow up here, how would he know about my grandfather or what he did in the war? Only the SS and the Russians knew. So there are two possible answers: he's Russian or German.'

'Which do you think it is?' Arkady asked.

'German,' Peter said. 'East German. To be more precise, the Staatssicherheit. Stasi. Their KGB. For forty years Stasi created identities for spies. Do you know how many people worked for them? Two million informers. More than eighty-five thousand officers. Stasi owned office buildings, apartment houses, resorts, bank accounts in the millions. Where did all the agents go? Where did the money disappear to? In the last weeks before the Wall came down, the agents at Stasi were furiously creating new identities for themselves. When people stormed its offices, they were empty and the master files had evaporated. One week later Boris Benz rented his flat in Munich. That's when he was born.'

The third floor was servants' quarters turned into medicine cupboards and nurses' rooms. Panties were drying on a line that ran from corner to corner.

Peter said, 'Where could the Stasi go? If they were important, they were going to be put in jail. If they were unimportant, with "Stasi" on their papers no one would hire them. They couldn't all rush to Brazil like a second wave of Nazis. Russia doesn't want thousands of German agents. What's this?'

A narrow stairway was blocked by buckets. Peter moved them aside, climbed the stairs and tried the knob of a door built into the ceiling. A sash snapped and dust cascaded down the steps as he pushed the door open.

They pulled themselves up into the tower. The casement windows were buckled, parts of the roof had fallen in, and from one corner grew a stunted lime tree, a life-long prisoner of the tower. The view was wonderful: lakes and rolling hills reaching to Berlin, green country in every other direction. Two storeys below was the balcony with the nurse in the wheelchair. She had pushed off her sandals and rolled down her stockings to her calves. She raised the leg rests and angled the chair for more direct exposure to the sun, then lolled back like Cleopatra, the cigarette in her mouth an exclamation mark to total ease.

Peter said, 'Ask yourself, where does an Ossie find the money to buy eighteen new cars? Or live in Munich? For a man with no history, Benz was born with impressive connections.'

'But why bother your grandfather?' Arkady asked. 'What did he get except war stories?'

'Stasi was more than spies; they were thieves. They targeted people with valuable goods. People weren't just arrested; their savings were taken as "reparations to the state", and their paintings and coin collections ended up in the home of a Stasi colonel. Maybe when Benz disappeared, he took something and doesn't know quite what. There's so much still hidden in this country. So much.'

Peter's was a perfectly German, exquisitely logical answer to the identity of Boris Benz. It wasn't Arkady's answer, but he admired it nonetheless.

Peter asked abruptly, 'Who is Max Albov?'

'He's given me a place to stay in Berlin.' Surprised, Arkady tried to go on the offensive. 'That's why I was calling you. You have my passport and I can't stay in a hotel without it. Also I want to extend my visa.'

Peter tested a post before leaning against it. 'Your passport is the leash I have on you. I'd never see you again if I gave it to you.'

'Is that so bad?'

Peter laughed, then cast his eyes over the trees. 'I can imagine myself growing up here. Running in the hall, climbing the roof, breaking my neck. Renko, I worry about you. I followed you to that flat on Friedrichstrasse yesterday. Albov arrived before I left for Potsdam and I identified him by his licence. From the checking I've done, he's a slippery type. A defector twice, no doubt connected to the KGB, an ersatz businessman. What could possibly bring the two of you together?'

'I met him in Munich. He offered to help.'

'Who's the woman? She was with him in the car.'

'I don't know.'

Peter shook his head. 'The correct answer is "What woman?" I see now that I shouldn't have left; I should have camped on Friedrichstrasse and watched. Renko, are you safe?'

'I don't know.'

Peter accepted that. He took a deep breath. 'Berlin air. It's supposed to be good for you.'

Arkady lit a cigarette. Peter took one. From the balcony below came audible snoring mixed with the garden sound of flies. 'The Workers' State,' Peter said.

'What about the house?' Arkady asked. 'Are you going to be a landowner, are you going to move in?'

Peter leaned on one railing, then another. He said, 'I like to rent.'

Chapter Thirty-Three

The day was fading when Peter dropped Arkady at Zoo Station. Over the city was a momentary hush, a pause between afternoon and evening. Minute by minute, Arkady was learning what he would do to stay with Irina. The answer seemed to be *anything*.

She would be going to dinner with American collectors. Arkady bought flowers and a vase and walked through the Tiergarten in the direction of the Brandenburg Gate, its columns and pediments as high as a five-storey building. He saw how impressive a promenade this could be, a boulevard that ran the length of the western half of the city and continued through the Gate into the old imperial squares of the east. He had it practically to himself. When the Wall was up, this hundred metres of tarmac had been the most carefully observed spot on earth – from one side by watch towers, from the other by tourists who climbed a platform to gawk.

At the base of the columns was a white Mercedes and a man bouncing a soccer ball on his head. Wearing a camelhair coat tied as casually as a dressing gown, he balanced the ball on his forehead, dropped it to knee, to instep, tipped the ball to his other foot and flipped it up again. A professional player like Borya Gubenko didn't lose his skills if he kept in shape. He bounced the ball from knee to knee.

'Renko!' He waved Arkady closer, keeping the ball in steady motion.

As Arkady approached, Borya kicked the ball high into the air. Arms out like a tightrope walker, he caught it on his foot, cradled it on his instep and flipped it up to his head. 'I've been doing more than just hitting golf balls in Moscow,' he said. 'What do you think? Think I'm ready to run back out there and defend the goal for Central Army?'

'Why not?'

When Arkady was close enough, Borya stepped back to let the ball drop, then stepped forward and kicked it full force into his stomach. Arkady dropped. As he landed, he heard the vase break. His legs went different ways. The ground spun and he couldn't get his balance even lying down. There was a ring around his vision and spots in the sky.

Borya knelt and put a gun to his ear. An Italian pistol, Arkady thought. 'I owe you a lot more than that,' Borya said.

The gun wasn't necessary. He rose, opened the passenger door of the Mercedes, lifted Arkady by the collar and the back of his belt – the same way drunks were toted out of football games – and threw him into the front seat, put the ball in the back and slid behind the wheel. The car's acceleration shut Arkady's door.

*

Borya said, 'If it were up to me, you'd be dead. You never would have left Moscow. If people saw us kill you, so what? We'd pay them off. I think there's a self-destructive streak in Max.'

Arkady breathed shallowly. He hadn't had the wind knocked out of him for so long that he had forgotten the utter helplessness. Flowers and vase were lost. His stomach still felt concave. He was aware that Borya was taking a scenic route along the Spree river, more or less in the direction of the sunset, maintaining just enough speed so that Arkady wouldn't jump out. Borya could have killed him by now.

Borya said, 'Sometimes smart people overcomplicate. Great plans, no execution. What's the classic example?' He snapped his fingers. 'In that play.'

Arkady said, '*Hamlet?*'

'*Hamlet*, perfect. You don't admire the ball forever, you kick it.'

'Like you kicked the Trabi off the road in Munich?'

'It could have solved our problems. It should have. When Rita told me you were still alive and that Max had brought you here, I honestly couldn't believe it. What's going on with you and Max?'

'I think he wants to prove he's the better man.'

'No offence, but Max has everything and you have nothing.' Borya broke into a smile. 'In the West that's how it's scored. He's the better man.'

Arkady asked, 'Who's the better man, Borya Gubenko or Boris Benz?'

Borya's smile spread into the grin of a boy caught

stealing cookies. He fished out a pack of Marlboros and gave one to Arkady. 'As Max says, we have to be new men for new times.'

Arkady said, 'You needed a foreign partner for the joint venture and it was easier to create one than find one.'

Borya stroked the wheel. 'I like the name Benz. It has a more reassuring sound than Gubenko. Benz is a man people want to do business with. How did you figure it out?'

'Obvious things. You were Rudy's partner, but on paper Benz was Rudy's partner. Once I knew Benz was a paper identity, you were the most likely candidate. It struck me as odd that the clinic at your Munich house believed me for a second and let me in the door when I claimed I was you. I don't sound very German. Then you made the mistake of videotaping a restaurant window when you were taping Rita. Your reflection wasn't a perfect portrait because you were holding the camera, but on a big screen an old football hero still stands out.'

'The tape was Max's idea.'

'Then I should thank him.'

Heading south towards the Ku'damm, they passed a service station with signs in Polish. Borya said, 'What the Poles do is they steal a car, a nice car, cut it off the motor, drop the car on a legal motor, maybe a piece of junk that barely runs, and drive to the border. The border guards check the number on the motor and they let it through. It's like a joke: how many Poles does it take to steal a car? If you have any money, you just pay the guard and drive through.'

'Getting a painting across the border, is that more difficult?' Arkady asked.

'You want to know the truth? I like that painting. It's a rare work of art. But we don't need it. There's a difference of opinion here. We were doing very well with the slot machines, the girls—'

'That's the personnel part of TransKom, bringing prostitutes from Moscow to Munich?'

'It's legal. It's an opportunity. The world's opening up, Renko.'

'Then why smuggle the painting?'

'It's democracy. I was outvoted. Max wants the painting and Rita loves the idea of being Frau Margarita Benz, gallery owner, instead of a madam, which is what she was. After I missed you in the Trabi, I wanted to hit you here. I was outvoted again. I have nothing against you, but I wanted to leave Moscow behind. When I heard you were here, I exploded. Max says you're going to be quiet, you have a personal involvement and you're not going to get in the way. That you're on the team. I'd like to believe it, but when I follow you I see you jump in a car with the German police and go for a day trip to Potsdam. Put me anywhere in the world and I recognize the local militia. You're two-facing us, Renko, and that's a mistake. This is a new world for both of us and we should take advantage instead of tearing each other down. We can't be Neanderthals the rest of our lives. I'm happy to learn from the Germans or the Americans or the Japanese. The problem is the Chechens. They're going to spoil Berlin the way they spoiled Moscow. They pick on Russian businesses. It's a shame that they bring down their own people. Walking around with automatic weapons as if they were at home, kicking their way into restaurants, busting up shops, kidnapping children – horrible stories. So far the German police don't know what to do because they've never seen anything like it. They can't infiltrate because none of them can pass for Chechen. Not close. But it's short-sighted on the part of the Chechens because they have so much money that if they invested it here legally they could make a fortune. I could show them how to get into the positive side of business. Rudy was an economist, Max is a visionary, but I'm a businessman. I can tell you from experience that business is based on trust. At the golf range I trust that my suppliers are selling me good liquor, not poison. The suppliers trust that I'm paying them in real money, not rubles. The most civilizing idea in the world is trust. If Makhmud would just listen, we could live in peace.'

'That's all you want?'

'That's all I want.'

They drove through the now familiar hordes of the Ku'damm, under neon grails of AEG, Siemens, Nike and Cinzano below a sky of pale lavender. The ruins of the Kaiser Wilhelm Church looked out of place because it was the only building in sight that wasn't new. Hard behind it stood the glass wall of the Europa Centre, starting to blaze with office lights. Borya parked in the Centre's garage.

In its shopping area, the Europa Centre had more than a hundred shops, restaurants, cinemas and cabarets. Borya led Arkady past the entreaties of sushi bars, first-run westerns, cultured pearls, Swiss watches and nail salons. His eye had a speculative glint, as if he were considering expanding on his golf range.

'Makhmud trusts you. With you along, he might listen.'

'He's here?' Arkady asked.

'It's one thing for Max to say that you're as good as on the team. If you do this for me, this little thing, then I'll know you're okay. He's right upstairs. You know how he is about his health.'

They climbed three flights. Arkady had imagined that any meeting with Makhmud Khasbulatov would take place in the back of a car or in the corner of a dimly lit restaurant, but at the top of the stairs was a brightly illuminated carpeted foyer and a counter lined with a selection of organic shampoos, sunglasses and chelated vitamins. For sixty Deutschmarks the attendant issued them towels, rubber slippers and metal-bead chains with locker keys.

'A bathhouse?' Arkady said.

'A sauna,' Borya said.

The changing room had lockers, showers, hair dryers, complimentary mousse. Arkady hung his miserable few clothes on the hangers, locked up and slipped the chain over his hand like a bracelet. Borya had to stuff his wardrobe in. Most men when they stripped looked mis-shapen or diminished. An athlete like Borya Gubenko had undressed before other people all his life. He wore physical ease. Arkady looked starved alongside him.

'Makhmud comes here?' Arkady asked.

'Makhmud is a health nut. Wherever he is, here or Moscow, he spends an hour a day in a sauna.'

'How many other Chechens are here?' At the South Port car market, Makhmud never had less than half a dozen.

'A few. Relax,' Borya said. 'I just want you to talk to Makhmud face to face. For whatever reason, he likes you. Also, I want you to see that everything I do here is legitimate.'

'This is a public place?'

Borya pushed open the sauna door. 'It couldn't be more public.'

Arkady was used to utilitarian bathhouses, to pale Russian torsos and the smell of alcohol working its way out as sweat. This was different. A veranda with a tropical forest of plastic plants opened on to a circular indoor swimming pool surrounded by marble steps. Swimming, floating, stretched across chaise longues were naked bodies so pink they looked as if they had just rolled in snow. Male, female, boys and girls. The scene would have been hedonistic if it hadn't been so serious. They looked as fit as Olympians and as stiff as mummies, some with the embellishment of a towel, some without. A man with a goatee and a belly of grey hair walked up the steps as gravely as a senator. Chechens were easy to find. Two of them leaned on the balustrade watching a woman swim slowly back and forth in bathing cap and goggles, nothing else. Although Chechens would never allow their wives to go naked in public, they had no objection if Germans wanted to.

Toddlers with hair as fair as goose down ran out of a dining area, their shrieks echoing off the copper baffles above the pool. Arkady heard the bang of dominoes being slapped on a dining table. Probably more Chechens there.

Borya took Arkady the other way, past two smaller sitting pools and through the wooden door of a dry sauna. Inside was the senatorial German. They climbed benches to the warmest air. The German paid them no attention. He sat by a wall thermometer and rubbed sweat like soap over his body. Every few seconds he checked the temperature. Sweating seemed to take all his concentration. The metal beads of Arkady's chain were already hot. The sauna was well insulated. He could hear no pool sounds at all.

'Where's Makhmud?'

'Somewhere here,' Borya said.

'Where's Ali?' If Makhmud was nearby, so was his favourite bodyguard.

Borya put a finger to his mouth. He could have been a sculpture except for the dew of sweat starting to appear on his temple, upper lip, the hollow where his neck sank into the armature of muscle that was his chest. He whispered, 'Dry heat takes too long. Let's try the Russian bath.'

He climbed down and Arkady followed. Outside, the Chechens at the balustrade watched the swimmer dry herself by the near edge of the pool. She wasn't young, but from the back she had a hard, athletic body to be proud of and she turned towelling down into an elaborate process. She pulled off her cap, releasing thick, blonde hair that she swung round to rake fiercely with her fingers, then brush back wet from a face that was broad, Slavic, not the least German, with eyes that were so bold and diffident they summed up and dismissed both the Chechens and Arkady at the same time. It was Rita Benz.

Borya pushed through a door labelled RUSSISCH DAMPFBADEN and Arkady followed, plunging into an aromatic cloud. The bench on his side was empty. He sat, put his hand out and touched a limestone rim. A fountain. The only light rose as a smoky glow from four glass floor tiles around the fountain's base. He couldn't see Borya on the other side.

A sauna was an oven that slowly baked the sweat out; a Russian bath was so saturated by moist steam that perspiration bloomed in an instant. The scent of cypress helped open the pores. Sweat flowed down Arkady's forehead, ran over his chest, accumulated between his toes, filled every crevice of his body; he felt like one great conduit of sweat. He thought about Rita and the first time he had seen her in Rudy's car. The way she had looked at him now was the way she had looked at Rudy then.

'Ali?' Makhmud's voice came out of the corner.

Arkady was already moving towards the door when Borya hit him. His head bounced off the wall and he toppled off the bench and to the floor.

He didn't so much lose consciousness as pass through a brief eclipse. Then his eyes were open and he half crawled, half swam off the floor and perched unsteadily on the edge of the bench. Aside from his poor balance and a compression problem in his ears he was in one piece. The question that victims of concussions always asked was what happened? A second ago he had been in the Russian bath with Borya and Makhmud. Now he seemed to be alone.

The steam was pink. To Arkady that meant his head was cut and blood was running into his eyes. He found a knot on his scalp, but no cut. He wiped his face with a towel. The bath was still a cube of rose-coloured steam.

Arkady looked down. The glass tiles on the floor were red. As he manoeuvred around the fountain he saw a red foot dangling from the opposite bench. The foot led to a small, desiccated body that he pulled towards the light.

Makhmud seemed to be eating a towel. So many puncture marks bled from his neck and chest that he looked as if he had been the target of an automatic weapon, but the taped grip of a knife stuck out of his withered stomach. Arkady remembered that he had worn a towel tied prudishly around his waist. Borya had carried his towel in his hand. Arkady felt his wrist. The chain and key were gone.

There was a knock on the door. When Arkady didn't answer, the door opened and Ali stepped halfway in. Steam rushed out. He looked fat and strong and his hair hung in ringlets around his eyes. 'Grandad, don't you think you've been in here long enough?'

Arkady said nothing. He felt the fact register in Ali's mind that steam should be white. Ali moved all the way in and shut the door. His pudgy hand groped through the mist. Arkady stood on the bench so that his feet wouldn't be visible in the light and walked around to the other side.

'Where are—'

For a moment there was nothing but the sound of water running over the rims of the fountain. Then he heard Ali lift the dead man and the suction as he pulled out the knife. With Makhmud off the glass tiles there was more light in the bath. Arkady saw Ali's feet turn around. 'Who's here?' Ali asked.

Arkady was silent. Two more Chechens were outside the door, and more were at different areas around the spa, he thought. Ali had only to call. 'I know you're here,' he said.

There was a flurry in the mist, a flutter of water particles spinning as Ali slashed at steam. He was partially impeded by the fountain. Arkady tried to slide by towards the door and felt a hot line draw across his back. He retreated. Ali had also felt contact. His next move was a thrust into the wood by Arkady's hand.

Arkady kicked out and Ali rocked. The fountain shifted, too. A hand grabbed Arkady's foot and dragged him down on to the bench, then to the floor. Ali took a handful of hair and pulled Arkady's head back, but the motion made him slip on the slick floor and lose the knife. Arkady heard it rattle on the far side of the bath.

They crawled over each other towards the sound. Ali had enough weight to force Arkady down and reach ahead. He got to his feet, a red buddha rising through clouds, with the knife in his hand. It was a boning knife with a long, narrow blade. Arkady hit him. Ali slid back and came forward again. Arkady feinted another punch and Ali leaned forward to keep his momentum. When the punch didn't come, he started to slide. He swung the knife and grabbed Arkady on the way down. They skated clumsily together for a second and landed under the fountain.

Ali heaved free and sat against the bench. He looked down, where his stomach was sliced open on a curve from his left hip to his right rib. He tried to hold his stomach together, but it was running out like the contents of a spilled cup. Ali sucked air. He couldn't get enough to talk. He had the expression of a man who had willingly jumped from a height to find to his horror and disbelief that this time there was no safety cord. He thought Arkady was helping him up, but Arkady was taking the key chain off his wrist.

Arkady gathered his towel and slippers and left the bath. The two Chechens had moved down to the pool, though Rita was gone. He was aware he was covered in blood. He dived into the nearest sitting pool, which was frigid, and climbed out, leaving red curls unravelling in the water. He rinsed in the second, heated pool and dried himself as he went to the changing room.

Ali's locker contained his shiny suit and a Louis Vuitton bag with a machine pistol, three clips and a Vuitton wallet fat with high-denomination Deutschmarks. Arkady dressed at normal speed and on the way down the stairs passed office workers who were hurrying up for after-hours relaxation and didn't seem to find it unusual how badly a Russian's clothes could fit. He returned his slippers to the cashier on the way out.

Chapter Thirty-Four

At Friedrichstrasse the garage door was still wedged open. Arkady climbed the stairs to the fourth floor. He left the lights off while he found his holdall and changed clothes. Ali's shoes pinched; he would have to get new ones tomorrow.

Timing was everything. If Borya heard that two bodies were found in the bath, he would be reassured. If he heard that both were Chechen, he'd be warned. The police would put together a description of the man who had left in Ali's suit. Beno and the other Chechens would already be looking for him.

Arkady was no expert on small arms, but he recognized the machine pistol as a Czech Skorpion, an automatic with a snout sticking out of an oversized slide. The clips each held twenty rounds, which the pistol could empty in two seconds. Perfect Ali fireworks; with a Skorpion, no one needed to aim.

When the door opened behind him, Arkady pushed home a clip and turned to fire.

Irina was in the doorway, so frozen in place she balanced between the light of the hall and the dark of the room. Arkady looked to see whether anyone else was in the hall, then pulled her in by the wrist and shut the door.

'I thought I heard you,' she said. Her voice came out as small as a pre-recorded tape.

'Where's Max?'

'Why do you have a gun?'

'Where is Max?'

'Dinner was over early. The Americans had to catch a plane. Max went to the gallery to see Rita. I came here to see you.' She pulled her wrist free. 'Why is it dark in here?'

When she tried to reach the switch, he pushed her hand away. She tried to open the door and he kicked it shut.

'I can't believe this, Arkady. It's happening again. You didn't come back for me, you came for someone else. You used me again.'

'No.'

'Yes, you did. Who are you after?'

Arkady was silent.

'Who else?' she asked.

He said, 'Max. Rita. Boris Benz, except that his real name is Borya Gubenko.'

He felt her pull away. She said, 'I used to think that the day I left you was the worst day of my life. This is worse, though. You've come back and outdone yourself. I've wasted my life on these two days.'

'You—'

'Five minutes ago I was yours. I ran down here. What do I see? Investigator Renko.'

'They killed a money dealer in Moscow.'

'What do I care about Soviet laws?'

'They murdered my partner.'

'Why should I care about Soviet police?'

'They killed Tommy.'

'People around you get killed. Max wouldn't hurt me. Max loves me, he'd do anything for me.'

'I love you.'

She hit him. First with the flat of her hand as hard as she could, then with her fists. He stood like a man leaning into the wind and let the pistol hang. He let it slide down his leg to the floor.

'I want to see your face,' Irina said.

She found the switch and turned it on. At once he could see something was wrong from the shock in her eyes. He put his hand up and felt a tender swelling from his temple to his brow. It had ballooned since he had left the bathhouse.

She looked at Ali's shirt on the floor. The back was soaked through, red as a flag. She unbuttoned the shirt he was wearing. He pulled it off and she turned him around to look. He heard her breath stop. 'You're cut.'

'It's not deep.'

'You're still bleeding.'

They turned on the bathroom light. In the cabinet mirror Arkady saw that Ali had slashed him from the right shoulder blade down to his belt. Irina tried to swab the blood from his back, but a facecloth was inadequate. Arkady set the pistol in the basin of the sink, undressed and stepped into the shower. She set the water on cool and cleaned him around the long red slice.

His muscles bunched and shook from the temperature of the water, then eased at the touch of her hand on his back. Her fingers found a scar on his rib, and, as if tactilely remembering, went to a puckered mark on his leg and then up to a slick ridge in the middle of his stomach, as if he were a map with four limbs.

Arkady turned off the water. He emerged from the shower while she pulled off her skirt and slipped in two steps from her pants. He lifted her up. She held on to his neck, wrapped her legs around his waist and arched herself so he could enter.

She opened herself even as she held him tight. Her mouth was hot. Her eyes were wide, as if afraid to close. Outside they were locked. Inside he travelled to the heart of her. They rocked, his back against the wall.

She cried with sharp intakes of breath. In the mirror, he saw the wall wiped with his blood. They looked like they were climbing together from a black pit to the light, on one pair of legs that had never been so strong before. She held on, her fingers curling in his hair.

'Arkasha!' She leaned back while inside he drove closer to a yielding balm. She held on as desperately, her mouth on his again, on his cheek and against his ear whispering with a voice as hoarse as his until the last inner resistance dissolved.

As his legs failed, they dropped slowly to their knees on the tiles of the floor, then he rolled on his back with her astride.

There was a moment of softness. She pulled her

blouse up over her head. Her breasts were bare, the tips dark and hard. He felt himself grow large again.

He filled his mouth with her breast. Her hair hung in a curtain around her face. Her tears sluiced down her neck and between her breasts to him, a mixed taste of salt and sweet. And forgiveness. This was the absolution from and for herself. When she threw her head back, he saw below her right eye a delicate blue flaw, her own Moscow scar. As she rode, her eyes closed as if he were rising inside along her spine up to her throat.

She twisted to be beneath him and spread to take him even further in, her legs high, in flight. He drove her along the tiles. Inside, she carried him deeper, as if they could shed their bodies, shed the lost years, shed the pain. Save each other. Two persons in one skin.

They lay on the bathroom floor as if in bed, her head pillowed on his chest, her leg resting over his so that he felt her bush of hair against his thigh, a subtle contract of trust. So what if their flanks were red from the blood on the tiles? If Orpheus and Eurydice had emerged intact from hell, what would they look like?

Even in shadow, Irina looked exhausted. 'I think you're wrong. Max isn't a killer. He's smart. As soon as reforms started in Russia, he said it wasn't reform, it was collapse. He was unhappy because our relationship hadn't developed the way he'd hoped. He wanted to come back a hero.'

'By defecting again?'

'By making money. He said the people in Moscow needed him more than he needed them.'

'He must have been right.' If he had been wrong, Max could never have returned to Germany.

'He wants to prove he's smarter than you.'

'He is.'

'Oh, no, you're brilliant. I said I'd never let you close to me again, yet here I am.'

'You think Max and I can work out our misunderstanding?'

'He helped you get to Munich, he helped you get to Berlin. He'd help again if I asked. Just wait.'

They sat on the floor by the living-room window with the lights off. They were classic refugees, Arkady thought, he in trousers, Irina in his shirt. Dried, the cut on his back looked like a zipper.

Where could they go? The police were searching for Makhmud's and Ali's killer. Assuming their guidelines were like the militia's, the Germans would broadcast his description, watch the airport and train stations, alert hospitals and pharmacies. Meanwhile, Borya's people and the Chechens would search the streets. Of course the Chechens would also be hunting Borya.

After midnight there was little traffic. Before Arkady saw cars down on the street he could identify their voices. The asthmatic rattle of Trabis, the clockwork ticking of diesel Mercedes. A white Mercedes went by at the speed of a trolling boat.

'Do you want to help?' he asked.

'Yes.'

'Get dressed and go up to your floor.' He gave her Peter's telephone number. 'Tell the person who answers where we are, then stay there until I come up.'

'Why don't we go up together? You can call.'

'I'll be with you in a minute. Keep calling until you get an answer. Sometimes he doesn't pick up right away.'

Irina didn't argue. She pulled on her skirt and went barefoot into the hall. The brief glimpse of light was blinding.

Below, the white Mercedes passed by again. Arkady heard the organ note of the Daimler before he saw it slowly approaching from the other direction. Max and Borya had to protect each other from Chechens as much as hunt for him. Max would be the one coming up, but Irina was right, he wouldn't hurt her.

The two cars passed each other in front of the building and drove on.

In a few years, when developers were done, Friedrich-strasse would be pulsing like a regular artery with department stores, fast-food outlets and espresso bars. Arkady felt he was keeping watch in the graveyard of the old East Berlin.

The two cars appeared again from the same directions as before. They must have circled the block. The

Mercedes parked across the street. The Daimler swung into the building garage.

There wasn't a lot of protection in an unfurnished flat. Arkady set his holdall directly in front of the door so that anyone opening it would focus first on the bag. He lay down on the far side of the floor facing the door to present as small a target as possible. Through the floorboards, Arkady felt the lift engage. He doubted Max would be alone. The crystal sconces in the lift were bright. Arkady wanted Max's irises and those of any friends dazzled, tight as pins.

The pistol came with a folding wire stock that Arkady straightened and put against his shoulder. He pushed the safety-rate selector to full automatic and laid the three other ammo clips in front of him like extra cards. The hall light edged the black rectangle of the door. In this frame the door seemed to vibrate.

In the hall, the lift stopped. He heard the doors slide open, pause, then shut. The lift went on up to the sixth floor.

There was a knock. Irina slipped in and shut the door behind her. Her eyes found Arkady. 'I knew you weren't coming up.'

'Did you call?'

'A machine answered. I left a message.'

'You're missing Max,' Arkady said. 'He's going up right now.'

'I know. I used the stairs. Don't try to make me leave without you. I did that before. That was my mistake.'

Arkady didn't take his eyes from the door. Max might

be temporarily confused to discover Irina gone, he thought. The lift stayed on the sixth floor for ten minutes though, longer than made sense unless Max was quietly coming down the stairs. But when the lift activated again it went straight down to the garage and seconds later Irina said she saw the Daimler leave, with the Mercedes following.

Chapter Thirty-Five

Irina said, 'I always imagined who you were with. I saw someone very young, for some reason. Small and dark, bright, passionate. I thought of places you would walk, what you'd talk about. When I wanted to torture myself, I imagined an entire day at the beach – blankets, sand, sunglasses, the sound of waves. She tunes a short-wave radio looking for romantic music when she happens to hear me. She stops, because the station is Russian after all. Then she moves the dial and you let her; you don't say a word. So I imagined my revenge. She gets a trip to Germany. By coincidence we share the same compartment of a train, and as it's a long trip we talk, and naturally I discover who she is. We usually end up on an icy platform in the Alps. She's a nice woman. I push her off the platform anyway for taking my place.'

'You kill her, not me?'

'I'm mad, I'm not crazy.'

From the floor of the flat, the street had a sound like surf. A wash of headlights moved across the ceiling.

Arkady saw a car park one block north on Friedrichstrasse. He couldn't tell the make, though he could see that no one got out. A second car parked a block south.

As the hours passed, he told her about Rudy and Jaak, about Max and Rodionov, about Borya and Rita. To him it was an interesting tale. He remembered his walk with Feldman, the art professor describing the revolutionary Moscow that had been. 'The squares will be our palettes!' We ourselves are palettes, Arkady thought. Possibilities. Inside Borya Gubenko was a Boris Benz. Inside an Intourist prostitute known as Rita was the Berlin gallery owner Margarita Benz.

Irina said, 'The question is who can we be? If we get out alive. Russian? German? American?'

'Whatever you want. I'll be putty.'

'Putty is not what comes to mind when I think of you.'

'I can be American. I can whistle and chew gum.'

'Once you wanted to live like the Indians.'

'Too late for that now, but I can live like a cowboy.'

'Rope and ride?'

'Drive cattle. Or stay here. Drive on the autobahn, climb the Alps.'

'Be a German? That's easier.'

'Easier?'

'You can't be American unless you stop smoking.'

'I can do that,' Arkady said, although he lit another cigarette. He exhaled and watched the smoke.

He screwed the cigarette out on the floor, put his

finger to his lips and motioned her to move away. It had taken him a moment to realize that the shift in the smoke was air stirring under the door. Stairwells produced suction, though he wouldn't have felt the draught if he hadn't been lying down.

He put his ear to the floor. See, he *could* live like an Indian. He heard the easing of shoes in the hallway.

Irina stood against a wall, not trying to hide or get small.

Around his holdall, Arkady saw the light at the bottom of the door, a white bar fading at one end.

He pressed his stomach into the floorboards. If he were any flatter he could slide under the door himself. He glanced at Irina. Her eyes watched him like hands keeping a man from falling off a cliff.

The door swung open. Light fanned in and a familiar bulk stepped across the threshold.

'You could get killed that way, Peter,' Arkady said.

Peter Schiller kicked the bag aside. He snorted at the sight of Arkady. 'Is this a shooting range?'

'We were expecting other people.'

'I'm sure you were.' Peter saw Irina, who returned his stare undiminished. 'Renko, we have Russians running all over Berlin. We have two dead mafiosos at the Europa Centre, cut up by someone who looked like you. What happened to your back?'

'I slipped.' Arkady got to his feet and shut the door.

'Arkady was with me,' Irina said.

'How long?' Peter asked.

'All day.'

'Lies,' Peter said. 'This is a gang war, isn't it. Benz is connected to one of them. The more I know about the Soviet Union, the more it sounds like one endless gang war.'

'In a way,' Arkady conceded.

'This afternoon you said you didn't even know this woman. Tonight she's your witness.' Peter walked around the room. He had the size and vigour of a Borya, but he was more Wagnerian, Arkady thought. A Lohengrin who had stumbled into the wrong opera.

'Where is Benz?' Arkady asked.

'Gone,' Peter said. 'He boarded a plane to Moscow an hour ago.'

It wasn't a bad time to leave Berlin. Maybe Borya was abandoning the entire Benz identity, Arkady thought. After this Boris Benz might never be seen again. Eliminating Makhmud was certainly a more important accomplishment than hanging on to the German asset of Fantasy Tours. All the same, he was surprised; Borya wasn't the type who settled for less than everything.

Peter said, 'Benz boarded the plane with Max Albov. They're both gone.'

'Max was coming here,' Irina said.

Arkady remembered how the lift had paused on his floor before continuing to the sixth. Max must have been packing. 'Why would he go to Moscow?'

'They got on a charter flight,' Peter said.

'How could they get on a late-night charter flight at the last minute?'

'There were lots of seats available at the last minute,' Peter said.

'Why?'

Peter looked at both Arkady and Irina. 'You haven't heard? You don't have a radio or a television here? You must be the only ones in the world who don't know. There's been a coup in Moscow.'

Irina softly laughed. 'It finally happened.'

'Who took over?' Arkady asked.

'A so-called Emergency Committee. The army rolled in. That's all anyone knows.'

A coup was the predicted catastrophe, the long-due sum of Russian fears, the Moscow night that followed day, yet Arkady was stunned. Stunned to find himself stunned. Max and Borya must have been surprised, too.

'With all that confusion, why would Max go back?' Arkady asked.

Irina said, 'It doesn't matter as long as they aren't coming here.'

'So you don't need this anymore.' Peter took the machine pistol away from Arkady, scooped the clips off the floor and stuffed them in his belt.

'We're safe,' Irina said.

'Not quite.' Peter motioned with the pistol for them to move to a corner. Arkady had put the safety on; now Peter pushed it off.

The room was still dark. Peter could see them against the glow of the glass better than they could see him, but Arkady caught the gesture for them not to move. In the hall the lift door opened. Irina took Arkady's hand. Peter motioned for them to lie down, then turned around and fired through the wall.

The Skorpion wasn't a particularly loud weapon, though its 7.62mm heads went through plasterboard as if it were paper. Peter walked along the wall, sawing waist-high, reloading as he went. A couple of rounds sparked off studs and nails. Shouts of outrage and confusion answered from the hall. Peter sprayed the second clip at knee level. Someone in the hall finally understood what was happening and fired back. A saucer-sized chunk of the wall exploded into the room. Peter used the shining hole as a target. He turned his back to the wall, disengaged the empty clip and inserted the last. An arc of holes answered through the walls. Peter walked to the high point of the arc, aimed low and fired, standing as close as a carpenter to the wall, surrounded by shafts of light. He moved to the side when a single shot responded, took his stance again, put the barrel in the hole and widened it with four more shots. He set the rate to manual and listened for moans, then placed a shot straight through the wall at his feet. Reset to automatic and finished the clip in a spray. In ten seconds Peter had put eighty rounds through the wall. On his way to the door, he let the Skorpion fall and reached around to the holster at the back of his belt for his own gun in case he needed it.

He didn't. Four Chechens lined the hall. Covered in blood and lime, they seemed to have suffered an industrial accident. Peter sorted through them, holding a cautionary gun to each head with one hand while he checked the carotid pulse with the other. A couple of the dead men held Skorpions of their own, for all the good it had done them. Arkady recognized Ali's friend from the Wall café staring up through a layer of dust. He didn't see Beno.

'They were parked outside when I got here,' Peter said. 'Two in each car.'

'Thank you,' Arkady said.

'*Bitte.*' Peter relished the word, like a mouthful of satisfaction.

People are confused when they wake to the sound of automatic fire. In an area of the city with so much construction, the first reaction is bourgeois outrage that anyone would break the law and drive a nail before dawn.

On the street, Arkady saw blue police lights floating far off down Friedrichstrasse, approaching without sirens since it was the middle of the night. He and Irina followed Peter around a corner to his car. As he started to drive, Peter monitored the police radio.

The responding officers had to locate the right address, then search four floors to find the bodies. There were no witnesses in the building. Arkady knew that possibly someone in a flat across the street had noticed them leave the building, but what was there to describe except two men and a woman seen from hundreds of metres away at an angle in the dark?

Peter said, 'There's nothing we can do about your

finger- and footprints; they're all over the flat, but they won't be easy to match. Your friend says she has no criminal record in Germany and there are no prints on you at all.'

'What about you?'

'I wiped the pistol and the clips, and I didn't use my own gun.'

'That's not what I meant. What about *you*?'

Peter drove for a while before he said, 'There's an official review every time you use a firearm. I don't want to explain why I shot four men that I didn't formally identify and warn. Through a wall? They could have been four visitors asking directions, collecting for Greenpeace or Mother Teresa.'

There was dust on Peter's fingers. He wiped them on his shirt.

'I don't necessarily want to explain how I was helping my grandfather. This is a Russian gang war. I'm not going to let it turn into a public scandal about him.'

'If they do trace this to me, Federov knows your name,' Arkady said.

'With the coup, I think the consulate in Munich has more on its mind than me or you.'

On the police band, a dispatcher ordered ambulances to Friedrichstrasse. The urgency of the voice contrasted to the calm of the Tiergarten, the park's rounded massing of shadow under morning stars.

Peter said, 'You've lied to me from the start, but I have to admit that I've found out more from your lies than the lies I've heard before. What is it about you, I wonder? I still expect the truth.'

Arkady said, 'If we go to Savigny Platz, I might be able to show it to you.'

While Arkady sat on an arbour bench, his back tightened. He needed aspirin or nicotine, but he had no pills and didn't indulge the telltale glow of a cigarette because the hedges around him stayed dark as the sky slowly lightened to grey. From the bench he couldn't see Peter and Irina, parked a block away. He could see the lights of the gallery, which looked as if they had burned through the night.

In Moscow, under the same roof of clouds, tanks were rolling through the streets. Was it a military putsch? Was the Party reclaiming its role as the vanguard of the people? Had the work of national salvation begun in earnest, with both hands? Just as the Party had protected Prague, Budapest and East Berlin before? There should at least be a rumble of distant thunder.

Except on Friedrichstrasse, the Germans seemed to have slept soundly through the night. German television had closed its eyes at the accustomed time. Arkady assumed that the planners of the coup would, at the minimum, detain a round thousand of the leading reformers, take control of Soviet television and radio, close the airports and telephone lines. He had no doubt that City Prosecutor Rodionov deplored the necessity of a coup, but, as every Russian knew, grim tasks were best done quickly. What Arkady did not understand was why Max and Gubenko had rushed back. How could an international flight land if the airports were closed? This would be a good time to listen to Radio Liberty. He wondered what Stas was saying.

A fine sprinkling of rain arrived. Then the rustling of unseen birds in the hedges, like the excitement of extras in the wings. Over the hedges spread the window lights of early risers, a sea sound of traffic, the browsing of street cleaners.

The two/two time of high heels passed on the other side of the hedge. Rita came into view, in matching poppy-red raincoat and hat, walking briskly between the garden squares that made up the plaza, right hand in her pocket. Arkady had seen her at least start to sign a dinner bill; he knew she was right-handed. When she unlocked the ground-floor door, she kept her hand in the pocket and looked back at the street before she entered.

Ten minutes later an armed guard came out, yawned and stretched and went off with loggy steps in the opposite direction.

After another ten minutes, the gallery lights went out. Rita reappeared, locked the door and started back across the Plaza, holding a canvas bag by the handles with her left hand.

Arkady caught up with her on the bag side in the middle of the plaza and said, 'That's no way to treat a five-million-dollar painting.'

She was startled enough to stop. He appreciated the

purity of her first reaction, which was fury. The contents of the bag were wrapped in plastic. 'I hope that's waterproof,' he said.

When Rita started walking again, he grabbed a handle of the bag. 'I'll shout for the police,' she said.

'Shout. I think the life of the German police is incredibly boring – at least it would be without Russians. The police would love to hear a story about you and Rudy Rosen, though the details might not help your business much. So Max and Borya left you all alone?'

Arkady liked Rita's resilience. She was used to dealing with men. A softer, more reasonable expression came over her face. 'I'm not going to wait around for Chechens to show up.' She offered a neutral smile. 'Can we talk out of the rain?'

He thought of slipping into an arbour, but Rita led him across the street to patio tables sheltered by an awning. It was the same restaurant as in the videotape, and she went to the same table at which she had raised her glass and said, 'I love you.' The inside of the restaurant was black. They had the patio and plaza to themselves.

Despite the early hour, Rita's face was made up in a mask that was ferocious and exotic. The red raincoat she wore had an oily quality that went well with her lips. Arkady unzipped her coat.

Rita asked, 'Why did you do that?'

'Let's say that you're an attractive woman.'

They sat, each with a hand on the bag under the

table. Because her coat was open, her pockets hung straight down, out of her immediate reach.

Arkady asked, 'Do you remember a Russian girl called Rita?'

Margarita said, 'I remember her well. A hard-working girl. One thing she learned was that she could always do business with the militia.'

'And Borya.'

'The Long Pond people protected the girls in the hotel. Borya was a friend.'

'But to make real money Rita had to get out of Russia. She married a Jew.'

'No crime.'

'You didn't get to Israel.'

Margarita held up her right hand to show her long nails. 'Do you see these building a kibbutz in the desert?'

'And Borya followed.'

'Borya had a perfectly legal proposition. He needed someone to help him recruit girls to come and work in Germany, and he needed someone to watch over them while they were here. I had experience.'

'There's more to it than that. Borya bought papers that created a Boris Benz, which was convenient when he went searching for a foreign partner in Moscow. This way he could be both. When you married Boris Benz, that enabled you to stay here, too.'

'Borya and I have a special relationship.'

'And if the wrong person called, you could play his maid and say that Herr Benz was holidaying in Spain.'

'A good whore is a good mimic.'

'Do you think the Boris Benz identity was a good idea? It was a weak point. Too much depended on it.'

'It worked fine until you came along.'

Arkady looked around at the empty tables without taking his hand from the bag. 'You made a videotape here and sent it to Rudy. Why?'

'Identification. Rudy and I had never met. I didn't want to give him a name.'

'He wasn't a bad character.'

'He was helping you. After Rodionov told us, it was just a matter of how to get rid of Rudy to the best effect. He knew about the painting. We let him think if he got it authenticated he could make his own sale. I gave him a slightly different painting. Borya said that if there was a big enough explosion we could get rid of Rudy and give Rodionov a reason to wipe out the Chechens, both at the same time.'

'Did you think Borya was going to stay here at some point and become Boris Benz for good?'

'Where would you rather be, Moscow or Berlin?'

'So in the videotape when you said, "I love you," you were saying it to Borya.'

'We were happy here.'

'And you were willing to do things for Borya that his wife never would, like going back to Moscow and delivering a fire bomb to Rudy. I had to ask myself why an obviously well-to-do tourist would stay somewhere as shabby and far out of the city as the Soyuz Hotel. The answer was that it was the hotel closest to the black market and the shortest ride with a fire bomb that didn't have a timer. You were brave, taking a chance you wouldn't blow up too. That's love.'

Rita wet her lips. 'You're so good at questions, could I ask you one?'

'Go ahead.'

'Why don't you ask about Irina?'

'Like what?'

Rita leaned forward as if she were whispering in a crowd. 'What Irina got out of it. Do you think Max paid for her clothes and all her little gifts because she made good conversation? Ask yourself what she was willing to do for him.'

Arkady felt his skin start to heat.

'They were together for years,' Rita said. 'Practically man and wife, like Borya and me. I don't know what she's telling you now. I'm just saying what she's doing for you she did for him. Any woman would.'

His ears burned. A hot meridian spread across his face. 'What are you really trying to say?'

Rita's head rested sympathetically to one side. 'It sounds as if she hasn't told you everything. I've known men like you all my life. Somebody has to be a goddess, and everyone else is a whore. Irina slept with Max. He bragged what she would do.' Rita invited him to lean towards her and lowered her voice even more. 'I'll tell you and you can compare.'

As soon as he felt tension on the handle ease, Arkady lifted the canvas bag. 'Shoot now and you'll put a hole through the painting. I don't think it's insured for that,' he said.

'You prick.'

Arkady grabbed the pistol when she brought it over the table. It was Borya's .22. He bent her wrist and twisted the gun free.

'You fuck,' Rita said.

Borya had betrayed her, run to Moscow and abandoned her with this puny gun. Arkady removed the rounds from the breech and clip and tossed the empty pistol in her lap. 'I love you, too,' he said.

Chapter Thirty-Six

At an airport souvenir shop, Arkady bought a beer tray and a cotton shawl embroidered with the rats of Hamelin. In a lavatory cubicle, he covered the painting in the shawl, wrapped the tray in bubble plastic, put it in Rita's canvas bag, and then rejoined Peter and Irina in a corner of the transit lounge.

Arkady said, 'Think of all the paintings and manuscripts confiscated from artists and writers and poets for seventy years, hidden away by the Ministry of the Interior and the KGB. Nothing is thrown away. Poets may get a bullet in the back of the head, but the poem is stuffed in a box and buried in a cellar. Then, at a magical moment, when Russia joins the rest of the world, all that evidence becomes valuable assets.'

'But they can't sell it,' Irina said. 'Art more than fifty years old cannot legally be taken from the Soviet Union.'

'But it can be smuggled out,' Peter suggested.

Arkady said, 'Bribes will do. Armoured tanks, trains and crude oil have been moved across the border. To bring a painting out is relatively easy.'

'Even so,' Irina said, 'the sale isn't valid if Russian law is broken. Collectors and museums don't like to be involved in international disputes. Rita couldn't sell *Red Square* if it came from Russia.'

Peter said, 'Maybe it's a fake from Germany. There were fantastic forgers in East Berlin, all out of work now. Has this painting really been examined?'

Irina said, 'Completely. It's been dated, X-rayed and analysed. It even has Malevich's thumbprint.'

'All of that can be faked,' Peter said.

'Yes,' Irina admitted, 'but it's a curious thing about fakes. They can be the best forgeries on earth, with the correct wood, paints and technique, but they don't look right.'

Peter cleared his throat. 'This is becoming spiritual.'

Irina said, 'It's like knowing people. After a while you learn the fake from the real. A painting is an artist's idea, and ideas can't be forged.'

'How valuable did you say the painting is?' Peter asked.

'Perhaps five million dollars. That's not much here,' Arkady said, 'but in Russia it's four hundred million rubles.'

'Unless it's fake,' Peter pointed out.

Arkady said, '*Red Square* is real and it's from Russia.'

'But they found it in a Knauer crate,' Irina said.

Arkady said, 'The crate is fake.'

'The crate?' Peter sat up. Arkady could see him mentally rearranging. 'I hadn't thought from that direction before.'

Arkady said, 'Remember, Benz wasn't interested in the art your grandfather stole. He had his own. He was interested in the crates your grandfather built – with Knauer carpenters, if you remember.'

'That's good,' Peter said appreciatively. 'That's very good.'

Arkady laid the shawl on Peter's knees. Peter sat up straighter. 'What are you doing?'

'The cultural atmosphere is a little unsettled in Moscow right now.'

'I don't want it.'

'You're the only person I can leave it with,' Arkady said.

'How do you know I won't disappear with it?'

'There's a kind of justice in making you a guardian of Russian art. Besides, it's a trade.' Arkady patted the jacket pocket with the passport and visa Peter had returned to him and the ticket he had bought with Ali's money.

There had been no difficulty in getting on the regular Lufthansa flight to Moscow. There was nothing like a military coup at a destination for decimating a passenger list. What Arkady still didn't understand was why leaders of the new Emergency Committee were allowing planes to land at all.

Stas limped off the Munich flight with a tape recorder and a camera. He was full of perverse good cheer. 'Such a glorious idiocy. The Emergency Committee didn't arrest any of the democratic leaders. Now it's a stand-off. The tanks are in Moscow, but they just keep circling around. Standards for oppression have really dropped.'

'How do you know what's happening?' Arkady asked.

'People are calling us from Moscow,' Stas said.

Arkady was amazed. 'The telephone lines are open?'

'That's what I mean about idiocy.'

'Does Michael know you're going?'

'He tried to stop me. He says it's a security risk and an embarrassment to the station if we're caught. He says Max called from Moscow to say that it's business as usual and there's nothing for me to be so excited about.'

'Does he know Irina's going?'

'He asked. He doesn't know.'

Though boarding had started, Arkady dove into a telephone booth. A recorded message on the phone repeated over and over that the international circuits were busy. The only way he could get through was to call continuously. As he was about to give up, he noticed a fax centre.

Polina had said she would take Rudy's fax machine. At the desk, he wrote her telephone number and the message 'Looking forward to seeing you. If you have a painting of Uncle Rudy's, could you bring it with you? Drive very carefully.' He added his flight number and arrival time and signed the message 'Arkady'. Then he asked for a fax directory and wrote a second message to Federov: 'Followed advice. Please inform City Prosecutor Rodionov of return today. Renko.'

The assistant's eyes opened as wide as a doll's. 'You must be anxious to get home,' she said.

'I'm always anxious when I go home,' Arkady said.

Irina waved him to the gate, where Stas and Peter Schiller were regarding each other like examples of different species.

Peter grabbed Arkady and pulled him aside. 'You can't leave me with this.'

'I trust you.'

'My short experience with you suggests that's a curse. What am I going to do with it?'

'Hang it some place with a constant temperature. Be an anonymous donor. Just don't give it to your grandfather. You know, the story about Malevich wasn't a lie. He did bring his paintings to Berlin to keep them safe. For the time being, do what he did.'

'It seems to me that Malevich's mistake was going back. What if Rita calls Moscow and says you took the painting? If Albov and Gubenko know you're coming, they'll be waiting for you.'

'I hope so. I wouldn't be able to find them, so they have to find me.'

'Maybe I should go with you.'

'Peter, you're too good. You'd scare them away.'

Peter shifted reluctantly.

Arkady said, 'Life can't be all fast cars and automatic weapons. You finally have a task worthy of you.'

'They'll kill you at the airport or on the way in. Revolutions are for settling scores. What's an extra body? At least here I can throw you in jail.'

'That sounds inviting.'

'We can keep you alive and extradite Albov and Gubenko.'

'No one has ever successfully extradited anyone from the Soviet Union. And who knows what government will be in place tomorrow? Max might be Minister of

Finance and Gubenko might be Minister of Sport. Besides, if there's a decent investigation into Ali and his friends, I think you'll be glad I'm far away.'

A soft gong announced the last boarding call. Peter said, 'Germany goes straight downhill every time Russians show up.'

'And vice versa,' Arkady said.

'Remember, there's always a cell waiting for you in Munich.'

'*Danke.*'

'Be careful.'

Peter scanned the boarding queue as Arkady joined Stas and Irina. From halfway down the ramp, Arkady could see Peter's head over the crowd, still carrying out the duty of a rearguard. At last glimpse, Peter took a fresh grip on the shawl and slipped away.

The canvas bag fitted in the overhead compartment. Arkady sat on the aisle, Stas by the window, Irina in between. When they took off, Stas's face took on an even more ironic expression than usual. Irina held on to Arkady's arm. She looked exhausted, blank, not unhappy. Arkady thought the three of them resembled refugees so confused that they were going the wrong way.

A number of passengers seemed to be journalists and photographers burdened with hand luggage. No one wanted to spend two hours at baggage reclaim while a revolution was going on.

Stas said, 'The Emergency Committee starts off by

saying Gorby's sick. Three hours later, one of the ring-leaders drops from hypertension. This is a strange coup.'

'You don't have visas. What makes you think they'll let you off the plane?' Arkady asked.

Stas said, 'You think any reporter here has a proper visa? Irina and I have American passports. We'll see what happens when we get there. This is the biggest story of our lives. How could we pass it up?'

'Coup or no coup, you're on a list of state criminals. So is she. You could be arrested.'

'You're going,' Stas said.

'I'm Russian.'

Though Irina's voice was soft, it possessed finality. 'We want to go.'

Germany stretched below, not the straight roads and quilted farms of the West, but narrower, more winding lanes and shabbier fields the further east they flew.

Irina rested her head on Arkady's shoulder. The feel of her hair cushioned against his cheek was so normal it was overpowering, as if he were briefly travelling through an alternative life he had missed. He never wanted to come down.

Stas talked nervously, like a radio at low volume. 'Historically, revolutions kill the people at the top. And usually Russians overdo it. The Bolsheviks killed the ruling class and then Stalin killed the original Bol-sheviks. But this time the only difference between Gorby's government and the coup is that Gorby isn't in it. Did you hear the complete statement of the Emergency Committee? They're seizing power to protect the people from, among other things, "sex, violence and glaring immorality". Meanwhile, troops keep moving into Moscow and people are erecting barricades to protect the White House.'

The White House was the Russian Parliament building on the river at the Red Presnya embankment. Presnya was an ancient neighbourhood given the honorific 'Red' for building barricades against the tsar.

Stas said, 'That won't stop tanks. What happened in Vilnius and Tbilisi were rehearsals. They'll wait until night. First they'll send in Internal troops with nerve gas and water cannons to disperse the crowd, and then KGB troops will storm the building. The Moscow commandant has printed three hundred thousand arrest forms, but the Committee doesn't want to use them. They expect people to see the tanks and slink away.'

Irina asked, 'What if Pavlov rang a bell and his dogs ignored him? They'd change history.'

'I'll tell you what else is strange,' Stas said. 'This is the longest I've ever seen so many journalists stay sober.'

Poland spread as dark as an ocean floor.

Food trolleys blocked the aisles. Cigarette smoke circulated along with theories. The army was moving already, to offer the world a *fait accompli*. The army would wait until dark to carry out its attack so that there would be fewer photographs. The Committee had the generals. The democrats had the Afghan vets. No one knew which way the young officers just back from Germany would lean.

'By the way,' Stas said, 'in the name of the Committee, City Prosecutor Rodionov has been rounding up businessmen and confiscating goods. Not all businessmen, just those against the Committee.'

When Arkady closed his eyes, he wondered what kind of Moscow he was returning to. It was a rare day that offered so many possibilities.

Stas said, 'It's been so long. I have a brother I haven't seen in twenty years. We call once a year, at New Year's. He called this morning to tell me he was going to the Parliament building to defend it. He's a little fat man with kids. How is he going to stop a tank?'

'Do you think you can find him?' Arkady asked.

'He told me not to come. Can you imagine that?' Stas stared out of the window for a long while. Vapour had condensed into balls of water between the double panes. 'He said he'd wear a red ski cap.'

'What is Rikki doing?'

'Rikki went to Georgia. He put his mother, daughter, TV and VCR in his new BMW and they went tootling off. I knew he would. He's a lovely man.'

The closer they got to Moscow, the more Irina looked like the girl who had left it, like someone returning to a fire with a particular glow. As if the rest of the world were an unlit, interim place. As if she were coming back with a vengeance.

Arkady thought he could be swept up by her and follow. Happily, once he was done with Borya and Max.

How much of all this was his private score, to atone in some small measure for Rudy, Tommy and Jaak? The dead aside, how much was because of Irina? Dealing with Max wouldn't erase the years she had known him. He could call them émigré years, but seen from a height Russia was a nation of émigrés, inside and out. Everyone was compromised to some degree. Russia had a history of such confusion that when a few moments of clarity arrived, everyone naturally rushed to the event.

In any case, Max and Borya were more likely to be the thriving specimens of a new age than he was.

As they crossed into Soviet air space, Arkady expected the plane to be ordered to turn around. When they approached Moscow, he thought it would be directed to a military base, refuelled and sent home. When seat-belt signs lit, there was a general, last-second extinguishing of cigarettes.

Out of the window were the familiar low woods, powerlines and grey-green fields that led to Sheremetyevo.

Stas held his breath like a man diving.

Irina held Arkady's hand as if she were the one bringing him home.

Part Four

MOSCOW

21 August 1991

Chapter Thirty-Seven

Arrival in Moscow was never a rose-strewn path, but this morning even the normal bleakness was accentuated. After Western lights, the baggage area was dark and cavernous, and Arkady wondered whether there had always been as much numbness in the faces, such a closed-down look to the eyes.

Michael Healey was waiting at the customs booths with a colonel of the Frontier Police. Radio Liberty's deputy director wore a trench coat of many belts and watched passengers through dark glasses. The Frontier Police was KGB; they wore green tunics with red tabs and faces screwed to perpetual suspicion.

Stas said, 'The winged shit must have taken the direct flight from Munich. Damn.'

'He can't stop us,' Irina said.

'Yes, he can,' Stas admitted. 'One word and the best that can happen to us is to be put back on the plane.'

Arkady said, 'I'm not going to let him take you back.'

'What are you going to do?' Stas asked.

'Let me talk to him. Just get in the queue.'

Stas hesitated. 'If we do get through, there's a car waiting to take us to the White House.'

'I'll meet you there,' Arkady said.

'You promise?' Irina asked.

In this setting, Irina's Russian seemed different, softer, with more dimensions. This was why beautiful ikons had plain frames.

'I'll be there.'

Arkady walked ahead to Michael, who followed his approach like a man pleased to find gravity working in his favour. The colonel seemed to be primed for more prosperous targets; he gave Arkady only passing notice.

Michael said, 'Renko. Good to be home? I'm afraid that Stas and Irina won't be able to stay. I have their tickets for the flight back to Munich.'

'You'd really point them out?' Arkady asked.

'They're ignoring orders. The station has paid them, fed them, housed them, and we're entitled to a little loyalty from them. I just want to make it clear to the colonel that Radio Liberty refuses any responsibility for them. They aren't assigned to this story.'

'They want to be here.'

'Then they're on their own and they can take their chances.'

'Are you going to cover the story?'

'I'm not a reporter, but I've been around reporters. I'll help.'

'You know Moscow?'

'I've been here before.'

'Where is Red Square?' Arkady asked.

'Everyone knows where Red Square is.'

Arkady said, 'You'd be surprised. A man here in Moscow got a fax just two weeks ago asking him, "Where is Red Square?"'

Michael shrugged.

Ahead of Stas and Irina, photographers top-heavy with gear and hand luggage clattered forward. Stas slipped fifty-Deutschmark notes into his passport and Irina's.

Arkady said, 'The fax came from Munich. In fact, it came from Radio Liberty.'

'We have a number of facsimile machines,' Michael said.

'The message came from Ludmilla's machine. It was sent to a black-market speculator who happened to be dead, so I was the one who read it. It was in Russian.'

'I suppose it would be, a fax between two Russians.'

'That's what fooled me,' Arkady said. 'Thinking that it was between two Russians and that it was about Red Square.'

Michael seemed to have found something to chew on. His dark glasses maintained a smooth gaze, but his jaw was busy.

Arkady said, 'But just when you least expect it, Russians can be exact. For example, the fax asked where was "Krassny Ploschad"? Now in English a square can be a place or a geometric figure, but in Russian the geometric figure is a *quadrat*. In the English language, Malevich painted *Red Square*. In Russian, he painted *Krassny Quadrat*. I didn't understand the message until I saw the painting.'

'What are you getting at?'

' "Where is Red Square the place?" makes no sense. "Where is Red Square the painting?" makes a great deal of sense when you're asking a man who thinks he will have the painting to sell. Ludmilla couldn't use the wrong word, no Russian could. Her office is next to yours, as I remember. In fact she works for you. How is your Russian, Michael?'

Siberians killed rabbits at night with torches and clubs. The rabbits would sit up and stare red-eyed at the beam until the club came down. Even through glasses, Michael had the transfixed attention of a rabbit. He said, 'All that proves is that whoever sent the fax thought the person on the other end was alive.'

'Absolutely,' Arkady agreed. 'It also proves that they were trying to deal with Rudy. Did Max put you and Rudy together?'

'There's nothing illegal about sending a fax.'

'No, but in your first message you asked Rudy about a finder's fee. You were trying to cut out Max completely.'

'It doesn't prove anything,' Michael said.

'Let's leave that up to Max. I'll show him the fax. It has Ludmilla's number on it.'

The customs queue shuffled forward again and Stas Kolotov, state criminal, stared directly through the glass at the officer, who compared eyes, ears, hairline, height to the picture in the passport, then riffled through the pages.

Arkady said, 'You know what happened to Rudy. It's not as if you'd be safer in Germany. Look what happened to Tommy.'

Stas got his passport back. Irina pushed her passport through the slot and presented a glare so defiant it invited arrest. The officer never noticed. After a professional frisk of the pages, her passport was returned and the queue moved forward.

'Michael, I don't think this is a time to call attention to yourself,' Arkady said. 'This is a time to ask, "What can I do for Renko, so that he won't tell Max?" '

Despite Stas's urging, Irina stopped at the far side of the booths. Arkady mouthed the word 'Go', and he and Michael watched Stas lead her through the exit.

It turned out that Michael did have something to say. 'Congratulations. Now that you got her in, she'll probably be killed. Just remember, *you* brought her back.'

'I know.'

A German television crew was negotiating the price of bringing in a video camera. The Emergency Committee, a colonel of customs informed them, had only that morning banned the transmission of video images by foreign reporters. The colonel accepted an informal bond of a hundred Deutschmarks to ensure that the crew didn't violate the Committee's laws. The other camera crews ahead of Arkady all had to make their own financial arrangements with customs and then race to their cars. Arkady's Soviet passport was a disappointment, a no sale. Like a cashier, the customs officer just waved him through.

An open double door led to the waiting hall and a reception line of emotional families waving cellophane-wrapped bouquets. Arkady watched for dry-eyed men with heavy sports bags. Since Sheremetyevo's metal detectors were haphazardly manned, the only persons sure to be unarmed and unprotected were arriving passengers. He held the canvas bag to his chest and hoped that Rita's call saying that he had the painting had got through.

Arkady recognized a small figure in a raincoat sitting alone in a row of chairs halfway down the waiting hall. Polina was reading a newspaper – *Pravda* by the look of it. Not a difficult guess, he admitted, since most papers had been banned the day before. He stopped for a cigarette by the flight board. Amazing. Here was an entire nation that could go about its business and keep its eyes down. Maybe history was nothing but a microscope. How many people had actually stormed the Winter Palace? Everyone else was searching for bread, trying to stay warm, or getting drunk.

Polina pulled her hair away from her eyes to give Arkady a sharp glance, dropped her newspaper and marched out. Through the window, he watched her join a male friend who was sitting on a scooter at the curb. The friend came to attention and moved to the rear seat. Polina sat in front, stomped the starter pedal with more fury than weight and drove off.

Arkady walked up the hall, took the seat she had left and looked at the newspaper, which said, 'The measures that are being taken are temporary. They in no way signal a renunciation of the course aimed at profound reforms . . .'

Under the newspaper were car keys and a note that said, 'White Zhiguli licence X65523MO. You shouldn't have come back.' Translated from Polina-ese, this meant, 'Welcome home.'

The Zhiguli was parked in the front rank of the terminal car park. On its floor was a square canvas covered in red paint. Arkady removed the beer tray from the plastic wrap, replaced it with the painting and put it into Margarita's bag.

He took the motorway south to Moscow. As he reached the dark of an underpass, he rolled down the passenger window and sailed the beer tray out.

At first the road seemed normal. The same unrepaired cars rolled at high speed over the same potholes, as if he had been gone for a single morning. Then, set back from the motorway behind a row of alders, he saw the dark outline of a tank; once he'd spotted one, he saw more tanks like dark watermarks on a screen of green.

There were no tanks on the road itself, in fact no sign of the military at all until the side road at Kurkino, where an endless line of armoured personnel carriers filled the slow lane. Soldiers wearing campaign caps rode in open hatches. They were boys with eyes streaming in the wind. Where the main road crossed the ring road and became the Leningrad Road, the caravan exited and headed into the city.

Arkady sped up and slowed down while a sleek, metallic-blue motorcycle with two riders stayed a steady hundred metres behind him. They could simply put a bullet in his head as they drove by. Except for the painting, on which they wouldn't want a scratch.

A light rain cleaned the street. Arkady looked on the dashboard. No wipers. He turned on the radio and after Tchaikovsky heard instructions on how to remain calm. 'Report the agitation of provocateurs. Allow responsible organs to carry out their sacred duty. Remember the tragic events of Tiananmen Square, when pseudo-democratic agents provoked unnecessary bloodshed.' The accent seemed to be on *unnecessary*. He also found a station operating from the House of Soviets that denounced the coup.

At a red light, the motorcycle pulled up behind him. It was a Suzuki, the same model he and Jaak had admired outside a cellar in Lyubertsy. The driver wore a black helmet, leather jacket and trousers sculpted like armour. When Minin hopped off the back, raincoat flapping, hand on hat, Arkady floored the accelerator, raced through the cross-traffic and left the bike behind.

The Voikovskaya metro station was surrounded by Muscovites who had emerged from rush-hour trains to study the clouds, arrange their raincoats and gather resolve for the dash home. Calmer souls loitered at the entrance to buy roses, ice cream, piroshki. The scene was surreal because it was so normal. Arkady began to wonder whether the coup was taking place in another city.

Cooperatives no bigger than shacks had set up business behind the station. He queued at one that sold Gauloises, razor blades, Pepsi, canned pineapple, and bought himself a bottle of carbonated mineral water and a tall lavender aerosol can of 'Romantic' deodorant. He went on to a secondhand shop that sold watches without hands and forks without tines and bought two collections of odd keys on wire loops. He tossed away the keys and kept the wires, which he added with the water and deodorant to the canvas bag.

Back in his car, Arkady returned to the avenue and cruised until he picked up the motorcycle again outside Dynamo Stadium. Traffic was becoming more congested. When the Sadoyava Ring was blocked by a procession of armoured personnel carriers, he made a left and followed them until he could slip through at Fadayeva. He first smelled, then saw the black exhaust of tanks idling in Manege Square along the west wall of the Kremlin. Crossing Tverskaya, he had a glimpse of Red Square, its brow of cobblestones blocked by lines of Internal troops spaced like hedgerows.

Shoppers emerged from Children's World bearing stuffed animals. On the pavement women held up stockings and used shoes for sale. A coup? It might be happening in Burma, darkest Africa, the moon. The majority of people were too exhausted. If there was shooting in the streets, they would still queue. They were sleepwalkers, and at this sunset Moscow was the centre of sleep.

Across the square from the toy shop, the Lubyanka looked equally somnolent. However, at the back of the building, a line of vans rolled out of the bay.

Arkady drove into his courtyard, squeezed the Zhiguli between the vodka cases around the church and opened the gate to a woodcart alley that ended on a bluff overlooking the canal. Carrying Rita's bag, he entered the back door of an apartment house and climbed the stairs to the fourth floor, where he had a view of the courtyard and the blue motorcycle lurking behind a delivery van a block away.

Arkady sympathized with Minin. On any other day, he would have cars and radio communications. What did he remember about his assistant? Impatience, a tendency to rush ahead. Minin got off the motorcycle, his face folded with doubt. He was followed by the driver, who pulled off his helmet to release long black hair. It was Kim, looking for Arkady now.

He went out of the back door and across an overgrown area that dwindled down to a dirt path threading between the back walls of workshops and brought him to the street on the far side of the motorcycle. Looking towards his house, he saw Minin push the buttons of the code box.

The Suzuki leaned on its kickstand, front wheel at an angle. The motorcycle had a blue plastic body that swept from windscreen to the exhaust like the cowling of a jet engine. Access to the exhaust pipes was tight; on the other hand, anything added wouldn't easily be seen. Arkady lay flat on the ground and felt the long scab on his back crack under his weight. The Suzuki had a four-into-two-into-one exhaust system running from header pipes to the silencer. When he shook the water bottle and sprayed them, the pipes spat back. Although he emptied the bottle on the pipes first, he still burned his fingers when he reached in, ran the wires around them and attached the deodorant can. Nevertheless, he twisted the wires tight. Jaak would have been proud.

By the time Arkady got to his feet, Minin and Kim had disappeared. He wiped his hands on his jacket, shouldered the canvas bag and followed their trail to the house. He saw the curtains in his window shift.

Minin had composed a grin. He let Arkady enter the flat and close the door before popping out of the bedroom hall with the huge Stechkin he had waved outside Rudy's flat. A Stechkin was a machine pistol like a Skorpion but not as ugly. In fact, it was the best-looking part of Minin.

The cupboard opened at Arkady's back and Kim stepped out. He had a face as flat as a jack of spades, and he held a Malysh, the same weapon he had carried to protect Rudy so long ago. He must have had it tucked inside his leather jacket. Arkady was impressed. It was like facing artillery.

Minin said, 'Give me the bag.'

'No.'

Minin said, 'Give it to me or I'll kill you.'

Arkady held the bag to his chest. 'The painting inside is worth millions of dollars. You don't want to put holes in it. It's fragile. If I even fall on it, it will be junk. How would you like to explain that to the city prosecutor? Also, I don't want to undermine your authority, Minin, but I can't think of anything more stupid than putting a target between two automatic weapons.' He asked Kim, 'Can you?'

Kim moved to the side.

'This is your final warning,' Minin said.

Arkady kept the bag cradled to his chest while he opened the refrigerator. Something like moss had grown out of the top of the kefir bottle. He shut the door on the smell.

'I'm curious, Minin. How do you think getting this painting will safeguard the Party's sacred mission?'

'The painting belongs to the Party.'

'So much does. Are you going to pull the trigger or not?'

Minin let the gun hang. 'It doesn't matter whether I shoot you. As of today, you're dead.'

'You're working with Kim. Aren't you a little embarrassed to be riding around with a homicidal maniac?' When Minin didn't answer, Arkady turned to Kim. 'Aren't you embarrassed to be riding with an investigator? One of you ought to be.' Kim smiled, but Minin was actually sweating with hate. 'I've always wondered, Minin, what do you have against me?'

'Your cynicism.'

'Cynicism?'

'About the Party.'

'Well.' Minin had a point.

'I thought, "Senior Investigator Renko, son of General Renko". I thought you'd be a hero. I thought it would be a great experience to work shoulder to shoulder with you, until my eyes came clear and I saw the sort of corrupt individual you are.'

'How?'

'We were supposed to be investigating criminals, but you always turned the investigation against the Party.'

'It just worked out that way.'

'I watched to see if you took money from the mafias.'

'I didn't.'

'No. You were more corrupt because you didn't care about money.'

Arkady said, 'I've changed. Now I want money. Call Albov.'

'Who's Albov?'

'Or I will walk out with the painting and you will have lost five million dollars.'

When Minin said nothing, Arkady shrugged and took a step to the door.

'Wait,' Minin said. He went to the wall phone in the hall, dialled and walked the receiver into the living room. Arkady examined his bookshelf and pulled out *Macbeth*. The gun that should have been behind Shakespeare was gone.

Minin had a moment of satisfaction. 'I was up here while you were in Germany. I searched everything.' Someone came on the line because Minin spoke rapidly into the receiver and explained Arkady's lack of cooperation. He looked up. 'Show me the painting.'

Arkady lifted the painting out of the bag and pulled it halfway out of the plastic wrap.

'There's been a mistake,' Minin said into the phone.

'There's no painting, just a canvas. It's red.' His forehead squatted. 'That's it? You're sure?' He held the phone out to Arkady, who took it only after slipping the painting back into the bag.

'Arkady?'

'Max,' Arkady said, as if they hadn't seen each other for years.

'I'm glad to hear your voice, and I'm certainly pleased you brought the painting with you. We spoke to Rita, who was upset and sure you were going to turn her over to the German police. You could have stayed in Berlin. What brought you back?'

'I would have stayed in jail. The police were searching for me, not Rita.'

'True. Borya did set you up. I'm sure the Chechens would also love to know where you are. It was very shrewd of you to return.'

Arkady asked, 'Where are you?'

Max said, 'The situation being what it is, I don't want to broadcast that. Frankly, I'm worried about Rodionov and his friends. I hope they have the resolve to finish this business quickly, because the longer they wait, the bloodier it will be. Your father would have wiped out the defenders at the White House already, wouldn't he?'

'Yes.'

'I understand that you want to make some sort of arrangement about the painting. What?'

'A British Airways ticket to London and fifty thousand dollars.'

'A lot of people are trying to leave town. I can give you any amount of rubles, but foreign currency is tight right now.'

'I'm giving the phone back to Minin.'

As soon as he had handed over the phone, Arkady took a serrated knife from a drawer by the sink. While each act was reported by Minin, he opened the window and pulled the wrapped painting out of the bag. The wrap's plastic bubbles started popping as Arkady sawed.

'Wait!' Minin said and offered the phone to Arkady again.

Max was laughing. 'I get the point. You win.'

'Where are you?'

'Minin will bring you.'

'He can lead me. I have a car.'

'I'd better talk to him,' Max said.

Minin listened grimly before he returned the receiver to the hall. 'You don't have to lead me,' Arkady said. 'Just tell me where he is.'

'There's going to be a curfew tonight. In case there are any road blocks, it's better if we all go.'

Kim broke into a grin bursting with personality. 'Hurry up. I want to come back and find the girl on the scooter.' It was the first time he had opened his mouth and it wasn't what Arkady wanted to hear.

'We saw Polina,' Minin said. His tone was judicial, though his tongue left a brief dab on his lips. 'You look like shit. You look like you've been rolling on the ground. They didn't treat you too well in Germany.'

'Travel is wearing,' Arkady said. Switching the bag

from hand to hand, he slipped out of the soiled jacket. The back of his shirt was black with old blood and red with new. Kim sucked in an audible breath. From the cupboard, Arkady selected a wrinkled but cleaner jacket, the one he had worn to the cemetery. From its pocket, he pulled his heirloom, his father's revolver, the Nagant, an ancient firearm with a hammer and wooden grip as curved as apostrophes. The four rounds, thick as silver nuggets, were in the pocket too. One arm through the handle of the bag, he swung open the cylinder and loaded it. He said, 'How many times have I told you, Minin? Don't just check the cupboards, check the clothes too.'

Minin and Arkady waited in the courtyard while Kim went for the motorcycle. The sky was dark. Lamplight and rain intensified the blue of the church and lent the windows of the house a pastel oiliness.

Arkady wondered whether the television hypnotist was on tonight. He said, 'I have a neighbour who collects my mail and puts food in my refrigerator. There was no mail and no food.'

Minin said, 'Maybe she knew you were away.'

Arkady let the inadvertent admission gape for a while. The church gutters were stopped up, as usual, and the overflow fell in bright threads. He said, 'She lived right below me. She always heard me walking around, and she probably heard you.'

Minin's face played in and out of the shadow of his hat.

'Why don't you just say you're sorry?' Arkady asked. 'She had a bad heart. Maybe you didn't mean to scare her.'

'She interfered.'

'Pardon?'

'She overstepped. She knew she was sick, I didn't. I take no responsibility for the consequences of her actions.'

'You mean you're sorry?'

Minin put the barrel of the Stechkin where the bag covered Arkady's heart. 'I mean shut up.'

'Do you feel left out?' Arkady asked more softly. 'That I'm depriving you? That they're having a revolution without us, you or me?'

Minin tried to be silent, but he shifted with the feet of an ardent spear-carrier. 'I'll be there when the action starts.'

Kim arrived on his motorcycle and followed them through the low arch of the alley. At the car, Minin jumped in on the passenger side. 'I'm not going to let you slip away again. And I'm not going to ride with that lunatic any more.'

Arkady considered compromises. If he refused to go, he wouldn't find Albov. Also he had pressed Minin about as far as he could. 'Put the gun in your left hand,' he said.

When Minin did as he was told, the selector catch of the Stechkin was above his top knuckle. Arkady reached across and turned the catch down from automatic to safe. He said, 'Keep your left hand where I can see it.'

The Zhiguli had a manual gear lever. Arkady rested the canvas bag by his left foot and laid the Nagant on his lap.

Kim led the way up Tverskaya in the central, official lane. Rain had chased most shoppers off the pavement. At Pushkin Square, a crowd carried banners in the direction of the parliament building. Many were kids, of course, but an unusual number were Arkady's age or older, men and women who had been children during the Khrushchev era, been allowed the heady oxygen of that short-lived reform, but had said nothing when Soviet tanks invaded Prague, and had lived in shame ever since. That was the essence of collaboration. Silence. They wore woollen caps over thinning hair, but miraculously they had discovered their voices.

In Mayakovsky Square, the traffic stopped for tanks moving to the parliament building by way of the Sadoyava Ring. 'The Taman division,' Minin said approvingly. 'They're the toughest. They'll roll right up the Parliament steps.'

But Moscow was such a big stage that most people seemed unaware of any coup. Couples walked hand in hand towards the cinema house. A kiosk opened its shutters and, oblivious to the rain, a queue of customers formed.

Tracks wove in and out of shining macadam. Tver-skaya became Leningrad Prospect, which turned on to the Leningrad Road. Kim raced ahead. At speed, at least, Arkady wasn't afraid of Minin shooting him. 'We're taking the airport road?' he said.

Minin said, 'You're falling behind. I don't want to miss the fireworks.'

Along Chimki Lake there was a sudden calm, a shadow among the urban lights, the monotone of drops on the water. A line of slitted headlights appeared, more tanks moving at a walking pace. Beyond them was the horizontal haze of the ring road.

The motorcycle began to trail sparks, as if it were dragging its silencer. The can Arkady had wired to the exhaust pipes was one-third propane gas, which expanded two thousand one hundred times. Ignited, it expanded like a blowtorch. Flames fanned up the plastic sides and through the ports and over the rear tyre in jets of fire that seemed to drive the bike forward. Arkady saw Kim looking at his rearview mirror, where the light would first appear to be coming from, then from side to side, then finally down, where the entire plastic sheath was igniting like a meteor around his legs and boots. The bike oscillated from lane to lane. That must be an impulse, Arkady thought, to try to outrun fire. Though the road was crossing an arm of the lake and there was no place to turn off, Kim jumped the shoulder of the road.

'Stop! Stop the car!' Minin pushed his gun against Arkady's head.

The motorcycle touched a side rail and rolled as a tumbling flame. Kim stayed with it through a long slide, then the bike spun again, spewing a helmet from the blaze. As Arkady accelerated by, Minin pulled the trigger. The Stechkin didn't fire. He remembered the safety and switched hands, but Arkady picked up the Nagant and held it on him.

'Get out.' He slowed to fifteen kilometres, enough to knock Minin off his feet when he landed. 'Jump.'

Arkady leaned, opened the passenger door and pushed Minin. But as the door swung wide, Minin swung with it and hung on to the outside of the door, pressed against the glass. He broke the window with the Stechkin, got his elbows in and aimed. Arkady tapped the brake. As Minin fired, the side window behind Arkady exploded. The door swung out and Minin's hat flew off. The motorcycle burned far behind. The lights of the ring road flyover appeared ahead. Arkady kicked the door open again with his right foot and with his left pushed the accelerator all the way down. Minin's weight and the air resistance forced the door back in. Minin began firing as soon as the door swung inward, spraying the rear and side windows as Arkady steered across the shoulder of the road and hit the corner of the flyover.

The dark under the ramp was enormously quiet. When the Zhiguli came out of the other side, the passenger door hung like a broken wing and Minin was gone.

Arkady had no guide left, but he was fairly certain

by now that he was returning to a place he knew. He brushed glass off the bag. Air tunnelled sideways through the hanging door and out of the shattered windows.

Arkady remembered that Soviet cars always evolved, doing with fewer and fewer luxuries.

This was the new model.

Chapter Thirty-Eight

The first time Arkady had come through the village, women were selling flowers on the side of the road. Not tonight. This place seemed abandoned, its windows dark, as if the houses themselves were trying to hide. Sunflowers bobbed in the rain. A cow, startled by his headlights, bolted from a garden.

On the road, water was pooling in tread tracks. Tanks had kneaded mud to a soft consistency, and where they had moved two abreast they had rolled over fences and fruit trees. The Zhiguli had front-wheel drive, and Arkady ploughed ahead in low gear as if he were steering a boat.

The fields on the other side of the village were flatter and the way was straighter, though more chewed up. Half a kilometre on, the right shoulder of the road was crushed by tracks emerging from a field. Mud stood stacked like bricks, showing how the tanks manoeuvred on to the road, advancing one tread to pivot on the other. It would have looked like a military parade, Arkady thought, except that it had started from a potato field, with as few witnesses as possible.

The rest of the way was smooth enough for him to use only running lights. Fields stretched in rows from grey to black and, with the rain, the road looked like a causeway between bodies of water.

There were no bonfires this time to guide him. Coasting between animal pens into the yard of the Lenin's Path Collective, he saw the rusting tractors and reapers waiting like so many theatrical props, the garage where he had discovered General Penyagin's car, the slaughterhouse, the shed full of consumer goods. In the middle of the yard the lime pit in which he had found Jaak and Penyagin was swollen by the rain.

Arkady got out, pushed the revolver under his jacket into the back of his belt and held the bag chest-high. With every step, milk that was a combination of rainwater and septic lime filled his shoes.

On the far side of the yard, past the barn and shed, were headlights. Closer, he saw that the car was a Mercedes and that the lights were aimed at a figure climbing out of one of the command bunkers, the one that had been locked during his first visit. Borya Gubenko struggled under the weight of a flat, rectangular wooden case. His shoes were encased in mud, his camelhair coat was hemmed with mud. He lifted the case up to the back end of a Lenin's Path lorry, the same one that had sold Jaak a short-wave radio.

On the floor of the lorry, Max arranged the case against others standing on end. 'You almost missed us,' he called to Arkady. 'We were packing to go.'

Borya seemed less pleased. He was drenched, his hair stuck to his brow, as if he'd played a full day of goal in foul weather. He looked past Arkady. 'Where's Kim?'

'Kim and Minin had road problems,' Arkady said.

Max said, 'I'm sure. I would have been disappointed if they had made it. Anyway, I knew you'd come.'

'I have to get more.' Borya gave both Max and Arkady a hard look and trudged back to the bunker. The case that had just been loaded bore fading stamps: FOR REFERENCE ONLY AND CONFIDENTIAL MATERIALS OF THE ARCHIVES OF THE USSR MINISTRY OF THE INTERIOR.

'How is Irina?' Max asked.

'She's happy.'

'What I'd forgotten about Irina was her impulse for martyrdom. How could she resist you?' Max seemed bemused, a little distracted. 'I didn't get a chance to say a proper goodbye in Berlin because Borya was in a rush. He's unromantic. Once a pimp, always a pimp. He's still hanging on to his prostitutes and slot machines. He wants to change, but the criminal mind is so limited. Russians don't change.'

'Where is Rodionov?' Arkady asked.

'He's keeping the prosecutor's office in line for the Emergency Committee. The Committee is such a collection of Party hacks and all-out drunks that Rodionov shines by comparison. Of course the Committee will win because people always recognize the crack of a whip. The trouble is that the coup is so unnecessary. Everyone could have been rich. Now we're going to go back to a system of counting crumbs.'

Arkady nodded at the crates. 'Those aren't crumbs. Why are you moving them if the Committee's going to win?'

'In the wildly remote unlikelihood that the attack fails, people are going to trace the route of the tanks very quickly. Once they're here, they'll go right to the bunkers and we'd lose everything.'

Arkady looked in the direction Borya had taken. 'I'd like to see.'

'Why not?' Max jumped off the lorry, happy to oblige.

The space inside the bunker was narrow, designed for a dozen men to sweat out a nuclear holocaust and live like apes around a vented generator so that they could radio troops that had been crisped in the field. The generator, throbbing like a Trabi, powered red emergency lights. Borya was covering a painting with an oilcloth.

'It's tight,' Max said. 'We had to get rid of the radiation counters. They didn't work anyway.'

He played a torch across it. The eye imagines a mine with veins of malachite, lapis or gold twisting into the ground. This was even brighter. Some of the paintings were crated, but most were not, and the beam lit a canvas covered with the primal stripes of Matiushin, in colours as fresh and vivid as the day they were painted. Max moved the beam across a palm tree by Sarian, Vrubel's swans, radiant suns of Iuon, an angelic cow by Chagall. An ogre by Lissitzky overlapped erotic sketches by Annenkov. Above a kaleidoscope by Popova was a fighting cock, all whirling feathers, by Kandinsky. Arkady felt he had stepped into a mine of images, as if a culture had been buried.

Max shared his pride. 'This is the greatest collection of Russian avant-garde art in the world, outside of the Tretykov Gallery. Of course the Ministry didn't know what they were confiscating because the militia doesn't have any taste. The people they stole from did, however, and that's what matters, right? First the Revolution confiscated all the private collections. The revolutionaries themselves wanted the most revolutionary paintings. Then Stalin purged his old friends and the militia got its second harvest of great art. And it kept on harvesting, right through Khrushchev and Brezhnev, hiding it all away beneath the Ministry. That's how great collections are built. Let's give Rodionov credit because when he was given the task of cleaning up the Ministry archives he recognized *Red Square* and it led him to all these, which are great art but not in the class of *Red Square*. He also had the sense to know that while he could smuggle the painting out himself, he needed someone more sophisticated both to get it out and legally put it on the market. You have the painting?'

Arkady said, 'Yes. Do you have the money and the ticket?'

Borya looked around with the experienced eye of a man who knew how complicated transactions could be. 'It's crowded here. We need more room.'

Max led the way into the slaughterhouse. The torch picked out butchering blocks, meat grinders and waist-high tallow pots out of the dark. The pig still hung on the wall hook, exuding an odour of swamp gas.

Max shared cigarettes. 'I'm not surprised to see you.

What I do find hard to believe is that you're willing to make an arrangement. That simply isn't like you.'

'Yet here I am and here's the painting,' Arkady said.

'So you say. I think that fifty thousand dollars is high, considering there's no one else you can sell it to. You don't have the provenance or the Knauer crate.'

'You agreed.'

'Tonight of all nights, it's difficult to get money together,' Max said.

Borya stared out at the rain. 'Take the painting.'

Max said, 'You're always in a hurry. We can work this out between intelligent men.'

'What is it with the two of you?' Borya asked. 'I don't get it.'

'Renko and I have a uniquely intimate relationship. We're practically partners already.'

'Like last night in Berlin? When you came down from the flat, you said Renko and the woman weren't there. I'm starting to think I should have been the one to go up. Now that I think about it, I've done all the work.'

'Don't forget Rita,' Arkady reminded him. 'She must have overwhelmed Rudy.'

Borya's shrug became a smile. 'Rudy wanted to get into the art business with us, so we let him. He thought someone was coming from Munich with a fabulous picture for him to authenticate. He didn't know who Rita was because he didn't have a very active sex life.'

'Unlike Borya,' Max said. 'Some people might call Borya indiscriminate. Bigamous, at the least.'

'So Rita brought him one,' Borya said. 'Max painted it. He called it a "special effect", like in the movies.'

Max said, 'Kim added his own incredibly crude bomb because Borya demanded that everything in the car burn up.'

Borya said, 'Kim can do all kinds of things with blood.'

'Such a rich life Borya has had,' Max said. 'Rita and Kim. In TransKom we had a venture that could have become a true multinational company if we'd just stayed away from gambling and whores. It's the same with this Emergency Committee. They could all have been real millionaires, but they couldn't tolerate even the least reform. It's like having a partner who's in the last stage of syphilis, when it attacks the brain. Now we're just salvaging what we can.'

'I had a friend named Jaak, a detective. I found him here in a car. What happened?' Arkady asked.

'Bad timing,' Borya said. 'He ran into Penyagin. The general was checking the communications in the other bunker, and your detective asked why there was a battalion of tanks and troops sitting in the field. He thought it was going to be like Estonia all over again, there was going to be a coup and he was going back to Moscow to sound the alarm. It was lucky I was around. I was checking a shipment of VCRs in the shed, and I stopped him before he got to the car. But Penyagin was in a dither.'

Max said, 'Borya doesn't like grandstand critics.'

'Penyagin was supposed to be head of CID. You'd think he'd have seen a body before,' Borya said.

'He was a desk man,' Arkady said.

'I guess so. Anyway, Minin was supposed to investigate, but you showed up first.' Borya stared at the lime pit. Like a man who can't trust his good fortune, he said, 'I can't believe you came back.'

'Where is Irina?' Max said.

'Munich,' Arkady lied.

'Let me tell you where I'm afraid she is,' Max said. 'I'm afraid she came back with you and went to the White House, where she'll probably be gassed and shot. The Committee may be a collection of Party nobodies, but the troops know their job.'

'When is the attack?' Arkady asked.

'At three a.m., the middle of the night. They'll use tanks, it will be fast but messy, and they won't be able to spare reporters even if they wanted to. Do you know what would really be ironic? If this time I saved Irina.' Max let a moment pass. 'Irina's here. Don't deny it. You still have a little glow. She wouldn't let you come back without her.'

Strangely, Arkady couldn't deny it, though a lie would have served. As if a word could make her disappear.

'Now do you know what you wanted to know?' Borya asked Max, who nodded. 'Let's see the painting.' He snatched the bag away and opened it while Max played the torch through the plastic wrapper. 'Just like Rita told us.'

Max lifted the painting out. 'It's heavy.'

Borya protested, 'It's the painting.'

Max unwound the wrapper. 'It's wood, not canvas, and it's the wrong colour.'

'It's red,' Borya pointed out.

'Red is all it is,' Max said.

Arkady thought it looked like one of Polina's better efforts – vibrant crimson instead of dark maroon, with more consistent brushstrokes.

'I think it's a fake, but what's your opinion?' Max turned the torch directly into Arkady's eyes.

Borya kicked Arkady's legs out from under him, then, with no loss of momentum, moved in and planted a second kick in his chest. Arkady rolled into the dark. On his side, he freed the Nagant from the back of his belt. Faster, Borya produced a pistol and fired into the floor, spraying Arkady with cement.

Arkady shot. Max had been standing in the black behind the torch. Now he held a shield of phosphorescent white brilliant enough to light the entire slaughterhouse. Polina's canvas had ignited as the slug passed through and Borya squinted, stupefied by the blaze. When he understood what was happening, he turned back to Arkady and fired wildly four more times.

Arkady shot and Borya dropped to his knees, into the soft folds of his coat. The breast of his coat showed a bright rosette. Arkady fired a second time in the same place. Borya swayed, rose and lined his eye on the sight. His eye wavered. As he started to topple, he put his hands on the floor, still clutching his gun, trying to keep the world from spinning. His head rolled and he relaxed and slumped across the floor at full length, as if he were diving for a penalty kick.

On the floor, the canvas produced a white light that broke into noxious smoke against the ceiling. Max's sleeve was on fire. He was framed in the doorway for a moment, a man attached to a torch. Then the doorway went dark as he ran.

The room filled with a chemical cloud that made Arkady's eyes smart. Flames ran down the blood grooves of the floor. His chest stung, though he didn't feel particularly hurt. Borya's kick had folded his knees in a new way and his legs were numb. He dragged himself over the floor to retrieve his jacket and Borya's gun, a little TK pistol that was empty. He crawled to the door, pulled himself up so he could exit erect, staggered out and leaned as stiff as a ladder against the wall until sensation returned.

Except for the glow from the slaughterhouse and the headlights of the car, the yard was black. The surface of the lime pit seemed to seethe, but it could have been an effect of raindrops. There was no sign of Max, not even smoke.

The Mercedes raised its headlights and Arkady's shadow jumped the pit. He stepped back and started to slide, so he stood his ground and fired the Nagant's last shot, though his eyes were so overloaded he could barely see his hand, much less the car. The lights swung to the side, raced across the yard and on to the road that led through the pens towards the village. Rear lights danced from rail to rail until they disappeared.

More on one foot than two, Arkady made it to the step of the lorry. His knees still felt rearranged. When he opened his shirt, he could see that his stomach was pocked by cement, no worse than bird shot. He wished he had a cigarette.

He buttoned his shirt and pulled on his jacket, then removed the ignition keys from the lorry and locked the back doors. Hobbling to the bunker, he closed it against the rain.

In the last glimmer from the fire, Arkady staggered across the yard to the Zhiguli. The car had the gaping windows and crumpled fender of an abandoned wreck. Max had a head start. On the other hand, the Zhiguli was made for Russian roads.

Chapter Thirty-Nine

The radio picked up nothing. He might have been travelling cross-country in Antarctica.

He would have seen more in Antarctica. Snow reflected light, potato fields absorbed it. Man didn't have to search for black holes in the universe when there were potato fields.

By the time he was on the main road his leg had stiffened so much from Borya's kick that he no longer knew whether he had the clutch in or out.

The ring road was a starry line of lights. Above the city, tracers dotted the sky. He tried the radio again. Tchaikovsky, of course. And a warning that a curfew was in effect. Arkady turned the radio off. The air rushing through the broken windows made him feel as if he were re-entering earth.

On the Leningrad Road, armoured personnel carriers stopped pedestrians but let cars drive through, so that there were long spaces of sparse traffic and empty pavements, then crossing spotlights and military vehicles proceeding slowly on a circular road. The Zhiguli, bent door and all, drew no attention. At night a driver noticed that Moscow was a series of concentric rings, and how much the city resembled orbits of light in a void.

The metro and buses were shut down, but people started to reappear out of the dark singly or in groups of ten or twenty, heading south. Troops were non-existent at one corner, massed at another. In the Red Presnya district, Belovaya Street was blocked by tanks; the idling of their engines sounded like deep thought. Regular militia was off the street.

Arkady parked and joined the pavement traffic. A stream of men and women poured towards the river. Obviously some knew each other because there was quiet murmuring. Mostly they were silent, as if everyone was saving their breath for the walk, and as if that breath, visible in the rain, was sufficient communication. No one mentioned or looked askance at Arkady's bloody shirt. To his relief, his leg functioned, knee and all.

Arkady let himself be swept forward. As the pace quickened, he found himself running with the crowd down a sidestreet that had been turned into a dead end by Army lorries parked bumper to bumper. But the canvas cover of one lorry was pulled back and people helped each other up, as if climbing a country stile.

On the other side of the lorry, the wide Red Presnya embankment road curved between the river and the White House. It was a relatively new building, a four-storey marble box, with two wings that seemed to float lightly in the glow of thousands of people carrying candles. Arkady's group squeezed single file between buses and bulldozers that had been set up as a barricade.

Along the way, he heard every rumour. The Kremlin

was ringed by tanks ready to move down Kalinin Prospect to the White House. Riot troops were stationed outside the Bolshoi. The Committee was bringing gas canisters by barge to the embankment. Commandos had found tunnels to the White House. A helicopter assault would land on the roof. KGB agents inside the building would machine-gun the defenders at a secret signal. It would be like China or Romania, but worse.

People hovered over small warming fires of rubbish, and around votive candles stuck in makeshift altars of wax. These were people who in all their lives had gone to no public demonstration that hadn't been organized and herded. Yet their feet had brought them here.

There weren't that many ways to reach the White House because the bridge over the river was barricaded at both ends. Arkady spotted Max among people arriving from Kalinin Prospect. From a distance he didn't look much the worse for their encounter. He nestled one hand in his jacket pocket but moved with an assurance that parted the crowd.

At a corner of the White House a tank that had come to its defence was festooned with flowers. The soldiers on board were boys with the hollowed eyes of determination and fear. The turrets swung towards Kalinin Prospect, where Arkady heard the drumming of automatic fire.

Students played guitars and sang the kind of sappy songs about birches and snow that usually drove Arkady insane. Around another fire, rockers took sustenance from a heavy metal tape. Ancient veterans linked their arms and puffed up the ribbons on their chests. A battalion of street cleaners, women in black coats and scarves, stood like a row of witnesses.

Arkady manoeuvred to keep Max in sight since he seemed to know better which way to go. He skirted a barricade being assembled from construction timbers, mattresses, iron fences and benches. Its builders were men with attaché cases and women with shopping bags who had come directly from offices or bakeries to the battle line. A girl in a raincoat scaled the makeshift palisade to tie a Russian tricolour to the highest plank. Polina looked down from her vantage point without seeing Arkady in the crowd below. Her cheeks were flushed, her hair free, as if she were riding the crest of a wave. Her friend from the airport climbed after her, more carefully, as the sound of weapons fire resumed.

Max moved towards the White House steps. As Arkady tried to catch up, he saw there was a defence plan of sorts. Within the barricades, women had established themselves as an outer ring that soldiers would have to break through first. Then came shock troops of unarmed citizens, a mass that water cannon or armour would have to dislodge. Behind them, younger and stronger men were organized in divisions of about a hundred. At the bottom of the White House steps Afghan veterans stood in groups of ten. Above them was an inner cordon of men wearing dark ski masks over their faces and shouldering weapons. At the top of the steps flashbulbs popped around microphone booms and still and video cameras.

'You?' A heavy-set militiaman grabbed Arkady's arm.

'I'm sorry.' Arkady didn't recognize him.

'You almost ran me over last week. You caught me taking money.'

'Yes.' Arkady remembered; it had been after the funeral.

'See, I'm not just someone who stands in the street and takes bribes.'

'No, you're not. Who's in the ski masks?'

'A mix – private guards, volunteers.' The officer's concern, however, was Arkady. He gave his full name, insisted that Arkady repeated it and shook his hand. 'You never know another man until a night like tonight. This is the drunkest I've ever been and I haven't touched a drop.'

Everywhere was a common look of astonishment, as if they had all ventured individually to drop their life-long masks and show their faces. Middle-aged teachers, muscular lorry drivers, wretched apparatchiks and feck-less students wandered with expressions of recognition. As in *I know you.* And among all these Russians, not a bottle. Not a one.

Afghan veterans with red bandannas around their arms patrolled the perimeter. Many still wore their fatigues and desert caps; some held radios, others carried sacks of Molotov cocktails. Everyone had said how they'd gone to Afghanistan, become drug addicts and lost the war. These were the ones who had lost their friends in the dust of Khost and Kandahar, fought on the long retreat on the Salang Highway, and avoided the anonymous ride home in zinc-lined coffins. They seemed very competent tonight.

Max's hair and one ear looked singed and he had changed jackets, but he seemed remarkably untouched after having one arm on fire at the collective. He stopped by worshippers huddled around a priest who was blessing crucifixes at the base of the White House steps, then turned and saw Arkady.

A loud-hailer announced, 'Attack is imminent. We are observing a blackout. Extinguish all lights. Those with gas masks, prepare to put them on. Those without should tie wet cloths over their noses and mouths.'

Candles disappeared. In the sudden dark there was a stir of thousands of people slipping on goggles and tying scarves and handkerchiefs over their faces. Undeterred, the priest pronounced blessings through a gas mask. Max had slipped away.

The loud-hailer appealed, 'Please, reporters, do not use your flashes!' But someone stepped out of the White House door and the response at the top of the steps was an explosion of flashbulbs and spotlights. Arkady saw Irina among the reporters and Max climbing towards her.

The embankment was blacked out, but the scene at its centre was an illuminated theatrical production. The steps spilled over with lights and journalists trading shouts in Italian, English, Japanese and German. There were no official press passes for the coup, but reporters were professionals used to mayhem and Russians were accustomed to disorder.

Max was stopped halfway up by two men in ski masks. Half an eyebrow was gone and his neck had a raw sheen, yet he seemed unruffled and in control. Cameramen rushed up and down the steps on either side. He enlisted the guards in conversation, employing a confidence that commanded any situation, an ability to flow around any obstacle.

'...you can help me,' Arkady heard him say as he caught up. 'I was on my way here to join my colleagues from Radio Liberty when my car was deliberately run off the road. In the explosion one man was killed and I sustained injuries.' He turned and pointed to Arkady. 'There is the driver of the other car. He followed me.'

The guards had cut eye holes in woollen ski caps that were a contrast to their satiny suits. One was hulking and the other small but they both had sawn-off rifles that they held casually in Arkady's direction. He didn't even have his father's gun, and by now he was so exposed he couldn't retreat.

'He's not from the press. Ask for his identification,' Arkady said.

Max took hold of the situation like the director of a film. It looked like a stage set: wet marble steps, vying spotlights, the fairy lights of tracers in the clouds. 'My identification burned in the car. It doesn't matter because a dozen reporters here will vouch for me. Anyway, I think I recognize this character. His name is Renko, one of Prosecutor Rodionov's gang. Ask *him* for identification.'

Dark eyes stared through the masks. Arkady had to

admit that Max had defined the moment neatly; here his identification could condemn him.

'He's lying,' Arkady said.

'Is his car a wreck? Is my friend dead?' In the clamour of the steps, Max's whisper was all the more effective. 'Renko is a dangerous man. Ask him whether he killed someone or not? See, he can't deny it.'

'Who was your friend?' the smaller guard asked through his mask. Though he had no face to go by, Arkady thought he had heard the voice before. The guard could have been militia, like the traffic officer at the bottom of the steps, or a private bodyguard.

'Borya Gubenko, a businessman,' Max said.

'*The* Borya Gubenko?' The guard seemed to know the name. 'He was a *close* friend?'

Max answered quickly, 'Not close, but Borya sacrificed himself to get me here and the fact is that Renko brutally killed him and tried to do the same to me. Here we are, surrounded by the cameras of the world. The world is watching these steps tonight and you can't afford to let a reactionary agent like Renko near anybody. The main thing is to get him out of sight. If you should trip and accidentally shoot him in the back, it would be no loss to the world.'

'I don't do anything accidentally,' the guard assured him.

Max began to sidestep to continue his climb. 'As I said, I have colleagues here.'

'I know you do.' The guard lifted off his mask. It was Beno, Makhmud's grandson. His face was almost as dark as his mask, but it was lit by a smile. 'That's why we came, in case you tried to join them.'

The larger guard pulled Max back by the tail of his jacket.

Beno said, 'We were looking for Borya too, but if Renko took care of him then we can concentrate on you. We'll start by asking about four cousins of mine who died at your apartment in Berlin.'

'Renko, what is he talking about?' Max asked.

'Then we'll talk about Makhmud and Ali. We'll make a night of it,' Beno said.

'*Arkady,*' Max appealed.

'But since it's going to get dangerous here in about an hour,' Beno said, 'we'll do our talking somewhere else.'

Max wrestled free of his jacket and ran diagonally down the steps. On the bottom he slid on wax, crashed through the line of veterans, regained his feet and fought his way through the circle of worshippers around the priest. The larger Chechen raced after him. Beno waved calmly to a group in the crowd and pointed in Max's direction. In his white shirt he was easy to follow.

Beno regarded Arkady. 'Are you staying? It's going to be bloody.'

'I have friends here.'

'Get them out.' Beno slipped his cap back on and adjusted the holes over his eyes. He took one step down. 'If you don't . . . good luck.' Then he plunged, a darkling figure, into the crowd.

Arkady climbed the rest of the way to the jostling

lights at the top of the steps, arriving just as a spokes-man emerged protected by guards carrying bulletproof shields. Ringed by cameras, the spokesman was outside just long enough to announce that snipers had been seen on the roofs of nearby buildings. He ducked back inside, but the journalists stayed in clear sight to check notes.

Irina had appeared with the spokesman and remained outside. 'You came,' she said.

'I said I would.'

Her eyes were set deep with exhaustion and brilliant with exhilaration at the same time. 'Stas is inside on the second floor. He's on the phone to Munich. They still haven't cut the wires. He's broadcasting right now.'

Arkady said, 'You should be with him.'

'Do you want me to go?'

'No, I want you with me.'

As more tracers fanned across the sky, the loud-hailer insisted futilely on an absolute blackout. Cigarettes re-appeared, along with gas masks – a perfect Russian blackout, Arkady thought. As the sound of patrol boats approached on the river, the lights of a convoy appeared on the far bank. The women in the outer line had started to sing, and parts of the crowd picked up the song and swayed, so that in the dark they looked like the surface of a sea or a plain of grass in a wind.

'Let's wait with them,' Irina said.

They walked down the steps, through the defence ring of the Afghan veterans and past a row of candles freshly lit. Other veterans in wheelchairs had arrived and had run chains through the spokes of their wheels. Women shielded them with umbrellas. Now *that* must have made a parade on the way here, Arkady thought.

'Keep walking,' Irina said. 'I didn't get down here before. I want to see.'

People were sitting, standing, slowly circulating as if at a fair. They would all have different memories later, Arkady was sure. One would say that the atmosphere around the White House was quiet, grim, purposeful; another would remember a circus air. If they lived.

All his life Arkady had avoided marches and demonstrations. This was the first one he had ever willingly come to. The same could be said, he suspected, of the other Muscovites around him. Of the construction workers who formed the unshaven and unarmed inner troops. Of the mousy apparatchiks who set down their briefcases to hold each other's hands and form a human ring – so many that there were fifty rings of them around the White House. Of the women doctors who somehow, out of empty hospital storerooms, had scavenged bandages.

He had an urge to see each of their faces. He wasn't the only one. A priest moved along a row giving absolution. He noticed artists who were making white pencil portraits on black paper, passing them as gifts.

The mystery is not the way we die, it's the way we live. The courage we have at birth becomes hoarded, shrivelled, blown away. Year after year, we become more alone. Yet, holding Irina's hand, for this moment, for this night, Arkady felt that he could swing the world.

A piece of paper was pushed into his other hand. Look at this face, it was familiar, it was the one he was born with. Sound grew as a vortex in the rain. Overhead a helicopter shook the air and shot a flare that dropped, a matchhead in a well.

Acknowledgements

I must acknowledge the guidance I received in Moscow from Vladimir Kalinichenko, Alexander Stashkov, Yegor and Chandrika Tolstyakov; in Munich from Rachel Fedoseyev, Jorg Sandl and Nougzar Sharia; and in Berlin from Andrew Nurnberg and Natan Federowskij. Generous assistance was also given by Nan Black and Ellen Irish Smith, courage by Knox Burger and Katherine Sprague.

Once again, the compass of this book was Alex Levin. The errors are all mine.

HAVANA BAY

Martin Cruz Smith, former journalist and magazine
editor, is now a full-time writer. He is the author of
nine previous novels, including *Gorky Park, Polar Star*
and *Red Square* – the Arkady Renko trilogy which has
sold millions of copies worldwide. *Havana Bay* is his
long-awaited new Arkady Renko novel which Macmillan
publish in hardback on 22 October 1999. What follows
overleaf is the first chapter . . .

Chapter One

A police boat directed a light toward tar-covered pilings and water, turning a black scene white. Havana was invisible across the bay, except for a single line of lamps along the seawall. Stars rode high, anchor lights rode low, otherwise the harbor was a still pool in the night.

Soda cans, crab pots, fishing floats, mattresses, Styrofoam bearded with algae shifted as an investigation team of the Policía Nacional de la Revolución took flash shots. Arkady waited in a cashmere overcoat with a Captain Arcos, a barrel-chested little man who looked ironed into military fatigues, and his Sergeant Luna, large, black and angular. Detective Osorio was a small brown woman in PNR blue; she gave Arkady a studied glare.

A Cuban named Rufo was the interpreter from the Russian embassy. 'It's very simple,' he translated the captain's words. 'You see the body, identify the body and then go home.'

'Sounds simple.' Arkady tried to be agreeable, although Arcos walked off as if any contact with Russians was contamination.

Osorio combined the sharp features of an ingenue with the grave expression of a hangman. She spoke and Rufo explained, 'The detective says this is the Cuban method, not the Russian method or the German method. The Cuban method. You will see.'

Arkady had seen little so far. He had just arrived at the airport in the dark when he was whisked away by Rufo. They were headed by taxi to the city when Rufo received a call on a cellular phone that diverted them to the bay. Already Arkady had a sense that he was unwelcome and unpopular.

Rufo wore a loose Hawaiian shirt and a faint resemblance to the older, softer Muhammad Ali. 'The detective says she hopes you don't mind learning the Cuban method.'

'I'm looking forward to it.' Arkady was nothing if not a good guest. 'Could you ask her when the body was discovered?'

'Two hours ago by the boat.'

'The embassy sent me a message yesterday that Pribluda was in trouble. Why did they say that before you found a body?'

'She says ask the embassy. She was certainly not expecting an investigator.'

Professional honor seemed to be at stake and Arkady felt badly outclassed on that score. Like Columbus on deck, Captain Arcos scanned the dark impatiently, Luna his hulking shadow. Osorio had sawhorses erected and stretched a tape that read NO PASEO. When a motorcycle policeman in a white helmet and spurs on his boots arrived, she chased him with a shout that could have scored steel. Somehow men in T-shirts appeared along the tape as soon as it was unrolled – what was it about violent death that was better than dreams? Arkady wondered. Most of the onlookers were black; Havana was far more African than Arkady had expected, although the logos on their shirts were American.

Someone along the tape carried a radio that sang, '*La fiesta no es para los feos. Qué feo es, señor. Super feo, amigo mío. No puedes pasar aquí, amigo. La fiesta no es para los feos.*'

'What does that mean?' Arkady asked Rufo.

'The song? It says, "This party is not for ugly people. Sorry, my friend, you can't come." '

Yet here I am, Arkady thought.

A vapor trail far overhead showed silver, and ships at anchor started to appear where only lights had hung moments before. Across the bay the seawall and mansions of Havana rose from the water, docks spread and, along the inner bay, loading cranes got to their feet.

'The captain is sensitive,' Rufo said, 'but whoever was right or wrong about the message, you're here, the body's here.'

'So it couldn't have worked out better?'

'In a manner of speaking.'

Osorio ordered the boat to back off so that its wash wouldn't stir the body. A combination of the boat's light and the freshening sky made her face glow.

Rufo said, 'Cubans don't like Russians. It's not you, it's just not a good place for a Russian.'

'Where is a good place?'

Rufo shrugged.

This side of the harbor, now that Arkady could see it,

was like a village. A hillside of banana palms overhung abandoned houses that fronted what was more a cement curb than a seawall that stretched from a coal dock to a ferry landing. A wooden walkway balanced on a black piling captured whatever floated in. The day was going to be warm. He could tell by the smell.

'*Vaya a cambiar su cara, amigo. Feo, feo, feo como horror, señor.*'

In Moscow, in January, the sun would have crept like a dim lamp behind rice paper. Here it was a rushing torch that turned air and bay into mirrors, first of nickel and then to vibrant, undulating pink. Many things were suddenly apparent. A picturesque ferry that moved toward the landing. Little fishing boats moored almost within reach. Arkady noticed that more than palms grew in the village behind him; the sun found coconuts, hibiscus, red and yellow trees. Water around the pilings began to show the peacock sheen of petroleum.

Detective Osorio's order for the video camera to roll was a signal for onlookers to press against the tape. The ferry landing filled with commuters, every face turned toward the pilings where, in the quickening light floated a body as black and bloated as the inner tube it rested in. Shirt and shorts were split by the body's expansion. Hands and feet trailed in the water; a swim fin dangled casually on one foot. The head was eyeless and inflated like a black balloon.

'A *neumático*,' Rufo told Arkady. 'A *neumático* is a fisherman who fishes from an inner tube. Actually from a fishing net spread over the tube. Like a hammock. It's very ingenious, very Cuban.'

'The inner tube is his boat?'

'Better than a boat. A boat needs gasoline.'

Arkady pondered that proposition.

'Much better.'

A diver in a wet suit slid off the police boat while an officer in waders dropped over the seawall. They clambered as much as waded across crab pots and mattress springs, mindful of hidden nails and septic water, and cornered the inner tube so that it wouldn't float away. A net was thrown down from the seawall to stretch under the inner tube and lift it and the body up together. So far, Arkady wouldn't have done anything differently. Sometimes events were just a matter of luck.

The diver stepped into a hole and went under. Gasping, he came up out of the water, grabbed onto first the inner tube and then a foot hanging from it. The foot came off. The inner tube pressed against the spear of a mattress spring, popped and started to deflate. As the foot turned to jelly, Detective Osorio shouted for the officer to toss it to shore: a classic confrontation between authority and vulgar death, Arkady thought. All along the tape, onlookers clapped and laughed.

Rufo said, 'See, usually, our level of competence is fairly high, but Russians have this effect. The captain will never forgive you.'

The camera went on taping the debacle while another detective jumped into the water. Arkady hoped the lens captured the way the rising sun poured into the windows of the ferry. The inner tube was sinking. An arm disengaged. Shouts flew back and forth between Osorio and the police boat. The more desperately the men in the water tried to save the situation the worse it became. Captain Arcos contributed orders to lift the body. As the diver steadied the head, the pressure of his hands liquefied its face and made it slide like a grape skin off the skull, which itself separated cleanly from the neck; it was like trying to lift a man who was perversely disrobing part by part, unembarrassed by the stench of advanced decomposition. A pelican sailed overhead, red as a flamingo.

'I think identification is going to be a little more complicated than the captain imagined,' Arkady said.

The diver caught the jaw as it dropped off from the skull and juggled each, while the detectives pushed the other black, swollen limbs pell-mell into the shriveling inner tube.

'*Feo, tan feo. No puedes pasar aquí, amigo. Porque la fiesta no es para los feos.*'

The rhythm was . . . what was the word? Arkady wondered. Unrelenting.

Across the bay a golden dome seemed to burst into flame, and the houses of the Malecón started to express their unlikely colors of lemon, rose, royal purple, aquamarine.

It really was a lovely city, he thought.

*

Light from the high windows of the autopsy theater of the Instituto de Medicina Legal fell on three stainless-steel tables. On the right-hand table lay the *neumático*'s torso and loose parts arranged like an ancient statue dredged in pieces from the sea. Along the walls were enamel cabinets, scales, X-ray panel, sink, specimen shelves, freezer, refrigerator, pails. Above, at the observation level, Rufo and Arkady had a semicircle of seats to themselves. Arkady hadn't noticed before how scarred Rufo's brows were.

'Captain Luna would rather you watched from here. The examiner is Dr Blas.'

Rufo waited expectantly until Arkady realized he was supposed to react.

'*The* Dr Blas?'

'The very one.'

Blas had a dapper Spanish beard and wore rubber gloves, goggles, green scrubs. Only when he appeared satisfied that he had a reasonably complete body did he measure it and search it meticulously for marks and tattoos, a painstaking task when skin tended to slide wherever touched. An autopsy could take two hours, as much as four. At the left-hand table Detective Osorio and a pair of technicians sorted through the deflated inner tube and fishnet; the body had been left tangled in them for fear of disturbing it any more. Captain Arcos stood to one side, Luna a step behind. It occurred to Arkady that Luna's head was as round and blunt as a black fist with red-rimmed eyes. Already Osorio had found a wet roll of American dollar bills and a ring of keys kept in a leaky plastic bag. Fingerprints wouldn't have survived the bag, and she immediately dispatched the keys with an officer. There was something appealingly energetic and fastidious about Osorio. She hung wet shirt, shorts and underwear on hangers on a rack.

While Blas worked he commented to a microphone clipped to the lapel of his coat.

'Maybe two weeks in the water,' Rufo translated. He added, 'It's been hot and raining, very humid. Even for here.'

'You've seen autopsies before?' Arkady asked.

'No, but I've always been curious. And, of course, I'd heard of Dr Blas.'

Performing an autopsy on a body in an advanced stage of putrefaction was a delicate as dissecting a soft-boiled egg. Sex was obvious but not age, not race, not size when the chest and stomach cavities were distended, not weight when the body sagged with water inside, not fingerprints when hands that had trailed in the water for a week ended in digits nibbled to the bone. Then there was the gaseous pressure of chemical change. When Blas punctured the abdomen a flatulent spray shot loudly up, and when he made the Y incision across the chest and then to groin, a wave of black water and liquefied matter overflowed the table. Using a pail, a technician deftly caught the viscera as they floated out. An expanding pong of rot – as if a shovel had been plunged into swamp gas – took possession of the room, invading everyone's nose and mouth. Arkady was glad he had left his precious coat in the car. After the first trauma of the stench – five minutes, no more – the olfactory nerves were traumatized and numb, but he was already digging deep into his cigarettes.

Rufo said, 'That smells disgusting.'

'Russian tobacco.' Arkady filled his lungs with smoke. 'Want one?'

'No, thanks. I boxed in Russia when I was on the national team. I hated Moscow. The food, the bread and, most of all, the cigarettes.'

'You don't like Russians, either?'

'I love Russians. Some of my best friends are Russian.' Rufo leaned for a better view as Blas spread the chest for the camera. 'The doctor is very good. At the rate they're going you'll have time to make your plane. You won't even have to spend the night.'

'Won't the embassy make a fuss about this?'

'The Russians here? No.'

Blas slapped the pulpy mass of the heart in a separate tray.

'You don't think they're too indelicate, I hope,' Rufo said.

'Oh, no.' To be fair, as Arkady remembered, Pribluda used to root through bodies with the enthusiasm of a boar after nuts. 'Imagine the poor bastard's surprise,' Pribluda would have said. 'Floating around, looking up at the stars, and then bang, he's dead.'

Arkady lit one cigarette from another and drew the smoke in sharply enough to make his eyes tear. It occurred to him that he was at a point now where he knew more people dead than alive, the wrong side of a certain line.

'I picked up a lot of languages touring with the team,' Rufo said. 'After boxing, I used to guide groups of singers, musicians, dancers, intellectuals for the embassy. I miss those days.'

Detective Osorio methodically laid out supplies that the dead man had taken to sea: thermos, wicker box, and plastic bags of candles, rolls of tape, twine, hooks and extra line.

Usually, an examiner cut at the hairline and peeled the forehead over the face to reach the skull. Since in this case both the forehead and the face had already slipped off and bade adieu in the bay, Blas proceeded directly with a rotary saw to uncover the brain, which proved rotten with worms that reminded Arkady of the macaroni served by Aeroflot. As the nausea rose he had Rufo lead him to a tiny, chain-flush lavatory, where he threw up, so perhaps he wasn't so inured after all, he thought. Maybe he had just reached his limit. Rufo was gone, and walking back to the autopsy theater on his own, Arkady went by a room perfumed by carboys of formaldehyde and decorated with anatomical charts. On a table two feet with yellow toenails stuck out from a sheet. Between the legs lay an oversized syringe connected by a tube to a tub of embalming fluid on the floor, a technique used in the smallest, most primitive Russian villages when electric pumps failed. The needle of the syringe was particularly long and narrow to fit into an artery, which was thinner than a vein. Between the feet were rubber gloves and another syringe in an unopened plastic bag. Arkady slipped the bag into his jacket pocket.

When Arkady returned to his seat, Rufo was waiting with a recuperative Cuban cigarette. By that time, the brain had been weighed and set aside while Dr Blas fit head and jaw together.

Although Rufo's lighter was the plastic disposable sort, he said it had been refilled twenty times. 'The Cuban record is over a hundred.'

Arkady bit the cigarette, inhaled. 'What kind is this?'

' "Popular." Black tobacco. You like it?'

'It's perfect.' Arkady let out a plume of smoke as blue as the exhaust of a car in distress.

Rufo's hand kneaded Arkady's shoulder. 'Relax. You're down to bones, my friend.'

The officer who had taken the keys from Osorio returned. At the other table, after Blas had measured the skull vertically and across the brow, he spread a handkerchief and diligently scrubbed the teeth with a toothbrush. Arkady handed Rufo a dental chart he had brought from Moscow (an investigator's precaution), and the driver trotted the envelope down to Blas, who systematically matched the skull's brightened grin to the chart's numbered circles. When he was done he conferred with Captain Arcos, who grunted with satisfaction and summoned Arkady down to the theater floor.

Rufo interpreted. 'The Russian citizen Sergei Sergeevich Pribluda arrived in Havana eleven months ago as an attaché to the Russian embassy. We knew, of course, that he was a colonel in the KGB. Excuse me, the new Federal Security Service, the SVR.'

'Same thing,' Arkady said.

The captain – and in his wake, Rufo – went on. 'A week ago the embassy informed us that Pribluda was missing. We did not expect them to invite a senior investigator from the Moscow prosecutor's office. Perhaps a family member, nothing more.'

Arkady had talked to Pribluda's son, who had refused to come to Havana. He managed a pizzeria, a major responsibility.

Rufo went on. 'Fortunately, the captain says, the identification performed today before your eyes is simple and conclusive. The captain says that a key found in the effects was taken to the apartment of the missing man where it unlocked the door. From an examination of the body recovered from the bay, Dr Blas estimates that it is a Caucasoid male approximately fifty to sixty years of age, one hundred sixty-five centimeters in height, ninety kilos in weight, in every regard the same as the missing man. Moreover, the dental chart of the Russian citizen Pribluda you yourself brought shows one lower molar filled. That molar in the recovered jaw is a steel tooth which, in the opinion of Dr Blas, according to the captain, is typical Russian dental work. Do you agree?'

'From what I saw, yes.'

'Dr Blas says he finds no wounds or broken bones, no signs of violence or foul play. Your friend died of natural causes, perhaps a stroke or aneurysm or heart attack, it would be almost impossible to determine which for a body in this condition. The doctor hopes he did not suffer long.'

'That's kind of him.' Although the doctor appeared more smug than sympathetic.

'The captain, for his part, asks if you accept the observations of this autopsy?'

'I'd like to think about it.'

'Well, you accept the conclusion that the body recovered is that of the Russian citizen Pribluda?'

Arkady turned to the examining table. What had been a bloated cadaver was now split and gutted. Of course, there had been no face or eyes to identify anyway, and finger bones never did yield prints, but someone had lived in that ruined body.

'I think an inner tube in the bay is a strange place to find a Russian citizen.'

'The captain says they all think that.'

'Then there will be an investigation?'

Rufo said, 'It depends.'

'On what?'

'On many factors.'

'Such as?'

'The captain says your friend was a spy. What he was doing when he died was not innocent. The captain can predict your embassy will ask us to do nothing. We are the ones who could make an international incident of this, but frankly it is not worth the effort. We will investigate in our own time, in our own way, although in this Special Period the Cuban people cannot afford to waste resources on people who have revealed themselves to be our enemy. Now do you understand what I mean?' Rufo paused while Arcos took a second to compose himself. 'The captain says an investigation depends on many factors. The position of our friends at the Russian embassy must be taken into account before premature steps are taken. The only issue we have here is an identification of a foreign national who has died on Cuban territory. Do you accept it is the Russian citizen Sergei Pribluda?'

'It could be,' Arkady said.

Dr Blas sighed, Luna took a deep breath and Detective Osorio weighed the keys in her palm. Arkady couldn't help feeling like a difficult actor. 'It probably is, but I can't say conclusively that this body is Pribluda. There's no face, no prints and I doubt very much that you will be able to type the blood. All you have is a dental chart and one steel tooth. He could be another Russian. Or one of thousands of Cubans who went to Russia. Or a Cuban who had a tooth pulled by a Cuban dentist who trained in Russia. Probably you're right, but that's not enough. You opened Pribluda's door with a key. Did you look inside?'

Dr Blas asked in precisely snipped Russian, 'Did you bring any other identification from Moscow?'

'Just this. Pribluda sent it a month ago.' Arkady dug out of his passport case a snapshot of three men standing on a beach and squinting at the camera. One man was so black he could have been carved from jet. He held up a glistening rainbow of a fish for the admiration of two whites, a shorter man with a compensating tower of steel-wool hair and, partially obscured by the others, Pribluda. Behind them was water, a tip of beach, palms.

Blas studied the photograph and read the scribble on the back. 'Havana Yacht Club.'

'There is such a yacht club?' Arkady asked.

'There *was* such a club before the Revolution,' Blas said. 'I think your friend was making a joke.'

Rufo said, 'Cubans love grandiose titles. A "drinking society" can be friends in a bar.'

'The others don't look Russian to me. You can make copies of the picture and circulate them.'

The picture went around to Arcos, who put it back into Arkady's hands as if it were toxic. Rufo said, 'The captain says your friend was a spy, that spies come to bad ends, as they deserve. This is typically Russian, pretending to help and then stabbing Cuba in the back. The Russian embassy sends out its spy and, when he's missing, asks us to find him. When we find him, you refuse to identify him. Instead of cooperating, you demand an investigation, as if you were still the master and Cuba was the puppet. Since that is no longer the case, you can take your picture back to Moscow. The whole world knows of the Russian betrayal of the Cuban people and, well, he says some more in that vein.'

Arkady gathered as much. The captain looked ready to spit.

Rufo gave Arkady a push. 'I think it's time to go.'

Detective Osorio, who had been quietly following the conversation, suddenly revealed fluent Russian. 'Was there a letter with the picture?'

'Only a postcard saying hello,' Arkady said. 'I threw it away.'

'*Idiota*,' Osorio said, which nobody bothered to translate.

'It's lucky you're going home, you don't have many friends here,' Rufo said. 'The embassy said to put you in an apartment until the plane.'

They drove by three-story stone town houses transformed by the revolution into a far more colorful backdrop of ruin and decay, marble colonnades refaced with whatever color was available – green, ultramarine, chartreuse. Not just ordinary green, either, but a vibrant spectrum: sea, lime, palm and verdigris. Houses were as blue as powdered turquoise, pools of water, peeling sky, the upper levels enlivened by balconies of ornate ironwork embellished by canary cages, florid roosters, hanging bicycles. Even dowdy Russian cars wore a wide variety of paint, and if their clothes were drab most of the people had the slow grace and color of big cats. They paused at tables offering guava paste, pastries, tubers and fruits. One girl shaving ices was streaked red and green with syrup, another girl sold sweetmeats from a cheesecloth tent. A locksmith rode a bicycle that powered a key grinder; he wore goggles for the sparks and shavings flying around him as he pedaled in place. The music of a radio hanging in the crook of a pushcart's umbrella floated in the air.

'Is this the way to the airport?' Arkady asked.

'The flight is tomorrow. Usually there's only one Aeroflot flight a week during the winter, so they don't want you to miss it.' Rufo rolled the window down. 'Phew, I smell worse than fish.'

'Autopsies stay with you.' Arkady had left his overcoat outside the operating theater and separated the coat now from the paper bag holding Pribluda's effects. 'If Dr Blas and Detective Osorio speak Russian, why were you along?'

'There was a time when it was forbidden to speak English. Now Russian is taboo. Anyway, the embassy wanted someone along when you were with the police, but someone not Russian. You know, I never knew anyone so unpopular so fast as you.'

'That's a sort of distinction.'

'But now you're here you should enjoy yourself. Would you like to see the city, go to a café, to the Havana Libre? It used to be the Hilton. They have a rooftop restaurant with a fantastic view. And they serve lobster. Only state restaurants are allowed to serve lobster, which are assets of the state.'

'No, thanks.' The idea of cracking open a lobster after an autopsy didn't sit quite right.

'Or a *paladar*, a private restaurant. They're small, they're only allowed twelve chairs but the food is much superior. No?'

Perhaps Rufo didn't get a chance to dine out often, but Arkady didn't think he could even watch someone eat.

'No. The captain and sergeant were in green uniforms, the detective in gray and blue. Why was that?'

'She's police and they're from the Ministry of the Interior. We just call it Minint. Police are under Minint.'

Arkady nodded; in Russia the militia was under the same ministry. 'But Arcos and Luna don't usually go out on homicides?'

'I don't think so.'

'Why was the captain going on about the Russian embassy?'

'He has a point. In the old days Russians acted like lords. Even now, for Cuban police to ask questions at the embassy takes a diplomatic note. Sometimes the embassy cooperates and sometimes it doesn't.'

Most of the traffic was Russian Ladas and Moskviches spraying exhaust and then, waddling as ponderously as dinosaurs, American cars from before the Revolution. Rufo and Arkady got out at a two-story house decorated like a blue Egyptian tomb with scarabs, ankhs and lotuses carved in stucco. A car on blocks sat in residence on the porch.

''57 Chevrolet.' Rufo looked inside at the car's gutted interior, straightened and ran his hand over the flecked paint. From the back. 'Tail fins.' To the front bumper. 'And tits.'

From the car key in the bag of effects Arkady knew that Pribluda had a Lada. No breasts on a Russian car.

As they went in and climbed the stairs the door to the ground-floor apartment cracked open enough for a woman in a house-dress to follow their progress.

'A concierge?' Arkady asked.

'A snoop. Don't worry, at night she watches television and doesn't hear a thing.'

'I'm going back tonight.'

'That's right.' Rufo unlocked the upstairs door. 'This is a protocol apartment the embassy uses for visiting dignitaries. Well, lesser dignitaries. I don't think we've had anyone here for a year.'

'Is someone from the embassy coming to talk about Pribluda?'

'The only one who wants to talk about Pribluda is you. You like cigars?'

'I've never smoked a cigar.'

'We'll talk about it later. I'll be back at midnight to take you to the plane. If you think the flight to Havana was long, wait till you go back to Moscow.'

The apartment was furnished with a set of cream-and-gold dining chairs, a sideboard with a coffee service, a nubby sofa, red phone, a bookshelf with titles like *La Amistad Russo-Cubana* and *Fidel y Arte* supported by erotic bookends in mahogany. In a disconnected refrigerator a loaf of Bimbo Bread was spotted with mold. The air conditioner was dead and showed the carbon smudges of an electrical fire. Arkady thought he probably showed some carbon smudges of his own.

He stripped from his clothes and showered in a stall of tiles that poured water from every valve and washed the odor of the autopsy off his skin and from his hair.

He dried himself on the scrap of towel provided and stretched out on the bed under his overcoat in the dark of the bedroom and listened to the voices and music that filtered from outside through the closed shutters of the window. He dreamed of floating among the playing fish of Havana Bay. He dreamed of flying back to Moscow and not landing, just circling in the night.

Russian planes did that, sometimes, if they were so old that their instruments failed. Although there could be other factors. If a pilot made a second landing approach he could be charged for the extra fuel expended, so he made only one, good or not. Or they were overloaded or underfueled.

He was both.

Circling sounded good.

GYPSY
IN AMBER

For my father and mother

Acknowledgements

This book could not have been written without the help of the Gypsy library and the notes of Reverend Frederick S. Arnold.

The Romany *chi*
And the Romany *chal*
Love *luripen*
And *lutchipen*
And *dukkeripen*
And *huknipen*
And every *pen*
But *moripen*
And *tatchipen*

The Gypsy woman
And the Gypsy man
Love stealing
And loving
And fortune-telling
And lying
And every *pen*
But killing
And truth

– old Romany saying

Chapter One

God had made Man in His image, Roman had heard. He wondered which god would claim the body on the aluminum table.

'Caucasian female, age approximately twenty to twenty-five. Hair brown, eyes blue.' The medical examiner spoke into a microphone clipped onto the lapel of his white smock. A wire from it led to the tape recorder in a roomy pocket.

'The body has been dismembered into six separate parts,' he went on in a monotone. 'Otherwise it appears to be that of a healthy female. All the teeth are present, although there are silver fillings on each of the upper right molars. There is a small, old diagonal scar under the chin. No digits are missing. There is some bruising of tissue on the knuckle of the fourth metacarpal, where a ring has been removed while alive or shortly afterward. There are no other scars, birthmarks or moles.'

There were four men around the table. Roman wasn't a weak man; he'd seen death before. But the others, including Isadore, had professional objectivity to fall back on. He didn't, and the disassembled horror of the sterile room was a revelation to him. He'd never considered that put back together, the human body resembled a misshapen octopus more than anything else.

The examiner had pulled back a flap of scalp and sawed through the skull for the brain. One cuff raised an eyelid to reveal a blue eye that stared at Roman with a madly askew iris.

'There is no sign of hematoma.'

The brain, a convoluted ruby, was weighed and deposited in a glass jar. The examiner's assistant wrote out a label, licked the back and applied it to the jar.

Sergeant Harry Isadore looked out of place, a long-suffering snowman. His cheeks and nose were contrasting hues of blue and pink, and he slapped his thick hands together to encourage circulation. He had dressed for a warm summer day, and going into the mortuary on First Avenue had loosened his sinuses.

'You've got to admit it's easier this way,' the assistant said as he pushed the legs and arms to one side.

The examiner opened the chest cavity and removed the heart and lungs and studied the interior of the cavity for fractured ribs. As a team, he and the assistant cut out the intestinal tract, the liver, spleen, pancreas and kidneys. When they had finished examining them, they placed the organs in glass-top fruit jars and sealed the tops with wax. The assistant wrote out more labels while the examiner drew blood for a typing, two men cataloguing a treasure.

The police reported the girl had come from the Cadillac Eldorado driven by Nanoosh Pulneshti. Nanoosh had started from Montevideo, Uruguay, gathering pieces for Roman. In Cuzco he bought Incan statuettes, in Manaus a crate of gold Empire service brought up the

Amazon by a nineteenth-century rubber baron; in Maracaibo he stole silver candlesticks from an abandoned Jesuit fortress. He crossed the Rio Grande without passing through U.S. Customs, and three days later Nanoosh was on the Palisades Parkway approaching the George Washington Bridge. One of those everyday accidents occurred between the Eldorado and a U-Haul bringing antiques down from Newton, Massachusetts, to the Armory Show. Both Nanoosh and the U-Haul driver had died as the car jackknifed over the van. It would have been a simple case for the highway patrol except for the neat, scarcely bruised pieces of the girl they found strewn over the roadside.

'No spermatozoa,' the assistant said after looking at a smear under the microscope.

'Can you give me a closer age, Doctor?' Isadore asked.

The examiner prodded the jaw open again while the assistant held the head steady.

'From the wear on the teeth' – he cut a thin line into the gum – 'and the immaturity of the roots of the third molar, I would venture closer to twenty years than twenty-five.' He pushed the jaw closed and shrugged. 'She's not a virgin, but she's never borne a child or had an abortion. No evidence of drugs. Hardly any cavities. She must have been a clean liver.'

Isadore had brought Roman down to identify Nanoosh in his stainless-steel filing cabinet. Roman didn't know what the point was in asking him to witness this gruesome theater. He refused to watch, looking instead at the curved tile floor with its black, grooved borders.

'*Rigor mortis* has set into the entire body. Since the face is still rigid, the victim may have been dead for from eighteen to twenty-four hours. However, there also seems to be little lividity, and the *in situ* report states that specimens of dry ice were found at the scene of the accident and it's possible the ice was used to preserve the body. So the time range can be stretched to about ten to thirty hours to account for the possible effect of a lower temperature on the muscles.'

Roman cried for Nanoosh, for the arrogance and daring reduced to a filing drawer. But this was another kind of reduction beyond grief, the butcher's secret.

'There are nine great wounds of dismemberment. Since there is a lack of bruises or lacerations to indicate a struggle, it is likely that separation of the head was first. The wound entry is from the back of the neck at the second cervical vertebra. The sinews and muscles are cleanly cut, and strands of the victim's hair are embedded in the flesh. Separation of the spinal cord, not to mention the jugular, indicates death was instantaneous. The weapon used was sharp, clean and heavy and used with great force. There is no indication of a second blow. The wound entries for dismemberment of the arms are at the armpits. The arms would appear to have been drawn back, and again there is no indication that more than one blow was used. In each case, the greater tubercles have been crushed. Likewise, the olecranons in the separation of the biceps from the forearms.

'The patella was shattered in each leg in the separation of the thighs from the calves. Separating the thigh from the pelvis was not such an easy matter. The thigh appears to have been spread back, and the wound entry is in the front at the origin of the *rectus femoris*; but the neck of the *fovea capitus* seems to have resisted, particularly in the right leg, and several blows were necessary to disengage the femur from the pelvis.

'There are no in-and-out wounds to describe the assailant's weapon. There are no marks indicating a point on it. The assailant appears to have had a basic knowledge of anatomy and great strength. There are no hesitation wounds.'

At the end of all this the examiner paused and glanced at Isadore. His assistant was at the ready, rolling forward a tray with its container of formalin, alcohol and carmine to embalm the parts. Isadore stopped the tray. He took a toothpick and ran its flat end under the girl's polished fingernails. He held the toothpick up to the light and inspected it.

'Nothing. She didn't suspect a thing. She thought she was with a friend.'

'Is that all, Sergeant? We'd like to clean up.'

'Hold it.' He gestured for Roman. 'One last thing.'

Roman stood next to Isadore above the cool table with its display of meat.

'Is she Gypsy?' Isadore asked.

There was no way of avoiding it now. Roman looked, concentrating on minute points, refusing the whole. Finally, he looked at the fingernails Isadore had just held.

'No. There'd be a brown moon around the cuticle at the very least.'

'Then how do you explain it?' Isadore asked.

'Explain what?'

'How she could think your friend Nanoosh was her friend?'

Roman didn't know what to say. Isadore was Roman's friend, too.

Chapter Two

There were five faces visible in the window of 'R. Grey –
Antiques' when Isadore parked in front of it that morning. One was of a Siennese madonna, the perfect oval of
her face outlined by her black hood, the hood set in a
golden halo. The wings of joyous seraphim touched her
shoulders as she ascended to heaven.

On the other side of the window was a Florentine
banker captured in all his intelligent avarice. A rich fur
hat mimicked the hands that weighed gold coins, and a
greyhound's luminescent eyes watched the glittering
money. In a corner was the inscription in red 'Bottega
del Ghirlandaio'.

Next to the sixteenth-century banker was another who
could have been his brother, except that this head was set
on shoulders of Dunhill pinstripe, and it was alive.
Isadore recognized the senior member of the board of
the American Stock Exchange as the man ran his hand
tenderly down the carved frame. A look of anxiety was in
the senior member's rimless glasses, and Isadore got an
inkling of the painting's value. The fourth face was
Roman's, and it was as Byzantine and mysterious as the
madonna's. The fifth was that of Beng, Roman's solid
black cat that paced from one painting to the other.

The stock market was down. Isadore didn't know how

much until Roman put his arm around the broker's shoulders the way a sweetshop owner would put his arm around a penniless boy. Beng disappeared from the window, a sign that the bargaining was over. If it had been any other Gypsy, Isadore would have been alert for a traveling wallet. With Roman he knew the customer would end up signing a check eagerly another day, and in the meantime Isadore couldn't help enjoying the tableau. The Gypsy was one of his few indulgences.

When the broker had left with one last lingering pause in front of the window, Isadore gave himself a second to erase the smile from his lips. It wasn't a funny day. He got out of his car, slowly, for once not wanting to talk to the dealer, taking in the narrow, expensive East Side street with its picture townhouses where newsboys delivered the *Times* and *Woman's Wear Daily* in foyers.

The door to Roman's shop did not have an automatic lock, making it a curiosity in the New York antique trade.

'*Sarisban*,' Roman said. 'I saw the long arm of the law skulking across the street, so I put some tea on.'

He was in the back of the shop barely visible past a Chinese screen, but Isadore could see him grinning as he set two cups and saucers beside a teapot.

'Morning,' Isadore replied. He wasn't in the mood to reciprocate their usual greeting. Roman came to the front of the store with the cups. He had an exaggerated frown.

'Official business again. I never knew police work was so dull until I met you, Sergeant.'

'Hot tea, Christ,' Isadore muttered. 'On a day like

today. It's already eighty out there.' Just holding the saucer made Isadore sweat.

'You're turning into a dilettante on me,' Roman told him, taking a healthy sip from his cup. He pushed a chair over to Isadore with his foot.

'Incidentally, what are those paintings worth?' Isadore asked. He refused to sit, another compromise with his job. He would have put the cup down on the table next to him, but he didn't want to leave a ring.

'Whatever I can get. Michelangelo's teacher may have done the portrait if that gives you an idea.'

'And you just leave them in the window?'

'I put them there so the customer could see them in daylight. I don't usually handle paintings, so I don't have any place to hang them.'

'Yeah.' Isadore looked around the interior. It had the haphazard jumble of a pawnshop; but he'd learned the prices of some of the pieces, and Roman had explained the salutary effect of the mess on the clientele's imagination. Inlaid chests lined the walls under suspended side chairs, partially unrolled tapestries and showcases of Oriental porcelain. It always reminded him of a museum tilted on its side.

'These paintings just sort of came into hand like everything else?' he asked.

'Is that all it is?' Roman said. 'You want to see the bills of sale? Why didn't you say so when you came in?'

'No.' Isadore sighed and sat down. He rested his cup on his lap. 'Look, what was Nanoosh Pulneshti doing for you?'

Roman tried to read the cop's face, but Isadore was staring at his tea.

'Nothing. Nanoosh is a friend of mine, you know that. What's the matter, is he in trouble?'

'Not anymore. He's dead.'

Isadore looked up, trying to catch Roman's reaction. It was too late; all he saw was brown mask calm. If it had been another Rom bringing the news, Roman would have cried openly. For a callous moment Isadore found himself resenting the limits on friendship between Rom and *gajo*, but he went on.

'He died in a car accident. Witnesses say he was trying to get onto the exit ramp for the George Washington Bridge the same time as a van. You know what happens: Neither one wanted to give way, so they're both dead now.'

'Nanoosh was a good driver.'

'Maybe the other driver was at fault. So what? The thing is, we found another body in Nanoosh's car. A girl, she'd been murdered. Brunette, pretty, I don't think she's Gypsy. Young, blue eyes.'

'What are you driving at?' Roman asked. Isadore kept his face averted to keep from clueing him.

'You might know who she is. I want you to take a look at her; it's as simple as that.'

Roman shrugged. Beng threaded his way through a set of Meissen.

'I don't know what you're talking about, Sergeant. Besides, how do you know the girl wasn't killed in the accident?'

'Take a look at her and you'll know. The bastard was carting her around the whole day, Roman. Maybe he was a pal of yours; but Nanoosh didn't have a driver's license, the plates on the car were bad, and he had a knife.'

'What's wrong with that?'

'They're wrong to me. I'm not trying to pin this on him just because of that, though. We found a whole bunch of stuff from his car all over the road. Silver plates, candlesticks, statues. And the girl. His Cadillac was split open like a beer can.'

'Then you didn't find her in Nanoosh's car.'

Beng had settled beside a ceramic view of the Rhine and glared at Isadore.

'Not in it, no. You don't put a seat belt on a corpse.'

'And the other car?'

'It was a small truck, a U-Haul. That was open, too, but no luck. It was checked from top to bottom right before the crash by an insurance examiner. That's the problem, Roman; no insurance examiners are around when your friends are delivering antiques to you. You operate differently.'

'There were antiques in the van?'

'Yes.'

'That's interesting. You don't think so?'

'No. Damn it, Roman, this isn't a game. I came here to tell you that the delivery boy in your little operation has killed somebody. I know how you got that chandelier over there and that tapestry. I haven't been able to prove it; but I know, and maybe I wasn't trying hard enough because it was only a matter of you milking a few snobs.

This time it's murder. Nanoosh was bringing his cargo to you, body and all.'

'There are over a thousand antique dealers between Wall Street and Eighty-sixth Street.'

'But you're the only Gypsy. He was coming here, this shop.'

'The only Gypsy,' Roman repeated. He looked at Isadore with some sorrow. 'That's why you came here. Are you going to arrest me because I'm the only Gypsy?'

'That's not what I meant, and you know it. Do you deny that you operate outside the law for the stuff you sell? Come on, be honest with me.'

'As a friend? No, I won't deny I operate outside your laws. As a suspect I deny everything. Now I get a question. This accident didn't happen in New York. It happened in New Jersey – didn't it? – while Nanoosh was getting on the bridge for the city. What have the New York police and you got to do with it?'

It took a moment for Isadore to answer, but there was no chance of evasion. Roman already knew the answer.

'They gave it to us because I'm the Gypsy expert,' Isadore said. 'They thought you'd talk to me.'

Roman left without a word and went to the rear of the store. Isadore sat in his chair feeling angry and foolish. The shock of Nanoosh's death hadn't worked, and the threat about the merchandise had failed as miserably as the first time he tried it when Roman opened the store years ago. Beng leaped from the porcelain to the top of a secretary desk. The cat looked at Isadore complacently, then shut its eyes and went to sleep. Its whiskers looked almost white against its fur. Isadore, the Gypsy expert, remembered that Beng was named for the devil of the Ganges. Otherwise, he knew as much about the cat as he did about its owner. Roman came back and dropped an ice cube into Isadore's cup.

'You should have told me before you wanted your tea another way,' he said. He wiped his dark hands on a handkerchief.

'If you want some help, here it is,' he went on. 'Nanoosh was a Gypsy, just like me. He broke laws. He stole cars, and he liked girls, too. Gypsy girls. But he was no killer. You have my word.'

A Gypsy's word, Isadore thought. That was like a contradiction. On the other hand, Roman Grey was a contradiction.

'That's not enough.'

'That's all you're going to get. Nanoosh didn't waste his time with *gaja*; he trusted only Gypsies. As for *gaja* women, he despised them; he said they were milk, and a *gaja* man was a thief who made his own rules. He wouldn't touch either of them. If you want to find out who killed the girl, you look for her kind of man.'

'So far as I know, you're an accomplice to murder,' Isadore said. He was out of his chair, and his face was flushed. He looked for some place to put the cup down.

'I don't have anything left to say to you, Sergeant. That's a Hancock Worcester you have in your hand, try not to break it.' He took the cup from Isadore.

'I could pull you in right now. You've already admitted dealing in unregistered antiques.'

13

'That's too bad,' the Gypsy said. 'You were one *gajo* I trusted.'

Isadore's hand had reflexively gone to his chrome cuffs for the arrest when the shop door opened. A girl came in. She was dressed in Saks' version of a fringed Indian dress, and she wore a beaded headband around her brown hair. She was beautiful and vaguely familiar. It wasn't just that Isadore had the sense he'd seen her on a dozen television commercials. She was what all his son's dates tried to look like.

'Roman, did you know how many calories there are in goulash?' she demanded.

Roman winced and relaxed slightly. He leaned on the secretary.

'Thousands,' she said, 'literally thousands. If I had any, it would be dry toast for a month. That's what they feed prisoners.'

'Dany, it was your idea,' Roman said. 'You wanted to cook a real Hungarian dish.'

'But goulash?' the girl asked Isadore. 'Have you ever seen those Hungarian girls? No wonder they all look like sausages. You never see French girls eating goulash.'

'I don't think my friend is interested in your peculiar view of nationalities,' Roman told her.

'A friend?' The girl's attitude changed from distress to pleasure. She seized Isadore's hand. 'I'm so glad to meet you. Roman never introduces me to any of his friends. He thinks they'll disapprove,' she said in a stage whisper. 'I never would have thought you were a Gypsy.'

'He's not,' Roman said. 'Dany Murray, meet Sergeant

14

Harry Isadore. He's a policeman.' Her attitude went back to distress. She retracted her hand.

'I haven't said anything wrong, have I?' she asked Roman.

'Nothing they can send me up for, unless there's a law against consorting with gibbering clotheshorses.'

'Maybe I'll be going,' she suggested.

Roman nodded. She kissed him quickly on the cheek and just as quickly wiped it off with her hand.

'He hates lipstick,' she told Isadore. On her way out the door she stopped long enough to say, 'Poached eggs,' and was gone before Roman could answer.

He rubbed his face and turned back to the policeman. He could see that Isadore had thought of something new.

'Well, Sergeant, aren't you going to arrest me?'

'No. It's just that there's another *gaja* girl I want you to meet.'

Chapter Three

Sergeant Isadore inhaled and coughed. He was trying to give up cigarettes by smoking small cigars, but he kept forgetting. As he pounded himself on the chest, he wondered whether his son was going to keep his student deferment. Perhaps if he keeled over in Captain Frank's office, they'd let Morris stay home as a hardship case. That was a hell of a price to pay to keep a son home.

'You ought to give up smoking,' Frank suggested balefully.

'I know,' Isadore said. He stubbed out the cigar in the stand-up ashtray the city provided.

'Now tell me again. Is it Roman Grey or Romano Gry? Which one is the alias?'

'Both,' Isadore said. 'I mean they're both his real names. Gry is his name with other Gypsies. Grey is for *gaja*, non-Gypsies.'

'This is a simple case, Sergeant. But I'm beginning to see what makes it complicated.' Frank had the almost hairless head of a newborn bird, and it lolled from side to side as he spoke. 'If I remember correctly, we've spoken about him before.'

'He's cooperated with the department before, Captain.'

'Sergeant, I'd call donating some chairs for the Policemen's Ball swell, but I wouldn't call it cooperation.'

'Yes,' Isadore agreed. 'Well, we don't have enough information to make a charge stick. He can account for his whereabouts for the past four days, we can't get any complaints from his customers, and actually we haven't established any provable link between Pulneshti and Grey.'

Frank squinted at the one-by-two-inch photo of Grey stapled to his file. 'Looks like some kind of mulatto to me.'

'The Grys are famous for being dark,' Isadore pointed out. 'They're Lovari Gypsies like Pulneshti. Grey has quite an interesting background. Orphaned and brought up by a judge in New York. That's where he got the money to start his store.'

'How about that? Can you tell me anything about the girl or Pulneshti? Something dull like the murder?'

Isadore swallowed a cough. 'Nothing positive. The FBI can't match her prints, and it takes some time to check all the runaways and missing persons. The lab tests verified no hard drugs, so we're hitting the missing persons harder. Pulneshti has a record of grand and petty larceny, mostly cars, but we don't have any record of next of kin.'

Frank snapped his middle finger on the Grey file. 'No help here?'

'No. He says he's sure we'll catch the guilty party.'

For a man whose avocation was sarcasm, Frank was not alert to the possibility in others. He merely grunted.

'We're trying to cut down the area of search,' Isadore continued. 'We sent a description of the car around the national wire, and we have a zoologist looking at it tomorrow to check out the bugs on the car and the radiator. That could help us determine where the car's been, and it certainly looks as if it's been everywhere.'

Frank's face was starting to screw up with an inner pain.

'It's a little unorthodox, I know,' Isadore said, 'but it's not like tracing an ordinary person. Gypsies don't carry credit cards, they don't stay at motels, they don't have bank accounts, and they don't talk to the police. Even when they do talk, it's in their own language. None of the usual techniques work.'

Frank looked at Isadore for a long time. They'd started out in the Police Academy together, and Isadore had always gotten the better marks; he was the one who was expected to rise to inspector. Instead, Frank had followed orders, never hounded a case too long, always remembered St. Patrick's Day, and now he was ahead by two grades and a few thousand dollars. Still, they had an understanding.

'Harry, we've got to wrap this case up fast. It's practically done for us. Pulneshti was probably the killer, and he's dead. But the commissioner is resigning. The Irishman at the Central Investigation Department wants the job. So does the Jew at the Detective Bureau. The district attorneys and the captains are lining up with their boys, and I've got to jump soon. I thought I could lay low until this girl and the Gypsy came along in Jersey. Now someone transferred this homicide to you and me and don't know who. It sounds like that college boy at the bureau, but CID is closer to the Jersey patrol. If you handle this right one of them is going to take the credit. Unless they expect you to blow it and then they can pin it on the other.'

'Why don't you call one of them and find out?'

'The phone's tapped, that's why. I tried to get messages through, but they're both traveling all over town with their flying squads. Do you understand? You have to wrap this up fast and neat, and if it means putting this other Gypsy in the can for a while, I'll back you up. Until we find out who comes out on top.'

Frank pushed the files across the desk to Isadore.

'You're the man with the imagination, think up something,' Frank said. 'Anyway, from what you tell me, we're dealing with born criminals.'

Chapter Four

On West Eighty-second Street above a *bodega* with a
Puerto Rican flag flying over cans of papaya juice and
bottles of saffron was an even more colorful window. It
had a yellow hand with red lifelines dealing the ace of
spades. Hanging out over the street was a sign with
smaller versions of the symbols and the words 'Madame
Vera. Fortunes told in your hands, in the cards. Love or
Career. What is Fate?'

Madame Vera had moved to the *ofisa* a month before.
She and her family of twelve had driven over the Manhattan Bridge from their old *ofisa* on Flatbush Avenue in
Brooklyn in two new but battered Chryslers. When they
arrived at their new business address, the girls immediately
unloaded a stack of folding chairs from the trunks. The
men brought up tables, and the boys struggled up the
stairs with *gonyas*. Each *gonya* consisted of a strap that
went over the shoulders with enormous bags at each end.
Inside was all the wealth of the family in heavy necklaces
of American eagles, double eagles, old Mexican pesos even
richer in gold, but mostly Austrian four ducats with the
head of Emperor Franz Josef. As the tables and chairs were
set up, the men strode up and down the stairs with
bedrolls and the eiderdown quilts called *dunbas*.

While the men relaxed with cigarettes, Vera and her

sisters and daughters prepared the *ofisa*. They hammered nails into the walls, strung wires from the nails, and hung dark-red curtains from the wires so that in a matter of minutes the railroad flat was divided into living quarters and tearooms where the women could do their *duikkerin*, fortune-telling. Three crudely painted oilcloths were hung. One displayed a hand with the tracery of a map, another a buddha and a cross, and the third a phrenologist's chart. Along the walls were tacked horoscope magazines and newspaper clippings on Django Reinhardt and Yul Brynner. Altogether, it took an hour to prepare the *ofisa* for its customers.

Customers demanded such a setting. They climbed the stairs anxious about dreams or curious about a number to play. Only a few asked about their future. Holding their hand, Vera would usually satisfy them with, if they were old, 'a dispute over property that has caused great anguish' or, if they were young, 'your passions have been misunderstood and got you in great trouble.' The different ones with real secrets could be read, too, though. The way they spoke, whether their eyes could stay with hers, the corner of a mouth were all letters in an alphabet that merely needed to be put into words and then sentences.

The family would stay in the *ofisa* until Vera made her *bozur*. Vera would know the victim as soon as she entered, a woman alone whose children visited once a month, just like the last one in Brooklyn. Vera had spent more time than usual in sympathetic conversation before abruptly asking whether this woman suffered from peculiar pains lately. Like all the victims, she agreed eagerly. Vera examined her palm carefully and saw 'something bad.' She sent the woman home and told her to sleep naked under her three warmest blankets holding an egg over her belly. The next day the woman returned with the egg wrapped in a napkin. Vera broke the egg open and lying in the yolk was a tiny hideous head with human hair grinning up at them. The devil's head was proof of the evil – possibly cancer – growing inside her. It was the sign of a curse.

The root of the curse was the money in the woman's savings account. Vera explained that at some time it had passed through the hands of a murderer and the evil would only stop growing when she had taken the curse off. She wanted no payment for herself; this was too important a matter. As a test, she told the woman to draw a ten-dollar bill from her account and bring it to her with another egg in a napkin.

When the woman came back, she tried to give the bill to Vera, but the Gypsy refused to touch it. She asked the woman to place the napkin in a corner of the *ofisa*. They waited an hour, and when they broke the egg, looking up at them was another ugly devil's head. There was no longer any doubt about the curse.

Vera told the woman what was necessary. The next day she went to her bank and drew out every cent in her savings account in large denominations, fifties and hundreds, 'so that it will fit in the little bag,' as Vera put it. The Romani word for the little bag of money was *bozur*, and Vera would have to hold it when she took the curse off.

The woman tied up the *bozur* herself. While she gaped,

Vera began talking to the bag and to the special spirits she was in contact with. Soon the talking turned to pleading, the English turned to Romani and then to complete unintelligibility as the Gypsy collapsed on the floor, rolling her eyes and moaning under the force of the *bozur*. She ripped her blouse and scratched her face. As she yielded a particularly eerie howl of agony, her hands slipped the bag into her several thicknesses of petticoats and a second, absolutely similar bag appeared. At last, Vera passed out on the floor.

When she was revived, she had bad news for the woman. The curse could be drawn off, but only if the money were destroyed. When the woman hesitated, the Gypsy pointed to the devil's head that leered at them from a glass case. Vera had the bucket and coals ready when the woman gave in. The victim threw the *bozur* in herself, a phony *bozur* with paper cut in the shape of bills, and the two women knelt and prayed as the flames shot up. Finally, Vera told the woman that she was saved but only on the condition that she never tell anyone how.

Of course, the following day the bank manager called the woman's sons, and they got the full story from her but by then Madame Vera and her family had moved their *gonyas* and *dunhas* into a new *ofisa*.

Today, however, a prospective victim would have been disappointed. For once, fate had cheated Madame Vera.

'*Nanoosh, te aves yertime mander, te yertil tut o Del,*' Roman said. He was in the center of the long *ofisa*. Dark curls hung over his face, and his suit was torn and damp with sweat.

'Nanoosh, if you will forgive me all I have done to you, I will forgive all you have done to me.' The chorus came from the figures huddled along the walls of red burlap.

'*Te avel angla tute, Nanoosh, kodo khabe tai kado pimo tai mange pe sastimaste,*' Vera Pulneshti said. Tears ran over the deep lacerations on her cheeks.

'Nanoosh, if you will forgive me all I have done to you, I will forgive all you have done to me,' the family repeated. In a small pile in the center of the room was whatever jewelry they had been wearing when they heard of Nanoosh's death. Roman's cuff links were mixed with earrings and necklaces. In the gloom, they reflected the votive candles lit on a small altar that carried a photo of Nanoosh and a miniature figure of a Black Virgin.

One of the children, a girl with a mat complexion, passed around a tray of tea sweetened with strawberry jam. It would be all the Pulneshtis were allowed to eat until after the burial. Roman took a glass, holding it with his thumb on the rim and his forefinger on the bottom. Vera refused a glass for herself and held onto Roman's arm.

'He was such a good man. You remember how you respected him. Everyone respected him,' she said hoarsely. It wasn't exactly true. Nanoosh was a gambler, good at the races but bad at cards, and he owed everybody. But he was great fun at a party, and he played the guitar like a Gitano, and it was his sister's duty to see him praised.

'Those things I said to Nanoosh the last time you were

here? That was love talking, you understand. And now he's dead.'

When Roman tried to comfort her, she pushed him away. She waddled ferociously to the makeshift altar and snatched the picture to bring back to Roman. It was a Polaroid snapshot of Nanoosh sitting on the fender of a limousine.

'He was a great Rom,' Roman said soothingly. The other men in the room grunted agreement.

'Is this the face of a murderer?' Vera asked. 'Can this man have killed some stupid *gaji* and cut her into pieces? No! Are you going to tell me that, Romano Gry?'

'I didn't,' Roman said. 'The police are fools, but they'll find out that Nanoosh had nothing to do with it.' He believed what he said, Isadore was like all *gaja*, collectors hoarding pieces of a style or a crime. Sooner or later, it would become obvious that Nanoosh was a piece that didn't fit. Whether Isadore found out who did commit the crime, he didn't care.

'Then why did they come to you?' Vera asked, advancing on him. With her eyes burning between the tangle of her hair and the red stripes on her cheeks, she was undeniably formidable.

'You know how they are. They wanted to know where Nanoosh was going and they thought I could help them.'

Vera's heavily sagging front had Roman's back against a window. He had heard that not even the most skeptical client left her *ofisa* without a twenty-dollar scare.

'Ah! Then they thought you could help,' she said.

'He was bringing some things to me, you know.' He

looked around to see if one of the men would pull Vera off him. There wasn't a chance; she had the whole family cowed. Her son Tibo in the corner could lift a small car to remove its transmission. Around his mother he was a mouse. Even the Welfare Department paid Vera just to keep her out of the office.

'Look, I've fixed it so that you can pick up Nanoosh and give him a decent burial,' Roman told her.

'A decent burial!' she shrieked. Vera turned to the rest of the room so that everyone could appreciate her histrionics equally. 'Listen to Romano. A decent burial! My brother is called a murderer, and this man says he will have a decent burial!' She spat on the floor. 'You live like the *gaja* so much that you're turning into one. What about Nanoosh's *mulo*? What about tonight when his spirit walks around that cold morgue knowing that the shame of a murder is on him?'

There was nothing ridiculous in what she was saying. Nanoosh's spirit was freed from his body, dead but not gone, a *mulo*. The *gaja* might despise the Romany, but no Rom ever forgot his dead. For him, roaming over the earth were not only the half million Gypsies who drew breath but also the countless Gypsies who had gone before, restless spirits still wandering through cities and deserts, still real. In the dark room hung with Vera's maroon curtains this was a fact.

All the same, Roman suppressed a smile. Vera was flaunting her dramatic talents. She shuddered, displaying her strong profile. Her large hook nose was almost as fine as Roman's.

'Nanoosh made only one mistake,' she announced. 'He thought that Romano was a true Rom, a *phral*. Perhaps it's better he never knew that he was wrong. As you all know, a Gypsy girl is not good enough for this man here. He doesn't dress like a Gypsy or eat like one or smell like one to me. We are not worth his bother. He's changed. I'm sorry, Nanoosh, forgive me for telling you.'

Roman sighed. 'Okay, Vera, what are you after? Just tell me.'

The fortune-teller let her bosom stop heaving and wiped a tear from her eye. 'I only want you to help the *mulo* of your friend. Nanoosh can never reach paradise with the taint of murder on his name. The police asked you to help. I think they're right, the ignorant bastards. You do that. You prove that Nanoosh was an honest man, that he didn't kill anybody.'

Roman didn't see how he could ever prove Nanoosh was honest, but he said, 'I'll see what I can do.'

'That's better,' Vera said. On cue, one of her daughters came out of the shadows with a paper plate. On it was a pastry dripping with pistachio and honey. 'We can't eat until the *pomana*,' she said, 'but you should. You have a lot of work to do.'

'Thanks.' He noticed that Vera was her old self now that she had gotten her way.

'Why are you grinning like a fool?' she asked.

'For the best of reasons,' Roman answered.

Chapter Five

Nanoosh's burial was at a cemetery in Linden, New Jersey, where New York Gypsies had for years buried their dead. Isadore watched at a distance, but Vera was unable to restrain herself from sinking to her knees in the freshly turned soil and reaching down to her brother's coffin. The mourners spoke in Romani, and Isadore was able to catch only a few phrases. As the gravediggers began throwing the dirt on the coffin, the Gypsies threw money so that a rich mix of earth and money lay over Nanoosh. The Gypsies got back into their Cadillacs and headed north to New York. Roman walked over to Isadore, who was waiting in his Ford.

'You want a ride back?' Isadore asked.

'I was hoping for it,' Roman said. He got into the car. 'Did you hear anything?'

'You know I can't speak it that well.'

They rode up U.S. 1 past Roselle and Hillside on New Jersey's sprawling checkerboard of suburbs and industrial slums. Isadore's hat was pushed back to reveal a white untanned line. He drove conscientiously with both hands on the wheel as he discussed his son, whom he was taking to watch the Mets at Shea Stadium on the weekend.

'I want to prove that there's more to life than protest meetings,' Isadore said.

'The Mets are really up there, aren't they?' Roman asked absentmindedly. 'They're ahead of the Jets, right?'

Isadore's mouth dropped open in shock. 'Jets? That's a football team. Boy, you really aren't in contact with the real world, are you?' He glanced at his passenger with a very fast, very safe jerk of his head to see if he was being kidded. 'You do know that baseball is the national pastime, don't you?'

'Baseball, football, Jets, Mets . . .' Roman looked out the window at a large sign going by. It claimed that New Jersey had more paved highway per acre than any other state in the nation. 'Anything more on the girl?'

'No fingerprints on file, so we have to wait on the dental records. That means we have to find out where she came from. We'll find out, just like we'll find out where the car was coming from. Nanoosh had it full of goods from South America. The captain said it didn't mean anything because there was no report from customs on Nanoosh. I think I've finally convinced him that Gypsies have been crossing borders for a long time without going through customs. As soon as we get an answer from our zoologist on the bugs found on the car we'll know exactly where it's been. Amazing what those experts can do, find an ant caught in amber that's been dead, extinct for a million years, and they can tell you all about it. We'll trace the car and we'll find the girl.'

'So you still think it was Nanoosh.'

'Damn it, Roman, who else could it be?'

They drove on for another mile bordered by streams colored by chemicals.

'Which means that I'm the best suspect you have,' Roman pointed out.

'Something like that.'

Isadore chewed on his lower lip for want of a cigarette. He was suffering, Roman saw. He had a murder, and he was a good cop, and he should be making an arrest, at least for the record.

'Look at it from my viewpoint, Roman. Antiques and objects of art have to be declared when they enter the country. The United States has agreements with these countries your friends go through, and if you don't take their stuff out through legal channels, it's contraband. You're the head of a contraband ring. Nanoosh is your accomplice, and he kills a girl. Maybe it was an accident, but he chopped her up afterward.' Isadore glanced at Roman again. 'Nanoosh was your accomplice, and he butchered her.'

The Ford looped around a tractor and continued on.

'I can just forget about it, say it's closed. New York has one unsolved murder a day. Just statistics, one more statistic. But the girl was mutilated. How can I face my son if I do that? Answer me.'

'What would you like me to do?'

'Help me,' Isadore was almost pleading. 'I don't think you knew anything about the girl, but just tell me what you know. I can get you off the contraband rap pretty light. Those bills of sale you have aren't too bad.'

The chubby hands gripping the wheel were turning white. Ahead of them Newark was rising mirage-like on heat waves. The glass slab of an insurance company towered over a ghetto. The dull cube of a brewery floated in a yeasty fragrance in the center of the city. The Ford followed the stream of cars toward the tunnels for Manhattan.

'Tell you what,' Roman said. 'Get on the turnpike for the Palisades and we'll try to see what happened.'

Isadore thought it over. Taking the Gypsy in would please Frank, and it might even ease his own conscience. He was still telling himself he was considering it when he got on the turnpike at Kearny. The turnpike led through the steel bubbles of oil refineries to Fort Lee and the Palisades Parkway. A stench of oil that was like the stench of a decaying animal made them shut the windows of the car. Roman lit a Gauloise to kill the smell. Isadore refused one.

The Palisades Parkway was tidy and landscaped in comparison to the turnpike. The George Washington Bridge made a neat paperweight at its southern end. White on green notices urged drivers to park and enjoy the view of the Hudson. Isadore made a U-turn through a gap in the median strip marked 'For Official Use Only' and pulled up on the side of the road.

'What do you expect to find?' Isadore asked.

'I don't know.'

They got out and walked along the gravel skirt, moving in slow motion against the lane of cars at their side. Isadore pointed to white scrapes in the concrete. In a direct line across the river was the medieval arcade of the Cloisters.

'That's where the van turned over. You'd see some

31

blood around here, but the state cleans up after highway accidents now. I can show you photos if you want to see what the stains and the cars looked like.'

Roman kicked the gravel around with the toe of his shoe. At once, he realized how silly it was to think he would find something in the stones that the police had missed. Riders took mildly curious stares at him as the cars continued to roll by a few feet away toward the bridge. He wandered off onto the grass bank. If there were something the cops had missed, it would be gone by now. The grass was freshly mown. He rubbed his hand over his chin. Stubble was already growing back from the morning shave. Some people couldn't keep as freshly mown.

Isadore walked back to the car. He didn't mind watching someone discover how hard it was to play a real detective, but he didn't want to embarrass a friend. He came back with a manila envelope closed with twine.

'These are the pictures, Roman. They'll help you.' He opened the envelope and took out twenty eight-by-ten glossies.

'Thanks.'

The first shots had been taken from the top of the police tow truck, and they showed a hundred yards of road. The van was nearest, on its side. The Cadillac was sprawled about twenty yards beyond it, upside down. Instead of bodies, X's marked where they had been picked up. Far down the road and on either side were pieces of furniture and plates, and ropes and padding. Roman remembered that it had been a sunny day. The gold plates shone. Among them were other X's marking where different parts of the girl's body had been found.

Most of the other photos were close-ups of the cars and of the bodies with blankets drawn back as they rested in useless ambulances. Worst were the pictures of the anonymous girl, each part of her in its plastic bag on a separate picture complete with six-inch celluloid markers so that the mind couldn't help guessing – as if it were a game – which part was which. Roman looked from the photos to the road. A sports car without a muffler was racing over the spot where her head was picked up.

'See,' Isadore's finger pointed to the first photo of the road. 'Plates, bits of statue, the girl. All in the same area.'

'And the antiques.'

'And one big difference between the way you operate and the way Hoddinor Sloan operates. His antiques were going to his stall at the Armory Show. An agent from his insurance company got in the van in Nyack to check the whole shipment inside and out. That's why the van was using the Palisades instead of staying on the Merritt. The agent even followed the van on the parkway for a few miles, and we have witnesses in other cars who happened to see him all the way to the accident. It's too bad nobody checks you out.'

Isadore waited in the car while Roman policed the side of the road with the photos. Finally, the Gypsy gave up and joined him.

'Well, what's your answer?' Isadore asked. 'Are you going to help?'

'This Sloan,' Roman said. He seemed surprisingly

33

undiscouraged as he knocked another cigarette out of his pack. 'Has he picked up his antiques?'

Isadore rolled his fingertips on the wheel once and turned the car into the traffic. 'No. Why should he sweat it? He probably made a profit off the insurance, and his antiques are a mess. Besides, there's some question of who can release them. We have it in town, but New Jersey is still carrying it on paper. Typical foul-up.'

'He hasn't looked at his antiques himself?'

'We sent him some photos through the Massachusetts police. He identified them and said they were total losses, which you don't have to be an expert to see. I spoke to him on the phone, and frankly, he's a bastard. Didn't even ask how the driver was.'

'What about the driver?'

Isadore sighed. He tapped a paper bag that hung under the police radio. Up to now Roman had thought it was a litter bag. It was Isadore's file. Inside were business envelopes stuffed with notes.

'That's the one,' Isadore said.

'Locher' was written in longhand on the envelope Roman held. He opened it and took out sheets of paper held together by a paper clip. In six pages Isadore had a concise record of Harold 'Buddy' Locher from birth to death at twenty-nine. There were medical, psychological and vocational descriptions, most of them concerning his life in the Army. He'd mustered out as a corporal ten days before at Fort Hood, Texas.

On the back of the last page Isadore's longhand made its second appearance. 'Locher left the service to avoid a third tour of Vietnam. He claims (see Psych.) to be a mechanic, not an infantryman. Arrival in Boston one day before accident looking for friend who was out of town. Got job driving where friend worked on friend's route because short of drivers. In Boston one night sleeping at friend's place. Witnesses verify he was alone. Picks up loaded van in Boston, van checked in Nyack, N. Y., see all the way to bridge exit and acc. No motive or opportunity.'

Roman looked through the middle pages before stuffing the notes back into the envelope. 'Very thorough. No motive, no opportunity.'

'Right. You're beginning to learn I don't just sit on my ass and harass Gypsies. Locher was a little nutty, if that's what you can call being afraid of dying. Even if he was a homicidal maniac, though, he didn't have a chance to prove it.'

They coasted off the George Washington Bridge and curled onto the Henry Hudson Driveway. There was an envelope on himself, Roman knew. Skimpy on the background but heavy on suspicion. Suspect for being a Gypsy but not acting like one, which was a different kind of double jeopardy. Would Isadore be amused that for a long time he had worked at piecing his own past together?

Everyone knew about the Jews killed by the Nazis. No one knew or cared about the five hundred thousand Gypsies slaughtered in camps because 'for reasons of public health and particularly because the Gypsies have manifestly a heavily tainted heredity, and because they are inveterate criminals who constitute parasites in the bosom of our people, it is fitting to prevent them from reproducing themselves and to subject them to the obligation of forced labor in the labor camps. We must pursue this program fearlessly and unreservedly, keeping in mind that sterilization is but a half-measure. It is in conformity with the principles of a state with morals on a high level and particularly the Third Reich.'

The letter from the *Gauleiter* of Steiermark to the *Reichsminister* was one Roman remembered well. It created the high-sounding paper trap that caught his parents and killed them either in a camp or some cattle car rolling from Romania with other *Rassenverfolgte*, racial undesirables. His father and mother had been foolish, of course. They were English Gypsies, and they thought they could ignore the war and take to the road for the wedding of a friend outside Constanta. It was the time of the Phony War and Gypsies always ignored *gaja* affairs. They were in the middle of the celebration toasts when the *Sicherheitsdienst* threw a ring of truck lights on them and divided them into men and women and children and loaded them up for the short drive to the railroad junction.

There was no very good reason for his escape. The truck he was in was at the end of the line, and the security police didn't see any need yet for the rear guard of motorcycles they would use later when those rounded up knew where they were going. Because the truck was so crowded, the five-year-old boy sat with the driver and guard in front. Halfway to the station, the truck slowed down and the guard pushed him out onto a grassy bank.

Then it sped up to rejoin the dark caravan, and that was the last time he ever saw his parents. Yojo and Mara Gry didn't exist anymore.

He walked back down the road to the deserted campsite because he didn't know where else to go. Roman sat in the middle of a scene that looked like an abandoned circus, the painted vans and tents and hungry, tethered horses and even a trained bear sprawling over the meadow in bewilderment, waiting for Gypsies. The only ones to come were an old couple of Turco-Americans who were late. They understood immediately what had happened and they stayed only long enough to stuff Roman in the back of their ancient car. Lazlo and Yula Kronitos had returned from the United States with the money they'd made on *bozur* so that they could roam through Anatolia comfortably. Instead, they headed through North Africa and then to Portugal, paying their way with the infinite gold coins of Yula's heavy necklaces, taking the boy with them. From Lisbon they sailed to New York, where they gave Roman to their son, and when the ship left to return to Europe, the old couple was on it. The boy had been a 'heavenly obligation' in Yula's eyes, and they had discharged it.

It was not difficult to gain American papers for Roman. He retained his father's *gaja* name, Grey, because it fitted well. He spoke English. Besides, the authorities had long given up the battle of keeping birth certificates for Gypsy children born on the road. When the police did question his false papers of baptism, the Gypsies turned to another defense. Roman became the court ward of a downstate New York professor. It was a traditional ploy for a Gypsy family to seek the protection of a sympathetic and wealthy *gaja*. To be one of these was to be a *rai*. 'Part sucker and part father' was the way James Oliver described the title he had gained. Oliver was a Poughkeepsie judge who'd left the bench to study Sanskrit. His interest in Gypsies began when he discovered the closeness between Romani and the lost language, and he was a regular godfather at Gypsy baptisms. It was not difficult to infiltrate a Gypsy boy into his large empty house along the Hudson.

'What are you?' Oliver would muse aloud to the olive-colored boy who sat across from him at the dinner table. 'East Indian? English? Not Turkish, I would guess despite your friends. Rom, naturally, but Lovari or another tribe? The English Grys are famous for being dark and clever, so I suppose that fits. Then Rom, let's settle for that. But when you leave, do you think you might be part *gajo*, too?' And Roman would shake his head vigorously.

Oliver took a poorly hidden delight in tutoring the bright boy in the things he considered important. His tenure in the court had given him a distaste for politics and the law. What he appreciated decorated his house, thousands of books in a dozen languages and a priceless collection of antiques. 'It's not so horrible that you've broken something,' he told Roman as they stood amid the bright remains of a crystal goblet, 'as the fact that you don't know what it is you've broken.' Roman learned, mainly because what he broke he had to put back together under the careful direction of the professor.

Roman was nine when he ran away for the first time. He'd spent weeks out before with Gypsies coming through the Hudson Valley, but this time he was away for a year, wandering with a family of Kalderash as far as Mexico City. When he returned, he found a place set for him at the table. 'Take the apologetic look off your face,' Oliver said. 'I wouldn't expect a *vadni ratsa* to stay in a pen.' Roman picked up a piece of bread and smiled with relief. A *gajo* who understood 'the wild goose' was a *rai* indeed.

The table was always set for him no matter how far or long he traveled, and when he was searching for the grave of his parents, out of concern for their *mule*, there were long absences. It was after walking over a field in Bavaria where the grass was growing again over the lime pits that he found a letter waiting at Munich General Delivery. Professor James Hancock Oliver had died of tuberculosis. Efforts to reach Roman by mail or through American consulates had been in vain. Would he return on receipt of this letter? He was the main beneficiary of Mr Oliver's will. It was only rereading the letter a hundredth time – he was sitting beside the warm, dull Danube and cursing the *gaja* mails; if it had been a Rom who died, he would have known about it in a day no matter where he was – that he realized he'd wasted another father while he was looking for his first. He was twenty years old, and he was rich in exactly those things he didn't want. Otherwise, he had nothing.

*

'I'm going down to department headquarters, Roman,' Isadore said. 'Are you coming in with me or not?'

'Sure, Sergeant. I'd like to take a look at the Sloan antiques.'

'Why? Sloan didn't.'

Roman laughed. 'I guess that's why.'

Chapter Six

The department warehouse was so crowded with crates of liquor, televisions, transistor radios and all the other criminal evidence of an affluent society that the guards in charge had long ceased trying to maintain order. The Sloan antiques made a small pile that was roped off from a tower of dusty clothes on one side and an unsteady stack of typewriter cases on the other.

'There you are,' Isadore said. He was unconsciously dusting his pants as he walked. 'Officer Swoboda will have to keep an eye on you, you understand. I don't know what you think you're going to find. Afterward, you'll come up and see me?'

'Thanks, Sergeant. I'll just look around.'

'You do that,' Isadore said. Roman watched his round, disconsolate shape disappear through the door.

Officer Swoboda, one of those who had forsaken the warehouse fight, a man counting the months to his pension, stood over Roman as he knelt beside the wrecked furniture. No attempt had been made to reassemble the antiques, just to lay corresponding pieces together. Roman could do nothing about the mutilated girl, but he could do something about this.

'Excuse me, Officer, have you got any epoxy here?'

'Yeah, but that's department property.'

Roman pulled a twenty from his money clip. The guard looked at the closed door dumbly. Roman rubbed the bill between his fingers so that it crackled. Officer Swoboda's hearing proved to be his most acute sense. He fetched the tubes of epoxy and stood poised for any more errands.

Roman ignored the policeman while he cleared an adequate working space. The silver was in the best shape, a small tea service by either Coney or the Huguenot Apollos Rivoire who changed his name to Revere. The slender spout had been badly crippled by the accident but was easily reparable. It was a charming set, and it was hard to imagine any collector with the taste to own it who wouldn't come to tend to it alone.

There was no way of writing off the pair of Queen Anne side chairs, no matter how badly one wanted the insurance money. They had lasted two centuries of fairly constant use because they were solidly constructed of heavy mahogany. The scratches were purely superficial. A quick inspection showed that even the drake feet were originals. On the other hand, there was little to put back together of an inlaid shelf clock. The works were displayed like a twisted skeleton through the shattered case. From the carving of the center plinth and finial, it wouldn't have been the best example of Federal Massachusetts workmanship, but it was still a shame. Roman could picture it gonging madly to its death as it tumbled over the highway.

Another fatal victim was a tambour desk. It took imagination to see what it must have looked like. A trim

Hepplewhite from the shape and inlay work of a broken leg. The cherrywood veneer on the shelves was largely scraped off, and the tambour section with its delicate sliding doors had separated from the lower half of the desk from the impact of the collision. He examined the insides of the drawers, checking the joining. It was here as much as the exterior that the real craftsmanship could be found. To be a joiner two hundred years ago was to be a member of a skilled profession that looked down on carpentry as a doctor would look down on a quack. The dovetail joins had held firm with an integrity Professor Oliver would have admired.

A box contained shards of Tiffany glass. A mediocre cut-down Windsor rocker was a tepee of turnings now. The sides and bottom of a dower chest gained Roman's eye for ten minutes. It had the tulip and sunflower motif of Pilgrim Connecticut, square and innocent. Roman finished his examination with a feeling of disgust. He would have liked to find something incriminating about the Pilgrims.

He looked up. Officer Swoboda was puzzling his way through the *Daily News* crossword with a well-used eraser.

'That's it?' Roman asked. 'That's the lot?'

'Yup.' The cop didn't look away from his work.

Roman picked his jacket off the floor. It was dirty, and he was sweaty. The stubble on his cheek was a purple shadow. It took constant care to keep himself from looking like a mugger. He was halfway out the room on his way to Isadore when he remembered the pictures.

'Wait. I saw something else. Big.'

Swoboda got up to lock the door behind Roman. As he stood, a canvas dropcloth slid off his perch to the floor. His chair had been the battered top half of a highboy.

'What about that epoxy?'

Roman ignored him and dragged the rest of the dropcloth away. The whole highboy was there. In parts, but there. It was an unusual Chippendale with slender cabriole legs and ball-and-claw feet. A fanciful scroll top matched the crotch walnut veneer fronts and the engraved brass handles.

'I'll need it,' Roman said.

The old dowels were broken, and the double chest would never stand up again. He didn't care. He would be the good embalmer and prepare it for its funeral. He spread milky epoxy onto a piece of the scrollwork and pressed it back onto the top.

'I also need some skilled help,' Roman told the guard. 'If you'll just hold this here.'

He rigged supports from the chairs and typewriters to hold other parts of the highboy together as he did his pasting. The target of his energy soon started retaking its shape. The highboy was a graceful chest-on-chest, New England, about 1750, made from extra-light dried walnut. There was no other way the slender legs could have held under its height. He put the bottom back on a drawer.

'It's a shame you don't love them,' he could hear Oliver saying as he worked, the way the old man always talked as they repaired a cabinet together. 'Think of the years and the art it took to make this.'

'They're only things,' he would say in return. 'Things are the *gaja* disease. Not for me.'

'But such a beautiful disease.'

The bottom apron of the brittle walnut chest had snapped off. Roman found it in a drawer. It had a boldly scalloped shell on it, with the open claw of the foot and the high scroll the final signature of a young, experimental Goddard highboy.

'Hey, that's kind of pretty,' the policeman said.

'John Goddard, Newport, Rhode Island, will be glad to hear that,' Roman said. He pushed himself off the floor and straightened up. It had taken more than an hour of nonstop labor putting the highboy together, and he looked as if he'd put on his clothes straight out of the washer.

'You done? You going to leave it like this? It'll fall apart.'

It seemed unlikely, but there might be the first stirrings of an appreciation in the policeman. Roman gave him the benefit of the doubt and another twenty-dollar bill.

'Just stand still. If Sergeant Isadore asks where I am, tell him I had a case of Gypsy feet,' Roman said on his way out.

It was after a taxi and a shower and while he was shaving that he thought about the highboy. Since he needed three shaves a day to stay presentable, he spent a lot of time in front of a steamed mirror. He prided himself on the profitable concentration he'd developed during these periods of inactivity. The only danger was in forgetting the small scar on his neck.

There was a chance Sergeant Isadore might think he put the highboy back together for fun. Maybe. In any case, it was the only excuse he could think of for spending so much time on the double chest. From the outside everything was normal. Even the nails in the pine backing were originals, hand-wrought flattened spikes. The drawers slid out easily on deftly repaired runners, and that was the first trouble. They shouldn't have slid. The rope and padding he'd seen in the photograph should have held firm over the empty drawers all the way through the accident. Unless there were something in the drawers, something heavy rolling around and slamming against the front of the drawer until the rope broke. A sixty-pound torso would have done the job.

Inside, the drawers were spotless. The dovetails interlocked as cleanly as fingers, or they had until very recently. Now each drawer had one or two dovetails gaping, warped out of contact next to other joins that were as tight as the day they were glued. He'd seen damage like it only once before, when a girl had stuffed an antique dry sink with solidified carbon dioxide, dry ice.

Roman thought the policeman would finally catch on to the last thing he was doing, but he didn't. While Roman was fumbling with the drawers, he accidentally ran the sharp metal bevel of his ring along the wood of each drawer's sides and back. Inside the hardwood exterior of any antique the drawers were made of soft pine and gouging the wood was a common method of determining whether wormholes were twisting and genuine or straight and artificial. The wormholes did something else. Their capillary action would soak up any stain that was washed off the surface of the wood. He found what he was looking for in the last drawer. The wormholes there were clotted with a rusty deposit. Roman knew the difference between blood and an oil stain.

The razor took off the first layer of epidermis, then the second and the third, provoking a bright bud of red before he noticed that he'd run into the scar again.

Chapter Seven

Hoddinot Sloan's house was in the Federal style. Neo-Virginian against the Massachusetts countryside, with fluted wooden columns and cornices in white on red brick, a row of french doors opening onto a well-tended garden, all of it hidden from the road leading to Newton by a line of elms. Hoddinot Sloan also seemed in the classic Federal style. A fine nose was balanced by white eyebrows. His blue eyes seemed irritated, but the distinguished gray hair was unruffled. His thin mouth was a blend of distaste and civility.

'Will you please explain your mission again?' he asked politely as he barred the door.

'Certainly. The Metropolitan Museum is compiling a study of the best private collections of early American furniture. This is for the unlikely event of part of the museum's collection being destroyed, but you know how things are in New York. If something of this nature happens, the museum wants to know exactly where it can replace damaged articles. Naturally, your name came up. I called a few times, but your line was busy. Since I was in this part of the country, I thought I'd take a chance and drop in anyway.'

Sloan looked his visitor over warily. He definitely didn't look as if he were connected with any museum.

With the Mafia, more likely. Sloan had never seen such dark eyes. The pupils were so large there was almost no room for the whites. The man's complexion had an unsettling tone somewhere between chocolate and red wine. His suit bunched up over a laborer's shoulders. Not the sort of man who was interested in antiques, unless he was Armenian; that could be it. Though Armenians were only good with rugs, he believed.

'Your name?'

'Grey. Roman Grey.'

It wasn't always Grey, Sloan decided.

'You have a letter or some identification?'

'Of course.' Roman took an envelope from his jacket and handed it to Sloan. The first thing Sloan did when he took the letter out was to check the letterhead. It actually was from the museum, a surprise, and repeated what the man had said and asked for any cooperation. It was signed by the director of the museum's American Wing.

'Oh, come in, come in,' Sloan said reluctantly. He read the letter a second time as Roman entered the foyer. The interior of the house matched its outside with cream gray moldings, a grandfather clock by Willard, a complete set of four matched side chairs, the patina of old furniture and old money. Sloan eyed his visitor apprehensively as if he expected him to seize the clock under his arm and bolt through the door.

'You know something about antiques?' Sloan asked.

'A little.'

'Really,' Sloan said, not bothering to hide his doubt.

'You don't mind if I call the museum to check this letter, do you?'

'Please, go right ahead.'

Sloan didn't usher Roman into the living room; he just motioned him in with a jerk of his gray locks. It was clear he wanted to keep an eye on the intruder. The letter went into Sloan's tweed jacket like evidence. Roman stationed himself in plain view beside the fireplace and admired the mantel's plaster carving. What did a room like this do for Sloan, he wondered. Set him off from the rest of the world, just where he wanted to be.

Sloan redialed with some exasperation and finally slammed the phone down. 'Some idiotic recording. The offices are closed, and they'll be closed all weekend.'

'That's too bad, but it's always like that on Fridays. And everyone's away on vacation, you know,' Roman said. He'd held his breath for only a second during Sloan's call.

'Too bad for you,' Sloan said. 'This will have to wait until next week at the soonest then. Besides, I am personally in no mood to have a stranger snooping around my house. If I felt like meeting people, I'd be in New York for the Armory Show this instant.'

'Yes. I was rather surprised that you weren't.'

Sloan hesitated, not sure whether the question was impertinent. 'I would be if some moron hadn't rammed into the truck carrying my exhibit and destroyed the lot. So you'll have to excuse me.'

The distinguished head jerked toward the front door. Roman looked around the room. If he didn't get in now, he never would. The phone call on Monday would finish him.

'I can understand your being upset,' he said as he moved slowly to the foyer. 'The more one appreciates fine antiques, the more one is hurt by their thoughtless destruction.'

'Yes, yes,' Sloan said impatiently.

'What I don't understand,' Roman said, 'is how a man of your obvious good taste could put a récamier in this room. It's like putting a grand piano on a raft. Weights down that corner of the room a little bit, don't you think?'

Sloan froze with his thin mouth open during the first part of Roman's comment. The well-groomed hair bristled. By the time Roman was finished, though, the collector's eyes were mobile and curious.

'I know what I think,' Sloan said. 'Perhaps you should elaborate on your odd remarks.'

'Forgive me, I didn't mean to offend.' Roman smiled broadly. This was the time to turn on the charm. 'It simply struck me that way. But look at this marvelous Sheraton side chair you've selected to go by the window. The airiness of the center splat carving, the reeded legs and spade feet make it look as if it could float. The New York cabinetmaker who created it might have made it for this room. And then this récamier. It may just be my prejudice, but I think that the Empire style was a mistake, the worst one Napoleon ever made. Where could a day-bed get such delusions of grandeur? The styles of Egypt and Rome don't mix, and it doesn't matter how much good mahogany you waste trying. It's a shame that

American furniture makers had to pass through an uninventive phase like this.'

Sloan listened intently. 'Very forthright of you, Mr Grey. Since you are so interested, perhaps you'd tell me whether the paint and gilt on the récamier are original?'

Roman nodded and lowered himself to the floor. He could see Sloan raising a corner of his mouth wryly. A line of sphinxes ranged along the apron of the sofa keeping their secret to themselves. This was the part where he was supposed to run his hand over the finish and make a guess. Instead, a penknife appeared in his hand. The tip of it followed the gilt around the blocky leg of the récamier underneath. Quickly, before Sloan could have second thoughts, he gouged a tiny sliver of the gilt out, holding it as if it were on a tray while he got to his feet and then put the blade on his tongue. He closed his mouth and rolled the flake against his palate. When he was satisfied, he rubbed his tongue with a handkerchief.

'It's the original, but it's not gilt. To begin with, it's a Boston récamier, and Boston furniture makers always were restrained in their use of gold, so I had my doubts. No, it's orpiment. Lovely yellow, but it hasn't been used for some time because it's poisonous, a sulfide of arsenic. Lasted as well as it has because it's in Venice turpentine. Since the orpiment is original, I think we can assume that the paint underneath is also.'

'Amazing,' Sloan said, genuinely impressed. His estimate of his visitor was going through some rapid changes. 'It took me a week to come to that conclusion. A friend left it for an opinion, and this reaffirms what I thought. And what you said about the Empire period, I quite agree with. Napoleon was a nasty man, and he inspired a nasty style. Amazing, though. I never saw that done before. Have you been poisoned by any chance?'

Roman smiled. Sloan was a good deal warmer than he had been before. 'No. I would appreciate some water to wash my mouth out, however.'

'Naturally, naturally,' Sloan said. 'While I get it for you, let me show you to the rose garden. There are a couple Houdon bathers there you might enjoy. This way.'

The rose garden was on the other side of the house, the shady side so that the flowers could last out the summer. Roman eased himself into an iron chair facing the marble bathers and thinking about Hoddinot Sloan. If the fish was not on the hook, he was very interested in the bait.

'Here we are.' Sloan emerged from a door farther down the house at what must have been the kitchen. He was bearing a salver with a bottle of white wine and two glasses. 'Might as well wash our mouths with a good year.' He set the tray down on the table between them. 'What do you think of the bathers?'

'Much more attractive than Madame Récamier.'

Sloan laughed. Real teeth, Roman noted. For a man in his late fifties Sloan kept himself up as well as his house.

'That was quite a trick. Where did you pick it up?' Sloan asked. It was meant to sound like a cross between curiosity and congratulation instead of envy.

'Simply an old method,' Roman told him. 'The difficulty is in differentiating from the other sulfides used in painting. Of course, arsenic has a definite taste of its own. Excuse me.' He spit a mouthful of Vouvray onto the grass.

'Bitter almonds, isn't it?' Sloan said.

Roman nodded. 'Something like that. How did you know?'

'Mystery books. I must read a hundred a year,' Sloan confessed with a touch of pride. 'I just wish some of them were harder to figure out. But about this problem with the sulfides, are there any other ways of finding out which is which?'

'Oh, yes. Putting a sample into a spoon and holding a match underneath is one way. The smells are often quite characteristic. And as a last resort, you can burn it. I'm sure you can read a flame for pigments or zinc.'

Sloan smiled reassuringly while his eyes betrayed ignorance. The two men were equals now, even friends, until Sloan could appropriate the odd visitor's knowledge. The remark that it was simply an 'old method' was too vague for him to accept.

'You collect yourself,' the host prompted.

'Study. I'm afraid I don't have the money to surround myself with beauty the way you have, so I content myself with scholarship. From time to time, I advise beginning collectors.'

Sloan gave another of his smiles of understanding. There were so many people trying to buy their way into society with the purchase of a Chippendale chair or two, usually at inflated prices. His visitor was getting more and more interesting.

'I'm sorry,' Roman said. 'Here I am taking up all your time when I was about to go. Thanks very much for the wine; the Loire grapes are my favorite. Now I will be on my way. It's a long drive back to the city.'

'Wait,' Sloan said as if something had just occurred to him, although he'd been thinking about it for the past minute. 'Have you got a room in Boston?'

'No,' Roman admitted. 'I just dropped by today because this is my last week with the museum. They'll be sending someone else out next week.'

That was enough for Sloan.

'Then I insist. You must stay here for the weekend. The director is an old friend of mine, and the least I can do is cooperate, and I'd find it a pleasure to show the collection to someone I know would appreciate it. I'll have the guest room readied. The servants will bring your luggage from your car. You have no other plans for the weekend?'

It was more an order than a question, but Roman displayed the decent amount of hesitation.

Sloan winked. 'She'll wait. They always do.' It was meant as a masculine insight, though it had that inevitable element of upper-class fantasy for the sexual life of 'other types.' How many times had Roman run into that myth when he was on the road with a *kumpania*, the *gaja* gaping on the sides of the road, nudging each other and not bothering to whisper about the Gypsy girls with their precocious breasts and bright petticoats – 'The darker the cherry, the sweeter the meat' – totally unaware and probably not caring that there was no female more chaste than a Gypsy? The girl who gave away her virginity gave away her seat by the Romany fire.

'Okay,' Roman said. 'If you'd really like me to.'

After another glass, a maid came and showed Roman to his room. His suitcase was already in it, opened on the bed, and his toilet kit was in the bathroom. He washed under his arms and shaved and laid himself out over the bed. The whole thing would have been easier to reconstruct if he'd been Isadore. He stared blankly at the dun-colored ceiling so tastefully in place with the Georgian decor of the room. Nanoosh. A Chippendale highboy. A body in several parts, making a murder out of an accident. A funeral with Madame Vera.

Hoddinot Sloan. A man very interested and fairly knowledgeable about antiques. Wealthy, from what? The murder of whales, slaving, rum? It didn't matter; money, it was universally acknowledged, got a polish with age. A snob, a man who found it difficult to deal with people. The tweed jacket and the lemon turtleneck, the banker's profile, the signet ring with the crest, were just more furniture to surround himself with. A possessive man, a man who should have gone to New York outraged at the loss of the van's delicate cargo. An ultimate *gajo*, who for some reason was not acting like one.

What had he said? That he was not in the mood for meeting people. Sloan wasn't the sort of man who stayed home to be alone with his thoughts. He was expecting something. Not someone, or he would never have invited a stranger to stay. The ploy with the récamier was barely enough to secure an invitation as it was. Sloan's greed had swung it. It wasn't strong enough to get him out, to go down to New York, but it was enough to have a stranger in his house for some information on the free. An unpleasant man, Hoddinot Sloan.

A maid knocked on the door to report that dinner was being served. Roman dug a fresh shirt out of his suitcase, put it on and topped it with a tie.

Chapter Eight

'There you are,' Sloan said with an air of discovery as Roman entered the dining room.

There were three places set at the table, Royal Worcester on San Dominican mahogany. The dining room was similar to the others Roman had seen with the addition of a patriotic wooden eagle.

Sloan removed a bottle of white wine that had been perspiring in a silver basket and filled their glasses. As a bit of before-dinner conversation, he asked Roman whether he could identify the various pieces in the room. It was a simple, tedious task, but Roman did it with a smile. After all, what else could Sloan imagine that they had in common? Loving? Hating? A slaughtered girl? It was an intimation of Roman's social standing that Sloan didn't bother to suggest who the third diner might be until she appeared.

'Oh Hillary, we were wondering where you were. This is Mr Grey; he's staying over for the weekend. My daughter.'

Hillary had a cool hand, like the glass of wine. Roman had seen her picture in the living room in a frame from Biddle, Banks and Bailey. As she sat down, she still seemed to be in a sterling silver frame. Her hair was long and so fair as almost to be white. She'd inherited her father's eyes of ice blue and a full mouth from someone else. She was dressed in a chic blouse, pants and an embroidered leather vest. Roman guessed her age at nineteen.

'Something new,' she said as a greeting.

'I'm glad to meet you, too,' Roman said. Before she could take umbrage, he gave her a wide smile of brilliant teeth against his dark face.

She looked from Roman to her father trying to figure out the connection. 'Well, Father, I thought I knew all your friends.'

Sloan blushed. 'Mr Grey is here to compile a list of the collection for the Metropolitan Museum.'

'Ah.' It was neat and informative. She'd not only put her father down with an ease that showed practice but also put the visitor in his place. There was an embarrassed pause while she innocently smoothed her napkin over her lap.

'Let's eat,' her father said suddenly, as if it were a good idea.

The supper was overcooked scrod and a salad, the sort of meal designed for a middle-aged man watching his weight. Roman grew sympathetic to Sloan's digestion as the girl led the conversation from one sore subject to another in a soft, sweet voice. She was like a surgeon probing with a scalpel not to dispel pain but create it.

'My father's a very good collector. I'm so happy your museum is becoming aware of that fact. I bet there's not another man in Boston with his eye for value. Remember the time' – she turned for aid from her father – 'when that old Irishwoman asked you to look at that chest. You know, she'd been a maid to one of the Cabot families her whole life, and all she got out of it was a dirty old bureau. She was practically in rags, you told me. Anyway, Father took one look at it and knew it was a, what, a William and Mary, that's right. He paid her fifty dollars for it, brought it here and cleaned it, and sold it two months later for three thousand dollars.'

She slid a fish knife down the flaccid spine of the scrod.

'My friends are all against the war. I mean, half of them are in Canada, and the rest are trying to break a toe or something before their physical rather than let themselves be turned into cannon fodder. So far as I'm concerned that's a lot braver than just letting yourself be inducted. The silly boys aren't as original as they think, though. Father was just as smart as they are now and it was a lot more unpopular in World War II. It took real nerve claiming a bad back then, don't you think?'

By the time she was finished she'd picked her father as clean as the fish. Sloan's eyes had the watery look of a man who was knocked out and merely refused to fall. The unusual aspect in the girl's attack, what made it so effective, was an absence of any feeling. She didn't act from betrayal or pique the way a daughter should. It reminded him of the absent presence in the framed pictures. There were no photos of her mother in the house. The ones of Sloan and the girl together belied the idea that he ever held her on his lap for anything but portraits. He was the sort of father who sent his daughter from one boarding school to another, probably showing up late if at all on Father's Day and then making contact with the other fathers instead of with Hillary Sloan. Now he was paying for it.

She wasn't just a girl anymore. Roman could feel her physical presence, the line that led down her cheek to a stylishly long neck to the casually unbuttoned blouse and the fact that no bra restrained her breasts as she twisted back and forth from her father to the fish. At the same time he was aware that she was studying him. It was unusual enough for a man like him to be sitting across from her whether he was from the museum or not. The few electric shocks she directed at him – 'I've always supposed that immigrants understood better how bestial this country is' – got no reaction, and this mystified her further.

Roman began feeling sordid for having insinuated himself into the Sloan household to hear a dinner conversation that, except for its degree, was taking place in a million other American homes at the same time. He had to remind himself that it was necessary. The *vilos*, the old witches of Romania, could work magic on a person only when they had something of his – a fingernail, a hair. Something to make him concrete. Roman didn't spend on magic, but he understood the truth of the system. He needed the frigid, arrogant pulse of the Sloans, or else he would be blind the way he had been on the highway trying to decipher a stretch of road and a handful of photographs. He was no detective. This was the only way he could work, the way the Romany had always worked.

Hillary was talking about a rock festival. Sloan listened

with a frown of disapproval. As she spoke, she raised her arms above her head, the imprint of her nipples through her blouse adding another level of intimidation. Sloan looked aside.

Roman watched with interest. Few *gaja* understood the physical language between people, and the girl herself probably didn't know what a good job she was doing of undermining her father. When her luxurious stretch was done and she saw that Roman had not diverted his eyes to his lettuce, she stared straight at him. His eyes still didn't fall.

'That's a beautiful vest,' Roman commented. 'Kid leather had a religious significance during the Middle Ages. Especially black kid.'

'Oh, she has one of those, too,' Sloan said, eager to tell what he had given her.

'Really? You're an expert on any number of things,' Hillary said. He watched the pupils of her blue eyes narrow with dislike. 'I guess that's a lesson. Those who can't afford things know the most about them.'

'I'm afraid that's the truth.' Roman smiled disarmingly.

The dessert came, glass bowls of sherbet. Sloan took small, disheartened scoops of his. His daughter took one large spoonful, praised it extravagantly, and let the lemon-colored ice melt into a puddle of conspicuous consumption. Roman enjoyed his completely.

'Have you got reservations up in the White Mountains?' Sloan asked. It was a last attempt to establish his role as patriarch.

'Reservations at a rock festival would be a little illogical, Father,' Hillary said, as if she were explaining affairs to a slow child. Her nostrils dilated, and her fingers rose a quarter inch from the table.

'Cigarette?' Roman asked. His hand held out his pack of Gauloises to her. Because that was what she had been thinking of and what her minute gestures told Roman, she took it before she could stop herself. 'They're strong things, but they're all I have,' he said.

To give back the cigarette would be a confession of weakness. Hillary accepted his light.

'*Très chic*,' she said with a motion of the Gauloise.

'*Très* cheap,' Roman told her.

Sloan attempted to drag the conversation back to the festival. His daughter led him on effortlessly. There had been a change in the relationship between the girl and the visitor. She showed off for Roman. He sat back and watched them, taking in the polite Sloan ferocity, their Royal Worcester, their inlaid mahogany prosperity, their worm-eaten ancestry, their hair and fingernails.

As an exercise in imagination, he placed a dismembered body on the table in between the father and daughter and tried to see if it fit.

Chapter Nine

It wasn't a good night for sleeping. The bed was made of
pillows, and the Sloans spun around a lightless antique
shop. He couldn't make out what they said. Finally, he
slept on the floor.

Breakfast was Continental, croissants and coffee. He
had that to be thankful for. The cook made his pot
double strength, and he poured a stream of sugar into it.
It was before eight, and only he and the staff were up.
When he was finished, he went out into the garden.

Sloan's taste for things Virginian showed in the land-
scaping. No native evergreens were allowed to intrude,
and the few maples were barely tolerated. The garden
with the marble bathers was divided from the rose garden
by a trellis. There was a second trellis halfway down the
side of the lawn serving as camouflage for a potting shed.
He wandered down to it and found nothing more
suspicious than varmint poison. Rather than come back
through the yard he crossed to the Sloan driveway. A
yellow Buick station wagon was parked in it. He followed
the driveway to the front of the house. On the west end
were two rooms he had not yet seen, an office and a
workroom with neat rows of paint cans and, hung on
hooks from the walls, legs and arms salvaged from
discarded possessions.

'Looking for something?'

Hillary came around from the gardens. She was in a green one-piece riding outfit with jodhpur wings and high boots. Her hands were on her hips. The effect of the green and her white-gold hair was what she wanted it to be.

'Yes, you,' Roman said. 'The house is lovely, but I was hoping for some company. Maybe I'm just an early riser.'

'Maybe,' Hillary said, but didn't bother keeping up the tension. 'I can't say that I like it. We used to have a house in Cambridge. When my mother died, we sold it. The neighborhood was changing, Father said. We bought this. I still don't like it.'

'How long ago was that?'

'Twelve years. Before I forget, he sent me to fetch you. He's at the breakfast table.'

Hoddinot Sloan appeared to have recovered from last night's dinner. He dabbed half a croissant with marmalade as he welcomed Roman.

'Sleep well? That's a pencil post four-poster in your room, you know.'

'I'm sure he does,' Hillary commented. She poured twin braids of milk and coffee into her cup.

'Which is more than I can say for you.' Her father went on. 'I've tried to interest Hillary in the study of antiques for years. All she can think of is horses and hippies, a fairly individual combination but not one likely to stimulate the brain.'

Far away at the rear of the lawn a gardener laid out sprinklers. When they stretched from one fence to the other, he bent down to a water nozzle hidden in the grass and turned it on. A series of rooster tails erupted from the grass. The works, Roman thought, had also been turned on beneath Sloan's own manicured exterior. Last night's dinner had not been a normal one; he wasn't a man to invite an audience to his own execution.

'Father disapproves,' she said. She crossed her arms, drawing the knit riding suit tight around her chest. Sloan still didn't know how to handle the outlined maturity of her body. Sex, as usual, was the ultimate weapon. 'Do you jump?' she asked Roman.

'Occasionally. On hot sand, things of that sort.'

'No, no, jump horses. That's Hillary's hobby,' Sloan said.

Hillary giggled. 'I thought it was quite funny.' She began laughing again. The happier she was, the younger she looked.

'Ridiculous,' Sloan said. The last shred of croissant vanished into his mouth. 'Come on, Grey. We have a lot of work to do.'

While Hillary went down a path to the stables, Sloan escorted Roman into his private office. Sloan had chosen second-rate antiques for the room, good enough to lend a pleasant air but nothing whose value would be ruined by wear.

'Very wise,' Roman said. 'A lot of people would have just put these into storage.'

Sloan pointed to the files. 'I never waste anything. I got these at a dollar apiece. Simply replaced the runners and cemented strips on the drawers, and they're good as new. I've been offered a hundred apiece for them now. Tell me, how do you plan to categorize the collection?'

Roman explained that he intended no comprehensive catalogue, just a detailed list of those pieces that were of exhibition value. Sloan volunteered that he had photos of every piece that went through his hands with records of any restoration that had been done to them.

'It's a matter of protection,' he added. 'I don't want anyone accusing me of bad faith. I tell them exactly what they're buying. I may not tell people what they have when they're selling to me; that's part of the game. Otherwise, they shouldn't be in it.'

Roman nodded obediently, and Sloan went on.

'I'll tell you this, no one can accuse me of shady practices like so many New York collectors.'

'Are there many people like, uh, that in Boston?'

Sloan sniffed. 'Mostly Irish here. I thought it was a good time to leave the city when the Kennedys bought it.'

Sloan's bigotry rose like a whale through the calm surface of a sea. It blew off its supply of bile and in a few moments returned to the depths of his personality. The conversation moved back to antiques.

'It must have made you very sad when your Armory shipment was destroyed. Perhaps it wasn't total,' Roman suggested. 'If you could restore the files and you have photos, you might be able to restore some of those pieces.'

Sloan shrugged the suggestion off. 'I doubt it. Besides – you'll find this hard to believe – they're being held as evidence or something by the New York police. Some murder or a body, I haven't got it straight.'

Roman raised his eyebrows with wonder.

'It is presumptuous, I agree,' Sloan said. 'But apparently the man who ran into the van was hiding a dead girl in his car. If it hadn't been for the accident, he probably would have gotten away with the crime.'

'Didn't the police tell you anything more?'

'No.' Sloan sighed. 'An affair of passion most likely. That's what these cases usually are. Emotional things.'

Sloan opened his desk and took out four loose-leaf folders. The pages were full of notes and snapshots. He gave them to Roman to carry as they moved to his workshop. A sharp blend of turpentine and sawdust permeated the room. Dowels of varying thicknesses stood in an ascending line like the pipes of an organ. A large rotary saw stood on one side. On the walls were the dismantled trophies Roman had seen through the window: cabriole and reeded legs with hall-and-claw, hair paw, pad and spade feet. A bright fluorescent light in the shape of a halo hung from the ceiling.

Roman put the notebooks down and took out his own notebook and pen. Sloan dragged a dropcloth off a small serving table. It was New England Sheraton rather than Philadelphian, from about 1800. At any auction it would draw a very good price and Roman had to admit it was museum class.

'I purchased this for, let's say five thousand. I'll sell it for much more,' Sloan told him. 'Can you tell me how I was able to buy it for so little? Also, can you tell me where you have seen work by the same artist here?'

Sloan was insatiable. A mania for tests was in the best of *gaja*, and it was something that Roman could never comprehend, an 'it's how you perform today that counts' attitude that explained their frustration with sex. Served them right. Roman ran his hand along the fine carving of the legs and the glossy mahogany of the drawer fronts. He didn't have the patience to keep Sloan in suspense.

'Samuel McIntire did the carving, and you can see the design is basically the same as the mantel in your living room. I admired it the first day I was here. That puts us in Salem. McIntire didn't do the lid on this top, however; that's the trademark of William Hood. They collaborated on this piece. How did you get the bargain?'

He opened the drawers. Except for lathing on the bottom of the sides to correct a droop, they were the originals.

'The back. The back was broken in,' Roman said.

Sloan's mouth dropped as far as it decently could.

'How did you know that? You haven't even pulled that table away from the wall to see the back.'

If it had been yesterday when he needed to impress Sloan, Roman would have answered with some dramatics. Today he was a bored magician.

'I'm afraid that's all it could have been. Obviously everything else is in perfect condition. Besides, a few of the old traditions persisted in Salem into the nineteenth century. The witchcraft trials, you know, and some of the old fears. It wasn't rare for a descendant of one of the accused ladies to have his house and all his furniture broken in some way after he died. It was supposed to ruin any hiding place that his spirit might try to reside in. Being thrifty New Englanders, they usually chose to do the damage someplace where it wouldn't show. They must have been a strange people.'

'Indeed,' Sloan agreed. He pulled the table out. A new pine panel covered the back. 'To think that a ghost would hide away in a table.'

'A highboy would be more comfortable, wouldn't it?'

Confusion clouded Sloan's face and then passed.

'Oh, yes. I see what you mean. Much more comfortable.' He laughed. 'Anyway, as you no doubt suspect, I'll stain the pine to match the rest of the table.'

'You'll use handwrought nails.'

'Naturally. Look, they're in. Tight as a coffin.'

The serving table filled the first page of Roman's notebook. There were others to come from Sloan's collection, and both men had worked up an appetite by lunchtime.

Chapter Ten

Lunch was a *salade niçoise* and a bottle of Tavel. The delicate fare was starting to make Roman's stomach growl in disdain. Sloan directed the conversation to the fictitious collectors whom Roman advised.

'Without naming names, of course,' Sloan said. 'I understand the discretion involved. Even with *nouveau riche*. You use only New York dealers?'

Roman said that wasn't necessarily true. It was enough encouragement to keep Sloan talking until Roman's salad bowl was empty.

'Starving, aren't you?' Hillary asked.

Sloan's face turned red. 'Get those animals out of here. I've told you a million times about those horses. The gardener hasn't got time to clean up after them.'

Hillary looked down and smiled. She was seated on a bay Morgan, and she held the reins of a second horse in her free hand. She was a good enough horsewoman to have crept up silently with the two. It was when she was arrogant that she was most her father's daughter, and then both of them seemed to be set in clear plastic.

'I'll get them off the lawn on one condition. Mr Grey comes with me. He could use some exercise after being cooped up all morning with old chairs and tables.'

'Mr Grey has a job to do. There are a number of things, porcelain, glass, that he has yet to see.'

Hillary slouched in her saddle. 'I can wait.'

Sloan's hand, the one with the signet ring, ran through his silver hair. He looked back and forth from his daughter to Roman, who assumed a pose of complete impartiality.

'You don't want him to see too much, do you, Father? He might get tired. Some riding in the open air might freshen him up.'

Sloan lost some color in his cheeks.

'Well, how about it?' he asked Roman with the little grace he could muster.

'I think you'll have a surplus of fertilizer unless I do.' Roman laughed. He approached his horse, a handsome bay with a star, and patted his neck. He always liked the hot sheen the coat of a good horse had.

'Okay.' Sloan gave in. 'A short ride. I'll expect you back in an hour.'

'By the way,' Roman said, 'if you feel like it, you might want to set up some paints. We can discuss different methods of analysis when I return.'

Hillary led the way off the lawn on her horse while Roman walked his. When he felt they were out of sight, he swung onto the horse's back. They waited until a truck went by on the highway and crossed. A dirt road led to a stable and corral. They took another one into the woods.

'What are you here for?' she asked.

'What?'

'You heard me. What do you want? Why are you getting so friendly with my father?'

She ducked under a branch as if it were an insult hardly worth noticing.

'I'm making a list of antiques. Collectors who cooperate find me full of charm.'

She looked at him shrewdly through golden lashes. 'You claim to be a psychologist then.'

'No. You learn how to deal with people in my profession.'

'Oh, come on. I'm not as dumb as my father. I'd say if a man like you didn't want something really badly from my father, you'd just blow him and his whole house down. I see you more around nightclubs or lions than a collection of antiques.'

They came through a copse of trees to a meadow. The high grass steamed with insects in the afternoon sun. A thrush moved over the field in short dashes. Roman's knees clamped the sides of the horse comfortably, though he would have preferred to do without the saddle.

'It's true I get violent over antimacassars,' Roman confessed, slapping his horse's neck. 'What's his name?'

Hillary tilted her head to look at him. 'You're changing the subject.' After a minute of silent riding, a genuine smile edged onto her lips. 'His name's Blaze. Not very original, is it?'

'And yours?'

'Brownie. They're good horses all the same,' she said proudly. The grasshoppers wildly evacuated their path as she scrutinized her riding partner. 'Questions now, Mr

Grey? Something innocent first and then lead up to the biggies? But I can't ask you questions, like what brings you into the bosom of the nation's dullest family?'

'I give up.' Roman sighed. 'I came for the secret of your scrod with mock cream sauce. If I can't get that, I'll settle for the *salade niçoise* made with Velveeta.'

'Seriously. I can't get it out of my mind why someone like you is interested in my father. Has he got himself involved in something?'

Roman looked around. The girl's questions were almost lost in the din of the insects. It wasn't the noise that made the hair on the back of his neck stand up but the feeling that they weren't alone.

'You think your father's done something wrong?'

'Another question is not an answer.' Tiny beads of sweat appeared at her hairline. The sun had lacquered Roman copper. 'I happen to know you're from the police.' She paused. 'Or the Mafia.'

Roman slapped his hand over his face. She flushed and rode on with her jaw set firmly. He took his hand off his face to wipe the tears away, and she saw her suspicions were correct. He had been laughing. 'God, I can't wait until I see Isadore,' he said. 'The Mafia, what'll be next?'

'Very funny,' Hillary agreed grimly. 'So you're just a poor man interested in antiques and mixing with the upper crust. You must ride pretty well then.'

He was still wiping his eyes when Hillary stopped Brownie beside a raspberry bush and fed him some of the berries. Blaze nuzzled her hand until she gave some to him as well. They'd gone on another ten yards when

Blaze's ears perked up. He reared, stamping his two rear legs. The horse twisted the reins out of Roman's hands and looked back, the pink sides of his eyes showing. The stirrups swung into his legs like ballpeen hammers. Roman caught one blurred look at Hillary's satisfied beam before the horse bolted.

Blaze was a strong young Morgan sixteen hands high, and he was going at top speed when he crashed into the woods. Roman simply tried to stay on. It was impossible to see through the branches that tried to pull him off. Suddenly the horse stumbled. Roman slid to one side just as the horse ended his fall against a tree, crushing his rider between himself and the trunk. Blaze regained his footing and plunged forward. Both of Roman's hands were tangled in the Morgan's mane. He was still on, but his chest refused to expand. There was a dark edge to his vision of the approaching trees. He batted his eyes trying to clear them. He felt the horse starting down an incline before he saw it.

The underbrush became sparser as Blaze slid down the incline regaining velocity, and the black ring closed in on Roman's sight. He could make out a stone fence at the bottom of the bank. The horse would never make the jump with him hanging on like a sack of cement. A shriek that wasn't his own reverberated in his ears. Blaze's flanks bunched in response to his training as they reached the end of the bank and the fence. There was no edge of Roman's vision now, just total darkness.

As Blaze coiled, Roman rose on his knees. There was little point in hesitating. He turned his heels in, squeezed them hard, and rolled all his weight forward onto the horse's withers. He called 'Jump,' blindly and Blaze answered, throwing his sixteen hundred pounds into the air. The surge carried Roman weightlessly up, and he heard two sharp clicks, the sounds of Blaze's front hooves grazing the edge of the wall.

Roman flattened himself against the horse's powerful muscles as it landed and came to a halt. When he straightened up, the knot that had been around his throat was off. He could make out lights and shadows. While the jumper stood and shook with fright, Roman spoke to him and smoothed the febrile trembling in his neck.

Roman turned at the sound of a second horse coming down the bank. He could clearly see Hillary bringing Brownie expertly over the fence. She rode up looking very scared. Blaze shied when she joined them.

'Oh, Mr Grey, I – '

'I know,' Roman said. He slid off the horse to his feet and approached Blaze's head, patting him all the way. One dark hand rubbed Blaze's star, and the other delicately searched his nostrils until he brought out a tiny sprig. He sniffed it. 'Rosemary, right? It would pep up the dullest horse, let alone a healthy one.'

He took the horse by the reins and walked him to let him cool. Hillary got off Brownie and walked by his side. Her lips were tight, and he could almost hear her trying to think of something to say. He didn't know what he wanted to say. She seemed authentically frightened now, but there was a point in the woods when she could have caught up and helped. He didn't even hear her until he was going down the bank.

'I just wanted to scare you.'

'Weren't you afraid I'd sic my mob on you?' he asked sardonically.

'I guess I made a mistake.'

'I'd call it a tantrum. And now I'm throwing a tantrum.' A noise of disgust came out of his throat. 'Maybe this will teach me not to go riding with flirts on horses named Blaze.'

He sat down where he was under a tree.

Roman struggled to stifle a painful laugh of rue. Hillary sat down with him and stared. The horses wandered deeper into the shade of the tree, a large old oak.

'I almost get you killed and you think it's funny. You are the strangest person I've ever met,' she said.

'You lead a sheltered life.' He stuck a blade of grass in his mouth. His jacket was torn, but it was plain he wasn't losing any blood.

'Now I know you're not here just to look at Daddy's antiques.'

Roman frowned. 'Daddy? I thought it was something more formal, like Father or *Pater*.'

'In moments of stress I revert,' she confessed. 'Not often, I guarantee you.'

'I'll take your word.' He rejected the blade and chose another. 'You've got him on the run with that threat about me seeing too much. What is it, phony labels?'

Hillary picked a blade of grass for herself.

'I saw the paper through the window this morning,' Roman went on, 'and I saw the ink when I went into the workshop with your father.'

She took the blade from her mouth and tossed it like a tiny green spear. 'Isn't he the phony? Christ! If he'd been on Blaze, he would have fainted. And if he'd caught me afterward, he would have killed me.'

'You're kidding, aren't you?'

'Oh, I don't know.'

'What about your mother?' He thought she might react with her police suspicions. She simply shook her head.

'No mother, not even a picture anymore. She had "bad blood," according to my father, who is the one person in the twentieth century who still uses that phrase. The truth is she was coming home from a charity ball one night and she drove the car into the Charles River, taking her lover with her. Now, when I come home at four in the morning, which is usual whenever I'm at home, my father tells me that I have "bad blood." I haven't got a generation gap with him, I've got a historical gap.'

She drew the pack of Gauloises from his shirt pocket and lit one for each of them. As Roman accepted the cigarette in his mouth, his eyes half shut, she studied him. The bridge of his nose was sharp enough for a knife, and his skin looked as if it had been patiently oiled by a tanner. Instead of being trim, his waist was a solid continuation of his barrel chest, and yet, in all, there was something uniquely appealing about the combination.

'The language you were speaking to Blaze when I came up. It was Gypsy, wasn't it?' she said softly.

Roman was surprised. 'How did you know?'

'A teacher introduced me to some once in Switzerland. So your name isn't really Grey, is it?'

'Yes. Not the color gray; there isn't such a color to Gypsies. The closest translation would be "horse," actually.'

'Oh,' Hillary said in a chastened voice. 'Many famous Gypsy jockeys?'

'"Jockey" is a Gypsy word.'

They nodded at each other, compressing smiles on their lips.

'Give me some other words,' she said. 'I'm interested.'

'Okay.' He looked up at the underbellies of the leaves. 'Since you seek enlightenment, a *camo djili*:

> *Paownie birks*
> My *men-engri* shall be;
> *Yackors* my dudes
> Like *ruppeny* shine:
> *Atch meery chi,*
> *Majal* away,
> Perhaps I may not *dick tute*
> *Kek komi.*'

His voice was husky, conversational, but there was an energy in it she hadn't heard before. Hillary was suddenly aware that the strange language he was speaking was his first tongue, the one he thought in.

'I liked it. What was it?' she asked.

'A love song. It goes, in a slightly bowdlerized version:

> I'd choose as pillows for my head
> Those snow-white breasts of thine.
> I'd use as lamps to light my bed
> Those eyes of silver shine.
> O lovely maid, disdain me not,
> Nor leave me in my pain,
> Perhaps 'twill never be my lot
> To see thy face again.'

Hillary was more affected than he'd expected. She turned away and stubbed her cigarette out on the ground.

'What's the matter?' he asked.

'That's pretty trite stuff,' she said brutally.

'Gypsies are pretty simple people,' Roman said, taken aback. 'You're a modern, sophisticated girl. A Gypsy isn't. A friend of mine has been telling me all about primitive insects found in amber. That's what Gypsies are. Anachronisms, throwbacks. Living fossils and they don't know. Appreciate them while you can.' He didn't like lecturing; but he liked her now, and he wanted to get through.

'Now you're being trite. Come on, my father is waiting for you.'

He raised his eyebrows in surprise. Blaze whinnied amiably as they approached. At least someone had a sentimental soul, Roman told himself. Hillary looked in every direction but his.

They were riding back through the field where Blaze had bolted when Hillary put her hand on Roman's thigh.

'The song was fine. Really. We can stop here if you like.'

She'd already reined Brownie to a halt, and he stopped Blaze.

'Don't worry. You didn't hurt my feelings.'

'I'd like to, very much. Wouldn't you?' she asked.

She was sincere. Her blue eyes held his frankly. The golden body that rode so lightly would be very real and pleasant under him.

'Yes, I would. But I won't.'

He dug his heels into Blaze's sides, disrupting the kingdom of the grasshoppers, leaving before he changed his mind.

Chapter Eleven

The room was in dark except for one flame, a fat verdigris glow that lit only the nostrils, cheeks and brows of the two men so that they looked like nothing more than grotesque levitating masks. The strong stench of rotten eggs permeated the room.

'It all depends on the amount of zinc,' Roman said. 'That and whether you use earth pigments or chemical compounds.'

'This is safer than tasting?' Sloan asked.

'Not as a steady atmosphere. On the other hand, sulfur and lead won't do your stomach any good.'

Sloan squinted into the fumes of the flame he held in the teaspoon. Roman turned aside to breathe. They had been burning paints in Sloan's workshop for two hours. He had to give the man credit: Sloan was a fast learner.

'You can make the pigments also?' Sloan asked.

'Sure, if you want to take the trouble. Buying it in the store is simpler and cheaper.'

'Naturally, naturally,' Sloan agreed. 'But I'm restoring the récamier. I'm not going to be able to buy orpiment in any store, am I?'

'No,' Roman admitted.

'Well then, how difficult is it to make? I'll have to have some.'

'Not difficult at all.'

'How?'

Roman felt one heartbeat pass through his chest like a train in the dark. There was no way to avoid an answer.

'Simple. All you need is sulfur, arsenic and a covered crucible. Heat it and let it cool. The orpiment will gather on the cover.'

'That's it?'

'Yes. And don't mix it with lead or copper carbonate because neither will go with a sulfide. And don't taste it.'

'It's that powerful?' Sloan urged.

'You wouldn't be able to poison anybody with it,' Roman said lightly. 'It would be impossible to disguise the taste. Some artists have died, though, without wanting to.'

Sloan blew the flame out, and the room was black for a moment until Roman put the light on. The dealer was not trying to hide his satisfaction. He'd learned more in one afternoon than he had in a year. The future unfolded as a calendar of profits in his mind. Roman opened the door and stepped into the office. The stink of sulfur had insinuated itself there, too, and he went on to the living room without waiting for his host.

'I suppose you're hungry,' Sloan said when he caught up.

Dinner was a cold salmon. Roman paid more attention to the brandy. He'd had his fill of the *gaja* household and its diet. What he wanted now was a hot stew bright with paprika with the loud arguing of hungry Romanies, not gelid civility. He withdrew into himself as Hillary tried to gain his attention with her wit. If he had pumped the father and daughter dry, they had pumped him, too. Sloan attempted to draw him into a dispute over the merits of the Reveres and got nothing but grunts. It didn't matter to Sloan. He would be rid of his guest tomorrow, and he had what he wanted.

Roman retired early, going to his room and making a bed for himself on the floor. He put an ashtray beside him and smoked one Gauloise after another in the dark. Below he could hear them still carrying on. Sloan wanted to know what she and the Armenian had been doing in the woods for so long. She said he wasn't Armenian, and who was her father to talk about fooling around? He said he didn't care what Grey was; he wanted her to stay away from him. They weren't yelling. From the tone of their voices, a conversational hum, many people wouldn't have been aware that they were arguing. But it was far hotter than any talk Roman had heard between them before. The strain of living together for even a short time was beginning to split their charade at the seam. The wooden beams of the old house carried their mutual hate like a wire transmitting electricity.

She excused herself and left to drive to Boston to see some friends. Sloan said good-night and reminded her that she knew what he'd do if any of her friends showed up around his house. Roman expected Sloan to go to his bedroom soon after that, but instead he moved to his office. The sounds of drawers opening and feet pacing went on for two hours. At last, Sloan slammed the office door shut, locked it, and went upstairs to bed. Roman waited another hour for his host to fall asleep.

He got up and opened a window that looked out over the back lawn. The stars were very bright, dimming only where they came close to the nearly full moon. Scorpio sprawled up from the trees. Cassiopeia, the Queen of Ethiopia, reigned over duller subjects. Roman's cigarette imitated a shooting star as it spun out the window to the grass.

No gardener on a night shift appeared. Roman sat on the sill with his stockinged feet hanging over the two-story drop to the lawn. He let go and came down on the grass on all fours. He had a moment of fear when he lost his breath, but it returned as he moved back into the shadow of the house. The last thing he wanted was to be staggering about blind and gagging outside a locked house. He was in the garden where Sloan had first offered him a glass of wine. The marble bathers held each other for warmth under the moon. He moved around the trellis to the rose garden and past to where the house spread to accommodate Sloan's workshop and office. Roman stopped in front of the image of himself in Sloan's office.

Sloan's arrogance showed in the precautions he took against theft. There was no electric alarm system, just two impressively heavy bolts on the sides of the window. During the time Roman spent in the office while Sloan sorted out paints and spoons, he'd had ample time to remove the latch screws. The sturdy bolts were shot and secure, but Roman lifted the window easily, the bar carrying the latch with it.

Roman passed through the office into the work-shop. Because Sloan kept his silver there, he'd kept a closer eye on Roman in this room. The paints were still out, and sulfur clung to the air. He picked out the saw with his pocket flashlight. It was a relatively new machine, large enough to split a tree with, no doubt an instrument of pride to its owner. A ring of curling teeth rested in the thin slot. Roman took the saw out of gear and turned the wheel slowly in the light's beam. There was no sign of blood. The teeth had been cleaned very recently.

He turned the light onto the floor. The sawdust was new, and there were no stains under it that he could see. He crouched next to the wheel and examined the slot it lay in. The cleaning hadn't been as thorough here. The back end of the groove was spotted brown. It would take sawing a board dripping with stain to produce them, if it were stain.

In another half hour there was nothing else to find in the shop besides the metal stamps Sloan did his forging with. A sample read: 'Mills & Deming, 374 Queen ftreet, two doors above the Friends Meeting, NEW YORK, Makes and fells, all kinds of Cabinet Furniture and Chairs, after the moft modern fafhions and on reafonable terms.' Mills and Deming had been master cabinetmak-ers, but they didn't print their labels with a border that only became popular in the second half of the nineteenth century.

He went into the office. Through the window he saw how the sky had shifted. It was about 2 a.m. None of the files was locked, and he didn't bother with them. There wasn't enough time. Every drawer in the desk was locked. Roman took a ring of thin metal rods from his pants pocket. Working fast, bending a variety of rods of differing lengths, he created a key for each set of tumblers.

He found the typical *gaja* idea of valuables. There were papers to the house, stocks and bonds, insurance policies, bills of sale, loan notes, memberships in clubs, newspaper clippings with the Sloan name, five hundred dollars in cash, checkbooks, deposit slips and a list of Sloan's customers. There was nothing of recent business that demanded Sloan stay up two nights in a row.

The letters were in the back of the bottom drawer. They were unlike any of the other papers, written in longhand, the address in a girl's rounded manner. There was no return address. There were fifteen in all, and he chose the latest one, postmarked a week ago. Roman could hear Hillary now, '. . . who are you to talk about fooling around?'

Dear Hoddinot,

Today passed as slowly as if it were a year. You joke about life being more enjoyable the slower it goes. It's not very funny to me. As it is, I spend all my time thinking about us.

Writing again. The head librarian came by to make sure I was filing. She's jealous because starting Monday, I have a week's vacation and she doesn't want to do the work herself.

Back again. She's finally gone to lunch. At last I can get down to it. I'm sorry it takes so long to work up to things, I'd meant to make it short and sweet. The fact is I meant what I said on the telephone. This is the end. It took a long while to sink in, but now I finally realize that we aren't getting anywhere. Or, I should say, I'm not getting anywhere.

As a matter of fact, I'm just beginning to figure out what a fool I've been. Never being seen with you in public. Sneaking into New York to some sordid hotel and never telling my friends where I'm going and who this fascinating older man is who's going to marry me. Calling you late at night so the servants won't catch on. And why? Because society isn't ready for me yet. I have to be introduced properly to become an eligible wife for Hoddinot Sloan. As if meeting you for weekends in New York was helping me get introduced in Boston! I guess I'm just sick of hearing you say that we just haven't set the date.

This isn't easy. Ever since you came into the library that day I've been in love with you. Maybe you're in love with me. All I know is that Monday I leave for the Virgin Islands, and when I come back, I have an interview to become a stewardess. I'm good-looking and fairly smart, and they say I shouldn't have any trouble. I know how you feel about stewardesses, but let's admit it, thanks to you I'm no virgin anymore.

So I finally agree with you. I'm too young, too lower-class, too gauche to ever fit into your society.

Let's just call it quits and part friends. Don't worry
about me; all your secrets are safe.
Love,
   Judy

Roman turned to the first page. The letterhead had an
embossed script reading: 'Judy Mueller.' He folded the
letter neatly and put it back with the others. Scorpio was
searching the middle of the sky as Roman climbed up the
trellis to the second floor.

Roman's eyes adjusted to the more complete darkness
of his bedroom. There was a subtle change in it. The
hundred and twenty-five million optical rods that marked
man as a night animal reflected faint patterns of light and
shadow. The four thin posts of his bed were partially
broken, snapped where they rose from the frame and
joined over the center of the bed to form a pyramid.
Something was moving, though Roman was sure nobody
else was in the room.

He turned the flashlight on toward the top of the
pyramid. A string hung from it, and the light followed it
down to within a foot of the bed, where, slowly describing
circles with the open cone, was the frozen ivory grin and
matted hair of a devil's head.

Chapter Twelve

It was afternoon by the time he got back to New York. Nobody had seen him off at the Sloans'; he'd left before they rose. Because it was Sunday, there were few cars on the streets, and Manhattan's sky was relatively clear. The sidewalks seemed populated entirely by young couples in leather pants and psychedelic shirts walking Afghans and Great Danes. Their parents no doubt had all locked themselves in their apartments with their air conditioners.

When he unlocked the door to his apartment, Dany was there, lying on the sofa, eating unionized grapes, and leafing through fashion magazines. Roman kicked his suitcase under a side chair and threw his jacket and tie over it.

'Hi. I thought you were going to do some shooting on the island this weekend.'

'We got it done in one day. The rest of the gang stayed up there, but I decided to come back. In case you did.' She held up a center spread hosiery ad. 'Don't you think I have better legs?'

'Models are insane.'

Dany frowned. He always said that when she asked for his opinion. She had the feeling that he meant it.

He stole a grape from her and ate it. She did have better legs, but he refused to encourage the vanity that served as a soul for a professional model. She was in nothing but an old happy jacket of his, her tan limbs and tilt of the head inviting a phantom photographer with a motorized Nikon to pop up from the other side of the sofa.

'Find what you wanted?' she asked.

'Yeah.' He scratched the stubble that was taking over his chin. Even in a tuxedo on the steps of the opera, he'd look as if he had come to hold the place up.

'What was it?'

'A family. The all-American family.'

He went to the bathroom to shower off the sweat of the ride and shave. He picked up a roll of adhesive tape and came back into the living room in a towel.

'Jesus Christ,' Dany said. A grape stopped an inch from her lips. 'What the hell happened to you?'

He raised his arms. 'Tape me up, will you?' Last night's activities had irritated the tear. During the shower he'd kept his eyes away from the bruise that ran from his shoulder to his navel. Now that he saw it it hurt.

'A truck run over you?'

'A tree, believe it or not.'

She circled him until a wide white band covered part of his chest.

'Looks like a bruised plum,' she said, running her finger down the discoloration. 'I'm sorry. That wasn't much of a welcome, was it?'

She kissed him, first on the cheek and then on the mouth. Roman's arms found themselves inside the cotton happy jacket. The pain was subsiding.

'Speaking of bruised plums,' he said.

'Stop that. You're tickling me.'

Hillary's come-on in the field had left its residue of desire. The happy jacket dropped to the floor beside the towel. He pressed Dany into him, conscious as always of the contrast in colors, a contrast that became more marked as contact became more intimate.

'You've gained some weight,' he told her. 'You'll lose your job, but I like it.'

'And what will you do when I lose my job?'

'Get you a crystal ball and teach you how to tell fortunes.'

'I'd never be able to tell fortunes. I don't even know what I'm going to be doing a minute from now.'

He grinned broadly.

'Well, that, of course,' she said.

'Then why fight fate any longer?'

It was four thirty when Roman woke up. The room was in what shade they could get by closing the drapes on an afternoon. Dany, asleep and content, rested her head on his bruised arm. The sheet was down at the foot of the bed so that the air could blow over their bodies. Her breasts sagged slightly to the sides over her rib cage. They were supposed to be a bit too big for her business. What was it that made Americans demand large breasts in their fantasies and flat breasts on their models? To a Romany a woman's breasts were not a sex object. They were out in the open too much, suckling children in a room full of friends or before anyone's eyes on the public road. On Dany, he had to admit, they were sex objects. If she ever succeeded at what she hinted, if they ever did marry, would she suckle her children in front of her friends from Long Island?

Painstakingly he slid his arm out from under her and rolled off the bed. He went into the living room and closed the bedroom door. When he'd put the towel back around his waist, he sat by the telephone with the phone book and opened a fresh pack of cigarettes. He called Pan American first. A recording stalled him for a minute, and then a girl came on the line.

'Hello,' Roman said. 'This is the First National Bank travel bureau, Mr Baldwin calling. We would like to check on a reservation made for a Miss Mueller. M-u-e-l-l-e-r. Judy Mueller, for last Monday to the Virgin Islands.'

'That would be St Thomas?' the girl asked.

'That's right. She was supposed to join a tour down there, part of the travel package that we handle. She never did join it. That isn't really that unusual. Often younger clients prefer to disappear on their vacations. But the tour director has just called me to say that her flight is about to leave for the States and Miss Mueller still hasn't shown up. I wonder if you could check your records and tell me whether she made her flight down to the islands.'

'Could you tell me the number of her flight?'

'I'm afraid that part of the office is closed on Sundays.'

The girl was obviously pondering the request on the other end.

'This is very irregular.'

'I understand. But the tour director is very concerned, and so am I. We feel some obligation to our customers to make sure of their well-being.'

There was another wait.

'Could I have your name, please, miss?' Roman said. 'I'd like to know it the next time I see your supervisor.'

'Wait a moment while I ask the computer,' she retorted crisply.

Roman was putting out a cigarette when the girl came back.

'We have no Miss Mueller on any flights for St Thomas last week. What's this all about?'

He hung up.

That was a blank. Pan Am was the only airline he knew of that flew to the Virgin Islands; it was the one Dany had taken the year before. She was tight with her money, though; she would have shopped around. He went back into the bedroom.

'Hey, Dany. Come on. Let's go.'

She struggled up on her elbows. 'You don't have to lift my eyelid. You know that wakes me up.' She rubbed her face. 'God.'

'I couldn't tell if you were breathing there for a second. You should be glad I checked. Look, when you went to the Virgin Islands with that decorator – '

'He was doing the backgrounds for the bathing suit number. You know that.'

'With that decorator, you flew Pan Am. What other airlines go down there?'

'From here?' Dany tried to think through the bleariness of sleep. 'Trans Caribbean, but only on Sundays.'

'Thanks.' He kissed her eyes closed and pushed her head back down on the pillow. She knew she wouldn't be able to go to sleep again.

He found the number for Trans Caribbean and called. A voice that was a copy of the Pan Am girl's spoke to him. He was disappointed – he'd hoped for some rich fluty West Indian tones – but he went through his Mr Baldwin routine enthusiastically. The girl paused at the same points as her Pan Am sister, but she went to check her records, too.

'Hello? Mr Baldwin? I checked and we did have a reservation for a Miss Mueller. It was paid in advance as you said. But I don't think your tour director should worry. Miss Mueller never boarded the plane; she didn't check in at all. I'm afraid she was a "Stay Away,"as we call them here.'

'Yes.' Roman agreed and hung up. He guessed so, too.

'Trouble?' Dany asked. She was at the doorway, picking up the happy jacket with her toes rather than venture in front of the window even though the nearest possible peeping Tom was on the other side of the East River.

'Not exactly. The trouble's gone.'

'Antiques?'

'Yeah, antiques.'

He had a lost look that came over him very rarely. She crossed the room and pressed his head between her breasts. The maternal gesture revived Roman because it amused him. Maybe she would nurse her kids in public after all.

'I think you should drop the antiques,' Dany said, 'and get into something interesting.'

Chapter Thirteen

'Bugs?' Captain Frank said. 'You're supposed to be getting this murder case out of the way, and you're talking about bugs? I'll tell you about bugs.'

He went past Sergeant Isadore to the door and locked it and came back to his desk.

'I'll tell you about bugs,' he repeated. 'Yesterday I came back here late and what did I find? A CID taping a mike in the men's room, that's what. And a plainclothes going through my wastebasket. That's all. So don't you tell me about bugs.'

Isadore pressed his lips together tightly. His round face took on the rigidity of a steel trap shut tight on a small animal. The animal was his tongue.

'Zoologist! He's been too sick to come in? Fine. Keep him away from here. You could have arrested that what's-his-name. Instead you let him get into the warehouse and practically start an antique store. I bet they got a good laugh out of that at CID. Why not give all our suspects a chance to play with the evidence? They can take it out if they like, like a library.'

By the time Isadore got a chance to exit, his ears buzzing, he was happy not to hear about bugs either. He turned his anger on Grey. The Gypsy had broken his promise to help. When he got to his desk he found a note that someone called 'Number One Son' had called. If this son showed up, he'd arrest him too.

Isadore stared at the gray Formica top of his desk trying to get hold of himself. Coffee rings merged with cigarette burns which led like exclamations to the crumbs of the Danish he'd had for breakfast. He picked up a crumb on the tip of his finger and ate the evidence. He couldn't arrest his son. As for Grey, he was only acting like a Gypsy. Why had Grey fooled around with the antiques? Was there evidence in the evidence? It was the sort of question that gained baking soda a permanent place in Isadore's heartburn.

An hour later he was at the warehouse of the Astor Movers off Astor Place in the East Village. The friend whose place Buddy Locher had taken the day of the accident was there, having just delivered a van from Boston the day before. The warehouse was nothing more than a pair of truck bays between a used clothes emporium and a hat and felt goods manufacturer. Everything lay under a layer of dust as thick as gray velvet.

Isadore's nerve broke. It was a bad day and a sour case and a man couldn't be expected to do everything at the same time. He went to a corner newsstand and bought a pack of cigarettes. He lit up on the way to the warehouse. The first drag developed from an innocent experiment to a wicked, lung-stunning inhale. He walked into the empty bay.

'Yeah. What is it?' a man in a dirty mover's uniform asked as he came down a ramp. The uniform stretched over equally beefy arms and stomach.

'I want to –'

'Hey!' the man said. He pointed at Isadore's cigarette and then at a sign posted beside the bay. 'Can't you read?'

NO SMOKING IN THE VANS, IN THIS BUILDING OR ON THE JOB, the sign said.

'Everyone's a Surgeon General,' Isadore muttered but he walked out to the street to step on the cigarette. He went back and explained in a deliberately calm fashion who he was and why he'd come.

'You don't want me,' the mover said accusingly. 'You want the kid.' He went to a metal door, kicked it and yelled, 'Hey, Hale. Get down here. Some cop wants to see you.' Isadore resisted the impulse to ask whether garbage collecting was good training for moving works of art, but just barely.

'The kid' impressed Isadore more. His name was Howard Washington Hale. He wore his blond hair long but neatly trimmed, and his uniform was crisply white. He was even polite.

'I knew Buddy in the service, but he was a little different,' Hale reported. 'Not dangerous, just nervous. He didn't send me a letter to say he was coming to Boston, and I bet it was just because he was so relieved to muster out.'

'How long have you been out?'

'Six months. I wish I'd been there when Buddy got into town, but there was a party out of town and . . . you know. Don't tell Mr Astor.'

Isadore's jaw dropped. 'There is a Mr Astor?'

'Sure, you just talked to him.'

Isadore talked to Hale until the boss reappeared, slamming the door open with one butt of his stomach.

'You still here?' he yelled at Isadore. 'I got a schedule to keep. This isn't civil service.'

Hale shrugged his shoulders. 'Any more questions?'

'No, thanks.'

Hale got into the van. Somehow the kid kept it clean even in Astor's warehouse. There was a plastic saint on the dashboard. Isadore remembered it had been among Locher's effects. Astor threatened some cars in the street and waved the van out. Isadore watched it drive to Broadway and wait for the light.

'What is it now?' the mover asked Isadore with anguish.

'Nothing. Thanks, you've been very cooperative, Mr Astor.'

Astor flared. 'Okay, okay, so it used to be Astorini. You going to make something out of it? You and the FBI. You want to see my membership card in the underworld?'

Isadore picked a straight line to his car and tried to follow it. The line was intersected by a bum asking for a cigarette. Isadore handed over his whole pack.

He drove toward the end of Manhattan where the department tow truck dropped vehicles bound as evidence. A pair of young patrolmen were looking over the cars headed for public auction. They passed right over what now looked like a busted accordion but had at one time been an Eldorado. Isadore went to the small van that said LEASED TO ASTOR MOVING on the door. There was no top to the door; it had been sheared off with the top of the cab. He went through the interior for the third time. He didn't expect to find anything he missed at the accident, but Grey's accusations about picking on Gypsies annoyed him. Except for the marks of the collision, the van's cab was spotless, and so was the rear where the antiques were carried. Isadore got out with a sense of absolution and walked to the Eldorado. He'd find a rich field there loaded with possibilities as soon as his expert showed up. His essential optimism was showing through.

Isadore began groaning twenty feet from the Eldorado. He trotted over the damp cement, and by the time he was standing over the crumpled fender he was mentally pounding his breast. No zoologist would help anymore. The Eldorado's body was, for some strange reason, as clean as the van's.

'Yeah,' one of the attendants said when Isadore asked. 'CID said to hose the place down. Said it was getting to be a health hazard.'

It made sense. The Detective Bureau used the lot much more than CID. He and the attendant got the hood open. He looked at the smashed honeycomb of the radiator. The bugs there were washed away, too.

The interior of the car was still dirty, but it had been checked thoroughly. All the contents down to tobacco and pieces of garbage had been sealed in cardboard boxes. The door hung open like a broken wing. The upholstery hardly existed. The lab had taken samples of all stains, and there hadn't been much that wasn't stained in Nanoosh Pulneshti's car. The ashtrays were gone, along with much of the carpet. The dashboard was marked with inscrutable scratches. There was little left of the windshield Nanoosh had gone through. There was nothing left for him to find.

Almost nothing, he admitted. Dirt had collected under the brake pedal, and as a pathetic last note a fungus was growing in it. It reminded him unnecessarily of the humidity of the past few days. In the wreckage of death, life persisted. Isadore was not a callous man.

There was no point going to the driver's side. The door there hadn't opened since the accident. He angled over the floorboard to get a closer look at the fungus. It was a fringe of tiny mushrooms with thin stems and pointed caps. It was a new one on him, and he used to take his boy out mushroom hunting in the Catskills.

'A *pajarito*,' Lieutenant Ebert said. He held Isadore's catch into the light with tweezers. The lab technicians had been as stymied as Isadore when he came in with his handkerchief wrapped in a bundle. Ebert was from Narcotics. 'How about that? Where in the world did you get it?'

'Then it's not local?'

'I'll say it isn't. You could sell a little treasure like that for five hundred dollars in the East Village. It's from Mexico, the state of Oaxaca just west of Guatemala. The Mazoteca Indians grow some of the best hallucinogenic mushrooms in the world there, *pajaritos*, *derumbes* and big, fat *Santo Jesucristas*. First time I've seen one of these in the city.'

The Gypsies hadn't been smuggling the stuff in, Isadore knew, because nothing else like it had been picked up after the accident. These *pajaritos* were just growing, smuggling themselves in.

'What's the germination period for these? I mean, how long would it take them to grow and how fast to die in New York?'

Ebert scratched the bristle that served as hair on his head. Being a 'nark' meant he had an active outdoor life and a tan that showed through his crew cut.

'All depends. Fungus's pretty basic stuff. It'll pop up easy enough, but here, in New York, it should die pretty quick. Especially *pajaritos*. I've been down there with the immigration patrol. Cool, damp mountains in the Sierra Mazoteca. See' – he held his hand out – 'these are already dehydrating. So I'd say these could last, once they've started growing, four, five days.'

'How long could they have been in the dirt before they started growing?'

'Oh, I get you. Considering the change in climate, it would have to be real soon. Less than a week for that, I'd guess, but then nobody knows for sure. Like my friends on the street say, mushrooms are crazy things.'

Isadore returned to his desk and sat down with a pencil and pad, feeling a little bit like a girl on the rhythm method. If the *pajaritos* – 'little birds,' Ebert translated – were about four days old, tops, and the germinating stage was no more than a week, that put the Eldorado in the southern end of Mexico just eleven days ago. This was Friday. The accident had occurred four days before. Which gave Nanoosh Pulneshti less than a week to drive through Mexico and most of the United States. Gypsies were known to be exceptional drivers, but this was pushing it. A week hardly gave Pulneshti enough time to run over a dog, let alone commit, dismember and pack a murder.

He walked around the room. It was mostly empty, just a lieutenant in the corner learning to type. The rest were home having supper. Why wasn't he? On a large corkboard were pictures of kids reported missing by their parents. A file below it held nothing but the names and descriptions of kids who had run away from home or just vanished. Kids who weren't home for supper. He went through the file for the tenth time, picking out those who might bear some resemblance to the body in the bigger file at the morgue. Strict selection winnowed the number down to five.

A high school student from Roanoke, Virginia. A nurse from Brownsville, Texas. Another high school kid from Memphis. A dropout from Little Rock and a social worker from Wheeling, West Virginia. It had to be someone on the road from Mexico, that much he was sure of. If Pulneshti did it. And if Pulneshti didn't do it, he knew less than when he started. The trouble was that Isadore was beginning to suspect that Grey really had learned something.

It took some cajoling, but Erskine Lippincoot of Lippincoot Frères had a weakness for working with the police. When Sergeant Isadore called him on Saturday morning, he took some pleasure in announcing to his weekend guests that he often assisted the authorities in matters dealing with antiques and that they would have to excuse him for a few hours. Duty called, and the Lippincoots had never vacillated in performing civic acts.

Isadore was waiting at the warehouse when Lippincoot arrived in a chauffeur-driven Mercedes. He wadded his gum into a ball and wrapped it in paper as Lippincoot revealed himself in a white twill summer suit and ascot. The two men had never met before, but they recognized each other without difficulty.

'Perhaps you could explain this to me again,' Lippincoot said as they entered the warehouse.

'I'll try,' Isadore said. 'We have some antiques here from an accident. One expert has, uh, already gone over them, but we can't get his report. I'd appreciate it if, with your expertise, you could examine these pieces. Since you are acknowledged to be the top dealer in town and you've been kind enough in the past, we thought you'd help. You see, if you don't find anything, then I'll know that the other man didn't find anything.'

'Odd,' Lippincoot said, presenting a formidable row of wrinkled brows. 'Who is this other man? I'm sure I'd know the name.'

'Unfortunately, I can't tell you.'

'Very odd.'

'It's just to relieve my mind.'

Lippincoot's brows met and rebounded. He'd come all the way from Sag Harbor to relieve some sergeant's mind.

'Here they are,' Isadore said.

Lippincoot's irritation subsided under the pleasure he always took in fine antiques. Mentally he classified each piece and dismissed the policeman. The tragedy – and masterpiece – of the set, of course, was the highboy, reconstructed so artfully as to almost hide the fact that it was beyond repair.

'Marvelous work, really marvelous. The owner came down to put it back together?' It wasn't the sort of work a police carpenter was capable of.

'No. The other expert. In about an hour,' Isadore said. He couldn't help wondering how long it would have taken Erskine Lippincoot.

'Hardly likely.' Lippincoot opened a drawer gently. The expressive brows rose further. 'That's odd. Why did he do that?'

'What's odd? Did what?'

'The fellow scratched the inside of the drawers, that's all. It's something you might do to authenticate a piece, not put it together. I use a little silver knife for that sort of thing myself.'

'On purpose, he did it on purpose?'

'Of course. The man who put this antique together wasn't about to stumble through it. Pine's very soft, and he probably could have managed with any sharp object. I remember, it was during the war, we were in France, and I had nothing but a nail file . . .'

'Pull them out. All the drawers.'

'Oh, no,' Lippincoot protested. 'This is dried walnut that's two hundred years old. Very brittle and just held together with epoxy. It could fall apart if we began manhandling it.'

'Pull them out,' Isadore ordered in the tone of voice

he used on rookies. Somewhere in that circumference of fat was a steel core, Lippincoot realized, and he obediently pulled the drawers out one by one and laid them on the floor.

'Odd.'

Understatement was starting to wear on Isadore, but he inquired politely what provoked the remark.

'You cut to see if wormholes are genuine,' Lippincoot informed him. 'These are. They're regular capillaries, wormholes, and that's where you run into some of your troubles with refinishing. Sucks moisture in, thus. And there's a definite residue in some of these. Recent I'd even say, though it's hardly noticeable.'

'Residue of what?'

'Oh, blood, of course. I am an expert, you know.'

Lippincoot was unwavering in his opinion. Asked whether there was any evidence in the drawers of dry ice, the dealer said just the warping in the joins.

'An insurance agent checked it?' he wanted to know. 'That doesn't mean anything if the man's late for lunch or something. You don't look for smuggling in a Chippendale chest, you know, just to see if someone had knocked a hole in the side. You can't place too much in what insurance agents say, you see. As a group, they're very...'

'Odd,' Isadore supplied.

There were a round dozen girls missing from the New England area, Isadore discovered when he got back to the office. Half of them were suspected of skipping off to cut cane in Cuba. Four others for color of hair, build or easily identified marks were disqualified. That left a private school teacher from Middlebury, Connecticut, and a librarian from Boston. There were no fingerprints on either that he could match with the corpse. It took an extra day, but he had Middlebury and Boston get hold of the girls' dentists and check out the dental profile. By Sunday afternoon he knew the corpse to be one Judith Jean Mueller.

Chapter Fourteen

A submarine bobbed in the brackish water. Its batteries had run down, and its crew propellers were still. Radio signals failed. Its skipper, a twelve-year-old boy, looked at it in frustration. He turned the knobs on his transmitter back and forth. With technology a failure, he went off into the park to find a long stick.

'I suppose you've told all Nanoosh's relatives, the ones you couldn't find before. They're pleased,' Isadore said, gesturing with a hot dog.

'If I could find them, I'd tell them, and they'd probably be ecstatic. Thanks to you.'

'Tell them they're welcome.'

The two men were sitting on a bench beside the boat pond. Behind them rose a treelined edge of Central Park and above that the luxury apartments of the East Side in a skyline like a dingy graph.

'It makes more sense. One thing always did bother me,' Isadore said, licking a dab of mustard from a finger. 'Why in the world would a Gypsy who was racing across the country stop off to commit a murder?'

'People have told me it's possible.'

Isadore winced. 'You know what I mean. Now Sloan makes sense. There's a reasonable combination of motive and opportunity there. In fact, a lovely one.'

'Boy gets girl, boy loses girl, boy kills girl.'

'Uh-huh.' Isadore wasn't sure whether he was being teased or not. He turned with Roman to look at the boy, who was batting the water with a branch that was too short. 'The Mueller girl was reported missing by her roommate. The roommate knew everything about Miss Mueller's romance with Sloan except his name. He was some wealthy, older society guy who seduced her and then went back on his proposal. The marriage proposal, that is. The roommate never saw him, just his car when he parked outside and honked. It was a lemon Buick station wagon. She never got the license plate, but she remembered that she saw a scrape on the right rear fender when the Mueller girl left that last night.

'It didn't take long to find the car. The scrape came from an accident reported a week before when Sloan's daughter was driving it. As soon as the Boston police took the roommate around to Sloan's place, she saw the car. It was the same one.

'And then everything cracked. The roommate told us Mueller and her boyfriend went off for weekends in New York. We didn't get anything from the desk clerks, but Sloan was so cheap he used his credit card. That gave us enough to tackle Sloan last night. He denied everything, naturally, until we found the letters in the desk. Then he said it was all a mistake. They were close, but the girl was exaggerating: He made no promises about getting married, and of course, he never killed her.'

The submarine had submerged. The boy was throwing rocks in the water from frustration. The two men moved farther down the bench to avoid getting wet. Isadore wiped his hands with his paper napkin, folded the paper neatly, and put it in his pocket.

'Did he?' Roman asked innocently.

'It's pretty plain that he did. Nice girl, good reputation, a little bookish, ripe for some character like Sloan. Sooner or later she finds out that she's been had, and in a last scene she threatens to let the affair out. If she's not good enough for the society page, she'll make sure he isn't either. A man like Sloan, it's the most important thing in the world. He kills her in a rage, cuts her up in his little workshop and stuffs her in the chest of drawers.'

'Highboy.'

'Highboy, lowboy, who cares? Packs her off to the Armory Show in New York in a panic. He figures he can always pull the chest out of his exhibit once it's at the Armory and dispose of the body. The main thing is to get it out of Massachusetts. Maybe he'll toss it in the Hudson; he doesn't know, he's no professional. Then he hits the jackpot. The insurance company calls him up and says there's been an accident, his pieces have been badly damaged. By the way, they say, he might be interested in knowing that the accident caught a desperate murderer who was carrying a mutilated body around. The murderer died in the accident.

'Talk about luck. He was wondering what the hell he was going to do with that body, and the body takes care of itself. What's better, he's not sending anyone else to jail because they're dead already. God is smiling on Hoddinot Sloan. All he has to do is lay low and take the insurance money. He might even make a profit. Isn't that what Calvinism is all about?'

'You're a learned man, Mr Isadore.'

'I know what makes sense, that's all, and this makes sense. Murders always do in some crazy way. And murderers are such cocky bastards. The Boston police told me Sloan practically fainted when they told him the roommate decided she'd seen him pick the Mueller girl up that last night when she disappeared,' Isadore said.

'He denied it?'

'No. By that time he was screaming for his lawyer. And when his lawyer got there and Sloan discovered he could only handle codicils, he screamed for another one. I'm taking the train up this afternoon. If I'm lucky, I'll get to be the one who tells him about the blood on the saw. It's the Mueller girl's type. I just wanted to let you know what happened before I went because I gave you sort of a rough time. It's okay?'

'Sure,' Roman said. Isadore really did care whether they were still friends.

'Besides, you gave us a lead with that chest, you know. Made me look at it a second time. How come you didn't tell me about it?'

Roman shrugged. 'I found it; but I didn't know what to do about it, and I didn't even know what I'd found. I'm no detective like you.' He paused. 'Sloan's the man, huh?'

Isadore tried to read something in the Gypsy's black eyes and gave up. 'Right. Anyway, I'm happy about the way things worked out. Don't tell me you're not?'

Roman laughed. 'It's in your hands now, Sergeant.'

'Hey, I've got to go. My train leaves in an hour, and Number One Son is driving me to the station. I've got to give him plenty of time.'

Roman watched Isadore's slouched figure move away down the border of the pond and up the stairs that led to Seventy-second Street. In the water, the boy was wading toward his ship with hands out as if he were walking on a tightrope.

Roman walked away from the park toward his apartment to get ready for a party. Vera's *kumpania* would not only be celebrating the clearing of Nanoosh's name but also the marriage of her daughter Laza to a boy from a *kumpania* in Queens.

Dany was in a pout when he got home. She had been insinuating herself more and more into his life, waking him in the morning with a phone call, rushing off to a model's call, visiting his shop at lunch, rushing off for another shooting, coming back to cook supper and make love. If she wasn't any closer to getting married, she was making him feel very guilty.

'I don't think they'd be so upset because of one *gaji*,' she said. 'How am I ever going to meet your friends, anyway? I mean, I know some of the men, but I've never met any of the women.'

Roman painted his face with lather. It was impossible trying to tell her that he was separating her from the Gypsy women for her own good. A *gaji* who married a Rom was treated as a slave by every Gypsy woman. She would have to fulfill every Gypsy duty and custom, from

113

changing from Givenchy's to crude petticoats to learning the exacting, sometimes humiliating business of *duikkerin* fortunes. Not that he needed the money, but the women would demand it. He and Dany were better off as they were. He only wished he could find something to change the subject. As he started to shave, a thin red line appeared along his scar.

'Damn it, Dany, you shaved your legs with my razor again. I gave you your own.'

'It was dull.'

'Then change it.' He slipped a fresh blade into his razor. She was hovering right outside the bathroom door; he could sense it. Usually, he had no trouble handling her moods, turning her anger into a joke they could both laugh at. There were times, though, when he seemed to be paralyzed, and her obvious, even childish manipulations would drive him mad. 'It's not just a party,' he told her between strokes. 'No strangers are allowed at weddings. Not even priests. Another time would be better. You want to like them, right?'

He looked up and saw her in the mirror. She was biting her false fingernails, a bad sign. He hid by ducking into the sink basin and washing off the lather. When he was dry, he slipped a fresh shirt on and went into the living room. On the table were the bottle of anisette and felt bag weighted with gold eagles for Laza's new *gonya* he would take with him.

'So, you are going to the party and just leaving me here,' Dany crowed triumphantly. She sat with her arms crossed beside the door.

'Come on, Dany, be fair. I called you and told you about this, and you said it was fine because some speechwriter had asked you out.'

'The one who said he wanted to improve my mind?' she snorted.

'That's right, the one who wanted to improve your mind.'

'Very funny,' she said with the recurring air of triumph.

He let his arms sag, unequally because one of them held the heavy bag. The only *gaji* in the world that had the power to confuse him was this obstinate, intriguing, practically unread (not including *Vogue*), soap-operatic, almost skinny, silky, passionate, damp-eyed model.

'There are a hundred parties in town that you could go to tonight if you wanted to,' he said.

'I'll stay here if you don't mind. I think I'll read in bed.' She saw that that was going down pretty hard, so she added, 'And maybe there's something on television.'

'Whatever you want.'

When he left and while he was waiting for the elevator, Dany opened the door again and slammed it.

Why was he feeling like Hoddinot Sloan?

Chapter Fifteen

Vera was happy because Laza would not have been able to marry for some time if Nanoosh's name had not been cleared. Roman explained to her on the phone that Sergeant Isadore solved the crime, but as far as she and her *kumpania* were concerned, they had asked Roman to save Nanoosh's *mulo* from limbo, and in a week that was what happened. Their low opinion of the police accepted no other interpretation. Now they could celebrate.

All the curtains inside the *ofisa* were pulled aside so that the party covered the entire floor from the back to the front of the building. Folding tables were placed together and decorated with colorful cloths. On them were plates of cold cuts, barbecued chickens, meat-stuffed pancakes called *bokoli*, pink beef with a sharp scent of rosemary, pork roast with liquorice aniseed, a holiday goose redolent of sage and marjoram, more chickens, and from somewhere an enormous glistening suckling pig. Surrounding these, as if the point of honor was to leave no inch of the table bare, were smaller bowls of yogurt with sesame or lettuce or cucumbers or tomatoes. Women shoved these together to make room for slippery white beans in vinegar, chick-peas in sesame paste and green beans in sour cream. The men spiced their thirsts with lentils and cheese and small, salty ripe olives.

Children reached for honeyed pastries, meat balls rolled in nutmeg and chilly squares of eggplant that ringed fragile mountains of fresh black bread. At one end of the long line of tables a brother of the groom pumped beer from the kegs around him like a happy madman trying to explode a cache of dynamite lost in the profusion.

'It is a very good match,' Vera announced into Roman's ear. 'Dodo came to me the other day about his boy as if he had a present. Him with those two apes of brothers with the chicken in their hands.' She pointed with a hunk of pork. 'They offered only five hundred dollars, if you can believe it.'

Roman shook his head with simulated wonder. What did make him wonder was how Vera was able to speak above the din of spontaneous singing, dancing, bragging and two competing record players, one with the rhapsodies of Balogh Istvan and the other with the flamencos of Manitas de Plata.

'Romano, I ask you. Five hundred dollars for a sweet girl like Laza! Sweet-tempered, hardworking, beautiful like a plum, knows how to *duiker* like a grandmother, can go into J. C. Penney's and come out with an electric stove and nobody sees her. For a boy like Kalia. Dumb, bad-mannered, ugly. I pity his mother. All he thinks about is cars, and he gets caught stealing those. As a favor, just so as not to dishonor Dodo in front of his own brothers, I ask four thousand dollars. It's the least I can do for Laza.'

One of his friends gave Roman a fresh beer and tried to take him away by the arm, but Vera hung on.

'So we sat down and discussed it,' she shouted.

'Perhaps Kalia wasn't such a bad boy after all. Remember how he made that car out of nothing but stolen parts, and for just being sixteen he seems to be pretty lucky at the racetrack. Laza, even I'll admit, has a taste for expensive things, and sometimes she has to pay for them. I mean, it wasn't all black and white. Dodo offered a thousand, and I came down a little to thirty-five hundred for courtesy.'

'For courtesy.'

'Yes. Then it was mentioned that Dodo's *kumpania* was one of the oldest and most respected in the country and had really a very good lawyer that they would lend us since we would be related and offered fifteen hundred. Someone also mentioned Laza couldn't cook old shoes, which I denied, but Dodo and his family have been guests of mine before and I came down to two thousand seven hundred and fifty.'

'Very wise,' Roman said. It was easier to talk now since they were being crushed together by people clearing a circle for dancing.

'Then, naturally, there was the human aspect,' Vera said with a tragic, tolerant sigh that shamed the fact that her feet were barely touching the floor from the squeeze. 'It seems that Laza and Kalia do feel some affection for each other and wanted to marry. So, for twenty-five hundred dollars, I gave in.'

All of Vera's *kumpania* of more than forty Romanies and Dodo's *kumpania* of fifty and a hundred or more guests were jostling in as many different directions in the crowded *ofisa*. Men who had not seen each other for days and others who had just come back from years of wandering through Europe were seizing old friends and inventing toasts. Their wives were just as forceful shaping huddled atolls of gossip. The *shavs*, small boys and girls, wended their way through legs to the tables to fill themselves with sweet pastries. A large hand came through the mass and snatched Roman away from Vera like a card in a magician's hand.

'Romano! Romano! So this is our detective!'

Kore Tshatshimo, a giant with ringlets hanging over a genially misshapen face, slapped Roman on both shoulders and then smothered him in an embrace that took his breath away. Roman squeezed him back until he could feel Kore's ribs shifting. Kore howled with pleasure.

'The same,' he said. 'All this talk about you going soft. I said that the day Romano Gry becomes a *gajo* is the day I put on a skirt. Ha, remember that time we were in Rio and the soldiers tried to make us show identification cards. Ah? Yes?'

'I can't forget.' How could he? That was the time Kore kicked a patrol car into the Atlantic.

'And you and Nanoosh took their uniforms and put them on and went and arrested those girls,' Kore said before remembering that Nanoosh was dead. To cover any sacrilege, he offered a toast. 'To Nanoosh.'

They drank, and Kore brightened up.

'You know, it's a good thing you got that killer. Laza's been trying to run away with Kalia for the last month, I hear. Vera couldn't get her married off soon enough. Besides, I think it's a good thing, a marriage now.

Everyone has been very unhappy about Nanoosh. This will take their minds off it.'

'A toast to happiness,' Roman said, knowing a cue when he heard it. A procession of mugs passed through his hand along with the toasts. Since he was a hero, everyone wanted a drink with him, and Kore wanted to match everyone's toast. All the men had contributed liquor, so a blend of cognac, carbonated wine, anisette, vodka, brandy and beer rolled through his stomach and up to his head. On a table that had been stripped of its food, the guests were depositing their gifts in columns of gold coins and dishevelled wads of paper money, the start of Laza and Kalia's *sumadjii*, a portable heirloom and treasure.

Dodo and Kore sat Roman on a chair for a *patshiv* to be sung in his honor by one of Kalia's brothers. He was a lean boy with a Spanish guitar. A grizzled old man stood behind him with a violin, waiting for the boy to begin. The boy waited with his eyes closed until the crowd in the *ofisa* had become silent, and then he sang.

It started as a high, emotional keening, the boy's head thrown back in sorrow as he told of the shock of Nanoosh's death. The Romani tongue, a dark Indian opalescent stone lacquered with singing for the Persians, slaving for the Magyars, and dying in every corner of the earth, filled the room and their hearts. Guttural but light as a bird swooping through the night, traditional and unpredictable, something that delighted in melody and then ignored it for a stronger impulse made the ring of men and women and the children sitting on the floor all hold their breath. This was their story, their history coming from the young boy and the old man, and when the *patshivaki djili* came to its exploding, victorious close with the identification of the murderous *gajo*, two hundred people were clapping and crying.

One song was not enough. It was the old man's turn with a *djili* centuries older than himself that came out in practically a whisper. With a show of extreme reluctance, an elder with a white mustache that came down to his collar allowed himself to be pushed into the middle of the circle. His hands lifted over his head, he began to dance, at first awkwardly, and then, as the spirits coursed through him like new blood, with a recall of vigor and grace that drew shouts of appreciation from his grandchildren. When he tired, another ancient took his place. When all the elders had danced, the *shavs* took over, slapping their hands together and shouting, inspired by the admiration of the girls who watched.

'All this is really for you, Romano,' Kore said with great solemnity but a little unsteadily. By now even his bulk had been saturated with alcohol. 'Imagine, trying to say a Lovari would kill a girl. That is a *gaja* vice. A Rom might hit a woman, but kill her? Never! Unless, of course, he was Gitano.' Kore, like most Kalderash and Lovari, had a great distrust for the Spanish Gypsies.

The music stopped, and into the middle of the circle stepped Vera and Dodo. Kalia's father held a bottle of Courvoisier. Around the neck of the bottle was a string of gold pieces which marked the brandy as the *pliashka*. The bottle was opened and poured into two glasses from which Dodo and Vera drank soberly. When they embraced, their children were married. Later there would be a ceremony by a sympathetic priest, but it would be only for form. The Romany signified their recognition of the union now with cheers from the women and drinks for the men.

So far Kalia and Laza had been invisible. The groom had been driving up and down Broadway with some of his closest friends while the bride stayed at another *ofisa* with a friend and an aunt. At this point she was brought to Vera's and escorted to the kitchen to wait for Kalia. It was a necessary part of the tradition that she be carried off struggling by her husband.

The drinking and talking and singing carried on for another hour until Kalia arrived. The signal was passed back to the kitchen, where Vera hurriedly unbraided Laza's long hair. The girl stared down at the white silk dress bought specially for the occasion. With a tenderness that surprised Laza, Vera sang very softly:

> *Kay hin m'ro vodyi?*
> *Ujes hin cavo,*
> *Ujes sar o kam,*
> *Ujes sar pani,*
> *Ujes sar kumut,*
> *Ujes sar legujes,*
> *Pen mange,*
> *Caveskro vasteba*
> *Kay hin m'ro vodyi?*

In another language it would mean, 'Where is my heart? The child is pure, pure as the sun, pure as the water, pure as the moon, pure as the purest. So tell me, how could the child steal my heart?'

There was a knock on the kitchen door, and the girl went out alone. In a line waiting for her were her brothers and cousins forming a shield. Coming across the room toward them were Kalia and his brothers and cousins. The two small armies met and engaged in a spectacular Hollywood stuntman sort of battle that Kalia's side was ordained by custom to win. He grabbed Laza around the waist and started to drag her away. She screamed and pushed him away violently, but he refused to let go. They fell to the floor once, and when he still pulled her to the door, Laza tore at her hair with fear and scratched her face while the spectators moved out of the way of the shrill elopement. The bride made one last desperate effort to break loose, and then Kalia had forced her through the door and was dragging her down the steps to her accompaniment. At last, he threw her in the car and drove off.

Kore took a cigarette from Roman, lit it and let out a judicious blue plume of smoke. 'Very good. She did her family honor. It's not often you see nice kids like that, Romano.'

Roman wondered whether a marriage like this would appeal to Dany's hysterical instincts. Kore had picked up a keg on each shoulder and danced while Roman accompanied him with claps. Dodo and his brothers joined in with a song. Vera laughed at one side, her necklace of coins slapping against her bosom. Dodo's brothers forced toasts of beer and Tokay onto Roman. As he danced, Kore's amulet, a seashell inscribed with stars, fell out of his shirt and danced on a chain. For a passing moment it became a devil's head.

Roman wasn't drunk. He was thinking more clearly than he had all day. Something in the back of his mind was eating the brandy and beer like a demon. It was evil. Its outline was large and ominous. 'There are no hesitation wounds,' he remembered. It was capable of bending the posts of a bed, let alone dance with kegs on its shoulders. It had killed the girl and Nanoosh, and it could have killed him too if it had wanted to. It was not an outline of Hoddinot Sloan.

For the first time he admitted to himself what he shared with Sloan. The dry, pretentious, unpleasant *gajo* was also in love. Why else would he save the letters and wait up for hours for a phone call from a girl he had murdered?

Chapter Sixteen

Celie Miyeyeshti was an important woman by a number of definitions. To begin with she was a mountain of a woman whose petticoats made pleated foothills. When she sat, her great-grandchildren raced to put at least two folding chairs side by side. Among Romanies, the word 'important' was the most common polite description of someone with weight, and Celie Miyeyeshti was the most important woman in New York.

Besides that, she was a *phuri dai*, a woman acknowledged to have such extraordinary powers of perception and such understanding of the unwritten laws of Romany that children and formidable members of the *Kris* alike would modestly bring their problems to the garish, mammoth crone on her folding throne. No one knew how old she was. Her passports gave a variety of guesses, just as they differed on her nationality. She traveled in the rear of her Fleetwood Cadillac limousine with jump seats for anyone who cared to stuff themselves into the vast car with her as she dispensed wisdom – where to rent an *ofisa*, when to attempt a *bozur*, what crime was great enough to assemble the *Kris* – with an air of mystery that was almost sexual. Early in the morning, when Laza and Kalia had consummated their wedding and the bloodstained proof of virginity had been displayed, Celie would face the weary couple. She would break a loaf of bread and put a pinch of salt on each piece and offer them to Laza and Kalia, saying, 'When you are tired of this bread and this salt, then you will be tired of one another.' Laza and Kalia would exchange their halves and eat them as the children threw handfuls of rice over their heads, and yet another round of celebration would begin.

'Get this Romano a chair,' Celie ordered. A tiny girl slid a chair behind Roman.

'Thank you,' Roman said. He wiped the sweat off his forehead and looked at Celie. Somehow she remained cool in the Spanish mantilla and virtual breastplate of necklaces of strung coins she always wore to parties. Gold seemed to permeate her; it winked from twenty teeth when she smiled.

'You should learn to relax,' Celie said. 'If everything is over, why aren't you relaxing? What did you want to ask me?'

He wondered what it was that gave him away. No matter, he was good at reading people but she saw things that he wouldn't in a thousand years. She knew that for once he wasn't sitting next to her to banter about her girth.

'I don't know,' he said.

Over by the tables, Kore and Dodo were pretending to be an Oursari and his bear. The boy who had sung the *patshiv djili* was singing an emotional *canto hondo* he'd learned in Granada. Two women were arguing over who had made the better *bokoli*. Children attacked each other with bread clubs. When one threw a disputed *bokoli*, the din became worse. A circle of elders began singing the old songs, and in a few minutes when their second wind came back, they would start dancing, too.

'Come,' Celie said as she heaved herself out of her chairs, 'this is no place to talk about death.'

Roman followed her as she plowed her way with dignity back through the *ofisa* to the empty kitchen.

Dany finished chewing one side of her lower lip and started on the other. Her oversized glasses rested on the end of her nose, the lenses glazed by the blue of the television screen. Without them, anything beyond ten feet was a blur. Contact lenses made her eyes tear, which created new problems. She wouldn't wear anything but contacts in public and Roman did nothing but make fun of her as she alternated, while they strolled in front of Harry Winston's, between lighthearted smiles and Kleenex.

That was another reason to hate him, to add to all the others she'd thought of during the evening. On the television, an enormous iguana was terrorizing Japan. It was a boring stupid movie, and it scared her, and that was another reason for hating him for leaving her alone.

She shifted on the sofa, pulling a pillow over her stomach. It was a warm night, so she was in nothing but his old kimono, and since she'd turned all the air conditioners on full blast, she was freezing. She glanced at her watch. It was two thirty, and she had enough precious gems of enmity to stock her for a month.

Roman had promised that he'd come back early, and she was amazed at her own acuity of hearing each time the elevator moved. Dany knew what she was going to say. She wasn't going to say a thing, just let him stew in guilt. Later, in the morning, she would let him make up. As the hundred-foot iguana ate a tank in the middle of downtown Tokyo, she held the pillow tighter.

The elevator stopped on the floor. It had to be Roman because the apartment was on the top floor and his neighbor was in Europe. It was too late to turn the set off, so she grabbed the book on the floor and began reading the last pages of Spinoza. There was no key in the door, and she was putting the book back down when the bell rang. She jumped and laughed at herself. He'd know that she was up waiting for him.

Dany took her time, checking herself in the mirror, tying the sash tight and assuming a look of displeasure. She took the chain off the door and opened it. Before she could close it again, the heel of a hand shot through, staggering her. She tried to keep her balance, holding onto the antenna of the television, when the hand came down a second time over her mouth. As she tried to pull free, another hand gripped the back of her neck. The antenna snapped off as she was dragged back onto the sofa.

There were five of them, all dressed brightly in thick pullover ski masks, windbreakers and ski gloves. The heat of the night was already making them sweat in their costumes, so their eyelids batted.

'The lock, the lock,' the one holding her whispered.

The chain was shot, and they turned back to her. Dany reached back to scratch, and her hands were grabbed and twisted down behind her back. Something bit into her wrists as they were tied together, and she was thrown onto her face. She was smothering in the pillow, and at last her head was wrenched back by the hair, and she inhaled once before a balled-up nylon stocking was pushed into her mouth. One of Roman's socks was tied over her eyes.

It was ridiculous, she knew, but what she thought of was that the kimono was pushed up on her back during the struggle and her rear was uncovered. She knew that she should fight some more no matter how futile it was but that would expose her completely. She squeezed her legs together and concentrated on not throwing up on the gag. On the floor, she could hear the crack of her glasses being crushed by a heel.

'Take it easy,' the whisperer said into her ear, his hand resting familiarly on a bare buttock. 'Just take it easy and nod. Now, is he coming back?'

Dany shook her head. She was crying and cursing herself for being so weak. The worst they could do was rape her, she told herself. Then a hand closed on her nostrils, clamping the cartilage hard, and her blinded eyes shot open as she realized what they could do. The grip on her nose loosened, and she sucked in air.

'I'll ask you again. Is he coming back tonight?'

As soon as she started to shake her head again, the hand regained its grip. She couldn't escape it. A fingernail dug through the skin. In a black vacuum, she saw with utter clarity that she was being killed. She'd swallowed the nylon gag back into her throat. When she tried to roll off the sofa, two more hands held her ankles. It took her forever to understand that the brittle snap was the cartilage bending in that inescapable grip. That the twin pops were the feeble protests of her eardrums. The sofa seemed to open up, like a cushioned coffin.

Death was a stream. An iguana changed colors as it gained on her. It grasped her toes and climbed up to rest on her soft instep. Floating, she couldn't shake it off. When it had regained its breath, the lizard started climbing up over her ankle, to her calf, tickling her as it dragged itself over the back of her knee. Its sharp feet dug into the meat of her thighs as it continued its journey. When it raised itself over the shuddering flesh of her buttocks, its footsteps became strangely louder, crashing, deafening. Then she felt the cool touch of its split tongue on the base of her spine and she could stand it no longer. She escaped from her body.

'Hey, she's having convulsions and throwing up.'

'Make the gag tighter.'

She couldn't escape. Somewhere in her mouth and nose, clots of her were caught. The crashes became louder, more distinct.

'She's choking on the stuff.'

'I can't stand it. Cover her somebody, please.'

'She'll survive.'

The footsteps were inside her, running with dull, heavy thuds, racing and shaking her with each step. Then, with amazement, she recognized her heart. And the acrid taste of vomit in her mouth, and the fact that she wasn't dead. Something warm touched her.

'I'm sorry, I had to cover her,' a girl said.

'Whisper, God damn it, whisper. She can hear you,' said the voice that she identified best. 'Turn up the TV.'

It was wonderful to hear the shrieks of the horror movie again. She couldn't have been under for more than a few minutes. Her ears hurt but unusual sounds, besides the screaming of film extras, came through. The noise of a drawer being opened and the disjointed clatter of its contents on the floor. A curtain being carefully, maliciously ripped apart. An antique chair caromed off the wall by insane force.

When was he coming back, they'd asked. He was already late. He was probably rushing home now, she thought. They were tearing the place apart because they didn't have their hands on him. She began praying that he was drunk, that his friends were holding onto him, keeping him, that he was flirting with a girl, anything. The chill sound of glass being scratched filled the room. Nobody else would hear it. The people downstairs were away on vacation too.

'It's your fault. You said he was home.'

'The lights were on,' a male voice answered.

'Don't throw the china. Use a hammer.'

They knew she was awake because they all were whispering again. It was difficult to tell which was a man and which a woman.

'It's Sèvres.'

'Give me that hammer.'

The china cup exploded like a gunshot. As the unseen phantoms went on with their destruction, the rest of the fragile set went off like a child's string of firecrackers. She huddled in the blanket, shivering, her tongue pulled away from the stocking, hoping that they were done with her.

'There's a safe behind the bed. Let's open it.'

She heard them pull the bed back, and then there was a relative silence as they attempted to find the correct combination. Failure was marked with the report of a hammer and the renewed zeal with which they attacked the rest of the apartment. She was getting better at images now. She could picture the knife that penetrated the cushion of a chair and ripped out the stuffing in manic jerks.

How long had they been there, she wondered. Her fright gathered when she realized that there must be almost nothing left to destroy in the apartment. Every chair or table or mirror or piece of china, everything had been smashed but her. They would be left standing with their hammers and knives and hands with only one target left. The strange cacophony had longer and longer pauses. Before, she'd wanted it to end. Now she was willing for it to go on forever.

The room was silent, except for the panting of people who had been working very hard on a summer's night in woolen masks. Somehow she knew the colorful masks and gloves were still on. How nice it would be to go skiing with Roman in New England, in the White Mountains. She'd never done that.

The sofa sagged. Someone was sitting next to her. She

132

felt the heat on the side of her face when he bent to speak to her.

'We have to go. We're going right now,' the whisperer said in a pleasant, conversational tone. The hope leaped in her even while she tried to fight it. She made her body as absolutely still as possible. A hand ran along her ribs.

'We have to go,' he repeated. 'But we can't just go. Do you know what I mean. We can't just go.'

The hope died stillborn.

'Give me the razor,' he said, and she knew he wasn't talking to her anymore. It was stupid, of course, because the sock was around her eyes but she closed her eyes anyway so that she wouldn't see what he was doing because she was a stupid girl, as Roman always said, and that was the way she'd die.

At least she knew enough to pass out when he started.

Celie balanced the glass of hot tea between the fingertips of her hands so that it looked like an offering to a bizarre buddha. She blew a wisp of steam away and gave the glass to Roman.

'You're a smart boy, Romano. I always said that. You may be right, and I may be right, since we're both so smart. But let me tell you something wise. Stay out of it. It's *gaja* business, not yours.'

'You said that before.'

'Because I know when you're not listening to me. Nanoosh is safe. That's all that concerns you.'

'He threatened me with the devil's head.'

'Bah. That doesn't frighten you, and I know it. It shows how much he really knows about the rites.'

'It shows that he thinks he knows. That's what makes him dangerous.' He thought back on Sloan, the coward who paced for hours in his office waiting for his phone call, who went to bed to have bad dreams. The man who left the devil's head had come in through the bedroom window the same as Roman. Roman would have heard him if he had entered the house by a door. It was a man who was as at home in the dark as Roman. 'The only reason he didn't kill me was that I was at the house. It would have been too coincidental for the police. He knows what I am.'

'You think that this evil thing is after you in particular? I have news for you, *gaja* evil is more impersonal than that. You can step aside and let it go on its way, and it will forget all about Romano Gry.'

'And what do you suggest I do tomorrow night? Not think about it?'

The sound of the party wasn't enough to overcome the silence in the kitchen. A pin from Laza's dress was on the floor, and Roman pushed it aside with his foot.

'All right,' Celie said finally. 'You are such a *phral* of this policeman, why don't you tell him?'

It was quite a concession for Celie to make. No Rom spoke to the police. Only her dispensation would allow Roman to in the eyes of the *kumpanias*.

'No good,' he said. 'Isadore has a suspect, I have someone I've never seen, a phantom. He has his evidence and motive. All I can say is that there will be another murder. Do you think that courts admit Gypsies with stories about devils and dark ceremonies? I've seen the murder weapon, and so have you. Isadore wouldn't know what I was talking about. Besides, Isadore could take the killer to a ball game and not know it. If I saw him, I would know him in an instant.'

'Then let the *gaja* fight their own battles,' Celie said. 'If they don't know how to, that's their problem. *Phew*, now you've ruined my evening.'

He'd never seen Celie angry before, and shrugging his shoulders didn't help.

'Let me tell you another secret, since you're so interested in them,' she said. 'We are in America, right?'

'Right.'

'You even go around with an American girl, don't you?'

'Uh-huh.'

'Do you consider yourself American? Because if you do, I consider you a great fool. How long has this America been around, two hundred years? Well, the Romanies have been around for five thousand years. Longer than any nation. And why? Because we know how to survive. The Aryans tried to kill us, the Persians, the Tatars, the Magyars, the Africans, the Germans, everybody. But we stay together, and we move on, and we keep one thing in mind, to survive, and that is our greatest secret. As soon as you stop thinking of yourself as a Rom and as something else then, Romano, you are already a dead man. And when they come to my door to tell me about your brave death, I will say *bater*, so be it.'

Roman looked down at the pin. He forgot whether it was good luck or bad to pick it up. It was after three, and he'd promised to be back long ago, and he was tired. Celie had been battering him for an hour.

'I wouldn't have told you what you wanted to know if I'd suspected what you wanted to do,' she said. 'You are a favorite, so you were able to hide it from me. It wasn't fair. So I am not going to let you go until you promise that this is the end. Because you have involved me, I can demand this. You will do nothing. You will let the *gaja* murder themselves and catch themselves. I forbid you to have anything more to do with it.'

The ageless black eyes looked into his.

'Do you promise?'

He sighed and put the glass on a counter. The side of the glass was smeared with jam. A tart aroma rose from it, a heady aroma he'd smelled a thousand different times and places before.

'Yes,' he answered.

Kore had a new song he wanted Roman to hear when he walked out of the kitchen. Yojo was opening a fresh bottle of brandy. Roman begged off and was about to leave when the newlyweds returned. Laza glowed in response to the awed giggles of her former playmates. Vera spread her arms wide to reveal a bedsheet spangled with bloodstains.

Roman didn't get home until after four, and then he found his promise already broken.

Chapter Seventeen

The apartment looked as if it had been picked up and shaken in the teeth of a monster. Slashed paintings and broken mirrors lay on the floor amid china shards. Chairs had been denuded of their legs and splats. A torn curtain dragged on the floor, stirring a little from the air wandering in from the broken window. In the haphazard destruction, it took Roman a moment to pick out her arm.

A memory emerged of a childhood enemy who had one winter unexpectedly pushed him into a deep creek – the same frozen, heavy, helpless shock. He pulled the blanket off her, moving quickly as an antidote to fear, untying the blindfold of his own sock and the scarf around her wrists. Her hands were cold, and one arm was daubed with blood. Something was hanging from the corner of her mouth, and he watched with horror as a whole nylon stocking came out when he pulled.

It was impossible to tell whether she was breathing and he put his hand between her breasts, and the frozen sensation thawed into sweat when he felt her heart beating shallowly in sleep. The vandals had left a decanter of brandy in the kitchen untouched. Roman lifted Dany's head to pour a glass into her mouth. She choked, and he sat her up, holding her upright against his shoulder. The nearer she dared come to consciousness, the closer he held her until finally they were rocking together on the sofa in the middle of the shattered room with the night air coming through the paneless windows.

'What a dump,' Dany said in an imitation of Liz Taylor doing an imitation of Bette Davis. It was an hour later, and she was coming around. They were sitting on the bed, the scene of least damage. The bathroom medicine cabinet had been emptied into the tub, and the contents of the refrigerator had been emptied everywhere. She was eating a reasonably clean breakfast roll for her empty stomach.

'How's the arm feel?'

'Fine. I don't even notice it. It'll heal in a couple of days. As a matter of fact, I don't even know why they did it.'

She inspected the herringbone pattern of razor cuts on the inside of her forearm. Roman had painted them with iodine, a ritual that reassured her.

'The main thing as I see it,' she said, 'is that we're going to have to walk around here in shoes for a while until all the glass is picked up.'

Roman shook his head in amazement. It had taken her thirty minutes to stop crying enough to talk at first. Now she was handling it as if it were a slip on the pavement. It was a show, and he appreciated it all the more.

'You know, I wouldn't have even noticed the hair that was pulled out,' she said and rubbed her head. 'I thought it was just part of the overall headache. Does that make me a poor victim?'

'Lousy.' He watched the smile on her face disappear. 'What's the matter?'

'The reason they didn't do anything to me. Except scare me to death. They wanted you, to kill you.'

'Well, they missed and got you, and it's my fault. I'm not going to leave you alone like that again. I swear. There's a police sergeant who owes me a favor. He and I will find out who these . . . people were.'

'No.' Dany grabbed his arm. 'They won't come back. Forget about them. I'll look through the peephole and won't open the door without the chain on from now on. Please. If you want to do something for me, don't do anything. You don't know how much it scares me when you talk like that.'

'Okay. Okay.' He patted her knee. 'I'll let the cop do his job. How's that?'

Dany was relieved. He'd never given in to her before. She threw her arms around him and kissed him.

'Wait, wait a second. You have to tell me what to tell my friend.' He thought the ordeal might be too upsetting to relive, but Dany had no qualms about talking, like a child who's only afraid of the dark when he's alone.

'I can't remember exactly what they said. I was too scared,' she admitted. 'All I know is that I think there were five of them, and I think two were men and three were women. I can't say how big or little.'

She spoke for a long time without adding much in the way of facts. She'd been blind and terrified and usually dead to the world. One thing she felt was an impression that they had come for one thing, to get Roman, and without him they were vaguely at a loss. The destruction had been vicious and general, although there was something about china that she couldn't remember. And the safe, they hadn't been able to get into the safe.

When her eyelids drooped, Roman brushed the crumbs off the bed and laid her head down on the slashed pillow. He turned the lights out, and as he walked back to the bed, he dropped his clothes on the floor. This was one time when they wouldn't make a difference. When he got into bed next to her, Dany moved her head from the pillow to his shoulder.

'It's a funny thing,' she said sleepily. 'Just goes to prove how dumb I am. When I woke up the first time after he held my nose, I kept thinking how hot they were in their ski masks, and how nice it would be for us to go skiing. You'll have to take me to the White Mountains.'

She was asleep by the end of the sentence. Her hair brushed over Roman's mouth. He had never been more awake.

He hadn't told her what he found as he searched the apartment. The blood and hair had not been taken for no reason at all. They were necessary for the image, the little broken warning that he looked for as soon as he saw what they'd done to her. It wasn't hard to find. In the wreckage, the untouched case stood out like any lone survivor. It was a small custom-designed chest about a foot high, made in Philadelphia about 1750 for the various eyeglasses of a wealthy buyer. Franklin's bifocals were not popular yet, and the case had drawers enough for six pairs. The drawers and chest were made of cherry wood, and the inside was lined with velvet.

In the first drawer he pulled open was a tiny pink leg. He recognized it as coming from a porcelain Victorian doll in his collection. The leg had been ripped from the hinge. It was wrapped in one of Dany's hairs and smeared with her blood. He took the other leg from the second drawer, the torso from the third, the right arm from the fourth and the left arm from the fifth. The head was in the top drawer. Each of them had been similarly tied and painted.

The callers had left another memento, probably less intentionally. The scarf they had tied Dany up with was an unusual one. It was a long, thin braid of black silk, and one end was tied around a gold four ducat with the placid profile of Franz Josef. He was not surprised that it had cut off her circulation.

He patted Dany's sleeping, content head. It wasn't so dumb of her to wake up thinking about skiing in the White Mountains. After all, that's where Hillary Sloan and her friends were heading, according to the brown spotted piece of map he found next to the doll's head. He didn't have to accept the invitation, the doll said, but then Dany would take his place.

Chapter Eighteen

Roman entered New Hampshire on the F. E. Everett Turnpike outside Lowell. He felt respectable just using a road with a name like that.

'You should be happy. You don't sound happy at all,' Isadore had said on the phone from Boston. 'The agent admits he didn't look in the chest. The girl's blood matches the type on the chest and the saw in Sloan's workshop. Sloan has no, repeat, no alibi.' He was upset when Roman told him about the visit to his apartment. 'I'll get onto it as soon as I get back. As for the murder, though, the only possibility is that they saw your name in the paper. Captain Frank gave everything but his mother's maiden name to the press. You and Lippincoot were called consultants. Didn't you see the papers?' Roman let Isadore in on the fact that he didn't read the papers. 'Well, the kids do,' Isadore said, 'and you know how it is. One weird case like this sets off a whole army of kooks. It's not revenge, I'll tell you that. Sloan didn't have a friend in the world. Would you believe this guy turned out to be a forger?' Roman said he was shocked. 'I'll bet. Sloan is almost as upset about that as the murder.' Roman asked whether Isadore could drop everything he was doing and join him on a trip. 'You're crazy. You don't know what you're asking. I know you're upset about last night, and I'll do everything I can. No, I can't spare any men either. This isn't my jurisdiction up here, and New York is still up in the air over politics. Just wait until I get back. Look, Sloan's new lawyer just ran in looking like his coat's on fire. I'll call you back.' Roman accepted Isadore's excuses but remarked that, as a consultant to the police, he'd suggest that the sergeant look at the rings left on wood by a rotary saw. The same saw would leave anything but clean cuts on flesh. He also suggested that Isadore go to the library branch where the Mueller girl had worked and look up the records on readers who had taken out an unusual number of books on Gypsies and Indian mythology recently. 'Leave the crimes to me and I'll leave the fortune-telling to you,' Isadore suggested. Roman could hear two other men talking to the sergeant at the same time. One of them was Sloan's lawyer, and apparently he'd shown the Boston papers to Sloan, and Sloan did read the papers. 'Hold it, hold it, Roman,' Isadore shouted. 'You didn't tell me you were at Sloan's house.' That was when Roman hung up.

He felt better than he had in a week. He was free of promises and cooperation. A motorcycle passed as he gladly made room for it. The kids had been passing him all morning on cycles and cars. Many flashed the peace sign at him, and he returned it. Past Concord, he slowed down for a roadblock. State troopers were checking every bike and car. One with sunglasses motioned Roman to drive off the road; but when he started to, the trooper motioned him impatiently to get moving, and he saw through the rearview mirror that the center of interest was a large cycle. The troopers made the riders get off and stand for a frisk. They were looking for drugs.

The land changed to mountain country. A month later an older generation would tour it for the foliage. No troopers would wave them down as instant suspects. Sloan's lemon station wagon would have been undisturbed; now that sort of life was ended for him no matter what happened.

The traffic slowed down again. There was no roadblock, just too many cars for the two-lane road. It was fifteen miles to Moultonboro, a small town on an isolated plain in the Ossipee Mountains. The rock festival started the next day on the plain between Moultonboro and the smaller town of Sandwich. The road was full of kids, driving and walking. A couple with a little boy and girl on their shoulders were moving particularly slowly, and he pulled over to give them a lift.

'Fantastic. Thanks,' the guy said. The girl was in the back with the children and silent. It didn't make Roman nervous, but the young man shot inquiring glances backward.

'It's the car, not you,' he whispered to Roman. 'Pollution. She wouldn't have got in, but the babies were tired.'

'Stop whispering!' the girl shrieked. 'That's what I mean by male chauvinism.'

'You whisper with your friends,' he said meekly.

'It's the traditional right of slaves to whisper,' she said. 'Every time I think your sensitivity is heightened you go off getting palsy with some strange man.'

'He's giving us a ride, Honey.' He leaned over the seat

to talk to her. It was as if Roman weren't there to hear them.

'Honey! My name isn't Honey, buster.'

'The kids.'

She told him what he could do about the kids. The rest of the ride to Moultonboro the car was as silent as a tomb. When he left his riders off outside town, the guy stuck his head in the window.

'Guilt is a terrible thing,' he said.

Everyone who was coming to the festival seemed to have already arrived. The plain north of Moultonboro was crowded with tents and, from what Roman could see from the makeshift parking lot, the heads of people weaving their way through the tents searching for their own square foot to spend the night. Far away the band platform was being assembled. Half built, it looked like a gallows. An attendant rushed up to take ten of Roman's dollars. The producers of the festival said they were expecting more than two hundred thousand spectators. It didn't look as if they were going to lose any money.

An encampment of Romany blended in with its setting. This camp overwhelmed it. He could see kids everywhere. A ripple from the fifties' baby boom rose like a multi-colored bathtub ring on Ossipee. The ground was beaten grassless and dusty. It was not only another nation but another world, one without shirts, with scarves, without combs, with leather armbands, a high distaste for the money system and more expensive 35mm cameras than he'd ever seen in his life. They were appealing more to him all the time. The fact that they were beating the

145

ecology of the plain to death with their bare feet would have gladdened the heart of the blackest cynic. The flaunting of naked bodies was against every custom he grew up with. A Rom would never even indicate to his family that he was going to the bathroom, sexual lines were so strict. But there was an exuberance to these children struggling to break away from their *gaja* lifestyle that had to be sympathized with.

Breughel would have enjoyed painting the scene of self-proclaimed peasants in their bell-bottom pants, leather vests, headbands and beads. The kids were a show in themselves, and they enjoyed the show, gawking and commenting at warpaint on faces and surrounding the hundreds of impromptu blanket bands. A disjointed music covered the field from guitars, Jew's harps, sitars, harmonicas, drums and sticks. The only thing like it Roman had ever seen was the great market at Marrakech and just as in Marrakech, hawkers moved through the crowd loudly vending their selections of hash.

A girl bare to the waist stared at Roman, and he realized something was wrong. He stuffed his tie into a back pocket and threw his jacket over his shoulder. The crowd spilled over onto Route 25, and there the kids were racing underneath kites. Most of them were of the plastic variety. Some were impressive Chinese kites of battleship dimensions with brilliant scalloped tails curling behind.

The number of naked kids increased as he ventured closer to Squam Lake. The physiques of the girls were tributes to American nutrition. The boys, on the other

hand, were in distressingly poor shape, and they resented
Roman's presence more.

> I had been happy if the general camp,
> Pioneers and all, had tasted her sweet body.

Roman turned to face a thin, heavily made-up girl in
a purple robe. On her shoulders was a brace that balanced
in front a large tome of Shakespeare's complete works
and in back a poster reading 'Peace.' Altogether, she bore
a strong similarity to some of the kites he'd seen.

'Do you know what it is?' she asked. Her eyes were lost
in a welter of mascara. He confessed he didn't.

'*Othello*,' she said. 'You look like Othello to me.'

'But I don't feel like Othello.'

'Wouldn't you like to try?' she asked.

When he looked back at her a few minutes later, he
saw he was more right than he thought. A gust of wind
had caught the poster and was driving her toward the
lake. She was trying to get out of the brace, but it was
plain she wasn't going to make it. Roman had the
manners to look the other way and walk on.

Afghans, St Bernards and Irish setters provided a
homey atmosphere as they nosed around kids stoned on
pot. A monkey passed Roman at his own level before
Roman saw that it was standing on the head of a dwarf.

Even the confrontations when festival guards had to
identify themselves seemed to be just another part of the
show. A boy with electrified orange hair had violated a
commune's stew, and a guard on a motor scooter stopped

to escort him to the highway. Immediately a ring of a hundred people gathered, most of them with Nikons or Leicas. Some of them sported heavy movie cameras. The boy pulled his shirt on, and the guard tried to comfort him, explaining there were still some things you couldn't do at a rock festival. The boy got more upset, and finally, when it appeared he would cry, he hauled off and slugged the guard in the face. A thousand people were watching the familiar pantomime by now as the two grappled in the dust. There were some shouts of 'police brutality,' but they were halfhearted. A car prodded its way through the spectators, and the boy was slung in the back.

'That wasn't so bad. Thirty feet of action,' the man next to Roman said. He was a lean perspiration-soaked individual with a dark crew cut and a wrinkled sports shirt. A film camera was balanced on a shoulder saddle. 'Hell, they make you pay fifty dollars to bring the camera in, you want to get something in return.'

He told Roman where the public phones were. Roman had to wait fifteen minutes in a line before he got to the phone, and then it took the operator another five minutes to get a clear line to Boston and another five to find Isadore.

'What are you up to?' Isadore demanded. 'What's with this trip? I've been calling your place all day, and Miss Murray just knows you aren't there.'

'I'd tell you, but I don't want the local constabulary on my back.'

'Wait for me then.'

'Too late now. It would take you too long to get here. What changed your mind?'

'Who said I changed my mind? We're still holding Sloan. It's just that what you said about marks interested me. It reminded me of something else, too. There were scratches all over the dash of Nanoosh's car. There was only one that looked familiar at all, round scratches that you get from one of those little magnetic saints. Did Nanoosh have one of those?'

'Of course. Wasn't it in his car?'

'Damn it. It was on the road, and we thought it came from the van. Now that I remember, though, there weren't any marks like that on the van. Then I saw it again. Roman, are you going to tell me where you are?'

'No, but I assume you're having the call traced. I've been timing it, and it's been three minutes, and the operator hasn't interrupted yet.'

'Don't fool around, Roman. I never was happy about the way that roommate changed her story on Sloan. I think there just may be a connection between that and what happened last night. So if you think you know who those people were at your place, just tell me. At least wait where you are for me to show up.'

'You're stalling,' Roman said.

'You're goddamn right I'm stalling.'

He placed the phone gently on the receiver and walked back out to the festival ground for a second tour. Isadore didn't understand, and even if he did, it was too late. He was threatened, Dany was threatened, and even if both of them escaped, that left a killer running loose. He was happy for the first reason because that left himself loose to act. There was another reason, too. In a petty but strong way, it offended him that the *gaja* dressed their threats in magic. The devil's head and the bloody doll irritated him instead of cowing him. The *gaja* world was for combustion engines, bank accounts and profitable rock festivals. The other world, the one of the immaterial, of vampires and ghouls, was the Rom's unlucky birthright.

A group of kids shaved and dressed as lamas shuffled by with chants of 'Om!'

Isadore needed evidence, he didn't. One look at Sloan was enough. The collection of antiques and snobbery was a wall against inadequacy. If he'd actually murdered a girl, he simply would have fled, not butchered and shipped her coolly in his own antiques. Isadore didn't know the evidence when he had it. The rotary saw would have bathed the workshop in blood if it had gone through the neck of a person whose heart was still beating, as the coronor claimed. Instead, the cuts had been made by a weapon without a point. There was only one knife Roman knew of like that, the *bhotani*, the executioner's sword.

The lamas did a slow sort of Mexican hat dance with their feet. They were a pink, soft lot with vacant stares. The excitement in the area came from what appeared to be a circus.

Chapter Nineteen

A clown in a startling jacket of patches walked on high stilts juggling large, varicolored balls over the heads of the crowd. His face was painted with red eyebrows and a red mouth. He executed an about-face and strode back to a second performer on stilts. The other one had the same painted face and a court jester's outfit of a belled cap, curly-toed slippers and checkerboard jacket and leggings.

Roman worked his way to the front of the spectators. A chubby girl in a long peasant dress was juggling Indian clubs while two other girls kept time with small cymbals. From time to time one of them danced with streamers, turning herself around like a Maypole. The lamas didn't have a chance. They muttered an 'Om' or two and went on their way, leaving the audience to the circus.

At the end of the music, the clown let himself fall forward off his stilts, tumbling and landing on his feet artfully. The much smaller jester was content merely to jump down. Before the crowd could break up, the jester explained that what they had seen was a troupe of jongleurs. The jongleur, he said, was an ancient and respected profession. During the Dark Ages, jongleurs not only entertained the nobility of the time but also served as tutors for their children. They were harbingers of news from the outside world and repositories of knowledge. It was the jongleur who kept the lamp of reason burning during the dangerous Middle Ages. Testament to this, he said, was the high number of nobility who left their castles to roam the land as jongleurs themselves. Richard the Lionhearted was the best-known example.

'This is the new Dark Age, a dangerous, ignorant time. So we have chosen to revive the profession of the jongleur as a most honorable and necessary trade. We too roam the land. First as entertainers' – here there was a rattle of cymbals – 'and second as seekers of knowledge. Naturally, we are dependent on your generosity for what we eat and drink.'

It was a charming and informative presentation, and when one of the girls came around with a peaked hat held out for contributions, Roman put in ten dollars.

'Nice dance, Hillary. What else do you do?'

He thought she was going to run, but she controlled herself.

'Sometimes I sing.'

'I'll wait around to hear you.'

Her friends had seen him. They weren't bolting either. The jester talked some more as the troupe prepared new entertainment for their audience. The clown pulled musical instruments from the front of a Volkswagen microbus that had been spray painted in psychedelic colors. Then he went to the rear of the bus to untether a billy goat that had been lazily chewing grass around the wheels. He led the goat to the center of the ring.

'The traditional pet of the jongleur is the goat. Pan,

the symbol of fertility,' the jester said. The girls struck their tambourines. The goat's ears perked up, and it stood on its rear legs. It walked awkwardly, its front hooves bouncing off its chest.

'To the superstitious people of the Dark Ages, the horned goat was the manifestation of the devil. You probably remember how in *The Hunchback of Notre Dame*, Esmeralda was arrested for consorting with Satan simply because she danced with her pet goat. For this reason, Gypsies were often tormented by peasants of the time for training goats to dance, although, in fact, the Gypsies were as ignorant of supernatural secrets as their persecutors.'

The clown jumped in front of the goat. He waved a painted wand, and the goat's eyes followed it, the horned head bobbing and its rear legs hopping to keep up with the baton. The jester forsook his spiel for a flute, and the girls sang a medieval air. It was pretty and earnest, and Roman could tell the kids watching accepted it as part of their own new world. When the song was over and the goat was being taken back to the microbus, the jester skipped into the ring. The girls roamed through the audience, and Roman was taking his wallet out when he received a jab in the side. It was the crew-cut cameraman who had been at the scuffle.

'Keep your eye on this. They do it every show.' He pressed his hollow cheek to his eyepiece.

The big clown brought out a wooden bull's-eye nine feet across and set it against a tree. He stationed himself with his back to the bull's-eye, his arms and legs cutting the colored lines into quadrants, looking straight ahead at the jester twenty-five feet away. The kids emptied their pockets so they wouldn't be searching for change when the action began. The jester made a rambling speech overloaded with quotes. Roman paid no attention to it, fixing his eyes on the narrow fingers that played with a silver fan of knives. The girls returned, and the jester looked indulgently on the money they poured into a chamois sack.

'And now the last member of our troupe as I promised you: death.' The jester toed a mark and let his weight rest on his back foot. He selected one knife from the rest. Roman could feel the crowd growing from the pressure on his back. With no more fanfare the jester's arm came forward and the knife appeared three inches from the clown's belt. The clown didn't budge. The jester chose another knife, weighted it and threw. It appeared two inches from the other side of the belt. Roman looked at the target's face. There was no anxiety. A third knife popped up next to his shoulder.

'Not bad,' the cameraman commented. 'Not professional but not bad.' A boy next to them frowned for quiet. The cameraman gave him an obscene gesture and went on. 'Of course, the knives are coming out from the back of the bull's-eye and the little guy is palming the ones he pretends to throw. An illusion, you know what I mean.'

Roman had picked a spot halfway between the jester and the clown where there was a solid background of dark leaves. For an instant that was practically invisible he caught the flutter of a metallic bird. A new knife perched beside the clown's throat.

'You know these kids pretty well,' Roman said.

'Hell, I see right through them,' the cameraman muttered.

The jester raised his empty hands. The clown stepped away from the bull's-eye and did the same, if possible even more calmly than the jester. 'They're so hopped up on drugs they couldn't...' He described what they couldn't do, in detail.

'Thank you, gentlefolk,' the jester said, 'for your good vibrations and even more for your money.' The cameraman spluttered an expletive of agreement. 'See you tomorrow, and may hallucinations of sugarplums dance through your heads.'

The girls drifted into the applauding crowd for a last donation. 'See what I mean about drugs?' the cameraman said. He let his heavy machine slide off his shoulder and hang by a scrawny arm. His short-sleeved shirt had turned completely gray with perspiration. 'Say, how'd you like to join me in a few drinks back in Sandwich. We could scare up some action, some groupies. The boys are all queer, but some of the girls aren't so bad.'

'I see you're a married man,' Roman said, looking at the ring on the man's hand. 'It must be fun having something in common with your kids.' He turned back and watched the clown pull the knives from the bull's-eye. The cameraman was flushed, but he couldn't read anything hostile in Roman's dark face because Roman had erased him from his mind.

'You know the trouble with you jigs,' he said at last. 'Nobody's good enough for you.' When he didn't get a reply, he slapped a cap over the lens furiously and left, pushing his way through the departing crowd.

Hillary deliberately collected from the far side. The chubby girl was near Roman. She had a timid smile and a heavy application of makeup. He put a fifty-dollar bill in her tambourine.

'Wow, thanks!'

The crowd had almost dispersed, and she waved the bill at the jester to get his attention. She blushed immediately, regretfully, but the jester had seen her and came over. He had one of the knives in his hand. He was thin, and his dark eyes moved over Roman speculatively.

'I thought you might want to contribute something,' he said as menacingly as he could.

Roman smiled, although he was anything but happy. For a short while he hoped he was wrong and that the jester was the one he was looking for. The first threatening overtone destroyed that wishful thought.

'Oh, no,' the clown said. He'd eased his way through the last of the crowd without Roman's noticing. He stood, taller than any of them, with his arms out in a gesture of friendship. Roman saw evenly planed, handsome features through the red-and-white greasepaint. The clown pulled his belled cap off, and a mane of blond hair fell to his shoulders. He smiled as broadly as Roman, the red mouth curling in satisfaction. 'Don't you know the correct greeting is *sarisban?*'

Roman put on his own mask of delighted surprise. The clown motioned Hillary to join them.

'You're a friend of Hillary's. She told me about you,' the clown told him.

'No,' Hillary said. She tried warning Roman away with her eyes. 'We met only once.' The clown glanced at the jester and the plump girl, enough for them to leave and start gathering the props spread over the ground.

'Imagine, a real live Gypsy,' the clown said. The first cloud of the day passed overhead, casting a shadow over the small circus. His blue eyes glowed in the sudden dark.

'And very superstitious,' Roman added. He took in the ironic hilarity on the clown's face. He could imagine him without any difficulty slipping soundlessly into a second-story window. 'Somehow I feel we've met before too.'

'Don't you have to go back to New York now, Mr Grey?' Hillary asked pointedly.

Roman ignored the question. 'I've never seen a rock festival before.'

'You'll miss it,' Hillary said. 'It's not until tomorrow. Now we have to pack up.'

Roman smiled and watched the other performers gathering the colorful litter of props. The bright balls reminded Roman for some reason of the broken shells of a giant bird and the jongleurs of hatched, ungainly young. Hillary and the clown would be the beautiful ones, of course, the violent aristocracy. The rest were merely a chorus for whatever tragedy those two would make of themselves.

'It's not every day we get to talk to a man like Mr Grey, Hillary,' the clown commented.

'It's not every day I see such educational entertainment either,' Roman said.

Hillary bit her lip. The clown laughed and winked at Roman as if they were in a male conspiracy. The force of personality came off him like a hum off a tuning fork.

'Hillary never mentioned that she was part of a traveling troupe.'

'She's very shy.'

'I suppose so. She hasn't even introduced us.'

The two men waited until she said, 'Howie, this is Roman Grey.'

They shook hands. The clown's grip was as strong as Kore's. 'No last name?' Roman asked.

'No,' the clown said lightly. 'No addresses or credit cards. Isn't that like Gypsies?'

'But we have made names. For ourselves and for other people.'

'Secrets! I love secrets,' Howie said enthusiastically. 'Maybe you can teach us some.'

'Mr Grey was going, weren't you,' Hillary said. It wasn't a question.

'Impossible. He came to see the festival, and he's a friend. He can stay with us tonight. Can you imagine it. Secrets!' The way he said it made the word sound itself like a secret.

'He wants to get home.'

'He wants to see a real rock festival,' the clown argued persuasively. His arm went around Hillary, out of sight.

Roman watched her pupils dilate with pain. 'Don't you agree?'

'It would be interesting,' she said slowly.

'Great, it's settled then. Just give me a chance to get this paint off, and we'll be going.'

'Where?' Roman asked. 'You never said.'

'There,' Howie said. He pointed to the lake. Roman saw a small, thickly wooded island in its center. Its reflection in the water gave it the shape of an amused mouth, and if it had been red, it would have been a perfect copy of Howie's. Roman really would have preferred his enemy to be the knife thrower, not the man who amiably waited for the knives without flinching.

Chapter Twenty

Close up, the summer afternoon gave the island an inviting haze. An oar scraped rock, and Howie jumped in the water. It splashed around his knees as he easily pulled the boat onto the beach over a hiss of rocks.

'Ararat,' Howie said. He stood on the beach, the rope held lightly in one hand, his weight on one leg, and he reminded Roman of nothing so much as Michelangelo's David with perhaps the curl of the lips a trifle more pronounced, the shoulders Americanized and broadened. He was dressed completely in pure white buckskin that reflected the sun.

The rest got out. Without his costume and paint, the jester was a thin boy with the large head of a prodigy. His name was Gerry, and he dressed in a flower shirt and bell-bottoms belied by his accountant-close haircut. The plump girl wore a waistless peasant's dress and a bow in her hair. Her name was Rosalind. Isabelle kicked at the water spitefully. She had an angular, heavy-cheekboned face, and her black eyes had the warmth of dead coals when she looked at Roman. Hillary stared back at the festival, the breeze towing at her gold hair.

'I'm so glad you came,' Howie said earnestly as he took Roman by the arm. 'The others didn't think you'd show up, Hillary most of all. I said, if anybody would, you would. The girl wasn't too hurt, was she?'

'More frightened,' Roman said. The others were hurrying to the camp deeper on the island. He and Howie followed slowly, like lifelong friends.

'Good. You don't know how much I admire you. You're what, ten years older than I am, but I related immediately to you. I am something of a student of Gypsies, and this is a real treat for me.' The way to the camp was padded with moss. Bright orange salamanders watched them fearfully. 'That's where I first saw Sloan and the girl together, you know, at the library. She kept a whole list of the new mysteries especially for him. That struck me as one of the twists, by the way, creating a mystery around a man who was such a devotee of them. Anyway, I saw him there' – Howie cocked his head at the memory – 'and he saw me, too, but he didn't recognize me. Isn't that odd? I'd brought antiques to his place two or three times. That's how I met Hillary. But, see, he didn't recognize me because to him all people who looked like hippies were the same. He couldn't be bothered to separate them into individuals.

'This is what fascinated me. I could kill his girlfriend, and he still didn't suspect who could have created this mystery all around him. But with you, all I had to do was – what? – cast a shadow in the woods and you knew I was there.'

'That was why Hillary was asking me all the questions, wasn't it?'

'Yes. That was the first time I got a good look at you.

Hillary thought you must be from the police.' Howie grinned. 'Of course, after your fast exit on the horse, I told her how silly she was.'

'And you went off to get your devil's head.'

'Exactly.' Howie laughed with delight. 'See how much easier it is for people like us? I met a police sergeant on Friday. He was as far from the truth as Sloan. He will even convict Sloan for murder on circumstantial evidence, and neither of them will ever understand what was done or why, two men operating in the dark and never knowing the rules of the game. While you, in an instant, would know Sloan was innocent. That was why I tried to warn you off. After we read about your connection with the police, we had to get more serious.'

'You knew I'd come alone.'

'Sure. I know you pretty well.' Hillary and the others watched them come into the camp. The two men walked arm in arm. Gerry had a fire started. Isabelle was rooting through a pair of rucksacks for cans of food. Roman looked around for Rosalind and spotted her beside a tree. Tethered to it was another goat, a black one.

'Do you like it?' Howie asked with an expansive gesture. 'This is how we get away from the madding crowd. I haven't whipped them into a *kumpania* yet, but it's a start.'

'It is still in the Tom Sawyer league,' Roman said. Howie laughed appreciatively.

Roman caught a look going from Isabelle to Gerry.

'What do we do with him?' Gerry asked. His hand was frozen in the act of slicing kindling.

'What do we do with him?' Howie asked back. 'What kind of question is that to ask for a guest? We invited him, and he came.' He strode across the clearing in his buckskin with his arms wide.

'We treat him like a guest,' he said with a touch of humility that was so good even Roman was tempted to believe it. 'He's one of us, an outsider. We should all stick together. Do you know how much you owe to the Gypsies? The rhymes, the songs. How many children's fears have been handed down by them.' As he looked around, his long hair swung. He put a finger to his nose.

'Take this, for example. "Hickory dickory dock." You know it. "The mouse ran up the clock. The clock struck one and down he run. Hickory dickory dock." That's an old Gypsy rhyme that actually went, *"Ekkeri akkery an."* It's a counting ditty. And there are many others, aren't there?'

'You're too generous,' Roman said. 'Hillary, are you the hostess?'

'I guess so,' she said without enthusiasm.

'Like before.'

She paled.

'At your father's house, I mean.'

'Oh. Oh, yes,' she said.

'No, not like then,' Howie said. 'This is fun. We all know each other now. We'll have a picnic and then some entertainment. First you entertain us,' he said to Roman, 'and then we entertain you.'

'How is he going to entertain us?' Rosalind asked

ingenuously. Roman had reached the opinion she was partly retarded.

'With the best kind of show,' Howie said. 'He's going to try to escape. You don't think he came here deliberately to get his throat cut, do you?'

He came up behind Roman and slapped him on the back. Roman was struck again by how handsome Howie was, not only the features seemingly cut from flawless marble but the same cerulean blue eyes of a statue. So when he smiled, the effect was ghoulish, like seeing a statue smile.

'What's it going to be? A little fortune-telling? Divide and conquer? I wonder if you can tell what we have in store for you?'

'The fortune-telling comes later,' Roman said. 'My medium works better on a full stomach.'

'Beautiful.'

'Roman, don't. It's not funny.'

Everyone looked at Hillary. A gelid quality glazed Howie's eyes for a moment. Gerry coughed nervously and mentioned something about food to fill the silence. It snapped Howie back.

'Right, food. I've had to do all the work so far. Now I've someone who can really help me.'

'Gerry's pretty good with knives,' Roman said.

'With still targets. I taught him how to do that,' Howie said. 'But hunting with a Gypsy, that'll be a kick. Of course, we won't be able to give you anything sharp, you understand.'

'I somehow imagined there was a condition like that.'

Gerry glared at him anxiously, long enough for Roman to grasp Isabelle's violent hate.

'Great, then we'll all go and watch. It'll be just like Mr Wiz –'

'Howie, I don't think I can come,' Hillary said.

Howie took a deep breath. 'You'll come,' he said in a voice that was almost different from the one Roman heard before. 'You'll all come.'

The salamanders scurried from the damp moss into the filigree shadows of ferns. A daddy longlegs moved giraffelike down the bark of a beech. Roman and the jongleurs moved in single file past their tiny spectators down to the lake again. Hillary brought up the rear. Howie didn't mind; he was in good spirits again.

'And Kaliban, there's another Gypsy who never got his due. Half man and half beast. He only had one talent: he knew how to curse. Isn't that so?'

'You did spend a lot of time in the library,' Roman said, raising an eyebrow.

'And here we are, Kaliban. The vast deep, full of sea changes. What are you going to show us?'

They came out of the woods a little down from the boat. On the faraway bank the mass of kids played at shepherd like Marie Antoinette. In between, a trail shimmered on the water from the sun.

'Fish are usually what you find in water,' Roman said.

'But the word is *matcho*,' Howie said. '*Matcho*, fish. This is a good chance for the rest of you to learn the oldest living language in the world.' The others spread out over the shore watching, except for Hillary, who squinted at the sun: 'Without a hook, remember.'

'I'll try.'

Roman walked along the shore until he found a flat rock jutting over the water. He squatted on it and rolled his sleeves up.

'He's going to do it with his bare hands,' Rosalind said excitedly, Gerry told her to be quiet.

Roman lowered his hands in the water. It was late in the afternoon but still hot. Beads of sweat slid down his cheeks. His hands descended at a rate that could be noticed only if one of those watching looked away and then looked back. It took five minutes in all. An underwater plant caressed the back of his hand. He waited another five minutes as the people on the shore became edgy. Something nibbled at a finger, and he felt the stiff bristles of a sunfish. The sunfish left as something bigger chased it from the shade. Roman hoped the others could keep still long enough. A smooth back grazed his palm. The trick was not to grab too fast or too slow.

'He's got one,' Gerry shouted. A bass flipped on the ground, squirming in the dirt. It had lost its dark glow in dust by the time Gerry pushed his knife through the gills and began sawing the head off.

'Howie's got one, too,' Rosalind said.

Roman had been too busy concentrating to see Howie wade into the water. He had his eye on a catch, too.

Suddenly his arm was in the water. It came out empty. The knife in his hand was pink, though.

'You missed,' Gerry said as Howie waded back.

'No, I got him.'

When they left the lake, the headless fish in Gerry's sack, none of the jongleurs looked very happy.

'It was a joke,' Hillary explained.

'That's right,' Howie said as he walked with Roman. 'I don't want to do any of the work for you,' he said confidentially. 'You've always heard of a man digging his own grave. But a man getting his own last supper, that's a little different.'

'It shows imagination.'

'Oh, you're humoring me, you dog you,' Howie said good-naturedly. 'I can see how you put Sloan through the hoops. Frankly, I think we have a lot in common. I even wish we could meet in different circumstances.'

'Maybe we will,' Roman suggested.

'That's the spirit.'

Roman showed the jongleurs how to reap food from the island as Howie stood by and named almost everything they found. Wild onion, *purrum*. Watercress, *panishey sbok. Pedloer*, nuts. Roman agreeably supplied *yakori bengeskro* for elderberries. All the time, Hillary fell farther and farther back. Once she had to go off by herself and be sick.

'Are you going to keep up with us?' Howie asked when she came back.

'I can't,' she muttered.

'We can turn back now,' Roman suggested. It was the last thing he wanted to do.

The marble lids clicked over the blue eyes once. 'We'll go on. It doesn't make any difference.'

Roman led the others through the woods, picking up speed gradually as Howie and Hillary followed. The forest changed from lowland woods to pines. The moss stopped and a cover of pine needles began. Above, the sharp green tips tilted to the east. The incline became steeper, and he hurried because he saw ahead of him what he'd been searching for, the top of the island. Gerry and the girls scrambled after him with their sacks, but while he moved effortlessly through the trees, they kept slipping on the needles underfoot. They were relieved to see him stop on a bare knoll. Then they saw Howie with him. Somehow he had outdistanced them all.

Roman looked around. The whole island was spread out below a ring of pines.

'What do you think you're doing?' Howie asked sadly.

'Did you ever hear the old story about the man Beng took to the top of a high cliff and offered all the gold in the world?' The island fell away in stages to the west. Near the west shore were the burned remains of a house. South, a stand of birches like washed-out graves lay between the pines and a swamp.

'That's not a Gypsy story.'

'Nobody said it was.' There were no other campfires besides their own. No boats that he could see. East, there was a bare patch past the pines and then the sycamores and dogwoods around their camp.

'I could kill you right here,' Howie said matter-of-factly.

'You could. I don't think that's what you want.' He inhaled the pine resin deeply.

'What's going on?' Gerry asked as he reached them. The girls with their sacks of herbs looked as if they were on a real picnic. Their cheeks glowed with exercise. Howie was about to answer when a cardinal that had waited in the pine beside him until its heart was bursting shot out of the tree. It headed for the swamp, fluttering like a red handkerchief.

'*Cherriclo*,' Roman said. He left the knoll for the long slope going west.

'Bird,' Rosalind said and followed with the others.

Howie waited for Hillary. She was just reaching the top, her hands against her sides. 'You're slowing me down.'

'I can't go any faster.'

'You're always slowing me down.'

Hillary watched him decide what to do. Obviously, he was considering a great number of alternatives.

The trail Roman set below wound through a maze of pines. V's of brown needles kicked up over their feet as they followed the stocky agile figure in the lead. They caught up where he waited for them on a rock shelf. The pine forest had precipitously ended, and they looked out over a different, leafy wood.

'I never knew there was so much on such a small island,' Gerry said.

'Look.' Roman pointed to a gray shadow. Two ears

169

twitched, and it was a rabbit. 'That's *kaun-engro*, which is cleverly translated as the thing with the big ears.'

'Can we catch him?' Gerry already had his knife out.

'I doubt it, but we can try.'

The rabbit bounded to the side, and they followed on the ledge. Roman took the lead as the ledge became hemmed in by pines. A second outcrop of granite rose at its back, and they were forced to move sideways, looking straight down to the twenty-foot drop. Roman thought they'd have to back up when the ledge vanished, but he found it went around a bend in the outcropping.

'This would be a very good time for you to take off, wouldn't it?' Isabelle said.

Roman looked at Gerry, who said nothing. 'After you,' he told Isabelle and squeezed himself against the rock enough to let her pass. She went first around the bend.

Her hand came back and grabbed Roman's. When she was steady, he went around the bend with her. The rock ended at a seam of dirt and a sinkhole. Isabelle had almost fallen in. 'There's a moral here someplace,' Roman said. They edged their way between the wall at their back and the hole. It was ten feet deep, and the bottom was dotted with animal droppings. In the lower woods was a badly rotted line where a tree had fallen.

'That was here once,' Roman said. He looked up. There were two large pines directly overhead on the upper rock. 'The animals have taken over now.'

'Snakes?' Isabelle asked.

'They prefer rocks, and they don't leave droppings like

that. More like pigeons. It would be a fox or a rabbit. Wait a second.'

He went past the hole to the rock shelf on the other side. The granite had hundreds of crannies filled with small plants. Roman used them all to get down to the lower woods. Gerry watched anxiously, but Roman didn't have the cold sweat that warned him of Howie's presence. He tamely inspected the side of the shelf below them.

'Great, there's a small opening here. From the prints I'd say we have – '

'Say it in Gypsy,' Rosalind urged.

'I'd feel safer if you were more explicit,' Isabelle said.

'Hedgehog. Those who want the Gypsy version can see me after class.' He had Gerry toss down a book of matches. 'I'm going to start a fire with some brush and smoke them out. Use the sacks to catch them. Try not to knock each other into the hole.'

The operation wasn't a complete success. They were half-blind from smoke when the hedgehogs finally came out, which was all at once and in all directions. They were lucky to catch two. Gerry was better at dispatching them.

As they walked through the lower woods to the black timbers Roman had seen from the hill, some change had taken place in the jongleurs. They carried their sacks with enthusiasm. Isabelle had stopped fixing Roman with blank stares. The larger change had been in him. He strode over the grass floor happily. His chin had a blue of stubble, his shirt was dirty and minus a button, and his hair hung in ringlets. He whistled a spirited *djili* to set the pace. Tiny emerald leaves of ivy crawled over the burned house, and a new sycamore was growing out of the enriched ground.

A margin of lilacs marked what once was the lawn. Rosalind ran ahead with a yell of excitement, swinging her sack. The rest trotted after her. She stopped before they did, staring up at the house, and then they halted in their tracks.

Howie stood in front of the black wall, an exclamation point all in white. The wind hardly bothered his hair, although the ivy behind him shuddered delicately.

'The picnic is over,' he said.

Roman was the only one to take the last few steps up to him. 'It's hardly begun.'

Howie tilted his head back to the sky. 'Getting dark. God, they're long, aren't they?'

'What's long?' Gerry asked.

'The days,' Roman said. There were, after all, moments when he understood Howie in a way the others couldn't. The moon had risen in the still bright sky like a ghost. 'There's one more thing. Here.'

He went down into the gutted cellar of the house. The cement floor was an inch deep in water at places. He went to the part hidden under the shell of the first floor. Everything he touched left a blur of soot. He found what he wanted in the darkest, innermost corner of cement and beams. He killed it before it woke up.

They watched him come out of the cellar. Gerry had his knife drawn, but Roman's hands were together. He drew one away to reveal a crumpled ball of fur, leathery wings and a face that was mostly flaring nostrils. Howie pulled back the lid of its left eye. It was missing.

'What does that mean?' Gerry said.

Howie sighed. 'It means that the man who has it has the power of invisibility.'

'I still see him.'

Howie's blue eyes scanned Roman. 'Now I really see him.'

Chapter Twenty-One

The fire sprawled redly through its border of rocks like lava in the dark. A few of the hardwood skewers had dried out and added to the blaze while bones made irregular shadows in it. A pot, empty of soup and askew, reflected the glow. Roman lit a Gauloise in the flames and blew out a long plume of smoke.

'A last cigarette,' he said. 'What a nice tradition.'

'It is about that time,' Howie agreed.

'You didn't eat anything. Neither did Hillary.'

Howie didn't answer. He looked at his hands, held out in front of him. They were large and strong, but there was nothing brutish about them. They were almost hairless. He lifted his eyes and watched Roman. Everybody else was.

'What is death like for a Gypsy? "Ban, ban, Kaliban? Has a new master, get a new man?"'

'You're asking the wrong Gypsy. Ask Nanoosh.'

Howie was momentarily puzzled. 'Oh, the Gypsy who died in the crash. But we only have you, and that won't be for long.' His voice was sad, but his face was as empty of emotion as a mask. 'I think you're out of secrets.'

'The entertainment, I'd almost forgotten,' Roman said. 'The least I can do.'

'Fortune-telling?' Isabelle asked.

'He's kidding,' Gerry said.

'He's serious,' Howie said. He clapped his hands together. 'He's going to try it. Come on. Kaliban, *duikker* for your life.'

'Where's his crystal ball?' Rosalind asked.

'He doesn't need one,' Howie said.

'Not now,' Hillary said. 'This isn't the time for card tricks or jokes, please.'

'Quiet, quiet in the audience,' Howie said. He stood up and strode back and forth as he talked. 'Ladies and germs. Hah-hah. Tonight only an appearance by royal command. A chance to gaze at the hand of fate, to pick a card from the deck of tarot, an opportunity to reach back in the past or forward into the future. Who will be the first to tax the mental powers of the victim? Pardon me, sir, the maestro. Yes, the chubby girl in the back row.'

Rosalind put her hand down. She tried to look as cunning as she could as she posed her question. 'How did Gerry meet Isabelle?'

'They're brother and sister,' Roman said.

'Very good, very good,' Howie said and led the clapping. 'Not a toughie, but he fielded it pretty well.'

'How did you know?' Rosalind asked. She was impressed if nobody else was.

'Gerry is her younger brother, and she's always had to look out for him. That's why she wishes I were already dead' – he shrugged – 'so I couldn't show up here. She loves him.'

'He embellishes,' Howie announced.

'Let's try something a little tougher than that,' Gerry

said. His face was red, not only from the heat of the fire. 'You tell us about Judy Mueller.'

Howie didn't say anything. He squatted in the shadows and watched Roman attentively. Rosalind's head jerked toward the goat tied by its tree. It was still there by the evidence of its orange minus-sign eyes.

'The girl. I can't tell you much about her life. I'd guess it was pretty dull if she could fall for your father, Hillary. No offense, I hope.'

He lit another cigarette. 'Howie would say that the only extraordinary thing about her was her death. He wouldn't be wrong. She was surprised, but then you all were, weren't you? Except for Howie. You thought it was a joke. You were going to scare her off so she wouldn't marry Mr Sloan. So you took the yellow station wagon and honked the horn. Howie, you followed them before, so you knew what to do. She got in, and you took off. Hillary was along, so she wasn't scared.

'You took her into the woods. The whole thing was going to be a prank. You were all walking along. Nobody was holding her hands, nothing. Suddenly, from nowhere, Howie cut her head off. The rest of you stood around, not saying a thing, while he took her clothes off and chopped her up. Then, just in case you thought it was a whim on his part, he brought out the plastic bags, and he told you, Hillary, that your father was sending some things down to an antique show in New York. He'd know.

'Well, you know all the rest, but there was one thing about Judy Mueller you didn't know. She'd thrown your father over, Hillary. You didn't know her as well as you thought. You didn't have to kill her; she didn't have to die at all.'

There wasn't a sound when he finished until Gerry said, 'You're lying!'

'High marks,' Howie said.

'You made it up,' Hillary said.

'It was in her letters to your father. Of course, if you and he had had human communication, you would have known.'

The revelation had been lost on Rosalind but not on Isabelle. Her black stare covered Howie.

'That's over, though. She's dead, and you can't bring her back,' Roman said. 'Isn't there something you'd like to know about the future? Something happier than all that?' He looked around. They looked in a state of shock. 'No? How about you, Hillary? Wouldn't you like to know if you're pregnant?'

Her eyes reminded him of the horse before he bolted.

'Come on, this is just after-dinner entertainment. The Gypsy's last act. Howie must be curious himself by now. He's the father. Right, Howie?'

Howie hovered in the shadow, a suspended mask.

'Go on,' he said.

Roman had Rosalind give him a tambourine from a sack. He used a charred skewer from the fire to draw nine lines on it, three descending like ladder rungs down the middle, the others describing a broken circle around them. He picked a handful of stones off the ground, selected nine and threw the rest away.

'Let me explain first that we should be using beans but . . . ah, well.' He put the stones in Hillary's hand. She let them fall, but he caught them in the drum. 'If they stay within the lines,' he said, 'you are. And if they don't, you aren't. You'll excuse me for skipping the mumbo jumbo.' He tapped the bottom of the drum with his fingertips. The stones danced with a life of their own. He felt the suspended breaths around him. He gave the skin one final tap and stopped. The stones came to rest, all nine of them inside the lines. 'Congratulations.'

Hillary didn't say anything.

'You are pregnant?' Isabelle said.

'That's great,' Gerry said. Howie didn't reply, and the burst of enthusiasm became strained.

'Would you like to know what sex it is?' Roman asked. 'We can find out if you want. It's easy.'

Hillary glared into his eyes as if he were a stranger. In a way, he was. His face glowed with a bronze wetness from the heat of the fire, and his thick black hair was coiled. With his shirt open, she saw a seashell hanging on a cord over the black hair of his chest. His eyes were lined with red.

'It would be fun,' Rosalind said.

'Have you got an egg in one of the sacks?' Roman asked Gerry. Gerry said he thought so and took out a carton. He made a joke about breakfast and took an egg out. He gave it to Roman.

'Fine. Now, you have to hold this under your shirt against your belly for five minutes with the flat end toward you. Then we'll break it open at the other end. If the yolk shows, it's a boy. If the yolk doesn't show, it means it was attracted to the female growing within you, and it will be a girl.'

She just held the egg in her hand, so he pulled her shirt out and placed her hands inside it. There was some flour and salt beside the fire that he had used for the fish. He had Rosalind give him some baking soda from a sack. Gerry asked what he was making now, but Roman silently moistened the flour and soda and salt. When it was soft, he brought the bat out of his shirt and sprinkled some of its blood on the dough. Then he rolled it into a strip and wound it around a stick and placed it over the fire.

'Okay, Hillary, let's see what you have.' He pulled her hands out of her shirt gently and disengaged the egg from her fingers. He held the warm egg close to his face, waiting until Gerry's nervous coughing ended.

> *Anro, anro in obles*
> *Te e pera in obles,*
> *Ava cavo sastavestes!*
> *Devla, Devla tut akharel!*

He watched Hillary's pale eyes as he repeated it.

> The egg, the little egg is round
> Just as the belly is round,
> Little child come in health!
> God, God is calling you!

He struck the egg above the middle with a sharp stone and took off the cap of shell. He seemed puzzled, and he slid two fingers into the raw egg, searching. Hillary shook as he drew his fingers out, and after a moment when her mouth was open but mute, she screamed. Hanging from Roman's fingers, dripping with albumen and blood, was a small, hideous human head grinning.

'You dirty son of a bitch,' Howie said.

Roman threw the head into the fire. The albumen crackled, turning first white and then black. The smell of hair rose out of the flames. Roman quickly drew the stick with the dough out. It had risen and curled around the skewer like a snake.

'It's an old trick,' Howie shouted. No one paid attention to him. They had seen the head come out of the egg. Roman pulled the dough off the stick and gave it to Hillary.

'Eat some. It has bat's blood because the bat is the purest of all birds in that it suckles its young. You have to protect your own child.'

She numbly took the dough and bit off an end. She chewed and swallowed and took another bite.

'Now, Howie, it's your turn,' Roman said. 'You have – '

If there had been more light than the fire, he might have seen it coming. All there was was a flash of color that reminded him of the frightened cardinal and then a soft penetration that spread from the temple over his face and down to his body.

There was another howl that almost woke him up and a sense of being handled. It was the sound of crying that finally came through the fog and brought him back. The first thing he saw was the moon, no ghost anymore but a tangible entity. From its position through the leaves he knew he'd been unconscious for ten or fifteen minutes. His pulse roared over one side of his head. He expected that much; what worried him was that he couldn't move his hands. They were tied to his side and around something else. It wasn't a tree because when he moved, it moved. Then he felt the rough textured hair against his hands and a rank animal smell. He looked where the black goat had been and it was gone and he knew he didn't have to look any further. It was bound to his back and from the limp way it followed his shifting body it was dead.

'He's awake,' Gerry said.

They were still around the fire although from Hillary's face her mind was far away. Rosalind sobbed over the goat's collar. They all looked scared, except Howie. As he stood, a red scarf with a weighted end dangled from a pocket.

'You're very sensitive,' Roman groaned. 'Haven't you ever seen a devil's head before?'

Howie smiled in a new way; his beautiful head merely cracked for a second around the mouth. Roman rolled around until he had enough leverage to sit up. A sticky fluid ran down the back of his neck.

'Secrets, real secrets,' Howie said. 'No more of that

181

bajour junk.' He stood between Roman and the fire, his silhouette hiding objects that cast strange shadows over the ground.

'You had to kill the poor goat to tell me?'

'It's part of it. So is this. Recognize it?' Howie took something small from his pocket.

'It belonged to Nanoosh.'

'Correct!' He held it up for the others to see. It was a plastic dashboard religious statue like a million others, but it was black. 'His *Develeskie Gueri*, right?'

'The Black Virgin,' Roman said. He tried sliding his hands out of their bonds. It was no good.

'What religion, Kaliban? Christian?' His voice boomed into the dark. 'Isn't her name Kali?'

'There is a patron saint of the Gypsies known as *la Kali*,' Roman said. 'There's a pilgrimage for her once a year in France.'

'Yes, at Stes.-Maries-de-la-Mer. There are Kalis, Black Virgins, in Poland, Portugal, at Chartres, in Czechoslovakia, wherever the Gypsies are. Through all the cities they have gone through, like Calcutta, Karak, Karachi, Carakalu. Isn't it true that there is another name for Gypsies besides Romany and that name is Kalo? Isn't that true, Kaliban?'

'Would someone please tell me what Howie is talking about?' Roman said.

'What are Gypsies, anyway?' Howie went on. 'The Dravidians, the people who inhabited India before the Aryans. Reduced to becoming wanderers, untouchables, thuggees. To pretending that they worship this Kali' – he shook the plastic figure – 'when the real Kali is right here.'

He reached behind him and slammed down on the ground in front of Roman a statue two feet high. It was the representation of another black female but in a grotesque manifestation. Her breasts hung loosely under a green necklace of bodies and skulls. Around her waist she wore a belt of mutilated hands. Two of her many arms held up a demon's head and a broad-headed sword. Her teeth were tusks, and her forehead was marked by a third eye. Most striking of all, though, was her tongue, still glistening with the goat's blood.

'Kali!' Howie said. 'Consort of Shiva. Her lust for blood grew from her battle with the demon Raktavira whose special power was that every drop of blood that touched the ground brought forth a new demon. She defeated him by drinking his blood as it flowed, creating a thirst that could never be satisfied. And a ceremony that demanded the death of a black goat and a man.'

'The old stories about Kali and the thuggees?' Roman said. 'The English wiped them out a hundred years ago. There aren't any more human sacrifices or men with strangler's scarves or executioner's swords.'

'Then what are you doing tied to a goat, and what is this' – he drew the scarf out and threw it aside – 'and what is this?' He reached back for the other hidden shadow and brought out a short crescent-headed sword. He sank it headfirst into the ground beside the idol. The fire's glow curled around its twisted handle of silver and bronze.

'That is an Indian executioner's sword, probably of the last century,' Roman said as if he were appraising a Queen Anne side chair. 'It is sometimes called *bhotani* because it is from the city of Bhotan. Other times it is called *bhowani*. Or Kali or the Black Mother. There are smaller versions in junk shops all through New York City, but it's difficult to find a real one. Where did you get it?'

'Thailand, while I was in the service. That's when I first became interested in Kali and you.'

'Me?'

'That's how we were going to scare that dumb librarian, with the statue. I knew that wouldn't be enough. I knew everything was going fine when the cops gave me Nanoosh's Kali. They thought it was Buddy's.' He paced behind the idol and sword, gesturing with his arms. 'But you had to try to screw things up, and Gypsy or no Gypsy, that wouldn't do. So we had to hunt you, us and Kali.'

'Interesting,' Roman said. 'An interesting theory. Let's say one or two facts are true.'

Howie laughed. 'You're in no position to talk about theories.'

'Why not? According to you, Gypsies have worshiped Kali for thousands of years. What would you know in comparison to what I do? The names of evil: Mot, El-Zebub, Lucifer, Baal, Seth, Leviathan. Kali's names: Parvati, Uma, Gauri, Ambika, Durga, Chamundi, Minakshi, Devi.' He looked at the others. 'Does he know enough for your brother to become a murderer, Isabelle?'

'He's trying to save his life,' Howie said. 'He admits

what I said is true. Kali is the goddess of destruction, the Clawed Hands, the Blood Drinker. This is her sword and that' – his hand, the fingers spread, reached toward the idol – 'is her face.'

'And that's one side of her, as it is for any god. If you knew her for thousands of years you'd know she could be all colors. The sky is black at night, but if your eyes were good enough, they could see the different lights of a million stars. Death is part of her because death is part of life. Was that your big secret, Howie? Maybe you can get that library card renewed.'

Howie's eyes narrowed to shadows, and his hand fingered the butt of the sword. He gained control of himself, and the hand dropped.

'I almost forgot you were tied up,' he said hoarsely.

'A worshiper of Kali, but you're afraid to kill me? Why?'

Gerry moaned and looked at Howie. Rosalind stared, mesmerized by the stubby sword. Roman spoke to them, trying with his voice and eyes to blunt the image of a bruised man tied to a dead goat.

'Howie surprised you when he killed the Mueller girl. There weren't any marks on her arms, so I know you didn't help him. The trouble was that you saw him do it. Now he needs you to kill somebody so you won't be witnesses anymore; you'll be killers, too. That's why he drummed up this story.' The sweat poured over his face. In their eyes he glistened. 'Let's see, I guess you're the man of the hour this time, Gerry. Then Isabelle, I suppose you're next to take a couple whacks. Then your turn,

185

Rosalind. After that, Hillary, and then you'll all dump what's left in the lake. If I hadn't shown up, it would have been some kid at the festival. That must have been something to look forward to.'

'Not all of us can tell fortunes,' Hillary said, breaking her silence.

'Everyone makes his future. All of us but Howie. *Te aves vertime mander, te yertil tut o Kali.* You have no future.'

'You're threatening me,' Howie said with amazement.

'She is.' He nodded, and Howie followed the gesture to the idol by his side. Roman went on, completely without malice. 'She does according to her wisdom in destroying what is useless or what has lived its destined time.'

'There's only one person here who's lived his destined time,' Howie said. He yanked the sword out of the ground and dropped the plastic statue in the fire. It bubbled, losing its shape and releasing a bitter odor. He watched with satisfaction and strode past the fire to the others.

'Now?' Gerry asked.

'We're not going to have any ceremony.' Howie thrust the sword at him, handle first. 'Here.' He forced it into Gerry's hands and forced the fingers around it. 'It'll be easy. One swing.'

'I don't think I can do it,' Gerry said. He seemed to be in physical pain.

'Damn it, get up. You don't even have to look. Just swing the thing and I'll hold him still. Get up.' He grabbed Gerry and pulled him to his feet. Gerry looked at Howie in terror, and his knees folded. He dropped the sword as he hit the ground and curled up.

'You little twit, get up or I'll use it on you,' Howie said. His rage was slipping away from him, reshaping his pale face. Hillary saw it. It was the face from the egg.

'I can't,' Gerry cried.

'He's telling the truth,' Roman said.

Howie's head snapped around. 'Another trick?'

'Poison, another old Gypsy talent, remember? Some mushrooms I picked up during our outing. I dropped them in their soup. It'll hit them all if they try standing, a little later if they stay still, but all of them. They should get to a doctor as fast as they can.'

Isabelle stood up. She took one step before she gasped and sat down, holding her stomach. She tried cursing Roman and couldn't do that, either. Howie snatched Rosalind off the ground with one hand. He jammed the sword in her hand and pushed her toward Roman. She collapsed near the fire. Howie ranted, going back and forth, kicking and threatening them. At last he gave up and stood in the middle of them, furious.

'The doctor,' Roman repeated. 'Unless you want three more bodies to dispose of. Now that could get tricky.'

Howie pulled Hillary to her feet. Roman hadn't given her any of the mushrooms, and she wasn't sick, not physically at least.

'You do it,' Howie yelled in her face. 'He knows too much.'

'He always did.' She refused the sword and turned away to the figures on the ground. 'They're dying.'

A sound that was nothing less than a growl came from Howie's throat. He pushed her away and grabbed the nearest retching body. Roman stayed as still as he could. Howie was going to take them to the boat. He wouldn't row them across, but he would be gone from the camp for a minute or two. Even with a dead goat on his back that would be enough time to get away.

Howie watched him, reading his mind.

'It looks like I'll have to do it again all by myself. When I'm finished, when I . . . you and the goat are going to look like Siamese twins.' Rosalind hung from one hand, and he picked up the idol with the other. 'And if you want someone to keep you company until I get back, here's your goddamn Kali.'

He threw the heavy idol as easily as a beanbag. Roman tried to turn to make the goat catch the burden of the blow. He didn't succeed. The idol smashed into his ribs, and he rocked, finally falling forward with the goat on top of him.

Out of the corner of his eye he saw the moon, cruelly cut by leaves. The moon began contracting, first to the size of a silver dollar, then a quarter and then a dime. There was no air in his lungs, and none was coming in. *Dude* was supposed to be good luck, he was sure of it.

On the other hand, he thought as the moon disappeared, there were always exceptions.

Chapter Twenty-Two

'Did you really poison them?'

'Enough to make them sick.'

Hillary had rolled him on his side so that the goat's weight was off him. A draft of air poured into his lungs. Hillary's face was as faraway as the moon.

'Where are the others?' He was gasping so hard he doubted that she understood him.

'We took them to the boat. I ran back while Howie was putting them in.'

He stared up at her because everything else but the fire and the moon was dark. She thought the startling eyes could see more, and she began pleading with him.

'Please don't kill Howie. You've got to promise you won't. I still love him.'

'Kill him? I . . .' There was something comical about her asking favors from a half-blind man lying on the ground tied to the corpse of a goat. The silent laughs scratched his ribs.

'He's coming back?'

'Right now. But you've got to promise that you won't do to him what you did to the others.'

'Get them out of the way. So they wouldn't have to make a choice, choose.' He wasn't making sense, and he struggled to get hold of his tongue. He couldn't afford to lose her.

'Promise?'

Promise? Everyone wanted him to make promises as if he had some power over the way things happened, him tied to Dany and Celie and a poor goat that was worse off than himself only by a matter of minutes. He fought the conspiracy of his ribs and temple and lurched up to his knees. The goat's hooves dangled in all directions like a bagpipe. Every time he moved the carcass sagged in a new place trying to drag him down.

'Help me, Hillary, for God's sake.'

She looked at him dumbly. He swore and repeated the plea in English. 'It's a promise,' he added.

Even standing bent over with Hillary supporting him, he was dizzied by the height. He really was Kaliban now, half man and half animal. He spread his legs cautiously, expecting them to fail.

'Untie me.'

She seemed to notice his predicament for the first time. He almost collapsed as she fumbled with the rope.

'Would the sword help?' she asked.

'The sword?' He never thought Howie would leave the *bhowani* with them. 'Of course. Where is it?'

'On the other side of the fire.' It lay in full view only twenty feet away, reflecting the fire like a crescent-shaped mirror.

'Quick, get it.'

Hillary hesitated, mildly curious why he hadn't seen it, and in that moment he heard Howie returning – not

Howie returning because Howie moved silently but the unnatural vacuum of sound that precedes any predator. The katydids were the last to hush, and when they did, Roman pulled Hillary back.

'Forget it. Hold my hand and get into the woods, fast,' he whispered.

Her slim white hand took his brown one and obediently led him away from the fire into the woods. Once among the trees he was totally blind. They were still within her sight of the camp when he abruptly knelt and pulled her down.

Howie stood at the edge of the camp directly opposite them. He was so motionless it was hard to believe that he hadn't been there all the time. When he moved, it was in long, unhurried strides to the fire, and he slowly looked around in a circle. Then he saw the sword. His eyes scanned the camp once more, and he noted the absence of the goat and the rope. He picked the sword up and laughed so loud Roman thought he could only be feet away. Hillary watched from the grass like a fawn.

'I know you can hear me,' Howie yelled. 'I know you're right here. You ran so scared you even forgot the sword, you know. You might have had a chance if you took the sword.

'Hillary, you made a bad mistake. I don't know how you think I'm going to take this, your betraying me like this. I'm not happy, you know that. Anyway, two of you are going to be a lot easier to find than one. The three of you, pardon me.'

He laughed again.

'Can you see me? I bet you can.' He turned quickly and relaxed again. 'Hey, antique dealer, have you got any more tricks or did you run out? How's the bat eye working? A few words in Romany? No?'

Hillary started sobbing. Roman squeezed her arm until his fingers ached.

'Okay, play hard to get. It's all the same to me. But I think you'd like to see what I have in store for you two.' He walked past the fire toward them. For an instant Hillary thought he saw them, but he bent to pick up the idol. He walked back to the fire with it.

'Gypsy, you watching? You too, Hillary. This is what I'm going to do with you.' He held the idol out with one hand and brought the sword down with the other. The idol was made of hardwood, but the blade sank an inch through its chest and necklace. He pulled the sword out and dropped the idol. He attacked its head, slicing off the tusks and tongue and then, when it was on its back, began hacking away at its neck. The more he worked, the more furious he became, so that when the idol was covered with gashes, his face was dripping with sweat. He wasn't satisfied until there was nothing recognizable left of the idol, no hands or breasts or legs, and then he stood exhausted with his hands hanging down, his face ash white, and stared at his victim. He picked up the decapitated head.

'What is he doing?' Roman whispered.

'He put the head in the fire, and he's still hitting it,' Hillary said. Her voice sounded as if it belonged to a five-year-old in a distant room.

Howie slashed away until the fire and the head were indistinguishable, and then he went on cutting at the flames and slapping the broad head of the sword down so that there was less and less of the campfire all the time. At last there were only a few embers left, and he tracked them down, smothering them with the sword until they were all dead and, blow by blow, he had faded into the surrounding dark.

'Coming to get you.'

They huddled as near the ground as they could get. Roman's ear was on the ground, but he couldn't hear a step. A cool breeze smoothed the grass around them, making them stand out as hillocks.

Howie would be on them now if he'd taken the right direction, and he had excellent night vision. No sword came down. The first insect began talking again. Roman took his hand off Hillary's arm. He wasn't surprised how cramped and sweaty his palm was.

'What do we do now?' she asked.

His map of the island was incomplete. The camp was on the eastern side, and he knew the land between it and the water. He knew the southern shore and an area between it and the island's high point to the west. They'd been through the pine forest and the woods to the house, but Howie had been very careful to lead them back to the camp by the shore trail. The center woods, the birch groves leading to the swamp, the swamp itself and most of the shore running from east to north to west were terra incognita.

'How well do you know the island?'

'Not well. I've been sick the last few days. I'm okay at night.'

'Have you been to the swamp?'

'We picked some berries there.' The timbre was coming back to her voice as she talked. 'It's deep.'

'We have to find some place to rest and get this off my back. Can you think of some place I didn't go today?' The swamp was out. Stumbling through it blind with no hands was just saving Howie work.

'No. We stayed in camp mostly. Howie was the one who went out and got food.'

Roman closed his eyes to think. Having them open and seeing nothing was worse. They couldn't talk where they were for long, and when they moved, it had to be someplace in particular. Wanderers made noise. The south shore was the most logical path, and that, he was sure, was where Howie was waiting. They needed time as badly as Howie needed to finish quickly and make his escape. It was a long swim back to the bus.

'Hillary, do you know Polaris?'

'Of course.'

'Can you see it?'

He felt her lean away. 'It's that way. North.'

They started off, Hillary following the star through the trees. She moved confidently leading Roman by his shirt. It hadn't sunk into her that he couldn't see, and he knew it. Occasionally a tree would hit the goat and shake him; but the ground was level, and he kept his footing. Only once, they heard Howie calling out. He sounded so far away their spirits were lifted.

The ground became rougher, and Roman's feet scuffed against sharp rocks. A tall nettle reached his face and left minute red lines. Isadore might be at the festival; he might even meet the boat as it arrived. Roman forced the picture from his mind because it was wishing, not thinking. He tried pushing away guilt for the trick with the egg. That wasn't as easy. Hillary would have been safer hunting him than running with him, and now that he'd deceived her he would have to go on doing so. She was operating on lies.

'Look, isn't it beautiful,' she said. They'd stopped. He heard the lapping of water and the amplified music of the kids traveling over the lake.

'See the Bear. And that's Cassiopeia on the other side.'

Hillary looked up. Where Cassiopeia should have been was white cloud. She nodded happily.

'See if you can find a sharp stone,' Roman said. He sank down and pretended to search the ground. Howie would have given up the south shore by now. Roman was sure that if he could get his arms free from his sides, he'd be able to breathe normally. The moon passed between clouds and gave him an encouraging moment of sight.

'How's this?'

Roman told her to put it in his hand. He ran his thumb over the edge. It was glass.

'Great. Go ahead, cut the rope.'

He leaned over and presented the bound goat. The ropes tugged his chest as she began sawing. It wouldn't take long for the glass to slice through. He listened to the whine of the mosquitoes busying themselves around the carcass. The short hairs on the back of his neck stood up; then all the hairs down his spine were erect.

'Hillary, are there any big rocks in the water?' She said there were, as calmly as if they were discussing a landscape. 'We have to get in the water. Don't make any splashes. Get behind the rocks and hide.'

She immediately headed for the water without waiting for him. He managed to get hold of her belt with one hand and followed. The water rose to his knees and then his chest as she led him in. His face felt colder. The water's buoyancy made it easier for him to carry the goat and practically impossible for him to hide.

'How big are they?'

'Big enough.'

There wasn't time to argue. The lake bottom fell away, and they were treading water. He lost his grip on her and regained it. A rock hit his chest, and he shouldered his way around it.

'See, here we are,' she said.

He trod as fast as he could. The goat, like an oversized hump, kept forcing his face into the water. He angled his hands up from his sides as much as he could and found a hold on the rock. When his shoe discovered a projection to rest on, he hugged the rough side of the rock as if he could get into it. Hillary was as composed as a sleepwalker.

They waited in the water for ten minutes while the chill settled into their bodies. Then, before he could tell Hillary they were going back, a white birch moved in the bright moonlight from the other trees and onto the beach. It carried a shining branch over the spot where Hillary had tried to cut the ropes. As the white shape glided back and forth, Roman saw she had taken them only twenty yards into the water. The struggle to the rocks had felt like a mile when they'd hardly moved at all.

He remembered the ground when he'd pretended to search for a stone, a film of sand over rocks and hard soil. If there was more sand, the tracks into the water would be unmistakable. The apparition never turned to the water. It simply retreated and, bent over with the brilliant arm in front, dissolved back into the trees.

They waited another ten minutes and came ashore. Roman spit out the water he hadn't swallowed in the struggle back. The goat was twice as heavy as before. The ropes were tighter. Hillary hugged herself and shivered. Her dank hair hung over her shoulders, and her shirt was pressed over her breasts and belly.

'That was close. I'm amazed he didn't see us.'

'Us? You don't have to worry,' Hillary said, 'you're invisible.' She wasn't kidding. Roman's teeth chattered.

'Have you still got the glass? He won't be back for a while.'

'I'm sorry, I lost it in the water.'

The goat wouldn't budge no matter how hard she pulled. Finally, they started moving again only to stop and take off shoes that squished on the ground. She laced her sneakers neatly together and hung them over her neck to dry. In bare feet, they crept back into the woods, the girl leading what was at first sight a helpless beast of burden.

Chapter Twenty-Three

'The Bear is about five inches over the trees,' Hillary said sleepily.

'Fine. Just three more hours until daylight,' Roman said.

'Can I go back to sleep?'

'No, you'd better stay awake now.'

The moonlight was bright and constant. The clouds were gone, and they wouldn't be back until dawn. Roman and Hillary were on the eastern fringe of the pine forest overlooking a meadow that ran to the woods in the center of the island. They'd been there for an hour watching Howie move below. He was searching the island in a circular patrol that was tightening around the high ground. Each sweep was shorter. In the beginning there had been a fifteen-minute space between his appearances. It was down to about every five minutes.

Roman leaned forward. The rope was hooked over a stub on the tree, taking some of the weight off him. They'd never come as close again to freeing him from the goat as they had on the beach, but altogether they'd been very lucky. Twice Howie had passed within inches of them, once in the birch stand when he'd suddenly manifested again and once in the woods below. He was a smart tracker. All of his screaming had been in the first hours of the hunt, and he'd been patiently silent since. From Hillary's description, he stopped and took careful surveys each time he came by. He'd know if there was something different about a tree or whether a bush had exactly the same outline.

Roman had him pegged now. The pure whiteness had thrown him off just as the idol's blackness had confused the others. Howie was Priculics. During the day, Priculics was a beautiful young man. At night he was a huge black dog that killed and devoured anything he met. He'd hunted Faust, and now he was hunting them, padding through the woods on all fours with his beautiful shining teeth.

'Roman.'

He shook his head. He'd fallen asleep. It was the strain of trying to see when he could barely make out the blur of trees.

'Roman, it must be wonderful being a Gypsy.'

'Why?'

'You don't have to be scared of anything. I've been afraid all my life. With you, nothing can happen.'

'Shhh.'

The white form slipped by sixty feet away. It was moving faster now. Howie's patience was wearing thin. When he was gone, Roman and Hillary moved up to the next line of trees. Moving over the meadow, they'd be too easy to spot. Anyway, Roman liked to know where Howie was.

The search area was localizing around the knoll. On the other side of it the pine forest ended in a cul-de-sac where it fell off to the lower woods. Roman decided that they would move in the direction of the knoll one more time, and then they would have to make a break for it back toward the shore.

'They're all asleep,' Hillary said. The far shore was completely dark; the kids had tucked themselves in. Roman wondered idly whether Isadore was wandering around the blankets. 'It's so peaceful, like the end of the world,' she said. 'I don't mean destruction. I mean as if their world ended over there and we had this island right off the edge.'

'Finisterre.'

'Right. And we'd make our own laws. Like we'd have things rise instead of fall and water could run upstream.' She crouched next to his knee for warmth. 'Is it silly to want that?'

'Everybody wants that.'

She was answering him when he put his finger over her lips. The white blur was moving through the trees again closer than Roman had expected. Hillary's body was close to Roman's, and he heard her heartbeat go from a placid rhythm to terror. Howie was looking up at them, studying the shadows inside the apron of branches. Something smaller moved down the hill like a bouncing ball. It was a rabbit. As the tall white blur moved on, Hillary stifled a laugh of relief. Her heartbeat returned to normal. Roman would have put his arm around her if he could. His sleeves and the front of his shirt were smudged with red where the ropes had rubbed the skin raw. She helped him to his feet, and they ran together to the next jagged line of pines. His back and legs were stiff from their cramped posture, and he moved gracelessly in her wake.

Hillary had just slid under the bows of their new hiding place when she screamed. The cry pierced the night like a bubble. Roman tossed himself beside her. A saw-toothed trap was shut on her foot. He recalled what she'd said about Howie leaving the rest of them in camp while he supplied food. That's what Howie had been doing all night, checking his traps. The teeth of this one had only closed over the toe of her sneaker. She took her foot out and left it hanging.

'I'm sorry,' she said and hiccupped with fear.

'That's okay, but we have to get out of here.'

It was too late. They saw Howie as soon as they crept out of the trees. He was running down from the knoll full tilt. When he saw them, he waved the sword and yelled unintelligibly. He approached as easily and mindlessly as the wind, his face lit by the moon with triumph. Roman and Hillary tried running downhill, but Howie caught up with them before they even reached their last hideout.

Roman, of course, was the first one he reached. Howie brought the sword down with both hands on his back. Roman kept running and Howie struck two more times, the blade sinking deep into its target. Still Roman ran with his head down as the blows came down, almost jarring him off his feet. The crescent tip sliced over his head once, cutting off part of the goat's horn. Hillary hobbled far ahead on one sneaker, turning back up the hill. Roman fell to his knees and rose in one motion as Howie chopped and grunted in frustration. The face Roman saw was barely recognizable. Howie's lids were drawn back from bulging eyes, his lips stretched over his teeth. Roman tried dodging between the pines. Howie shrieked with pleasure and knocked him through the stiff branches, the sword flashing like quicksilver as it met Roman coming out. Roman's cramped legs started to give out and slip on the blanket of needles.

As Howie rose up for a final blow, Roman dived at his feet. Howie's swing had already started. It missed and Howie went with it, plummeting face first. The needles rolled under him, allowing his hands nothing to grip. The sword spun on and on halfway down the hill before it hit a tree and came to rest.

Roman watched the disconsolate figure slide down the hill to gather its weapon. He saw the sword clearly, even its twisted handle of silver and bronze, as it lay in its cushion of needles. Howie took the sword away from the tree and stood looking back up the hill for the Gypsy without success. Roman saw him very clearly.

Roman started up toward the knoll. By the time he reached it his arms were free, and he was toting the goat over his shoulder like a sack. Once again the whole island lay around him. Howie was desperately climbing the hill far behind.

'You're alive.' Hillary stepped from a tree timidly, afraid to believe her eyes. 'You're alive,' she said with more certainty. 'He couldn't kill you. I saw it.' She touched his face.

Roman unslung the goat from his shoulder. The carcass was nearly cut through, and one whole side was crosshatched with gaping slices. There was little bleeding because the animal was already dead. The ropes that bound it to Roman were cut through in several places. He rubbed his arms to encourage the circulation.

'Ouch,' he said as he massaged a raw sore. It shook her, and he added, 'I know I'm invulnerable, but even a Gypsy likes sympathy. Howie's going to be here soon so we'd better go.'

'Where are we going to hide now?'

'We've stopped hiding.'

She wanted to ask what he meant, but he was leading her down the west slope of the pine forest. He continued to carry his grotesque burden. Not that it held them up. They had gravity going their way, and they slid on the seat of their pants through a rustle of needles. He led her through the dark maze as easily as if it were day. Once or twice she thought she saw a contented smile on his face.

The roller coaster ended when his arm shot out and grabbed her. Hillary skidded on her back to a stop. Overhead the pines were an angular wall bordering a blank sky.

'What is it?' She sat up and found herself on the edge of a rock shelf. Her feet dangled over a twenty-foot drop through the tops of dogwoods and sycamores.

'It's a part of the island you've never been to before. We don't run anymore. We face Howie.'

'You mean we're in a corner.'

'If you try to hide, that's where you end up; that's

what corners and Finisterres are for. I should have faced Howie after I went to your house. I didn't. Well, Howie's coming down this hill any minute, and I'll have to face him.'

'You don't seem very sorry.'

'It's easier for me. You should split now. If things go wrong, you can hide until he leaves.'

'I have to watch.' She shook her head.

'He may get lucky.'

'Howie doesn't have a chance. I always knew that.'

He thought she was babbling about magic again until he caught the pinholes of pain in her eyes. She was talking about something he knew very little of, that he wanted to know nothing of.

'That's it then.' He took her hand, and they edged their way along the granite shelf, dragging the carcass with them. Howie hadn't been along earlier in the day, but it was possible he knew the outcropping. Roman thought of the face with the sword and doubted that it made a difference. The fringe of a sycamore below touched their feet while the pines at their back tried to push them over. They moved cautiously until the higher shelf rose behind them. Ten feet farther on, the rock at their level curved around a dark void.

A short step beyond the curve brought Roman to the lip of the hole. His bare foot felt the roughness where Isabelle had almost fallen in. He located the eighteen inches of solid ground between the hole and the wall and stepped lightly to it. The hedgehogs, if they'd returned home, were silent.

Hillary took his hand, and he guided her beside him. There was barely enough room for the two of them, and she had to make herself as comfortable as she could in a niche in the wall. Roman stretched across her to reach the goat's rope. He pulled its carcass carefully between her feet and the hole to him.

'What are you doing?'

'Howie set a trap for us. We set a trap for him.' He ran his hand along the rope. The part that had been cut into short sections he'd left by the knoll. Even the part he had was badly damaged. It only had to service once, he told himself. He tied a loop around the goat's shoulders and gave the other end to Hillary.

'Roman, remember your promise.'

It seemed pointless after all the other promises he'd broken. Still, he said, 'I know, that's what I'm trying to do.'

He searched the granite wall at their back until he found a handhold. Hillary thought he must be climbing on air; but he moved quickly up the rock, and the next thing she knew he was asking for the rope. She threw it up. The goat began rising.

He worked fast, with an exhilaration he was ashamed of. He selected a strong branch for the gallows and tossed the rope around it twice. The free end of the rope he secured around the trunk of the pine. The goat lay on the ground under the branch and the slack rope. Roman checked the branch once more for snags and pushed the carcass out gently. As it cleared the upper rock, the body changing from horizontal to vertical over the lower shelf, Roman played the rope out slowly, and the suspended goat sank until it hung with its hooves just inside the shadow of the hole. He secured it at that height with another knot at the trunk. He took off his shirt and used it as a muffle to break some of the smaller branches.

Hillary was near panic. She'd stopped thinking of the animal when it was on his back. Hanging beside her gave it human proportions, the warning of the overdone suicide. She fastened on Roman's whisper gratefully and took the branches as he handed them down. She thought he left, and then he was next to her again.

'You didn't tell me.'

'You set a trap for what you want to catch,' he said. He laid the branches over the hole, partially covering the dangling feet.

He tried judging the outline of the carcass. It sagged badly where the lower legs were barely joined to the body anymore. He covered the defect by dressing the animal in his shirt.

'I didn't think – ' She caught her breath. The goat swayed and touched her leg.

'I know. Just stay as still as you can now. I'll come through first and then Howie. You don't have to do a thing. Here.' He took something from his pocket and gave it to her. She knew immediately from the feel what it was.

'That helps.'

Roman didn't have the stomach to say anything. There

were lies and there were lies, and if she thought the bat's eye helped, she could have it. He steadied the goat and gave it one last critical appraisal. In the shadow of the pines all that would be visible would be a body with his shirt on.

'Thank you, Roman. I know what this means to you,' Hillary said. He was gone, though. The clothed carcass jiggled beside her in the breeze.

The moon swelled and grew fat as it descended. The air became fresher, making the pine needles shiver as he moved up the hill to the knoll. Howie would be some-where nearby because there'd be gore on the sword and he'd think they couldn't go far. Roman made a complete circle of the knoll, and then he went to the top. The new wind was especially strong there, coming from the east. He settled on his stomach and waited. It wouldn't be long. Time was running out for Howie.

Howie was worried. It was obvious even at a distance. He was running back and forth where he had caught them. His mouth was open and gasping. Roman waited until the wind slacked off, then he started speaking just loud enough for his voice to carry. 'Hickory dickory dock, the mouse ran up the clock.'

Howie stopped and stared up the knoll.

'The clock struck one, and down he run, hickory dickory dock.'

Howie was coming up. Roman waited until he was fifty yards away, and he moved backward off the knoll. He swung down through the pines. He stopped when he could still see the knoll and started talking again.

'*Ekkeri akkery, ukeryan, fillisi follasi nakelàs jan, ekkeri akkery ukery an.*'

Howie's head appeared over the knoll, and then his shoulders. His blond hair was ragged with briars. There were dark circles under his eyes. He carried the sword low. During the long night it had become heavy. He looked warily around.

'*Hokkani bukkani dook,* the rat ran up the clock.'

Howie saw him. The white figure crossed the knoll in two strides and came down the hill. He paid no attention to the trees, slicing at the branches as he plunged down in as straight a line as possible at the retreating man.

Roman twisted through the pines. He heard Howie fall and collide with a tree. Then the feet were following him again. He disappeared by cutting at a right angle from his path. The feet stopped. He let Howie get impatient for the voice before he spoke again.

'The clock struck one,' the feet were sliding through the needles already, 'and down he run, *bokkani bukkani dook.*'

Howie burst through the trees. Roman swung around a tree and ran to his left. Howie stumbled, swinging at him, but his fall carried him right behind Roman. Roman cut back to his right, sliding on his thigh. A branch separated cleanly by his head as Howie swung again. The sword began slowing Howie down. Roman gained a foot, then a yard, and Howie's thrusts became more and more futile. Roman cut even more sharply to his right, and Howie fell, not able to grab a tree immediately because he was more concerned with holding onto the sword. Roman had completely disappeared. Howie stood up and leaned against a tree. This was an area of the island he'd never been in before. He took one step and held onto the tree tighter. Five feet in front of him was a rock ledge, and beyond that was nothing.

Roman stood on the ledge where the wall rose behind it. He waited until he was satisfied nothing had fallen into the lower woods. Then he repeated, '*Hokkani hukkani dook.*'

Howie's head snapped around. The Gypsy was closer than he'd dared hope. He held the sword straight out at his waist and padded along the ledge.

Roman took five steps back. A pine needle cracked in the dark where Howie was coming from.

'*Avata ratti dosch.*'

Another needle broke. Howie was becoming less anxious about being quiet. He saw the wall block the stone shelf off from escape through the pines. He hesitated because he didn't know whether Roman had taken the exit.

Roman crouched where the shelf curved. He couldn't see Howie in the gloom of the pines' shadows, just the frequent reflection of the sword as it turned over and over.

'*Cocalor dan, dand ba ran.*'

He turned the corner, brushing Hillary as he slid by the hole. The goat was spinning ever so slowly. He stopped it and positioned himself behind the carcass and the branches at its feet. He took one look at Hillary. Her eyes had the bright glaze of something that was being tortured to death.

The silhouette of the corner of the wall steadily grew as Howie came around it. He inched his way forward holding the blade in front. His foot distinguished the edge of the shelf from air, and he turned the corner.

'*Hokkani bukkani dook.*'

Howie almost lost his balance as he heard the voice and saw the shadowy figure directly in front of him. He exhaled faintly and moved forward again, watching the white shirt. As he stepped past Hillary hidden in her niche, the sword appeared as a coil of light high above his head.

'Don't!' Hillary broke out.

Howie halted and turned. They touched and looked directly at each other's face. Hillary screamed.

Roman saw Howie changing the angle of his cut so she wouldn't be protected by the wall. There was no way he could reach them over the hole. He pushed the goat. It swung too lazily to Howie, and he saw it coming. He had plenty of time to set himself and swing at its belly. The blade sliced through the intestines like butter. There was no backbone left; it had already been chopped through. The lower half of the carcass dropped through the branches into the hole. Howie staggered forward, propelled by the momentum of his swing. His front foot slipped over the edge of the hole and he grabbed the swinging torso. He managed to pull himself nearly out when the strain finally snapped the damaged rope. He and the top of the goat vanished together down the hole. His last act was to throw the sword aside so that he wouldn't land on it.

They sat and waited on the ledge for two hours. In all that time there wasn't a sound from the hole. At last the dark began washing out of the sky, not so much as if day were entering victoriously as if night simply let go. The lower woods were still in shadow when the tops of the pines veered toward the dawn. Roman let himself down in the hole. It was obvious Howie could outwait them all.

He was on the bottom, his arms locked around the goat. The sword lay harmlessly beside them along with the legs it had cut off. Howie didn't move as Roman passed the sword up to Hillary, and didn't start as Roman turned him over. His last surprise was in his face. Roman quickly shielded him and rearranged it, closing the eyes and drawing the corners of the mouth down. It was more than he could do for the girl on the aluminum table, but Howie still looked like a broken bust put back, subtly, completely ruined. Roman pulled the goat out of his arms. Its absence left two spongy holes in Howie's chest where its horns had cradled. The animal's gold, gun-slit eyes caught the first light of day as it broke over the pines.

'Howie sacrificed himself,' Hillary said.

Chapter Twenty-Four

'Now that makes sense,' Isadore decided. 'He wanted to get the girl's money; that's why he framed her old man. Don't give me any of this hocus-pocus stuff.'

Roman and Isadore were making slow progress down Centre Street to department headquarters. Every time Isadore wanted to make a point he stopped and jabbed a stubby index finger into Roman's arm. Pedestrians took second looks at the round policeman and the dark man with the patch on his head.

Roman snapped his fingers.

'I never thought of that.'

Isadore scowled. 'Sure. Well, you better think of this: Your testimony's the only thing between those kids and a healthy sentence. They're only out of trouble as long as you are, at least until the trial is over. So stay clean.' His finger beat a tarantella on Roman's shoulder.

Roman countered by whistling a mazurka. It gave him a headache, but it kept Isadore from asking any more questions. They went into headquarters and got on an elevator.

'Lousy home life,' Isadore relented. 'That's what did it. They wouldn't have swallowed any of that stuff if they had good homes.'

The psychological explanation seemed to be a respectable compromise between Roman's demon theory and the usual economic motivation. 'Don't give me any more tales about the devil. It's not the sort of case breakdown that the captain likes.'

'You're right.'

'I can't say that a werewolf in the shape of this Howie tried to start a new wave of human sacrifices. It looks a little funny on the file cards. You'll have to bear with us if we say Howard Washington Hale, thirty-two, mental discharge from the Marine Corps, schizoid, superior intelligence, tried to work a new racket. Okay?'

'You're the detective,' Roman said as he ushered Isadore into his own office.

'I keep reminding myself.'

They sat down, and Isadore pushed over a sheaf of papers for Roman to sign. Roman went over the statements word by word. Isadore glanced covertly at the men at the other desks. He took off his jacket, cleaned his fingernails and picked his teeth, but Roman didn't hurry. Isadore even took his hat off. A few of the other officers were sitting up and smirking by now.

'Will you sign one of these goddamn things?' Isadore whispered. 'You're making a fool out of me. You're on our side, remember?'

Roman didn't fool about papers. He took his cigarettes and pushed them across the desk to Isadore. Isadore refused and shoved a stick of gum in his mouth. The damn Gypsy had the funniest quirks, he thought.

Isadore meditated upon society in general, on fathers and sons, Gypsies and non-Gypsies. The curious thing, he decided, was that the person who had come out best was Grey's fellow antique dealer, Sloan. Charges dropped, daughter safe, troublesome girlfriend out of the way, insurance money paid.

'This one isn't for me,' Roman said.

He handed one of the papers to Isadore. It was a bulletin from Boston, and Isadore wondered if some supernatural signal had prompted the thought about Sloan. The dealer was poisoned, a suicide in his workshop an hour after he was released. According to the first report, the dealer's mouth and throat were covered with gold paint. Roman had written in the margin the word 'orpiment.'

'What does that mean?' Isadore asked.

'It means he became an antique. You see, some people do believe in magic.'

He started signing the papers. Isadore picked up the bulletin and got up to go to the teletype room, hoping that nothing else strange and illogical had happened. He crossed his fingers.